Crusaders

Richard T. Kelly was born in 1970. He is the author of *Alan Clarke*, *The Name of This Book is Dogme95* and the highly acclaimed biography *Sean Penn: His Life and Times*. He also edited *Ten Bad Dates with De Niro: A Book of Alternative Film Lists*. *Crusaders* is his first novel.

Further praise for *Crusaders*:

'Ambitious, truthful, perceptive and heart-breaking . . . It is a book with a heart and a soul and courage and conviction.' Susan Hill

'Extraordinary . . . Kelly brings the less salubrious parts of his semi-fictional Newcastle cinematically to life. He also has a pitch-perfect ear for dialogue, an empathy with "ordinary" lives and a special ability to convey menace.' Adrian Turpin, *Financial Times*

'An ambitious and convincing account of political chicanery, ideological quandaries and gang violence in 1990s Newcastle . . . In *Crusaders*, the north-east has found a new champion.' Daniel Starza-Smith, *New Statesman*

'Kelly's flair for character and dialogue keeps his state-of-the-nation epic whipping along but, above all, his seamless mesh of the personal and political leaves you swooning with admiration . . . *Crusaders* gets to the cantankerous heart of modern Britain.' Ian Ramsey, *Tatler*

'Kelly describes social deprivation with a red-hot sense of injustice . . . The dialogue is superb.' Alastair Sooke, *Daily Telegraph*

'A wonderful novel and . . . a thrilling realisation of what a novelist can do.' Andrew O'Hagan

'*Crusaders* is The Great British Novel of this decade.' David Peace

also by Richard T. Kelly

non-fiction

ALAN CLARKE
THE NAME OF THIS BOOK IS DOGME95
SEAN PENN: HIS LIFE AND TIMES

as editor

TEN BAD DATES WITH DE NIRO

CRUSADERS

A Novel

RICHARD T. KELLY

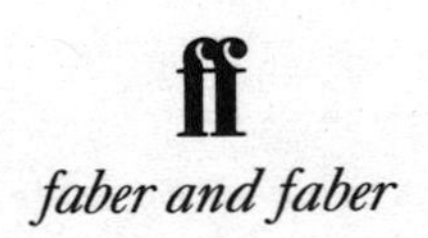

faber and faber

First published in 2008
by Faber and Faber Limited
3 Queen Square London WC1N 3AU
This paperback edition first published in 2008

Typeset by Faber and Faber Limited
Printed in England by CPI Bookmarque, Croydon

A CIP record for this book
is available from the British Library

ISBN 978-0-571-22805-8

2 4 6 8 10 9 7 5 3 1

For Trevor, Kathleen and David

Since every man is a microcosm, in whose heart may be read all that sends armies marching, I must admit I am no better.
I. F. STONE, 1956

The intriguing thing about Pilate is the degree to which he tried to do the good thing rather than the bad. He commands our moral attention not because he was a bad man, but because he was so nearly a good man.
TONY BLAIR, MP, EASTER SUNDAY 1996

AUTHOR'S NOTE

The tale told in these pages takes place in the recent past and across the north-east of England, amid some real and recognisable cities and towns. But the reader is advised that there is no ward in the west of Newcastle by the name of Hoxheath, nor is there a parliamentary constituency called Tyneside West. There is no Grey Theological College in Cambridge, nor an Excelsior Working Men's Club in Sunderland, nor a nightclub called Teflon on Newcastle's Quayside – and so on. That said, a good many place names in the book are taken from life, as are certain personages. The mixture is intended only to lend credence to the fictional characters and predicaments described herein.

CONTENTS

PROLOGUE

St Cuthbert's Day: Sunday, 20 March 1978

He had set himself a mission and felt beholden to it. He told Audrey as much when she came in her coat to the threshold of his room, asking would he join her for morning service at St Aidan's. He wasn't impervious to her plea, and the skies were looking doomy, but he had determined for this day that he would climb up to the Monument.

He had seen it from afar, perplexedly at first, for there seemed no earthly reason why a Greek temple sat foursquare atop a wooded hillside over Sunderland. His mother, the amateur historian, spoke vaguely of some civic debt to 'Radical Jack', Earl of Durham back in the days when the northern cities were granted Members of Parliament. Altogether John approved of the symbolic aura, and wished to associate himself with it. He had plotted a course through those woods guarding the hill's upper reaches, an awkward style of approach, likely to ensure solitude.

That morning he donned his anorak and cycled ten miles north by A-roads, wary of cars that zipped by, blaring their tetchy horns. Keening easterly he passed through drab stretches of industrial estate before hazarding upon a long tree-lined path. Freewheeling down its slope he could see the great grey Monument, perhaps two miles distant, gravid blue-black clouds massed and settled above. He crossed the Wear by a footbridge, chained his bike to a bench by the Old Fellows pub, and trudged up a winding road that levelled out between wide fenced fields. Sedentary horses studied the intruder, then snorted and galloped away. John felt light rain on his face as his target steadily enlarged. Finding his way barred to the enclosure below the wood he took a circuitous road left, and climbed over a stile onto a grassy incline where the ground grew steep and moist underfoot – he began to feel embers of heat in his cheeks, exertion in his calves. But on and up he trudged, and soon he was stepping through a kissing gate into the cool gloom of Penshaw Wood.

Foliage made a dense canopy as he hastened along the trail. The sudden shrouded sense of hush, the deadened ash-greyness of surrounding trees, unsettled him somewhat – these and the silence, disturbed only by birdcalls and sounds of scampering in the undergrowth. A shadow lengthened in his mind. Somehow he was certain that another was present, dogging his steps – beside or behind him, in or out of the trees. He shook his head the better to clear it of such claptrap, for already through the treetops he could glimpse the apex of the temple's lofty pediment.

Then he made out something up ahead of him, wet and dank and crumpled in a pile next to a muddy puddle. Warily drawing near, he peered down. It was an anorak, dark blue, akin to that he wore himself, but smaller – as would fit a child – and slathered in muck. The protective coat, so roughly discarded, seemed the very evidence of something ugly, some misdeed. He spun and looked all about him in the gloom, feeling a hard pulse behind his ribs. No, he was too much alone here. His composure splintered. He began to jog, then to run.

The trail wound on interminably, indifferent to his escape; until some light seeped through the trees where a passage was seemingly dug out, and he scrambled up this boggy track – breaking out onto a hillside carpeted by high bright-yellow rapeseed, stretching for half of a mile under moody skies and a cordon of telegraph posts.

Recovering his breath, he stepped over a stile in a wire fence and made the trek up a stony path, his eyes now fixed on journey's end. It was taller than a dozen men, surely a hundred feet long, its porticos in a square of four-by-seven – a colossal achievement, as if transplanted from Periclean Athens. At closer quarters he saw the difference, the darkness – for those columns were blackened by coat upon coat of industrial cinder, made indelible by decades. In dismay he saw some crude scrapings into the stone, clearly the work of knives or chisels – 'I Lishman 1955', 'S P Evans 1972', 'Donk', 'Jass', 'Nipper', 'Buns', their claims on posterity more recent than Radical Jack's.

He hoisted himself up onto the broad stone base and paced the perimeter of the atrium. There was no roof, and rain had puddled between the uneven cobblestones. The aura was that of some queer semi-derelict outdoor theatre, amid a blasted heath, under a bleak sky, a place fit to offer Greek tragedy to uncomprehending locals. Or Shakespeare, perhaps – *Julius Caesar*? But there was a kind of grandeur here, no question: he would dare to call it a transcendency.

His spirits reviving, John turned around on his heels, surveying the panoramic views. But to the north the Wear Valley was not – he decided – so very much to write home about: naught but the industrial stacks and housing sprawls of Washington. Southward, Chester-le-Street and Houghton-le-Spring yawned out for drear miles, to no greater effect on the imagination.

The traffic noise from the motorway below was muffled by elevation and the rising wind. A strange depleted feeling stole over John, one he had grown to recognise and regret but to which he could give no name. It was a kind of sadness, banal to the taste, and yet it masked an ache like hunger. He wanted something, while knowing the want to be insatiable, unrequitable. There was something out there in the world, never to be his.

He hunkered down at the foot of a column and took his diary from his anorak pouch, thinking he might scribble awhile, as had become his wont. His universe was described therein, and he felt its miserable limits keenly. He was much too proud of his opinions, he knew – the effort he invested in them, the degree to which he fancied they set him apart from his peers.

'Shyness too is a vanity of man,' he murmured into his chest, and, liking the sound of that, he uncapped his pen and inked with care onto the rain-specked page.

'Divvint be shy,' said a voice from above.

John snapped his head toward the sound and found the speaker standing but a few feet away across the cobblestones. He was short and squat, clownishly overweight, clad in a black mackintosh. Moon-faced and pasty, his cheeks were unshaven, his black hair plastered over his brow.

John was mortified. The wind had blown him so deep into self-absorption he had assumed total solitude. And yet this lump of a man had clambered soundlessly up onto the Monument's base.

'Sorry,' John stammered.

'Divvint be sorry.'

The man's eyes were small and dark, his slight smile unwelcome.

'Were you looking for us?'

'Sorry? No.'

'Aw. Thought you might be looking for us.'

The man's fists had been sunk into his mackintosh pockets, but now he pulled out a chubby paw and gestured in the air.

'It's some thing this is here, eh? Some thing.'

Pushing his diary back into his anorak, John lifted himself from the cobblestone floor, not taking his gaze off this loon, the swell of whose pale belly sagged, voluptuous, between his unkempt pullover and beltline.

'Y'knaa what this stone is? Do y'knaa? It's grit-stone, this. *Grit-stone*. They call it God's own rock, them that knaa.'

John was on his feet, but cornered. He was taller, but the loon heavier – did that mean stronger? Or slower?

'Y'knaa how I knaa that, but? The stone? Cos it's me job. It *was* me job, any road.'

'Yeah?' John risked a few glances about him, in directions he might flee.

'Aye. And do y'knaa how they got them stones shifted up here? Do y'knaa *that*?'

John shook his head, thinking, *Walk away? Jog? Run?*

'They were carried by angels. *Arch*angels, like. Michael, and Raphael. And Urial, and Gabriel. And Lucifer. The most *bee-yoo-tiful*.'

The loon appeared most proud in his wisdom. Panic was throbbing anew in John's chest.

'I divvint believe in God, me, y'knaa? I'll tell you what, but, I'm so sure about the other. The other, aye. Cos I've *seen* him, that one. Seen him, in the corner. Do y'knaa him? His name, like? You *want* to. Shall I tell ya? Shall I? Come here, you.'

When the loon stepped toward him John felt the blood move his body, and he turned and leapt the five or six feet from the base onto the grass below, pitching face-forward. He scrabbled upright, his knees and ankles shouting in pain, forcing himself to run – and in that moment he heard the garrulous bark of a dog, then a terrier was bounding up and over the crest of the hill before him.

A human head-and-shoulders surfaced behind – a redhead female, some heavy-coated wifey. The woman looked at John and then, uneasily, beyond him, while her dog gambolled hither and thither at her feet. John strode unsteadily toward her.

'Are y'alright, pet?'

'I'm champion, thanks.'

He hastened past her, down the slope and onto Hill Lane, the pathway into safer, sparser woods from whence the woman and her dog must have come. Ten yards onward, his composure restored, he chanced a look behind him. But there was not a soul in sight, only the blackened Monument, inscrutable once more.

Book One

THE REVEREND GORE

Chapter 1

THE OUTSET

Thursday, 12 September 1996

'Can you help me, boss? Please?'

The beggarman, pained and unclean, stood between John Gore and where he needed to be – the concourse of London King's Cross, antechamber of the gateway to the north. The unbidden presence posed a question greater than he knew, one that Gore would rather have sidestepped on this bright and brisk morning, this day of all days.

As a rule he didn't fret unduly about whether one's good money should be doled out on request to the needy or distressed. His settled view – albeit the composite of a hundred different thoughts down the years – distilled into something quite simple. Yes, by such charity one soul was assisted, if only for the day; but why should the one be so favoured, when legions elsewhere were suffering the same or worse? Where was the social gain in a sole transaction? On the horns of this dilemma Gore was inclined to hang on to his so-called spare change, and if it betrayed an economy of pity – well, he forgave himself that much.

At this very moment, however, he was damnably late for a train. And so it was a small matter to fish a few coins from his pocket and be done.

As he rummaged, Gore threw glances all about him, anywhere but at the beggarman – his skin dry as a lizard, baseball hat tugged low, bomber jacket and jeans coated in dust as if he had crawled free from a collapsed building.

Finally he proffered a pound and some lesser bits, glancing to the platform clock above their heads. He had four minutes and seventeen seconds until his train pulled out of London. And yet, still, an urgent thought occurred.

'You're not going to buy alcohol, are you?'

'Fucking too right I will, boss, I'm an alcoholic.'

The beggarman's alarming grin was full of pale recessive gums. Gore's fist closed on the coins. The clock was running – four minutes and nine, eight, seven.

'C'mon boss.' Plaintive anew. 'Offies aren't open, are they? I just wanna sandwich, cup of tea. *Something*, please.'

Pointless, Gore knew, to stage an inquest. He dropped the coins into the outstretched hand, nodded to stall the man's clearly well-rehearsed abasement, and hastened his steps for platform 7, a heavy travel-bag in each fist, his coal-black topcoat flapping at his ankles.

'God bless, eh, boss? God bless!'

He shot a glance back over his shoulder to see the beggarman grinning scarily again, miming the tilting of some imaginary drinking receptacle to his lips, gulping down imaginary mouthfuls, and finally – *Bravo*, thought Gore – tossing the imaginary beaker aside to wipe his mouth with a grimy sleeve.

Doors slammed all down the deep-blue carriages of the Great North Eastern train, those not travelling waving their fellows goodbye. Gore kept moving, seeing only First Class insignia in every window, until he gave up and clambered aboard at the next open vestibule. Slipping down the aisle of a deserted carriage, noting its comfortable seating and places set for tea or coffee, he marvelled anew as to why he had been such a mule in asking his employers to stump up no more than the Standard Class fare. His own ingrained nature, so wearily familiar to him: he refused – he would always say – to set himself above others; wished, indeed, to live as though the option didn't exist. But then here he stood, at the outset of a major endeavour – maybe his life's work. Did he not *deserve* the simple courtesy, the teapot fetched to table, the individually wrapped biscuit?

A partition door fizzed open onto a Standard compartment thick with restless bodies and low din. Bulging suitcases and sports bags were being hoisted overhead, rowdy children entreated to sit, brown-paper bags full of burgers and milkshakes ferried from hand to hand across the aisle. Ahead of him were a pack of six big men sporting black-and-white striped football shirts, trying to insert themselves into parallel four-seat berths. One of these gents, his scalp clean-shaven, strained his shirt with an expanse of belly so luxurious he might have been carrying twins. Gore motioned as to squeeze by, and found the lads bleari-ly acquiescent.

He stowed his bags and counted his way down the aisle, seat number to seat number, until he came to his anointed place: 32 Facing. There, already installed and staring up at him, was a rotund teenager in a lime-green tracksuit, his broad face ruddy and belligerent. Beside him, a much smaller and leaner accom-plice in a red model of the same tracksuit peered out from under a black baseball cap, drumming his fingers on the tabletop.

'Excuse me, boys,' Gore offered, extending his ticket, earning only a harder glare.

'C'mon, lads,' he tried afresh. 'I think you'll find that's my seat.'

The bigger boy stirred, thumping his little friend on the arm. 'Aw bollocks man, it's the *cloth*.'

The titch, snorting, pointed a dirty finger at Gore. Then the two of them lurched from the seats and pushed their way past him, hooting. Gazing after their retreating backs, Gore poked a finger into the clerical collar snug at his throat, running it round to the nape of his neck. Other passengers were watching him with curi-ous eyes. He lowered himself into the warm vacated seat. Moments later, the train shuddered all through its length and set to rolling out of London.

In the seats opposite were a young couple, their hands clasped atop the table, making conspicuous her twelve-carat sparkler and silver wedding-band. She was dark-haired and wary-eyed. Her burly husband bulged out of a yellow polo-shirt, his heavy-fringed haircut one his mother might have given him.

The woman leaned over to Gore. 'Eee but I'm glad you got sat there, Father. Them little *beggars* . . .' She looked to the window, as though it were all too much, then back to Gore, as though she could not let it pass. 'I'd say it was your dog collar what did it, mind. Where do they *get* it from?'

Gore only shrugged, as to say it was a mystery. And as three they shared a desultory smile, reassured for the moment by the restoration of the peace, the coincidence of shared values.

Here as always Gore was quietly amused to find people of his own age or older so keen to address him as 'Father'. True, he wore the clothes of his calling, but it seemed to him a larger issue of persona – something to do with his standing six feet and three inches, or the speckles of silver in his thick black hair, belying his thirty-one years. The frowning cast of his features, too, had always aged him, not to speak of his grave demeanour. The latter, though, was a choice of his, a matter of personal style: Gore had always been of the mind that a good minister of God needed a touch of the actor about him.

He unfolded his newspaper and bit his lip at a front page reporting strife at the annual conference of the Trades Union Congress in Blackpool. BLAIR TO SEVER UNION LINK? Scanning the write-up he gathered that a few coming characters in the Labour Party – to which he had subscribed staunchly since his fifteenth birthday – had been mouthing off about policy at supposedly private dinners. Most likely, Gore assumed, in the hope that their unthinkable thoughts be controversially made public by the journalists in attendance. It was all too clearly the behaviour of a government-in-waiting, growing bumptious in the queue for succession. Amid a list of MPs quoted in defence of their brazen colleagues, Gore searched for, and was unsurprised to find, the name of the man who would be representing him before this day was done – Dr Martin Pallister, Labour member for Tyneside West, newly promoted Opposition Whip for Education and Employment. The man, indeed, for whom his older sister was employed as strategist, spin doctor and all-round major-domo. Susannah had always been a purposeful soul, and in Pallister she seemed to have found a prime focus for her energies. They made a team, sharing the same taste in good dark suits and well-minted phrases. Gore himself had first encountered Pallister more than a decade ago, when they were both scruffy lefties of a sort. Now the MP and his sister had joined the big push to revise Labour's gospels. That they were clearly effective in same did not allay his view that they were a gilt-edged disgrace.

His meditation was broken by murmurs from behind the outspread paper, and his arm was lightly tapped. It was the husband.

'I'm gannin' to the buffet car, Father, can I fetch you back owt?'

'Oh, well, actually I'd love a tea if it's no bother.'

Gore's hand went to his pocket, but the man was shaking his head and clambering out of his seat. His wife smiled. 'I'm Tina Grieveson, Father, how'd you do?'

'John Gore. Pleased to meet you.'

'Aw, likewise I'm sure. Me husband's Stuart.'

'A most considerate husband he is too.'

Stuart Grieveson returned bearing three plastic cups, a wad of napkins and a fistful of miniature milks. 'How far you gannin' the day then, Father?'

'Call me John, please. I'm for Newcastle.' He noted the recognition wrought by his horizontal vowels.

'Aw, you're *from* the north-east then?'

'I used to be,' Gore smiled. 'Been away a good while. But I'm back now. For work.'

'Aw, really?' A thoughtful silence. Tina made as to spit something out. 'And is it – as a *vicar* then? That you'll be working?'

Gore gestured down his collared and black-clad frame. 'No, as a circus clown.'

Stuart eked out a smile that persuaded his wife to follow suit. Gore felt they were all suitably at ease, and so grew expansive. 'No, that's right. What I'm doing, I'm going up to what they call *plant* a church.'

'"Plant", you say?' asked Tina.

'You mean start it from scratch, aye?' said Stuart. 'Build it out of nowt?'

Gore nodded, gratified by this speed of uptake, for he had been braced to deliver a longer explanation. 'That's right. It's funny, I'll be giving services in a local school to start with. Until we find out whether I can pull a crowd. The Church has its doubts, to be honest. But it's the fashion right now, you see. Not new churches, as such, more like new *sorts* of churches.'

'Where'll you have yours then?' Stuart asked. 'What bit of Newcastle?'

'Out west. Hoxheath?'

Stuart let out a low whistle. 'Dear me. What they call inner-city preaching, eh?'

Again Gore sensed a familiarity of terms. 'Are you churchgoers yourselves?'

'Oh yes,' said Tina. 'It's Gosforth where we are in Newcastle, we belong to a nice big congregation.'

'That'll be a blessing.'

'Oh it is. We have quite a brilliant young vicar, I must say, fella by the name of Simon Barlow. He's your age, probably. You don't know of him by any chance?'

Gore forced a smile while nodding into the brim of his tea, though it was as if he had just swallowed rat poison. These two were Anglicans, then – his own people – but of a markedly different stripe. Barlow had been his contemporary at Grey Theological College, and 'brilliant' was a wildly naive assessment. He knew too that any church where Barlow declaimed from the pulpit was bound to be evangelical by nature, its pews filled by solid suburban couples whose lives nonetheless had seemed listless and grey until the day they met a guy called Jesus.

'Hoxheath, but, good lord,' exclaimed Tina. 'You'll not be short of souls to save round there. Them little charvers what were in your seat? Plenty more of that sort in Hoxheath.'

He was familiar with such reactions, thought them snobbish, the knee-jerk of those who imagined an afterlife populated solely by their own 'sort'. Rather than cavil, he resorted to a stock tactic – smiling gently to himself, stirring his tea, meaning his silence to intimidate.

Stuart, though, was made of impervious material. 'So how in hell did you get lumbered wi' this job? I mean to say – you must've done summat awful to get sent to Hoxheath.' And he chuckled.

'Well.' Gore set down his plastic spoon. 'I was serving my title, as we say, down in Dorset, quite happily really. Then the Bishop of Newcastle came to me and said he had a plan for Hoxheath – for a few estates that weren't getting reached by the older churches. He needed a man, so he asked me if I'd take it on. I didn't think twice, really. I mean, I took it as a privilege. A duty, if you like.' This seemed to chase the condescending smiles from the faces opposite, so Gore ventured a sharper angle. 'It's a challenge, of course, I know. But that's what life's made of, isn't it? We can't run from it, we in the Church. We have to be out in the world. Among the people.'

'Aye, right enough,' offered Stuart, after a moment or two.

'Anyhow – it's just the world of work these days, isn't it? You go where you get sent, wherever you're told to. I was told to plant a church.'

And Gore shrugged, as to say that was the size of it. Still, just the simple stating of his mission – *I was told to plant a church* – resonated at his core. He would never phrase it so for the layman – much too pompous to be let away with – but these were the times when he believed he was about the work his Father intended.

Pleasantry had receded, silence settled. Gore withdrew his pen and notebook from his coat, and started to embroider some jottings he had made toward a sermon drawing on St John's account of the Good Samaritan. '*If any man hath this world's goods, and seeth his brother hath need, and shutteth up his bowels of compassion against him – how dwelleth the love of God in him?*'

Such a well-minted entreaty, the quintessence of his tradition – the stripe running up his own spine. Mother religion, 'the heart of a heartless world'. And yet with what ease did a well-wrought phrase become a platitude. What should be the segue? He scribbled quickly. '*As fellow Christians we are commanded to love our fellow man as ourselves. But it's not easy. We have all faced a stranger in need and said, "Not today friend, I have troubles of my own . . ."*'

No, he thought, setting down the notebook. Not easy, by no

means. Easy to *say*, for sure. Easy to say 'You must love'. Easier still to say 'But it's not easy'. All talk came easily. Anything worth doing was onerous. 'He that will eat the kernel must first crack the nut.' The point was to do it. Also to succeed in it? Gore was unhappily conscious that for large swathes of his life he had sat on plastic chairs in small aggrieved groups, listening to just this kind of pained debate – from Labour Party branch meetings to parish church councils and back again.

As for his sermon – no doubt it needed work, but he sensed it would repay the effort.

Oh river city, industrial seat, Victorian marvel of Newcastle . . .

If no one else in the carriage seemed greatly fussed, still Gore felt a fond sentiment kindling in his chest as their train trundled onto the King Edward Bridge across the River Tyne. The sky outside was overcast but daubed with patches of serene blue, a pale sun straining to burn through tufted clouds. He craned his neck in search of the best vantage from the window. To his right, stalwartly arrayed down the river's gentle bend, were four other crossings – their fulcrum the great radial green steel arch of the Tyne Bridge, a sight that filled Gore with boyish delight.

The general view he considered only a little tarnished by the faceless candy-coloured uniformity of offices and apartment blocks that seemed to have sprouted in clusters down the riverside toward the Crown Court – itself a blank, brute mica-pillared parody of classical form. Long gone were the derricks and trolleys and giant cranes, the colossal black trappings of heavy industry that formed the river landscape in picture-books Gore had pored over as a boy. But the banks of Gateshead now behind them were like one big building site – mounds of tilled earth, lying in wait for some forthcoming venture of labour and capital.

The train swung right toward Central Station, a shed of iron and glass looming up ahead, and then they were trundling under its high arched portico. Gore was quick on his feet and to the luggage rack, taking up his chattels and disembarking into the hub-bub of the afternoon, shafts of sky-light falling on the tiled con-course, its burger shacks, sports bars and ticket hutches. He had not to go far before sighting his promised welcome party: it could only be Mr Jack Ridley holding up a white card with carefully etched letters in black felt-tip, 'REV. JOHN GORE'. Ridley stood stock-still amid the bustling commuters, as if he had been rooted there dourly for years while the old Victorian station was slowly remodelled around his ears. A stocky man of medium height, probably in his late fifties, he wore corduroy trousers and Hush Puppies, an olive-green car-coat and a flat cap, some scant reddish hair curling out from under it. Though there was an affable aspect to his squashed nose and chubby cheeks, he was unsmiling, and something in his even, assessing gaze was flint-like – if not obsid-ian – as Gore drew near.

'Jack? I'm John.'

Gore's glad hand received a cursory clasp. 'How do then, Reverend.'

'You'll call me John, I hope.'

'Shall we's gan? I'm parked a canny way off.'

Ridley had wrested one of Gore's bags from his hand, wheeled and set off before Gore could quarrel. Indeed he sensed already that there would be little arguing with this man – either that, or a great deal.

'How long have you been active in the parish, Jack?'

Ridley, now in bifocals, was peering through his windshield with displeasure at a lady motorist reluctant to nose out onto the roundabout. 'Helpin' out, you mean? Whey, since we started gan-nin' to St Mark's up in Fenham, me and the wife – before I was retired, even. Before the new vicar started and all. I'll always help, but, where I can. If I'm asked to. I'm still at it, any road.'

Ridley refocused his riled attention on the traffic. Gore took a moment to decide where he might start decoding. 'The new vicar being Bob Spikings? My mentor-to-be?'

'Aw aye. He's alright, is Spikings. Not the worst.'

'And you're not working any more yourself?'

'Oh I've never stopped *workin'*, me. No fear. They laid us off, but, back in – must have been nineteen-eighty-six? When they shut down the County Council, y'knaa? Tyne and Wear. On the orders of bloody *Thatcher*.'

This last was virtually expectorated. Gore weighed his options before opening the next front. 'What kind of work did you do for the Council?'

'What I've always done. "Technical services" they called it. I'd been a carpenter and joiner, had me certificate in electrics. So if they'd problems in the housing I'd gan out and fix 'em. If they *could* be fixed, mind you, cos you'd see some bloody shambolic things, I can tell you.'

'And so – you're working freelance now, is that it?'

'"Freelance"?' The scowl endured. 'I s'pose. I'd a tool shop for a bit, but I got sick to the back teeth of little buggers breaking in. *I* wasn't making any money but the locksmith and the glazier got a wad out of us.' He gave his car horn a testy smack. 'And even then, y'knaa, I'd get neighbours coming round, some problem they'd want looking at. And what with me at the church so regular, I'd only be having me bit tea and biscuits after the service and Spikings'd bring owa some owld biddy. "Have you met wor Jack? Aw he'll sort you out . . ."'

Gore was not at all certain he would have actively sought the help of such a dyspeptic individual as this man seemed. Not that he was the type who would take a penny in return, that much was clear. Nevertheless, Gore did somehow suspect that for any favour Jack Ridley might grant, one would never quite stop paying.

'Well, I want you to know, Jack, I couldn't be more grateful to you. For agreeing to help me out like you're doing, with the starting up and so on.'

'Never you mind, son,' Ridley grunted. 'It'll not amount to much.'

They paused for traffic lights at Marlborough Crescent, Gore peering out at a sprawling construction site bounded by tall wire fences and boards proclaiming multiple sources of public money. Drizzling rain speckled the windshield. Ridley rummaged in his dashboard and produced a tin of mints which he flipped open with one thumb and offered to his passenger.

'You're on your tod, right? Nee wife or bairns?'

'Thas' right,' said Gore, settling a mint on his tongue.

'Huh. You're on the young side, I'd say. For the job you've got here.'

'I think,' Gore ventured, 'the Church believes that planting is a job best suited to the younger minister. In terms of the physical effort.'

Ridley looked askance. 'Whey, I wouldn't have this job of yours for the world. And I'm still in canny nick. Nah.' He shook his head. 'It's nowt to look at, Hoxheath. Oakwell Estate's not bad, the one where they've put you. They wanted to, mind. Some of them holes? Crossman Estate? Dear me *how*. I mean, look at that bliddy great tower block there.'

Gore followed Ridley's jabbing finger out of the window. *That* – he granted inwardly – *is one fuck-off big high-rise.*

'There's folk older than *me* stuck up there. You can't tell me that's right.'

Gore had the unhappy sense of being a coerced party to an argument. He wished to rebut, but held his tongue. The plain fact was that he had accepted this job with alacrity, yet without requesting a preliminary tour of his catchment area. Newcastle, he had reasoned, was where he was from – or near enough, at any rate.

They had broached the west of town. Rain lay in puddles for the dispiriting drive down the main Hoxheath Road – one darkened civic building, a succession of shabby commercial facades, takeaways and bookmakers, off-sales and newsagents. PUB KICKING: LATEST read a fly-poster on a sandwich board. A bus shelter looked to have been assailed with a sledgehammer. Turning off the main drag, Ridley drove past a gated industrial-heating factory, the surrounding grass evenly coated with fast-food litter and leavings. A lone telephone exchange box was adorned with a red-paint graffito: CRESSA CHOKES ON COCKS.

Gore turned his gaze back to the road, just in time to see a dark shape weave into view twenty feet shy of the car bonnet.

Ridley's foot went to the floor, he and Gore lurching forward, Gore's stomach turning over. Ridley hammered on his steering wheel in anger as a hooded boy, maybe twelve years old, scampered back to the safety of the pavement. Gathered there were others of his kind – a pack of them, in identical casual clobber. One cheerily clapped his pal on the back. Ridley thumped his car horn, three sharp blares. The tallest of the boys swivelled and issued a boldly defined middle-finger rebuke.

Moments later, the Fiesta pulled up into a row of parking spaces by a built-up wall and a fenced pathway into the Oakwell Estate. As Ridley locked up and checked each of his doors, Gore surveyed the dense cluster of low-rise properties, cheek-by-jowl, identikit in their yellow-brick construction and red-tiled roofs. The system of layout was immediately apparent – the small houses arranged in set squares, criss-crossed by long narrow alleys, orderly as a sheet of graph paper, though the alleys proposed a touch of menace. The last of the afternoon sun was a blessing for the moment, but Gore had begun to wonder about the level of lamplight after dark.

In silence they stood together in the sitting room, the small sum of Gore's worldly goods stacked all around them in sealed wooden crates, his bicycle pointlessly wrapped in paper and propped against a radiator in the hallway. A gloss-painted door yawned open onto a narrow fitted kitchen, off-white units crammed together in an awkward L-shape. A floor-to-ceiling window looked out onto a patch of enclosed lawn. The place was cold as stone and Gore knew by his nose that it had been recently wiped clean with bleached rags throughout. He traced a semicircle with the tip of his shoe on the carpet, a rough and bristly industrial textile in charcoal.

'That'll be black so the fag burns don't show,' said Ridley, returning from an inspection of the fuse-box in the hall.

'Oh, but they do,' murmured Gore, pointing his toe-cap at a crop of small scorched holes. He climbed the staircase that led from the sitting room to the upper quarters, and surveyed the cabin-like rooms. A turquoise bathroom with sink and shower tub, mildew leaching into the corners of the splash-back tiles. One decently sized bedroom and two cubbyhole spares, all with magnolia walls, Allied carpets and cheap pine-finish furnishings. He drew back a yellow voile curtain and peered out. Ridley was crouched on the lawn below, fingering the stem of a wilting plant. Gore headed downstairs again, keen to discharge the needful goodbyes.

'My wife,' said Ridley, unmoving, 'asked us to ask you if you'd like to have your tea at ours th' night.'

'Oh, that's very generous. I just have a feeling, you know – I'd like to make a start, crack on with things here?' He gestured around him, not wishing to offend, nor to lose the chance of a break from the steady barometric pressure of Ridley's company. Ridley, though, took several brooding moments before responding.

'Aye, well, I see that. You've got your work cut out.'

In the smallest bedroom he bolted together the panels of his collapsible desk, then unwrapped and wiped clean a framed print that he nailed into place above the worktop. The picture was a Byzantine mosaic of Christ Pantokrator, one that Gore had toted with him from place to place since seminary days. Generally wary of the graven image, he made an exception for Byzantine art. This Jesus was face-front and symmetrical, his forehead long and furrowed, features lean and lips pursed in a blank, unreadable mien. There was just a certain something in the rational, near-anonymous execution that rendered the son of God no more exalted than the man in the street.

As he wiped the glass he heard a sharp crack from out of doors, like the report of a starting pistol. *Christ*, was his thought. *Not a gun?* Then came a sizzling sound, airborne. *Okay, a firework. Surely?*

From a box file he retrieved a carefully pressed photocopy he had made of his catchment area from an Ordnance Survey section, and he Blu-tacked this to the wall beside Christ.

At just after three o'clock he lifted the telephone receiver, found it functional, and dialled the mobile number he had been given, its sequence still foreign to him. But the call was snapped up on the second ring.

'Hel-lo?' Mildly irritable, over background buzz and chatter.

'Suze. It's John.'

'Oh! Hello there, St John. Hang on . . . God, it's today, isn't it? Are you here?'

'Yep, just got in. Just getting settled.'

'And how's your new gaff? Is it really, really awful?'

'It's fine, I've no complaints.' Gore was never sure why his sister had ever strayed north of Watford again, having made home in London all through her twenties. Yet here she was, a mere few miles from where he sat as the crow might fly.

'And have you spoken to Dad yet? Have you fixed to go and see him?'

'I haven't. Not yet. I will.'

'Look, you've got to see him, John. He's talking about going back to work again. With electrics and whatnot. And God knows what he could do to himself, the state he's in.'

'Suze, we've been through this, that's rubbish.'

'John, it's dementia. Or some sort of clinical daftness, I'm telling you. He's getting nearly as stupid as you.'

Further pleasantries were exchanged, but Gore could taste the usual tartness in their conversation, one that did not conclude with a pledge from either party to pay a call upon the other.

In fading light he pulled on his topcoat, addressed the Chubb, Yale and mortise locks of his new front door, and walked out into Oakwell's long corridors. Rain was still palpable, but merely a mist. Strung across the full lengths of many a tightly boxed back-yard were crammed lines of jeans, knickers and bright synthetic sportswear, lemon-yellow, lava-pink, slowly soaking.

He set out northward, planning a stroll of an orderly square half-mile that would return him to his door. Passing the heating factory, crossing Hoxheath Road, he turned east, past a scrappy patch of parkland in the shadow of a cluster of twenty-storey high-rises. Modular and Scandinavian, they had once proclaimed the future, perhaps, but they were forlorn and weather-beaten now. On the horizon east, St James's Park football ground sat impregnable as a castle above its environs.

Trudging on, Gore passed a small estate where brown-skinned children hopped and skipped in the street, and the signage appeared to be entirely in Sikh. The next estate was Blake, little two-storey abodes in stained grey brick. Toiling up a poor-looking road of grocers and bric-a-brac shops, he made note of the Netto supermarket, its trolleys chained in a row like a listless gang of labourers. The houses now were back-to-back terraces, split by long alleys, their high yard walls topped by cruel shards of glass. On the street corners lads in caps loped and loitered in pairs, seemingly restless but not going anywhere. Gore kept his head low and felt happier once he reached the vast precinct of the General Hospital, before turning south and heading down past a quiet stretch of semi-detached houses that restored him to Hoxheath Road. Past a dank-looking carpet warehouse and a bed-frame superstore, past a row of small shopfronts embattled behind grilles, and the office of Tyneside West Labour Party, VOTE PALLISTER in smart red capitals. To his right were long slopes of Victorian terracing declining in the direction of the Tyne's old grey waters, and a mass of riverfront industrial works now rendered into disused warehouse space.

The Scoular Estate proposed a minor advance on Blake: solid red-brick construction, some good iron fencing, some decent garden plots. Gazing up and over the rooftops Gore made out the green-and-gold cap of a mosque, and he detoured from the main drag for a closer look. In its shadow was a squat, unlovely pub – The Gunnery by name – and a so-called YOUTH CENTRE, a breezeblock hut with a flat roof and poky high windows like a changing room for school sports. Its front doors were bolted but a quartet of boys sat outside, smoking, on a railed concrete ramp. Even from twenty yards Gore could smell something acrid on the air.

And now, unavoidably in front of him, was the Crossman Estate. A more grimly gimcrack construction he could not have imagined: brick and clapboard buildings, erected with what could only have been a callous disregard for time and weathering – dreadfully rotted window frames, low wooden fences hardly worth kicking down, front doors with numbers chalked or painted on. Stupefying amounts of rubbish were strewn about the place – not merely foodstuff and discarded wrappings, but industrial pallets, broken-backed recliners, a knackered fridge, a punctured ball. Pigeons clustered and strutted about with an air of proprietor's ease.

It was sensory overload of a sort – more pure bleakness than Gore could fully assimilate. There had to be lives going on behind these terrible facades, the actual condition of which he was going to have to determine. But the evening chill felt much the harsher now, and he decided for the time being to suspend his enquiries into the condition of the English working class.

Chapter II

FACTS OF LIFE

On secular occasions when it was asked of John Gore quite why he chose the vocation of Anglican priest, he had two responses ready to hand – one for such inquisitors as seemed to respect the life of the spirit, the other for those who appeared, affably or otherwise, to be taking the piss. Parties of the former were favoured with his best recollection of a moment in his early twenties when, breaking rocks in the Auvergne region of France, he had – for want of a less worn expression – 'felt the call'. As for the piss-takers, Gore told them that he came from a little village in County Durham by the name of Pity Me, and so resolved from an early age to go forth and pity others.

It was a one-street town within the parish of St Cuthbert, and John grew to know its contours as well as the nose on his face. Northward sat the more populous Chester-le-Street, and ten miles on lay Newcastle, as much as he could then imagine by way of a metropolis. But to stray a mere mile south was to enter the environs of Durham City, with its grand Norman castle, hallowed cathedral and esteemed university college. Pity Me and its near neighbour Framwellgate Moor had been founded on Front Street in the nineteenth century, per the needs of the coalmining industry, for both squatted over St Cuthbert's share of the vast Durham coalfield. But local mining had dwindled to a halt by the 1920s, the workers forced to shift to nearby Bearpark or to Easington on the coast. By the time of John's adolescence, Framwellgate's 'Old Pit' was buried far beneath a fenced depot belonging to the County Council, and the villages were mere dormitory suburbs of the city.

The Gores lived but a stone's throw from Front Street in a tidy red-brick close, their semi within sight and earshot of a thundering bypass that carried cars and lorries down to Darlington and, further yet, to that other place called THE SOUTH. And yet John always bore the vague conviction that he had received a rural upbringing. From his bedroom window he would spy on two languid chestnut mares kicking their heels in a secluded field. Many a local estate bordered on woodland that could turn surprisingly thick, albeit scythed through by bridleways. This much John learned of County Durham from the seat of his Raleigh Grand Prix bike, and he grew fond of the way in which invisible borders were traversed and works of man receded, while fresh vistas and tracts of green space opened up – stretches of field and farmland, fences of post and wire, horses and shabby-fleeced sheep.

He found Durham rich, too, in place names that struck him as novel and fantastical – Craghead, Monk Hesleden, Quaking Houses. One evening over the family's tea he stated his intention to cycle five miles out to Sacriston, the invoking of which seemed to fill him with an instinctual piety. But his father Bill only creased his brow in a familiar manner that cancelled all debate. 'Whey, it's just a bloody pit village, John.' And from the far coast of the kitchen table Susannah let out a short scoffing laugh.

Only Granddad Alec ever saw fit to indulge the boy's fancy in this area.

'Have you ever been to *no place*, bonny lad?' Such was his stock query. John would giggle, only for Alec to make a great show of rueful head-shaking and produce from his pocket a square of yellowing paper, unfolded carefully into an Ordnance Survey. And there indeed, at the end of Alec's fingernail – and really no further than another five-mile jaunt up the road – was NO PLACE, CO. DURHAM.

Alec was broad-shouldered and forthright in any social gathering. Bill was whip-thin and pensive, prone to the silent chewing of a thumbnail. Alec's capacities looked to be distributed evenly about his sturdy physique, while Bill's seemed to have migrated entirely upward, to that furrowed brow beneath a helmet of prematurely silvered hair. And while Bill was perennially unkempt, living in cardigans and corduroys far past their good wear, Alec clad himself always in a three-piece of black gabardine with a pressed and collarless white shirt, the fine strands of his own snowy hair brilliantined back across his scalp.

John knew in his bones that Dad and Grandad were very different men, but the grown-up world mystified him such that he couldn't quite see why. The facts known to him were that Alec had worked in a coalmine for twenty years, his cheeks pockmarked by tiny shards of anthracite, before he was granted promotion to a managing role in the pit welfare fund. Whereas Bill drove a yellow van all round the locality, and made people's telephones work. Why one job for money bested another was unclear to John. He assumed only that if people worked hard then they got their just desserts, but Dad and Granddad seemed not quite to concur on this point, at least on those evenings that they spent supping beer and disputing matters in the parlour by the three-bar fire.

Their regular schism was over the Labour Party – which, if Bill was believed, embodied all things slovenly in the world, even though he had once subscribed keenly to his local branch. But Alec still lived and breathed Labour. And as far as John could see, the very facts of life in the region were Labour through and through. This, though, was precisely his dad's point.

It seemed to have a perplexing amount to do with houses – how they were built, and then allocated, by the Labour council. 'Rotten,' Bill decreed. 'All out for themselves.' John thought he would never hear the end of T. Dan Smith or Alderman Andrew Cunningham. If Bill was believed, scarcely a new home got built in the north-east but for Smith profiting by the very bricks and mortar. 'He pays them who decide what gets built,' Bill fumed, 'then the bloody builders pay *him* for the job.'

'How is that allowed?' was John's falsetto contribution.

'Aw, it's not against the law, son. Would you credit that? A blind man can see it's all wrong. But owld Smith, he gets away with it, see, cos they're *all* rats. All in each other's bloody *pockets*, man.'

This was where Alec would clear this throat heftily and remark that not all parties should be tarred by the same brush. Bill, though, was merely warming to the topic of Alderman Cunningham – the 'Baron', as he was known, and John pictured a caped and moustachioed villain trussing a damsel to a railway track.

'How many jobs has that bugger got, eh? He's running Labour in Durham. Running General and Municipal union. Twenty-grand house he's got in Chester-le-Street. And his bliddy *son*'s an MP. How'd he fix *that* up, eh?'

'He was *elected*, Bill. Him *and* his lad.'

'Whey, Dad, man,' Bill scorned. 'A bliddy *parrot* in a red rosette could hold that seat. Labour Party looks after none but itself.'

'So you'd have the Tories, would you? Eh? Is that what you want?'

This seemed to be Alec's *coup de grâce*, for Bill would lapse into the stoniest silence.

It was a flag-day in the Gore house when Dan Smith was packed off to prison along with the Baron and another crony, some Yorkshire architect. For Bill the joy was tempered by the return of Labour's avuncular Mr Wilson as prime minister. John had thought his teachers would throw a party, so keen was their pleasure. But 'Owld Wilson', Bill was adamant, had benefited by a miners' strike, of which Bill didn't approve. Bill thought the miners selfish, saboteurs – whatever the sins of the Tories. Precisely what his father *did* admire in this seamy world, John had no clue. He could see, though, that Alec let no slur on the miners go unchallenged.

The modest bungalow where Alec lived alone was the gift of the Durham Aged Mineworkers' Association. John's mother, too, had been a miner's child, and when she was no older than his age something had happened at Easington Colliery so dreadful that it could hardly be spoken of thereafter.

'They had an explosion, see,' Alec told John on one of the boy's Saturday visits, as he sat in a deckchair watching his granddad pull up leeks in the small walled back garden. 'It was all cos of some sparks come off the cutting machine, when they'd *methane* gas in the air. Dreadful it were. Eighty-one men, dead and gone.

And your mam's dad,' he sighed, 'Herbie, he was one of 'em. Did y'knaa that?'

John nodded dumbly. But he had not. And he wasn't sure he wished to know more, for the whole world of that work, the pit-shaft and the black seam, wore a grim, forbidding aspect.

John inherited Bill's gangling leanness, but his mother was portly, for she relished good meat and gravy and all sorts of pies and pastries, sugared or savoury. She was partial, moreover, to a sweet wine or a sherry, and the odd furtive cigarette. She wore her thick hair in a curly mop at the front and a bunch tethered at the back and there was a dolefulness to her eyes, accentuated by the bags and the slab-like frames of her spectacles. She was no beauty – a plump mole on her cheek and a lugubrious long philtrum under her nose. But her smile was warm, serene, and suggestive of intellect. Her regard for local history led her to found a Pity Me Society, though it never found sufficient members to justify a meeting. Thwarted, she transposed her energy to instructing John on the monastic tradition of the area – how the monks of Lindisfarne bore St Cuthbert's coffin to Chester-le-Street, so founding a community that would become the episcopal county palatinate. Weekly she marched her children down Front Street to Sunday School at the church hall of St Aidan's, and on bright mornings set fair for games it seemed to John a huge injustice that he be dragged once more to that dusty hall.

St Aidan's was a plain stone chapel built for the miners, set in leafy grounds behind the modern prefab hut where John was taught his Bible stories. At first he found these lessons about as appealing as the monthly visit to Terry the Barber over the road. But he tarried with his peers while a chubby young woman led them through illustrated books describing the travails of Abraham and Isaac, Joseph and his brothers, and other strangely bearded men in robes and sandals. The tales began to exert a charm – not least that of Joseph, who long suffered the disdain of those brothers, only to realise his destiny in Egypt. In due course John joined Audrey in the chapel, since Bill and Susannah had other things to do. He was not fond of hymnals, oblivious to boring stretches of the service, but keenly attendant to his own imagination, piqued as it was by images and concepts of pilgrimage and mission, of Potiphar's wife and the Pharaoh's dream, seven lean years and seven years fat.

Allegedly Bill too had been book-smart as a boy, but his schooling was curtailed at sixteen, whereupon he drew his first wage as an apprentice at Bearpark Colliery. He never took to it: not the place nor the people, nor the noisy, filthy, ill-rewarded graft. Instead he had the wit to sign up for and cycle to a night-school class, and won a trainee position as an installations engineer for Post Office Telecommunication.

In John's eyes his father appeared the consummate workman in helmet, overalls, belt and boots, climbing toolbox in hand from his Bedford utility van, emblazoned with a decal of a fat orange parrot in a vest exhorting passers-by to MAKE SOMEONE HAPPY. Whenever John peeked at the innards of that van he would boggle at the unruly forest of drop-wire, the hanging baskets of insulators, gravity switches, surge arrestors and sockets. The truly daunting fact was that his father operated solo, beginning work out by the pole on the street, up a ladder with a dispenser drum, and concluding it within the hour by the skirting of the customer's hallway. Granted, Bill was less adept at conversing with these customers, many of them wary of what he might do to their paintwork with his drill. John couldn't imagine how his fretful father managed such exchanges.

But these were only a portion of the complaints he would hear from across the kitchen table. It was a source of inordinate ire to Bill that, 'in this day and age', the nation's telephone network should still be part of the Post Office – that the poles up which he shinned each day were government property. 'You see that?' Bill would jab a finger at the black bakelite phone on the Gores' hall table. '*That's* not ours. We *rent* that. It's bloody *Soviet*, man.'

'Why don't you tell *them* then? Give 'em what for?' Such was the view of Susannah, very much her father's daughter, fifteen-year-old Saturday girl at Boots the chemist in Durham.

'Whey, you'll never ever change 'em, Sue. Not the jobsworth brigade.'

In Jubilee Year the Gores moved to a three-bedroom house on Durham Moor Crescent, closer still to the city. Bill's fierce proficiency seemed to be getting its due. In only one small respect was he a little unmanned before his family. On certain mornings after he had stepped from the house, as John and Susannah dawdled over cereals, the golden van remained stationary in the driveway for some minutes, until Audrey dropped the latch and dashed to the driver's window. Apparently Bill would sometimes climb into the front seat and jam the key into the ignition only to discover he had forgotten entirely where he was going. Audrey began to fret. She spoke of her worry to John now and then. She had tried confiding in Susannah, who merely informed her, with seeming sangfroid, that telephones emitted microwaves and could yet fry Bill's brain over time, if it were not already toasted.

One pale autumnal Sunday John strode forth ahead of Audrey, from Durham Market Place down cobblestones and past the shopfronts of Saddler Street, a short distance thence to the narrow steep-winding path of Owengate which drew the pilgrim toward the broad enclosure of the Palace Green. As he trudged directly up the middle of the road, he began to hear a deep-reverberating peal of bells. Then Durham Cathedral revealed itself, sat in colossal assurance over its surroundings, five hundred feet wide from east end to west.

This, by John's estimation, had to be what was commonly known as a work of art. And yet he could just as easily suppose the Cathedral had always been there, rising but gradually from the earth over a thousand years – like an iceberg, its sculpted summit a mere fraction of a truly awesome depth. The almighty clang of bells persisted, their shudder and judder lording over the Green, tearing the air, dispelling any rival claim. Everything in John hammered and resonated in kind.

Within the walls, cool and calm prevailed. All visitors were pacified, made respectful. John wandered down past the massive stone columns that flanked and dominated the nave, each minutely and geometrically patterned, supporting great arches that lured the eye up to a ribbed and vaulting ceiling. Craftsmanship and handiwork, impossibly fine! *This* was the model of how God should be glorified.

He sat awhile in the pews, peering at a huge circular rose window set high in the east end – Christ in majesty, ringed by solemn saints. The light so cast was rare within this great shadowy space, and yet it seemed to John there was no want of translucence, as if some form of light were emanating through the very walls. Everything felt heightened, every step meaningful. Some visitors lit penny candles. Many more sat stolid, heads bowed. John wished to give his feeling a physical expression, some gesture of respect. He went to a column midway down the nave, traced on it with a finger, then pressed his cheek against the chill granite.

He found his mother again, drifting down the nave.

'I always get the shivers a bit in here,' she murmured.

'Do you want my jumper?' John enquired.

'No, pet, I mean it just *feels* cold to us. The mood of it. It's beautiful and all that, of course. But there's no . . .' She shrugged. John could not concur. Audrey seemed to read as much. 'Well of course,' she added quickly, 'it's a very special place.'

She paid ten pence and lit a candle, then they walked back by the west side, Audrey pausing before an alcove in which was set a coal-black memorial feature, etched with gilt letters, winged cherubs flying up both sides. An extravagant basket of flowers was placed on a step below. Suspended to the left, above the creamy pages of a book of remembrance, was a brass candle-lamp, which John recognised as identical to one Alec kept on his mantelpiece in Langley Park. He followed his mother's gaze to the gilt inscription.

REMEMBER BEFORE GOD
THE DURHAM WORKERS WHO HAVE
GIVEN THEIR LIVES IN THE PITS

OF THIS COUNTRY AND THOSE WHO
WORK IN DARKNESS AND DANGER
IN THOSE PITS TODAY

John clasped his hands across his groin, straining to recall what little Alec had mentioned of that immemorial explosion at Easington. Eventually he chanced a glance at Audrey. But she was pressing a forefinger on the bridge of her spectacles between closed eyes, rubbing distractedly, and there was nothing he could read but that she was 'cold', tired, ready for home.

The Gore household had seemed at peace on a Sunday afternoon in high June, with Alec lodged in the visitor's armchair, mugs of tea getting supped and cold meat pie consumed. Alec sucked his dentures for a while, looked first at John, then to the settee where Bill and Audrey sat.

'I was thinkin', does the bairn maybe fancy coming wi' us to big meeting?'

Bill blew out his lips as to say the thought hadn't occurred. Audrey was nonplussed. 'I doubt our John's one for a miners' gala.'

John knew his father's dislike, and his mother's worry – that he dallied too much around Alec, failed to consort with his peers. But at least he wasn't knocking about with all the little terrors at the shopping precinct. And Big Meeting was known to be a grand day out. Still, when he raised his voice to express a preference, it felt nonetheless like a minor treason.

Saturday, 15 July 1978, and the done thing for Big Meeting, it seemed, was to go by bus and get there by nine. So John rode a mere handful of stops and disembarked near the County Hospital. There stood his granddad, imperturbable in black gabardine, toting two plastic carriers – one stacked with Tupperware boxes, the other with four pint-bottles of Federation beer.

'Got your bit bait, have you, son? What's your mam given you?'

John proffered up a single sandwich wrapped in tinfoil. It

seemed a small package in the sunlight, next to Alec's heavy load.

They stood and watched brass bands congregate at a car park in the shade of the railway viaduct. Chartered coaches and minibuses were arrayed in row upon row, their drivers in huddles, shaking off fatigue over a flask and a fag. Bandsmen were in stages of undress, vests visible between brass buttons, their gleaming instruments sat in cases on the gravel. Spot-checks and impromptu rehearsals were afoot, and the grainy ululation of bagpipes, emanating from one lone clan in kilts, rose above the parps of brass. The scale and seeming import of the day began to get its hooks into John – so many souls, ebulliently certain of why they were gathered.

'How, there's my team owa there.' Alec steered him toward a set of bandsmen congregated round the banner of Langley Park Colliery that several pairs of hands were carefully unrolling. John gave his firmest handshake to each man and woman, and his granddad accepted a bottle of beer – this at nine-thirty in the morning. As John rehearsed his surprise, Alec decanted half the beer into a Tupperware tooth-mug and handed this to John with a wink, before treating himself to a healthy swig from the lips of the pint bottle. John sipped cautiously at the sharp-tasting froth, and found it not unpleasant.

They moved off en masse through Durham's narrow streets, crossing the Wear by the broad Framwellgate Bridge, and climbing the steep cobbled Silver Street to congregate in Market Place square. John was mutely stunned, Alec a shade wistful. 'It's canny, but it's not what it was. Should have seen it thirty year ago.'

Kicking his heels as others made busy, John found himself for the first time making close inspection of the square's main statue, a huge impassive hussar rearing on horseback, plated with copper of a greenish corroded hue. The engraving identified CHARLES WILLIAM VANE STEWART, MARQUESS OF LONDONDERRY.

'You admiring his lordship?' Alec was at John's shoulder, sour-faced. 'If he could step down off of there I'd knock his block off. Biggest and worst mine-owner in all Durham, that one. Eh, Hughie?'

By Alec's side was a rheumy-eyed old fellow wearing a dark Crombie overcoat in defiance of the sun. 'Londonderry?' the old fellow responded. 'Aw aye. If he were still about the day he'd be packing *this* un off doon the bloody pit.' And with gnarled fingers Hughie rattled John's shoulder.

All around men had begun shouting, clapping and calling to order. Trumpets were being raised to lips, drums strapped onto chests, banners lofted and marchers arrayed. Two of Alec's comrades lifted poles, their wives clutched the stabilising ropes, and the name of Langley Park was hoisted high. John peered all about him at a tide of Durham place names, thirty or more, festooned in many colours. Langley Park was decorated with a painting of the 'Sam Watson Rest Home'. Other banners offered multiple portraits of whiskered and sober-suited gents, presumably local heroes – John counted half a dozen images of one Keir Hardie. Some favoured uplifting exhortations: 'Unity is Strength', 'Workers of the World Unite!' John was more taken by the biblical scenes on display: East Hetton Lodge, adorned with a vivid storybook painting of the Good Samaritan stooping to tend the unfortunate traveller, underscored by the legend 'Go Thou And Do Likewise'.

The march began as a short but congested journey down the hill. Soon it was obvious to John that progress would be hopelessly slow. The old snaking streets were crammed with bodies. As they shuffled, John took care not to tread into groups of men sat by the kerbside in shirtsleeves, nursing cans and bottles, calling out merrily. The ale had worked a little magic on his own spirits. He sensed a breakaway of some bodies moving up Saddler Street in the direction of the Palace Green.

'Are we going to the Cathedral?' he asked Alec.

'Nah, son, we're for the racecourse. Some do, later on. There's a service to get their banners *blessed* and that.' The scorn in Alec's mouth John thought odd and uncommon. They shuffled onward. Alec, though, seemed dissatisfied with the manner in which he had expressed himself. 'I'll tell you summat, mind. Y'knaa how after the war, the government, they bought up the mines for the country?'

John nodded, though he didn't entirely follow.

'Cos before that, they were just the property of the big knobs, y'knaa? And none of them buggers gave a tinker's toss for their men, right? But I'll tell you who else got fat off owning the mines in the old days, and that was Dean and Chapter of Durham Cathedral. What do you think of that, eh?' Alec's eyes were chilly blue as always, but his cheeks were mottled. 'Aw aye, there's two sides to Durham, bonny lad. Never the twain shall meet.'

The incremental progression carried them over the Old Elvet Bridge, and they paused in unison outside the Royal County Hotel. From a balustrade balcony two floors up a welcoming party waved down, some with conspicuous raised fists. John recognised Durham's Mayor, bloated in civic regalia, pressed in on all sides of the standing room by a congregation of men in grey suits and their good ladies.

'Are they all important?' John enquired of Alec.

'They reckon they are. The fat fella?' Alec pointed at a bespectacled gent with a bulbous, near luminous nose. 'That's Heffer, he's in the government. Ginger nut beside him, that's Scargill, big man in the union. They'll be boring us stiff wi' speeches later on.'

Langley Park turned its banner toward the balcony. The band formed up facing the same way, and struck up a tune. The lordly ones gazed down as the opening bars rose upward, bearing with them immediate cheers and applause from the gathering. The guests turned to one another, then joined in the singing, looking to Gore's eye for all the world as though they were lined up in church. One suit even put his hand to his breast, trying, it seemed, just a tad too hard. Everybody knew the words.

'Though cowards flinch, and traitors sneer, we'll keep the red flag flying here . . .'

It seemed to John that if there was drunkenness abroad now, it was not liquor alone that had lifted spirits. Even Alec's voice was lusty in the chorus, and he seemed, as Audrey might say, proud as Lucifer.

Durham Racecourse Ground was a well-trodden carpet of green under the sun, munificently set with stalls and fairground attractions. The heat of the day had risen, the atmosphere thick with noise and smell. John stood with Alec as Langley Park's banner was dismantled. Beneath the shade of a tree a short distance hence, a thickset chap with meaty sideburns was bent over, one hand on the trunk, vomiting onto the ground. Hughie shouted over cheerily. 'That's it ya bugger, get it out!'

Alec was quick to press coins in John's palm and urge that the boy avail himself of the entertainments. 'Nee fun for you, sittin' with a load of old pit yackers.' But John wasn't mad for chips or candyfloss, nor did he fancy testing his strength or aim. It didn't seem wholly appropriate. Instead, while the men munched their sandwiches, John sat and stole looks at Tommy, a lanky man, milky-eyed and jug-eared, his crinkled forehead topped by startlingly vertical tufts of grey hair. But it was Tommy's right hand that transfixed him, guiltily, for it had somewhere and somehow suffered the loss of the four fingers, now rendered down to smooth white nubs of skin. Finally John must have looked a little too long. Tommy caught his eye and raised the wounded hand in the air between them, sharp as a warning. John felt himself blanch.

'You after the tale of this then, kidder? Is that it?'

But there seemed no affront in Tommy's piping high voice. Nor did the others look bothered. 'Aye, gan on, Tom,' murmured Alec. 'Give him the story.'

'It were, what? Twenty-eight year ago now? I was on back-shift, right near the end of it, more's the pity. And this bliddy great coal truck – well, the dreg on it was fettled, see? It come down on wuh so fast I couldn't get out the road. So it went right owa this here hand. Quick as a wink. I can still feel it now when I think.'

John had flinched. With the fingers of his good left hand, Tommy took a consoling grip of the dorsum of his right. 'Now your grandda – him being the deputy – he ran and fetched us a bit bandage and that, from the first-aid box. Cos he was good like that, your grandda. And wor marras got us up and out, sharp as they could. Hugh here, he was banksman, see? He did the cage, got us to surface. Doctor from the ambulance station were ready for wuh. I knew, but, in me'sel. That was me done. Ruined, y'k-naa? Stupid thing, but. It shouldna happened.'

Tommy paused and trailed his good fingers over some tufted blades of grass. John felt a shiver run through him, heedless of the sun's warmth. He realised, mortified, that his eyes had moistened, and he ducked his face into his chest.

Tommy looked up. 'Aye, that was how ah felt and all, bonny lad. I'll tell you this, but. I passed out for a bit, after, while the doctor were seein' to us? When I come round, he were stood over wuh, all solemn, like. And he says, "Tommy, son, now listen, I've stitched you up, and you'll be grand. But I'm very sorry to have to tell you – you'll not play the violin ever again."'

Seasoned chuckles in the group. Tommy was pulling a music-hall face of dismay. 'I says, "Eee, doctor! Divvint tell us that, man, I'm down to give a recital in the club Tuesday neet . . ."'

John watched the old men, their sides heaved with suppressed jollity. The sudden levity he found yet more impressive than the earlier stoicism, and he rubbed at his wet cheek. Alec's eyes were on him. 'Are y'alright there now, bonny lad?'

John swallowed, nodded. 'It's just, it's not bloody fair is all,' he said into his chest. He had thought himself barely audible but when he looked up, Alec was grinning in a skewed manner at his old pals. 'Whey, d'you hear that, eh? He's a Labour man, this lad. Red-hot Labour in the making, why aye.'

A ways across the field a brass band struck up, a deep mournful swelling that brought forth applause. John felt himself stir. For the duration of the opening bars he was sure he was hearing 'The Lord is My Shepherd', or some variation on the same. But on all sides of him it was a different set of words that Langley Park were singing or mouthing. John listened with care, until there came a great final surge of brass, a crash of cymbals, and words that seemed the stuff of hymnal.

O saviour Christ, who on the cruel tree, for all mankind thy precious blood has shed
In life eternal trusting, we – to thy safe keeping leave our dead.

He looked to Alec, who nodded a grudging respect amid the louder acclamation.

In the dwindling days of that summer they gathered at Alec's bungalow, under the sober supervision of Armstrong's Undertakers Ltd. Bill was one of six who bore the coffin out into the street, Alec's Langley Park mates Hughie and Tommy among the others. Carefully they lowered and passed the casket into the compartment of a horse-drawn hearse, tethered to two placid pit-ponies dressed with black plumes.

Alec had fallen by his own garden-gate, angina pectoris the stealthy killer, and left behind no instructions for his interment. Bill addressed the needful formalities with a certain grousing scepticism. 'There's nee point the Church putting a mark on a man in death when it never laid a finger on him while he was living.' Yet he recalled one matter on which his father had been most specific, and that was cremation. 'He always said to me, "From naught I came, and to naught I'll return."' It was then a simple matter for Bill and Audrey to agree that the minister of Langley Methodist Chapel, one Charles Casson, should preside.

Lined up in a pew with his family, wearing the scratchy suit in which he had been confirmed, John found that the austerity of the Methodist service appealed to him. Yet he could not shake the obdurate suspicion that it did not quite become his grandfather, a man who had been so very much alive. There was no changing the protocol, though, not now. And when bade to do so, the congregation stood as one to sing 'Abide with Me'. They remained on their feet as Casson offered a prayer.

'Merciful God, we commend our brother Alexander to your perfect mercy and wisdom, for in you alone we put our trust.' All eyes settled upon the oaken casket set squarely upon the catafalque. *'Forasmuch as our brother has departed out of this life, we therefore commit his body to the elements – ashes to ashes, dust to dust – trusting in the infinite mercy of God, in Jesus Christ Our Lord.'*

Staring at that coffin, John felt an inner hollow he had carried all day now fast filling up with panic. For it seemed to him, very suddenly, that this whole function had been far, far too orderly – indeed premature, remiss – to have arrived so starkly at its terminus. It was in the stillness of this fraught moment that Casson raised his head from a seemingly ruminative pause. *'I heard a voice from heaven saying, "From henceforth, blessed are the dead who die in the Lord." "Even so," says the Spirit. "For they rest from their labours."'*

At John's side Bill nodded gently. A hatchway opened slowly in the wall behind the catafalque, and the belt-driven mechanism began to convey the coffin by inches toward its final destination.

Bill drove the family to the Working Men's Club where it was arranged that all friends and well-wishers be made welcome. To John's surprise the reception was a concertedly jolly affair. Everybody got drunk, or attempted the feat. His father, meanwhile, surprised him, for there were a few jokesters among the gathering and Bill consorted freely with them at the bar, joining in a loudly disputed game of darts. It dawned upon John that Bill had a social circle all of his own, some kind of sodality drawn from work and the local cricket club. After he had sat watching their game awhile, it was big rubicund George Bell who staggered away from the oche and offered his darts to John, insistent that 'the lad couldn't do worse'.

'You'll miss your granddad then, son?' Bell remarked as they loitered together, his arrows swapped for a large Bushmill's. John nodded mutely. Bill stepped in, seemingly desirous of speaking for his son. 'Aye, they were proper pals, him and his grandda. Weren't you? Went off to the Big Meeting together not three month ago.'

'Aye, aye?' Bell winked. 'All the comrades together, eh?'

'Well, he's a lefty, this one, see,' said Bill. 'Young communist. Fancies that Russia's a little workers' paradise.'

'Aww, divvint be telling us that,' groaned George.

John was riled by the seeming slur. It was perfectly true that he had borrowed a Pelican paperback of *The Communist Manifesto* from the library, and had expressed interest in nearby Chopwell village where the streets were rechristened in honour of great Soviet personages – Lenin Terrace, Marx Avenue. But in these pastimes he felt sure he was merely tugging at a red thread that had attracted his eye. 'I never said I was a communist,' he murmured.

'Good job and all, son,' said George. 'Mind you, your dad mouths off but they're a bit lefty in his union, all them posties.'

'Dad's not a postman.'

'Quite right, son, he's an *engineer*. But his union lumps in with the posties and the clerks and the lasses what do the switchboard.'

John looked from the bumptious Bell to his father. It might have been no more than the effect of his suit jacket removed and shirt sleeves rolled – that and the boozy jocularity – but Bill wore a combative look. 'Well, speaking of commies, you should know, John, *his* lot used to have commies *running* their bliddy union.'

That sounded wildly unlikely to John, yet Bell held up his hands. 'Oh aye. Twenty years back. *National* leadership, mind.'

'What, *real* communists?'

'That's what they called themselves,' Bill uttered between his teeth. 'All fixing ballots in their favour, like. What do you think of that, eh, John? "Vote for me, you might as well, because me and me pals' votes are worth two of yours anyhow." *That's* your communism, young John. People don't want it so it's got to be forced on 'em.'

John was feeling browbeaten, and found that he didn't care to be lectured on unfairness. 'That's what unions are for, though, isn't it? To stick up for people who don't know what's good for them.'

Bill was visibly more hotly incredulous. 'What unions are *for*, son, is wantin' more pay for less work and bleating if they're asked to put up with it. Don't bloody kid yourself, John, this lot these days, they're not "socialists". They're bloody *communists*, man. Them at Ford Motor Cars wanting seventeen per cent on their wages. Bloody firemen wanted *thirty*. You know your mathematics, right? Figure that one out.'

'Okay, that's maybe quite a lot,' John wavered.

'*Whey*, John, man. They want what they see others have got, but they want it by blackmail. Not by graft. The only way they know is to hold the country to ransom, cause people as much bliddy bother as they can. They've not done a bliddy . . .' Bill was now fighting for breath and words, as if the unfairness defied both nature and description. 'They want what they haven't *earned*, man. And bliddy Labour government, they *get* it an' all. Tell you, even *my* dad woulda given this lot what for.'

With that, Bill stepped back to the oche and threw his arrows with vehemence.

'Naw, you're alright, son,' Bell said sotto voce, clapping John's shoulder. 'Don't you mind your da. He's just a bad un for keepin' a grudge. Principled, like, aye?'

The dregs of the afternoon decanted into the evening, and John stepped out into the small lobby of the Club to locate the men's toilet. Seeing Bill stood alone, across the frayed carpet at the threshold of the door to the street, reminded him with a start that his father had been absent from proceedings for perhaps as much as half an hour. Tentatively John stepped in his direction. Bill glanced aside, yet seemed hardly to acknowledge the presence. His eyes were vacant, his mouth set, morose. He tapped on John's shoulder, very lightly. Then his hand flew to his face, his palm pressed into his nose, his fingers spread across his eyes and into his silvery fringe. John heard first a groan, then a sob – the detonation controlled but no less shocking.

Chapter III

THE HOST

Monday, 16 September 1996

Gore was about his ablutions, grey morning light seeping into his cramped Oakwell bathroom. He had awoken from a senseless dream, its narrative twists already forgotten, but found himself lumbered with an equally meaningless erection. It had persisted through his rising from recumbent, and still would not relent. Now, as he urinated, he bent at the knee and applied gentle downward pressure so as to steer his stream cleanly within the bowl. Wrangling thus he was reminded of the one about the relative use of a monk with a hard-on, and grunted in amusement.

His sole purpose for the day was to present himself at St Luke's Church of England Primary School. Soaking under the showerhead, noting the falling-away of the earlier tumescence, he affirmed his resolve to go on foot, the better to further his acquaintance with the neighbourhood. He towelled himself roughly and laid out his clerical suit. *Do it proper*, he decided. He was not clear what respect would be afforded the cloth around Hoxheath, but folk were as well to know his business on sight.

The morning was dry but brisk as Gore made his way down Hoxheath Road, sidestepping chicken bones and chewing gum. As he reached a convenience store – NEWS 'N' BOOZE, PROPRIETOR S. MANKAD – a grey-haired woman hobbled past him clasping a crutch in her right hand, her forward motion badly synchronised with the drags she was taking from a cigarette in her left. He stepped into Mr Mankad's, intending to pick up a newspaper. Two young women in tee-shirts – a butterball blonde and a lithe, prettier brunette – chatted idly across the counter. 'Ah says to him, "Get on with ye . . ."' The females cast languid eyes over the cleric in his austere garb. Gore smiled, said nothing, attended to the news racks. Only the tabloids were on offer, so he selected a *Mirror* and stepped back to the counter. In front of him now was a bleary man buying four lottery tickets from the blonde, seemingly suspicious that he had not been served correctly, counting both tickets and coins, sweating dissatisfaction. *Those, my friend* – Gore eyed the tickets – *are not about to improve matters.*

Four children barrelled through the door – uniformed, satchels on backs. 'Oi,' the shopkeeper barked. 'Just two of yous at a time, nee more, right?'

'Shut up, bitch,' piped one child, in what Gore heard as a stab at an American accent.

'You *what*? See if I get hold of yee, I'll wring yer neck.' Indeed she was coming round the counter, paunchily formidable, and the threat drove a couple of the kids straight back out to the street. Her brunette friend slipped toward the door in their wake.

'Listen, I've gorra get on, I'll see you, eh, Claire?'

'Eh, Lind, while I think on, can you do the morra afternoon?'

'Aw, Claire, I canna man, sorry, listen I'll see ya?'

Returning to her station, vexed, Claire beheld Gore with reproving eyes as she took his coins.

Hoxheath Community Park offered Gore a plausible short-cut and so he strode down a gravel path between tree-hemmed lawns. The municipal flower beds were meagre, maple and birch trees sadly denuding. Yet there was a pleasing hush, the buzz of the high street traffic quelled. Midway down the path Gore heeded cries and exhortations emanating from three boys, teenagers, bashing a football back and forth against the wall of a redbrick public convenience, whereon black graffiti professed MIGHTY MOUSE, NUFC and FUCK OF YOU BASTARD.

'What a gurl!'

'*Off*side, man!'

'Whey bollox, how *can* ah be, Mackaz man?'

Nearing, Gore saw that one boy – tubby, slower to shift – was hugging the wall, acting as goalie, and somewhat forlornly as his pals hammered in shots from close range, much too fierce for the lad to risk flapping a hand at. Watching the bounce of the ball, the boys lustily giving chase, Gore felt a keen urge for a kickabout. *Be careful what you wish*, he thought, as another snapshot ricocheted off the wall and raced into his path. Instinctively he trapped and side-footed the ball back toward the boys. The one nearest to him stooped, picked it up and bore it back to him. He was a stout lad, his nose hooked, cheeks plump and ruddy, hair clippered close, every inch the pint-size juvenile Geordie.

'Oi mistah, will ya tak' a quick corner for us? Just quick, like?'

Why not? Gore jogged twenty feet or so hence to a suitable angle, spilled the Mitre ball onto the grass and dragged it to a prime spot.

'Eh man! On the heid!'

From a short run-up Gore struck the ball crisply with the outside of his right foot. It hung and bent in the air, and the other boy, back to the wall, leapt to meet it, clearly intending a bravura scissors kick. He failed to connect and fell rudely on his backside.

'*Ahhh!*' said his friend, Gore's new acquaintance. 'You're *shit*!'

Gore decided it was time for him to jog onward.

'Sorry, Fatha. Not you, like.'

'My name's John.' He waved as he went on his way.

His watch read 9 a.m. He had timed the walk nicely, even allowing for the unscheduled stops, and yet he found himself thwarted at the final hurdle. St Luke's – a modern redbrick construction with a pitched roof of grey polycarbonate panels – was protected by iron fencing all round its perimeter, no point of access apparent. Gore had tramped the full length of three sides before finally he saw a gaggle of children running through a gate toward a fibreglass portico. He hastened his step and fastened himself to the shoulder of one diminutive pupil, thus passing under a plain crest proclaiming FAITH HOPE CHARITY, and through glass doors. Within he was met by a familiar mingled odour – bleach, Tupperware, sour milk, unwashed hair. A bell was ringing, small bodies rushing around his knees, but one plump lady – ginger and slightly cross-eyed – was approaching him from the relative quiet of a corridor to his left.

'Rev'rend Gore? I'm Alison, I'll take you to Mrs Bruce.' She led him back from whence she had come, glancing over her shoulder. 'Your pal's here already? I just asked him to step out.' She gestured toward a waiting alcove at the end of the corridor, by a red door marked PRINCIPAL. Jack Ridley was poised awkwardly half-in and half-out of a hinged glass panel, trying to nurse an enamel mug of steaming tea whilst filling a pipe.

'How do, John. Smoker's corner, this.' He gestured out of doors toward a doleful man in jacket and tie pacing the patio, taking joyless pulls on a cigarette. But this he dropped and stamped upon quickly, and Gore turned, hearing the same sharp heels on linoleum behind him. A woman in a suit was bearing down, mid-forties, her features small and sharp, her hair fiercely coloured reddish-brown.

'That's five after nine and all safely stowed but you, Ian. Get on your way there, eh?'

The shifty teacher pressed past Gore, tugging on his loose necktie.

'I'm Monica Bruce, Reverend. Pleased to meet you.'

'John. Likewise. This is Jack Ridley – my churchwarden, so to speak.'

'How do,' Ridley grunted. 'I should say I was just lookin' at that bit bother you've got out there.' He pointed past the glass, beyond the sprawl of concrete playground, toward a derelict stone building that overlooked it, cordoned by plastic barricades and KEEP OUT signage.

'The old school?' said Monica. 'Aye, we've had to close off that bit playground. Slates falling off the roof, see.'

'Well, I can see about getting that fixed for you,' said Ridley.

'Oh no, it's a long-term problem, that. We want to develop it, see. You can get this or that money, if you can be bothered. It's just the forms are all thirty pages long. I get weary.'

Ridley might have heard her, but his expression was

unchanged. 'Well, I'm saying, I can see about getting it fixed for you.'

Monica patted Ridley's arm lightly. 'Well thank you, Jack, but it's about more than just a roof. Shall I show you's then? The hall and whatnot?'

They followed her, Gore endeavouring to stay apace, Ridley more dilatory in their wake. 'I hope you don't mind,' Gore offered, 'my intruding on your premises like this.'

'Hardly. We serve the same master, don't we? Anyhow – I'll see that you're made to pay for it.'

Gore smiled. There was something bracing and sceptical about this woman that made the taking of offence redundant.

'The only thing from my angle,' she continued, 'is how *long* you're here. Not wanting shot of you, you understand. Not when you just fetched up.'

'It's a moot point,' he shrugged. 'I'm on probation. If enough people come and keep coming, maybe they'll build me a church. Then I'm out of your hair.'

'Ah, but how many's enough?'

'Enough that I don't feel I'm wasting my breath. Just not so many as I can't remember their names.'

They had reached the assembly hall. *Not bad*, Gore reckoned. Presentable powder-blue walls, cherry-red linoleum, scuffed but not shabby, tramlines taped out for badminton. Windows down the length of one long wall, on the other an array of mounted and felt-covered display boards, each consecrated by age-group to pinned-up paintings of smiling suns, bacon-rasher skies, fluffy clouds and suchlike. There was no stage but an upright piano was pushed into a corner. A lectern stood lonesome in the midst of the floor, and they ambled toward it.

'Mrs Boyle – Alison? – she plays the piano for us. She'll do the same for you. We always have a hymn at morning assembly.'

'Nice,' Gore murmured. 'You take your duties seriously.'

'Oh, it's the least we can do. Some of the parents, I daresay they still think a church school can make their kids behave. Like we were Jesuits. That's the image, but, isn't it? Discipline. Tradition.

And not such a *mix*, to be honest – backgrounds and that?'

Ridley grunted.

'Don't get me wrong, I want us all to get along. But I'm not daft about how people look at things.'

Considering his reply, Gore saw that Monica was peering past him. 'Oh blimey, now here's a right one.'

Gore turned. Toddling up the length of the hall, with an oddly pronounced, near-comical swagger, was a boy of maybe six years in age – a little tow-headed tank of a kid, pink-cheeked, his lower lip protuberant, bearing in his hand a sheet of colouring paper. *Pretty mouth he's got*, thought Gore. Monica clacked down upon him, her own cheeks colouring. '*What* are you doing out of the classroom, Jake Clark?'

Undaunted, the tyke grasped the edges of his page and held it up for inspection. 'I done this. It's mint, everyone says.'

Monica tilted her head at him, in the manner of the prosecuting counsel. 'Did teacher tell you to come show me?'

'Naw, man. Everyone *says*, but.'

'Why then get you back to class this *minute*. And it's "No, Mrs *Bruce*."'

The boy stood stock-still, lower lip jutting yet further.

'Well, get *on* with you. Don't you *dare* get the huff with me, young man.'

His chin and brow fell – then he glared up anew at the adults, with a vehemence Gore thought almost unnerving. A strangled cry came out of him and he ran at Monica's lectern, shoving it with both hands. It teetered and fell before their startled eyes.

'*Right!*' Monica lunged at the boy, who somehow sidestepped her. Gore hazarded a helpful move in their direction, but the boy was ducking his head down as if to charge, and thus he ran, hard and headlong into Gore's groin. Pained, Gore just about managed to get his hands onto squirming small shoulders and pull the boy into his grasp before Monica marched up, furious, and he released him to her.

'Your mother'll hear about this, won't she? You think she'll be pleased? Do you?' She wrenched the boy's arm and began to drag him away, calling back over her shoulder. 'You's stop here, I'll send the caretaker.'

Massaging his abdomen, Gore bent down and plucked Jake Clark's drawing from the floor. It was a black-paint mural of a hulking man-beast – a giant, comically proportioned, with a smaller, geeky stick of a creature by his side. Above the figures was a script in a wildly looping, childish hand:

the man are back watch out you

Monica's caretaker, a surly youth in jeans, directed the visitors without fuss to a walk-in storage cupboard. Ten feet by ten, windowless, the space was overfilled with stacked plastic chairs and boxes on shelves. Gore withdrew his notebook. Ridley put on his motoring spectacles. 'Well,' the older man pronounced, 'I count eighty chairs, and I daresay that'll do you. We don't get that many at St Mark's on a Sunday.'

'Don't you think, but – it's going to need more? In the way of . . . I don't know, *decor*? Trappings. Stuff to make an atmosphere.'

'We're Protestants, aren't we? We don't need palaver.'

'Well, we need more than *this*, Jack.' Gore shook his head. 'Something. Even if it has to be begged or borrowed.'

'Or pinched,' said Ridley, deadpan. 'Don't forget pinched.' Gore smiled as he dabbled an idle hand into an open box-load of New English Prayer Books. Ridley sniffed. 'We'll be wanting the Book of Common Prayer, surely?'

'I can't afford to buy new. This is a shoestring production.'

'Well, you've got your piano at least. For your hymns.'

'Hmm. I wonder, though. Do we really need them? Hymns?'

'You're joking, aren't you, John? People aren't going to show up just to hear you natter. They'll want a tune.'

'*If* they turn up.'

'Divvint be soft.'

Gore's spirits, though, were meagre. What sort of a church could this amount to? It felt more like amateur dramatics, the humdrum worries of set dressing and helping hands and ticket sales. A crisis of legitimacy was on the horizon and here they were, he and his churchwarden, grubbing about in a dusty closet.

'I don't know, Jack.' He sighed. 'I'm feeling – out of practice here.'

'Well,' Ridley coughed. 'I should say. Spiking telt us he's planning on giving you a go or two in his pulpit? St Mark's? Just to keep you in nick 'til you're ready to go here. A christening, he said. Or a funeral, maybe, summat you can't mess up for him.'

Gore, having listened with interest, winced.

'Them's his words, not mine,' said Ridley, looking away.

In all the reconnaissance consumed more hours than Gore had expected, and he was ready to make haste for home when Ridley suggested they adjourn to a suitable nearby pub for a quiet pint. He didn't think it politic to spurn any more of the older man's apparently friendly gestures, and so let him lead the way down Hoxheath Road in the *sfumato* of dusk.

As they skirted the Crossman Estate, Ridley seemed almost to avert his eyes, shaking his head as they passed the Gunnery pub. 'Nowt good comes out of there.' Fifty yards further on, he nodded to himself. 'We'll cut through here, eh? The Lord Nelson's on the other side.' They turned into a long alley running behind blocks of redbrick housing on the Scoular Estate, and rounding a corner they came upon a grim concrete quadrangle under yellow sodium light – a playground with swings, roundabout, see-saw and sandpit. But it was an overgrown mob of teenagers who perched on and around the swings, nursing tins of drink, a large plastic bottle being passed around. Some sort of ruction was in progress too. Gore grew wary as he and Ridley drew near. A blonde girl in a ragged-hemmed denim skirt, and her bloke – carelessly barechested, lean and muscled if pasty – were cursing one another over who did what to who and when.

'Ah said, neebody fancies your rotten cunt.'

Gore saw Ridley flinch as if struck – recognised, too, one of the boys in the pack, with whom he had cheerfully kicked a ball that very morning. *Mackers?* The boy at least had the grace to look sheepish, electric-blue beer can snug in his fist. But they were nearly through the trouble-spot, and Gore wished only to leave it well behind.

'Watch that language, you lot,' Ridley barked as they passed.

'Fuck off, y'owld fucker.'

Gore was resolved to keep walking. Ridley, small mercy, did not stop to quarrel.

'Oi, you, I'm not *finished* wi' you.'

It took Gore some nervy seconds to be certain the shouted challenge was only the resumption of hostilities behind them.

'*You* fuck off, I fuckin' *hate* you.'

'Pack it *in*, Jason man.'

Then a shriek, and Gore and Ridley turned as one. The blonde girl had been thrown onto her backside, legs in the air, helpless as a ladybug, a streak of white underwear visible. Her bare-skin bloke strutted round her, clearly delighted, and disinclined to help her to her feet. Gore decided in a flash that this could not be permitted, and brushed past Ridley's custodial hand.

'Come *on*, what are you *playing* at?'

He had no clue how he would enforce the warning, which seemed only to further amuse the tough now squaring up to him. Worse, he sensed that he was being encircled.

'What do *yee* want? *Yee* want some? *Uh?*'

Then Gore felt a hard shove into his back, and a near-simultaneous blow to the side of his head, sharp and dazzling. He staggered and pitched down onto the concrete. Shouts and sounds of rubber-soled motion flew all about him as his vision scrambled. For the duration of several heartbeats he was certain that unless he got to his feet swiftly then he would receive a boot to the belly, or skull.

The blow did not fall. He rose, unsteadily. The group had scattered, cleared off. The tough, though, was holding his ground, glaring, his girl cowed and wet-eyed at ten feet's remove from him. Then he issued the bold middle-finger affront, turned and stomped off in the direction of his mates, arms aloft like a prize-fighter.

Ridley was coming forward now. Gore stared at the girl, her face so pale, mouth fraught, the band in her hair so tight. 'We'll see you back home,' he said, rubbing at the sore side of his head.

'I only live up *there*, man.' She flapped vague fingers.

'Well then, we'll take you. Come on, you've had a nasty turn.'

She shrank from Gore's open-handed gesture, but tottered along half a step behind the two men.

'What's your name, pet?'

'Cheryl. I'm not yer pet.'

'Okay, Cheryl. I'm sorry. Now do you want that fellow reported for what he did?'

'For *what*, man? Nowt to dee wi' me.'

They walked on, Gore weighing various remarks, thinking better of each. She led them through a barren yard, down a weed-strewn path, and let herself into a front door. Within, through a dim kitchen, down a hallway, Gore could see someone buried in the grasp of a sofa before a television.

'Good night, Cheryl,' he murmured at the girl's negligent back.

He and Ridley walked on without speaking until they were free of the estate, Gore still massaging the top of his head, prodding its tenderness to gauge whether a keener pain was on its way.

'Been in the wars, the day, you,' Ridley grunted. 'Are y'alright?'

'Oh yeah, sure.'

'Bloody little squirts. You still want that pint or would you rather home?'

'No, a pint would be good now, thanks.'

'Aye well, that's it owa there.'

The Lord Nelson was indeed before them, floodlights and flower-baskets above its awning.

'You *sure* you're alright?'

'No, I'm fine, honest.'

'Well then, give over rubbing your bloody head, will you?' And with that Ridley pushed on in through the double doors.

It was a cosy hostelry, strewn with older-looking drinkers; as they stood at the bar Ridley was greeted by a few of same. Gore excused himself and went directly to the toilet, where under a bare bulb he inspected his right cheek. He had expected a livid stamp there, but saw only a pale pink imprint of the blow. He felt relief, but a late stirring of anger too. Should he have swung for that twerp, having found his feet? Or would he have been set upon much the worse? For sure he had received no help from the boy Mackers – one small gesture of goodwill gone to waste, then.

Upon re-emerging Gore was introduced to several of Ridley's acquaintances, all of whom appeared keen to meet the Vicar. An old dear with thick glasses and frizzy hair was sing-song insistent that they join her company. 'Sit down, you, and tell us a story.' Ridley waved her away amiably and set down two pints of bitter at a distant table.

'Friendly place,' said Gore.

'Not bad,' Ridley replied, tipping dominoes from a wooden box onto the tabletop between them. 'Used to be a lot of canny pubs round here. The Smithy. The Block and Tackle. All for the shift workers, y'knaa, from the owld works.'

'They must have been tough old places. Tough crowds?'

'Rough and ready.' Ridley shrugged. 'Good people, but.'

They set to their game. Gore quickly found himself in a quandary. 'Well, I'm knocking here.'

Ridley nodded with satisfaction at the concession, and sipped at his bitter.

'I don't want to keep you from your wife tonight, Jack.'

'Aw, she's used to us runnin' about all hours.' Ridley was staring at the dominoes cupped and shielded in his calloused hand. Carefully he laid down a double blank.

'I've been wanting to ask your advice, actually. About the church.'

'Oh aye?'

'Yes, I wondered. What kind of a church do you think it should be?'

Ridley peered flatly at him. 'What *kind*?'

'I just think it needs a theme. Something a bit different to the usual. I mean, it's not usual, this, what we're doing. Is it?'

Ridley shrugged. 'Well, it seems to me – if you were wantin' to do a bit good – you would want a church that does something about *them* little buggers.' Ridley jerked a thumb in the general direction of whence they had come. 'Get them off the street.'

'Right. We should focus on the young people?'

'Maybe. I say that like it means owt. You'll have a bother. They're all that bloody ignorant. Ignorant and proud of it an' all.'

'It looks like they could do with something better to occupy their time.'

'*Whey*, they've got it cosy, man. Slouching about, sucking up beer. You'll not see 'em out of their pits before midday. Unless it's to sign on.'

'Do you think there's the work *for* them, but?'

'Why aye there's work. They'll just not do it. Their parents neither. But they've still got money for the big telly, and room to park their backsides, thank you very much.' Ridley had won the game, and began to reshuffle the dominoes. Still, he was dissatisfied. 'I'll tell you this, John, far as I'm concerned? The Church ought to say what's right. There's nee point to it otherwise. I don't like rubbish being talked. Not if a blind man can see things have gone to hell. We're not to say, "Aw, people are just like that nowadays, lads have got it tough, police are all villains." All that.'

'You're not by any chance a Conservative voter?'

Ridley looked as if he might spit. 'I bloody well am not. Them's the buggers took wor job. I'm a *socialist* is what I am, man, always have been. Tell you what that *means*, but. It means you *work*. Support your family, do right by your wife, mother of your bairns. You do the best you can, and you pass it on to your kids, so you've the right to expect same off them. Off your neighbour and all. That's the way things *work*. Not shirking off when you feel like. Like them lads. Who divvint want to be men. Who've got some – some bloody *lout*'s notion of what it means to be a man. Which is making themselves generally obnoxious. A quick squirt up some lass then off you skip, free as a bloody bird, so you can squirt somewhere else.'

Gore, taken aback by Ridley's terminology, looked at his hands for some moments.

'You'll be sorry now you asked my opinion, I daresay.'

'No, no. It's better we speak plainly.'

'You sorry yet for coming? Up here? Gettin' stuck with an owld bugger like us, after your nice place in the country?'

Gore shook his head. 'I don't miss Dorset one bit. It wasn't a happy time.'

'Was it not?'

'No. I'm not a country person. Didn't fit in hugely. And there was the whole BSE thing while I was there, the mad cow disease? Had a terrible effect.'

'Oh aye, it will have done, I s'pose. Rotten business, that.'

'It was. But, it taught me a few things. The whole experience.'

'Like what?'

'Not to make the same mistakes twice.'

Ridley nodded, as to say that was a very good one right there. Then he was up and collecting his cap, lifting their not-quite-empty glasses to the bar. *Rightly so,* Gore acknowledged, deciding against the offer of another round. He had no reason to believe that Ridley's causticity would dissolve in more alcohol, or that any further explication of his past and the lessons drawn from it would receive an indulgent hearing.

Chapter IV

THE RIGHT ANALYSIS

1983–1984

'Maggie, Maggie, Maggie! Out, out, out!'

Tentative at first, mindful of a police horse clopping close by his shoulder, John enjoined his voice to the crowd.

'Maggie, Maggie, Maggie! Out, out, out!'

It seemed the cry of hundreds, thousands, clustered all about him on a central London thoroughfare, exuding the thrill of a warrant for ungovernable behaviour in the streets of the capital. And so John clenched his fist and punched at the air, once, twice, thrice, just like his fellow marchers – with the notable exception of his sister, traipsing along to his right, chin tucked into her chest as if to deter long-lens paparazzi.

'That's right, comrades,' some voice was barking through a bullhorn. *'Shout it out so Reagan can hear you in Washington. Let's send him a message, loud and clear, he's not the boss round here, and England's not the fifty-first state!'*

Susannah was wincing. John peered past her to where Paul Todd – his new best friend – shot him a complicit grin.

At dawn that morning of 15 October 1983, Durham CND had departed the city in a hired coach. En route down the M1 John sat alone at the back of the bus, his head stooped over a *Collected Marx & Engels*, hardly stirring until the cover of the thick paperback was rapped by a knuckle and he looked up to see the twentyish lad across the aisle – lofty and lean, beak-nosed and cheery, in a jacket and jeans of washed-out black denim.

'Y'enjoying the grand old man there, are ya?'

Paul Todd wore a small headset at his neck, and John dared to enquire what was the music, though fearing the answer might as well be in Chinese. 'Bauhaus' was Paul's enigmatic reply. But John had a half-notion that the term applied to certain German buildings, and Paul's smile invited him into a conversation. He was a mechanic, it transpired, at Sacriston Colliery, and John spoke as best he could of his familial share in pit history. Paul was keener to extract John's view on the *Eighteenth Brumaire* and the distinction between bourgeois and proletarian revolution. But it was affable talk that detained them for an hour or more until the coach traversed a grimy stretch of north-west London to reach Waterloo Bridge, the murk of the Thames, and the Palace of Westminster. Waiting on the broad pavement of Victoria Embankment was Susannah, in loose jeans and a waxed jacket, clutching a furled *Telegraph* newspaper, her hair in a glossy bob. She met John with a wan smile, Paul with a limp handshake. This was her final year of reading economics at University College, and John had been given to understand that student life bred scruffiness and ill hygiene. Yet such was Susannah's grooming that she might have been studying deportment these two years past. She had traded her spectacles for contact lenses and looked the better for it, if now prone to oddly pop-eyed blinks.

On foot the trio made their way amid a growing multitude toward the appointed meeting place, Embankment Underground station.

'How much was your coat?' Susannah asked, fingering the army jacket of black twill John wore over a white school shirt.

'It was second-hand,' John murmured.

'I don't doubt it. Just like old Foot in his donkey jacket, eh?'

'That was a great reason not to vote for him, I'm sure.'

'Oh, but Mr Foot kindly gave us a million others, just to be safe.'

John groaned inwardly. Old Foot had led Labour to a crucifixion at the last election, even Newcastle Central falling to the Tories. Bookish, a bit scruffy, a tad gammy, he had nevertheless stood and fallen on a manifesto John considered close to godly, albeit rough-hewn – indeed much like the monthly agendas of his local Labour branch, a long wish-list, perennial wants and more recent grievances, hugger-mugger.

'So who do you fancy for the next Labour loser then, Jonno?'

'The next leader?'

Susannah's eyelids popped as to say she meant what she said.

'It's got to be Kinnock.'

'Ah. It'd be nice for him to have a proper job at last.'

Get knotted, thought John. He had first heard Neil Kinnock on the radio in the week before the election, addressing a crowd in South Wales, hoarsely and yet with no little rhetorical fire. Kinnock was a miner's son, and John was sure he heard the plangent cadence of a pulpiteer to boot.

At Embankment the tumultuous scale of the day became clear amid a mounting din of shouts and whistles. All around were vociferous men, women, children and babies, vividly disparate banners and emblems – AFRICAN NATIONAL CONGRESS, NICARAGUAN SOLIDARITY CAMPAIGN, JAMES CONNOLLY SOCIETY – but above all a multitude of painted doves and rainbows heralding PEACE. John had never seen so many dark-skinned people in the flesh, and tried not to stare. On the fringes of the teeming congregation were stalls purveying badges and flags, booklets and pamphlets. John was drifting toward the reading matter when a hawkish skinhead in a purple Harrington stepped into his way, waving a wad of newssheets.

'*Socialist Worker*, pal?'

'I won't, if you don't mind, thanks.'

'Your loss, pal.'

He came to a fold-out table tended by a girl with sloe eyes, a bolt in one nostril and a sheaf of vermilion hair. He inspected her wares – no doves or rainbows here, just angry splashes of red. *Straight Left*, *Burning Questions*. The girl smiled sleepily at him, and so he fished out some coins. On his return Susannah eyed him archly. 'You're in there, I think, Jonno.' She snatched the pamphlet. 'Tsk. Communist Party nonsense.'

Paul took an interest. 'Aye, that's the Marxist-Leninist faction but. They split, see.'

Susannah snorted. 'Over what? Something that happened in 1920?'

'Whey, you sneer all you want, Suzie,' Paul smiled impishly, to John's delight. 'But it's very important to make the right analysis. You should give it a try yer'sel.'

From set-off it took the marchers two hours just to step and shuffle halfway along the envisaged route through the city. The slow progress assumed a permanence, yet the vehemence of the crowd had its own momentum, and whenever this flagged there came a rallying cry of sorts – someone with a bullhorn or klaxon, or the first line of a song. As they approached Victoria John espied that sloe-eyed pamphlet vendor stepping hither and thither a short distance ahead, urging *Burning Questions* onto fellow marchers. He was daring himself to sidle closer to her when the *Socialist Worker* skinhead hoved into view at her flank, gesturing unpleasantly to the girl and her would-be customers.

'Don't be swallowin' anything off of these *fucking* middle-class Stalinists.'

'Oh yeah,' she riposted. 'Says the Trot *wanker*.'

The skin seized her arm, she shoved at him, and – to John's outrage – he shoved her back. John felt his feet taking him forward into the affray. But a second skinhead had come on the scene and was already restraining his bristly friend, seizing him by the chest as his arms flailed the air. Too late John saw a sharp elbow rising to clout him in the nose. Static burst behind his eyes, he staggered and fell to the tarmac.

Strange hands tugged him to his feet, some grey-bearded bloke and his wife in a blue bobble-hat. Now Susannah had her fingers on his face – 'Let us *see*, Jonno' – and Paul was fending off someone whose apology was unaccepted. 'Let's get him offside,' Paul was urging, then they were levering him apart from the hubbub, the parade passing by. They ducked into a pub, darkened in the late afternoon, strikingly quiet, wainscoted and divided into nooks by partitions of frosted glass. John was plonked in a corner while Susannah purchased drinks, in spite of Paul's protests.

Musical female laughter drifted from a neighbouring nook. John found himself staring at the handsome youngish couple sat there, he wreathed in smoke, she running fingers through flaxen hair, an evident intimacy he thought very enviable. He glanced aside only to see Paul's attention similarly diverted.

'That fella, I *know* him. Martin Pallister. Teaches politics at Newcastle Uni.'

'How do *you* know him?'

If there was an insult in Susannah's tone, Paul didn't rise to it. 'He does summer schools and that, weekend courses for union lads. Listen, I might gan and say hello.'

'Let's all of us,' Susannah decided. 'No point just nursing the casualty.' They took up their glasses and trooped behind Paul.

'Martin?'

A fleeting wince. 'Aye?'

'Paul Todd? I was in with your lot at Redhills last summer?'

'Oh aye, Paul. How're you keeping, son?'

'Canny. Did you come down for the march the day then, eh?'

'Aye, sort of. But I got thirsty, man.' Pallister grinned. 'You bunked off an' all?'

'Well, the lad here got a bash in the face off of some Trot.'

Pallister's gaze fell on John. 'So you did. Poor kid. Well, now you've earned your combat stripes.'

Even as they drew up stools John was certain Pallister's manner wished them gone. The girl at his side he introduced as Polly, and the corners of her mouth flickered, but her throaty chuckle had been silenced by the invasion. As Paul tried to engage Pallister, John made a discreet inspection of the man. His build was compactly sportsmanlike, his eyes very blue, and he was fine-planed of jawline and cheekbone. He wore a jacket of black corduroy over a half-buttoned grey shirt, a silver chain at his throat, his crow-black hair spiked on top but shaggy at the nape, more befitting a rock'n'roller than a college lecturer. Clearly his nose had been broken once upon a time, yet it added some useful rough to his good looks. Engrossed in this admiration, John suddenly saw those blue eyes turn on him anew.

'You still a bit glakey there, son? So what did you do to earn the smack?'

Paul leapt in, as if perched in the front row of a tutorial. 'He got between some Trot skin giving out to a little Commie lass for being middle-class.'

Pallister sniffed. 'Not a bad analysis. Mine wouldn't be much different.' He reached for his packet of Silk Cut, set squarely on the table beneath a distressed silver Zippo. Paul produced papers and pouch from his pocket and began to craft a roll-up, his eyes never leaving his hero.

'CND's a sweet idea,' Pallister exhaled. 'But there's nee real politics to it. '"Give peace a chance", aye, right. But they'll never achieve owt. End of the day? They're in bed with Labour. Meaning they'll take whatever a Labour government gives them. Meaning nowt.'

Susannah wrinkled her nose. 'What "Labour government" would that be?' Pallister flicked a wry eye in her direction, and she seemed pleased. 'Sorry, but you want to mind your language too, my little brother's red-hot Labour.'

'Christian Socialist,' John corrected her, feeling it was time he imposed himself properly on the symposium.

'Dear me how,' said Pallister, breathing another blue cloud. 'That's called an oxymoron, son. You can't absolve the rich of their sins by holy water.'

John made a face. 'That's not what Christian Socialism's about, it means –'

'I *teach* this stuff, sunshine.' Pallister wore a slight grimace of his own. 'For a living. So I think I know what I'm saying.'

'Well, then you'll know the Bible made as many socialists as Marx ever did. I mean, the churches are what Labour was founded on.'

'Oh, *Labour*, aye – Labour's a party of preachers alright. All the churchy types sign up there. I'm talking *socialism*, kidder.' John was confused, Pallister jabbing his lit cigarette as if to skewer a stray and offensive argument. 'Look, you've gotta know your history when you say "Christian Socialism". It was a proper movement, eighteen-nineties –'

'I know,' John blurted, keen to be profligate with his learning. 'F. D. Maurice, the small band of brothers.'

Pallister paused, his stare a shade darker. 'Oh, you know all that, do you? And do you know what they achieved? Nowt. Just a load of dog-collars sniffin' round the East End of London. *Missionaries*, y'knaa? Reckoned they'd sort out the proles. But the working class was organising *itself*, see. It wasn't in need of sermons.' He stubbed the cigarette pointedly. 'So aye, you're right, the Church gave Labour a start. But Labour outgrew the Church. We all outgrow it, don't we? You will too. I bloody hope you do.'

John could feel the burn of Susannah's thin smile in his peripheral vision.

'You don't give Labour much credit, do you?'

'I've not forgot what they're like in power. Divvint get us started.'

Susannah leaned in. 'Exactly. What's Thatcher doing that Callaghan wouldn't have loved to? If he'd had the bottle?'

'Well,' Pallister chuckled, 'to be fair – I don't know if he'd have sent men to the Malvinas to fight for a rock and some seagulls.'

'I'm sure he wouldn't. Then where would we have been? Kowtowing to Argie fascists? No, that was true leadership.'

'Blimey, where's your tin hat, love? Is it under your chair there?'

'Sorry, *flower*, am I a bit too tough for you?'

'Not at all, *pet*. I just never met one of your lot before. Hail the blessed Margaret, eh?'

John studied his sister and Pallister as they glared at one another. However guiltily, he relished seeing Susannah take a turn in the lions' den. He was conscious, too, of how silent the delicious Polly had been throughout these charged exchanges.

Susannah emitted a short laugh. 'You make me laugh, your lot.'

'My lot?'

She had plucked up Pallister's cigarette packet, defying his raised eyebrows, and drawn out a smoke. 'You lefties. Talking like you're for all the good things, and against all the bad things, and it all got decided ages ago. What you're actually *saying* is utter shit.' She had coaxed the Zippo into flame, and she lit and drew, a little clumsily. 'I mean, what do you think politicians are *for*? It's just a *job*, man. Governments aren't there to make everything sweetness and light. They're not Jesus Christ and his bloody disciples.'

Pallister looked to have recovered his cocksureness. 'Well, me and the Reverend here might see it different,' he said, winking at John, who suddenly saw a certain appeal in the man's rather louche assurance. Then Pallister seemed to dismiss the altercation with a flick of the wrist. 'So listen, Paul, what's the good word then? Are the miners going out this year or not?'

Todd, startled, mustered a shrug. 'Whey, everybody reckons we'll get shafted on the pay round, but, I dunno – wouldn't be the best time for it.'

'There's never a good time, son.'

'Aye, well, if we do strike then it won't be much to look at, I don't reckon. I doubt we'll even need pickets. I mean, everybody feels the same. Y'knaa Durham, it's middle-of-the-road, always has been.'

Pallister scowled. 'That's weak analysis, that, man. Naw, I reckon you'll have a battle this time. Scargill's not Joe Gormley. He'll not get the engineers out to help him neither. Used to be the miners went out if the nurses weren't getting. You'll not ever see *that* again. Proper fight brewing now.'

'Ha,' Susannah enunciated crisply. 'And where'll *you* be when it starts?'

Her effrontery must have kindled some defiance in silent Polly, for she stroked a deft hand over Pallister's on the tabletop. 'Quite. Macho man.'

Pallister recoiled, a little too sharply. 'I'm not talking . . . *punch-ups*, man. Revolutionary politics aren't just about *violence*. It's about people united, pushing in the same direction. *That's* the power of it.' He leaned back in his seat, his grin reinstated. 'Saying that – a bit violence can go a long way.'

'Revolutions,' Susannah sniffed, 'aren't started by a lot of big talk down the pub.'

'Actually, *bonny lass*,' said Pallister, winking again at John over the rim of his glass, 'I think you'll find there's a few went off in just that very manner.'

Paul set down his drained pint. 'Another, eh?'

Polly, though, was collecting her belongings. 'Martin, I'm off.'

'*Don't* go, c'mon, stop on.'

'Nice to meet you,' she said to the table, lightly and devoid of sincerity. Pallister laid a hand on her but she shrugged it aside and pushed her way out of the double doors to the street. In the abashed silence that followed, Pallister rubbed the grain of his stubble.

'You headed back north tonight, Martin?' Paul tried, finally.

'Nah, I'm stopping over. Least I thought I was.' Pallister's grin had revived. 'I might end up out in the kennel. Look, I'd best get on.' He rose and swept up his smoking apparatus. 'Cheerio, Paul. Nice to meet *you*, sunshine.' He patted John's shoulder. 'Bye then, Mrs T,' he fired gratuitously at Susannah. Then he hustled out into the greying afternoon.

'Some bloke, isn't he?' Paul clucked his tongue.

'Seemed like the standard lefty lout to me,' offered Susannah.

'Some of that,' John murmured, 'was for your benefit, I thought.'

Witheringly Susannah beheld her brother. 'Oh Jonno, pay attention, will you? Quite apart from that poor cow sat with him – he was wearing a wedding ring.' And she leaned back in her chair, lip curling, the imperious effect undermined but slightly by one more pop-eyed blink.

For some months after his day-trip John would, in idle moments, toy with the fancy that he might once more run into Martin Pallister and his lovely girlfriend. He saw himself performing more capably in the cut-and-thrust next time. But it was not to be. Nor did Paul Todd make good a cheery pledge to ring him up. And yet, one day in the late summer of the following year, they met again.

John had taken the bus to Newcastle in search of a small token to offer at a family dinner in honour of his father's promotion to

Chief Supervisor, Durham Region. A new Montego was in the offing, and for Bill there would be no more knocking on the doors of old gadgies. Such was the largesse of the newly privatised 'British Telecom'. Thankful news in all, though to John the home front was of receding significance, for within the month he was due to take up a college place on the south-east coast.

Headed for Eldon Square, the enclosed shopping complex of gaudy arcades that squatted and snaked through the centre of the city, he dawdled down Blackett Street toward the familiar mooring of the Earl Grey Monument, its fluted stone column soaring a hundred feet from a fat plinth set on a base itself taller than a man. To one side a small assembly was in progress, two dozen bodies shuffling in close proximity. John came closer. Collection tins were being rattled.

'Support the miners there. Support the striking miners . . .'

The most voluble of the collectors was a handsomely aged sort, wearing a black donkey jacket over dungarees, his good head of greying hair swept back and piled up like some 1950s Teddy boy. Then the man raised and flexed his right arm, and John saw first a void at the end of his coat sleeve, then – for it protruded only slightly – the metal split-hook of an amputee.

A squall of audio feedback rent the air, and heads turned toward the foot of the Monument. There, a lean and beak-nosed lad, wearing a loose-necked tee-shirt with the legend NEITHER WASHINGTON NOR MOSCOW, was unravelling a microphone from a PA and amp adorned with peeling decal stickers. BAUHAUS, THEATRE OF HATE, SOUTHERN DEATH CULT.

Hello, Paul, thought John, *you've had a haircut.*

'How do, I'm Paul Todd, Durham Mechanics NUM –'

Paul thrust the microphone apart from him momentarily, allowed feedback to crackle and abate, then glanced down nervily at a handwritten page.

'I'm gunna just say a few words, about the strike, why we need your support. You've all seen the Tory press bang on about Scargill and ballots, cos that's all they know how. But we're in agreement, and we always have been. This is a straight fight. The lines have been drawn, aye?'

He didn't read eloquently, John decided, and his whole demeanour seemed glad of the amplification. But he surely had conviction.

'The other day I was down Wearmouth. Aye, it's got as bad as that.' A ripple of supportive laughter. John joined on to its tail. *'We saw a pair of scabs driven through the gates into that pit at maniac speed. Like pop stars. Proud of themselves, eh? And, right enough, we'll not forget their names, or their faces neither, I'll promise you that.'*

This elicited a shower of applause and a raucous hoot. John glanced over to see the Teddy boy cheering as he applauded, banging his left fist onto his right shoulder and chest. A proud sort of gesture, thought John, like some Politburo bigwig applauding the October parade.

A pair of police officers in summery shirtsleeves had drifted into John's field of vision from the corner of Pilgrim Street and were standing at a meaningful distance, stock-still amid passing shoppers. One now folded his arms. John was unnerved. True, they possibly seemed a scruffy lot, loitering so near to Berry's the jeweller and the day's peaceable commerce.

Meanwhile, someone near to his shoulder was unhappy. A brawny black-bearded man was jabbing the air, heckling Paul. 'See when all this started? Youse lot were talking big about mass action, rank and file, all this. Then you slink off and we don't hear a shaggin' *word* out of you's, not for *months*.'

John did not look for Paul Todd's reaction, his eyes fixed on the two police officers as they started to take purposeful steps toward the assembly.

The one-armed man had his good hand on Paul's back, seeming to steer him apart and away from the fray. John dogged their steps down Pilgrim Street until close enough to tap on Paul's shoulder, and was met with a hard look that relented with recognition. Paul introduced 'Joe Pallister' and John thrust out his right hand, then cursed himself for the worst kind of idiot. But Mr Pallister put out his good left, twisted, grasped John's dangling right and shook heartily in topsy-turvy fashion.

'Divvint worry, kidder, takes a while to get it. Took me long enough.'

Paul was stealing looks back up from whence they had come. 'John, we're away off down to Joe's shop, if you want to come with.'

They turned off smartly into the narrow east–west side street of High Bridge, and John scuttled along in their stead. 'That was a bit sticky back there,' he ventured.

'Keeps wuh on wor toes,' Joe tossed back over his shoulder. 'This one here but, he's in bother already.'

Paul was smiling mildly. 'Got me'sel into a barney a while back, see, John. On a picket. Done for breach of the peace, obstructing an officer.'

'God. What happened?'

'Got fined, banned from off the picket lines. And any Coal Board property.'

'God. Isn't it risky then? To still be – doing stuff?'

'No choice, man. We need bodies. If you saw all the coppers they've got in.'

They had slipped into the narrow wind of Pink Lane, where Joe pulled up in front of a small commercial premises and fished in his pocket. The cramped window display was full of worthy faded paperbacks, and a painted awning read NINE HOURS BOOKS. Inside, John keenly inspected the shelves and stacked front tables – remainders and second-hand editions of Christopher Hill and E. P. Thompson. He had not known the Trades Union Congress published so widely. Mr Pallister pressed a button on an answering machine that clicked and whirred. Hearing a woman's voice, he frowned and waved at his guests. 'You's gan on in the back, eh?'

Paul led John into a windowless boxroom set with a work desk and chair, one set of shelves and a metal filing cabinet. Paul did not sit, and still seemed preoccupied.

'So what all else are you involved with? With the strike?'

'Well, you've maybe heard, there's a lot goes into stopping them shifting coal about the place. From the private mines, the open cast. Blyth. Tow Law.' Paul grinned. *They're* not Coal Board property.'

'And how did you meet – ?' John jerked his head toward the door.

'Joe? At a demo. He's sound as hell is Joe. Martin Pallister's dad, y'knaa? But he's the real thing, Joe. Used to be foreman up at Alderton Works? Tell you, I've made some proper friends on this strike. Some right clever people. Lawyers, writers – it's funny, but it's true. I've lost friends and all.' He shrugged. 'Tell you, everything I thought before all this started? It was just wrong. I was *dreaming*.'

Joe entered, squeezing past his juniors, took the seat behind the desk and set down a biscuit tin on top of a ledger book. With his left hand he pushed the tin flush to his impaired right forearm and began to withdraw coins and notes carefully with the good hand, stacking the coins by denomination.

'Can I ask?' John ventured. 'Why's the shop called Nine Hours?'

'You never heard of the Nine Hours' Strike, kidder? Eighteen seventy-one, engineers striking for an hour off the working day. Started in Sunderland, spread to Newcastle. The bosses brung in foreign blacklegs, see, so the leaders went and petitioned Marx hisself. It were Marx translated their leaflets into foreign, to gan all round the continent.'

Marx himself! John was still marvelling quietly as Joe held up a pound note barely held together with tape. 'Damn it, what bugger give us that?'

As Pallister groused into his chest, John glanced at Paul. 'Are you okay for money?'

'Well, I divvint buy so many records . . . But I've not got kids. Me girlfriend's mam and dad have give us a hand. They're not mad keen. Michelle's not mad herself.'

A tutting sound issued from Joe, his eyes flicking upward. 'Women, see, *reactionary* tendencies.' But he was surely kidding, for his face had puckered in amusement, and he began to whistle a tune John recalled vaguely as one from *My Fair Lady*.

*

With a robber's stealth John turned his key in the latch, then stood in the hushed hallway at the threshold of the dining room, cursing himself. Ahead of him the kitchen was deserted, but the oven was still lit and shuddering. A bad sign. He peered into the dining room through the doorjamb. Bill sat alone at the table, lit only by the sideboard lamps, a mug of tea steaming unattended before him. Similarly neglected was an unopened bottle of champagne, shiny blue ribbon tangled at its neck.

There was a heavy tread on the stairs behind him, and he turned to see his mother, wearing the white silk blouse she wore for special parties.

'Where *were* you, John?' she hissed. He held up his hands in futile contrition. 'Just get in there and say you're sorry, will you?'

He sloped into the dining room, Audrey behind him. His father looked up, wan, his silver helmet-fringe looking to have suffered a comb.

'I'm sorry, Dad. I lost track of time.'

Bill let out a sigh that must have inflated within him over a silent hour or so. 'You *make* time, John. You can always make time. When you're bothered to.'

John realised to his great surprise that he would have rather his father had been blazingly angry. 'There was this demo for the miners. I met a mate, we got talking.'

'Oh, friend of yours, eh?'

'A miner. From Sacriston. Bloke I met in London on that CND march.'

A compound of meagre causes to Bill's hearing, John didn't doubt. His father put his hands round his mug and stared down for some moments.

'John, shall I tell you a story? Back in, must have been, nineteen fifty-one? My dad, your grandda, one morning he told us get dressed and took us down to Bearpark. To meet the training officer. I was sixteen. Wasn't doing so badly at school. But there I was, Bearpark Colliery. And we were talking about a job. A job for me. And next thing I knew, I was in. Nee bother. I was in, cos me dad was a great bloke.' John nodded, as he had been nodding, but Bill scowled. 'Like that was all I was *good* for. See? It wasn't what *I* wanted. It wasn't what anyone I *knew* wanted. Who'd want to work down there? Your granddad even, you think he'd have chosen that?'

John mustered a shake of his head. 'Sorry, what are you saying then? Them who are doing it now, they should just – go do something else?'

'John, it's just how the world is, man. People used to have jobs making wheels for wagons. They used to need an operator to dial America. Sometimes people just have to learn to do summat different.'

'What if someone came to *you* and said, "Sorry, that job you've done all your life? We don't need you any more, you're fucking finished –"' He saw the line of his father's mouth harden at last. But Audrey was standing, with the help of a hand on the table, looking wan and queasy. And then Bill was on his feet too.

'Are y'alright, love?'

'No I'm not. I've got to take me pill.'

'Do you need a hand, Mam?' John gestured uselessly.

'No, I said. But you two carry on by all means.' Audrey pushed her chair in under the table and walked, a little ungainly, from the room. John stared at the dining-table surface, at the redundant champagne, then at his father.

'She gets very weary sometimes,' Bill muttered. 'You know that, don't you?'

John nodded, feeling worse than flattened, for he would have readily resumed their quarrel but that the teeth had been drawn from it so sharply. He would await another turn, then, to fight the good fight down to its right and dialectical end.

Chapter V

TYNESIDE CLASSICAL

Monday, 23 September 1996

'I don't like to tell you your business, Father, but this is the sort of decision you want to get right.'

Gore nodded resignedly, accepting that the argument was lost, his afternoon wasted. For half an hour he had been in conference across a counter from Mrs Paulette Wicker, tiny and strident professional seamstress of John Dobson Street. The project at hand was the commission of a formal cloth for the altar of the new church of St Luke's. They had discussed material, agreeing that rayon was tasteless, linen much the best. They had discussed colour, though Gore found his preference for oyster overruled, since purple was really the nicest and most popular. They had even discussed design and lettering, and Mrs Wicker let it be known she was very partial to cuneiform characters, most especially fish. Then progress had abruptly foundered on the question of the cloth's dimensions, its exact width and fold and drop on each side. These were precision matters, and Gore now knew he was a fool not to have come armed with the information. But then how could he?

'So you mean you've not actually got an altar?'

'Not yet. Like I said, I'm starting from scratch. I thought I'd get the set dressings gathered first, you see.'

'Well, that sounds very *novel*. Tell you what, I'll keep a note we've spoken, and you come back to us when you know better what's what, eh? Cos we don't want to make a whoopsie, do we? Not at forty pound a yard.'

Shouldering his way down the pedestrian thoroughfare of Northumberland Street, Gore found his mood didn't improve. It was strange to have quit the funeral-parlour murk of Mrs Wicker's little shop and find himself among so many who were lively and purposeful. The street was a chattering hubbub of mercantile activity, the world and his wife and kids streaming in and out of Next, Fenwick, HMV, Dixons, Marks and Spencer – larking youths, overweight couples, pushchairs and wheelchairs, pensioners lugging bags with chrome handles. All had come to the high-street bazaar, heralded by synthetic pop music drifting from every doorway. It seemed almost a form of recreation, no purchase necessary. Gore was not himself enticed, not by any glaring window. So why were so many out here, in the midst of a working day, picking up stuff just to put it down again? By the time he reached Blackett Street he was musing over themes and keywords for a sermon. 'Adrift', 'rudderless', 'beguiled'. 'Zombies' was probably too rude. 'Commodity fetishism' too Marxian. What, though, was the true meaning of 'popular'? Might there be anything in the etymology he could make instructive use of?

Then he paused and looked all about him, from the Body Shop to Berry's the Jeweller and Gregg's the Baker. And he knew that if he could draw a fraction of such a crowd on a Sunday then he would count himself a lucky fool. Would any of these people count it an attractive proposition to sit and listen to him for an hour or more? To sit and be with each other, quietly and thoughtfully, without visible gain? To ask the question was to answer it.

He had reached the broad open square of the Monument. Earl Grey stood serenely on his Doric plinth, a small bird atop his Portland stone head, two hundred feet above the afternoon trade. Citizens clustered at the base, resting their feet, some unwrapping takeaway sandwiches. Gore was headed homeward, down the steep wind of Grey Street, past facades of fine stone, Athenian detail and symmetry, enduringly handsome despite the wear and tear and general distress of the years and the rain and the pigeons.

As he neared the entrance of the Theatre Royal he made out that directly before its stately portico of Corinthian columns a crowd of bodies were milling – clearly composed of members of the press as much as onlookers, for the crowd made a crescent that bore all the hallmarks of a photo opportunity, if not a car crash.

He inveigled himself into the back of the throng. All attention was facing forward, its unlikely object a portly man in a grey suit, his bootlace hair slicked over his scalp, a sheet of paper clutched in one hand that quivered as if in want of a drink. Beside him, a similarly nervy, somewhat androgynous young woman in a shapeless blue smock. Beside *her* – indeed towering over her, tucked into the base of a column – was an extraordinary oddity: a square-sided monolith, seemingly constructed of white Perspex, perhaps ten feet tall and five feet wide with a doorway cut into one side, immaculately blank and madly incongruous.

'What's going on?' Gore whispered to a man adjacent who toyed with the levers and triggers of a Nikon camera and flash.

'Better listen,' came the shrugged response.

'Well now, as you may know, I'm Bob Muir –'

A ripple of presumably sardonic cheers. Mr Muir's scalp flushed.

'Aye, aye, and I just want to say – briefly now, you'll be glad to know – I want to say a few words about why we're here, on behalf of the council.'

'Sweating like a rapist,' Gore heard the photographer mutter.

'So, as you see, we're here outside our marvellous theatre that we've given a bit help to in the past. And this street, you might know, is known all over, really, by all the knowledgeable people, for the fine architecture of Grainger and Dobson, which I'm told they call "Tyneside Classical". Brilliant, eh?' Muir cast a more hopeful eye about the gathering. *'And, really, we're in one of the best spots in the city right here, a conservation area, all your listed buildings and whatnot. Now, we know, of course, these great streets of ours have seen their better days. But it's a big hope for us on the council that we can find a way to give 'em back their former glories. Revive the spirit of Grainger, if you want. So – and, well, but before that we want to start it all off by – aw, hang on, sorry.'* Muir peered avidly at his piece of paper.

'Eh, Bob, I'll bet you mean to tell us you'll be listening to the *people . . .'*

The heckle – if heckle it was, for it issued affably from somewhere to Gore's right – seemed to tickle the crowd more than anything the councillor had yet mustered, and Muir looked piqued. 'Aye well, of course I defer to the Member for Tyneside West, knowing his expertise. You're a good mile out of your jurisdiction but, Martin.'

'Hey, Bob, man, I'm only here to help.'

Gore craned his neck and saw a familiar – an unmistakeable – figure, blue-eyed and blue-suited, rocking on his heels at the head of the spectators, fists in pockets, chomping on a wad of gum.

'Pallister gets his oar in as usual . . .' This muttered by another near to Gore, into the photographer's ear – presumably his scribbling sidekick.

'Right, so the name of this game is consultation with the people of Newcastle, what we want is, yes, to listen to local people and take their input onboard and – and do summat with it. So I'm delighted to unveil today this installation which we hope will get us kicked off. We were pleased to commission Anthea Morrow here, who's a fine artist and a canny lass, and we thank her for her thought and effort on this here – piece.'

'Can you tell us what it is, Bob?' Gore's neighbour had his biro poised.

'Oh aye, well, it's sort of a suggestion box, really, isn't it, Anthea pet?'

Ms Morrow looked sceptical. 'If you like. On a certain scale . . .'

'Yes, that's what it's for, anyhow it'll be stood here for a couple of months and – well, you can see – people can just walk in through the doorway there and write what they want to on the walls. Pens will be provided.'

'You mean *graffiti*, Bob?' enquired Martin Pallister, as if innocent.

'Aye, like in a pub netty?' offered one of the hacks, emboldened.

'Well, eh, no. Because, inside, you'll see, there's, like, questions already printed on the walls – proper questions about the city and that. So I fancy there'll be smarter things get said than what *you're* saying. Any road, let's just wait and see what the people say, eh?

Let's have a bit faith in that.'

'C'mon, Bob, you can't tell us lads aren't gunna walk in there of a Friday night and piss in it.'

'Eh now, fellas, I mean for God's sake show a bit of enthusiasm. And a bit of respect for what Anthea's done here.' Some faltering applause was mustered, and one or two hoots. 'Alright, whatever you's want, get your bloody photos then.'

As the gathering began to disperse, Gore kept his eye on Martin Pallister, for the MP lingered meaningfully, apart from the VIP contingent yet fraternising easily with the members of the press – as though the day were all about him, or indeed had anything to do with him. Why did they pay him such courtesy in turn? Because he was better-dressed, better-groomed than the hapless Councillor Muir? It was, by any standard, peerless effrontery. Discreetly Gore planted himself near enough to hear what sounded for all the world like a briefing.

'. . . No, fine, look – off the record? I'm not knocking the intention. But it's not just about intentions. It's got to look professional, hasn't it? You've got to put the proper frame round these things. If you want to get investors interested, developers onboard – which you have to. And they're not mugs, not in those games. See, what bothers me is how many bloody meetings it took 'em all to decide *this* was a good idea.'

Gore wasn't sure what to make of the little pantomime he had witnessed. Without doubt, there was disrepair in the heart of Newcastle – nothing much seemed thriving about it, between the greying gloom of these Victorian streets and the outright plastic horrors of the 60s and 70s, the likes of Eldon Square. Yes, the condition of Hoxheath was much the more dire. Yes, the council's efforts today had been, perhaps, a little under-rehearsed, under-resourced – maybe a bit shallow, a token gesture even? And yet Gore found his sympathies resting with the harassed Muir rather than the self-professed know-all.

It was dancing in his mind now, a fancy to step forward, introduce himself anew to Martin Pallister, shake his hand, enquire after Susannah – see what he got back for his trouble. On reflection, though, this was not a hand he was well-disposed to shake. Did he have anything properly pleasant to say? No, so say nothing. Hadn't this poser once presumed to tell the miners how to win a strike? How could a man face himself in the mirror after cashing in his former convictions for all the world to see? No, he could not and should not be taken seriously. Gore turned his face from the dwindling assembly.

Chapter VI

MULTIPLE DEPRIVATIONS

12 April 1988

With care John plucked one from the cluster of three-inch figurines set on the glass table, and raised it to his eye-level. He had guessed correctly: Anubis, the jackal-headed god, sculpted and cast in dark pewter, bearing his scales. He replaced it among its fellows, the crocodile king, the cat clutching a staff, the female hiding a scorpion in her coiled hair. Queer choices for the master of a Cambridge seminary. On the wood-panelled wall behind the master's desk hung a Buddhist prayer shawl of shimmering white silk, pressed flat behind glass. Such were the traces of a man and his tastes, but as yet John awaited the actual presence of Reverend Gordon Lockhart, and the clock was tripping past eleven. John had straightened his tie, buttoned up his corduroy jacket and returned to his chair when at last Lockhart entered in haste. He wore his white hair swept back from his temples, with a neatly trimmed white moustache and goatee beard. His eyes were mild behind large-framed spectacles.

'Mr Gore. I do apologise. Let us brook no more delay.' Lockhart opened a manilla file and spread papers before him. 'Let's see. You were seen by Canon Botsford. You've done your conference in Leeds.' He glanced up. 'You're finishing a degree in politics? And you want the two-year divinity course at the university, after which – you'd come to us for the certificate in ministry?'

John nodded. 'That's about the size of it.'

'And you're from Durham? You didn't fancy keeping near your roots?'

'No, I liked the course here best. Roots are for trees, I think.'

Lockhart smiled, not quite approvingly.

'But you're renouncing politics? Your devotion until now?'

'Not as such. I still belong to the Labour Party. I just – lost a bit of the taste for politics, at university.'

'How unfortunate. Any special reason?'

'I think . . . it was a lot to do with the miners' strike. My grandparents were miners – Durham, you know. So I was ashamed of the Party, really, for giving nothing to that fight. To people they were meant to fight for.' Gore adjusted himself in his seat. 'There was that, then there was just all the nonsense of student politics. Pushy people calling each other names. It was like being back in the school playground – only pompous as well as childish.'

Lockhart seemed mildly amused. 'Oh dear. So what did you do to fill your time instead? At college?'

John shrugged. 'Christian Union, two nights a week. I played a bit of football. Acted in a few student plays.'

'Ah, drama. What sort of parts did you land?'

'Small things, mostly. I was Angelo in *Measure for Measure*.'

'Oh, now there's a useful character. A study in our dual nature. "Heaven in my mouth",' the master recited jauntily, '"as if I did but only chew his name. And in my heart the strong and swelling evil of my conception."'

Lockhart appeared to revel in a certain showmanship of his own. Again John shifted in his chair. This was proving a livelier exchange than he had expected.

'Well, our production was a "feminist" version, apparently, so the director said. I never knew what he meant. But he asked me to make the character cold and violent and generally loathsome. So I did my best.'

'That sounds rather fun. In a vicarious sort of fashion. You enjoyed acting?'

John nodded. 'I don't know that I had any great skill. But I found that I understood the words and could say them aloud so they sounded vaguely interesting.'

'That', Lockhart nodded slowly, 'is a definite boon.'

John omitted to share with the master what he had found to be the chief blessing of amateur dramatics, namely that it had inducted him into female company. The Isabella to his Antonio had been a third-year chemist called Amanda, a lively girl with limpid green eyes, a bushel of kinky copper hair, and a cat-like body that John held closely but warily as he flung her hither and thither round the rehearsal room. After one such vigorous evening she led him through cold streets and up to her attic bedroom, fitted and straddled him like good collegiate sport, and relieved him of his virginity. In short, he had found acting an altogether worthwhile pursuit; and Lockhart, for as much as he knew, seemed to approve. He was smiling, at least.

'Still, you've decided not to pursue the actor's life. You'd already given up on elected office. Through all this you stayed steadfast in the Church?'

The crux, thought John, clearing his throat. 'Yes. The Church has always been where I've found all my interests. All my passions. That's never gone away. It was affirmed for me, really, when the Church report on inner-city poverty came out. At the end of 1985?'

'*Faith in the City*,' Lockhart nodded.

'Yes. That made me proud, that piece of work.' He smiled despite himself. 'My father agreed with the Tories that it was all Marxist claptrap. I mean, that's what he read in *The Times*, I think.'

In Lockhart's own slight smile John saw complicity. 'Your father disputed the Commission's findings?'

'I don't think he'd dispute that a lot of people have got madly richer and just as many are miserably poorer. "Multiple deprivation" was the phrase, I think. But I don't waste time arguing the hows and whys of all that with my father. Or my sister, or any of the two million happy shareholders in British Telecom.'

'You have a sister? What does she do with herself?'

'She works for a public relations firm at Westminster. They're very close to the Conservatives.'

'How funny. So she's the real political animal of the family. And you, meanwhile, seek ordination to ministry.'

John nodded, a little perplexed by Lockhart's antithesis.

'Well, I hope no one's lied to you about the way we do things. You've read the syllabus? There are, of course, the core areas.

Doctrine, Old and New Testaments, the Fathers, Church history. Ethics we're rather big on, with reference to philosophy and theology. All of that appeals?'

John nodded. 'It's really theology that's my main interest.'

Lockhart closed his eyes meditatively, nodding as if to distant music. 'Theology is fundamental to Grey.' The eyes reopened. 'Who do you read that you fancy?'

Strange terms, thought John. 'John of the Cross. Tillich, I suppose. Bonhoeffer.'

Lockhart's eyebrows flicked heavenward. '"Religionless Christianity".'

'I don't think Bonhoeffer meant Christianity without God,' John hastened to add.

'Oh no,' Lockhart murmured. 'No, I expect he had in mind the dead weight of the Church. Or some of its votaries.'

'I should say the school of negative theology is the one I feel nearest to. The idea of God I feel I can best approach through a sense of His absence.'

'Oh well, of course, yes,' said Lockhart. 'There's that idea too.'

John was picking up something whimsical, unacceptably ironic, about this man, reflecting ill on the solemnity he had tried to summon for the occasion. He was unhappily put in mind of his chance meeting in the street only weeks ago – Amanda, out with her crowd, stopping and smiling brightly. But when he told her his news, his plans, she had bit her lip, her smile turning piteous. 'Oh John,' she had said.

'In any case,' Lockhart resumed, 'we get all sorts here. But the course itself is a set menu. Lectures are compulsory. You may feel your life has been full of such stuff.'

'It's true, I've been a long time about my education.'

'Quite. But here we believe in a proper balance between theory and practice. The true objective is to train you for your pastoral duties in the world. You are not hermits. You're free to pursue your hobbies, whatever they are – it doesn't have to be bell-ringing. There are certain domestic duties that fall by rota. How are you in the kitchen?'

'I'm told I make a decent pot of stew.'

'Oh well then, you're in.' Lockhart was turning over John's handwritten statement. 'No, I think I can understand your various interests, your background. What faith has meant to you. *Specifically*, though – I see you are someone who believes they "felt the call".'

John flinched. 'Isn't that how everyone feels – who comes?'

'No. No, it isn't.' Lockhart stared at him very levelly, then back to the statement. 'You refer to a particularly charged experience.'

'Yes, I had a – it was a couple of years ago – it gave me a very strong feeling. Not really . . . explicable, I thought. Not rational.'

'Go on.'

'I was in France, a village in the Auvergne region. I'd arranged some leave from my studies, I was – I wasn't in a very good frame of mind.'

'Why was that?'

John held his tongue for some moments, knowing nonetheless that this disclosure would have to be complete.

'My mother had died, very suddenly. I mean – she hadn't been well, it was a condition, malignant hypertension. But rest had seemed the only remedy. And, I hadn't seen her for a while but I thought that she was . . . coping.'

'But she wasn't?'

John nodded. 'My father called – I was in my college digs, in a bad way that day, just gloomy over some' – he sighed – 'oh, some totally insignificant personal woes. But my father reached me and he – I mean, I knew right away from the sound of him that it was bad, then he said Mum had had an awful stroke, and I, I said, "She won't die, will she?" And he said, "She's gone."'

The line of Lockhart's mouth twitched. 'I'm sorry.'

'It was a very low time.' John paused. 'But – my father told us we had lives to get on with, that's what he and Mum had always wanted. That's what Susannah did, my sister. I chose to get involved in this voluntary project in France. A restoration of some historical buildings.'

Lockhart raised a polite eyebrow.

'I just wanted to get away, try to make myself useful. I was in a team working on the sacristy of a Gothic chapel, and rebuilding a wall round an old medieval fortress. They were both stuck up on the same hill.'

'And was it useful to you, this work? Did it serve its purpose?'

'It did. My French got better – if only from people shouting at me for shoddy work. I learned to answer back. Learned how to cut stone. That was good – hard, hard on the hands, all the blisters and bloody knuckles. But rewarding. In itself.'

'And this was where you had your – experience.'

John nodded. 'It was after we downed tools one evening. We were all straggling back down from the hill, over the hay-fields to this old barn where they put us up. I was . . . exhausted, really a crushing fatigue, all the aches and grazes you get working stone. But I was – happy, I think. And I stopped walking and looked around me. It was that strange blue-rose light you see after sunset. There was a breeze. And I saw my friends' shadows lengthening over the ground, and the grass seemed to glow like jade. Very curious. And I shivered, but then – it was like a warmth crept all over me. And I felt such a sadness, right in the heart of things. But an amazing sweetness too – like they were of a piece, made of each other, the sadness and the sweetness. And I just realised that there was nothing wrong in the world. Nothing wrong but me – us, any of us. Nothing wrong but we don't see the *rightness* of it. The rightness of creation.'

In reliving his account, John had begun to feel a little light-headed anew. Lockhart had bridged his fingers, his brow creased. 'It didn't occur to you that you were perhaps just suffering exhaustion. Or, I don't know, that you'd ingested something?'

John winced – this was not the consideration he had wished for. At the same time, he knew, the shaky, groggy vertigo he had felt in that field had been not so far removed from the aftermath of his one hallucinogenic experience in college, a week or so after Amanda ended their affair, when in the depths of dolour he had let a course-mate talk him into swallowing a hundred dried and bulbous psilocybin mushrooms. Yet he was ready to insist on a vital distinction.

'No, the feeling had come from nowhere, and it was incredibly strong – in fact it became – frighteningly so. Like a thrumming in my head and behind my eyes, violent colours. I was scared, to be honest. I had to keep telling myself my name. Eventually some sort of calm came back to me. Some clarity. The colours faded, the noise too. Then it was as if my chest was full of fibres, all being knotted together, against my will, too tight to bear. But the feeling was exquisite, more powerful than any I'd known.' He shrugged. 'Then it was over. My friends were shouting for me. I could feel the earth under my feet. A greenfly on my wrist. And all was well.'

He had felt laughter, too, as he recalled – surging up his chest cavity like cool water through a brass pipe, racing to break forth. It had emerged as a wracking sob, and his workmates had seen the need to support him in the slow trudge back to the barn. But this, again, was not a detail John thought to disclose.

'What I mean is, I knew very clearly that I had had an experience.'

'You felt a presence.'

'It was . . . I suppose I'd say it was a worshipful moment? I'd been feeling a lot of things oppressing me. Then they just lifted.'

'What sort of things?'

'Just mainly my own self-absorption, I suppose.' Lockhart shook his head, gently, quizzically. John was disconcerted to find more words come forth. 'I'm sure I'd been feeling quite bereft, as you do. But after I had this . . . this moment . . . it just reminded me, I suppose, that life is short, really. And I had best get on and try to do things.'

'Do you think that's what your mother would have wanted?'

'Actually it's more my father's sort of – credo. I don't really know what she would have wanted. We didn't have that discussion. I didn't really pay her that courtesy. Before it happened.' John found his throat and speech suddenly clotted.

'Would you like a drink?'

'No, thank you, I'm okay.'

Lockhart bridged his fingers. 'Have you considered that perhaps what you really want to do is to, well, make good a loss?'

'No, not at all, I can't see how that would . . .'

Lockhart winced and waved a hand. 'No, forgive me, I am a psychoanalyst *manqué*. I ought really to stick to what I know.'

John coughed. 'Sorry, I will perhaps take a small drink if I may.'

Lockhart nodded, rose and went to his drinks table, unstopping the decanter. 'I don't mean to harass you. The fact is, I was myself reluctantly called. And that is the more common way, I find. The early Fathers, you know, a good number of them were *nominated*. Pre-ordained? In spite of what path they may have wished to follow.' He handed John a small port and resumed his seat. 'No, the common element isn't really a calling. It's a sort of a wound we carry, I'd say. An intimate wound.'

John was silent, uneasy. Having felt his own inner ballast overturned, he had no notion of how now to take Lockhart's confession. The master glanced down at the papers before him, as if abashed, then looked longer, and was silent awhile.

'You were born the same year I was ordained. I daresay half your generation were baptised in an Anglican church. The next lot, it wouldn't surprise me if that number were halved again. You'll be aware, I'm sure, of the present catastrophe in church attendance. When they offer the figures now, I have to look away. Like a car crash.'

After some moments, John shrugged. 'I don't know, what are you asking me?'

'Just consider this. You're twenty-two. As a candidate for ministry you propose to devote your whole working life to Christ. The duties are taxing. The pay is not generous. I'm asking are you serious?'

'I do understand – the price of the ticket, Reverend.'

Lockhart raised his chin and smiled. 'Of course you do. Very good, John, very good. Well, I really look forward to welcoming you among us.'

The master steered him out of the door, and then John stood alone once more in the wan sunlight of the college quadrangle, its lawns, beds and paths segmented around a slow-trickling stone fountain. He was unable to entirely shake the sense that he had been weighed in the balance, found a little wanting. But if Lockhart were laying some kind of wager on his level of commitment, then – and in this John was determined – the master had yet no notion of the zeal with which he would be repaid.

Chapter VII

WISE COUNSEL

Wednesday, 25 September 1996

'Now be ready to bite your tongue here, marra,' said Jack Ridley.

In reply Gore merely rapped the hardbacked notebook in his lap. He was not entirely certain if Ridley's remark was by way of scold or friendly warning, just as he was not entirely certain of its maker. But they were on the road again, driving north of Hoxheath through Arthur's Hill for the mile or so to St Mark's Church in Fenham. It was the dog-end of the working day, the only time, Gore understood, when his Parochial Council could be quorate, given the diverse commitments of its members.

Ridley steered his Fiesta through a sprawl of handsome semi-detached housing, the pavements congested with teenage school-children in impeccable black sweaters and blazers. St Mark's Church was set back through gates, in tidily landscaped grounds. They walked up the pathway to the vestry, a modern glass-fronted extension bolted onto the chapel. Inside, the door to a meeting room was propped open. Therein the table was already populated, teacups laid out. The Reverend Bob Spikings moved quickly down the length of the room to take Gore's hand.

'Hullo there, John. So, you, uh, found us, then?'

Spikings seemed to Gore like some dreamy corporate IT boffin, apologetic and mildly harassed. He was bespectacled and tidily bearded, probably in his late forties, a peeling Filofax and a mobile phone set by his teacup. Gore paid only a half-measure of attention as he was escorted round the table for the naming ritual. Here was a retired lady hairdresser, there a technical manager with Findus Foods; a manager at the electric company sat with a former bus driver. A journalist had a pen and pad before him.

Spikings's petite dark wife Rose had taken the chair by her husband. Gore assumed his seat beside Ridley at the far end of the long table, nodding in the direction of Monica Bruce, and struck a contemplative pose.

Spikings called the table to order and offered thanks to the attendees, who nodded sagely in approval of themselves. Then hasty footfalls emanated from outside and a latecomer ploughed into the room, dressed in clerical suit, barking some last remarks into a phone clamped to his ear. He grasped a free chair, made his phone to vanish, and smiled broadly at the assembled. The man from Findus tapped his watch. Spikings cut in. 'Simon Barlow, everybody. Simon has his own eventide to be ready for, but he's come across town tonight to help us out.'

'Not a problem,' Barlow chirped. 'Happy to. Really sorry, everyone. John.' And he waved to Gore down the length of the table. Gore nodded coolly in return.

'John, you and Simon, uh, know each other, right?'

'Yes,' said Gore, 'from Grey College. We're maybe older and wiser now.'

'Bound to be, mate. That's the real world, isn't it? Lessons, all the time.'

Gore was curious to see what a few years out in the field had done for his old classmate. For sure, he had grown out the rather *Hitlerjugend* grade-two crop formerly favoured, but he retained a bristly and fastidious goatee. Still familiar, too, the sleepy, hooded hazel eyes, the glottal stops that were his Essex birthright, and the skewed grin that seemed to shoot up one side of his face. Gore glanced around the gathering: anyone who appeared cosy with the latecomer, either verbally or in body language, had to be suspected for a suburban crusader of Barlow's evangelical stripe. But for the moment the apostle Simon sat alone, generally resented.

Spikings pressed his palms flat on the table. 'Okay, now everybody's finally, uh, bothered to show up, I think we should kick off by talking timetables. The schedule for John's mission in Hoxheath. John, how long do you say – actually, how much time do we *all* think John should set aside for the groundwork? The prep and canvassing and so forth, before he calls a date for his first service?'

The ex-hairdresser had raised a troubled hand.

'Yes, Susan?'

'Sorry, Bob, but can we not start and say what sort of a service we're talking about?'

'What *sort*?' Spikings chuckled uneasily. 'That'll be up to John – I mean, within the usual, uh, parameters, of course.'

'Yes, but, we don't know who he *is*, see.'

Gore glanced at Spikings so as to assume the speaker's role. 'It will be the *sort* of service I'm sure you're used to, Susan. Reverent and seemly. I should say, though – as you all know, this is a low-budget production. And we've no idea yet who is our congregation, right? So I'll have to use a bit of imagination. I'm sure you can all trust me on that.'

Spikings was nodding emphatically. 'It's your show, John.'

'It's not ideal, but, is it?' muttered the bus driver. 'Having it in a school?'

Monica twitched. 'What's wrong with my school?'

Gore countered. 'Well, firstly, I don't have any choice, not as far as I know. Second, I can see this is a fine building you've got here. I'm sure we all think our older churches are very handsome, but these days I'm not sure they're wholly appropriate for who it is we need to reach.'

'He's right, you know.' It was Barlow, to Gore's surprise. 'No use droning on about lovely old buildings if they're crumbling down on all sides and there's no one in 'em but two old dears and a dog. That's not a *living* church.' Barlow leaned forward, clenching his fists in emphasis, a debating trick Gore knew of old.

Susan was riled. 'Well, Mr Barlow, *we* get more than two old dears, I can –'

'I bet you do. No, but look, I don't want to get us off on an edgy one, but – is this council just a talking shop? Are we just gonna sit here carping on at John about what he should do before he's done it? Or are we gonna try and give him some practical advice? Something he can work with?'

A kindly effort, thought Gore. Though it didn't sound entirely spontaneous.

'Fair enough, John's not done this before and you don't know him. But I do. Don't you worry, he knows his onions. Guys like John and me, we're trained, this is what we're *for*. But what we're talking here, surely, is nuts and bolts. Spadework.'

The manager nodded. 'Aye, getting round the doors, leafleting people and that.'

'Agreed. John needs volunteers, right?'

'Yes.' Spikings seemed anxious to recover his chairmanship. 'Yes, of course, we need a list of people ready to help John with the, uh, spadework.'

'Exactly,' said Barlow. 'John will give the orders. But we find him the troops.'

Spikings gestured to his wife, scribbling diligently on a pad. 'Okay. How?'

'Well, we should have a proper coffee morning,' said Susan.

Of course, thought Gore, *all things in the Church get done over hot beverages.*

'Then,' said Barlow, 'as our friend says, John needs to start pounding them streets.'

'Aye, you'll have to get on your bike,' Mr Findus chortled.

'Well, I've got rather a good one, as it happens,' said Gore.

'Can I just say?' The journalist spoke up. 'That might be something I could get in the paper. You know, "the cycling parson"? Bit of publicity.'

'Right. Minute that one, Rose. Action point, Phil to talk to the *Journal*.'

'Okay,' said Barlow. 'Now, not to usurp your role, Bob, but I suggest we get down to brass tacks. Targets. What do we practically hope for John in terms of turnout?'

The subsequent silence was awkward. Gore was himself curious.

'I find,' Spikings hazarded, 'that . . . thirty people? Is a, uh, perfectly good congregation. I mean, not too shabby.'

'Thirty,' Barlow repeated. 'That sound okay by you, John?' Gore nodded. Such a target would cause him no pain, at least for now.

'Okay, now we're moving. But let's not put a cap on the ambition. See, at my church in Gosforth right now we get about two hundred and fifty.'

Liar. How on earth . . .? thought Gore.

'Not so long ago, but – yeah, we were about thirty. Then, bit by bit, more people started coming along more regular. Why was that, eh?' The table was Barlow's audience now, in his hand. 'Because they were *invited*. By someone they knew. It's all about building networks, see?'

'A lot depends on where you're starting from, Simon.' Spikings too, Gore could see, was feeling a needle's prick in Barlow's veiled boast. 'You have more of a, uh, *middle-class* catchment.'

'It's not a *class* thing, Bob. That's not the attraction. It's about friends telling friends there's a place they can go and make *new* friends.'

'I take Simon's point,' said Gore, deciding to be generous. 'It's obvious people on the estates I'll be dealing with can lead quite isolated lives. We have a chance to get them together into a group, however small. Make them welcome. Treat them well.'

'Now of course you need a bit more muscle,' said Barlow, 'if you want to pull in two hundred. At mine we've got the live music, the crèche, the youth leaders –'

'Your success precedes you, Simon,' muttered Spikings.

'Well, but I do like to think it's something to do with the preaching. Bringing the gospel to people every day. Don't forget that either, John.'

'I'll preach the gospel, Simon.' Gore held his fire. 'Once there's people to preach to. Once they're sitting comfortable. First, they need a place to sit.'

Silence, and a few sharp looks exchanged. Susan raised a hand once more. 'Are you going to have a Sunday School?'

'Right!' said Barlow cheerily. 'Whatever happened to Sunday School, eh?'

'In due course, perhaps. If I can raise these volunteers.'

'Well, you want young people, I've got 'em, John. So I've got a few tips for you in that department.'

Jack Ridley cleared his throat fiercely at Gore's side. All looked to him. 'It's worth saying, Mr Barlow, they're having maybe a dim view of the "old dears", but I see a lot of the older folk round Hoxheath, they're not happy making the trip to Fenham of a Sunday because the buses divvint run in this direction. So they have to cadge lifts off their children. Their grandchildren even.'

Spikings nodded fiercely. 'Well, there you go. There's a, uh, demographic that needs targeting.'

Gore nodded. 'I was wondering too about diversity?' He assessed the blank faces and ventured afresh. 'Thinking laterally, are there other kinds of partnership possible? In the community? A youth club, a woman's centre? Is there a Muslim association?'

Mr Findus scowled. 'Try the health centre. The doctors are all Bengali.'

'Don't run before you can walk, John,' said Barlow smilingly, reclining in his seat.

Spikings intervened. 'John, you have a limited budget, remember. There's the Urban Fund, there's contributions, and that's about it. Oh! There's a thing we need to talk about, fundraising, minute that if you would, Rose.'

Barlow waved a hand. 'Honest, John, whatever money you've got, you want to spend it like it's the last you'll ever have. And not on half-baked social services that aren't in our remit. Not before you've got a single volunteer.'

Okay, Gore thought, *another time then*.

'I think,' said Spikings, 'we need to get that coffee morning in the diary without delay. It should be an early evening, really, shouldn't it? Where do we have it?'

'I would be glad,' said Gore, 'if we could have it at St Luke's. Get started, break the place in.'

'Not a problem,' said Monica.

Spikings looked to his wife. 'So. Tea and biscuits for parents, pensioners and all interested parties at St Luke's School. Lovely.'

As Gore followed Ridley out into chillier evening air, Barlow was climbing into the seat of his octane-blue Ford Mondeo, but on seeing them both he re-emerged hastily and strode toward Gore, arms thrown out alarmingly wide.

'John, what am I thinking, eh? Proper hello?'

Gore was yanked into a clumsy embrace that he suffered for the sake of form, until Barlow stepped back and beamed at him. 'Well, that was scintillating stuff, eh?'

'Thank you for contributing.'

'Oh, you couldn't have kept me away. No way, not when I heard about this number. "John Gore evangelizes Hoxheath." Whatever next?'

'I didn't think urban mission was your thing, Simon.'

'Wouldn't have thought it was *yours*, John. No, the whole planting thing I'm fascinated by. I envy you. It's a real test, though. Good luck to you, mate.'

'Thank you.'

'Oh, you'll need it, you know that?' He dropped into a conspiratorial mode. 'In terms of driving things forward round here? You've got a lukewarm engine under you.' He had taken Gore's arm, freshly touchy-feely. 'You still in touch with old Lockhart?'

'Not so much. He wasn't keen on my coming here. Leaving where I was in Dorset.'

'Dear me. Never thought the master and his blue-eyed boy would come to blows.' Barlow was making a most regretful face. Gore ignored the easy scurrility.

'I didn't know you'd come north, Simon. How did that happen?'

'Oh, I just fancied getting my hands good and dirty. Out in the field. Like you.'

'Not so much dirt about where you are in Gosforth, if I remember.'

'It's not as leafy as you think, mate. Nowhere is in Newcastle.' Barlow's estuarine emphasis – *'Noo-carsel'* – was violence to Gore's ear. 'Anyway, but. Now I'm here I can't imagine being anywhere else. No, you'll be seeing a lot more of me, John. "I will tarry at Ephesus until Pentecost, for a great door and effectual has opened unto me, and I have many adversaries." Let's you and me have a pint sometime, eh?'

That corkscrew grin vaulted and curled up the right side of Barlow's face once again, rolling back the years. He turned, waved a hand over his shoulder, and strode back to the Mondeo.

Chapter VIII

APOSTLES

18 September 1992

'What do we have here?' So asked Canon Burn, babyishly fair of hair if sadly scant of same. The question was rhetorical. 'A document dating from 1563. Eight years later it's appended to the Prayer Book. Today it's commended to us by section five of the Worship and Doctrine Measure . . .'

Gore sat in the Grey College seminar room, sucking a pencil, contemplating the morning light across a classmate's broad dark back. Before him, as before all ten of them, a facsimile of the Thirty Nine Articles of the Church. *All these years,* he thought, *and I'm still at school, behind a desk, scribbling.*

'These Articles, then, are a statement of our belief. But they don't govern us. They are parameters. We just agree that what they say is broadly compatible with scripture.'

'What a load of mush.'

Barlow, of course, rocking in his chair, arms folded like a full stop. Gore thought the barrow-boy manner an affectation, no less irksome than the jeering hazel-eyed gaze or the convict's starkness of cropped hair and beard.

'If they've not got *authority*, why do we bother with them?'

Burn's smile was thin. 'For the purpose of study, Simon. A value in itself. At the same time I should say I know clergy who've never read them.'

'Oh, I bet you do.'

Burn lifted his nose clear of the taunt. 'If we just consider Article Twenty-Eight . . .'

Gore glanced to the page. *Transubstantiation, or the change in the substance of bread and wine, is repugnant to the plain words of Scripture.*

Barlow stirred first. 'Yeah, right. Exactly.'

'Yes, and yet,' purred Burn, 'as we know, there are some in our communion who take just this view. Believing in the real bodily presence in the Eucharist.'

Barlow rubbed at his face. 'Why can't we just take one line and stick to it? Eh? Look there, see, number six? "Scripture contains all things necessary to salvation." Nothing half-baked about that, is there? Can't quarrel with it, can you? Anyone?'

Gore knew what had to follow, sure as the earth turned. It seemed a hollow laugh now, yet in their first term Barlow, son of a salesman of cleaning products, had seized on him as a kindred spirit – perhaps the one other ordinand who had not come from the home counties via Oxford or Cambridge. 'You and me are the hardcore men here,' Barlow had bashed at his ear. 'Let's get hammered some night, thrash out a few things.' This as if they were affable fans of the same football team. Over time it had grown clear that they took rival sides.

'Simon,' Gore now weighed in, 'the Bible forbids usury, doesn't it? When you go into Barclays to discuss your overdraft, do you kick over their tables? Come on, this is a pre-Enlightenment document. It would be backward to endorse all of it.'

'Who are you to tell me that?' Barlow spat, then sharply directed his shorn scalp at Burn. 'And you, you stand there nodding your head? Call yourself an instructor?'

Burn seemed to flinch – the room merely to roll its collective eyes, as ever when Messrs Gore and Barlow got into one of their little furies, for hours had been lost to the same bitter end over the last twelve months.

'Simon, the fact is there aren't two of us in this room who'd agree on every one of these Articles. Never mind *outside* of it. But the argument, the *complexity* of it – that's what we're about.'

Barlow's gaze was baleful. 'What planet are you from, son? You are *dead* wrong, it is *exactly* what we're *not* about. I mean, what about when you've gotta actually stand up in a pulpit, John? Are you gonna say the cross is the way to salvation? Or are you gonna say to people, "Oh, mercy, I tell you, this 'believing' lark, it ain't half *complex . . .*"? How's your ordinary churchgoer supposed to make sense of that?'

Gore took his pause, let Barlow's fine spittle settle. 'I won't have any problem telling people that the faith can mean something quite different to any one of them.'

'Oh will you? *Nice*, John. But you know what? You'll be preaching to an empty church. *Empty*, mate. You know why? Because people who like that sort of guff, they don't *go* to church. They don't read the Bible. They go to the *theatre*. And they read the *Guardian*. People who go to *church* on a Sunday want to hear a sound man. Someone who believes what he's saying when he baptises their kids.'

'I think,' said Burn distantly, 'we've strayed far enough –'

'No, look, John, just tell me straight. No one's listening anyway. Do you believe Christ was born of a virgin? Do you believe His tomb was empty? I know it only *says* so, in all the gospels, but I just want your personal view.'

'Whatever I say I believe, Simon, it yields no proof anyway.'

Barlow snatched up the Articles, waved them aloft. 'I mean, what's sacred, eh? What's left? Next you'll be saying we don't have to believe in *God*, not *really* . . .'

There was a silence of mere moments, yet sufficient for Barlow to scan the room, before – with a timing that Gore thought risible, theatrical – raising his palms aloft, as if beset by enemies on all sides. 'Oh, come on. Don't be scaring me now. *Somebody* say they believe in God.'

Lunch hour in the common room, a dozen ordinands congregated. The humbly worn seating area projected out to a generous terrace, ideal in summer, but today was colder and the French windows were closed. Scattered side tables offered newspapers and makings for tea, and Gore had got himself nicely settled for both when he sensed a presence over him.

'Hullo, Gavin.'

'John. Mind if I sit? I wondered if we might chat about the Augustine essay?'

'Sure.' Gore nodded and made room for Gavin Knott – slight, of nondescript height, his dark curls cut close, a hangdog aspect to his gaze. His 'casual' wardrobe was yet fastidious, black jeans ironed, grey chambray shirt buttoned to his throat. He appeared self-contained, sufficient unto himself, if not hugely cheered by the fact. He and Gore were partners in a weekly visit to the local hospital, where Knott was rather enviably effective in consoling elderly patients on the wards. Gore, at best, had achieved a shallow rapport with a Nigerian cleaning woman.

No sooner was Knott sat, though, than they had more company – Charlie Gummer, round in the middle, thin on top, bearing a furled broadsheet and a supermarket carrier bag. 'Hello Gloria, Judy,' he sang.

When first greeted in this fashion Gore had felt some hackles rise, before realising it was simply an irredeemable trait in Gummer, and part of the tolerant atmosphere of Grey, fostered from on high by Lockhart.

'Look, quail's eggs. Sainbury's had them discounted.'

Gore tried to look impressed. Gavin too was being asked to coo, but he was not comfortable. And yet Gummer was allegedly his pal, another of a High Church disposition, hence their Tweedledum-and-Tweedledee alliance.

Gummer settled himself on the banquette between them with a modicum of squirming. 'So, you and Essex Man at each other's throats again, John,' he tutted. 'You know, I don't agree with Simon, not on much. Sometimes I think he's a bit touched? Few pages stuck together, upstairs.'

Gore nodded.

'Though I will say, he's got nice eyes.' Gummer was beating his *Telegraph* against his leg. Now he thrust the paper at Gore. 'More grief for the Windsors, you see? Charlie's been at it too.'

Gore glanced at the front page, given over to some new revelations about the marital strife of the Prince of Wales and his wife. 'Does it really bother you?' he murmured, returning the paper.

'"Bother" me? Our future king? Excuse me, Judy, in case you didn't notice, the monarch is the head of our Church.'

'But this is the front page? When we were just chucked out of the ERM?'

'Oh that's just . . . *money*. And bloody Europe.'

'A recession, Charles, and all because a few rich men with more money than the government start –'

Gummer clapped hands over ears in the manner of the prudently deaf monkey. 'La-la-la-la-la! Boring!'

Fine, thought Gore, *live in your own little cloister*.

'Judy, *this* is a constitutional matter. Does he plan on being a divorced king? Marrying his divorced mistress? Or does he just think he'll keep her on as his bit? No, we *have* to deplore this. The public demands it of us. To be properly reverent about things. It's like the opening of parliament. That's where we're at our best, Judy. In purple.'

'In pantomime, you mean,' Gore murmured.

'John,' said Knott, nearly smiling, 'I seem to recall you saying that vicars ought to be a bit like actors.'

Gummer was rubbing his hands toward a trestle table piled with shrink-wrapped sandwiches. 'Right, then, I've got my victuals but what'll you girls have?'

'Not for me, thanks, Charles, I've a lunch date.' Gore was glad to rise and stride out into the air, free of the airless sun-bleached room, mired in matters that Barlow's beloved Man in the Street would surely think queer if not redundant.

The designated restaurant on King Street was a brasserie, wrought-iron tables and chairs set for alfresco diners under a stiff white canvas awning. Gore the anchorite felt he had come to the outside world in some style. Within its shaded depths, a crisp young man danced across the laminate floor toward him.

'I'm here to meet Ms Susannah Gore?'

'Twelve-thirty? She's not here but I'll take you to table.'

Today was a surprise summons. Either Susannah was feeling unusually guilty for time not spent or, more likely, desirous of displaying her fast-moving prosperity, her irresistible rise within the firm of Hook Millard. His sole fear was that she might have a problem she wanted to share: if so, they were liable to sit marooned in unhappiness. Their teenage jousting had fallen into disuse, but nothing more meaningful had filled its place, so markedly different were their adult worlds. For four or more years she had been in an on–off relationship with a Tory MP, one Sebastian Sellars, a suave sort of a pig – relations that John firmly if fruitlessly deplored. Now he was given to believe the affair was in a dormant phase. But she surely had to know he had no advice to give? There was, then, a more discomfiting thought. If he were her best hope for sympathy, did she have any real friends?

And here she was, slipping between tables, rather chic in a black polo-neck, a heathery-grey wool miniskirt, sheer tights and knee-length black leather boots. He rose, they embraced lightly.

'I like your outfit.'

'Of course you like it. It's sort of *dull*, isn't it?'

She set down a dinky paging device and lit a menthol cigarette. Gore inspected the menu, mentally reckoning the price of each entrée as a percentage of his current account balance. Susannah leaned across the table, hand over face in stage whisper. '*Divvint worry, kidder. You can have the steak.*' She sat back, pleased with herself, and by her brother's giggle. 'I'll just claim it back. Or will I? Yeah, I will. I'll put you down as a consultant. Say you were advising me. On what *Jesus* would have done.'

'Don't let me get you in trouble.'

'Oh, trust me, you're small fry to what some of those buggers spend. You should have seen our summer party. Smoked salmon and champagne all night for two hundred. But – it pays for itself. So you have your steak.'

'What do you mean, "pays for itself"?'

'Well, there's plenty of our clients happy to sponsor a nice little drinky. They like meeting MPs. It cuts both ways – MPs like meeting millionaires. Who knows what it could mean down the road? Maybe a few thousand jobs in their backyard.'

'It sounds like – what do you call it? Insider trading?'

'Never. It's just like-minded people having a nice little drinky.'

'So you like it, then? Lobbying?'

'Well, I was fucked off with PR. Having to worry about the size of bloody *billboards* all the time. No, it's good, lobbying. We just took a job for the Nigerian government, would you believe? French Water Board before that. I got threatened with Scottish and Newcastle Breweries, but I telt them, "Listen, I don't drink turps."'

'What can you do for the Nigerian government?'

'Just present a case. For something they'd like done. They've maybe got a project and they're not certain how we do things, how our market works. Same as if it's a foreign manufacturer, he's maybe worried if he sets up here then he won't get to run off his waste into the River Tees. Little does he know, eh? So, anyhow, then we might have a word with one of our MPs.'

'*Your* MPs?'

'We've got a few members we pay. Consultants. We're only starting a conversation they'd want to be having anyway . . . What's that look for?'

'Nobody *elected* any of you lot, Su.'

'Pet, what is an MP for? God, if people knew, all what *doesn't* get done in their names, by whatever monkey they sent up, I tell you, they wouldn't set much store on the whole . . .' – she sighed – 'I don't know, *box-ticking* part of things. Anyhow, there's no politics in what we do. Not party politics like you think. We're not . . . *contaminated* by any of that. The people I work with, they're just clever people. They might have Tory backgrounds or Labour backgrounds, none of it counts on the job.'

'Who do you know has a *Labour* background?'

'Oh, we've taken on Labour people since the election. A lad used to be in the press office, a girl from one of the think-tanks. They're good, too.'

Gore did not quite believe the heresy. But a high gleam stayed in her eye as entrées were served. 'Do you remember a guy called Martin Pallister?'

'I do. Lecturer. From Newcastle? I remember his dad too.'

'His dad? Well, Martin came to see me and I'm doing a bit work for him. On the side, really. Off the books.'

'What can you do for a college lecturer?'

'Oh no, he's come on a fair bit. Wants to be an MP. I've been advising him. We ran into each other a few years back – that course I did out in Surrey?'

Gore had vague recall of his sister spending a long weekend at some country hotel being instructed in assertiveness, not an attribute he remembered as wanting in her or indeed Martin Pallister.

'Don't worry, it's not sexual. Just a job. No, my sex life is a bore, dahling.'

'No one left on the Tory benches takes your fancy?'

'Please. They're a lot of wimps. Snuck into the Commons under Maggie's skirts. They look a poor lot now she's gone, I can tell you.' She had taken on a dreamy aspect, her osso buco neglected. 'Seb wasn't like that. Not gay, or weird. Not on the take, not really. Just a smart, handsome guy. The wrong horse, but. Wife and kiddie and that. Don't know where my head went to there.' Gore was silent, feeling much the novice. Susannah shook her head as though to dislodge clinging irritants. 'No. No, I was silly. It won't happen again.'

'At least you got out unscathed.'

She pouted at him, as if the comment were woundingly heedless.

'Well, you did. All in all? Didn't you?'

A quite unthinkable thought occurred to Gore, and he quashed it before it gestated, chewing at length on his lean, flavourless beef fillet. To his relief Susannah recovered her stride. 'What I need is a new job. Or new contacts. Your lot are coming up.'

'We only got beat six months ago.'

'Well, defeats can be blessings in disguise. Isn't that what Churchill's wife told him when he lost to what's-his-face?'

'Atlee.'

'Aye, him. No, Smith's hopeless, just a Scots lawyer. He's not Kinnock, but. He could maybe beat Major. *You* could maybe beat Major.'

'You're too kind.'

'I'm serious. The ERM thing is a fucking *disaster*. I suppose you enjoyed it.'

Gore shrugged. Yes, he had felt a certain sickly thrill in the Tory calamity, worsening with each hourly news bulletin, the bumbling schoolboy Chancellor fighting his feckless rearguard, buying sterling in billions while foreign speculators bet against him with lethal ease.

Their plates were being whisked away, Susannah lighting up moodily. 'Housing market's gone rotten too. Just when I had my eye on Islington.'

'It's all about houses, isn't it?'

'You bet it is, pet. Ask your Church about it. You know how much they've pissed away on property? Eight hundred *million*. They might have to sell the Metro Centre.'

The Church's interest in a Gateshead shopping mall was not of interest to Gore. He tried to let Susannah see as much. 'Don't sneer, bonny lad, that's your pension there. I was reading, actually, about the Metro, they've got a *chaplain*, of all things? Presumably he goes around telling people not to spend all their money. Made us think, but. Have you picked out your pitch yet? That could be one for you . . . You didn't want coffee, did you?'

'No, I have class at two. Ethics.'

'Oh, ethics indeed? Is that where Basildon is?'

She glanced at her slip of a Tag Heuer watch, and made what John considered a rather over-defined show of flipping her credit card at the small white dish on which the bill was lolling.

The custom of the evening was for a loose affiliation of more sociable ordinands to follow Compline by a visit to one in the rank of pubs on King Street. Arriving solo after the terse weekly phone call to his father, Gore pushed through the door of the Nell Gwyn to find the session in swing, and saw to his dismay that Simon Barlow had inserted himself into the heart of the sodality.

'Right then, Gore's here, let's have some proper crack about the vote.'

Charlie Gummer set down his tall frothy lager. 'Ears! Ears! La-la-la-la-la! Not women! No, I bar the subject!'

Gore turned for the bar, there procuring a warm pint of sour sudsy bitter and a bag of peanuts, but on his return he found the issue unabated.

'The whole thing,' Gummer was gesticulating, 'is just a ghastly American import. Like *Dynasty*. All this time, there's poor Rome patiently reaching out to us. Now we're just going to blow that all to hell.'

Gore set down his pint. 'Who cares about Rome? We're Anglicans. We ought to have the right enemies. I pay no more heed to the Pope than I do to Mystic Meg.'

'*Ooh*. Nice one.' Barlow banged the table. 'Them's fighting words.'

'Well, I tell you now,' Gummer declared airily, 'I'd as soon go off and start up a whole new church than have to share the one we've got with a load of dippy *birds*. Is that what you want for our Communion, John? Women bishops, ordaining priests? It's ridiculous. Where's our authority then?'

Barlow clattered the table again: Gore knew it for a shameless ploy. '*Right*. And Christ told Peter, "On this rock I build My Church." And after Peter was Linus, after Linus Clement, after Clement . . . Who was it, Gavin?'

'Anacletus,' murmured Gavin Knott.

'*Anacletus*. Doesn't that stir your blood, Gore? Doesn't it *move* you? Our heritage, our descendance? From them who walked with Christ?'

Gore chose to ignore the monkey. 'You're very quiet, Gavin.'

Knott's eyes flicked upward from his glass of red-ink Syrah. 'Well, if you're asking for my view of the question, I should say – I do believe there's a reason why God chose to – incarnate himself, as a male. To reveal himself in that form. And take only men for his disciples. I do, yes.' He nodded.

'What reason is that then?' Gore was truly curious.

'Oh, I don't say I *know* what it is.' And Knott chuckled, the rarest of sights. 'But it does seem He was content it be so.'

A hundred easy ripostes occurred, but Gore bit his lip. He saw no point in arguing with a wilful mystic, or playing the male feminist in this homosocial conclave.

On returning heavy-footed to his set of rooms he should have gone directly to his bed, he knew, and yet instead, enervated, he fell onto the chaise longue and there stared glazedly and gloomily at a hollow of plaster in the wall. At some point, though, he must have faded into sleep, for the next he knew he was peering with bleary eyes at the back of a hunched and bristly figure perched on the end of his bed. Lit only by the bedside-table lamp, its shoulders seemed to shake with contained mirth. The grace of a few more befuddled moments were needful for Gore to take this strange sight as reality rather than dream-state.

'Simon . . .? What are you doing?'

Barlow swivelled to face him. 'Your door was wide open, pal. Thought I'd better check on you. Someone might have done you an injury.'

Gore hoisted himself upright, dry-mouthed, not madly grateful.

'Reason I *come*, see, is cos I thought you might fancy a nightcap?'

Now Gore saw the bottle of Bulgarian red on the bedside table, next to a pair of his utility glass tumblers, both of them generously charged.

'Here.' Barlow thrust a tumbler at him. 'Have a sip. It's not too foul for what it cost.' He took a swig of his own, then smacked his lips with a livid tongue. 'God almighty. Gav and old Charlie, eh? Fattypuff and Thinnifer. I mean, yeah, the whole women thing is barmy. But I can't stomach the way that Charlie puts it. See, you reckon I rub along okay with that lot, don't you?'

'No, not necessarily.' Gore sniffed uneasily at the wine.

'Well, it's true, I'm all for the High Church mob if it helps stick it to all you liberal scum. And I like this Pope, I'll say that. He's the boss, what he says goes. But that's it. No, he puts me right off my supper, that Charlie.'

'Why?'

'Oh, don't come the innocent, John. You know how it is round here. All these mincers. Closet cases, making rules to suit their own *perversions*. Or is that all okay by you then, is it?'

'Not just me,' Gore groaned. 'The bishops. We have a position, it's been settled. You know what Lockhart says. "God intends a partner for each one of us." Who knows, Simon, He may even have a partner for you.'

'Oh, funny, yeah. Not *clergy*, but. If they want to be clergy, the gayers, they're supposed to mend their ways. Get straightened out. I tell you what *I* think's funny. Letting them decide what God wants for them. What's the bet they decide he wants what *they* want? Eh? Lovely. So no harm in a little bit of buggery then.'

'Do you have to use that word?'

'People shouldn't hide it, John, or try and talk around it. *God* sees it. Augustine calls it dead right. "Let your sin have you for its judge, not its patron."' Barlow took a sluicing swallow of wine. '*Any*how. That's not my *point*. My *point* with these High Churchers, what really winds me up is all this threatening to pick up their ball and flounce off to Rome. That's not how you win an argument, right? You stay the course, fight the good fight. My lot, we're not going anywhere, I'll tell you that.' And he grinned. 'You wish we would, don't you John?'

'You can do what you like.'

'Oh, very liberal, I'm sure.'

Barlow stood with a little difficulty and slouched across the rug toward Gore's fitted bookshelves, where he trailed fingers over a mounted print of Christ Pantokrator and the old brass miner's lamp that served as bookend to Gore's small paperback library. He peered closer. '"*Existentialist Biblicism*". Bloody hell. Very *thin*, these books of yours. I mean, why do you bother? With all these continental phonies?'

'I don't see the harm in reading.'

'Well, you say that, I'm not so sure. I think it waters down the faith.'

'What, you don't read?'

'I read scripture, John. Just scripture. And I find it sufficient unto the day. It's got all you need, scripture, if you look right. Amazing, it is. Have you never noticed that? I mean, what *do* you get out of scripture, John? If it's not the Word of God?'

Gore took a mouthful of jammy vinegar and gestured, grimacing, to his bookshelves. 'Barth tells us the text itself is not the revelation – it only becomes the Word if and when we hear God speak through it.'

'Oh, you *hear* God, do you? Personal, is it, then? Between you and Him?'

'No, I mean that I read the Bible as the word of men, of fellow believers. A historical text. And I find some clues there – themes, traces of things.'

'*Themes?* Like in a novel?'

'Great themes. Covenant, jubilee. Concern for the poor. The conquest of evil.'

'How about creation? Redemption? Judgement? *Those* themes, John.'

'Well, true, I'm not so keen as you on God the lawmaker. The judge in black cap at the end of days –'

'Don't talk crap, John. You're judging me now. You hate me just cos I've got the neck to say I might know right from wrong.'

'I don't hate you. I hate fundamentalism. I can't just believe one thing to the exclusion of everything else. I know I can't, because I know myself. I have oppositions inside me. Divisions. Cleavages.' And Gore smiled wanly, for a certain mad notion had begun to whittle within him, a scheme to drive out his unwelcome guest. 'God and Satan are in me, Simon. Male and female. Hetero, homo –'

Barlow only grimaced. 'Oh, piss off with that. What are you *doing* here, John? You've not come to learn, have you? Learn your trade, a proper working preacher? I mean, it drives me mad, it does, it's like you come into my church without wiping your feet. Moping about, talking rubbish. It's not good enough. These are dangerous times, *everything* we're about is under attack. And what's our defence? Eh? We're the next generation of ministers.

How many after us? Who's going to keep the gospel alive? Keep England in the faith?'

'"Old toad, old toad, help me down Cemetery Road . . ."'

'Shut up, idiot, it's your living too. I'm telling you, if we don't fight then this Church is dead. We've got to be out there, evangelising the nation. Or else we're irrelevant, we're just some little *sect*, trying to get on the telly so people give a toss. And that'll be your fault, Gore, you and your lot. I'm not afraid, see, I'm ready to preach the gospel like fire. You, you've got this . . . *literary* appreciation of it. Very nice, for you. But you don't see the power, *wonder*-working power in the words. '"Marvel not that I said unto thee, Ye must be born again." Let a man be reborn of water and the Spirit.'

Barlow was on his feet and bobbing and weaving, banging away to some inner drum, fit and measured for his pulpit. Despair crawled over Gore, that this awful man wouldn't leave him to his slumber – worse, that he might have a point. Still it would have pained him too much to grant such.

'It's not *your* Church, Simon – you didn't make it, you don't own it. You think your lot could ever get it back to what it was? Where? In a tent? Not in a million years. You'd drive away twice as many as you ever got in, I'd bet any money.'

'Oh yeah?'

'Yeah. Because you're a bigot. It's all just poison comes out of you. Anyone can see it a mile off. It'd be too much fun just to ignore you. You'd make me want to kiss a man on the mouth just to get you to fuck off.'

Barlow lunged at him. For a sick instant Gore thought they would fight. Instead – infinitely worse, before he could flinch – his head had been seized between Barlow's hands, a talon-like grip. The bristly head darted down and his mouth covered Gore's, wet and sour to the taste, his grainy cheeks rubbing and grazing. Appalled, writhing to free himself, Gore then felt teeth incising into his lower lip, and punched out at Barlow's chest, driving him off.

'For Christ's *sake*. Are you *mad*?' Gore shouted, struggling to his feet, rubbing at his mouth. But Barlow was grinning, standing proud, wagging a teacherly finger at Gore as if the disgrace were not his own.

'Must do better, John. Must do better.'

'Get out. Get out of my *room*.'

Unbowed, Barlow plucked his foul bottle of Bulgarian red from the table, swaggered to the door, slammed it jarringly behind him.

'I know how you feel. I'm the same, really. It's hard.' Lockhart bridged his fingers, staring directly ahead. Gore, sat in the wooden pew behind the master, followed his gaze down the length of the college chapel – deserted at this early hour – toward the altar that was set through a proscenium arch, bathed in the pale first light seeping through high windows, the back wall bare but for a text from Matthew in mounted letters. I AM WITH YOU ALWAYS, YET UNTO THE END OF THE WORLD.

'It would be nice sometimes, just to be left alone with the faith.' Lockhart sighed. '*But* – that's not the job, is it? Unless you want a post with the divinity faculty over the wall.'

'It's just . . . some of the people I'm here with, we have nothing whatever in common.'

'I see that, yes.'

'Well, doesn't it bother you?'

'I've lived long enough. What we *do* is disagree. Almost by definition. Ever since the Greeks and Latins. The Great Schism of the West. Martin Luther. It's just split after split, isn't it? We talk about holding the centre together, it's a lovely notion. But a pipe dream, really. It defies our history. What would it take? Fiat after fiat. Endless Acts of Supremacy . . . No, the more we try to unite, the sharper our differences seem. We're a bit like your Labour Party, I suppose. I don't think the public will swallow it.' Lockhart chuckled softly into his chest. 'And here I'm supposed to help you.'

True, thought Gore, it was a fool's predicament. 'It wouldn't matter. If I really felt certain I'll be effective. Out in the field.'

'Oh, I thoroughly expect you will, John. Really. I'm sure you'll make a good fist of whatever comes your way. Right now you're a bit low. Well, part of the job is absorbing that. Coming to terms with it. Just how low a person can feel. The sadness in life. It doesn't go away. The thing is knowing you can help others with it.'

'That doesn't sound like the greatest lot of use . . .'

'You'd be surprised. People don't generally give as much of themselves. Not as a priest has to. It's really a stern test, you know. Shouldering the sorrows of others . . . rarely a chore that works to one's own advantage. Quite the opposite. That's why it's so Christian. Why are you smiling?'

'You make it sound like martyrdom.'

'Oh no, not *martyrdom*. No, that's a concept I can't stand. That's a million miles away from the purpose of the faith.'

'Which is?'

An indulgent smile. 'Oh I thought you knew . . . Fellow-feeling, John. To foster our best attributes, none of which we understand well enough or practise sufficiently. You could have fifty million God-fearers and not a kind soul among them. No, God's kingdom on earth will be here when we're all just a bit kinder to each other.'

Gore touched the raw spot on his lower lip and nodded without cheer.

Chapter IX

PRINCIPLES

Friday, 27 September 1996

His father was peering at him patiently, clad in his old V-neck and slippers, a mild smile tugging his lips above a mug of instant coffee. Gore stole glances in turn, scrutinising Bill for signs of the creeping decrepitude to which Susannah had condemned him. But then Bill had always been anxious. Time could be as readily blamed for his sunken eyes and slowed reactions, just as it had thinned his silver hair and consigned him to a partial deafness.

The spinning carriage clock tossed light around the living-room walls. Audrey's Doulton ornaments were powdered with dust. The arm-cloths on the settee were sadly frayed, there were crumbs in the carpet, the kitchen linoleum loosening from its tacks. The want of a woman's presence was palpable. More doleful for Gore was the evidence of odd jobs ignored or started then abandoned. The coffee table was stacked with pamphlets of technical reading matter, and the dining-room table suggested some new fixation. Laid out upon an old bleached-out bath towel were stray bits of lighting equipment familiar to Gore from his days as a college thespian – a lantern and a Fresnel spotlight, a console of sliding switches, strewn yokes, clamps and safety chains, and a clutch of coloured filters.

Gore spoke up, as best and fully as he could, about his mission in Hoxheath. He wished to sound practical, purposeful, not like the feckless caretaker of some cowboy operation. His father only continued to smile and nod, but asked no questions, and seemed to make no assumptions. After a while it became clear to Gore that Bill was not truly interested, but had retained the civility to hear a man out.

He left the lounge to urinate, and found himself absorbed in the slow-peeling paper on the cloakroom ceiling. On his return, Bill rose, crossed the floor with a shuffling gait, unsettled a glossy brochure from the pile on the coffee table and tossed it onto Gore's lap. On its cover was an unnerving close-up of a chameleon.

'I found out what's been wrong with us at long last. Just from a read of that there. Have *you* heard of the British Disease? Your owld dad's got it.'

Nonplussed, Gore began to turn the page leaves.

'All of 'em at BT got sent one of these, every bloody employee. My old mate Don Cox sent it on to us. Now can you tell me, but, what the hell they're on about?'

Gore peered at the spare layout, reams of text trailing across whiteness, punctured by bold headlines and pull-out quotes. '"The Customer is King". Sounds like you, dad.'

'No, that bit I understand. Where's me favourite? Where's that bugger? There.' His finger alighted on EVERYTHING YOU KNOW IS WRONG. ADAPT OR DIE.

Gore shrugged. 'Who's responsible for this then?'

'Management consultants. We were behind the times, apparently. It's to do with communication, don't you know? Funny, that.' He took the brochure back out of Gore's hands and threw it on the table. 'Bloody nonsense. *That's* why I took early retirement, right there. You know as well as I, John, it was never owt to do with could I handle the work. It's the *discourtesy* of it, man. I won't be *spoken* to like that. It's like owld Tommy Cooper said. It's not the principle I object to, it's the *money*.'

Gore was pleased to laugh, for a gag from Bill was a rare grace.

'Y'knaa what I'm saying, but, don't you?'

'Wasn't that the idea?' Gore felt old reflexes stir. 'When it was privatised. Wasn't that the way it was headed from then?'

'Aw, it wasn't ever meant to gan this far. Naw, John. And before that, y'knaa, we were second class, we were. Fodder, man. We were taken for granted.'

The sentiment struck Gore as so wilfully blind he lost his savour for pursuing the point. Bill in any case was looking distant. Gore clapped his knees. 'Well, anyhow. You've time for more in your life now. Interests. Maybe you should get involved with town council.'

Bill made a sour face. 'Oh, I'm not stopping work, no fear. I'm barely sixty, son. Don't you worry, I'll not be asking you to look after me. You will get a proper job, but? One of these days?'

Gore ducked the jibe, a little riled, and jerked a thumb toward the junkheap of the dining-room table. 'So what's all that then, Dad? What are you up to?'

'Aw, this fella I know at the cricket club, he got laid off from Thorn over in Spennymoor. Bit younger than us. Anyhow, he's all into this lighting. "Design", he calls it. Sort of decoration, like, for places what get visitors? He got us interested.'

'Sounds a bit – arty.'

Bill sniffed. 'Nah, just common sense, really. This fella, he's done the odd thing at Beamish Museum. The other week we did the rig for a little concert they had up by the old priory at Finchale. He showed us the ropes. It's not hard.'

'A concert. How was that?'

'Brass band. Wasn't poison. We might do something at the Cathedral. An exhibition they've got, some lad does wood carvings . . .'

'You sure you want the hassle?'

'John, son, I'm not going to be one of them buggers sat in the pub at three o'clock on a working day. I'll not be taking up *bowls* neither.'

'You're entitled to have it a bit easier.'

'Aye, and you're a long time dead.' Bill was toying with a slender remote control for the television. 'Shall we watch a bit of the cricket ?'

'Who've Durham got the day?'

'Leicester. Getting trounced, last I looked. They're poor, man. Beat Yorkshire, mind you. That Brown's got wickets in him. Wants to cut his hair, but. Shall I put it on?'

'I'm not so bothered. Don't follow it much.'

'Whey, come on then. Shall we's walk?'

Gore gathered his things and they left the house. Susannah, he concluded, was quite wrong. Bill was more or less fine, about his business as usual. He had expected the needle of political difference to rub raw between them, but all that discord just seemed to have died a natural death. How had he come to think of his father as such an irritable man? He wondered now if his memory hadn't betrayed him, or whether he had simply failed to pay attention. Was that possible?

On they trudged, up Finchale Road, past Carrgate School and down a narrow lane to the Carrs, obscured from passing traffic behind houses and industrial works, twenty acres of dry acid heath and marshland, with trails for biking and dog-walking scored out in criss-cross between clumps of bracken and yellow-flowering gorse. At last they took a pause, turned, surveyed the distance they had come.

'You'll have seen your sister, then?'

'No, actually. Not since I got here. We've talked. But she's full of busy.'

'You ought to talk more, you and her. There'll come a time, y'knaa? When you'll just have each other.'

Gore frowned. 'That's a bit of a bleak way to look at it, Dad.'

'Well, it's not like the pair of you's are looking like settling. Families of your own.'

'I don't know about that necessarily.'

'Whey, you say yourself, she works all hours. You think she'll ever settle?'

'She gives most of her life to the member for Tyneside West.'

'Well, there's a dead loss for starters.'

'I know, but – Dad, I've not *given up* myself. I'm not a monk, you know.'

'Aw right. Do you still keep up with that woman in Dorset? The divorcee?'

'No, we lost touch. Didn't have the best of goodbyes.'

'Funny old life you have. Funny old job.'

Presently they walked on, in silence awhile.

'And when do you start then, John? Proper, like, this church of yours?'

'The first service is meant to be in a fortnight. Sunday October twelve. If we're ready for it. Not that I've got any choice.'

'Well now, listen, I'd a thought. I could maybe be of help to you? With your – y'knaa, your service? Maybe put a few lights up in that school hall?'

'Thanks, Dad, but . . . I think maybe that might look a bit flash. Put people off.'

'Whey never, it'd bring 'em in, I'd have thought. Just summat simple. It wants to look professional, doesn't it?'

'Honestly, thanks, Dad. Maybe just let me see how we get on first.'

'Okay, well. Just so you know. I know you mightn't think of us as . . . I don't know, considerate and that. But I'm here. You know that, right? I'd not ever see you wrong.'

'No, thanks, Dad, I appreciate it. I do. Should we maybe head back?'

'What, are you looking to get off?'

'It's only I fancy making the midday train.'

Bill shrugged. 'Aw well, I'm for walking on a bit me'sel, John.'

'How far?'

'Maybe on up to Spy Hill.'

'Bit of a hike, Dad.'

'Nee bother. Do us good. Anyhow.' He thrust out a hand. 'Thanks for your company, our John.'

They shook and then Bill was off and away, down the narrow lane, slow but steady, his own man as always. Gore was momentarily nagged, unsure – should he have said something more, something better? Ought he to put on a step, catch up? Would Bill care one way or the other? A rising wind whistled and whipped at his trouser legs. It was pointless, he knew, for he had made his choice and would stick to it. At last he turned and set to retracing his tread, visible yet across the flattened acid grass.

Chapter X

IN GREEN PASTURE

1995–1996

6 September 1995

Dear Gordon,

I trust this finds you well. For my part I am sufficiently settled into bucolic Rodley (!) as to set down some impressions. The scale of the task is already apparent. Your advice will be taken to heart.

As you warned, the good Reverend Trevelyan is something of a loose cannon. Replacing him, though, would be no small feat. For one thing he is a cussed farmer, preaching to fellow cussed farmers. You thought I could expect a rivalry? Not so. True, he beheld me at first with – if not quite the basilisk stare – then an evident wariness. He would grimace at any naivety of mine, and sharply set me right. But I have begun to feel it is a sincere desire of his, to impart certain definite lessons.

He is proud of his freehold, short of respect for church governance. I rather wondered what kind of wild-eyed dissent he would shout from his pulpit. But really he is a 'sound man', his metaphors drawn largely from fruit and veg. None of your trendy ways, and the congregation seem to approve.

You are wondering, I'm sure, what size is this congregation? I will confess, it's not uncommon that the 8 a.m. service be given for five or six. But a second sitting at 10 will sometimes muster twenty. Always a smattering of couples in good casual clothes – weekending, one suspects, from a London residence. Plus the odd pair of shifty B&B tourists, stopping off from the stroll after their 'Full English' breakfast.

We are a small team, our forces spread thin over the neighbouring villages, so I get about a fair bit daily on the bike. I will take the odd drink in the pub with Trevelyan – he advises that I get my face known widely – and there I hear the most vigorous views about the clash between the incomers and the 'born-here' tendency. The tourists aren't even rated as human. Where I am counted in the scheme of things, I wouldn't like to hazard. Nor is Trevelyan neutral on the matter. Another of his little lessons is that we must keep our sheep close. 'We're not London,' he likes to say. 'If we hear a cry in the street, we can't just pull the curtains.' Indeed, almost any local problem he defines as one that can't be solved by 'zooming back up to London of a Sunday'. The scold is sometimes directed at me, as if I were a symbol of the Big Smoke rather than one who finds London as appealing as the gulag.

Funnily enough, last Sunday one of those London couples approached me, two glum twin boys in tow, and asked if they could make a donation to funds? Typical moneyed behaviour. He had the look of a grazing stockbroker – pink shirt, white collar, sleeves rolled. I tried to gauge what he was after in return. My guess was: a slightly more 'contemporary' mode of preaching.

For the moment I am lodging with a peppery old lady who prepares the church newsletter. She is a hard one, but the black pudding she serves is a joy. The townie way, I'm told, is to turn vegetarian as soon as one sees just how cows called Daisy and pigs called Jemima get turned into meat. But not I. My conscience is bad when I consider the ill use of God's creatures. But I have to tell you, that pudding is godly stuff.

Yours in faith & friendship,

John

12 October 1995

Dear Sue,

I'm sure one letter a month from me is more than ample, so forgive me for taxing your patience. It's just that I fear I'll go spare here. The darkness after nightfall is unfathomable. The baying of livestock sends me up the bedroom wall. My old landlady regards me with barely veiled contempt. I should stop before tears of merriment stain your cheeks.

There are pluses. Good fresh produce from the farmers' markets. Then again, this you will love, ten minutes by car gets you to a vast Tesco, its car park full of Land Rovers, Londoners after their preferred bread and cheese.

Most days I'm given to understand that the village has already gone to hell in a handcart, everything under threat or already lost, from the bus service to the sub post office. Rumour has it the train line survives only so as to serve the leader of the Lib Dems, who has a place locally. Politicians, you should know, are not much admired here. So, please, come visit, and bring your Pallister, hard as I'm sure it would be for him to wrench himself from his duties to Scotswood and Hoxheath. I hope he takes no more of your time than is necessary, since you did the hard graft and got him elected. How can he afford you? Whatever do you and he talk about? You can't have read any of the same books. I have a list I can send you, should you ever find yourself stuck for chat in 'Old Labour' circles.

All piss-taking aside, you have my honest admiration for having started up on your own. I raise my glass to SEG Solutions Ltd. What really impresses me – I mean it – is that you are taking the lessons you have learned and moving forward. A much bolder thing than I am capable of.

Per your last letter, understand that I am unperturbed by your jibes at the persistence of my long romantic drought. Lodging with Mrs Danvers is hardly an ideal arrangement, a cramp on the style of a gay blade such as I. But you are quite correct to assume that there is 'no one special', has not been for some time, and there is no prospect of that changing. Okay?

Love,
Jonno

9 November 1995

Dear Dad,

I have of late rediscovered some of my old fondness for pen and paper. It comes easier, seems to me more friendly, than the phone. I do apologise, though, for not calling so frequently. To be honest, I have so little news. Not much changes here, though the entrenched locals will tell you different. Some of them I daresay you would get on with.

The graveyard is a testament to the old families of the village, and I sometimes think most of the faithful are already interred. My pastoral duties are not extensive in the week, bar the more or less predictable incidence of birth, marriage and death (and sadly not enough of the first two). These and the visiting, from which I shrink, since my small talk is fitful. I imagine you had similar problems back when you were tootling all over Durham for the old gadgies.

One man I've met whom I'm sure you would have time for is a dairy-cattle farmer called Roy Jeavons. He appeared steadfastly at each service, then one day he lingered afterward and we fell to chatting. Now we will have the odd pint of bitter. He is a keen reader, recognises the citations when I preach – even those from heathen literary sources. His farm is called Long Meadow, he's been there for twenty-five years, effectively solo since his dad's death ten years ago. His wife died not long after, very sadly – cancer. He has a daughter just twenty, Cath, and she helps him out. It's very evident she has stayed for him rather than strike out for college and a career, as most others seem to. He does his business on a computer that puzzles him somewhat, though Cath is a dab hand. But he is always being told to change his way of doing business. I can see the argument. It's harder to apply, though – would be hard for anyone.

His profits have halved in the last couple of years. I gather – though it's a sore point – that it's much to do with the fallout of the BSE business. The worst of it is in the past now, but he clearly took a hit. I know you wax sceptical about farmers, but really his margins are tough. I was stunned to hear his milk production is running at an actual loss!? He likes to cite a biblical reference beloved of my boss Trevelyan, 'The husbandman that laboureth must be first partaker of the fruits.' It occurs within a complex passage in Paul's epistle to Timothy. But its meaning is quite clear to some among us here.

I hope whatever you're getting up to is giving you satisfaction, and look forward to seeing you at Christmas.

With love and best wishes,

John

7 December 1995

Dear Sue,

Okay then – I'm a Tory now. You be vice and I'll be versa.

Not really. But still. There are Tory virtues afoot out here, I am among a conservative community. The farmers, for instance, are remarkably hostile to Europe. It seems to have a lot to do with pig crates. I find my voice fails me on the topic. In truth I feel myself going native just a bit – 'acting it', as is my wont – a 'poser' as Dad would say – fitting in, rather than preaching brave and lonely on a rock and taking a hail of stones for my pains.

As for your and my Party – I am not so sure there isn't a Christian revival going on. The old Christian Socialism, even. One saw it somewhat during the dour Scots ascendancy, Smith and Brown. But Blair, too, was clearly God-struck at some key stage. He speaks without apology about 'sin', 'right and wrong'. But it's not a bad place for Labour to be. Especially if, as Blair seems to wish, you're standing on a law-and-order platform. I admit he was good after the Bulger boy was killed in Liverpool. He sort of reminded people how bad it is to live on those estates where the norms have broken down. Clearly that is why you get this abysmal behaviour. I truly believe you can't do such things if you grew up being loved, feeling safe, and indebted for the same. But there's no point imagining everybody else is just like us.

Now: will it shock you then to learn that I have made a good friend of a real woman? Her name is Jessica Bradbeer, though she prefers 'Jessie'. I think it's a stab at informality, as her origins are quite posh. She moved to Rodley with her twin boys and husband, a moody stockbroker who fancied a go at farming organic veg. It seems he soon wearied of that rubbish and deserted her, drove back to London, his old job, and some new blonde. Jessie has kept the house and the boys, who are, alas, the image of their moron father. I suspect persevering here is a way of fighting the humiliation.

She has loaned me a hand with Sunday School and coffee mornings, though these are desultory. She's cooked for me a few times too – I sit in her cosy kitchen and she tries to teach me about wine. I know people pair off in life, and I daresay she sees something in me. The more fool her, you say. But it's not like there's anybody else around. If there were, she'd surely be more mindful I'm a son of the Grim North.

The trouble is that there is something particular about my circumstance here that forbids a response to her. I belong to the community, for better or worse. And, I suppose the truth of it is, I'm not really attracted to her.

Ministry here is not dynamic, so I'm writing a long article about metaphors of renewal for a theological journal. I will send it to you on completion, and you are, of course, welcome to kindle your hearth with it.

Love,
Jonno

1 February 1996

Dear Gordon,

Just a line to report some success, if you'll forgive a short blast of euphoria. I gave a Plough Sunday service two weeks ago, very gratifying work. Star of the show, I concede, was a cherished old wooden plough borne into the church on stout backs, and there it sat throughout the service, until finally it was blessed and borne back out. It was also a fine touch of Trevelyan's to have the lessons read by farmers – no natural performers, but then the words can derive a new power from being quite flatly intoned. I gave a sermon on the metaphor of the plough – the promise of spring, new season's light, green shoots, the shearing of the rag-tag tatter and overgrown darkness of winter. I tried, of course, to offer the analogy of personal transformation. The audience seemed to prefer the first part, but I felt nonetheless like I'd finally made my mark.

I was sure to have a pint in the pub and there received a few compliments, though a few more seemed adamant about telling me where I might have improved. One hilarious little fellow – not drunk, just dogged – kept insisting how important it was that Adam was a farmer. 'It's in your book. The first man tended the earth.' Perhaps rashly I pointed out that it is Cain whom Genesis singles out as the tiller of the ground, Abel as the keeper of sheep. But this man was fixed. 'Who give 'em that land, eh? Them sheep?' Apostolic succession seems a small claim by comparison. It didn't spoil my day, though, and shows all the more, perhaps, what we are up against.

Yours in faith & friendship,
John

2 April 1996

Dear Dad,

I'm sorry for my silence, things have just gotten parlous here. Really since the government came out with the stuff about BSE in humans, a kind of dread has descended. The rapidity and reach of it is quite frightening. Locally there's some talk about bad pesticides, but it seems the emerging consensus is on this hideous business of 'cannibal cows'. A ghastly notion. Maybe worse to think of the spines and heads mauled and clawed by hooks so as to make sausages and rotten old thing-burgers.

It has got especially dire in the case of my friend Roy. BSE is old news for him, and he always told me things couldn't have gotten any worse than they were four or five years ago. But seemingly his herd is on the old side, and there is more and more talk of a selective cull. This on top of Europe's noises about a ban on British beef. A man from Exeter came down to inspect the herd last week, and Roy was worried about one of the cows he said was 'shy-headed', continually kicking for no reason.

A 'restriction notice' would be a bad blow to him. I am not certain of the extent of his debt but he's scarcely able to pay his bills at the moment so you have to worry. I saw him subsequent to a meeting at the bank and I don't think I've ever seen a man so morose. Cath has been looking for other work, related to the tourism, but they are just as blighted. I suggested he apply to the Benevolent Fund, but I don't really think he appreciated the suggestion. There is a bitterness there, and only natural.

In the general low mood I find it hard to be effective in my duties. I am lucky to have a good friend in Jessie Bradbeer, though she has been quite strict with me too. I told her I believed I might function as a sort of 'stress counsellor' but she insisted the government needs to sort it out, with money, not warm words. Fair comment, perhaps, though leaving me dispiritingly short of other ideas.

With love and best wishes,

John

7 July 1996

Dear Gordon,

Thank you for answering last night and for being so understanding, as ever. I suspect I wasn't coherent. You appreciate I was very unnerved, and though the aftermath is calmer I now find matters profoundly depressing.

Roy has for some time been in the forcible position of selling off his herd for slaughter. That those cows are truly sick, I'm not sure I can believe, but that's the view from Exeter, and there seems no way to arrest the decline. I suppose I should have better understood the nature of depression, said more to him and sooner, however banal, if only to fill the airspace, assure him he had a friend in me.

But I got this frantic call from Cath and cycled like mad to Long Meadow. He was stumbling over his land, shotgun in hand, several of the animals already dead. I thought long and hard about trying to snatch that gun from him, but those weapons are frightening at close hand, and I couldn't say for sure what was his state of mind. Not that I think he would harm me, just that one can imagine the thing discharging accidentally. There was a moment, as Cath and I pleaded with him, that the barrel swung my way. Anyhow, together, we managed to get him back to his farmhouse.

The worst of it, in a sense, is that I have lost my voice in the services. There is a deep ill feeling among the congregation. On Sunday I was accused of trying to gloss over the crisis. This old fellow quoted Deuteronomy at me, 'Thine ox shall be slain before thin eyes but thou shalt not eat thereof.' People talk of God withdrawing his blessings. I frankly hate this Old Testament view. But I am required to take it seriously.

Yours in faith & friendship.

John

3 September 1996

Dear Sue,

I know this is not a part of life where you have ever had help or reassurance from me, but I would value your counsel, for things have got very fraught between Jessica Bradbeer and I. I admit it was late in the day that I told her of my intentions with respect to the Newcastle job – though in fairness I kept it from everyone, other than those who absolutely had to know. And I had raised the possibility with her, but she only laughed, seemed to think it ludicrous that one might choose the Grim North over Dorset – strange, since she's hardly had the happiest time here herself. She had been shaking her head over the stuff in the papers about the murder of that vicar from St Margaret's in Liverpool. But that was a very tough place.

So I finally told her all last week, just after she had made me a kind birthday present of a wristwatch. And I did expect her to be a bit vexed, when we have been such friends and she has few others in the parish. In fact she said nothing at first, just smiled rather crookedly. Then she told me she had a lot to be getting on with, and made as if to get on with it. I dallied for a few more pleasantries and at that point she became quite short with me.

Then on Saturday night Trevelyan and the parish council threw a little send-off for me in the hall. A nice number showed up. I must have made some impact. Trevelyan was possibly glad to see the back of me. But Jessica pitched up late with her twins, clearly agitated. So I knew something was coming, though I thought it ill-timed of her. Sure enough, the moment I went to a trestle to load my plate she was at my side. 'So you're leaving us', and so forth. 'Fresh conquests.' Everything that came out of her mouth had some barb to it. I didn't have the heart to argue, just told her I had responsibilities, and she laughed. I roused myself sufficiently to ask what on earth had got into her, but she fairly bit back, called me 'a rotten sod', loud enough for others to hear. Then there were some remarks imputing selfishness, and she made her exit, kids in tow. The parishioners studied their shoes for a bit. I suppose I've made a hash of matters. I know I'm someone who keeps his cards close to his chest. And I do regret it, but it's hard to change. Honestly – what do you think?

Love,

Jonno

10 September 1996

Dear Gordon

Forgive me that this is written in haste. I've never felt so downhearted.

I admit that through all my preparations I haven't felt the uplift I hoped for, but I was not at all prepared for this morning's news. I had been doing nothing but staring at the wall, how long I don't know, when I got the awful call from Cath, beside herself, saying they had found Roy in the woods near here. Absolutely dreadful. I have lost family before, but not a friend.

I will not be able to stay on and officiate at the funeral. I am moving, that is just how it is. It is just unfortunate. I don't know in any case what words I could have found. And I'm not sure my closeness to the congregation was such that they consider me the best or most fitting eulogist. It is possible, in any case, that I never really knew Roy at all. That anyone could be in such a slough as to do that, I don't know that I can fully comprehend.

Excuse me for stating it so baldly, Gordon, but from the outset I have sensed your disapproval of my moving on. You perhaps would rather not say it, but I suspect it's your view that I ought to stay my course here. And maybe that is so. I just cannot help but believe the Newcastle mission is what I am 'meant' to be doing, the work intended me. The notion itself has surprised me, never mind the vehemence with which I feel it. And yet in this moment I seem to feel the reason I was called – why I came to Grey. I don't wish to sound unhinged on this. It's just that I am morally certain in Newcastle I can uncover what my ministry is for. Have you no sense of the same, not even remotely?

Obviously I'd far, far rather have your support. But I will say, Gordon, that I don't object if it is withheld in this case. I will respect your view, hope you will mine, and, while respectfully differing, I remain,

Yours in faith & friendship,
John

Chapter XI

THE GUNNERY

Saturday, 28 September 1996

Gore didn't like to stare, yet he could hardly ignore the veritable elephant in this particular parlour. A hulk of a man, shaven-headed, absurdly muscled, was trundling tank-like through the modest crowd of late Saturday afternoon – not boorishly, but with a clear, calm surety that lesser bodies would step out of his way. Mid-to-late thirties, Gore reckoned, though the bluish sheen of his clean scalp perhaps added years to an ostensibly younger face. His faded jeans bulged as if to burst, his navy-blue polo shirt stretched drum-skin tight by the barrel chest and slab-like biceps that put Gore in mind of nothing so much as the marbled flanks in a Bridport abattoir to which he once accompanied Roy Jeavons.

'So, uh, what do you think, John?'

'Oh I think it's terrific, Bob.'

Spikings flanked Gore by the door of his church hall, wherein the weekly jumble sale had reached its peak hour of trade. Gore counted eighteen or nineteen stalls, a turnout of eighty or ninety bodies. The elderly were notable, as were the parents of noisy children. But it worked, by God – it was orderly and cheery. And none seemed more genial than the Incredible Hulk, now making a big show of buying from this stall and that, his over-biting grin like that of some cartoon shark circling a bony castaway on a buoy-like desert island.

'Well, glad you think so,' said Spikings. 'Car-boot sales are quite the thing now, but we're fighting back. This is nicer, I think. You do see some pretty, uh, ragged elements at the boot sales.'

As opposed to the Mighty Quinn over there, thought Gore. Now the

Hulk was whispering into the ear of a plump lady, she pulling a delightedly scandalised face.

'And this turnout, it reflects your congregation?'

'Pretty much. Attendance is up three years running now. Just a little each time, but my God you notice. It's not a *revival*, nothing like the righteous Mr Barlow would argue. He can talk, uh, such crap.'

Gore smiled. An old lady was touching the Hulk's arm tentatively, cooing at him, and he inclined his domed head the better to hear.

'... No, sometimes I think we're just getting people out of their houses. Otherwise they sit by the telly and worry about crime and what-have-you. And we're cheaper than a seat at St James's Park. I mean, that's how it is these days, John – you've got to see it from the punter's angle. Find out what people want, try to give it them.'

Drawing near, thin and eczematic under a sponge of frizzy red hair, was Spikings's verger, Henry March, to whom Gore had been introduced in the foyer as he dispensed raffle tickets.

'How we faring, Henry?' Spikings asked.

'Pretty good. Forty-two sold.'

'Splendid. Now half of that will go straight to your cause, John.'

Gore murmured thanks. Well and good – albeit not so diverting as the two small children running gleeful circles around the Hulk's trunk-like legs, until he stooped and scooped first one then the other into his great arms. Only then, as the kids squirmed and bounced, did a momentary wince twist that grin of his. *Bad back,* thought Gore. *Achilles heel?*

'It takes all sorts, doesn't it?'

'Sorry, Bob?'

'That fellow you've your eye on? Quite a sight, isn't he? His name is, uh ... gosh, I'm blanking. Clarkson? Bit of a character at any rate, locally.'

'That I can imagine.'

'Do you know, last year he called me up out of the blue. Said he was a businessman, wanted to come in for a meeting, about "church funds", he says. I thought, fine. Then *that* shows up. You can imagine my face. But I realised, I'd seen him here before, at eventide. And what he did – I was stunned – was hand me a big fat donation for a new communion table.'

'Gosh. That's not to be sniffed at.'

'Lord, no. Cash, too. You don't forget that. Very *intense* he was about it. Said he wasn't much of a churchgoer himself but the Church meant a lot to him. Heaven knows why. Didn't give the impression he would brook any argument. And it was decent of him, I must say.'

'He seems to have friends here.'

'I'll bet there's not one he's met before. Some people just have that way about them, don't they? The world is their friend. No, he's not doing any harm. Good job. I couldn't ask him to leave, could I? I might get seven bells knocked out of me.' Spikings chortled as they began to dander down one side of the room, until Gore's arm was gently taken and he encountered some keen selling from a lady presiding over a table of crockery and tableware.

'Nothing to tempt you, John?' Spikings prompted. 'Not even something for your new place?' Sotto voce he added, 'You only make one first impression.'

Gore picked up the most plain-looking vase on display, a yellow ceramic number, and parted with a fiver.

'That's the spirit,' purred Spikings, as his phone trilled about his midriff. The next table was entirely populated by soft toys, and Gore had all but turned his face away when he spotted a saggy brown donkey with long fleecy ears and excessively doleful eyes. A daft impulse seized him.

'Oh, I'll have *him*.'

'Fiver alright for you?'

'My lucky day.'

He sauntered out to the foyer, firing out broad smiles in every direction. Spikings was muttering into his phone, but he concluded the call and slotted the device into a pouch on his belt, easy as a workman's tool. 'Have you not got one of these yet? They're awfully useful.'

'I'm a bit suspicious. They seem to make you a slave. A bell rings and you have to answer.'

'I wouldn't see it, uh, quite so drastically. When one is called, it's usually meaningful. My, that's quite a prize you have there.' He indicated the fluffier of Gore's purchases.

'Oh, I'm all for the donkey,' said Gore, surprised by his own cheeriness. 'A useful and good-natured creature.'

Spikings feigned a short laugh, clearly a bridge to discourse over the wreckage of a remark that had baffled him.

'That's a line in Dostoyevsky.' Gore smiled. 'Big favourite of mine.'

'Right,' said Spikings, his warmer smile suggesting no new understanding, but plenty of reassurance.

'Bob, while I'm here I wondered too if I might ask you a favour?'

'Anything. Well, you know, within reason. At a price.' He patted Gore's forearm.

'I think I need a loan of a few good items. Proper things. For my service.'

'Oh! For sure. We have spares. What are you in need of?'

'Well, a good altar cloth, certainly. Maybe a ciborium?'

'Hmm. Can you bear to wait around? Henry could sort you out after the raffle.'

Gore elected to stroll out of doors, down the Nun's Moor Road for a breath of air. On his return, the sale was finished, stalls were being packed up. He could not see Henry March. Thus he stepped aside, through connecting doors, into the chapel. Spikings had spoken with quiet pride of his burnished brass lectern, a rather special choir stall and a fine old three-manual organ. Gore fancied he might steal a moment to peek around the nave before evening communion.

The sight that met him was that of Henry towering over some sheepish and unkempt old fellow in a stained sweatshirt. Voices were raised, most especially Henry's. Gore set off down the aisle toward them, but the old man broke away and stomped past, his face madly ruddy, eyes wild, beard yellow-grey. As Gore reached

Henry's side he turned and together they watched the tramp lurch out of sight.

'As if there weren't enough on,' Henry sighed, 'I find *that* kipping in the pews . . . Oh, and God I *knew* it, I mean, look at that. The dirty mare . . .'

Gore understood as the stink assailed him, and covered his mouth with his sleeve, recognising the thoroughly regrettable shape on the ground, the piece of wretched ordure to which Henry pointed a short distance hence.

The verger's voice became a pained hush. 'Bob doesn't want to hear about this, see. It's like it's part of the job, right? They're all part of "the community".' March waggled his fingers in the shape of inverted commas. 'So who's left holding the baby, eh? I don't mind the doors being unlocked, but this is what you get. Dossing and drinking and . . . urgh. I wouldn't mind if he'd gone in his own trolleys. Oh bloody hell, I'd better go get the pail and shovel. We're not paid enough for this,' he muttered. 'Oh, and you want something too, don't you?'

'In your own time,' said Gore.

It was noticeably colder as Gore wended his way home on foot, and the lights of Hoxheath's pubs seemed unusually warm and welcoming, however smeared the glass or grubby the curtains. Passing a few open doorways he heard sounds of inchoate rowdiness, but also bonhomie. Saturday night was Saturday night, however it was sliced – time for good cheer, for a little light relief. Turning his key in his door, he knew he had nothing to pass the evening other than reading, not even a stroke of meaningful work. Feeling a mite foolhardy, yet mildly hopeful, he dialled Jack Ridley's number, and got his wife on the line. 'Oh, he's eating his tea, John . . .'

When Ridley came on, he sounded like a man gripped by heartburn.

'Jack, I'm just calling on the off chance. When we popped into the Nelson the other week, I found it very useful, meeting everyone and so forth? And I fancied I might head out to a pub or two around Crossman tonight. I just wondered if you'd be at all interested in joining me for a pint? A rematch on the old dominoes maybe?'

'No, thank you, John, we're settled in for the night now.'

'Of course you are. Sorry.'

'You say you're off drinking round *Crossman*?'

'Just to show my face. I'm all for pubs, as you know.'

For some moments only ambient Ridley household noise came back down the line.

'Okay then, John. But mind yourself when you're out. And divvint drink too much, hear? Good night to you.'

Gore set down the receiver, much the worse for having taken it up.

He heard noises, made out shapes, figures, in a doorway, and his pulse quickened as he made haste past the Crossman Youth Centre. Thirty yards ahead lay its squat detached doppelgänger, the Gunnery pub. A few cars were parked in its forecourt, and Gore felt a chuckle escape him, for one of these was a fancy jet-black Lexus – alloy wheels, creamy leather upholstery, tinted windows, bold as a bull in a tea-room given the wrecks all around it. He had to stop and walk around this immaculate vehicle in wonder, and it struck him that anyone with a house-key and a bad attitude might be tempted sorely to wipe the wealthy smile from the owner's face.

'Had a good fuckin' look then, have ya?'

The challenge came from behind and Gore twisted sharply, only to see a youth's face, a puffy truculent buffer under lamplight – a bristling little version of a man, smoking sourly, acting like this were his property, his ride. It was beginning to seem to Gore that this boy and he had been twinned for a higher purpose.

'It's Mackers, isn't it? Mackers?'

'What's it to yee?'

'Well – I thought we were pals. Before your mate stuck one on me. Didn't I take that corner for you? In the park last week?'

'He's not me mate. You're alreet, you. Just leave off eyein' the motor, aye?'

The hard look was nearly funny. 'Fine,' Gore murmured and turned away.

The Gunnery pub was sullen under the sodium light, exuding a certain eventide menace, a keep-out to passing trade. There were perhaps a hundred instant reasons to stray nowhere near, and Gore pressed them out of his mind as he pushed through the doors. Within? Just another drab boozer – a glum, unwelcoming, seemingly all-male haven for heavyweight drunks. At the bar two indecently red-faced men, in similar anoraks and tracksuit bottoms, were loudly speaking ill of an absent associate. Woodchip climbed the walls to a dado rail, above which the plaster was painted – smeared – in the manner of a dirty protest. Pushed up in rows askew around the wall were framed monochrome photos of local industrial scenes. A scattering of pension-age drinkers looked extremely ill over those drinks. For the moment, at least, Gore decided, he would not be initiating any conversations.

He ordered a bottle of brown ale from a dilatory barman who glanced at his clerical collar but found no interest there. Where, then, should he settle himself, which spot was least uncomfortable? Past the bar and to the left was an enclave of alcove tables, but a raucous manly hubbub was issuing from same. To the right, a dim corner table presented itself, and yet he couldn't but feel it would present him in turn, conspicuous as a prize lemon. He stood his ground, toyed with his half-pint glass. How long would he stay? How long to drain a bottle? Where next? His night out was off to a sluggish start.

He was shifting so as to face the door rather than any hard look when he saw, coming round the bar from the seating at back, a face he knew. For this colossal man was not forgettable. *What was his name? Clarkson?*

Tonight he had packed his bulk into a good single-breasted suit of dark blue, with a crisp white collar flying open, so framing that bulwark neck of his. He thumped on the bar without malice, but the barman hastily snuffed his fag. Gore made eye contact, then his eye darted aside, for he saw the big man's eyebrows knit. Eye contact was a mistake, wasn't it? He didn't suppose his clerical suit gave him Red Cross immunity from aggro. Still, he glanced back – and Clarkson was looking at him most fixedly. Impulsively Gore raised his half pint, tried a smile. Now the Hulk was striding round and at him, purposefully, and Gore's pulse jumped. He had meant no affront, and tried now to fight a wild-racing notion that he was about to be hoisted up bodily, tossed out through the double doors. Clarkson was nigh, raising a ham fist almost to his shoulder. *He's going to punch my arm.* Gore quailed, rooted to the spot. The fist came down, the arm extending, and turned into an open hand, into which Gore reflexively inserted his own, and so found himself part of a pumping handshake.

'Reverend Gore, aye? Am I right? I'm right, aren't ah?'

'Aye,' Gore blurted. 'That's me. You are?'

'I'm Stevie, Father. Stevie Coulson. Good to know you.'

'You know my name?'

'Aye, I saw you with the Reverend Spikings this afternoon, I meant to come owa, but you'd nipped off, hadn't you?'

At last Coulson relinquished Gore's hand. But there remained something strangely grave and decorous in his bearing, like a diplomat greeting the monarch, or an undertaker on duty. *Surely not for my sake*, thought Gore. He couldn't see himself as the recipient of dignities from this powerhouse, with his hard-worn hands and fighter's face and broad over-biting smile.

'So,' Gore tried, 'you wanted to say hello? This afternoon?'

'I did. You did us a good turn, see. Th'other week? I say "us", what I heard is you took care of a young friend of mine.'

Gore made a lighting-fast mental account of his recent activities in the area. No ball was dropping.

'It were young Cheryl MacNamara.'

'Oh! Cheryl.'

'Aye, her mam's a pal of mine, see, and she were proper grateful you brought her in th'other night. So I'm grateful to you an' all.'

'Well, it was nothing.'

'Ah but see, Father, it's not everybody thinks like that. Now you'll have another of them there, eh?' He gestured to Gore's bottle.

'Oh, sure.'

'And you'll come sit yer'sel wi' us in the back, right?'

Resistance, clearly, was useless. And so, after all, Gore had company for the evening. He found that he was served sharply this time, and carried his two glasses carefully to Coulson's table, where the man sat at the head of four brawny broad-shouldered fellows. Three still had their own hair, one of these clearly the junior of the gang. The other skinhead wore a low brooding look of such enmity that Gore suspected he had wrecked the man's evening. In their jeans and tee-shirts they were scruffy next to the suited and booted Coulson, though stacked to one side of the party in the shelf of an alcove was a little hillock of leather coats, clearly new or nearly so, giving off the good aroma of a tanner's shop.

'Now this,' Coulson announced, 'is the Reverend Gore I telt you's about.'

'Hullo. Call me John.'

'This here's Simms. That man's Dougie? That sour-looking toe-rag is Shack. And who are you again?' This was directed at the youngster, but with a sporting cackle that the group echoed. 'Nah, that there's Robbie. New start, see. I say Robbie, he's Smoggie to me, cos he's Middlesbrough, aren't ya?'

Robbie bobbed his head bashfully – either an uncommonly forbearing soul, or a lad of limited faculties. Gore eased himself down onto a stool, shaking all hands as he went.

'Now divvint tak' a word of bother out of them, John. There's not one of 'em as hard as they give out. And they all work for me, so they know to behave.'

'You do your preachin' round here then, do you?' muttered Shack.

'Actually I'm what they call "planting" a new church . . .' And Gore stumbled into his stock speech, unsure of the true interest from his interlocutor, whose mouth stayed tightly pursed around his tab, the scar tissue under his eyes very pronounced at close quarters. Shack was not built to such fearsome proportions as Stevie, yet there was perhaps a surpassing hardness to him, a sense of more callous materials employed.

When Gore was done, Coulson very solemnly clapped his hands. 'Good man, you. I tell you what, Father, you set a good example and you'll find people sharp follow it.'

'Well, I hope. If anyone shows up.'

'Whey, you'll not have bother. Plenty good people round here, good honest families and that.'

'Aye, Stevie's got family round here,' announced the one called Simms, seeming to think himself a wit, for a grin lit his babyish features, these with the regrettable look of having been crushed into the middle of his face as if by a vice. Stevie shot Simms a dead-eyed look in reply. Gore could almost smell the sheepishness among these big men, a seeming acceptance that, for all their equivalent size, one alone was the dominant dog in the pack.

'What's your line of work, then?' Gore asked between sips of beer.

Coulson opened his hands as if this were a complex matter, one on which he was often questioned closely. 'What I am mainly, what I *call* myself now, I'm a security consultant.' He dipped into the top pocket of his jacket and produced a business card, designed in blocks of black and white, bearing the legend SHARKY'S MACHINE.

'It's a lotta things these days, security. You've the pubs and clubs and that. Then you've businesses, minding premises. And there's bodyguarding, if we have to.'

'Right. Gosh. How long have you been at it?'

'Whey, for what – ten, fifteen year? Started on the pub doors me'sel. Just a hired hand, y'knaa? Now look at us. I've got employees, man. I have to pay tax and national insurance on these lumps here.' His look of long sufferance was comical. 'Aye, I ought to put this boozer down on wor card, man, it's like wor second office, y'knaa? This here corner right here.'

'You should pay owld Peter ground rent, Stevie,' offered Dougie.

'Aye, or compensation, like,' Simms hooted. 'For wearing all the covers off the seats with wor arses.'

Stevie showed another hard face. 'Eh, Simms man, what sort of talk is that?'

Gore raised his glass, sniffing a chance. 'Don't mind me. We've all got arses.'

Mild jollity, and Simms gave Gore a thumbs-up. Gore saw too that Coulson, between casting imperious stares about the table, always met his own eye with a wink.

'So you gentlemen keep the peace all over town, is that it?'

Again Coulson appointed himself spokesman. 'Aw aye. You get a lot of bad uns about, John, specially in the bars and clubs and that. Worky tickets, y'knaa what I mean? You've always got some want keeping in line. Some want a right fettlin' an' all. For their own good.'

'Aye,' grunted Shack. 'It's a public service.'

'Some of them buggers, it's a bliddy pleasure.' Dougie smirked, as if imparting the trade secret that manners normally forbade. But Gore chuckled and reached for his glass. He was starting to enjoy himself.

'Have you got plans up your sleeve, then?' Coulson asked. 'For getting folk along to your church?'

'Well, I reckon at least it's a day out. Cheaper than a seat at St James's.'

'Eh, now you're talking.' Simms whistled through his teeth. 'Eh, *Stevie* gans to all the games free, but. Cos of his big mate. Did y'knaa that, Smoggie?'

So addressed as the idiot child, young Robbie made a startled face.

'Aye, Rob,' said Dougie, 'and did you know it's your bliddy shout?' He waggled his sudsy pint glass, and Robbie hastened to his feet, clutching his head. Simms watched him go and then, with surgical precision, poured the dregs of his beer onto the seat of Robbie's low stool. 'Ye canna get the help these days,' he snickered.

'Aye, but guess what, Fatha,' said Dougie, leaning into Gore mock-conspiratorially. 'Stevie gans to the Toon but he's a Mackem, y'knaa?'

'Oh? You're from Sunderland?' said Gore.

'Washington, County Durham,' Stevie replied somewhat reluctantly. 'Before it was part of Sun'land.'

'Aye, so. A Mackem supportin' Newcastle, like,' Dougie persisted.

'Fuck off out of it, Dougie man.' Coulson reddened, then rounded on Gore. 'I'm sorry for that one, Father, just popped out.'

'Not at all. I understand the, uh, passions of it. The rivalry.'

'Where *you* from then?'

'Framwellgate Moor.'

'Aw aye? A Durham lad and all? Do you follow football?'

Gore nodded gamely. 'I'm black and white.'

'Good man. Like Tony Blair, aye? *He's* Durham, but he's black and white. Most of Washington's black and white, man, it's sound. Washington, Consett, Chester-le-Street . . . I mean, you get a bit both, you'll have seen that, aye?'

Gore nodded, though he had never much cared for the distinction.

'Naw, it's alreet, Sun'land,' Coulson persisted. 'Got some canny bits to it, like where me nana lives. Me grandda, now he was true mackem. Worked on the ships. He used to come in at night and sit in his old chair with his cap on, just bloody *ragged*, man. I couldn't believe such a skinny fella could work that hard. He'd say to us, "Stevie, lad, them ships gan off into the sunset but me, I stop here. Bloody shipwrecked." It was all true, but – they mack'em and tack'em.'

'How soft is that?' Dougie crowed. 'Being proud of summat people slag you for?'

'Nowt wrong with it,' Stevie insisted. 'That was the start of the rivalry, that was, the Tyne and Wear. Fighting owa the ships.'

'Balls, man,' frowned Shack. 'It was cos of the bliddy civil war, wasn't it?' Coulson's men seemed to want to fight this one out. Robbie returned with a tray of pints, set them down and reclaimed his seat, his face then twisting in outrage as the others sniggered. 'Aw ye *buggers* . . .' Somewhat apart from the highjinks, Gore found that he had all of the boss's attention.

'I meant what I said, John, earlier. I can tell, see – you're a professional, you are. And a good man. I respect that. Here's to you.' Coulson raised his iced drink and clinked Gore's ale bottle.

'Well, I hear you're a man for a good turn yourself.'

'Says who?' Coulson's eyes narrowed partially.

'Bob Spikings?'

'Aw aye. I used to kip in that church of his some nights, y'knaa? When I was a lad?'

'You slept rough?'

'Aye. Y'knaa how it is. Got wrang at home, so I ran off. Ended up round here. This is near on twenty year ago, mind. But this here boozer, it was me first proper job for money. Then I met some people, thank God, they looked after us – you know how it is, when you're young, you need someone to shout for you, don't you?'

Gore nodded keenly, though he had no clue what Coulson could be talking about. In respect of youthful role models, he supposed they had admired different sorts.

'Are you still a churchgoer, Stevie?'

'Not so much. Not so much. There's only so much I can stay on top of. We're all backsliders, aren't we's? A bit, like?'

'Oh, we surely are.'

'As long as you're doing right by people, in the main, eh?'

'Without a doubt.'

Stevie nodded, satisfied. 'Cos I want to be square, y'knaa, by the man upstairs?' He raised his eyes, waved a finger. 'Against thee and thee only have I sinned.' Gore smiled, mindful not to rile his new friend's po-faced calm, and wishing he could place the biblical allusion. 'Naw, but I find it very peaceful in church. It's a good proper quiet you get. Private time. Time to think. We all can do with a, what'd you call it? A place like a *sanctuary*?'

Coulson lowered his chin to his chest, pensive for a moment. Gore contemplated the profile. A shaven scalp had always seemed to him a vulnerable sight, fragile, like an egg, and yet Coulson's looked as if it might deflect an axe blow. He had never encountered such a jumble of elements in one man, solemn and fierce and jocular. Nor such a gargantuan frame. *A bit of a character*, yes, no question. Now he met Gore's eye once more. 'Listen, would you do us a favour, John?'

'What can I do for you?'

'Owld friend of mine, her name's Eunice, Eunice Dodd. Lives local. She's getting on, see, and I've not been round a while. Used to pop in regular. Bit bad of me. She'd be ever so glad of a visit.'

Gore shrugged. 'Well, would you like me to call in on her?'

'Would you? Aw, good man, you. It's Biddle House on the Crossman Estate. Number seventeen.'

Stevie leaned back in his seat. Gore, too, considered the transaction a success, for the commitment seemed a simple one.

It was then he sensed that Coulson's good humour had been displaced somehow. Now, in repose, his great bulk seemed the very substance of displeasure. Glancing about their neglected tablemates, Gore saw that they remained jovial, save for the dour Shack, whose grim disposition seemed terminal. Like Stevie, though, Shack was looking to the bar, and Gore followed these baleful gazes.

Three men stood there, in showy coats and shiny shoes, evidently new arrivals, seemingly desirous that all of the Gunnery's meagre clientele be made aware of their advent. Certainly it was impossible not to hear that they were making a garrulous job of getting in their drinks, browbeating the barman for an apparent failure to oblige their preferences.

'Haven't you got it in bottles? Nah, draught's horrible. Piss.'

'What about that glass of wine, our kid? Have you not got a list?'

Then they stood back, these three, and surveyed the room, bold as brass knockers. The tallest, catching Gore's curious eye, raised his glass. Gore looked aside and made to drain off his ale. He had achieved a nice little bit of progress here, undoubtedly. It seemed prudent to quit while ahead.

'Well, that's me, I'd say,' Gore announced to the table, setting down his glass. 'Two is my absolute limit.'

Stevie's smile was clenched at best but Gore saw no grounds to take it personally – no more than Shack's odd distracted gesture of sniffing at his fingers before accepting Gore's hand as he offered it round the table.

Out of doors, twenty yards hence down the keenly nipping dark of Hoxheath Road, Gore turned on his heel momentarily and peered back at the facade of the squat pub. No question, it was fatally unappealing to the eye, but not nearly so bad within. And it felt like territory gained, a flag planted, if provisionally. His steps were sprightly, for he was consoled in himself, confirmed in his abilities, reassured a little in his purpose.

Stevie was properly put out. So much for the quiet evening. Banter had been building nicely, now it was flattened, and for the sake of three numpties, three smug ugly faces in a row. His mobile should have rung, his lookout should have done the job assigned him, but that was past. His professional vigilance had rebooted. Saturday night was work-night once again.

He had assessed and named them. Big Chief Numpty, the eldest, the broadest, likely the hardest, undoubtedly the one in charge. His probable deputy? Shoulders, broader there than in the chest, but potentially a handful. And then the Squirt – physically negligible, making up the numbers, therefore most likely to be hiding tools about his person. Hardly the world's most shit-scary troops. It was their very presence, though, that rattled him – here, of all places, at this unlikely hour. On whose intelligence? Worse, he had been warned, he could not say he hadn't, he had frankly discounted the threat, and now here it was.

Shack, at least, had seen it too. Why was it only ever Shack with his eyes and his wits about him? The rest of them talked like they were combat veterans. And yet here they sat, yacking still, horizons no higher than the next round, the next pub, Keegan's best eleven, what one would pay for a cordless drill at Argos. Lately he had thought a fair bit about the role of delegation in leadership. Nights such as these reminded him sharply that he remained the chief asset of his business. At 9.47 p.m. he stood, pushed back his chair, vodka-tonic in hand, and strode toward the trio at the bar. The two juniors made to drain their glasses in unison, a pleasing sign. The eyes of Shoulders darted to the door. As for the Squirt, both eyes and body seemed to jerk in that direction – a bag of nerves, Stevie decided, the sort who would fill his lungs before throwing a punch. But Chief Numpty stood firm in his black suede jerkin, meeting Stevie's eye. A roll of cash lolled before him on the bar, as if that was cool. How much was he acting it? How true the show of strength? This much Stevie was bent on establishing.

'Ye's not for another there, lads?'

'No chance pal, just dropped in,' said the Chief. 'Reckon we can do a little better than this old shithouse the night, right?'

'Where've you's come from?' North-west was what Stevie was hearing.

'Roundabouts,' said the Chief.

'What's it to you?' offered Shoulders, another Manc.

'Divvint let us see you back in here.'

Silence. The Chief seemed to be chewing over the challenge.

'What's the matter wi' *yee*, like?' piped the Squirt, in broad Gateshead.

'You fucken know, you little bollox, so shut yer yap.'

'Well, see, Steve, we saw that Lexus of yours outside, so we had to look in.' And Shoulders grinned, as if the knowledge revealed implied mastery.

Stevie levelled a finger. 'You'd better not have touched that, mind.'

Chief Numpty laid a comradely hand upon Shoulders. 'Look, here's what it is, Steve. We'd a friend of yours in our local the other night. Lad name of Mickey, yeh?'

Inwardly Stevie kicked the wall. These days he had more associates than he was comfortable with, and Mickey Ash was not the one he would have chosen to represent him in a tight corner.

'Where the fuck's your local then? Old Trafford?'

'*Waallsend*, Stevie, Waallsend,' said Numpty, in a gruesome stab at an accent. It was contemptible, yes, but Stevie's spirits were rising on the assumption that this shifty shower of shit was the best that Big Mister Skinner of Manchester could send in his direction. The threat had declared itself, but with merely a fraction of the heft he had been keyed up for. Were matters graver, then Shoulders would not have his hand so near the heavy glass ashtray on the bar – though the detail was certainly noteworthy.

'Aye, right, so you saw Mickey, so the fuck what?'

'Well, he didn't stop. Ran off again sharpish.' As if this Numpty would stand his ground in all weather, outnumbered by however many. 'Now, *he's* the one you wanna tell not to be back,' he added, terse. 'Best do that, Steven.'

'Am I your fucken messenger boy?'

'You've been telt,' offered the Squirt, squeakily excitable.

'And this'll be from Lawrie Skinner, right?'

'You've been *telt*, man.'

'I hear you. Just tell us who I'm telt off.'

'I speak for meself, Steve,' said the Chief, chest forward.

'Whey you maybe do, but you divvint think I'll listen to a word out of a long streak of piss like you?'

The Chief took a step closer, which Stevie thought intriguing. 'I'll tell you this, Steven. We see any more of your ratty little scrote pals round where they know fine well they're barred – we'll have to give 'em a proper spanking, yeh? Then we'll have to take it up with you. And we'll find you. If it means coming back to this shithouse. Then there'll be more of us, knobhead. And if *that* happens, Steven son, then *you* – are fookin' – *dead* – yeh?'

Stevie didn't weigh up the singsong threat: in truth he hardly heard it. He had decided to deck this insufferable cunt during the trashing of Mickey Ash. The mere talk, the rash swagger, had dispelled his worry about weapons inside those down-filled coats. And now – like a rank amateur – the cunt had only done him the favour of stepping into Stevie's sweet spot, just a little to his left, where any excuse for a right he might throw would take about a week to land, time in which Stevie could play at leisure. His choices made, Stevie switched his drink to his left hand, reweighed and confirmed his advantage, then took the executive decision to ram it home.

He jerked his left wrist, tossing what remained of the vodka into the face of the hated one, who was blinking and spitting still as Stevie dropped the glass and raised his fists. The glass shattered as Stevie threw the right-hand jab, breaking Numpty's nose – he felt the pleasing give – and dumping him onto his arse. As Shoulders ran at him, Stevie was atop his momentum, shoulders relaxed, all power in his hips, and he pivoted smartly, swung a left-leg roundhouse kick to the abdomen, booting the twat, who crumpled and crashed back into the Squirt – a poor outcome for the pair of them. Now Stevie heard scraping chairs behind him, knew without looking that his boys were up and at his back. Shack would shortly be wading in. He glanced to the door, for the front bar was fast emptying of its patrons, much too fast for the Squirt to push his way through to the street. So now he was groping in his coat, and – yes, there it was, predictable as rain – a flashing blade, of an evil length. Stevie revised his estimate quickly, but not dramatically. There was no conceivable outcome – not a cat in hell's chance – but that the Squirt and friends were bound for the General tonight. They would not be home for *Match of the Day*.

Book Two

BIG STEVE

Chapter I

SIZE AND AUTHORITY

Stevie didn't speak of his past, not with mates nor lovers nor comrades. As far as he was concerned he had been born unto himself, somewhere round the age of eighteen. The years before had amounted, he would say, to 'a sack of fucking misery', from which nothing useful or pleasing or consoling could be fished. There was, though, one sole fragment of an anecdote he would gouge from himself, if set before a receptive audience, strong drink taken, and one or more parties unable to stay silent on the matter of how Big Steve ever got to be so rock – when and how those quads and lats and biceps began their fearsome inflation. If Stevie didn't mind his inquisitor – thought him genuine, not some chancer probing about for a sore spot – then his tumbler of Johnny Walker was raised to the light, the amber inspected.

'To Jim Doggett. Who made us what I am the day.'

Invariably the toast was fudged and muttered in the seconding, the big lads almost pitifully solemn to Stevie's eye – believing, perhaps, that they were saluting some hard-wearing owner of a fighter's gym or, better yet, a professional trainer. Inevitably a lad who was no fool would decide it were a better thing to stick one's head above the parapet than to persist in vulnerable ignorance.

'Who's Jim Doggett then, Steve?'

'He was me stepdad.'

'Aw, right. Good bloke was he?'

'He was an owld cunt.' This said as calm as you please. 'I tell you what, but' – and Stevie would set down his glass – 'he had his uses, that Doggett. He taught us the world's full of his type. So you'd best know how to look after yersel. And you've gotta learn that yer'sel and all, cos nee bugger can give it you on a plate.' And Stevie would shake his head, as to say that much more – too much – could be related, were there only more hours in an evening. 'Aye, that Doggett. He raised his hand to wuh when I was just a bairn. And I knew it all then, right there.'

'He hit *you*?'

As chuckles went round the table, Stevie would give up a ghost of a smile, if only to deepen the mystery. 'Aye. 'Til I hit him back. Then that was the end of that.'

The story, such as it was, always passed muster if judged by the gravely nodding heads. Inwardly, Stevie knew, the truth was not so clean-cut. He was so familiar with the gauge of his temper, his capacity to shift from stationary to active, that it stung him – truly stung him, *lashed* him – to think of a past he could not alter, not by any measure of physical exertion. To bear such knowledge was to dwell in a jailhouse of impotent fury. And to have stood there and borne insult and injury, to feel his cheeks afire, to feel worse than worthless in the world – to think back on all of this amid calm and solitude was sufficient to make Stevie shudder and curse under his breath, like some ragbag beggar afflicted with Tourette's. At such times he was gripped by an inner crisis that truly frightened him – a sense of watching himself from a studied distance, dumb-struck, appalled. *Who are* you, *then?* Just like the prodding nose-to-nose challenge he had heard a thousand times in dank doorways – off of some big Mackem lump, some little Geordie shite. Or the mass taunt of an unwashed horde in a full stadium. *Who are ya? Who are ya?* To Stevie it was devilment, purest evil, and alone he would count the numbers up to ten and back down, until some kind of tranquillity descended.

He should have learned sooner, steeled himself quicker. It should not have happened.

'Get in, you! Get your shoes on!'

Thus Stevie's mam forever scolded him in his pint-sized days, calling him in from the mangy street where he played, since the Coulson yard was no fit size for sport. Rain or shine, Stevie didn't much care if he was properly shod, indeed would happily run about in his pants. His mother, though, frowned long and hard. Mary had a sweetly lean figure, wore her black hair in friendly bangs, but it was that pinched, niggardly frown that defined her. She was the daughter of a stern man called Len Corbett, a stalwart of the jute mills of Dundee, in whose home Mary was raised to act demure and take no liberties. But a few months shy of her majority she had slipped over the border and been very peremptorily charmed, first into bed and then wedlock, by Bobby – *né* Robert – Coulson. And under Bobby's roof there was leeway for liberties and laxities of all kinds. In the raising of young Steven, Bobby was soft as clarts, and while Mary expected to be heeded she didn't carry a stick so big as to enforce the principle.

It wasn't even Bobby's roof during Stevie's formative years, since for a time Bobby and Mary were forced to run up an account on his parents' hospitality. The baby was brought home to Mount Pleasant near Penshaw on Wearside, poor and unlovely terrain, all closes and bungalows, a few redbrick semis, those cramped concrete yards, and one big expanse of scruffy parkland onto which most properties backed out. But small Stevie liked the domestic set-up just fine. Nana Coulson was forever telling him he was a nice-looking lad, with a bonny smile full of good teeth. He never heard such praise out of his mam, but Nana was a wise bird and he believed her.

For Mary, lodging at the Coulsons was undesirable but bearable, and for Bobby it was a source of unmanageable frustration. His father George had spent three decades working for Chappell's the shipbuilder of Wearside, though the firm had lately been merged with a rival and George forced to hump his gear to a new yard. He was a joiner and worked among a hundred others, insulating holds and chambers between decks. Outside of George's earshot, Bobby called him 'the owld codger'. The slur always earned a sharp rebuke from Mary, who was otherwise unbothered by the upkeep of George's dignities, yet insisted that hard graft be always applauded. Bobby respected his dad, for sure, yet seemed somehow bettered by him.

Bobby worked on cars. He left school free of qualification, and began at a good-sized garage in Birtley, washing, polishing and vacuuming. He would return home in the evening smelling waxy and astringent, however grubby his gear or the tack-cloth wagging from his trouser pocket. A joker by nature – 'dafty', in Mary's parlance – he was stern and emphatic when he talked motors. 'Car's a man's pride and joy. He wants to look after it proper. Part of how he *carries* himself. Who he *is*.' Whenever George heard such talk he pulled a constipated face – 'You talk some flannel, you' – and Bobby would glower. It unnerved young Stevie to see the two men at odds across the table, and when his mam and dad finally secured a home of their own he could stand the loss of his Nana's cooing, for his dad at least was master of his house now.

The move took them two miles north to Washington, lately designated a 'new town'. Old Washington had been coal mines and colliery houses, but the new town had raised up purpose-built 'villages' and multiplied the population, with schools, shops and facilities. Whatever its novelty, Washington still wasn't postcard-pretty. But Bobby got work as a panel beater for a decent garage, Armstrong Motors. Mary seemed content to have a functional home she could keep clean. And Stevie had a brand-new school to mope along to, much as he loathed it.

Unleashed from school hours, Stevie would often dawdle to Armstrong's and watch his dad at work on some motor up on a jig. Bobby weaved round the cramped space in his oily gear, trading shouts, wielding a spanner and a gas-fired cutting torch, hefting panels, diligently bashing at dents with a dinky hammer. He seemed assured, meticulous, versed in the magic of what went where and why, capable still of banter in the act. Stevie felt himself a lumbering and dafty lad in his dad's mercurial presence. Yet he saw how some of Bobby's workmates jibbed him, with a notable edge. It seemed that Bobby truly fancied himself a mechanic. He would replace the odd belt or spark-plug, and there were electrical issues on which he pronounced confidently. But those opinions were generally jeered. 'You're no mechanic, Bob. You're a mouth, you are.'

Bobby persisted, and began to come home with his blue overalls and moon face streaked and smeared by black grease. Then there would be some disreputable excuse for a motor vehicle sat outside the front gate of their semi for weeks. Stevie spied as Bobby roamed about, 'improving it' in some inscrutable manner, removing and stripping the alternator, fiddling with the starter motor. Worse, at times these parts might be given a temporary home swaddled in rags on the kitchen floor. Stevie felt complicit in these offences, for he knew that he, too, was a messy clot in his mam's eyes, always straying into reefs of fresh mud, the first among his mates to try to scale a barbed fence or ford a swift-running stream. Bobby's charm extended to the purchase of a washing machine one Christmas, but such largesse was not a cure for all ills.

For many were the nights Bobby would roll home late, with a red nose and red cheeks, the key having clinked uselessly round the keyhole for some moments previous. Bobby thought he was at his most riotously funny when he was insensibly drunk. Stevie sometimes thought his dad *had* to be play-acting, so comically stiff-legged was he, his gaze drowsy, fighting for focus. 'Angels wi' dorty faces, yee and me, kidder,' he would say. Bobby was indeed cherubic, if flushed and sweaty, dark curls adhered to his forehead. Mostly, though, Mary didn't think Bobby was funny, and didn't want to play the game. Their exchanges could turn sharp. 'Hell's *teeth*, can I not have a bit *fun*?' his dad would roar with disturbing bite. 'Can I not? Not a bit?' There was no threat there, but maybe something worse.

Still, over a month of nights round the tea-table some of Bobby's low talk actually seemed to acquire a serious shape. For he knew a bloke who had a mate whose mate could, conceivably, get Bobby in on the ground floor of a brand-new venture. A pair of smart engineers from the firm of Lotus had struck out on their own, and were taking steps to found a new company, its nursery factory earmarked for Washington New Town on the strength of some government money pledged to the cause of 'local development'. They had worked up a prototype for a sports car, a coupé, of all things. On first hearing, Mary did not so much frown as snort. True, it was far-fetched, and for this vivid fancy Bobby talked of quitting Armstrong's. He told Mary most vehemently, though, that she should bloody well watch out, because things were going to change. 'You want me to get on, don't you? That's what you're always saying. You want a new suite, you want this and that, and what's-her-face is off to Benidorm. You divvint get ahead by standing still, eh? Well, I'm bloody not.'

Within months this Clan Motor Company was operational and said to be close to turning out cars. Bobby's mate's mate, good as his word, smuggled him in as an assistant mechanic. The car was to be called the 'Crusader', intended as a nippy little number, light and aerodynamic, a fibreglass body atop a sporty engine. Bobby was soon expounding on the attendant problems of heat and noise and the clutch's heaviness, though he was short on solutions. 'Still sounds dafty to me,' muttered Mary. 'Bliddy fly by night,' was George Coulson's verdict. 'Whey it's not meant for the likes of you's, man,' Bobby shot back. 'Not the *pair* of you's.' And the production line rolled in the autumn of 1971. Wearside was making sports cars, and it made a gleeful sense to Stevie, for his dad was a character and had found himself a characterful calling.

Their routine was sacred. Every Saturday Bobby would take him for snooker at the Excelsior Working Men's Club. They would contest a frame or two, then Bobby would mingle with his pals and Stevie would sit it out patiently, the bairn in the corner with a bag of Tudor crisps and a glass of iced Cresta. Such was Stevie's treat. And yet he grew to hate these outings. For, somehow, old Doggett was always there, holding court. And Jim Doggett, somehow, was Bobby's best mate.

It had been so since school, but Doggett became a bricklayer, a rated one, and in short order he was a site boss with hopes of advancement. He carried himself about the Excelsior as though he were boss-man of all he surveyed – smoking odious panatella cigarillos, drinking Johnny Walker whisky chased by a straight glass of ale, fond of producing a black plastic comb, spitting upon it, and dragging it through his pompous thatch of rusty hair and meaty sideburns. 'Hello, *tiger*,' he would wink at his reflection behind the optics. From Stevie's vantage this was the behaviour of an outright ponce, and yet Doggett seemed to think he had bottled the very essence of machismo. Bobby and others in his retinue would tease him a little, for Doggett was a bachelor, but the man himself merely grinned at them glancingly, shooting back without apparent irony, 'Aw lads, see, but, I'm saving me'sel for Miss Right.'

Doggett had a few such stock gags. To wit, 'That's a smart top you've on there, son' was his customary greeting to Stevie whenever the boy drew near, clad in whatever cut-off tee-shirt he had clean to wear with his flares. Doggett affected a fly-collar shirt and a black waistcoat, his packet of tabs tucked into a dainty pocket, and seemed to think himself the very glass of fashion. Stevie would have been first to confess he cared nothing for clothes, considered them girls' stuff in any case – but he was quite certain Doggett looked about as smart as a sack of fucking spuds, whatever fancy gear he squeezed his lard arse into. His breath stank and all, what with the rotgut Scotch and the foul smokes. Stevie just couldn't tell the bastard to his face. If Doggett was a bully, bloated with talk, nonetheless he carried some weight and threw it about, and Bobby, too, deferred to him plainly. It pained Stevie. He felt himself a foursquare lad – no squirt, no titch. He had no fear of his teachers, not even Finlayson, the blackbeard yob who taught physics and picked the football team. He had no fear of classmates who told him he smelled, or called his dad 'grease monkey', for what did theirs do that was so bloody great? Doggett, though, was a different case, and Stevie coveted a share in that kind of size and authority. At thirteen, he knew, he just didn't have it.

On weekends Stevie knocked around glum Washington and its centrepiece, a commercial high-rise called the Galleries, all new shops and businesses under one roof. He and his mob – moody

Brian Shackleton, ginger Glen Howey, titchy Richey Gates – were of the same mind that the Galleries were shit. And yet people came in droves, sad shuffling zombies. And there, too, for all their disdain, were Stevie and the lads, lined up like hollyhocks under the escalators, watching folk go by – older folk in the main, often squashed and unshapely, lumpen and odd-looking. Brian, who claimed to know a few things, called them 'in-breeders'.

'Cos they shag their own, man, their sisters and that.'

'Whey, they *never*, man.'

'I'm *telling* yuhs.'

Jesus no, Stevie decreed. That was not possible.

If the lads were chronically bored then they were lured – as if by the chlorine pong – to the swimming baths on the edge of a vast bleak parkland named for the Princess Royal. They would sit in the bleachers and watch to see if any lush lasses were in the water that day. There was one sleek miss who sometimes would rise out of the froth in a navy-blue one-piece. *Nowt wrang-shaped about her*, thought Stevie. He fancied he had strong and manly features where his pals' faces were feral or bashed-in. The boys called him 'Sharky' in honour of his glaring overbite, and he liked that. (Brian, annoyingly, insisted on 'Shack' for himself.) But looking at that girl Stevie suddenly felt himself a crude job of work, water-marked second-rate.

Mary had always feared Stevie would get in with the wrong sort. Bobby was blithe: 'Let him away.' Their variance on this matter could turn surprisingly bitter – 'Is that all you're good for?' – and such daylight fights conducted within Stevie's earshot began to sound more like the night-fights, those where Bobby had Tartan beer onboard and Stevie sat on the top of the stairs but inched his way down, the better to hear. In the midst of such rows his dad always rammed Rod Stewart onto the record deck, the *Atlantic Crossing* album, and after a few bars of 'Three Times a Loser' – the time it took to cross their living room – came the silence of Mary wrenching the needle off the vinyl. Such was the bad odour about the house, Stevie was hardly surprised when Bobby's great strife began to unfold, in the bleak winter months of '72 and '73.

It seemed that his mam and his granddad were correct in their dour forecasts. The Clan Company had been abruptly set on its uppers. Bobby was muttering that it was 'out of their hands' – all the fault of the miners, off work all winter. The government didn't care. 'They'd bail out bloody Leyland, mind, bloody Rolls-Royce.' Then there was some vexation over petrol shortage, some war of which England had no part. Next, it was the bloody taxman. But whichever way it was sliced, Clan were making perilously fewer cars. That was bad enough. Then they stopped altogether.

On the night of the day that the Clan factory was locked and shuttered and bolted, Stevie and Mary didn't see Bobby before they went to bed. Mary told Stevie the firm was 'liquidated', and that sounded like what had happened to Bobby too. The next day, once Bobby had crept past the worst of his hangover, Mary, still tight-lipped, made her point. 'You'll have to go back, Bob, you'll have to ask them.' It did seem hard to bear, but Bobby called upon Armstrong's Garage, and had he a tail it would have been tucked into his shuffling gait. Yes, they had room for a panel beater, but no, it was no longer a space fit to be filled by Robert Coulson. He took his packet of pay-off money and rented garage space at a filling station, offering a basic mechanic's service. Like any business, it didn't take off overnight. Stevie lay in bed after dark, thinking, *Hell's teeth but, what'll happen to wuh?*

Rarely did he feel he had his mother's attention, but amid his father's woes he believed he had fallen clean off her radar. She was reading the evening paper very intently, nipping out at odd hours 'to see someone', chiding silent Bobby that they weren't 'on the telephone' – this grievance and that. Until, to Stevie's great surprise, she came to his room and announced that henceforward she would be going out to work in the morning. She had been hired at a new plant for television sets near Durham. The firm was called Haan, they were Dutch, and Mary would be sitting on an assembly line. Outlandish though it seemed, his mam had rolled up her sleeves to save the day. He was dully aware that he and his dad would be made to pay for it. For starters, Bobby had to shift himself earlier to drop Mary at Haan's before he went into the garage. Some days he was sluggish, and Mary stomped out to the bus stop.

The first boon of the new start was a colour television acquired on a very favourable hire-purchase. 'There's nowt on it,' Bobby scowled, and yet he began to watch quite a bit of stuff from the grasp of the settee. Springtime brought an FA Cup final between Sunderland and Leeds. Bobby wanted to invite 'a few mates', but Mary, too, had a notion for 'some people round' that day. The resultant party was ill-assorted, and Stevie lurked by the door watching Bobby's pals sprawled over the carpet around a tray of Tartan cans, while Mary's associates squashed onto the settee and she poured them sherry. Granddad George occupied the sole armchair. At half-time the very telly itself became the locus of some sort of argument between his dad and the hated Doggett. 'It's not the same as making stuff with your own *hands*,' Bobby was insisting. 'It's just stuff out of *kits*, man. Like the bairn's model planes. Mary's not a clue how it works, ask her.'

'Do *you* knaa then, Bob?'

'Listen I knaa you wouldn't catch us grafting for Dutchmen.'

'Whey man, what does it matter they're Dutch? Money's the same colour.'

'Whey then let's just give all wor jobs to the Krauts, aye? Or the Japs, eh? Just like the ships, Dad?'

George Coulson appeared to want no part of his son's case. 'Government will always see the shipyards right,' he muttered.

'Then what are we gannin' into Common bloody Market for? So wor yards get shut? We used to *make* the ships for the Japs. Now they make their own. Out of bloody *kits* and all. That's what's doing *him* in.'

'I'm alright, thank you, Robert, you speak for yourself.'

'Dead right, George,' Doggett boomed. 'Shut your moaning face, Bob man, you ought to be proud of your lady.'

Come the final whistle, Sunderland's shock victory saw general delight, but Bobby had not recovered his pomp. Stevie felt rotten.

His old man was surely in a slump, in need of a change, a plan – akin to what his mam had pulled off, somehow.

He bunked an afternoon's school, very sure that the settee and telly would be his, for Bobby was at the garage and his mam was at Haan's until five. Instead he surprised her at the kitchen table with her tea in a cup and saucer, but the cold exchanges for which he was braced did not come. It was much worse than that.

'Steven, your father and I have had a falling-out. It's very serious, I ought to tell you. So your father's not going to live here for a while . . .' He was, allegedly, already at a bed-and-breakfast in Birtley. Stevie nodded, giving nothing away, inwardly disbelieving, for whatever the rotten household weather of late it was not possible that such ties could be undone. What would Nana and Grandpa think? And yet, one and two and three nights without Bobby grew into a week, then a second and a third. Stevie needed to question his father, even trekking out to the bed-and-breakfast place by bus. But Bobby wasn't there, nor at the garage.

And thus began the Little Visits of Jim Doggett. He would greet Stevie as if kindly. 'Alright there, son?' The next outrage was Doggett and his mother stepping out for the evening. Bobby had always liked to be 'out with Jim'. Now Bobby was out on his ear, and Jim began to settle indoors some nights too – the intruder, in like a shot, like Flynn, like shit off a stick. Oh yes, he had been saving himself. His grin as he came through the door let Stevie know that he considered Mary bought and paid for. He shared her tidiness, that was for sure. He ferried stuff with him from his flat on the other side of town – a dressing gown, toiletries. The steamy bathroom started to reek of him. But neither his seafaring aftershave nor Mary's virulent air-freshener could ever mask the odour of Doggett's obnoxious dumps.

How could this man be in his house? Bobby, whatever his failings, was surely more appealing? But how could his dad have just fucked off, without a fight?

One Saturday of early October 1976, Doggett announced he would take Stevie to see Sunderland play Everton at Roker Park, as if this were the finest fare imaginable. Stevie was not about to be bought off. That same morning, Bobby pulled up outside in a red Cortina Mark Three. He had a lady friend, Jeannette by name, but she remained in the car, and in any case she didn't look as if she would suit a tidy living room. The couple took Stevie to the Excelsior, this at quarter past eleven. Jeanette was loud, drank too much and too fast. To Stevie's eye, Mary's primness for once seemed appropriate. Alone with the boy, Bobby stressed his enmity for Doggett. But, he was clear, he would not fight. 'Let them *live* with it.' *But dad, man!* – Stevie wanted to shout – *They're living with it fine!* When Bobby dropped him home his hand was pumped a little too long. 'There'll always be a bed and a plate for you,' Bobby said, and Jeannette nodded, as if it were any of her business. Only when Stevie was indoors did Mary inform him that Bobby and his friend were moving to be near her people in Nottingham.

He stared at his bedroom ceiling for hours, feeling a stone-like cold seeping into his bones. Doggett, he was only the bollocks that he was, but Stevie could not forgive his mother – not after all that dark-haired decorousness in the past, that oh-so-sureness of the done thing. So his dad had failed to come up to scratch. So his mam had moved him along. He needed Mary to know what he thought of all that.

Glen Howey and Richey Gates fancied they were brilliant at shoplifting from the Galleries. Stevie resolved to show them what for. He knew enough to force entry to a parked car with a wrecking bar and, within, to locate and mingle the ignition leads. Often, though, a mile or two down a quiet stretch of road, he pulled up abruptly and told Glen and Richey to get out and fuck off. That was part of being a leader – a little bit of picking on your weaker associates. At such moments he felt like his gloominess made an inch-thick carapace against argument.

He and Brian Shackleton had stopped knocking around – in the interim 'Shack' had assembled a little retinue of his own, and would sneer at Stevie across Princess Anne Park. One Saturday night they had a minor scrap that ended a draw, though Stevie felt he had shaded it. They settled their difference over a bottle of cider. Shack knew a moody girl called Tracy who sneaked out late to share a drink and a smoke. 'You've got sad eyes, you,' she told Stevie quietly. He and Shack fucked her in turn behind the brick bus shelter that backed into Biddick Wood, the experience scarcely more sexy than had he pushed his three-quarter-length erection through a hole in the shelter wall, but he humped his way through it, and when the frisson came and went he felt himself well shot of it.

Housebreaking was Shack's hobby. Round Washington it seemed a simple matter to loiter down the back-to-back rows, looking for the promising gap – then one foot over the wall into the yard, another up and through the fanlight. To Stevie there was something delicious to invading some bugger's home, getting one over them. He steeled himself to stay cool in the act – not cocky, but carefree – and made a signature of helping himself to anything worth scoffing in the fridge. Looting was of less interest – there was rarely much that seemed of value. But this was precisely Shack's obsession, zeroing in on the bedroom drawers. Richey, who never had a clue, just stood and gawped at one or other of them.

The trio were inside a respectable semi in Fallowfield Way. Stevie had found a pot of crimson matt paint under the sink and was indulging a mad notion to daub a slogan – TEAM SHARKY – on the kitchen wall. Then hefty thumps sounded overhead, and he dropped the brush and hurdled the stairs. The action was all coming out of a kid's boxy bedroom, painted that same warm crimson, but therein was Shack sitting on Richey's back, trussing his hands with a skipping rope. 'Just a bit fun, man,' Shack cackled over his shoulder. 'Fuck *off*, man,' Richey groaned, hopelessly. Stevie was torn between panic and giggles. Then Shack was wrenching Richey's jeans down to his knees, toying with a half-size snooker cue.

'You scared yet, Richey?'

In retrospect, Stevie accepted, it was scarcely a surprise – perhaps a stroke of fate – when they registered the sound of the key in the door below, froze and heard chatter in the hall, then a step on the stairs. Stevie and Shack ran, Shack using his shoulder to crash past the gentleman of the house, his wife and child gawping as they positively flew out the front door. In the chest-pounding euphoria of being back at large, neither had thought of aught but their own skins. When they remembered Richey, the matter still seemed somehow comical. It was hard to blame the lad for squealing, though they did. That same night Stevie was inside the cop shop at Glebe giving a statement to a patient officer, who corrected him on certain points of obvious fiction. Stevie felt a nagging penitence. It had been dafty behaviour. But he could not – would not – say as much. He was not charged, only cautioned – Shack, though, had had his chips – but the liaison officer informed the school, who had a policy in these matters.

'What'll he do now then, Jim? Eh?'

'Don't be asking me, Mary. Not my fault he's ruined himself.'

'Don't you say that. You can do something for him, can't you?'

'Get away. I've a *team*, man. Working men. How are they supposed to put up with *that* dead loss?'

'Is that all you can say? You his father now.'

Amazingly, what Steve overheard next was a painful silence.

Thus on Doggett's site Stevie began carrying the hod, hoisting scaffold. Doggett's gaffer was meaner still than Doggett, and no one fraternised with the new start, not even at lunch break. On his first afternoon he trod unsighted into a square of fresh cement and was vexed with himself, yet the censure he received was as if he had killed a man. A few days later he nearly severed his thumb with a hacksaw, and that raised a few chuckles. A few days back from hospital he stumbled over a concrete slab, so unloading a hod of bricks half upon himself and half onto a long pane of glass propped stupidly against a wall. Truly, Stevie thought he might never hear the end of *that* outrage. On the whole, he reckoned this gainful employment was probably worse than borstal.

On a freezing day before Christmas of 1978 Doggett's brother Frank brought his family up from Darlington. Stevie was warned to 'behave', and the thought of more identikit Doggetts infesting the place was hateful to him. But Frank's young daughter Lucy was blonde, a bit lush, and conspicuously friendly. As the day passed into evening and the adults grew merry, Stevie took his chance to cosy up. She smelled just marvellous, and didn't turn away or disdain him but smiled very prettily. When she snuck off to the bathroom Stevie tailed her, and on the upstairs landing he took her into his arms without a battle. It was dark, the kiss was juicy – it was all magic. Then she tensed. Stevie did not believe he had read wrong. Then he knew his error in the creaky tread on the carpeted stair. They had been observed: Doggett, of course – now ascending, a vision of wrath, unleashing his belt from about his lardy waist.

Stevie wanted to laugh, until Lucy no longer hung on him and Doggett was lashing out with the buckle end. He managed to grab hold, but the great lump used his weight, forced Stevie to the floor. And now they had an audience. Doggett got him by the cuffs of his tracksuit bottoms and dragged him, bumping, down the stairs. The pants came half-off, exposing Stevie's red Y-fronts and – most evil – his cock, semi-erect, poking midway through the vent. The humiliation burned white-hot, but barely for a moment before Doggett had hauled and shoved him out of the front door. There Stevie girded himself to trade punches when he heard the latch drop, realising he was to be left in the biting cold. He paced, hearing Mary within, her 'Let him in' rebuffed in irate tones. Adrenalin rushing, he strode directly round the back, swaddled his fist in his tee-shirt and thrust it through the glass of the door to the kitchen. Before he could fumble his way in, Uncle Frank had barrelled out, thrown two meaty arms around his chest, cursed him for an 'animal' and thrown him to the ground.

He stomped two miles to his nana's and granddad's in Mount Pleasant, refusing to admit the cause. His nana was all for putting on her coat and hat and going round. But Stevie had made up his mind. This fracture had been a long time coming, if no less a misery having come. He rose at first light the next morning, took a loan of George's macintosh and got aboard the X30 bus to Newcastle.

For the first night and the next day he loitered in the bus station and around the arcades, looked into pubs, filched discarded *Chronicle*s and *Journal*s and checked the Wanteds. There was a job centre, but it was horribly bright and he couldn't face anyone behind a desk. He wandered west, to Fenham and Arthur's Hill, and passed a night on a park bench, shitting in a flower bed come the morn. The next night, he claimed a hard pew in an unlocked church. In the window of some villainous den of a pub he saw a card, ventured inside and sat near the toilets, staring at the framed shipyard photos until an approachable face appeared behind the bar. His name was Jeff, in his twenties, with a head of shaggy curls. There was indeed a room for a live-in barkeep, dirt wages but rent-free. Donnelly the landlord was an unsmiling sort but seemed contented with the deal he had struck. Stevie understood when he saw the room.

He surveyed the crusty curling carpet, the mouse holes in the skirting, the bleak vista out the window through the smoke-grey piss-yellow net curtains. It was a death's-door of a lodging. He refused to crumple, but this adversity was bitter. Over the days that followed he managed to serve the old soaks and tough nuts who were the Gunnery's regulars. But there was no friendliness here, save for the odd sozzled endearment from some batty old baggage. It was an effort of will to leave the room and face another shift, another shower of mean buggers. And yet he hated that room – the size of his world. The small shitter on the landing was his one other refuge, and in its lousy cracked and smeared mirror he confronted himself.

No one will ever see me cry, he told his reflection.

And a voice replied, *Why fight it? Why should you have to? Why should anyone?*

And another voice said, *This is your* life, *man. It's* you. *You're Steven Leonard Coulson, you've not got nowt else. That's why.*

Chapter II

DUTY CALLS

Sunday, 29 September 1996

Reverend Gore mounted the concrete steps of the stairwell to the third floor of Biddle House, Crossman Estate. At the entrance below, sheltered from the muddy rain, he had fumbled with wet fingers and gaffa tape to stick up his printed circular on red A4, the text set beneath a curlicue cross. Its corners flapped in the draught.

A NEW CHURCH FOR HOXHEATH!
WE WANT <u>YOUR</u> VIEWS!
COME MEET THE REVEREND JOHN GORE!
Open Meeting to Discuss a New Service (Anglican)
All Welcome
Main Assembly, St. Luke's School
7.30 Tuesday 1 October 1996

Once more into the breach, he pondered as he climbed – another try at shaking a hand, making a friend, even in this sinkhole. No, *especially* here, he cautioned himself. At least, he had call to expect a welcome from Mrs Eunice Dodd at number seventeen. If he had always shrunk from this sort of visitation, he had equally resolved to do better. And in this case, he had given his word.

His sole wavered on a step, for something foul was assailing his nostrils. Up ahead on the half-landing was a curled mound of dog excreta, evidently fresh-laid. Despite himself, Gore stood and stared, gloom stealing over him. Not the worst sign in the world, merely and deeply dispiriting. He stood, indeterminate, feeling a chill up his trouser legs, whistling up from the door at ground level that had refused to close. He was still gazing in absent dismay when he was struck a glancing blow on the crown of the head by something light but sodden.

Looking to his feet, he saw a stained egg-box and the strewn debris of cracked shells. Then he heard the jeering giggles, and his eyes shot upward. Two floors higher, a cluster of hard young faces bobbed over the balustrade edge. Gore was still watching, nonplussed, as a deep plastic waste bin was heaved to that edge, until some better angel urged him to take evasive action. Then garbage rained upon him – wadded teabags, gnawed chicken bones, spent nappies, tumbling down about his head and shoulders.

Jubilation from on high.

Umpteen hard responses occurred to Gore, yet the one that spoke strongest to him was *hold your ground*. He brushed some rancid flecks and specks from his chest and resumed his climb, hearing ahead the squeak of rubber soles and a door slamming. When he attained the third-floor walkway – open to the pelting elements, six front doors arrayed down its length – one boy stood there still, bold as headland, barring his path. Gore stood in silence. Then he began to speak softly.

'Hello. I've something for you.'

Did the boy have any curiosity? His face was imperturbable.

'I have, you know. I've got something for you.'

He was making it up on the spot, but inspiration came blessedly hard upon. He raised his right forearm, shrugged down his sleeve, and unbuckled his wristwatch – Jessie Bradbeer's one-time gift, accepted guiltily, now deemed expendable. He proffered it to the boy, whose brow crumpled briefly with suspicion before he snatched the token from the open palm. Gore nodded. 'Now I'll see you later maybe. I'm just here to see a friend of mine, see.'

And he stepped past the boy, past a cluster of dead or dying plants in pots, their soil uselessly drowned, past four front doors until he came to number seventeen, two laminate digits adhered to the red-painted surface, albeit crooked and peeling. He stared at the back of his fist, poised close, then knocked – first one rap, unanswered, then a second. 'Wait!' came a cry from within, and he heard erratic footfalls. Who might Mrs Dodd expect at this hour, he wondered. A neighbour? The door opened just a little. The face in the crack was pale, aged, but violently made up – arched brows, green eye-shadow, blusher and mauve lipstick.

'Yes? What you want?'

'Eunice? I'm John Gore, I'm the new vicar in these parts, Stevie Coulson asked me to call in on you.'

'Stevie! Eeeh! Whey come *in*, hinny, get yer'sel in out of that . . .'

As Mrs Dodd slipped the chain, Gore glanced aside and saw the boy, his antagonist, slipping away down the stairs and out of sight.

Fully unveiled, Mrs Dodd was perhaps in her late sixties, but her nest of fibrous jet-black hair was – Gore quickly decided – a wig. She wore a long green woollen skirt, a purple roll-neck sweater, and two strings of yellow beads slung about her wattle neck. Had he encountered her in the streets of London he might have taken her for an unpublished poetess. A cloying smell of attar rose suffused the cramped flat. Temperature, though, was blood-freezing. Eunice hobbled ahead, aided by a stick, and Gore tried to assist her in the brewing of tea, but she refused. He peered into the kitchen from the hallway, long enough to see she had no refrigerator and was heating water in a pan. The scarcity struck him as so plangent that he retreated to her parlour and a seat on a ruined sofa, draped in a tartan rug and crawling with crumbs. It took Mrs Dodd three trips back and forth from the kitchen to present a tea tray and a plate laden with just two bourbon biscuits.

'Aw, he was allus special, Stevie. Always give us a hand, that un.'

Gore nodded keenly, masking his sharp certainty that he had just tasted something wrong in the tea – maybe the water, maybe the milk, or whatever substitute Eunice had mustered.

'How did *you* meet him then, hinny?'

'It was in the Gunnery pub, really . . .'

'The *Gunnery*. Like a drink, do you? Good man.' She winked. 'Aye well that's where ah knaa him from an' all. Divvint see him so much now, of course. But he's a busy lad, isn't he?'

'He's a worker, for sure.'

'Aw, he's a treasure but, that un. I'm as proud of him as I am me own. Such a good soul. He'd allus see us right, a bit this and that. He'd gan to market for his bait, come back wi' a bit boiling bacon for wuh. That's when there was nowt on him, mind. He was *lean*. 'Fore he got to be that *big*.'

Gore nodded. 'He is a big, big man.'

'*Huge*. Here, I tell you what an' all. He helped us out with my Terry. When it come to it. After he went bad . . .'

Eunice began to speak of a man Gore took to be her ex-husband, but the details were fragmented, filled in only by knowing looks. At length he had to conclude that she was describing a petty villain – a man given to sell his wife's possessions for his own ends, without prior arrangement. A violent man too, it seemed, one from whom Eunice had been forced to seek legal separation so that she could claim custody of the giro cheque essential to her and their daughter.

'So he helped you then, Stevie? With Terry . . .?'

She shot him a look as to say this was an understatement. 'He had a word. I mean, I only *heard* what happened, mind. But they said he got hold of him, proper . . .' Eunice looked askance. '*Any* road, all I know is, I never saw that Terry again.'

'They had a . . . a fight?'

'*Might* have give him a clout, Reverend. *Might*. *I* don't know. All *I* know, we had things settled from then. Here, let us show you.'

She gestured towards a set of photographs in fussy frames on a precarious shelf over the hearth-mounted three-bar heater that sat dormant in the arctic room.

'Now that's our Dusty and her two boys.'

Gore's eyes fell first onto an image of Eunice, perhaps a couple of decades younger, looking pie-eyed beside a grinning Stevie, he clad in white karate pyjamas, his hair amusingly long and straggly. He forced himself instead to inspect the picture of a fretful dark-haired woman between two sheepish lads.

'It's not easy for her, not easy. But she tries. Them boys have got to share everything between them. Their shoes even.'

'I'm sorry?'

'Oh, she can't afford shoes for both. They take it in turns, you know?'

Could he believe it? It was almost too flabbergasting – too upsetting. It seemed, though, his cue to segue. 'I should say, one of the reasons for my church, I'm hoping, will be to try and do something about just that sort of – deprivation, people have.'

'Eh?'

'I'm saying it's a wicked thing, that that sort of thing should happen.'

'Aw aye, wicked it is.' She nodded keenly. 'Wickedness. Oh, that's what your lot are here for, no buts about it. Isn't it, though?'

'Well, we – yes, obviously – it's my job to minister to anyone who feels themselves – what we call "oppressed by evil".'

'That's it. Aye, that's it. I see him and all, I do. I see him in the corner of the room.'

She was offering him a sort of a slow-dawning complicit smile. But it was another mad alley he was disinclined to venture down.

'What I'd like to do,' he ventured, 'is get people out of the house, get them together. More of a neighbourhood atmosphere. Do you think that's a good idea?'

The smile was still there but with a new glimmer – as if indeed she had heard something of interest. And yet somehow he was not convinced she had taken in a single word.

'Well, I tell you, people round here, whey . . . you'll know how they talk around these parts, *whey* . . . There's some *very* bad families, you know? Some bad characters moved in. Wicked, aye. They've come in and they've spoiled it. *Gangs* and that, I don't know *how* they get started but they spread, they do. Like a rotten old stain.'

'That is . . . a shame,' Gore offered.

'Eh? Aye. And you tell the council what happens and they say they won't stand for it, they'll evict them. But council still has to re-house them. It does, doesn't it? How about that?'

'Yes, I suppose . . . not everybody is a good neighbour.'

'*Whey*. And then you've got the Sikhs and whatnot. I've no axe to grind, me. But them uns what wear the turbans, they've the look of *wolves* to me.'

Gore pondered his knees, wishing now that he had not surrendered his watch, for it would have been a valuable prop in these circumstances. When he looked up again Eunice was looking at him plaintively.

'Here, but, I've an aaful problem. Would you ever have a look for us?'

Oh God, thought Gore. 'Why, yes, of course. I'll try. What is it?'

'Well, it's damp, I think. Council won't bother themselves. Stevie used to do this sort of thing for us, see . . .'

They rose and she led him off the hallway into a gloomy and musty bedroom. *Yes*, thought Gore, *I smell rainfall, ingress, rot*. He pulled aside the narrow single bed with its cheap frilled orange bedspread, and the painted wall behind the headboard was indeed horrendous – hopelessly blistered, a picture of dereliction. He touched a finger to the plaster, finding it cool and moist. Gently drawing aside the curtain, he saw a hopeless little window-fan fixed in the glass, its blades barely fluttering.

'You see, hinny, if I could just get all the rotten off, and fresh paint on . . .'

'To be honest, Eunice, I think it needs a proper damp course.'

'Eee, when am I going to get that done? Who'll pay for that? Council?'

'Well, they ought to.'

'I knaa, I just wish I could get a man round . . . it's bad, you see.'

Gore looked at his hands. Obligation – it seemed to make a chain in life.

'I'll do it for you. I'll sort it out.' *Jack Ridley*, he was thinking.

And she took his hand in hers, surprisingly tightly. He worried she might do herself an injury. Her smile was tight and troubled, but a smile nonetheless. 'Now, that service of yours,' she said. 'I'll be there, you can count on me.'

'Oh, now only so long as it suits . . .'

'No.' The grip tightened yet. '*You* can count on *me*. Cos you're a good un, you.' She looked very serious. Gore smiled tightly and patted her arm with his free hand, grateful for the old lady's endorsement but keen she deliver no hostage to fortune.

Chapter III

IRON AND JUICE

1979–1983

'He's a canny lad, this one,' Eunice declared to anyone and no one as Stevie slid her gin-and-bitter-lemon under her nose. If in earshot then Donnelly the Gunnery landlord tended to snort. Stevie kept his own counsel. In no position to scorn a friendly gesture, he still despised the thought of being mothered. His efforts were trained on establishing some rapport with Jeff, his partner behind the bar on alternate nights. When Jeff peeled down to his black Rainbow tee-shirt a startling musculature was unveiled, even though he wore bookworm specs and a swottish air. Sometimes, when Stevie sought out his room between shifts, Jeff would be on the stairs perusing *Black Belt Magazine* or *World of Judo*. Stevie took care to let Jeff see his interest and Jeff, at length, took pity, proposing that Stevie accompany him east of town to a place called Morton's of Wallsend.

It was a timber-frame shed with a pitched roof and one frosted window. Within, on a concrete floor laid with rubber mats, were stacks of free weights, a row of clunking machines, and a dozen or so big grunting half-naked men. Stevie ignored the sharp commingled stench of cheese and embrocation. For these men looked like *he* wanted to look. They glowered back at him, some with eyes alarmingly close-set. But Jeff steered him about, urged him to try his hand, spotted him under the bench-press bar. Then he engaged the proprietor, a retired shot-putter, in a muttered conference, and a deal was cut on Stevie's behalf. After changing, they sat by a small service counter and Jeff bought them both gloopy refreshments of dried protein powder in milk. He waved away Stevie's halting gratitude. 'Do unto others, Steve lad, do unto others. It's about treating people decent. That way, they treat you the same. You'll do summat for me someday.'

Stevie pledged himself then to the discipline of iron. 'There are principles,' Jeff told him, near-comically hushed and earnest. 'They go from man to man. You won't get them out of books.' For that much, Stevie was glad. Morton's became his home from the Gunnery, and a model home at that – a safe haven. Its members respected one other's purpose and work-rate, there was no posing or picking-on, and a man was as anonymous as he cared to be. Why couldn't the world be like that? Stevie fell hard for the iron – the pull and the push, the sweet ache of the exertion, his confident management of it – but, above all, its visible benefits. Gazing from the fastened stacks of weights to the size and shape of his burgeoning cuts of muscle, he had a pin-sharp sense that some inner faculty of his was being weighed in the balance and found favourable. Jeff prodded him helpfully. 'Try to see in your mind the person you want to be. Hold that picture. Work toward it.' It became clearer to Stevie from whence Jeff had acquired his odd air of abstraction. Jeff also started to slip him wraps of bland little tablets, Dianabol, to have with his meals. 'They'll build you up.' And there was something to it, he knew as much whenever he took his turn in one of Morton's two dank little shower cubicles and inspected himself – bulkier by the day, it seemed.

Waiting his turn by the dumb-bell rack one evening he made the acquaintance of Dicko, a big burring Bristolian, ex-army, or so he said, shiny-scalped but with a walrus moustache and a fine fuzz all over his barrel-like, slightly bloated upper body. Dicko had a little entourage, and Stevie found them appealing, for they bantered about football and cheeked one another easily. They were pub-and-club doormen, the gym a grapevine of such musclework. And they exuded assurance, but they weren't vain arseholes, not like Jim Doggett. Stevie only wished he had the lip or the strut to fraternise.

Jeff didn't rate Dicko, but Stevie didn't cleave to Jeff's views on all things. On the odd free night, they would have a pint of Guinness after Morton's, and Jeff put his finger on what had been a growing unease in Stevie. 'Gets boring, doesn't it?' he offered. 'Same old work-out?' Stevie agreed keenly. 'It's good, like, but it doesn't *go* anywhere . . .'

So Jeff marched him to the local community hall and a weekly martial arts dojo. 'Just watch the groups for a bit,' he said. 'See what you might like.' Stevie sat on a low bench and studied the range of styles being practised – judo, aikido, ju jitsu, taisudo, tae kwan do. Grappling looked a bit queer – two blokes grunting into each other's necks – and he fancied kicking, but he wanted to be able to punch too. So he plumped for Shotokan karate, based on techniques of what the brochure called 'street defence'. For a while, he limped along at a lowly belt in an intermediate-weight class, for he found it surprisingly hard to rouse himself into attack mode. 'Visualise an enemy,' Jeff advised. Stevie pictured a wet comb dragged through a pompous thatch of rusty hair. The sessions then grew a little edgy, until Stevie came to sense that other lads shrank from pairing up with him.

One night in the Gunnery, voices were raised and an awful fight erupted, the object some poor-looking woman, but it was some poor bloke who got a pint glass broken over his nose. The assailant, not a regular, took to his heels, but Jeff and Stevie waited for the cops with the luckless victim, a long evil shard of glass sunk into his cheek like some mad scientist's transplant. Stevie, silent, felt a shiver of nausea. Truly, there was the thought and there was the deed. Jeff too looked ashen, and three days later he handed in his notice. He took Stevie aside, murmured that he and his lass had some plans together. But Stevie was shipwrecked, with no plans larger than a few half-formed notions. He had believed himself an apprentice hardman, but the leap to professional status now seemed very stark.

He was sat in Morton's rest area, alone as was his way now, hunched over the oaten dregs of a protein shake, the sweat of a session drying on his muscles and his Lonsdale singlet. On the outer edge of his vision a lean young squirt of a bloke – not in gym-sweats but jeans and windcheater – was perched on a plastic chair, eyeing him. Smirking, even. And he didn't want to be doing that.

'The fuck *yee* looking at?'

'Looking at you, pal. You're some pup.' He had a wispy moustache, this squirt, and he chuckled like an old lag, for all that he looked not long out of the schoolyard. 'I've *watched* you, man. You train like a loony. It's a waste, but. You've peaked, your body's had it. You need to tak' on more *fuel* if you wanna get proper big.'

His name was Luke Ridley and he claimed to know some science. Stevie asserted he knew better, for didn't he swallow magic little pills with every meal? 'Waste of money, pal,' this Ridley shot back. 'You only shite them back out. You've got to *stack*. Proper chemical supplements. Everybody else does.'

Funny how no one else had mentioned it. And Luke Ridley had lowered his voice. But, surveying the clientele at Morton's, it did seem bulgingly plausible. Luke suggested they step outside to his vehicle. As they walked, Stevie saw Dicko glance his way.

The tariff for Luke's 'supplements' was alarming, but he offered a starter's discount, plus aftercare. So Stevie consented to part with a fiver a week for an ampoule of Deca Durabolin, designed to go directly into the top of his right arse cheek. Stevie wasn't keen on needles but he believed in discipline, and in the wisdom that one could get used to anything, at least in pursuit of the higher call of becoming something other. So, cloistered in his tiny Gunnery bedroom, he grimaced and contorted and drove the needle home – his very own mad science project.

He was impatient for change and moped for a week or two, but really it was soon that he sensed a new tightness and bulge in the wake of his workouts. Euphoric, he reported back to Luke, who counselled that the manly way forward was a boosted dosage, and something of a cocktail thereof. Thus Stevie introduced his right buttock to Testaviron. There were remedial drugs, too, for the tail-end of each six-week cycle. 'They're serious *hormones*, these, man, you divvint wanna grow women's tits.' Luke giggled, cupping a pair of imaginary bouncers. Stevie saw the point, and didn't resent the investment. His pint-puller's wage was good for nothing else. But he fast found himself creeping ahead of his given schedule, and so called round one day to Luke's home address in Fenham, ringing the doorbell only to be faced by Mr Ridley Senior – a stern, stocky customer, with a squashed nose and a stony glare. Luke was not best pleased when he next saw Stevie, instructing him to never show such initiative again.

As the days fell away Stevie had growing discomfort in his back and his arse, and when he got himself naked and back-to-front before a full mirror he was appalled to see a livid Petri dish of buckshot acne. Now, on top of the ache of the needle's gouge, came the itch and sting of weeping boils. Worse, he was aware of a worrying contraction about his bollocks, and the lads at Morton's ribbed him for a perpetual protective cupping of his scrotum. He attacked his work, though, with rising vigour and fierceness, hammering the iron in longer, harder sessions. In his mind the purpose had passed from simple self-improvement to some impending but yet undated confrontation, the antagonist but half-glimpsed, if not imagined. He pictured, too, unknown but approving eyes, the nod of heads, solemn respect in any room he entered. In the midst of one frenzied workout he had to be ousted from his seat at the pectoral machine by Dicko, politely but firmly, and it was only when Stevie stared down at the dark droplets dotting the rubber mat that he realised his nose was streaming blood.

'Ragin' bull, this young beggar,' Dicko chortled.

On the day Stevie was drawn aside by Dicko and sounded out about 'working the doors', he felt his fortunes in ascent at last. First, though, there was a sort of interview to be navigated.

'Can you box?'

'Nah. Not really. I've done a bit karate, but.'

'Oh blimey,' Dicko shook his head. 'Not the old Hoo-Flung-Dung. You shoulda boxed, flower, then you'd move better.'

Stevie felt stung, defensive. 'I've got plenty moves on us, Dicko man.'

'Oh, I bet you have. But if it's me and you against Fat Mick and five mates and one of them's got a jack-knife, then I don't want to look over and see you working out what dance you're gonna do. I need to know you're gonna whack 'em. Hard. In the throat. The nadgers. Whatever it takes.'

Stevie nodded as to say he took the point, relieved at least that he had this affable furry ogre for his tutor.

Dicko had several pitches, but it was at a 'disco pub' in Gateshead by name of the Loose Box that Stevie presented himself on the appointed hour for his first night's shift, clad in a thick black cable sweater and steel-capped Dr Martens. Dicko surveyed him critically. 'Okay, flower, stand up big, listen to me, and keep your mouth shut.' As the punters arrived, the duo manned the narrow doorway and counted heads for an hour. Only when a bumptious pair tried to push their way forward did Dicko step out and make a wall of himself. Afterward, he grunted into Stevie's ear. 'Them that wave their arms about, they're just trying to fool you. Stare 'em out, talk it down, nice and easy.'

In time they were relieved, whereupon Dicko escorted Stevie up a flight of stairs for a tour of the disco – desultory groups of females and larger packs of drinking males, under spotlights and mirror-balls. The dance floor felt spongy under Stevie's boots, and Dicko, rolling his eyes, advised that it had been laid on top of the old pub carpet. 'In here you get yourself positioned right.' This, it seemed, was lesson number two. 'Assess the room. Get yourself good at observation. Observation means *anticipation*. You see something you don't like, send out the stare. Let 'em *know* you're watching.' Within minutes Dicko had spotted the makings of a push-and-shove altercation by the bar, and once again, from the vantage of Dicko's burly shoulder, Stevie was intrigued to see how fast the hostility fizzled down to nowt like butter in a pan. 'Don't be getting demob happy,' Dicko cautioned. 'Breaking things up is easy. Lot of these tossers are just waitin' for you to step in, they *want* it broken up before they get hurt.' He grinned. 'Now, there's others – *they* want to do you. But, y'know, proper fight, you don't feel nothing anyway. Not less it *really* hurts.' And he looked askance at Stevie. 'Not scared yet, flower?'

'I'm canny, man,' Stevie muttered.

The night was passing without major incident, even getting dull. Then Dicko had his arm around a raddled redhead and then, with a wink, he vanished from view. Stevie was alone, stationed once more at the door, breathing the sharp night air and thinking about the bus home, when the landlord of the Loose Box appeared at his side in a tizzy.

'It's Steve, aye? Look, Steve, we've got this bugger, he's bother and he's not leaving, but I want him out, right now, son.'

'Fuck. Right. Where's Dicko?'

'He'll be shaggin', won't he?'

'Hang on, I'll get him.'

'*Now*, Steve, this needs doing *now*.'

Bollocks, thought Stevie, for the landlord was tugging at his arm and there was no backing down from the belly-stabbing sense that this was make-or-break time. Still, he tried.

'What's his bother, this gadgy? Will he not just gan on, like?'

'I'd rather not *ask* him, son. What am I paying *you* for?'

Stevie strode into the disco, his legs shaky beneath him as he crossed the spongy floor, girding up his sinews as if to inflate himself and still the quake in his bowels. In his mind's eye he was headed in the opposite direction, out the door, free and clear. But headed where? The owner was pointing out the enemy – a shaven-headed pudding of a bloke with a dead-eyed scowl, probably forty years old and twenty stone in weight, a big lump cosseted by a few big-lump pals. As he bore down, the gadgy's mates were clocking him, cockily, alerting their leader, who barely half-turned his head from the pint of beer raised to his mouth. 'Aw aye, then,' he spat. 'Yee and what army, you little prick?'

Stevie threw a straight right at the side of that meaty face, which cannoned gloriously into the mouth of the glass. Another right to the head, then another, then a left hook to the ribs – Stevie's hands weren't fast but they had clout – and then the gadgy's legs were failing him, his cause forlorn, collapsing him to the floor. One of his pals made a poor feint of a move, Stevie lashed out a boot at his shins, and the howl was louder than the music in the room. Two men down, a third looking like he might shit his pants, the area clearing, and all eyes on Stevie – all in seeming awe but he. The gadgy was on all fours so Stevie booted him in his sagging belly, and he voided the watery contents of his stomach onto the carpet. Now there was a grasping hand at Stevie's shoulder and he beat it off, before he was seized about the chest by twine-like arms. It was Dicko, bearing reinforcements, and the fire-exit doors were being kicked open, bodies manhandled from the space. But Stevie was blazingly content, for truly he had felt it – the rush of hormones from the adrenals, his fear turning to propulsive hate, hate that even now overrode the raw burning pulse in his knuckles. He delegated the rest of the kicking to Dicko, and waved away the landlord's ferrety gratitude, as he supposed a professional would.

Donnelly exuded displeasure over Stevie's ever more erratic hours at the Gunnery, yet seemed somehow shy of saying as much. Finally it was Stevie who determined it was time to move on – for it had become his custom to call by Dicko's functional flat in Byker for a shit and a shower before a night's work, sometimes sleeping over on the shedding couch, sometimes with a docile female if Dicko's 'entertainment' of the evening had a friend. One day Stevie simply lingered over a pot of tea, long after the plates of egg and bacon congealed. Upon fetching his small Adidas holdall from the Gunnery, he had successfully swapped one small room for another.

Batman and Robin they became, two fairly carefree bachelors even with twenty years between them. Dicko, too, was on Luke Ridley's juice, only longer and stronger cycles, heavy fuel, Testaviron and Sustanon. Over mugs of tea one morning Dicko advised Stevie that Luke had gone south and they wouldn't see him again. Stevie was panicked but Dicko assured him they would not go short, for he knew a bloke who knew a bloke. As for Luke, it transpired that his grim old dad had been nosing around and found his stash. The set-to had resulted in Luke's expulsion from the family home. Stevie wished he had had a chance to say goodbye, to tell his unlikely friend that these things happened, and it was okay, dads were like that. Jack Ridley, for sure, had seemed an excessively miserable cunt.

Stevie and Dicko ate together, drank together, injected together, and double-dated. Dicko introduced him to a voluble redhead named Debbie, who seemed to like him hugely. Certainly her libido was pronounced and naked. She was not a bad looker, compared to her hefty mates, her complexion smoothed by copious pancake, her lips surprisingly delicious. At Morton's, though, Stevie overheard some crack about 'Drippy Debbie', and his nascent composure cracked. 'You, round the back wi' me now' was his riposte to the joker, but Dicko's hand fell on his shoulder. Analysing his anger in quiet he understood – once again, he had found himself starting from the back of the queue, and that had to stop. He dumped Debbie double-quick and she called him a bastard, but the charge ran off his back, for he knew he would need to be a bigger bastard yet.

It was she, running post-coital fingers through Stevie's hair, who had teased him for going bald. He knew it, glumly, had long sensed it getting patchy and stringy and poor, one more unsightly offshoot of the juice. He chose his course quickly, took a loan of Dicko's electric clippers, and shaved his scalp clean. Afterward, scooping sodden wads of clippings from the plughole, he felt a powerful *tristesse*. It was almost as though he had aged in an hour, been abruptly stripped of his youth, joined Dicko on a craggy far shore of maturity. And yet there was undeniable solace: that shaven pate bestowed on him a certain sort of a look, his strong-boned face and ravenous grin thrown very strikingly into relief. As he strutted past the mirrors in Morton's he practised impassivity, an occasional roil of his thickened neck, as though something immensely displeased were stirring within him. This man in the mirror had size and authority, and his thoughts could not be guessed. The outward Stevie was stern and fierce as an ogre. Inside he was grinning like a kid.

Come the summer of 1983 Stevie could feel the sun on his face. Newcastle nightlife was reviving, several bigger and brighter and much-fancied venues springing up near the river – Roxanne's, the Love Boat, Club Zeus, Brilliant! Some TV pop show was broadcasting live from a studio on Fridays, so there were pop stars round town, and tidy-looking girls in tow. Dicko drafted Stevie into a job beside him at a club called the Matinee where the light was fluorescent, the music was funk, and the bar purveyed sickly cocktails. On first inspection the manager was bluntly disparaging of Stevie's boots and bomber jacket – 'That's nee fucking good, son, you get yourself a black suit for here.' Newly suited and booted, Stevie started to enjoy himself about the bouncer's craft. His greatest laugh was the early expulsion of bare-legged girls overpowered by cocktails, some so helplessly bladdered as to require shifting by a fireman's hold. 'Just you mind they don't spew up down your back,' Dicko roared. Certain other lasses – not quite so insensible but rowdy nonetheless – Stevie simply hefted off their feet as they hammered his chest and berated him in the crudest terms, their gussets exposed to gleeful watching Geordies. When he set them down out of doors, right side up, he sometimes received a very breathless look, and then sometimes a phone number, or even a straight proposition. He preferred to think himself a gent in such matters, but there was a certain sort of female on whom the courtesy, quite clearly, was wasted.

Shagging then became a principle and a competition in which Stevie steadily surpassed Dicko, who in turn grew a little censorious – or was it envious? – of the younger girls Stevie brought back to the flat. The deed was not always a simple matter. Stevie's scrotum was shrivelled much of the time by the steroids, and on occasions, before tackling the girl, he had to give himself a helping hand in the toilet – a quick five-knuckle shuffle, drawing on his skills of visualisation. Sometimes, to his own disquiet, he pictured himself, post-workout – stiff all over his body, biceps tight. It was a weird thing, perhaps, but it worked. And once he was on, he was on – one hundred per cent hard man, dispenser of physical sensation.

There was, he found, an upper echelon of female – certain rather foxy creatures who frequented the Matinee, consorted with the pop stars, wholly unresponsive to his rough-and-ready routine. Perhaps it was something else they sought, judging by the flounce and effeminacy of the Flash Harries to whom they clung. But he wasn't wholly convinced. '*Everybody* likes a bit naughty' – that was the Guv'nor's catchphrase.

Eric Manners was a professional photographer who regularly pitched up at the club and called for a bottle of Moët. He wore a burgundy leather blouson, stone-washed jeans with a hint of pink, and kept his white hair piled on his head like day-old candyfloss, only nicotine-stained like the net curtains in the Gunnery. It was a nonce-like ensemble, and Eric the sort of fellow at whom Stevie was inclined to look askance. He was touchy-feely too, and known for a connoisseur's interest in the male body, since his framed monochrome photos of torsos were all over the walls of the Matinee. Yet he was usually squiring some fit lass, and over a drink Stevie found he had a wife and grown kids and could talk knowledgeably about football – Newcastle, not Sunderland. Very candidly he told Stevie that there was no job he would not take, and as such he did his fashion stuff and his arty snaps and then also shot the occasional spread for mucky books. 'I'm not ashamed, Stevie, I work hard for me packet. I just don't pay tax.' And he nudged Stevie and laughed. 'Do you know, son, what is the *sexiest* part of the body?'

Stevie hadn't mulled it over and yet his preference leapt to mind. It was the back of a lass's neck – that nicely hollowed and contoured shape if the hair was swept away, eliciting cascades of giggles when nuzzled. That was true loveliness. He was all for the tits and the fanny, of course, but not wedded to them. This he kept to himself and merely shook his head for Eric, who tapped his forehead. 'The *brain*, bonny lad. That's the bit does the most work. Way more than the owld fella doon there. See, your average bloke's brain is thinking about sex at least once every ten seconds. Scientists have proved that. Ten seconds. That's more naughty than your owld fella knows what to do with. And that's where the owld muckies come in, see.'

Manners laughed and touched Stevie's shoulder. Stevie didn't believe any of this pontificating was quite as scientific as Eric claimed – he was, after all, a bullshitter. But it was impressive to him that Eric had applied such thought to his game, that he was pragmatic, aware of the customer's needs. There was a solidity to him, and Stevie saw and respected it. After Eric invested in new video gear, he came to Stevie for a quiet word, with a modest proposal. To Stevie it seemed a worthwhile test, even a bit of a laugh, and the offer in cash was terrific. On the appointed day he climbed the creaking stairs to a second-floor flat on the Westgate Road, where Eric and his assistant were already engrossed in fiddling with the video camera, the fluid-head tripod, the clunky cassette recorder and a large white cotton bedsheet clipped to a frame by clothes pegs. Stevie's accomplice for the day was perched on a bed in a flannel nightgown – a dark-haired lass called Michelle who might have come directly from working the chip van outside the Matinee – no great looker, but no tart neither, and perfectly sweet-natured about what she was being asked to do. Stevie donned a pair of blue overalls as instructed, and Eric led them patiently through rehearsal, punctuated by Michelle's giggles. But Stevie was soon into his stride – he had easy access to the needful exhibitionism, now that his body was both tool and thing of wonder to him.

He and Michelle were bollock naked, atop one another and near enough engaged, when Eric called a brief halt for a change of set-up, asking them both to hold very still. The assistant fiddled with the white balance and the clothes pegs. Eric patted Stevie's shoulder. 'You're a pro, you are, my son.' Underneath him, Michelle made a cooing sound, ran a fingernail up his taut bicep. Not the girl of his dreams, not by any means – any more than the many lasses he had been diddling of late without the benefit of today's pay-wedge. But she was out there somewhere, that special girl, and his ongoing graft and application would surely only bring her closer.

Chapter IV

THE FOCUS GROUP

Tuesday, 1 October 1996

Gore believed he was making a passable show of immersion in the logbook before him, and so at intervals he let his gaze flick upward and fall upon the girl. A young woman, in truth – mid-twenties, he supposed – seated on her own, slowly wreathing herself in smoke as if resolved to inhabit fully the role of pariah. Thirteen souls had presented themselves thus far to the assembly hall, and most had tried to spread themselves evenly about the available seating – sixty-four red plastic chairs set out with exacting symmetry in eight rows of eight. *She*, though, had made like a shot for the back row. She wore a chocolate velour tracksuit, her brownish hair hennaed and pinned into slides, her face painted, traces of purple about her cheekbones detectable from thirty paces. With a slight frisson Gore placed his recognition of her – the newsagent, on the morning he first walked out to St Luke's. The prettier of the two . . . though this particular prettiness he sensed as brittle, bought across a counter in a shop, put in place carefully each morning. But allure was allure, however sulky or cosmetic.

He turned again to the ruled columns of the registration book he had asked allcomers to inscribe. Before him, Albert Robinson, Pensioner. Rod Moncur, Retailer. Sharon Price, Housewife. Sean Goddard, Porter (Hospital). Alan Day, Teacher. Lizzie Spence, Legal Secretary. Kully Gates, Community Worker – no doubt the intently bespectacled brown-skinned woman four rows back. Susan Carrow, the former hairdresser on his parish council, had sat herself briskly without signing her name. At the foot of the page, one Lindy Clark had neglected to make an entry in the occupational column, but gave her address as Oakwell Estate.

'Are we getting marked for wor handwriting?'

The jest came from the front row, where sat a pug-faced fellow with a toothy grin, his hair a mop of dark curls, an affable mien only damaged by an unfortunate resemblance to the murderer Fred West.

'I'll let you know, Mr Moncur. It's just for my reference, a database, you know?'

An elderly gent – Albert Robinson, surely – sat with his flat cap on, hands folded in his lap, now and then peering about him as if troubled. His face was milky and craggy, a cupid-bow purse to his upper lip, a trait Gore considered distinctively Geordie. He sucked on his dentures doggedly and loudly, as though an entire meal – rather than remnants thereof – were adhered to their sides. His visible scepticism was the outward gauge of Gore's own inner doubt. The clock said 7.23. He had taken some cares, and they now contributed to his feeling a little foolish.

The assembly hall of St Luke's was chill and unwelcoming, as if hostile to the intrusion. A periodic clanking and groaning emanated from the radiators arrayed down its length of the hall. Gore watched as the caretaker bashed at one with a hammer. 'I can't blame him for being peeved,' whispered Monica Bruce, now at Gore's side. 'They're not in his job description, nights. Not this night anyway. At least he showed up.'

'Quite. So where are our punters, do you think?'

'Well,' said Monica. 'I told the kids in assembly, be sure and tell their parents. You put your little posters up?'

Gore nodded. He had visited the library, the town hall, newsagents, he had pinned up on every available pinboard.

'We maybe would have been better in the staff room,' said Monica.

'This is the space we've got to fill. We might as well start trying.'

Evidently Moncur had been eavesdropping from the front row, for now he chipped in. 'We could always move to the Gunnery.'

'Oh, there'll be refreshment,' murmured Gore, gesturing to a table laid with cups, a sizeable urn and plates of biscuits.

'I must say I'm quite dry already,' said Susan Carrow, wincing, twee in a pink sweater, fanning her fingers before her face. Then Monica was striding down the aisle and stooping to the side of that girl, gesturing to the fuming cigarette. 'Linda, pet. Would you mind not?'

'Bet I'm not the only one wants a smoke,' she groused, eyes darting heavenward. But she offered a parody of an obliging smile before screwing the butt to death under her trainer.

Clacking back down the aisle, Monica nodded at Gore, then turned to the assembly and joined her hands. 'Good evening, all, thank you for coming, most of you'll know me already so you won't want to hear me ask for money. But the Reverend will be too shy, so I'd just like to say refreshments are provided and please avail yourself, and if you enjoy them then a few coins would be appreciated, because Reverend Gore's on a tight budget here. Over to you, John.'

Suppressing a slight irritation, Gore stepped forward, lines prepared.

'Well, yes, thank you for coming out tonight to be a part of what, if you'll, uh, forgive my borrowing the language of Tony Blair, I would like to call my focus group.'

He had hoped for chuckles. He heard only Albert sucking those plates.

'Or – a steering group, if you like. A working party.'

He was, he decided, on the wrong horse. Back to the stalls, then.

'These are early days and we've a road ahead, but my hope for this project, once we have it up and running, is that it be a resource, a *real* resource, for the community. And a platform for the community's concerns. A way to bring us all together. So I thought tonight, rather than me standing up here lecturing at you, we might just throw it open from the start, and you could tell *me* a little of how you feel about Hoxheath. The community. What you think are its problems. Strengths too, of course. I'm here to listen.'

Gore was careful to finish with a gesture of open palms toward the seated, as if to extend the talking stick authorising the speaker at a gathering of the tribes. But there was only silence. Faces were impassive, or perplexed.

'Sorry?' Sharon Price, a rotund woman in a tent-like blouse, her face florid under a dark bob, spoke up. 'Sorry, but I thought we were here to hear about a *church*.'

Gore nodded keenly. 'Of course. I just want to be saying from the outset, the church I have in mind here is a social church. I want us to help. So I need to hear from you what you think people need help with.'

Kully Gates was smiling. Sharon Price was not. 'Aw but this isn't one of them *schemes*, is it? There'll be an actual *church*, right? A service, on a Sunday? With hymns and that?'

'Yes, yes –'

'Cos I don't know about anyone else but I'm sick of people coming round talking *schemes* – communal programmes and that. Sick to the back *teeth*.'

Kully Gates had raised her hand, thoughtful, and Gore seized on her. 'Please,' said Gore. 'It's Kully, yes?'

'Yes. Reverend, I think we're maybe *all* a bit confused, because you're sounding just a bit like a social worker. Which is my area, you see. And I suppose we had come here to hear about – worship?'

'Right, got you. Let me start again from the top. This is a new church, a new *kind* of church. Any new start offers new opportunities. So on top of all the things we normally do in church, I'm looking for new ways for this church to serve the community. I suppose you could say – not just to regenerate people in God but to regenerate Hoxheath itself.'

'Aw blimey, here we go,' groaned Sharon Price. 'That word.'

'Which?'

'"Regeneration".' How many times we heard that?' She looked around for support. 'All the talk, them do-gooders coming round. We've had the – what all have we had? City Challenge. Hoxheath Initiative. Drive for Jobs . . .'

Gore suddenly wished he had a notebook. 'These would be government schemes?'

'Aye. People come to your door to interview you. They're all the same, they ask you, do you wanna have "regeneration" in

Hoxheath? And you say yes, don't you? It doesn't sound like owt to quarrel with. If they said, "Would you like dog shite on your doorstep?" you'd say no, wouldn't you? 'Scuse my language, sorry.' A few hollow chuckles. 'Aye, so you tell 'em what you're bothered with and they nod and drink your tea then off they gan and write it up and do whatever they were minded to do in the first place.'

Sean Goddard, sour-faced behind a Zapata moustache, was nodding. 'Right. You're promised new this and new that, but you never get it. The things we've got, *they're* not kept up. So how are we going to get new? There's never money. Have *you* got money, Reverend? I doubt it, not if you're asking us to pay for biscuits.'

Gore felt his neck prickling. Sharon Price leaned forward in her chair. 'Aye. Now *I* come here to hear about a church service, thank you very much.'

'Seconded,' echoed Goddard.

Kully Gates spoke up. 'Be fair, I don't think the Reverend's trying to rip anybody off.'

Sharon Price rounded on her. 'Aye well, you *would* say that, you're one of them do-gooders.'

'Leave her be, man.' This was Lindy Clark.

In the fraught silence that followed, Kully Gates got to her feet. 'I should explain, John. I work for a community project in Hoxheath. So I have sat on some of those schemes the lady mentions, committees and so on. I don't know *why* – no one elects me, but I do get asked. Because I'm involved. Now, we run a credit union, a crèche, we do a scheme for school leavers. All this. But people are . . . suspicious. They've been let down before.'

Albert Robinson cleared his throat. 'Aye. Now, you take our esteemed Member of Parliament. Mr Martin Pallister. Disciple of your Mr Anthony Blair. How much hot air did that one blow off? And what's he done?'

This seemed to Gore a fruitful digression. Albert continued, calmly, hands folded in his lap. '*He* was a big regeneration man, Pallister. That's how he got hisself known hereabouts. With the TREC lot, Tyneside Regeneration.'

'He's *alright*, man, Pallister.' Sharon Price was riled again. 'He's done some canny things – what new housing we've had round here was all cos of him. He's local an' all, used to live right next door to us – I can *tell* you he's alright.'

'Well, say as you like, madam. I'll tell you, he come and interviewed us once. Must have been 1989. Seemed canny. Said he wanted all this new building, all down the river. I said, "We heard that off T. Dan Smith and we're still paying." And what did we get off him? Apartments selling for a hundred thousand pound. And a business park wi' no business. Not for the likes of us. I tell you what I think. You watch. In time, they'll want us all out. Ethnic cleansing.'

Gore blinked. 'What, like in Bosnia?'

'Aye. We've got all them lot *here* now – Bosnians. How about that? But aye, ethnic cleansing, just you watch. You've got land here, nowt much to look at but canny views of the river. All that's in the way is the people. They'd love to turf us out and tear them all down, start again.'

'So what are we supposed to do?' Sharon Price sounded upset.

'Move out of Hoxheath,' rasped Sean Goddard.

'When? After you win the lottery?'

Susan Carrow, who had twisted in her seat and listened to the foregoing exchanges in mounting agitation, now faced Gore. 'See? All your talk about "community" this and that. There *is* no community.'

Moncur nodded glumly. 'True, people aren't neighbours to each other. Not like when I was a bairn.'

Gore stood flummoxed. This was as poor an impasse as he could have imagined. His sole hope was that the wave of suppressed resentment had broken and was now receding. Consensus was badly needed.

'Okay, let me ask you this. What would you like from my church? Just take it as read we'll have a service on Sunday, with prayer and hymns and a sermon. That's Sunday taken care of. What else? Anything?'

Rod Moncur thrust a fist in the air. 'Does it have to be Sunday?'

'Excuse me?'

'Your service, does it have to be Sunday? Could you not maybe do it one night in the week?'

Albert cut in, waspish. 'Sunday is the Sabbath day, my friend.'

'Aye, you say that, but Sunday's a hangover in my house, more often than not.' Moncur chuckled, then seemed peeved that others didn't join in. 'Not just my house. You know how it is, the weekend, you've got a lot on.'

Mrs Carrow was nodding. 'It's true, but. You've got the family coming round, the lunch to do. Bairns want to get out . . .'

Moncur nodded. 'And there's the match on Sky. Aye, there's a lot wants done on Sunday.'

Christ alive, thought Gore. *Am I supposed to hire a van and call door-to-door by appointment?* 'Well, Mrs Bruce and I have a particular arrangement. Monica?'

'If you're asking for a midweek service,' she declared, tartness to her voice, 'I'm telling you now, Wednesday is my parents' evening and that's sacred.'

Gore faced outward again. 'Let's agree to talk again. Maybe we have a month of Sundays, then try a change.'

Heads nodded. To his right Gore detected the stirring of Lizzie Spence, a slight bespectacled young woman in monochrome office uniform of coat, blouse and skirt. 'Will there be a crèche?' she asked.

'For children?'

'No, for grown-ups,' Lizzie scoffed. 'Of course for children. You don't have kids then? If you had kids you'd be wanting a crèche.'

'Right. It's an idea. Though, Kully, you say *you* run a crèche . . .? So I'm not so sure we should double up services.'

Sharon Price thumped her palm. 'They *want* doubling, man. They want to be times-ten what they are.'

From the distant back row Lindy Clark gave out. 'Aye, a crèche would be a canny idea. Could be a mothers' group too. Like a parent-toddler thing, y'knaa? So all the mothers could get together, help each other out.'

'Oh sure,' muttered Susan Carrow, abruptly waspish. 'Then see all the liberties taken . . .'

'Liberties like what?' Lindy shot back.

'Like girls dumping their kids off on others so's they can gallivant.'

'Well that's not what *I'm* talking about –'

Gore felt the barbs biting and chose to intervene. 'Well, it's certainly worth a note, I'm going to look into it.' Childcare had not been of any previous interest to him, but as of now, clearly, it would have to be.

Rod Moncur was animated. 'I tell you what would be great, *really* great, would be stuff for older kids to do. Could you sort out some of that?'

'What do you have in mind?'

'Well, in my day, the best thing was a Scout troop. I'd love it for my lad to have that. Great for keeping lads out of bother.'

'It's an idea. Do you think we'd get young people to come?'

'Don't see why not.'

Sean Goddard intervened, as if he had rarely heard such folly. 'What, you want to gan to the park where they all hang about smoking tack, ask if they fancy learning reef knots? Wearing a bloody woggle?'

Moncur was defensive. 'Bet you'd get *some*.'

'Oakwell maybe. Scoular. Round Crossman you'd not.'

'Ah, you live on Crossman?' asked Gore.

'Not bloody likely. I'm near enough to smell it.'

More gruff chuckles. The unanimity Gore found worrisome. 'That's a little hard on the place, isn't it? On Crossman?'

Moncur shook his head. 'You can't be soft about it. There's people are just wrong uns, and Crossman's full of 'em.'

Sean Goddard too had fixed Gore with a jaded eye. 'It's a hovel, man. You've got cars burned out, bloody syringes on the grass what a bairn could pick up . . . You can't get people brought up decent there.'

Monica was looking sidelong at Gore as to say that such was the bed he had made for himself. He bridged his fingers and chose his words carefully. 'I should say, my remit, my pastoral care, is meant to extend to five local estates – to Oakwell, Scoular, Blake, Milburn and Crossman. All of them are equally important to me, but the poorest maybe more so. Now, I know Crossman is rough, I've been there –'

'Oh you've *been* there, have you?' Sharon Price cut in, not kindly. 'Where are you at, Reverend, is it Oakwell? You wouldn't be so cheery if you'd been burgled three times in a year.'

'I've been burgled. It's rotten but it's not the end of the world.'

'Did they take your mother's heirlooms? Smash your wedding photos, do their business on your settee?'

Gore had no answer to these charges.

'No, I didn't think so, but that's how they're raised round Crossman.'

Kully Gates had raised a hand, frowning, and was twitching her fingers. Gore gladly gave her the floor. 'Come, please, you must remember, you have some people out of work for years. Their children don't know what a proper job is.'

Sharon Price wore an outraged face. 'Get away, dirty bitches sitting happy on thirty grand a year, just for having spawned some litter of thugs.'

'Oh well now, if you think that's how the system works –'

'Aye, I do, I know it.'

Sean Goddard cut in again. 'Look, I work at the General, right? I see 'em all come in. Little girls wi' big bellies. Lads drugged to the eyeballs, and this un's gone and stabbed another for looking wrong at him. I've seen 'em hit *paramedics* have tried to help 'em. *That's* your Crossman. There's only one cure for it.'

Love? Gore feared not.

'You send the wrong uns down a lot longer. Zero tolerance, like they call it in America.'

'Right enough,' seconded Rod Moncur.

'It's a bit drastic, though, isn't it?' Gore ventured. 'Criminalising a young person at that age?'

'It's not a bother to *me*, man, not if the kid's a bloody criminal. There's lads round here have killed old ladies for money for drugs. What do you *do* with buggers like that? They've got to be *punished*, they've got to *know* they've been punished, it's got to *hurt*.'

A female voice intruded, violently bored. 'If you think lockin' up bairns for years is how to stop your tellies gettin' twocked you're *crackers*.'

Shoulders and eyes all shifted en masse to peer at Lindy Clark.

'I'm sorry, but you should hear yourselves. You go on about the good old days like we were all so bloody kind to each other, then you're talkin' about locking up bairns and throwing away the key.'

'What's *your* idea then, missus?' retorted Sean Goddard.

'Summat more like what *he's* talking, eh?' She waved a hand at Gore. 'That's your religion, right? *Supposed* to be, any road. Being kind to people, giving 'em a chance. Or are you's all so righteous already?'

There was no reply, but the glowers persisted.

'Oh, I see. So righteous you's don't want to listen to *me*, do you?'

Lindy got to her feet, sealed up a small bag and strode purposefully down the aisle, rolling her eyes at Gore as she passed.

'Please, don't go . . .' he offered.

She did not reply but pressed onward and out.

All eyes were on Gore. He understood that one of their scant number had elected to expel herself from the group. Clearly the group had not, in any event, deemed her one of them. He had sympathy with her. And yet the group was all he had to work with. The circle would have to be closed up and soldered – for the moment, at least. He raised his hands.

'You know, I wonder – if perhaps we might pray?'

He pressed his palms together and, to his relief, saw all assembled do likewise. He set to reciting the familiar panacea of the Lord's Prayer, supported by a low mumbling echo. This unanimity at least he found manageable. After the Amen he looked from face to face and smiled.

'Right then. Who's for a nice milky brew?'

In the informal huddle round the tea urn Gore found Monica was at his side, fastening a brocade scarf at her throat.

'I told you, didn't I?'

'What?'

'Get your Sunday right first. Don't run before you can walk.'

'I found it interesting, though. The anger in people. It's useful to hear it.'

'What you'll find, if you're not careful, John, is you'll just be a punch-bag. For what's bothering them. They'll just come to you to have a pop. You'll get bruised for it but you'll be none the wiser. You can't please everyone.'

'Well, if I can't please thirteen people . . .'

'Thirteen wasn't so bad, in the end.'

'Oh no, of course not. I'm only sorry we had a walkout.'

'Oh! I'm only sorry she showed up. Miss Clark. She's only funny, that one.'

Gore looked quizzical.

'All funny notions about herself. She was a bit more covered than usual tonight, mind. Her mam's dead of the drink. I don't think neither of 'em knew who her dad was. And now she's a kiddie of her own, and she's not got the foggiest how to manage far as I can see.'

'She has a child?'

'Does *she* have a child? You remember that little terror what tried to geld you the other day?'

Recall came sharply to Gore. It was all a little bit too interesting.

'You saw, though. She fancied that crèche. Oh aye, offer her a perk and she was in like Flynn. Thinking everyone else can look after her kid. She wasn't born yesterday. Nor was I.'

'What about the father? Of her child?'

Monica narrowed her grey-green eyes at him, a look Gore read clearly as saying: don't be silly, vicar.

'Dare I ask where he is?' he persisted.

Monica's mouth set primly. 'He could be any number of places.'

As he crossed the darkened threshold of number seventy-three Gore immediately saw the red light of his answerphone blinking through the gloom. Shrugging off his coat, he rewound the tape and heard a message from Bob Spikings.

'Oh, hello, John. One of these days you must get yourself a mobile. Anyhow, Jack may have mentioned my idea, about, uh, keeping your hand in? I wondered if you'd consider taking a turn in the pulpit for me at St Mark's? I'm afraid it's not the, uh, happiest *of all occasions . . .'*

Funeral, thought Gore. He rewound and listened again, carefully took down Spikings's number and dialled it. Spikings quickly confirmed his suspicion. There was a young man to bury, the circumstances violent. The deceased, one Michael Ash, had been stabbed to death in the seat of his car, in a car park near the city centre.

'Dreadful,' said Gore, after some moments.

'Horrible, yes, I know, I know. Only thirty years old. From an alright home too. But, uh . . . I think there's grounds for suspicion he was possibly the, uh, architect of his own misfortune. Wasn't robbed of anything, you see. The understanding is he was, oh, mixed up in drugs – you know? You consider the nasty way he went, and there's really no other explanation. Anyhow, I can't say I know the parents all that well. So this might be an opportunity for you to, uh, preside . . .'

Gore accepted, as he knew he must, with unease. The dull and sorry truth was that he could imagine few words – none from his usual store – that could be of any solace to the Ash clan.

Chapter V

FAIR TRADING

1986–1989

Stevie commonly found that words failed him. He was happier by far trading in nods and handshakes, for they served just as well. He knew, though, that certain matters had to be broached verbally, if they were not to sit and fester. For some weeks he had wanted words with Dicko. The need sat awkwardly inside, and he shifted it from locker to locker, just as he hopped from foot to foot on the opposite flank of the neon-splashed entrance to Club Zeus. The cold was biting, November of 1986 on its way out, and they were present and correct and properly attired. But something was wrong with the picture. And to fall out – to fight – with Dicko, toe-to-toe, was a bitter thing for Stevie to consider, even if, pound for pound, he reckoned by now that he could burst his old mate.

A fortnight hence Armstrong the manager had summoned Stevie to his small office, Stevie restive before he sat, knowing the issue would be their policy on recreational narcotics. Dicko, just like Stevie, was under instruction to act on any suspicion of possession or partaking, by search, confiscation and expulsion. It was no science, and such a drill had for months been yielding steadily mounting returns – ever more wraps of speed, fistfuls of pills, small slate-like squares of tack. Dicko assumed charge of their safekeeping, and at the end of each night he gathered Stevie's takings into a strong-box with his own, so as to pass them to management for disposal. But Armstrong, evidently, hadn't been having it.

'I'm no fool, Stevie, I know it's coming in the door, and if I'm not seeing it then the two of you's have to be doing me a disservice. Cos it's joint responsibility as I see it.'

'If you're that bothered,' Stevie shrugged, 'get the police.'

'We don't "get the police", son,' Armstrong snapped witheringly.

'What do *I* do then?'

'You keep an eye on your pal, Stevie.'

He would be nobody's pet rat. It was, though, undeniably the case that Dicko had developed certain tendencies. No fashionable door they had ever worked had welcomed unaccompanied lads ill-favoured in the facial department. Dicko, indeed, had a store of rejoinders to send the sad cases on their way. 'No, no, flower, this ain't for you, you want the wanking festival down the road.' Now, though, there were some notably queer-looking rabbits whom Dicko merely bade welcome with a nod and a muttered greeting, even as it was searing Stevie's lips to step forward with 'You're fuckin' kiddin', aren't you, pal?'

One such was a manchild with a moon face, spectacles and bum-fluff moustache, perennially togged out in a blue tonic suit, white polo shirt and loafers. One night Stevie determined to never let this nerd stray from his sight, and so watched him stand, surveying the dance floor, elbows on the bar, hailed and greeted by umpteen punters, though none lingered long. He sipped the same pint of lager for an hour, yet his trips to the toilet were continual. Finally Stevie tailed him on one such visit, and cleared the toilet of punters with a jerk of his thumb. Then he stooped and saw two pairs of shuffling loafers in the gap under a stall door. He straightened, and – with one, two, three brutal heaves – splintered the door from its hinges. His prey he seized by the throat, got his wallet in his fist, and found that this Mickey Ash had twenty little wraps packed tightly into a zip-pocket. But after shutting time he tossed these into the Tyne, for he couldn't face calling Dicko out.

As a team they had prospered, taking fewer gigs for better money, moving into a smarter two-bedroom rental, a new build on the Oakwell Estate out west. Dicko treated himself to a black Nissan, though Stevie still shunted about in a knackered Ford. But the camaraderie seemed to have been leeched out of their friendship, something arctic in its place, like the wind off the Tyne in late November. To Stevie's mind the draught emanated from one corner. It was all the fault of the drugs.

In Hoxheath he took on a few casual commissions, cash in hand, commensurate with the hassle. Over a quiet pint in the Gunnery he fell to chatting with the new landlord, fairly tearing what was left of his hair over some radgy Asian called Kumar who was selling drugs in the back bar, and was rumoured to carry an axe strapped to his thigh under loose-fitting pants. Stevie pledged to sort the little problem, and he didn't have to wait, for that same night Kumar stalked into the pub, a rangy lad with a shaved head and a manic stare. Once Stevie had his throat he was putty. 'I'll *give* you a bit of it, man,' Kumar protested, and Stevie slapped his face with a stinging report before booting him out onto the seat of his baggy trousers. 'Come back with your axe, eh, bonny lad?' he called out into the night, and was cheered to the rafters within. This, Stevie knew, was not how matters would be coming to a head with Dicko.

The needful conference didn't come at the door of Club Zeus but after closing time and a nightcap, when they were ensconced once more in the Hoxheath gaff, kettle on. Stevie had no savour for Dicko's company and was minded to retire. But Dicko bade him sit.

'Look, Stevie, I'm about right for moving on.'

He had decided to return south, to Bristol from whence he hailed. 'I'm sick of it, son. It's small time, this. Anyone shows a bit of initiative, wants to get on, there's always some numpty wanting to slap 'em down.'

Watching the shot-putter's frame slumped in a comfy chair with mug of tea, Stevie decided that this was indeed a man en route to the knacker's. He was gratified, too, that it was Dicko who seemed to be the one struggling to unload a burden from his chest.

'Stevie, the job we do's a serious old job. We earn our keep. We should be paid proper. And if we're watching others we shouldn't have others watching us. It can't operate that way.'

Stevie didn't like what he was hearing, and decided to ignore it. 'Well, I'm right sorry you're off, Dicko man.'

'I'm sorry to leave you in the lurch with this place, flower.'

'Nee bother. Reckon I'll keep it on.'

'You planning on moving that blonde bird in?'

Karen was Stevie's current girl, a somewhat unlikely conquest, a regular at Zeus amid a gaggle of similar girls. She was a cashier at a building society, long of leg, all teeth and yellow mane, her complexion too the colour of turmeric from regular sun-bed sessions. She had seemed stand-offish, until Stevie gave her some old chat and found that her poise was about as true as her tan. 'Me big *maaan*,' she would drawl as she draped herself over his chest after a third cocktail.

No, Karen would not be moving in.

The final goodbye when it came was brisk and tense. Stevie helped Dicko fill his car, unsure – though, frankly, unbothered – as to whether his old comrade saw him as Judas. But their parting handshake, Stevie was sure, had an edge to it.

Batman and Robin was a tough act to follow, and Stevie didn't bother to seek a new partner, simply permitting his regular venues to pair him with new hired hands. There came then a succession of mad young blokes, and Stevie began to feel like Clint Eastwood, breaking in the rookies. His technique had reached a level that in working a room – amid the heat, the boozy aggression and egotism – he glided serenely above it all. It pained him, though, to find there was little he could tell his younger counterparts, or, rather, little to which they listened. Some had the vexing habit of telling *him* what for, then moving on. It dawned upon Stevie that the venues were no longer the real sources of employment – rather, they preferred to contract private firms. Stevie didn't want to be Dicko the Second, the big lunk overtaken by events. So he asked around, made some calls and was taken on without fuss by Titanium Security, appointed supervisor to a 'mobile unit' of three. Since the units seemed to favour in-house tags, he chose 'Team Sharky'.

The first assignment was a pub in Battle Field that wanted to shed its belligerent element so that the place be more amenable to college students, whom the landlord fancied his best customers. Stevie duly steamed in, grabbed some collars, banged some heads, made the toerags unwelcome. But the students who began to slouch through the doors he found he didn't care for one bit. The landlord told Stevie quite sharply that he didn't want them searched, gallingly, since there were more than a few – bright-eyed, talking an incessant stream of shit – to whom Stevie would have gladly handed out a pasting. It began to gnaw at him that he was no longer his own man. He retained his patch at Club Zeus, yet on inspection of the Titanium pay-slip he saw that his nut – less tax and National Insurance – was less than previous. He could see *that* much.

As the summer of 1988 dwindled, Stevie came late and a bit drunk to a dinner-date with Karen. In his heart, he knew, the princess had metamorphosed into something of a nag. He had been dazzled by hair and suckered by fragrance, for she was less than the sum of her parts, full of pointless wishes and demands. On this night she would not take even her customary glass of Mateus Rosé, and when Stevie told her pointedly that she was as much fun as a hole in the road, she appeared to puff like an adder and spat, 'That's cos I'm fuckin' pregnant, man.'

He had never pictured himself as a father, nor Karen as a mother, not given the sum of her outgoings on cosmetics and vodka-based cocktails. For her part, she let him know that her mam and her friends thought this turn of events a tragedy, and her boss at the building society had looked fit to choke. 'Am I the last fuckin' one to knaa then, Karen?' Stevie growled, the kettle of his temper starting to rattle. He had to remove her from the restaurant by some duress, and their exchanges back at her flat were no more tender.

The months that followed were joyless. While Karen bulged steadily, Stevie paid the rent of two men, his shifts too relentless for him to find a new lodger. He was out front at Zeus one cold Friday night in January, an hour shy of opening, and he could feel a stinking cold coming on, his back stiff, feet leaden, mouth like sandpaper. Then he saw them, coming on foot from a way down the Quayside, four men in hats and hoods walking abreast, built like weightlifters. Before they reached the door Stevie had radioed his back-up for the night, Anthony, a short but tenacious lad from Cullercoats. And then the leader of the foursome declared himself.

'All change, Stevie, all change, son. You not been telt? This is our door now, me and these uns.'

'You reckon? Maybe I should get Armstrong down.'

'He's not the boss, Stevie. You'll not get owt off him. New ownership, see. So you and your midget want to step aside now, get on your way, like, there'll not be any bother. If you *want* bother, we'll fucken burst ye.'

As Stevie glanced from lunkhead to lunkhead, saw the fists clenching and the ears peeled for the word 'Go' – as he accounted for Anthony's position, and the usual computations whirred through his brain – the desire to simply turn and walk away rolled right through him, boldly as never before. He would swap his kingdom now for ten hours' sleep and a mug of tea, no stress and no fuss. It was, by any reckoning, a tenth-rate kingdom that could be usurped by four such ratbags. But it was in this sure sense of how the tale would get told in all the pubs round town that Stevie suddenly felt his pride revolt.

The team leader he annihilated with four lightning rights. Even off-colour, he had his club-hammer hands. Now they would see his stamina too. He bawled at Anthony, who made himself useful, if only by drawing some fire. They threw bodies onto Stevie, but none could get behind him or manage to restrain him. He took a succession of uppercuts and belly-blows but never fell, and with fists and feet and elbows he made himself the last man standing. A police vehicle was pulling up by the time the last of the foursome limped away, cursing.

When they were gone, Stevie sought Armstrong for a private interview. He wasn't going to pound on a fellow so much punier, but he made sure he got him against a wall, his frame occluding all light and means of escape. 'Steve, you know me,' Armstrong babbled, 'I wouldn't have had it like that for the *world.* It's not me, man, my hands are tied, the owner got himself a new partner, he put some money down, *he's* the one said how it had to be.'

They made it through that night. It was a sort of a buzz. But when the adrenalin receded, Stevie felt despondency creep back. Who was there to trust?

He was loyal to the shed that was Morton's of Wallsend, no turncoat for the fancy new gym near St James's Park where space got wasted on Aerobics for Women. He was cooling his muscles on the seat of the pec-deck when a pair of chestnut brogues planted themselves on the mat before him. He looked up into the small smile of a flash character, musky with aftershave, his tanned temples shining about his widow's peak. Even indoors he wore his camel-hair coat.

'Another heavy shift, eh, Stevie?'

Roy Caldwell had a Scots burr that conjured in Stevie some trace of his granddad Corbett. Dicko had introduced the two of them once, and he knew the guy to be a purveyor of cheap steroids, though some of the other lads had taken to calling him 'Mr E'. But a peddler, that much was for sure.

'Eh, but there's not a harder man than you in here, is there, Stevie?'

'You wanna suck us off or summat?'

'Ha. No, son, point of fact I fancy talking some business. About you and your team. "Team Sharky". Isn't that right?'

After Stevie had showered and quit the shed, Caldwell was waiting outside in pale sunlight at the wheel of a black BMW. 'Shall we take lunch at Altobello? Aye, I think we shall . . .'

They drove down the Fossway, through Byker and onto the City Road toward the Quayside. At the restaurant they were seated across a crisp white tablecloth. Caldwell ordered Frascati and fizzy water. 'Nothing too good for the working class,' he declared breezily. 'It wants a bit more of this, Newcastle. Good upmarket places. For the right people.'

Stevie had pledged himself to silence. Caldwell only smirked, and surveyed the airy cream-hued dining room. 'You see that lot over there?' He gestured toward an expansive table of eight men in suits. 'The good burghers of Newcastle. See, I spy a pair of politicians, two big union guys. A contractor. Him in the specs is an architect, I'll bet. Gadgy with the sideburns is the crookedest builder on Tyneside. Wouldn't you like to know what they're cooking up? Would you look at them, but? Little piggies with their snouts in the trough. Bald-headed bastards . . . No offence, son, I see you shave your head, not like that bunch of Bobby Charltons.'

Stevie ordered the spag bol without cheese, Caldwell the osso buco.

'How long you been doing the doors now, Stevie?'

For the first time in his life, Stevie reckoned it up mentally. 'Nine year come March.' That was quite a passage – a long old shift on his feet, and he seemed to feel the cold more these days.

'Tough old gig to stay on top of, eh? Still like your work, do you?'

'S'alright. I'm used to it. There's nowt scares us.'

'Right. And the money?'

'S'alright. I've enough for what I want.'

'"Enough", but. Is that really enough? Man of your talent? Wouldn't you rather have a bit more lying spare?'

Stevie shrugged. 'The job's the job.'

'Aye, well, it is and it isn't.' Caldwell sighed. 'It's coming along a bit at night, this town. I see it, in my line. You must see it too.'

'What's your line then?'

'I've a portfolio of interests. Entertainment venues. Leisure pursuits. Like I say – I get a different feel now, for the going out in Newcastle. It's not just drunken beggars with their bellies out down the Bigg Market. Not any more. You've better places, with a nice wee buzz about them. Lads and lassies all together. There's money in that. That's why I just bought out one of the boys in Club Zeus.' And Caldwell held Stevie's eye. 'Fact is, it was some of my lads called on you at Zeus the other night. My soldiers . . .'

Stevie placed both fists on the table. The surroundings were not conducive, and he had to suppress his rush, keep his voice even.

'Threaten me, would you? Think you can do that, ye bollox?'

'Stevie, please. It was totally wrong, I know that now, and I want to apologise to you. Sincerely. It was tactless and stupid of me, and I'm truly sorry you were put out.'

Dead-eyed, interested, Stevie watched Caldwell shift in his seat.

'The thing about that place . . . I've looked at it top to bottom, I know what it needs. New management for one thing. You running the door – that's a definite. You're a fierce bit of kit, no question. I think you can play a bigger field, but. You're wasted there. What I'd want, really, is you watching over a load more of my interests. See, in my line you've got to have soldiers. And I see you as a *general*, Stevie.'

Stevie sat back, content that this was a genuine show of respect, though Caldwell's eyes retained a critical distance.

'I mean, what's your collateral in life, Stevie? You're just living on that muscle of yours. If you'll excuse me – you should use your headpiece, son, get the profit you deserve. You should have your own firm.' And Caldwell wiped his mouth with a napkin, shaking his head as to say this much was academic. 'Here's my proposition. I help you set up. *Invest* in you. I don't just want to be paying you commission to stand on a door, see. Paying you to look the other way.'

'I don't look the other way, I look straight ahead of wuh.'

'Right. I hear you. But hear me out, son. What are you taking home a month now? I'll double that just for starters. I'm talking about you being your own boss. My end is, you sell me your services, across the board. I'm wanting a monopoly on your time, near enough. But like I say, I've got a lot of interests.'

'I'd be working for you?'

'In effect. But you'd have your own name on the door, and a proper share of the profits. You'd hire your boys, up to you, I'll trust you there.'

Stevie frowned down at his plate. It was far too much to compute at one sitting, tumbling out of a tanned shyster who had paid to have him hospitalised all but forty-eight hours ago. As business, though, he had never heard a more gratifying offer.

Caldwell settled the bill and they strolled by the Tyne. It had turned into a bonny day, sunshine and a kind breeze off the water. Caldwell flared up a cigar with a Zippo, using his good camel-hair as a windbreaker.

'How can you smoke that, man? Do you even *like* it?'

'I like how it bothers people. I like that a lot.' Indeed his eyes seemed watery with delight.

'How'd an old bloke like you get involved in all clubs and that?'

'Less of the old, eh? It was this buddy of mine. He'd sunk a bit of money into these big parties out in the country. Fields, y'know? Mad young kids coming in from all over. Crazy operations, they were. But, you know, it attracts all the wrong attention . . . As I see it, there's no reason why your regular clubs can't cater to that market, if they're big enough. It's no' the open air, I agree, but there's not the cow-shite lying about neither. Least the kids can get a taxi home. Same god-awful music and all else they're after.'

'Drugs, you mean, aye?'

'Do you've a problem with drugs, Stevie?'

Stevie shrugged, looked away, studied the dappled surface of the shirring Tyne waters.

'Well – to me, I tell you, it's a very pure transaction. I run a sound operation. I'm a businessman. I pay tax, VAT, National Insurance . . . I've a few young friends work with me, and I'd want for you to get friendly with 'em and all.' Caldwell jammed his cigar in his mouth and rummaged in his coat, coming up with a silvery tin of small printed cards. 'Now, you can either handle all that or you can't. But whenever you decide, give us a ring.'

That night he slept at Karen's, she gravid and snoring at his side, he mired in revolving thought. By morning light, under the thrum of the showerhead, he knew at least that he wanted the money. Drugs were drugs. Hadn't he hammered them into his veins for years now, albeit to a higher purpose? He didn't say he liked all that issued from the trade. But such was the world – it seemed to exact a certain price on men and their relations. The world hadn't started out from fair, so hardly a shock that it didn't finish up there neither.

*

They were presentable, at least, these young friends of Roy's – black leather coats and proper shoes the uniform. Thus did Stevie find himself grasping the hand of moon-faced Mickey Ash, who had ditched the specs and the bum-fluff moustache while seeming to swim inside his shiny baggy leather. But Mickey caused him no grief – not like those punters who sidled up to him and asked if he could 'sort them out'. They were out on their chins, no two ways about it, and he trusted Roy knew that was how it had to be, if only for sake of face. Shack and Simms and Dougie would take a different tack, but Stevie was resolved not to care. And wherever he witnessed trading unlicensed by the house, it was his pleasure to fall upon the offender like the proverbial hod-load of bricks.

One night Roy lingered at the doorway of Zeus just prior to opening, ostensibly to smoke a cigar, and so they wandered together toward the water's edge.

'You keep your eyes peeled, right, Stevie? For faces?'

'Roy, you divvint have to tell us, man, I'm a professional.'

'Just keeping you abreast, son. You know the Irish lot? The Codys? Mate of mine says they've been making noises in pubs. The usual bollocks, but, you know . . .'

'I'm not bothered. I've telt you, man, none of that scares wuh. Fear's a thing on its own. The only thing to fear is fear.'

'Aye well, you've got that going for you, and they've got guns and knives. If you're impervious to that lot, my son, then I owe you a pay-rise.' And Roy chuckled, amused by himself, plugging his lips once more with his plump Havana. Stevie hawked and spat into the Tyne, something he meant as a gesture defiant of the fates.

Chapter VI

OUTREACH

Thursday, 3 October 1996

Spikings parked his Subaru into the kerb halfway up the incline of the modest close in Arthur's Hill. He clicked off the CD player that had been burbling Debussy, and shifted in his seat to face Gore.

'How you feeling? Bit daunted?'

'Not so much. I've done this before.'

'Oh I know. The prep is hard, though, don't you find? More than the actual service, even. It's rather an exercise in telepathy, I always think.'

Gore's eyebrows vaulted.

'Well, you sort of have to – think your way into their head. If you're going to say anything useful on the day. They're just too . . . shattered, to think straight. How do you sum it up, but? The life of a loved one? I don't know. But they expect you to manage it.'

They were out of the car and tramping up the hill, the sky slate-like as befitted grave business, though Spikings chattered on. Gore trusted the lesson would be complete before they rang at the doorbell.

'Funerals now, you can't see them as one more job. Yes, we do a lot of them, it's what we're for. One of the things, anyway. But that's a trap. We can get a bit trite. Punters expect better.'

Spikings dug in his anorak, produced a scrap of paper, checked a scribbled address. They were at the right driveway, a respectable semi.

'I mean, look at the effort goes into weddings these days. *Any* wedding. Not just the toffs. Gary and Tracy. Same with funerals. You have to treat it as a – well, uh, you know – as a special day . . .'

They reached the front porchway.

'Well, you'd best go first. Don't worry, I've got your back.'

The door was opened slowly by a dormouse of a woman.

'Mrs Ash? I'm Reverend John Gore. You'll know my colleague Bob here. Please accept my very deepest condolences for the loss of your son. I'm so terribly sorry.'

It was a lower-middle-class home, the kind from which offspring fled early or else never left. In the double reception room the carpet was wall to wall, the wallpaper blue Anaglypta, the dining table G-plan, the ornaments Edwardian ladies, the curtains chintz and hung under a frilled pelmet. Hazel Ash brought coffee in a pot, and unstacked a nest of tables between the clergymen and she and her husband Clive. Gore rested his notebook on his knee, keeping notes discreetly in a careful hand.

The Ashs, though, had little to say of their son past the time of his schooldays when, it seemed, he would get good reports in science.

'Mike or Mick?' Gore asked as the thought occurred.

Hazel's mouth flickered. 'Some of his pals might have called him Mickey, *I* never cared for it.'

A photo album was produced. Gore turned the leaves gingerly, for the story told therein felt sadly skimpy. The boy Michael had worn thick NHS spectacles, soon replaced by metal frames. Adolescence was marked by a wispy effort at a moustache. Early twenties saw him affecting a tonic suit and porkpie hat, as if looking like a spiv might make him a 'character', relieve him of shyness. It was, then, with some surprise that Gore beheld the latter pages, holiday group snaps, a lively balmy bar-room – Spain, Gore supposed – and a very presentable blonde clutching Michael's arm. He was tanned and even toned in a white tee-shirt, the facial hair resurrected as a trim goatee. Everyone in shot was red-eyed and grinning maniacally.

'I always liked that one,' Hazel sighed. 'They all look so happy.'

Out of their brains on drugs, thought Gore.

A stray Polaroid not affixed to the page slid onto his lap. He flipped it and so met with Stevie Coulson, grinning his outsized grin, one slab of an arm slung around bashful Michael. Gore's finger trailed over the image. It seemed a promising lead, and he inked ASK STEVIE in the margin of his own book. There remained a few common-coin queries that, under the circumstances, seemed impossibly delicate.

'What was Michael's work?'

Husband and wife looked to one another. Hazel looked aside as she spoke. 'Well, there were a few things, this and that, over the years. He was always very into the music.'

'Aye, mad for the music, he was.'

'That was it, mostly.'

Gore didn't wish to persist, but he needed something better. Hazel Ash seemed to read as much in his poised pen. 'A couple of his pals from school had this sort of pop group, and he drove the van for them a bit. Then he was – like their manager. For a bit.'

'He *said* he was,' Clive sighed. 'Divvint knaa what *they* thought.'

'I wonder – would it be possible for me to speak to them? Those pals?'

'We're not in touch with them, Reverend.'

Gore set down his coffee cup carefully. 'Mr and Mrs Ash, what I'd like to agree with you, get your feelings on, is the . . . the balance of the content of the service. Between the treatment of . . . what we would call the soul of the departed. And the degree to which we just remember and commemorate the life Michael led.'

Clive Ash looked to his trouser leg and brushed it needlessly. 'Well, I say, he was a decent lad . . . If you could just say a bit about what he done at school. Is that it? What you're asking?'

Spikings was wincing. 'I suppose, Mr Ash, that what John is talking about is heaven.'

Gore nodded. 'It's a small matter but very important. Some believers wish for a very clear statement about their loved one and . . . the next life? Others are happy just with more of a gesture. To the idea that their loved one is – in God's hands.'

Mr and Mrs Ash looked at each other again, longer this time.

'We just don't know, do we?'

'I think you should just say what you think's best, Reverend.'

Shortly thereafter the clergymen were striding stiff-legged back down the hill. Gore was glad of the cold air. Spikings seemed a little bemused, so much so that Gore enquired after his thoughts.

'No, no, you were fine, John, I just wondered if you were going a bit far in the direction of asking them to, uh, judge their dead son.'

Gore bit his lip. Either the words were important or they weren't. If not, they were as well to get a brass band in, and some other cleric presiding.

That afternoon Gore watched as his dot-matrix printer very tortuously disgorged a sheaf of invitations to the Inaugural Sunday Service of St Luke's, Hoxheath. Then he took a seat and folded sheets into three, gazing out of the window at his straggly lawn. Should he try to cut the grass before autumn truly set in? Already a carpet of damp brown leaves had settled, dotted here and there by discarded takeaway food wrappers, evidently tossed over his wall from the alley.

The chime of the doorbell jolted him back to matters at hand. He gathered up his two hundred fliers, stacked into sets of fifty and bundled by rubber bands, descended the stairs and opened the door to Susan Carrow in a lilac coat and scarf, flanked by a trio of friends.

'Hello, Susan. There you go, thanks a lot for this.'

'Right you are. I'll do Oakwell, Brenda will do Scoular, Ann will do Milburn, and Jackie will do Blake. So then . . .'

'I'll do Crossman.'

'Right you are.' And off they trotted, his Christian soldiers.

Sufficient unto the day, he decided, once he himself had slipped fifty envelopes under doors chosen randomly but for that of Eunice Dodd. Heading home past the Netto supermarket he coaxed himself to replenish his meagre fridge and larder. An assortment of handwritten notices and want-ads were taped or pasted to the store's long window. He resolved to enquire at the checkout if he might add a flyer.

Collecting a wire basket, he made directly for a small selection of fresh produce. For some moments he toyed with a limp browning lettuce before he looked up and about him and recognised the figure of a young woman further down the aisle, stooped, her mien similarly sceptical over a tray of bruised apples. It was the hair, brunette but russet-hennaed toward the tips, cut in long bangs to near shoulder-length. That, and the tilt of her chin, the upturned nose in profile. Lindy Clark, no question.

Setting down the lettuce he drifted in her direction, stealing looks. What *was* it about her? There was something – a certain flair to how she assembled and carried herself. She wore a short jacket of red corduroy over a turquoise V-neck tee-shirt. Her long denim skirt fell to her ankles, split below the knee, and she was shod today in block-heeled sandals. A dinky leather embroidered handbag was slung over her left elbow, unzippered, slightly overflowing. As she bent again to the bad fruit, her tee-shirt and jacket rode up and thus did Gore see a tattoo impressed at the base of her spine – a coiled emerald cobra, rearing up to strike. It made him cringe, all these young women, their tender spots assailed by needle and ink.

Now Lindy Clark glanced aside and saw him – the briefest eye contact. Her eyebrows knitted, lips parted – then she turned and sashayed toward the cash tills. He put on a step to follow, strolling into the queue just behind her, his face but inches from that hennaed hair, gathered thickly on the back of her neck, at which she scratched absently with a red fingernail. It was hair dyed so often as to render the root shade a historical mystery.

She tossed her selections onto the conveyor. He knew he ought to say something, wished instead that she would, all the while studying the side of her face, the cheekbones somehow Slavic, the purplish-painted lips and eye-shadow. Her nose was pinched at the bridge yet flared at the nostrils, her two square front teeth a little discoloured. He detected now that her narrow eyes were grey-green, small wrinkles discernible even under thick-slathered liquid base. This because she was now looking straight at him.

'Wake up there, vicar.'

She motioned over his shoulder, and Gore spun to see a bloated man waiting to set a great deal of dog food down on the belt.

'Sorry, daydreaming,' Gore muttered.

'Aye, you looked a bit glakey,' said Lindy, turning back to the Asian girl manning the till and proffering a fifty-pound note, at which the girl peered sceptically for some moments before punching at her register. Lindy gathered her goods and chattels and walked off without another word. Gore bagged his handful of purchases, paid with correct change, and dashed from the store, down the ramp, looking left and right. She was thirty yards down the pavement, headed back to Oakwell.

'Lindy? Wait.'

She turned. Gore arrived before her, short of breath. 'Hi, sorry to hound you.'

'You're alright.'

'I just wanted to say – what you were saying at the meeting the other day – I wondered if we could have another chat about it?'

'A chat?'

'Yes. The child-related things, I was interested in your idea.'

She shrugged. 'Whatever. Tell you what, give us a hand with these back to mine and I'll put the kettle on.'

She hoisted up one of her plastic bags. Gore accepted the bargain.

'Get yer'sel sat, I'll just get these put away.'

Deftly she whisked an ashtray from a low coffee table and headed for the kitchen. Gore lowered himself onto a black leatherette sofa. Her place was better appointed than he had feared. In layout it was, inevitably, a double of his own, but one afforded the benefit of a feminine, contemporary sensibility. Here, too, were the cramped cubby-hole kitchen, the stairway leading from lounge to upper floor. But she had traded the cheap charcoal carpet for shiny wood-laminate, strewn over which were two overflowing crates of toys, a monster truck, a Japanese robot, mounds of plasticine, chalks and crayons and a screed of pages filled by black scrawl. The walls were smoothly papered in china blue, one of them lined by a sequence of wooden-framed photos of Jake – a swaddled babe, a toddler at play, a child in first uniform. One pine-effect unit of symmetrical squares was dressed with dried flowers, coloured bottles and stacked CDs. Vertical micro-blinds veiled the sliding glass to the garden. A hulking television and VCR were set squarely in one corner, atop the telly an alabaster Jesus turned into a camp joke by the addition of a doll's frilly pink tutu.

Lindy returned, setting down coasters, two mugs of tea and a clean ashtray. Then she slumped into an armchair, rummaged her bag, retrieved a lighter and cigarettes, and flared up. She was a poised and artful smoker, the fag cocked between index and middle fingers as she exhaled bracing plumes.

'You don't mind this, do you? Not like your partner in crime. Fanny Blott.'

'You mean Mrs Bruce?'

'She's a right fusspot, don't you think?'

Gore smiled, nodded, stroked the arm of the sofa. 'You keep a clean house.'

'Did you think I lived in a pigsty?'

'No, I mean – you should see mine.'

She nodded and relieved her cigarette of ash. 'Oh, I'm into me good housekeeping.' She had slipped into an abrupt Irish brogue. 'Cleanliness! Next to godliness, don't you know?'

She shrugged herself out of her short jacket. He found himself studying her bare arms, her slender carriage, the rise and fall of her chest. How invasive was his gaze? The thought sharpened as Lindy abruptly pulled up her legs and curled them under her body, an act somehow protective of personal space and sovereignty.

'So, you're on like a recruitment drive?'

'That's right. You saw what we got the other night, the turnout. That's the core, really.'

She exhaled. 'Mmm. Not good, is it?'

'No. Thanks for coming yourself.'

'Nee bother. Just half-fancied hearing what you'd to say.'

'From – seeing the posters?'

'Actually, y'knaa what? I saw you kicking a ball about with some lads a few weeks back. I thought, "He's a tryer, that one."'

Gore smiled. 'How did you find it then? The meeting?'

'How did *you* find it?' She snorted blue smoke. 'Good luck there, that's what I say. They're all a lot of snobs. You've noticed *that*, right? I mean, it's amazing. People with *fuck*-all to brag about really, and they still get to be snobs.' She clapped a hand to her mouth. 'Sorry. The gob I've got on me.'

Gore waved a hand. 'You should hear me cursing the air blue when I hit my thumb with a hammer.'

'Hammer? Bit handy then, are you?'

'Well, no, that's why I keep hitting my thumb.'

She smiled, showed some teeth. *Better*, he thought. 'But, what you were saying – you think people are a bit too stand-offish?'

Lindy sniffed and ground her cigarette concertedly into the ash-tray. 'I just think, like, some folk have always gotta have *somebody* to feel all superior to. You know? "Least I'm not as bad as all them lot."'

'Right. They look down at people poorer than them?'

'Whey, they divvint like blacks nor Pakis neither, even them that are doing okay for themselves.' She sighed and leaned back, nursing her mug. 'People like that, they're never happy. You're wasting your time, asking all what you can do for them and that.'

'You missed my call for volunteers at the end.'

'Well, sorry, I don't hang about where I'm not welcome.'

'Don't you think you could be a help like that?'

'Get away.'

Gore bridged his hands under his chin. 'Still. You came.'

'Like I say. I can see you're trying to help and that. Fine. I'll say this, but. What they said about being sick of do-gooders? They're not wrong. You do sound a bit like them. The trouble with you's lot is you're all a bit *nice*. You talk *down* to us. We're not *mongs*.'

'I'm not sure how else to talk.'

'Well, I know you're a vicar, that's your way, but we've heard it before, man. Young fuckers coming round grinning at you, barely out of school, but they really, *really* understand your problems. And it's, "Sign here." It's like . . . politics, you know? *Urgh.*' She shuddered. 'I've no interest. Bunch of liars and bullshitters.'

'Well, all I'd say, Lindy, is I'm quite happy to be judged on the strength of what I do or don't do. Rather than just talk.'

'Good luck to you, then.' She raised her mug. In the silence Gore stooped and scooped up one of the boy's drawings.

'Like that, do you?'

'It's very good. For six, right? Shows imagination.'

'Aw aye. Takes after his mam. I used to like it meself, drawing and that. Bit dark for me, what he does, mind. I'd worry, if I didn't know me lad better.'

'I've met Jake, you know? I met him at the school?'

'Aw aye? Was he behaving?'

'There *was* a little bit of a fracas.'

'A what?'

'He got a bit out of sorts, Mrs Bruce wasn't best pleased.'

'Naw? I never heard.' Lindy slumped. 'See, if she had her way she'd have him out of there. Six year old. And he's not a bad lad, he's just moody sometimes. They all get that. That's what school's for, but. Teach 'em to sit still and listen.'

'I think Mrs Bruce thinks that begins in the home.'

'What do *you* think?' Lindy was suddenly sharper, desirous of a prompt answer.

'I don't have children, so . . . what do I know?'

'You'll have an opinion, I'll bet.'

'Well, I'm going to be a governor of the school now . . . so I'll be researching in the field. I'll let you know once I've thought a bit more. Have *you* never considered that? Being a school governor?'

Lindy threw back her head and issued a throaty laugh. 'Get *away*.'

'Why not?'

'I don't win popularity contests, me. You've seen.'

'It's a way to get your voice heard.'

She was simply shaking her head at such preposterousness.

'But you're worried about your son?'

'Why should I be?'

'It just seemed strange to me. How he acted. Clearly you've a nice home for him, he has this . . . talent. I just wondered . . .'

'He's canny, he's always been canny. I dunno, he maybe gets it off his dad. I mean, his dad's a regular do-gooder. Just like you.' Gore smiled, only to see Lindy's face cloud. 'Well, not *much* like you. But he does his duties, don't you worry.' She lit another cigarette, tossing her head as if to clear it. 'No, Jake's always been canny. I tell you, honestly, he was such a love, such a comfort to us – even when he was tiny. I thought I'd wanted a girl, see. But I'd be looking at him sometime, bothered about something, money or a fella or whatever, and I'd be in the dumps just staring at him.' She looked at Gore earnestly. 'And sometimes it was like he *knew*. He'd reach up to us. Try to rub wor cheek, or give us such a bonny smile. It was just like he was talking to us, honest. And he's a happy lad, I swear.' She brightened suddenly. 'I've a *theory* about this, actually.'

'Oh yes?'

'Aye, see, I think you're either born happy or you're not. I've *always* thought that. Then I saw it on telly, the other night.' Animated, she moved from the armchair and joined him on the sofa. 'It was all about experiments on babies' brains, right? Little eight-week-old babies? To see what they've got going on in there. And it's proven, see, when they do the electric scan of the waves or whatever – brainwaves – there's some babies, their brains just *glow*. It's like they've got a big orange bulb in there, that's how it looks on the machine. Then there's others and you get nowt, not a spark. So I saw that and I thought, "There! *That* proves me theory."' Indeed she seemed triumphant. 'That's how I look at people now, when I'm going about. *He's* got a bulb. *She* hasn't. He's *definitely* got one. Him, his lights are out for good.'

'What's the telltale sign?'

'Easy. There's people not capable of a laugh. That's how you know. Like them lot at your meeting. Then there's people need their switch turned on first to get the bulb going. That's you, probably.'

Gore was unsure how to take this.

'I mean, I can get a laugh out of you, and I know it's not put on.'

'And Jake? He's got a big bulb?'

'He has. He did have, anyway. He's a bit low now, right enough.'

She looked away, her hands resting limp on her thighs, magenta varnish on irregular nails. She had such spirit, and yet a torpor could cross her like a cloud occluding the sun. Shadows were lengthening in the room. But Gore found that he wasn't giving up the sofa, or hastening to the crux of the visit. Looking about him, he was struck once more by her assortment of top-of-the-range electric goods.

'Can I ask how you manage? With a child, alone?'

'I work, man. More than one job. Simple as that.'

'What sort of work?'

'Aw, there's a place I waitress, there's bar work I do for a fella I know. I'll do a morning in the newsagent for me mate Clare.'

'Sounds quite a stretch.'

'The hours are an arse. But you add 'em together and it's a wage.'

'Enough to keep you? You and Jake?'

'Who's asking, eh? You an inspector for the nash and all?' Gore chastened himself. She lit another cigarette. 'I'm no benefit queen, me. Got that off me mam.'

'Have you ever wanted to do more? Look for something better?' He shifted in his seat. 'Since you're so bright.'

'Aww,' she said, and touched his arm lightly. Gore was pleased to have pleased her, until her sweet smile withered. 'You see? You talk to us like *mongs*. You should hear yourself sometimes.'

He blushed but she was gazing past him. 'Looks like rain,' she murmured. 'So what else you wanna know? Do you need to get on? If it's rain, mind, you can stop a little. Since you're on shanks's pony.'

'Maybe just a little longer, if that's okay.'

She rose. 'Well, I'm having a glass of wine. You want one?'

'Oh, I think not, thanks. More tea, maybe?'

She headed to the kitchen. 'I hear you'll have a pint, mind.' He peered after her in surprise. Then he heard her half-singing under her breath as she busied. 'Milk's done. Blast.'

'I'll drink it black.'

'Urgh.'

She returned with a jelly glass of white wine and a mug of black tea, resuming her discreet place in the armchair. Gore leaned forward from the sofa. 'Okay, this is the big question then.'

'Aw aye?'

'Can I expect to see you at my service next Sunday?'

Her eyes popped, theatrically. 'Oh Jesus, Mary and Joseph! Please, not God!' And she crossed her index fingers and waved them at Gore in the manner by which holy men in horror films sought to expel vampires. When finally she chuckled, Gore tried to join her. 'Now go on, Reverend.' She wagged a finger. 'If me mammy were here, God rest her, *she'd* want to talk all about this with you.' That brogue had resurfaced. 'She was a Catholic but she'd no quarrel with the Protestants. Sure it's all the same God. But meself and the Lord, we've never been so friendly.'

'Your mother was – Irish?'

'Aye,' Lindy nodded. 'Only they threw her out of Ireland. Like St Patrick threw out the snakes, right?'

'You were born here, though? Newcastle?'

'It was Liverpool, actually. We moved on to here when I was still a babe.'

'Why did she choose Liverpool? After Ireland?' But he knew by her face that he had erred once more.

'Hardly a choice, man. She liked it, but. Back in Offaly she was a disgrace. Liverpool, she was a bit of a chick. The seventies and that, all the music. Was only me that cramped her style.'

'She's passed on?'

A deep sigh. 'Aye, she's gone. Poor soul. Seven year ago. What a life.'

'Did she – live to see Jake?'

Lindy shook her head mutely.

Gore nodded. 'I'm sorry. I was twenty when I lost my mother.'

'Aw, sorry. Was she a nice mam?'

'Yes. I was lucky.'

'That's nice. Mairead was just fuckin' hopeless, really. Sorry, but she was. Drink. Made herself poorly.' She studied Gore now, as his gaze fell on her glass. 'I know what you're thinking. It's not the same. It's what you can manage. Me mam wasn't healthy – never, not right, mentally. I blame the Church me'sel. They're snobs and all. Make people feel rotten.'

'I'm not a fan of the Catholic Church.'

'Oh no?'

'No. It has a – bizarre view of women, for one.'

'And your lot are much better?'

'I'd make a case for us, yes. We're not a Church that judges.'

'You're squirming a bit there, but.'

'To be honest, it's the tea.'

'Gone right through you, has it? The bathroom's upstairs. Loo in the hall's knacked, sorry.'

The bathroom was scented with white rose, one small window shedding light upon a white vinyl floor and units. A mirrored cabinet was fixed over the sink. Gore urinated with care. After shaking and tapping, he yielded to an impulse and opened the cabinet. Within, a secret lair of feminalia – a mix of essentials and luxuries, a world away from his own spartan toilette. Here were Tampax, Clairol, Clarins and Lancôme, jumbles of make-up and moisturiser, bracelets and a tangled hairbrush, KY jelly, Givenchy perfume and two packets of contraceptive pills.

Exiting, he halted and peered down the hallway at two large rectangular cardboard boxes, set heavily up against the wall outside one of three boxy bedrooms. Upon his return to the living room he enquired after them. Lindy, now on her feet, waved a hand. 'It's all stuff out of a catalogue. For Jake's room. I forgot it didn't come made. Can't get arsed to start with it. Need a screwdriver and all. His daddy would do it, but his daddy's a busy man . . .'

'I'd be happy to knock them together for you. Really, any day that suits.'

Again she studied him with a wry, challenging purse of her lips.

'Well, aren't you good?'

'That's if . . .'

'Go on.'

'My service. Could I count on you coming?'

'Aw, get away. You're not putting the cosh on us, are you?' She shoved him with a palm, but affably. He found himself obscurely pleased by the rough touch – found himself, moreover, colouring into his chest.

'Well, you know, that's why I'm here . . .'

'There was me thinking we were getting along.' Her eyes narrowed but the look dissolved as she sighed heavily. 'Whey, whatever. I'll look in and see how you're doing.'

'It's Sunday after next. Probably ten-thirty start.'

'*Okay*, but you want to see you get that crèche going and all. I thought *that* was why you were here.' Her brow furrowed. 'What time is it?'

'It's quarter after two.'

'Aw! Me favourite!'

She plucked a remote control from the coffee table, flicked on the television set and fell into the sofa. Gore stretched his frame, wondering how to execute the cheerio, for Lindy was suddenly very engrossed. He walked to the window and looked out. It was raining still. So he sat down beside her and peered at the screen. A studio audience was getting itself terribly riled, stoked by a roving presenter with a microphone. On a dais, a harried-looking man in thick glasses, the unlikely object of such attention, was bemoaning – with remarkable if faltering frankness – that his wife had enjoyed a breast augmentation at his expense and had since denied him conjugal rights. The frame widened to reveal that the woman was beside him, head and décolletage bobbing in agreement, as to say, what would *you* do? Lindy issued a short scoffing laugh. 'Look at them cow tits. Who'd shag that?' She curled her feet up and under her. Gore could not conjure a meaningful comment.

The couple were succeeded on the dais by a young black woman who had birthed a child by a man unwilling to commit.

The errant father sat opposite, polished and arrogant, as if she should think herself lucky. Gore could imagine Lindy saying as much. *Say it*, he thought, and glanced at her profile. Her eyelids had closed. 'Lindy?' he murmured, and her breath came forth a little raspingly. Lightly he took up the remote control and switched off the television. For some moments he looked at her. Finally he decided there was no harm in leaving things be. Wreathed in thought, he rose and showed himself to the door.

As he reached for the latch, a key was turning, then the door swung open. There on the threshold was young Jake in a hooded black anorak, his hand in the grasp of a painfully pale and red-headed woman in her fifties, clad in a waterproof of her own. Before two pairs of wary eyes Gore was flustered.

'Hi, I'm John Gore, I'm the new vicar? I was just paying a visit on Lindy. *This* young man I've met. Hello there, bonny lad.'

'I'm his Auntie Yvonne,' she squinted, her accent Irish, in no way charmed or allayed.

'Yvonne?' came a croaking call from the living room.

'I was just on my way,' Gore smiled, and slipped past and out, feeling but a shade disreputable.

Chapter VII

THE REGULATOR

1992–1996

Stevie stood nursing his ale, stolidly surveying the three young women stripped to the waist as they chattered affably to each other in Dutch, presumably about the merits of this or that trick for hiding banknotes on one's person. He was more drawn by the range of brassieres on display under the moody light. Here, an innocent white cotton sports number. There, a lewd purple plunger, though its cups were not so bountiful as the black push-up model worn by the tallest of the three. The lass he would have most relished seeing in her skimpies was the fourth of the party, Roy Caldwell's girlfriend Nina, another Dutchie – twentyish, blonde but dusky of complexion, short but ripe at top and bottom. She, though, was only supervising procedures, and none too happily neither.

'You know your route, then?' Roy murmured, standing at Stevie's shoulder by the island that divided this conservatory-cum-kitchen/breakfast room of the Caldwell residence. Stevie nodded, thrusting his fists into his black leather coat.

'Leave them off on Collingwood Street, but *park* and get out, yeah? See they all get on. Three separate London trains, on the half-hour, first one at eight.'

'Ah hear ya,' said Stevie.

The boss charged his glass from a bottle of Rioja, Stevie topped his pint mug with brown ale. Across the terracotta tiles, grouped around a glass-top table, the girls – tippling from their own bottle of fizz – were packing wads of used notes in stomach belts about their bellies, the overspill laid down by Nina into nondescript new-bought tote bags. Such were the spoils of another week's trading. Swaddled in coats and cardigans the ladies' figures were unlikely to draw comment in this freezing November of 1992.

Stevie only saw as much of Roy as was prudent, but he had been keen to come over tonight and view the new gaff in the village of Darras Hill, Ponteland, eight miles' drive north-west of Newcastle. A desirable residence it was, a big new build with five bedrooms and an epic driveway that would have fully justified the installation of watch-tower or gun turret, if such were the buyer's requirement. Roy's company, though, Stevie never found wholly relaxing. He usually came away from it with more chores to fulfil. Tonight he was tasked with conveying the Dutch lady mules to Central Station, for Roy trusted him and him alone to ensure the job got done. Nina, clearly done with her own share of the chore, flounced past the men and out of the kitchen. Roy made an indulgent face.

'Pay her no mind. You don't happen to know anything about *ovens*, do you?'

It consoled Stevie that Roy, too, had his woes with women and households and domestic appliances on the blink. Stevie never heard the end of Karen's grievances – she and little Donna set up perfectly nicely in Chopwell, weekly visits and cash gifts, and it was hardly as though he were living high on the hog himself. Yet their relations were fixed at bayonet-point.

'Ach, she has to know how busy you are.'

'Nah. It's just her way. Never get this bother off anyone else.'

'Does she know, though? You've other wee girls on the go?'

'Not off me. She knows the score, but. I've always telt her, "First duty in my life is that firstborn child."'

'Sweet, is she? Your wee girl?'

Stevie grimaced. 'Takes after her mother.' His daughter presented her cheek to be kissed with the same Nordic air of reluctance.

'Aye well.' Caldwell foraged in his shirt pocket for his Zippo. 'You're conscientious, Stevie. Seems to me, but, you might want to . . . vary your habits a bit? I wouldn't have so many *haunts* if I were you. Same pubs, same bookies. If you've different beds you can sleep in, sleep in them. It'd suit you to be a little more elusive.

Except when I need you, of course.' He grinned. 'I'm not just talking your domestic, it's good business too. Keeps your luck fresh. Luck's a huge part of all this.'

Stevie nodded gloomily. Increasingly he turned it over in his head, this notion of luck – from whence it came, on whom it was bestowed, whether it ever served hard notice of its departure.

'You can put yourself in places where you're *liable* to be lucky, Stevie. If you're a creature of *habit* – then the joker's always got a chance of lying in wait for you. You get busted for nonsense. Cos the stars had time to line up against you.'

'Divvint start wi' that talk, man.' Stevie winced. It was bad enough that Karen was a head-case for charts and astrology, forever muttering darkly as if the topic were an improvised weapon she could wheedle into his guts.

'Okay, fill me in then. How are your boys? All the parts working?'

'Nee bother.' Stevie shrugged. The new starts in the minicab firms and the second-hand car lots were doing fine. The number of doorways of the bars and the clubs – graduate school – were ever increasing, and Stevie was taking on a few allegedly more experienced lads whom he might have queried harder in the past. But there seemed hardly the time for fine discrimination any more.

'It's just, it's like – everybody wants a piece of us, man,' he said finally.

Caldwell set down his wine glass. 'You're breaking my heart tonight, Stevie. Look. Expansion's not a luxury in business, it's a necessity. It's a matter of survival. Myself? I'd rather not bother. Much rather the simple life. But it's a fact, you can't get off the train when it's rolling. The *good* news is the life you get. Right? You can have a piece of anything, once you're big enough. And they all tell me they want my boys in. Well, not all of them, but, you know . . .' Caldwell placed a manicured paw on Stevie's coat sleeve. 'So, aye, I know it's more work for you, but it's worth it, right? *Isn't* it? Come on. Who's your pal, eh? Who's your buddy?'

Stevie threw Roy a forbearing look that seemed to delight the older man, for he grinned broadly. '*That's* right. Is there anything you'd not do for me, Stevie? If I asked you nice enough?'

'I wouldn't touch your old cock.'

Caldwell chuckled into the rim of his sea-dark Rioja. 'Aye, well there's other candidates there, son. Less of the old and all, eh?'

Weighing all things, Stevie knew he had no cause for grievance against his paymaster. Their association had carried him a mile north of Hoxheath to his own detached house in clean-swept Fenham. He had sorely needed a bigger drum for his goods, not to mention better security. With due regard for his new neighbours, he sought and secured a double garage, one bin for his handy new Lexus, the other for a pro set of benches and free weights.

Roy urged him always to make his money grow, even offering the services of some shady accountant. Stevie deigned to purchase a local off-licence on an untroubled stretch. He granted Roy's insistence that in business no stone should be left unturned, no opportunity spurned. Construction was booming about Newcastle – Stevie could see it with his own eyes, even in benighted Hoxheath, where ground was getting broken for some sprawling new City College campus. If builders raised scaffolding in such a blighted zone, the site was surely in need of protection from marauding charver kids – that much was common sense. He consulted Roy, who vehemently agreed this was a job for Sharky's Machine, that the boys should go round forthwith. But Stevie wanted the job personally. For when the company signage was lofted up on the perimeter fence, he recognised the name of Jim Doggett's old firm, albeit linked by ampersand to some new partner.

Stevie presented himself at the site first thing, his stomach growling in the wait to acquaint Doggett with his nemesis. Alas, he found only one harassed foreman, whom he browbeat at leisure for a quarter-hour, firmly boring through his hapless stammer that there were already contracts in place, shift teams, alarms, surveillance. 'Your site's bigger than that, man. And I'm telling you, there's neebody else can *guarantee* your security. Nee-fucking-body, y'understand?' He never raised his voice, much less a hand, and left knowing that he had made the correct impression. The tax was paid weekly when he dropped by, though he never saw sight or heard protesting word of Jim Doggett – the sole dissatisfaction in an otherwise happy transaction.

That was how it went in Hoxheath. Round Fenham way, Stevie wished to be better thought of by his neighbours. He had his own definition of fair play in life – it had been wisdom dearly bought – and he was resolved to act like it amounted to something. Offering a little cash to the good of St Mark's Church was a simple act of *auld lang syne*, for Stevie well remembered how its wooden pews had once been a bed to him. On certain afternoons, if at a loose end, he strode over to the church and through the doors and took a seat, where there was peace and solitude and pale soothing light. The iron, he was sure, had done more than pack his muscles – it had taken his head to elevated places, instilled some stirring thoughts. The silence and decorum of St Mark's he also found conducive to same. When other churchy folk were present, he was less sure of his welcome, for he could tell they assumed a great deal of his character from the shadow he cast. But he could face himself squarely in the bathroom mirror. *What I am,* he would tell his reflection, *what I do, I am a regulator*. It was a term he had gleaned from cowboy films, and it never failed to restore his spirits.

After a spring morning spent watching his three-year-old daughter behold him as though he were a burglar, Stevie dialled Roy's number from the Lexus and was given perplexing details of a new gig. In wheezing amusement Roy described the Damask Rose, a sauna-and-massage place on Westgate Road that had gone begging after the busting of an elderly madam who had failed to renew her subscription with the local constabulary. There seemed to be no qualms about new management stepping into her stead – a move that appeared to amuse Roy still. 'Don't know what possessed me on this one, Stevie son. Would you believe I was raised at the foot of the kirk?'

'All I knaa, Roy, everybody likes a bit naughty.'

'Is that right?' Caldwell cackled back down the line.

The first time that Stevie mounted the rickety stairs he had an odd flutter in his gut, for he couldn't picture what a bordello looked like in this day and age. In fact, it was a bog-standard second-floor flat, three poky bedrooms fitted with heavy blinds and painted in clashing colours as to offer a choice of mood to the punter. It was, he saw, an elementary task to appoint one beefy lad to patrol the narrow hallway. A mumsy woman was perched on a high stool in a galley kitchen, keeping a register, directing traffic, while a few polite and listlessly semi-clad ladies watched telly in a parlour. Stevie was vaguely fascinated by them – just girls, really, from Poland and Bulgaria – but he found he got on better with the mumsy manager, always ready with a joke and a plate of oven chips when he called to take the tax.

In the wake of one such drop-by, contemplating a solitary cod supper at the wheel, Stevie received a Roy summons to drive out of town by the Coast Road and join him and a pal at some bar in Whitley Bay. The tide was frothing on the blowsy seafront when he parked the Lexus. The venue, he discovered, was a private members' club, a queer sort of joint – mauve walls, tigerskin-print seats, and mounted paintings of bosomy females in loincloths basking with panthers or curled up in the coils of pythons. But it was private, for sure, and there, at Roy's bidding, Stevie shook hands with a flabby walrus of a man, one Jonjo Fitzgerald, who proceeded to witter on incessantly about Newcastle United – the genius of Kevin Keegan, the dead-eyed prowess of Andy Cole. Roy seemed to tolerate it, though Stevie had never taken him for a sportsman, and when Fitzgerald had drunk up and waddled out, Roy looked at Stevie like a cat with moist whiskers and informed him that Fitzy's day job was as a detective inspector with Northumbria Drugs Squad. That, Stevie decided, was the most surprising thing he had heard in all of 1993.

'What's a policeman, Steve, but a human man doing a job? He's more in common wi' you or me than Joe Bloggs out there empties bins for a living.'

'Detective *inspector*, but . . .'

'There's no' a lot of point getting pally with PC Plod. You're not much improving your influence there. Them boys, they'll talk to you happy enough, but you don't get much for your money.' Some indigestible thought had occurred. 'And some of them bastards, the young uns – awful devoted to the good old cause. Wee caped crusaders, dudley-do-rights. Fitzy there was just telling me about some boy got stuck on his team, some cunt-stubble. Didn't like what he saw, went behind Fitzy's back to his super. Next day he found these blades of grass in his desk drawer. Then, get *this* for cold – someone stuck a wee photo of his kiddie to the office whiteboard.'

Stevie frowned. 'What's that about, then?'

'Ah, well, it wisnae a picture *he'd* ever seen.'

Caldwell reclined into the tigerskin, raised an eyebrow, drummed fingers on his thigh of his good Italian pants. Stevie nodded. Truly, in a war of such nerves, there was but one side to be on.

'By the by, do you fancy the match on Saturday?'

Stevie smelled a rat. 'What, *United* match?'

'Aye, United–Liverpool. Fitzy wanks on, I know, but I've started going a bit myself. It's good entertainment. Good atmosphere. Cut above Tannerdice, I have to say. Do you fancy it?'

'Roy, man, I was brought up red and white.'

'Sunderland? They're muppets, aren't they?'

Stevie struggled for a rebuttal. His dad had been one to declare he was Sunderland until he died, but where was his dad now? The place looked a little smarter these days, at least north of the Wear in Fulwell, where his nana was eking out her days. But Wearside was the distant past, of which he remembered naught but rancour, unfairness and disloyalty. And, if he was honest, he liked how Keegan's United played.

'Aye well, it's top division football, I suppose.'

So he accompanied Roy to St James's Park and saw Newcastle trounce the Scousers with three identical goals from the imperious Cole. It occurred to him anew that a man could get used to anything.

*

1994 kicked off poorly – a rank odour round the pubs and clubs for months after the fatal shooting on New Year's Eve of a highly rated bouncer, one Viv Graham of Rowland's Gill, who was said to have got above his station. The council and police were soon insisting on a register of all doormen working in Newcastle. Stevie had twenty-odd men on the books of Sharky's Machine, serving thirty or more premises. Now there was the drear prospect of hard questions being asked of each and every employee – and, all 'diversification' aside, Stevie needed those doors. He now had real cause to rue a twelve-month suspended sentence for assault he had received in late 1990. The plaintiff had got all that was coming to him, certainly in respect of his loutish conduct inside Club Zeus, but the law had been blind to Stevie's motive and overly attentive to some admittedly wince-inducing CCTV footage. That prior conviction now, very abruptly, spelt the end of Stevie's term on the doors. The lads threw him a party in the back of the Gunnery, and they raised their glasses solemnly.

Stevie was pensive that night. For some time, he knew, he had been above the blunt graft of the doors, more engaged in Roy's tax collecting – in business. The old walk of life, its habits and denizens, had never been cosy. Always there had been the procession of gadgies making distant threats, big-mouthing in pubs about how Steve Coulson wasn't long for the world. Customary had become the calls or furtive approaches from associates to tell him that his name was being cursed to the heavens in the Loose Box, taken in vain at the Block and Tackle. Stevie knew he had attained such eminence that a lot of that shite was to be disdained for the small-dick Dutch courage that it was. Just sometimes, though, face-to-face it had to be. He would note the address, track the offender, see how much they liked it up them in front of their mates, if mates they had. Sometimes it was enough to appear, like a bear with a sore head and a low growl, right in the midst of whoever's slovenly excuse for a local, and to point a sharp finger.

'Fucking show us respect, you.'

'Aw but he respects you, Stevie, totally man. There was nowt meant by it, not a bit . . .'

Respect. It was all a lot of fucking *bollocks*. The whole stinking sham made Stevie's temples pulse. He had begun to feel the gravity of his mid-thirties, to count the furrows of his brow, to look into remedies for sciatic pain.

His friend Roy's unprompted response to these unvoiced woes was to put down money on a club called Teflon, a Quayside joint by the city end of the Swing Bridge. Stevie was to be manager, his name over the door. The move into management was logical, timely, not to say a blessing. How swift and glad was his embrace of the routine, assuming a black single-breasted suit and an open white shirt, strutting the buffed floors vodka-tonic in hand through the calm early hours of trade! And at a stroke he was a businessman, albeit one just as happy swapping the fine duds for his pub suit, his Gold's Gym sweatshirt and arse-frayed denims, at whatever time suited.

On the first day of 1996 that felt like springtime – a morning nipping at the extremities, yet blessed with a hazy sunshine, effulgent over Nuns Moor Park – Stevie took in the view at leisure from his bedroom window, prior to blending a protein shake and heading to his garage number two for a brisk half-hour's workout. He was due to rendezvous with Roy on the far side of Town Moor at eleven. It could be something or it could be nothing, but he would be locked and loaded as ever.

In the gloom of the garage he hunkered and stretched out on the cool vinyl of the bench, drew in breath, then launched his assault on the four-hundred-pound bar-bell – one furious set, then the strain of another, the torture of a third. He trained almost entirely at home now. Over the winter a fellow called Porter had been shot and killed by some radgy as he left the shed at Morton's. Stevie had a boxer's heavy bag suspended from the ceiling of the garage, and he pounded it for five solid minutes. He was steeled for combat, should the enemy appear.

Back upstairs he showered and dressed – black jeans and boots, clean gym vest and hooded sweat-top. When he donned his good leather coat, smelled the fine hide, felt its form wrap close about him, it was though he were assuming not so much an apparel or an armour as a secondary skin. The leather had a rigidity that Stevie considered akin to his mindset: pliant, but unpierceable. It was his right and proper raiment.

In the driveway he unlocked the Lexus and peered over the road, expectant of locating his lookout, the day's volunteer from his Charver Squad, as he called those lads. There indeed was the kid in the backward baseball cap, poised like a bush-cat up on the pedals of his bike. Stevie nodded, the kid coolly returned the favour. They were good kids, surprisingly susceptible to his attention and consideration. He gave each a mobile and solemn instructions, and he had yet to be let down. If anyone was loitering around his main places of business, he got the call. One more line of defence.

He took the North West Radial, a ten-minute drive, and pulled into a space near Exhibition Park. Striding into the grounds he felt a fine familiar stirring, a sad sort of fondness for the lovely biting cold of old Newcastle. There was no place like it. Other so-called hot spots had no atmosphere fit to compare, not that he had seen. He didn't romanticise the trouble-zones, the half-done demolition and the dog dirt and the Sunday morning snowdrift of burger-boxes down the street. But that was just people for you. He played his part in clearing things up, keeping the city upright and orderly, ready for business.

And now he could see Roy, loitering near the bandstand by the foot of a beech tree, clad in a dark cashmere coat, mobile phone pressed to his ear, his lately acquired black labrador Buster padding about at his heels. As he neared, Roy clocked him and nodded but continued his business. 'Aye, so a shade under five? The right side, *consigliere*. No, no problem, Barry, son. I am guided by you in all things. It's like all these things – could be something, could be nothing, I don't mind either way.'

'You buying a used car?' said Stevie once the phone was consigned to the coat pocket.

'No, no, son, I'm donating to the Labour Party.'

That sounded like prime Roy bollocks.

'You alright?'

'Nee bother.'

'You'd a visit the other day? At Teflon?'

That was correct. Stevie had thought it a matter on which he might keep his own counsel rather than trouble the boss. Now, regrettably, it looked to be the matter at hand. For a year or more there had been no problem with the law, at least nothing of the sort experienced by venues with less auspicious connections. Last week, though, there had been a snide visit from some DI, wanting to interview all door staff in relation to complaints from unidentified patrons. Who this buckshee copper imagined himself to be was a matter for more thought, but for the time being it was clear that a certain understanding was no longer being honoured quite so rigorously. Thus did Stevie conclude his report. Roy looked grim. 'I wonder, but. Fitzy's not talking to me. Someone's maybe pulling someone else. Somewhere in the bloody chain.'

'Some cunt-stubble?'

'Aye.' Roy sniffed. 'That, or Fitzy's had a bright idea. You'd be amazed how some of these pigs get used to your money. Like it was their own. *Greed*, I tell you – everybody's after a score.'

Stevie was sombre, knowing Roy's hatred of loose talk and disloyalty to be much as virulent as his own.

'I don't know, Stevie.' He was shaking his head, clearly genuinely perplexed. 'Who's meaning us mischief? There's maybe a fair old list. Them Codys I thought I was square with. This Skinner boy out of Manchester, he's maybe throwing money around. It could just as easy be one of ours, but. How are your lads?'

'They're sound, man. Sound. We have a drink every other week in the Gunnery, I always knaa what's gannin' on.'

'Aw, you're not still drinking in that fucking Gunnery?'

Stevie shrugged. The venue was hardly the point – rather, that there had in fact been some matters arising between him and the team. Dougie, he suspected, might just have heard by now that Stevie had consoled his estranged wife. Then the few overt trappings of his promotion had nonetheless ruffled some feathers. Shack had been first to bang on to him about wanting the same cut 'through the till'. But they weren't getting through the work he was stuck with, not the headwork anyway. Such was the division of labour, as Stevie saw it. He was the chief asset of the business still. Broadly understood, he had done right by them all. And Roy didn't need to know about a small falling-out between friends.

'Do a sweep, eh? Give everybody just a wee shake. I dunno, could be one of them middling dealer boys. I hear Mickey Ash wants to get married again, the wee git. Some blonde object he met on holiday. Musta give her a ton of free charlie.'

'Doesn't give up, that one.'

'He doesn't. So he's maybe thinking of retiring.' Caldwell sighed. 'Not the worst idea.' He stooped and rough-housed his big drooling dog about its ears. 'Who's your pal, eh? Who's your buddy?'

Stevie gazed at them without seeing. His agreeable mood was off, away into the long grass. Roy spoke without looking up. 'I've gotta be extra-wary, Stevie. You know that. But I've got you. Haven't I? I've got you, Stevie.'

There was a disconcerting edge to Roy's tone, or so Stevie thought he detected – a hint of an implied reproach, as bad as an outright slur. Yes, Roy had to take these matters seriously. All the same, he had to know who he was talking to.

'Roy, you'll never have to worry about us, man.'

'Oh I know, Stevie. I know *that*, son.'

Chapter VIII

INCORRUPTIBLE

Friday, 4 October 1996

Back in the saddle, thought Gore as he smoothed out his notes, upstanding in a strange pulpit, another man's perch. Below him in the pews of St Mark's was a respectable turnout of forty to fifty bodies. The onus was all upon his shoulders, for Michael Ash would have no eulogist today, no schoolyard mate or kind colleague to tell a benign story or summon up some other felt tribute.

That no one could be persuaded to speak for the deceased struck Gore as unutterably sad. Had the dead man left so meagre a mark? Or were people just embarrassed – of their own feelings, or the absence of same? He was familiar with a certain poor sensation of sham, imposture, that arose when orating over a stranger's coffin. But that unease had no claim on him today. He saw this awkward situation as one in which he could do no worse than what would otherwise pertain.

In the front pew were Clive and Hazel Ash, and a younger sister of Michael's, Gill, up from Manchester for the day. Earlier he had greeted them solemnly in the vestibule.

'And have the police made any progress? Have there been any arrests?'

'Police, whey, never,' muttered Clive. In his funeral suit the poor man looked shrunken, anger not quite surpassing some form of shame. His diminutive wife propped up his flank as though the customary duty of bearing up had been exchanged. In the churchyard beyond the vestibule Stevie Coulson's huge presence was conspicuous as he trundled to and fro among the mourners. Gore took note of just how many greeted Coulson warmly, as ever.

'Ee Stevie, what an awful thing, but . . .'

Mr and Mrs Ash were looking at Coulson too, a little oddly, or so it seemed to Gore. The look was not hostile, yet nor was it affable. Perhaps it was just the glassy, non-specific gaze of those who managed acute and incommunicable feelings. Or perhaps they felt as Gore did – that on such a dark day there was something newly stupendous about Stevie's frame, the rude life of it. Their son was gone, the gathering listless, and yet this man in their midst looked so very much alive. Funerals, Gore knew, were always like that.

'I'll never understand, but, *never* understand, *or* forgive, how a lad could be stabbed in the face.'

Gore placed a redundant hand on Clive Ash's shoulder. He badly wanted to give these people something for their unanswerable pain, without stammering or overstating. Face to face was far too intimate.

In the pulpit he cleared his throat and bade welcome to all, moving hastily from the set text to his own prepared remarks. The resonant echo of the high nave underscored his growing confidence.

'What can we say of a life cut short, so cruelly and inexplicably? We know, for it is written, we have but a short time to live, and like a shadow we flee. The wind passes over the ground and we are gone, and the place we leave behind will know of us no more. All this is true. And yet, there is a very singular painfulness that breaks upon us with the sad news of a death as untimely as Michael's. It is hopelessly inadequate to say that we live in violent times, for the evil of the violence visited on Michael cannot be tolerated. But when one of our number is taken in such a manner, it is a test of our faith. What comfort can we possibly obtain?'

Gore looked up and outward, certain he was being heard and heeded.

'For Michael there is the hereafter, the life beyond this life, promised us and won for us by Our Lord Jesus Christ. For ourselves there is this life that remains, and its challenge to us – the challenge to repair the damage wrought by violence, and to renew our oneness. We face that challenge together. The bells that heralded our service today summoned not only I,

the preacher, but yourselves, the congregation. Never send to know for whom the bell tolls. It tolls for thee.'

Again he looked up, and detected at least one nodding head.

'Those the famous words of the poet John Donne, who wrote so eloquently of how we are all one in the Church – how all mankind is of one author, and one volume. And for the loss of any one, we are all of us diminished. But when one man dies, a chapter is not torn from the book but, rather, translated into a better language.'

Gore turned open his Bible and read from Paul's eminently quotable First Epistle to the Corinthians. It was another strong suit.

'Behold, I show you a mystery. We shall not all sleep, but we shall all be changed – in a moment, in the twinkling of an eye, at the last – for the trumpet will sound, and the dead will be raised, incorruptible.'

Gore heard weeping from close at hand, and when he raised his gaze he saw Mr Ash, shaking and sputtering, unable to contain his misery, fingers clenched around the arm of his stoic wife.

'Please now let us pray.'

His work done and an amen put to matters at St Nicholas's Cemetery, Gore planted himself on the stony pathway bisecting the long graveyard and there accepted handshakes from mourners. Bob Spikings hustled past, Jack Ridley by his side, and offered a thumbs-up. Ridley then detached himself from Spikings and took up an almost proprietary stance a few yards from Gore. As people took turns with limp grips and mumbles into their chests, Gore had no special sense that the rites had signified much to any party, until Steve Coulson drew near – draped in black, shrouded in customary gravity – and took his hand in a vice.

'Father, I want to thank you very much, *very much* for that. It was true, all what you said. Very appropriate, like.'

A woman loitered at Stevie's side – blonde, suntanned, subdued, wearing a creamy trouser-suit, more of a wedding outfit to Gore's eye.

'Father, this here's Ally.'

'Glad to meet you. Can I introduce you to Jack Ridley, my churchwarden?'

Stevie's eyelids flickered. 'Jack I know. How you keeping, sir?'

'I'm well, thank you,' Ridley muttered. 'Excuse me, John,' he added no more happily, and walked off. The breach in manners seemed to Gore compounded by Stevie's remaining intractably polite before him.

'You and Michael were friends, Stevie? Hazel showed me some photos?'

'Oh aye? Aye, I knew him a good few year.'

'What do you make of this awful business?'

'Well . . .' His shaven crown shook slowly. 'Y'knaa what people are like when they start yackin', Father. Chinese whispers and that.' Gore saw that this Ally, too, was watching Stevie with interest. 'I doubt Michael ever did owt wrong. He was a good lad. You'll have heard that. Just in the wrong place at the wrong time, y'knaa? When your luck runs out.'

'Worse than bad luck, though. I mean, the violence of it.'

'John, you get people in this life would just as soon murder a fella as take his money. Pure evil. Absolute *scum*.'

Stevie's features had been disfigured fleetingly by a look of such virulence that Gore hastened to close a book in his mind. In the subsequent silence, Stevie clapped him on the back and peered round the sunlit graveyard. Then he fixed Gore anew. 'Aye, but you were canny back up there.'

'Thank you, Stevie.'

'Like I said. Professional. I do admire that.'

'It's what we're here for. What we do.'

'Aye, well, you do it proper. So when do we see your home debut then? Eh? Ally, the Reverend here's gunna start doing his own church at St Luke's School.'

Ally briefly animated her sloe-eyed features. 'Aw really? Nice.'

'You'll be full of busy then? When's the big day?'

'Sunday after next, October thirteen.'

'Well, I tell you what, I know me and some of my lads would like to come along, show you bit support.'

'You'd be very welcome, Stevie.'

'Aye, we'll be there. Lined up at the altar with wor tongues out, eh?'

Gore had to laugh. 'Well, there'll be a Eucharist, but no altar as such.'

'Why not?'

Gore mimed the yanking out of empty pockets. 'Skint. We'll be lucky if everyone has somewhere to sit.'

Coulson appeared overcast. Again the big mitt found Gore's shoulder. 'You're not serious, John. How bad is it?'

'We'll do our best but . . . We're bound to be a bit deficient in the decorative department. It's a poor man's church. An experiment.'

'We can't have that, Father.' The hand stayed on Gore's shoulder.

Ridley had drifted back, his eyes near-comically vigilant, as if to rescue Gore from assault. 'We're moving on now, John.'

Stevie persisted. 'If you need an extra hand, then me and my lads are here, John? You understand us, aye?'

Once again Gore felt the firm impress of this man's consideration as something to be fruitlessly resisted. 'Okay, Stevie. You're not coming on?'

'No, we won't, we've paid our respects.'

And with that Steve Coulson and the graceful Ally took their leave. Ridley looked sourly at their retreating backs. '"Me and my lads" . . .'

The venue for the reception, Gore decided, had not been the wisest choice – allegedly that of Ms Gill Ash. But he padded across the quiet dance floor of this Club Zeus with his slender bottle of Dutch lager, passing various elders who were wandering a little dazedly round the dim-lit and slippery laminate floors. The Ash clan had repaired to one dark corner, as if this were a final indignity from which to hide. Gore left Spikings to wait upon them and sought out Jack Ridley in a corner of his own, peering with suspicion at a pint of bitter with a freakish plug of thick foam. His flat cap was still atop his head, his fleshy face set in high dudgeon. Gore, though, felt he had unfinished business to raise.

'Not a bad day's work, all things considered.'

'You did canny.'

'Thanks. And I seem to have made a friend.'

'Like who?'

'Steve Coulson.'

'Steve *Coulson*? Aw, bloody hell.'

'What's that supposed to mean?' *Don't try to bully me with silence*, thought Gore. 'Jack?'

'Man alive. Well, for starters, you saw that blonde object he was carting round? Her in virgin white?'

'Ally?'

'Alison Petrie. Who was Alison Ash.'

'Not related to Michael?'

'Married to him. For six months maybe. Then she run off with a mate of Coulson's.'

This was information Gore wished he had gleaned in the course of his preparations. Now he did the extra headwork.

'*Dougie* Petrie?'

'Aye, Dougie Petrie. You know all Coulson's mob then, do you?'

'No, but I've met Dougie. So he and Ally aren't together any more?'

'Whey, divvint ask me, man. What I'm saying is Coulson helps hi'self.'

Silence ruled again, Gore a shade less assured than when he had revived the dispute. 'Is that why you're so opposed to him?'

Ridley looked elsewhere, seemingly lost in a mist of disgust. 'That bugger, he used to knock about with my son. Up to all sorts.'

'Like what?'

Ridley shook his head. 'John. You're an intelligent fella, for God's sake. What do you think a man like that does for money? What's the use of all that heft if it's not for badness?'

'Well, I know it's his job that he's got to be a big enough sight to stop people from – misbehaving.'

'"Misbehaving"? Oh, that's champion, that is.'

'Jack, I'm not stupid, okay. He'll have seen a bit of bother in his time.'

'Just a bit.'

So Ridley was on his high horse and would not be dismounted. Gore felt irritation rise, seeing the old man self-appointed as his invigilator once more. 'Jack, I should say that he made me an offer of help today. A very genuine one, I think. He seems quite *committed* to being helpful. As committed as anyone I've come across – yourself excluded, of course. And, frankly, I'm starting to think you have to take your community-mindedness where you can find it round here. So I'll not be spurning a hand of help from any man. Including Steve Coulson.'

Ridley stared stonily at Gore for some moments, then his mouth tightened and he shrugged as to say he had expected no better.

'I'll see you Sunday morning then, John.'

And he stood, abandoning his gaseous and mostly full pint to the table. Gore took a vexed swig of his beer, which foamed upward as if in a tetchy lather of its own.

Book Three

THE CHURCH OF ST LUKE'S

Chapter I

THE INAUGURAL

Sunday, 13 October 1996

On the concrete patio outside St Luke's offices John Gore stood unattended, sentry over precious little, save for the blind windows of the terraces past the gates and the low-hanging blue-black clouds above. It was a shade past eight and the augurs proposed a drab autumnal day in Hoxheath. Gore was quietly sure that rain – just the threat of same – would ward off whole cohorts of his imagined congregation. Thus by the most banal of means would a horde of high hopes and best efforts run to waste.

A scrap of memory revived in him – Audrey, years younger, chuckling through a tale of Bill's blunt courtship, how he could only be persuaded to squire her to the cinema if it were chucking down like stair-rods, for it was only when outdoor pursuits were wholly unviable that fancy diversions like movie-shows might – narrowly – be justified. Gore was yet unsure what kind of diversion he offered the public today.

He heard footfalls in the corridor behind him but did not turn until Ridley drew near. For once the old man was not assembling the parts of a contemplative smoke.

'We'd best crack on then, John.'

'Okay. Right. What's to do?'

'Chairs are all locked up for starters, aren't they? We need to get in them stores, start shifting.'

'Chairs. Right . . .'

Ridley had already turned away, so leaving Gore to chase after the broad back of his olive-green car-coat.

'Weather's not looking too favourite, is it?'

'Aye, well.' Said tersely. 'It'll do what it'll do, and we'll get on with our lot, eh?'

Gore heard an implied rebuke, understood it was past the time for him to get lively.

By ten to nine the two men, aided by Monica Bruce and Susan Carrow, had set out a hundred plastic seats in ten rows of ten, cloven by an aisle, Monica's lectern planted at the head of proceedings. Mrs Carrow, surveying this design, was yet unsatisfied.

'Do we really *need* that aisle?'

Gore frowned. 'I'd have thought so. It opens the space.'

'If we don't get so many along, it might be better a bit cosier.'

Monica cut in. 'We've no idea of numbers yet, so let's see, eh?'

Gore crouched down to the bulging Nike hold-all he had packed carefully at home, unzipping and beginning to withdraw his sacramental items in turn, each swaddled up in cotton tea towels. Aware that all eyes were observing his pains, he glanced up at Monica.

'Now, we want a table of some sort, to lay these out.'

'What sort of a table?'

'We call it a credence table, but anything you've got, really.'

'What *size*, but, John?'

'Oh – just something from one of the classrooms, maybe?'

'I've not got *keys* to the classrooms, John.'

'What about your caretaker?'

'He's off. Not due back 'til he thinks you're done at noon.'

'What about your office?'

'There's only my desk and a little coffee table, they'll not do you.'

'We're going to need *something*, Monica.'

'I *see* that, John, that's why thinking ahead comes in handy.'

Watching Monica clack away disagreeably, gazing anew around this sparse hall – the distressed floor, the glum windows, the childish art – Gore could do nothing to arrest the sudden plummet of his heart into his boots. Was anyone coming to his church today? The fear of a miserable failure was pressing down onto his shoulders. In his breast pocket, printed and folded, was the text of a sermon fastidiously drafted. He had lost hours of this last month to it, time and mental energy he now felt sickly sure that he had squandered. It was plain as a pikestaff – he had neglected the material, the organisational, the humdrum. He ought to have pounded the streets of Hoxheath by day and by night, with a bullhorn and a sandwich board larded in scripture.

Now there was fresh commotion at the entrance, and so entered Mrs Boyle, the plump ginger pianist, in her wake a ragged crocodile of nine- and ten-year-old children, most looking highly disgruntled to have been squeezed into uniform of a Sunday and frogmarched onto school grounds.

'Good day to you, John, I've brought some of my choir, they'll give us a help with hymns. Children, this is Reverend Gore, say good morning . . .'

A few half-hearted chirrups. Gore trusted that they sang at least in unison. Unsure whether the initiative was a boon or a further waste, he stood watching Mrs Boyle wrangle the children into cross-legged compliance, until Monica tottered up to him with a wooden-topped side-table, large enough – perhaps – to bear a slender vase.

'Right, John, this'll have to do you.'

Gore tapped his chin. He hadn't the heart to start laying out the sacraments on such inadequate provision. Instead – impulsively, for no reason but to cheer himself up – he retrieved from the holdall one of his more indulgent borrows from St Mark's, a free-standing crucifix, cast in pewter, hand-finished. He set it upright on Monica's table.

'What do we need but the old rugged cross, eh?'

Gore turned from Monica's frown, thus to behold new pilgrims drawing near – one of his councilmen, Phil from the *Journal*, chaperoning an unshaven young man in a striped V-neck sweater, vines of photographic apparatus gathered about his neck.

'John, can I introduce you to Matt Watson? He's one of the cubs on the paper, he'll take a few pics, maybe get a little write-up for you?'

'Thank you for coming out.'

'No bother.' Matt yawned. 'I'm due at a lads' football match at eleven.'

And now Rod Moncur was coughing at his shoulder, no doubt with a further query for which he would have scant interest and no answer.

'How, John, I think we're needing some people to move the piano?'

'Right, sorry, could you ask Jack Ridley?'

'I did, he said to ask you.'

Gore winced, considered the matter, chose to ignore it, and stooped again to take from his hold-all the thurible he had borrowed from Spikings, carefully unwinding its silver-plated components from cloth and tissue. As he stripped a briquette of incense and crumbled it around the pan like good seasoning, he saw a scuffed pair of Hush Puppies come to a halt before him.

'Do you have a match, Jack?'

Ridley rifled his pockets and shoved a box of Swan Vesta under Gore's nose. He struck a flame, touched it to the incense and held it there patiently until winsome trails of fragrant smoke were curling upward. Then he closed the silver cup over the pan, grasped snaky chains in a fist, hoisted the thurible aloft and proceeded with solemn tread to pace up and then down the aisle between the chairs, rocking the burning vessel gently from side to side. *Stagecraft*, thought Gore. But Ridley dogged his steps.

'What's the use of this, John?'

'Just a bit of atmosphere, Jack, don't you think?'

'Don't ask me, I just know Fanny Boyle's piano wants shifted.'

'It's on wheels, isn't it?'

'Aye, and both castors at one end just buckled. It's going to need four pairs of hands to lift and shift.'

'Oh, *fuck* it,' said Gore, his shoulders slumping, the thurible grazing the floor at the end of its tether. Monica, too, was cursing somewhere behind him, then – louder, heels clacking sharply – 'I'm sorry, hinny, we're not open yet.'

'Nivver worry, pet, I'm here to see the boss.'

Gore turned to see Stevie Coulson striding determinedly down the length of the hall, his great taut arms looped round and hefting a sturdy wooden frame that had to be all of six feet wide and three in height. All eyes in the room were naturally drawn to the strenuous approach of the colossus in big boots and old jeans and leather coat, until at last – scalp shining, perspiring slightly, his shark-like grin creasing his face – he laid down his tribute at Gore's feet.

'Mornin', John, full of busy, eh? Listen, I picked this up off a lad I know keeps antiques. Will it suit, do you think? For your communion and that?'

Gore felt the first unforced smile of the day stealing over his features. Before him was, indeed, a communion rail – a first-rate model of same, an antique piece, Gothic, hewn from old oak and joined in good order.

'Well, I'd say – it'll suit handsomely, Stevie.'

'Champion. Now you didn't manage to sort yourself an altar, did you?'

'We planned on managing without . . .' said Gore, realising anew the inadequacy of that plan, for he could now see past Stevie's brawny shoulder to where his strapping associates Shack and Simms were struggling into the hall, veins pulsing, faces ruddy with exertion, bearing between them a pool table of a size appropriate to a public house. They oriented themselves toward Monica's lectern and lowered the table to the lino with such delicacy as they could muster.

The room now looked to Reverend Gore as one – a look of surpassing perplexity. In a trice Gore saw that he alone seemed to have cottoned to Stevie's masterstroke. He stooped to his kitbag, drew out his borrowed altar cloth, unfolded it and shook it out. Then he cast it wide over the green baize of the pool table, spreading it smooth with the flat of his hand. Thus vestured, the table looked fit for an altogether finer purpose.

'Magic, eh?' said Stevie, clapping the shoulder of Shack, who dragged the back of a scarred hand across his brow and plucked a lone cigarette from behind his ear. Gore sensed Monica moving forward, lips pursed, and he laid a hand on her lightly. Blessings were not to be spurned, not in any respect, and gratitude for same had to be made plain and unconditional. Shack sparked his tab, just as Moncur came capering toward Gore once again.

'Reverend, y'knaa there's people stood waiting outside? What with the weather I was thinking –'

'People? Already? How many?'

'Two or three dozen at least, I'd say.'

Jack Ridley grunted. 'You want to get yer'sel dressed then, John. You're not giving the service in them jeans, are you?'

Gore reached to the floor for his bag, empty now save for vestments. As he straightened, a notion occurred.

'Steve, could you and the lads give Jack a hand with a piano?'

The clock edged past ten. Gore stood at the lectern and surveyed the hall, counting forward and back, sixty heads. He studied faces as they settled. The elderly predominated – they and the very young, under supervision and most wearing tired looks of duress. Fine – he had felt the same at their age. Monica, he knew, was keeping her own mental register of which pupils' parents had heeded her calls. As for those he could claim as his own, he noted Eunice Dodd shuffling in among the latecomers, and the last of these was Lindy Clark, in a down-filled coat with a fur-lined hood, holding the small hand of her son. From her seat she threw Gore a forbearing smile, and he was gladdened.

He had donned a simple surplice, an alb of white linen, ankle-length, closed at the throat. The hall curtains were half-drawn, patchy morning light diffused, incense still in the air. The piano was shifted, the choir in waiting, prayer books and orders of service snug in every lap. A pair of restless boys were bombing up and down the aisle, until Steve Coulson planted himself in their way and stooped for a quiet word. The kids slunk back to their seats, and Gore's unlikely sidesman resumed his patrol of the hall perimeter, nodding to his seconds. *So strange*, thought Gore, momentarily fixated upon Stevie's polished black boots crunching across the scuffed red lino. *My church has bouncers.* The notion that they might be pressed into action made mirth bubble up inside him. Say Albert Robinson were to heckle some irreverent part of the sermon? Might Stevie wade into the seating, seize the old man's lapels, propel him from the hall?

He hastened down the aisle to where Coulson had paused, statue-still, arms folded. 'We're ready to go, Stevie,' he whispered. 'Will you sit ?'

'I won't, John, if that's alright. I get a bit sciatic pain from wor back, y'knaa? These chairs'd be murder.'

So the Reverend returned to his lectern, smoothed open his order of service, felt the room fall into focus. Then he cleared his throat and launched into the welcome, thinking, *Light, keep it light, John, nothing too churchy.*

'As is written in Psalm ninety-five, let us sing unto the Lord and make a joyful noise unto the rock of our salvation. Now I don't know how your voices are fixed first thing in the morning – I can tell you mine has never won any prizes, I daresay there are cats in the street better able to carry a tune. So – I'd be ever so glad if you could help me lift the roof off this place, and I should say we're very grateful this morning for the presence of Mrs Boyle and her Year Seven choir. Would you all please stand, then, and we're going to start with one I'm sure you all know, though you have the words, and that's "All Things Bright and Beautiful" . . .'

Hands aloft, Mrs Boyle urged her children up from the floor, then plunged her fingers to the keys. Jaunty chords filled the air, chased by thin trebles and falsettos. For the first few bars the only other voices Gore could discern were his and Mrs Boyle's, and so he gazed about him, with a stage grin fit to tear his face. 'Come *on*,' he mouthed, and, to his surprise, people began shiftily to open their throats. A respectable drone soon emanated. That's *it*, thought Gore. *It's only church, you remember how it works. We sit, we stand, we sing, we pray. Then I read you a story and tell you what it means.*

'I wonder – are we gathered here this morning because we call ourselves Christians? I hope and trust that we are – that we hold this much in

common. And if we do call ourselves Christians, we have to be concerned with the welfare of our fellow man and woman. And endeavour to love them, as we love ourselves.'

A child's pained yelp rent the air.

'By all means disagree, bonny lad, but perhaps we can discuss it when I'm done . . .?'

A ripple of laughter. The child's mother was fussing, but restoring order. Gore regained his place.

'Yes, to love one another. Because, in the words of the apostle John, "If any man hath this world's goods, and seeth his brother hath need, but shutteth up his bowels of compassion against him, how dwelleth the love of God in him?" Well, how indeed?

'There may be many in our lives whom we say we love. Sometimes, in the abstract, it's possible to love the whole world and everyone in it. We've all had those moments, haven't we? When it feels like the sun is shining on us alone, and good will to others comes pouring out of us. But most days, we know, aren't like that. On a grey day like today, when maybe nothing much is going so right – are we ready then to love a man who lies before us in destitution? And love him not just with a pat on the head and a wince of sympathy, but with a little of the food and raiment that he needs?

'It's a tough one, isn't it? I can't say my conscience is clear, any more than you, I dare say. We can't be perfect, we can't always share in others' woes. It's hard enough with friends, never mind strangers. We can always say – can't we? – that we have "troubles of our own". And we do.

'But is it not just possible that in telling ourselves that – in averting our eyes from a stranger's pain – is it not possible we're cheating ourselves of a greater reward? I don't mean some gold star from God on high. I'm talking about something far more powerful. I mean, the joy of feeling His love working through us.

'If we call ourselves Christians then we say that love is the law. And we are bound to that law. God's love . . . is burning in us anyway, whether or not we choose to heed it. But why should we cheat ourselves out of experiencing that blessing, by not yielding to it? Why refuse ourselves the ecstasy we might have in letting God's love work through us in our actions? That's why John tells us, "Children, let us not love in word,

neither in tongue, but in deed."

'Words grow stale unless they're renewed by action. So many tired old words we hear too much of. What do we mean, for instance, when we talk about "our community"? We're always hearing – aren't we? – about this or that "community". What is the community of Hoxheath? It's more than just your neighbours, clearly. More than the people we know by sight in the Netto, or the Gunnery. It's everybody in our locality, isn't it? The people with whom we have the daily stuff of life in common – the same concerns, same hopes and fears. And we do *have those things in common as long as we walk the same streets and breathe the same air. Since we have those same feelings, shouldn't we try to act on them together? Each of us has a part to play in Hoxheath. A duty to act. But also a reward to be reaped. Because it's nice to be together, isn't it? Things we hold in common make us feel safe in the world. Feeling safe in the here and now gives us grounds to hope for more. And hope, dear friends, is the future . . .'*

They shared the peace. 'Greet ye one another with a kiss of charity,' Gore intoned. 'Peace be with you all who are in Christ Jesus.' He watched them slowly shift from their seats, begin to mill about, albeit tentatively. 'You don't have to kiss, of course,' he hastened to add. 'A handshake is fine. But you won't be taxed for a hug so long as you're sure of who you give it to.'

That seemed to break the ice, though Gore saw Albert Robinson flinch as he was folded into an aged female embrace.

Had he his preference he would have closed proceedings with the Lord's Prayer and sent a docile crowd on its way, but he had resolved to offer Holy Communion and offer it he would. After measures of silence, coughs, and shuffles – two, four, five, finally seven bodies rose and filed forward to the fine new communion rail, making of themselves an orderly queue as Gore busied himself with the vessels at his makeshift altar. Then he turned to where the supplicants were kneeling, thoughtful, in turn, and passed from person to person, commending that the bread and wine might be to them His body and His blood. The last face gazing up at him was Lindy Clark's, her fur-lined hood an aureole for her painted face. She looked evenly at Gore as he pressed the wafer into her hand, and after the sip of wine she crossed herself at her breast, her lip curled.

Afterwards, over tea and biscuits at the back of the hall, Gore tried to fight down a creeping euphoria. But the sight of apparently contented people taking their turn at the tea urn and settling into unforced conversation with their neighbours was a madly heartening one. *I built this*, he told himself, *I bloody made this work.*

Matt Watson hoved into view. 'Vicar, could I pinch a shot of you and the lads by the pool table? Before it gets carted off?'

Gore shrugged – why not? – ran hands through his hair and took steps toward his altar. Then he felt two hard shoulders tackling him behind his knees, butting up under each thigh, and powerful hands upon his armpits, hoisting him into the air as easily as if he were newborn. He was aloft the paired shoulders of Shack and Simms, and he teetered wildly, but found his balance with his palms upon their backs. There were laughs and cheers from all about the hall, though he saw perplexed faces too among the lingering tea-drinkers. But Stevie Coulson was reaching a glad hand up to him, Gore grasped it firmly, and the big Nikon camera flared like a muzzle-flash.

Chapter II

CLEVER DEVILS

Wednesday, 16 October 1996

'My name's Gore, I'm here to be on *Tyne Talk* with Chris Carter?'

He stepped back, surveyed the tiled foyer of Tyne FM Radio, dense with the comings and goings of clipboarded runners, motorbike messengers and newly arrived 'talent' such as himself. Within moments a beanpole blonde girl in black emerged from the elevator, only to seize Gore's arm and usher him back through the fast-closing doors.

'So did you read about my service in the *Journal*?'

'The *Journal*? Aw no, it was your sister, I thought? Aye, we got a call from your sister at SEG? Telling us all what you were doing.'

Of all the liberties, thought Gore. He bit back displeasure. 'Right. And this is live, this show?'

'Aye, dead informal, just a roundtable. People with all different views on things . . . You're in here.'

She was pressing him out of the corridor into the Green Room – in fact, white – where one soul had already taken up jaded residence on a seemingly inflatable sofa of fire-engine red.

'Reverend, this is Gaz Lyons, Newcastle's top nightclub promoter.'

'How man. Sally, you couldn't fetch us a double espresso, pet?'

'Sorry, Gaz, it's only the machine coffee we've got on this floor.'

'Get us two of them then, would you? Bit too much naughty last night.' Lyons belched, clapping a hand to his mouth. He was perhaps in his early forties, Gore decided, though his hair was a plaited tower of bleached dreadlocks. He wore combat trousers festooned with zippered pockets, and a padded coat that looked to be of some light-but-durable textile, fit for outer space – a sort of futuristic clown, albeit heavily medicated, in need of better skincare and earlier nights.

Sally returned, in her care a tubby man with a dark floppy fringe, wearing an anorak over his suit, grizzling into a mobile phone. As he marched testily into his very own corner and paced as if caged, Sally crouched beside Gore and Lyons.

'You know Don Watson? He runs Barzini's Pizza? You'll have seen 'em, right, they're everywhere now.'

Gore shrugged, trying without success to recline into the squeaking red sofa. Lyons was idly punching numbers into his own miniature phone, a force field of disinclination raised all around him. Abruptly he began a conversation, punctuated by wearied groans and guffaws. Gore gathered that a business associate was on the other end, for the talk seemed to be all of bothersome matters that one would rather the other dealt with.

'Aw, you do it, will ya? Just for once, man. I can't be bothered dealing wi' Steve Coulson this week. Don't make us. Prick.'

As Lyons set down his phone and peered into the murk of a polystyrene cup, Gore studied him with renewed interest.

'Sorry, do you know Steve Coulson?'

'Do *I* know Steve Coulson? Bloody hell, man. Do *you*?'

But Sally was in the doorway again, hopping from foot to foot.

'Welcome back to the morning session, with us today three special guests, each in their own special way offering new and improved services on Tyneside.'

Gore adjusted his headset and sat poised at the proposed six inches from his microphone. Lyons and Watson were separated from him by a cable-strewn expanse of red baize. The egregious Carter bossed the table, and in commercial breaks he asked very solemnly of his guests that they endeavour to sound as jolly as possible whenever they resumed. Once the red light blinked them back on air, Carter's own voice was pumped full of hale and hearty. Gore had to admire such polished fakery.

'Reverend Gore – just before the break we said a bit about this new church of yours in Hoxheath. What interests me is this. Who are you trying to *reach* with a new church? What's your demographic? Have you done, say, any market research?'

'Uh, that's a good question, Chris. For starters I'm very confident we're already reaching a lot of the older people in the parish, who've got a longer tradition of churchgoing in their lives. Then I'm sure we can also reach the younger adults, young families, who probably had a religious upbringing themselves, of a sort, and might want the same for their kids. Beyond that? I'd say we want to reach *anyone* out there who hasn't heard the Christian message.'

'Gaz? Did you have a religious upbringing?'

'Aw, I don't remember, man.'

'Right. So a new church on Tyneside, how does that grab you?'

'Whey . . Nee disrespect, I just think the whole idea of church is a bit funny, y'knaa? For me, like? I reckon for young people now, gannin' to clubs is like what gannin' to churches used to be for the old uns.'

Carter seemed to take that seriously. 'Interesting. Reverend, do you think – do you worry – that people in Hoxheath could care *less* about the Christian message? Has it anything to offer them? Really?'

'Well, I do think every one of us could stand to be told that we should do unto others as we'd have them do unto us. That seems to me good advice whoever you are. But, sure, I'd be just as happy to meet people who've never thought twice about any of it. I should emphasise – everyone's welcome at my church, we won't turn a soul from our door. What we really want is just a real community forum for Hoxheath.'

'And that's nice, but our listeners will want me to remind you there are parts of Hoxheath that are pretty . . . well, notorious. For crime, for drug abuse, for long-term unemployment. People might wonder what sort of community you've got there to speak of?'

'Chris, it's important to challenge stereotypes –'

'Some are true, but.' This was Don Watson, meeting Gore's eye across the table for the first time, looking very settled in his chair and his view.

'Maybe. It's true in Hoxheath there are people who've had a lot of trouble in their lives. It's hard to earn a living in parts of this city. And when people can't earn a living they can end up doing some very desperate things.'

Don Watson placed some of his bulk over the edge of the table. 'Can I say, Chris? That's what we call a bleeding heart. One thing you learn sharpish in business, nobody does you any favours in this life, so you'd best get on with it. Another thing you learn is to call things by their name. A crime's a crime, and a criminal's a criminal, know what I mean?'

'Yes, Reverend, you sound very affable but some people will say isn't the Church supposed to take a tougher line on, well, *sin*?'

'Um, I'll probably sound quite stuffy here . . . but there is a body of thought within the Church concerned with what we call structural sin – sins that arise because people were sinned *against*, in some way. That possibly sounds a bit academic.'

'You've lost me,' Watson grunted.

'Well,' Carter leapt in, 'let's try and take some of your calls before the break. Jack from Fenham, are you there, Jack?'

A throat was cleared down the line. *'Thank you. I'm listening to that fella you've on there, Mr Lyons? And he was talking about nightclubs being like churches? I want to tell him this. I've never been to a church where there's drug dealers handing out drugs to kids like they were sweeties, and fights on the pavement outside, and lads vomiting their guts –'*

'Sounds like a canny night, that.' Lyons wheezed in amusement.

'Okay, but have you been to a *nightclub* before, Jack?'

'No, and I shan't, thank you, not if Mr Lyons is any advert for it.'

'Okay, thank you, Jack.'

As Gore was escorted back to the foyer by Sally, he made a mental reckoning of his performance and decided to call it a moral victory of sorts, redeemed in part by that late show of support.

'That was really good,' Sally offered. 'Good response, lots of calls.'

'Thank you for having me.'

'Aw, well, they asked us to tell you we'd be glad to have you back, anytime. You've got something to say, you know?' And she nodded, keenly, perhaps a few more times than Gore could take as sincere.

The following evening found Gore once more before his parish council, and he strode into the room feeling himself justified. He poured his coffee, took his seat by Jack Ridley and tipped back his chair in a proprietor's manner. Bob Spikings, too, wore a fulsome air. 'Well, I think I speak for us all when I say the, uh, top item on the agenda has to be a big hand for John on the success of the first service of St Luke's.'

It was a tinny, hesitant round of applause – even Ridley a little tardy – though Simon Barlow appeared most vigorous and earnest in his acclamation. Spikings nodded. 'Quite right, John, and, uh – with any luck, you'll soon have no more need of us. Then we can all get our Thursday nights back. I should say, too, there's the matter of your performance on the radio yesterday, which I'm sure those who heard will agree was first-rate. And, uh, tremendous PR. The media is golden, as we know, and you really, uh, handled yourself well.'

Gore smiled thinly.

'Can I raise a point? About the service?' It was Susan Carrow, in her yellow pullover and snow-white blouson and citrine scarf, the ensemble clearly tailored to her ash-blonde hairdo yet bestowing on her the look of a lemon meringue, and today, it seemed to Gore, a sour one to boot.

'Can I just say? I was a bit put out – as were others – by those three – I hardly know what to call them . . . those three *muscle-men* who were strutting about the place?'

An emphysematic snort came out of Jack Ridley.

'I didn't think their presence was at all appropriate. I mean to say, one of them was *smoking*, and then another I heard using language that the children present shouldn't have had to hear. And of course *I* was hardly going to tell them off because I was *frightened*, frankly, as were some of the children . . .'

Spikings turned to Gore, who made sure to emanate bemusement. 'Mrs Carrow's referring to Steve Coulson and some colleagues of his from the security firm he runs, who very kindly came down and gave us a hand in the shifting of heavy items. I should say, too, that those who took communion on Sunday did so at a rail that was donated by Mr Coulson.'

Spikings stared determinedly downward at his paperwork. 'Well, yes, of course – we know Mr, uh, Coulson here at St Mark's, and he's given generously to this church also.'

'Well, I'm sorry,' volleyed Mrs Carrow, 'but him and his pals have the look of *thugs* to me, and I can't say they comported themselves any better. And I'm not the only one thought as much, because people talk, you know . . .'

Gore leaned forward. 'Susan, I didn't hear any complaints, so I –'

'Oh, that's cos you were off getting your photo taken –'

'And frankly I don't appreciate some of your own language.'

Mrs Carrow did not appreciate the rejoinder, and Gore was still returning her piqued stare when Simon Barlow coughed and took charge of the silence in the room. 'Hang on, sorry, have I got this right, John? You had *bouncers* for sidesmen? At your first service?'

'Geet big skinhead navvies,' Susan Carrow nodded. 'With tattoos.'

'And this Coulson bloke,' Barlow continued, dawning marvel in his eyes. 'He gives *money* to this church?'

'That's sort of how I met him,' offered Gore. 'Well, in fact, we actually met in the Gunnery pub.' He had the sudden blushing sensation of having volunteered more information than was helpful.

But Barlow's eyes were gleaming, dissimulating pure pleasure, and he bashed the table surface with the flat of his hand. 'Outstanding. *Outstanding*, John. *That's* the spirit, eh? You can't say *that's* not ringing in the new. That's worth another round of applause in itself. Honest, John, I'd never have thought it. Talk about thinking out of your box.'

Susan Carrow still looked to have something tart stored in her mouth. 'Well, I hardly see the cause for congratulation.'

'Oh, but Susan, Susan – it takes all sorts. *All* sorts. Who are we to judge, eh? Hasn't John always said that? I know I've heard him. Didn't the Lord find a great servant in the harlot Rahab? Was she not justified by works and works alone? Was faith not a mighty current in her? Too right it was.'

Gore thought himself long inured to Barlow's crackerjack displays of exuberance. Today he found himself wondering if the man was off his medication. But whatever the source of his sustenance, Barlow was beaming at Gore as if thinking him good enough to eat. 'What *will* you do next, John? Eh? Whatever next?'

'That is a good question, I should say.' Spikings seemed anxious to reclaim the chair's privilege. 'What are your plans for the rest of the week, John?'

Gore bridged his fingers. 'Well, my thought was to maybe start doing some voluntary hours at the Citizens Advice Bureau. On Westgate Road?'

'Come off it, John, where'll you get the time for that?' Scratchy scepticism was back in Barlow's voice. 'You can't, not if you're doing your pastoral duties properly. We've been through this, haven't we?'

Spikings was nodding. Mrs Carrow seemed to draw sustenance from these reproofs. 'What about a Sunday School? Didn't we talk about that last time?'

Barlow clucked his tongue. 'Hang on, Susan. Let's step back a minute, take a closer look at the turnout John got Sunday. How many kids from the school were there? Monica?'

'Ten, a dozen maybe? Not so many. I can't force them, as you know.'

Barlow was doing an impression of *The Thinker*. 'Hmm. And can I ask, Monica – how exactly is RE taught in your school? How's the faith made present?'

She shrugged. 'I start and end the day with prayer. We follow the curriculum, of course, far as it goes. Teaching the belief systems –'

Gore watched a familiar vulpine cast form on Barlow's features. '"Belief systems". What's that about? See, in my day RE was about introducing the kids to a certain guy called Jesus Christ. Wasn't it the same for you? I mean, I'm sure you're only doing what the *powers that be* say is adequate. But come on, a church school should have a clear Christian ethos? Shouldn't it? I know it's hard to get the staff now, but *hey*.'

Gore leaned forward. 'Simon, please, what's this – what's your point?'

'A dozen kids? Sorry, is that not pitiful? Monica, you can't sit there and tell me you couldn't have given John a better start?'

Gore was sure Mrs Bruce would retort in a manner fit to blister the paint from the walls. And yet she looked to have sustained a blow to the heart. Barlow nodded, apparently content he had hit his target. 'These kids, see . . . I'm all for them getting their A-B-C and their one-two-three. Just let's not pretend that's the end of it, yeah? Making them into clever little devils. *Church* education means fostering the head and the heart and the *soul* of the child.' And he clasped his big paws before him, a plangent gesture reminding Gore of Gordon Lockhart. 'Anyhow. Another day maybe. Yeah, so what about that ruddy Sunday School then, John?'

'Much done, much still to do.' Gore rocked backward in his chair, very sure he had lost sufficient hours of his life already bearing witness to Barlow's grandstanding. 'I've been pursuing this idea of a crèche with one of the mothers who came to my first meeting.'

Spikings gestured to his diligently annotating wife. 'Good, good. And that's who, sorry?'

'Her name is Lindy Clark.'

A mordant exclamation fell from Monica's lips. Gore rolled his tanks over the objection, thinking it wholly predictable. 'Ms Clark has a child of her own, and several jobs she has to do just to keep the boy, but she's very kindly been putting some thought into this matter for me.'

'Ms Clark,' said Susan Carrow, fresh stocks of contempt in her voice, 'is a little tattooed lah-di-da with no thought in her head but for herself.'

'Susan, please.' Spikings, and indeed his wife, seemed genuinely pained by the outburst. Gore made a point of chuckling under his breath, looking disbelievingly to the window, then the door. 'No, John, that all sounds well and good, well and good. The thing I've always said, the really *good* thing about this job, is that you *meet* people.'

'Oh, all *sorts* of people, Bob.' Simon Barlow made plain his own amusement. Gore made out just a little malice in the tone. In the silence he threw open his hardbacked notebook and scribbled a few short notes. He trusted his council understood that it was nothing to do with anything they had uttered – other than that Barlow, in the midst of his prior fit of quasi-scriptural raving, had reminded Gore of an excellent notion for a sermon.

Chapter III

STEVIE COULSON IS BUSY

Saturday, 19 October 1996

He spun the wheel of the borrowed transit van, fiddling the dial of the dodgy radio, questing for some good and proper driving tunes though wary of the player's limited capacity, for its housing had been sorely misused as an ashtray on some previous loan. For the moment he could get nothing but angry swarming fuzz. Beyond the windshield rainclouds were massing, but the promised deluge was staying its hand. Traffic at least was kindly as he turned off the Scotswood Bridge and onto the Derwenthaugh Road that would wend him down through Blaydon and Rowland's Gill. In short, not the absolute worst of days, though the day's labour wore an onerous cast. Giving up on the music, he whistled and sang a few bars of 'The Blaydon Races', a regular salve to his spirits.

'We flew across the Chain Bridge, reet into Blaydon Toon . . .'

My God, he thought, *if the fella wrote that could see old Blaydon now.*

The suspension groaned, and a hell of a clatter broke from the back of the van as Stevie pulled up to stop-lights on the A694. He cursed himself for not having made a better fist of securing the cargo. No point in stopping, though, for he had neither chain nor twine to hand. He kept his thoughts nailed to the promise of three o'clock, this outing but a chore en route. In and out like shite off a stick, that was the target – and if the traffic and the skies behaved themselves he would be installed in the Strawberry for at least a pair of pints before kick-off. *Whey aye.* He took the next right turn and was soon motoring through Highfield and Hooker Gate, Derwent Valley territory, the familiar depths of Chopwell Wood to his left.

It was the sticks, Chopwell, no question, and Karen never let him forget. But the development into which he had placed them, brand spanking new-built at the time, was a perfectly sound one, had kept so over the years, and remained perfectly handy for the Metro Centre, where Karen was presently engaged on the perfume floor of Debenhams. True, she faffed on about moving, but such ambitions were not Stevie's business. For – what was it? – all of five or six years, they had had no real grounds for dispute. Five it must be, Stevie reckoned, for tomorrow Donna turned six.

His card, he knew, was a poor choice, and he ought to have found one with the number on it. But he believed that the gift, in its size and splendour, would more than compensate. The darker suspicion behind his hope was that Donna wouldn't care less, preferring to join her mother in some witchy chorus of daddy-disparagement, some more sticking of the Stevie voodoo doll. This Donna just bore no relation to the gurgling moppet he used to paddle about between his big hands – some double it was, who shrank from him now. He bore the slight, didn't brood on it, as was his discipline. For he had every intention of proving to his daughter that some things in life were steadfast and unconditional – even if, at times, they racked up a man's temper.

He swung the van through wrought-iron gates, past the floral-fringed sign that proclaimed HALCYON HEIGHTS, and pulled into a spot beside Karen's silver Saab, outside the narrow two-storey mews house. It too languished under its own idiot name, HEATHERDOWN. Stevie had never seen fit to scribble such nonsense onto an envelope.

Karen opened the door onto her porch, clad in ski pants and old sweatshirt, streaky hair in a scrunchy. Almost all he could see of her now was her bold chin, her sharp nose, in or out of his business. She had yet to apply her face this morning, but the one she turned upon Stevie was not entirely bilious. She had wheeled away again toward the small kitchen at the rear of the house before she noticed Stevie was not at her heel.

'Are you coming in or what?'

But Stevie had repaired to the back of the van, and only now did he cross the threshold – edging his way, grunting a little, one arm over and one arm under his cumbersome prize, five feet long and four feet high including the stand. He lowered it down next to Karen's coffee table.

'Right, there you gan, girl.'

She was hewn from rock-maple, with enamel ears and a white-blonde mane, a saddle cloth of red suede and a bridle of soft tan leather. Such connoisseur touches had gone some way in persuading Stevie to part with six hundred notes.

'She's a palomino, they say. Donna can give her a name, like.'

But Karen's shoulders were slumping. 'Aw, for crying out loud, man. Where's that gunna go? She's not into horses anyhow, man, never has been, I told you just to get her that outfit for her dancing.'

Stevie took a breath. Donna was taking some pricey classes, one such this very morning, though he saw no obvious talent.

'Divvint be awkward, Karen. It'll gan up in your little room.'

'Which one's that, then?'

'Get away, you're canny for space.'

'*You* get away, man. We're on top of each other, me and her.'

'Well then, you're lucky it's just you and her. I mean to say, Kazza – two netties, the garage, you've more than you know what to do with.'

'Aw aye. And what if I had another bairn?'

'Then you'd be off my bliddy hands, wouldn't you?'

She beheld him scathingly. 'Aw whatever, stick it up there then. Just mind the walls on the stairs, will you?'

He rubbed his chin slowly, stared at her askance.

'What?' she said coolly, wheeling away into her kitchen, to Stevie's satisfaction, for he knew she knew she could not withstand a contest.

Once he had lugged the hardwood horse into the cramped utility room, he rejoined Karen in the kitchen, accepting a rattled mug of instant coffee while she smoked her Consulate. The kitchen was tired, units out of style, paintwork grubby and defaced by felt-tip scribbles. No handyman had stayed very long in the years since he had deposited the girls here – that much was signposted. He rifled his coat pocket and set down a plump stuffed Conqueror envelope on the worktop.

'That's you, then.'

'Cheers,' she said, cheerlessly.

'Y'knaa you want a bulb in that light? In the spare room?'

'It's not the bulb, it's the dimmer switch is knacked.'

'Well, then you want to get it fixed.'

'You said you would, Steve.'

'I never did. I'm not a sparks, Karen, I canna go messing with wires. I'll have a word with Dougie.'

'Dougie, yeah, aw aye . . .' Her voice trailed off.

'What?'

'You know what. He'll come round, he'll want the kettle on. He'll be sat there on the sofa, farting and scratching hi'self for half an hour, then he'll tell us it's a bit trickier than he thought so he'll be round again in the week.'

'What do you *want* then? I'm busy, Karen.'

'Oh, I know you're busy, Steve. I've seen your name over the door at that Teflon.'

'Aw right, you've been, have you? Bit lively for you these days, I'd have thought Kazza? Surprised my lads let you past.'

'How do *you* manage still? All the years on you, they must have to wheel you into there some nights.' She had fixed him over the trail of her cigarette, was chewing her nail as if she found something tasty there. 'Oh, I know you're busy. Saw your picture in the paper and all. Done your good deed for the year, have you? *What* a laff.'

'Just givin' a hand to a bloke.'

'Aye, he's on the radio and all. The vicar? Bullshitter he sounded. Mind, what did he ever do to deserve you? Does he *know* about you?'

'Does he know what?'

'What do you think? That you hurt people. For a living, like.'

'He knows I've a *business*, Karen, that's what –'

'*Howay*, Steve, who do you think you're *talkin'* to, man?'

'It's not his business. I tell you this, but, Karen, he's glad of the hand, that bloke. He's not on his high horse about people. Not like you. Not biting the hand what's putting food on your table.'

'Bollocks, Steve, we get by, we do, so never you worry. Not *my* problem what *you* do for your conscience, you can do what you like.'

'Ah, can I now? Can I really, Karen?'

'Aye, you can. That's all what this is, man, all it's *ever* been. "Aw, *my* bairn'll always be alreet." Aw *bollocks* . . .'

He wanted badly now to hoist up the kitchen table and hoy it out the window. He had many exes, few to whom he believed he had been so honourable, none who hated him more. Sometimes – even this time – he could look at her and still see the girl who clutched at him, so fearful, throughout her contractions. That was life, the worm, working its way through your innards. When he thought on it for much more than a moment, the gall made him sick – made him want to retch out everything he'd ever eaten.

Bollocks to this, move yourself. Eyes on the prize, three o'clock, Strawberry by two.

He set down his unfinished coffee.

'I tell you what else I read. All that about Mickey.'

He scowled, rubbed his neck. 'Did you now? I was at the funeral. Where were you?'

'Bet they were made up to see you.'

'We're all grown-ups.'

'That poor little bastard.'

He could see them anew, the six of them on that impulse jaunt to Gran Canaria. Was it 1989? He and Karen, Mickey and Ally, Dougie on his tod. And Donna just a baby – docile, and she needed to be, with beery sunburned faces peering down into her travelling cot. Perhaps the last time he and Karen had sex, or spoke to one another with care. He shook his head. 'There's some proper ratbags come into town.'

'You think you're any better?'

'I fucking do. I fucking *know*.'

A current of metal-edged pain coursed through the meat of his right calf, and he shuddered, cursed himself for having stood there slouching, continuing these worthless exchanges.

'Is that a *flinch* you've got, Stevie?'

'Not a fucking flinch, man. Sciatica.'

'Poor you. Told you, see? It's you what's getting on. An old man with a bad back. Ready for the knackers soon, just watch.'

He revolved his head about his neck, tilted his brow at her and growled. She was doing a good job of seeming blithe. 'And you needn't give us that look neither, I'm past frightened of you.'

It was impressive, after a fashion, for she knew what he could do, she had seen it. She should have seen him only the week gone by, when he did it again, squiring her old friend Ally to a nice bar, she in a backless dress, until some mindless clart had offered her a load of old chat. She seemed so sure he would never lift a hand to her. And no, he wouldn't, he wouldn't. Sometimes, though, he was standing on the precipice, and the long way down, the vertigo, the crushing impact – they almost seemed worth it.

'You wanna get on without us, Karen? Gan on then. Doing so fuckin' well, are you? Does Donna think you're brilliant? You sure? How brilliant would you be if she had to give up all her classes? Is some other daddy-man gunna come along –'

'Fuck off out of it, Steve man.'

'I don't see him, Kazza. Nah, you're maybe not the lass you were.'

'Fuck *off*, you.' She swiped the dregs of her coffee mug at him.

Stevie grinned, having bit and bit deep. 'That's right, flower, let it out.'

Now she darted at him like knives, poked at his chest. '*Bastard*.'

'Aw, don't hurt us, Kazza, please, don't hurt us . . .'

Now she was hammering with both of her fists, panting, and Stevie was content but no longer tickled, and he seized both of her wrists with no small force and held them hard, until she was pacified, incapable, and she broke under his stony gaze.

'Steve man, *don't*. *Stop* it. *Stop* it, you rotten *bastard* . . .'

Oh right – now the tears. What the fuck? Didn't she know, by now, how it all ended, once she chose to get started? So why start?

And now he was supposed to apologise? Poor Kazza. He released his grip and her knees seemed to buckle.

'I'll be back the day after the morra to see her, so have her ready.'

'She's *sick* of you, you fucker.'

He heard the last only as he closed the front door behind him. Out in the air he took a couple of breaths and screwed his equilibrium back into the sticking place. HALCYON HEIGHTS. *Aye, right.* This experience was hateful, and hated, and its true value really needed to be reassessed. But some other day than today. St James's for three, the Strawberry for two.

Much to his consternation he saw that he had left the van doors yawning open. *You* are *going soft, son.* Slamming them shut, he observed a motorcycle, bearing rider and pillion passenger, puttering through the gates of the close and up the driveway. A dirt-bike, really – Yamaha? Bloody rowdy old exhaust. Boy racers, haring about where there could be small bairns playing. Who did they reckon they were trying to impress? Stevie was half-inclined to go over and knock them off their perch with one push. *At ease, big man,* he soothed himself, digging for the van keys in his tight denim pocket.

The bike made a showy swerve to a running stop five yards in front of him, and two inscrutable black visors turned to face his way. Messengers? The passenger was clutching something close to his leather chest.

And then Stevie heard a clinking, snagging sound. The passenger shook his hand as if stung, threw out his arm, at the end of which, clear as day, was the tube of a barrel. Ice-coldness flushed from the crown of Stevie's head, straight through his bowels to his feet. He flinched, threw his hands in the air, then wildly over his face. *No, never, couldn't be.* Again that mad snagging clink, and between his fingers he saw the passenger shaking the gun furiously like a spent bottle, muffled curses coming from behind the black visor. Then a thump on the driver's back, the engine revved, the exhaust snorted, and the bike tore off back from whence it had come.

His mind cringing still, Stevie felt his feet move bravely beneath him. He was jogging, then running, down toward the gateway. But when he reached the road the bike was already a quarter-mile hence. He pressed his palms to his temples. What had he seen? What the fuck was it? Had anyone seen it? He whirled about him, looking for the twitch of curtains, for concerned faces at windows. But the double-glazed windows of Halcyon Heights were blind. *The gun*, he told himself – heard himself telling Roy, telling Shack, reporting back – *The gun, it jammed. I'm fine, aye, but only cos it fucking jammed, man . . .*

He tasted bland sizing in his mouth, swallowed, then smartly crouched and bent, and the sky rolled over him as he vomited forth his breakfast, once, twice, onto somebody's discreet paved driveway. He held the crouch for one or two minutes, until he was sure he was voided, then straightened, spat, and strode unsteadily back to Karen's door.

Chapter IV

AMONG THE YOUNG MEN

Sunday, 20 October 1996

No time for faint hearts, Gore told himself, no fannies in a fit. True, he had expected a cakewalk today, money for old rope. But he was tense and out of sorts, even as he grasped the trusty lectern, texts arrayed before him in good order. Stakes were higher second time out of the traps.

Last week's turnout had been matched, possibly surpassed – media, word of mouth, what Lockhart had been wont to call the '*Songs of Praise* factor'. A pair of showy flower baskets had come from some anonymous well-wisher. But rain too had come early and relentless this morning, congregants had shuffled indoors looking damp and harassed, and a rank air of discomfort lifted from the seats. A pair of fluorescent light-poles had packed up, settling deeper gloom upon the hall. Worse, a few volunteers from Sunday past had absented themselves. Though Steve Coulson's associates Simms and Robbie had pitched up in the transit with the pool table, they also carried a mumbled apology for the absence of the boss.

Gore might have written off these minor impediments as the devil's share, were it not for the presence of the small crew from local television, now loitering intently behind the last row of chairs, their director whispering urgently to his lighting cameraman, making frames in the air with his hands. Gore at first suspected an escalation in his sister's campaign of unsolicited PR. But the director claimed only a sincere interest in what he had lately seen in the papers.

He was as ready as he could be in the circumstances when came the unheralded entry of Susannah Gore herself, swishing in just one minute before ten in navy woollen coat and scarf, sitting herself serenely near the back, a handful of seats down from where puffa-jacketed Lindy Clark was trying to settle her Jake. Two more taxing eyes upon him, then.

And the remainder of the audience? Some dutiful couples and their kids, then a bloc that could have been an over-sixties outing, bussed in and bribed with tea, struggling nobly with digestive disorders, waiting for the preacher if a preacher was booked – as opposed, say, to a jolly seaside stand-up. *Lest I get carried away . . .* thought Gore, minded anew of a stock sermonising gag – the one about the woman who called on her priest to confess to the sin of vanity, the hours she wasted before the mirror in thrall to her beauty, only to be told, 'You're not sinful, child, you're *mistaken*.'

The opening hymn – 'The Lord's My Shepherd' – was no disgrace. Susan Carrow, having insisted, read clearly if flatly from the Gospel of St Matthew, damning the scribes and Pharisees, 'for they say and do not.' Gore gave out some scant announcements, asking that any drivers with a spare seat, or any ladies able to devote some hours to a crèche, might dally and consult with him afterwards. He was consoled when, at last, he reached his sermon, sure that a strong performance would marshal his spirits.

'In Joshua we read of how, after the death of Moses, the Lord restated to Joshua the selfsame promise he had made to the lawgiver. Namely, that all lands lying across the Jordan, down to the Euphrates – wheresoever Joshua set foot – were promised to the children of Israel.

'And so Joshua sent forth two messengers to venture ahead, prepare the way, spread the word. They came first to the great walled city of Jericho, and the king there was alerted to their presence, and wished them harm. But it was a woman called Rahab – a harlot, a common prostitute – who offered Joshua's men a refuge within her own home, safe from the king's soldiers. She resisted the king's orders, and enabled the Israelites to escape, at no small risk of peril to herself. But mark you the aftermath. For when Jericho fell, it was Rahab and her kin alone who were spared the sword.

'Now, the Apostle James tells us, "By works is faith made perfect. Was not Rahab the harlot justified by works? When she had received the

messengers, and had sent them out another way? For as the body without the spirit is dead, so is faith without works." And that is a message I consider endlessly, undyingly relevant.

'Let's be clear. Any one of us, whatever our station in life, whatever our past indiscretions or failings – any one of us is capable still of the very best and finest actions in this world, if and when the right moment comes. It's not just a case of who's been most pious for longest – we can't store up moral treasure on this earth that way. No, sometimes . . . I think it's only when the circumstances *fall into place that we really find in ourselves the grounds of a burning faith, one that drives us to action. How easily we can come to think ourselves lost, our efforts doomed or pointless. Cometh the hour, though – cometh the hour – and the soul will rise.'*

After a modest Eucharist, the hall fast emptied save for a thirsty two dozen or so, a good few so immobile as to need their tea fetched to them where they sat. Gore stood supping his brew with Jack Ridley in contemplative silence, trying unsuccessfully to locate his sister amid the bodies, when Monica Bruce weaved up to them.

'Sorry about them lights, John, they'll be right for next week. I've got to shoot off, but you's can see to the lock-up, can't you? Now how are you's fixed for your supper the night? I'd like to have you both round to ours.'

Gore could muster no immediate excuse, for his diary was bare.

'How about you and your missus, Jack?'

'What are you making?'

'Shepherd's pie.'

Ridley licked his lips. 'Champion.'

To the TV crew Gore granted a short, upbeat, anodyne interview. As he glanced at the small tight circle of congregants drawn in to witness, he saw at last his sister, smiling crookedly, coolly amused. When he stepped aside from the lens she took his arm, kissed his cheek, commandeered him. 'Well, hello there, Reverend. Is it nice to be a local celebrity?'

'It's got its problems, I have to say.'

'You seem to cope. I must say, though, this room could do with a lick and a promise. Nice little service you give, but. Very thoughtful lesson. Good of you to tell us what we can all learn off of the common whore.'

'My pleasure. Take it away and use it.'

'I will. You read that Bible like you wrote it, mind.'

'Is this the best you can do? I thought you were in the praising business.'

'That's you, kidder. I speak as I find, me.'

Gore could see Lindy Clark, hovering behind Susannah, desirous of a moment, her coat zipped, her son tugging her towards the outdoors. He saw his sister's dissatisfaction, too, in not enjoying one hundred per cent of the available attention.

'Hello, Lindy, hi there, Jake. This is my sister Susannah.'

'Hiya.'

'Was that useful today?'

'Canny enough. Has anybody said owt about the crèche?'

'They haven't. Not yet . . .'

She sighed. 'And I thought I'd be seeing you again. At ours?' Gore detected the flicker of Susannah's eyebrows. 'Weren't you gunna come round to do them shelves and that? I don't mind, I can get 'em done for us nee bother, but they need doing and you said you would, so . . .'

His sister, he knew, was unabashedly weighing Lindy in the balance. He couldn't imagine how she might score, but he worried – for the puffa jacket, the vivid cosmetics, the little boy wrapped around her legs and fishing down the back of his trousers. He was not sure that Lindy herself would care more than a speck – until he saw her eyes flit sharply in Susannah's direction. Susannah, though, was glancing repeatedly between her slender silvery wristwatch and the exit.

'Look, I can't stop, John, but I'll call you, okay?'

'You haven't got my number.'

'It's in this from when you called me.' Impatiently she flashed a mobile phone lodged in her palm like a gemstone, waved at him, then turned in a swirl of dark coat-tail and was gone.

'Lindy, yes, I know, I'm sorry. Can it wait until next Saturday?'

'I suppose. Aye, fine. That's a date then? Come for around three-ish and I'll give you your tea.'

'Okay. Saturday then.'

'Aye, right.' Lindy smiled fleetingly at him, then she too was being yanked in the outward direction.

He was feeling perplexed, somewhat dispensed with, as Kully Gates stepped forward, her hands slotted demurely in the pockets of her multicoloured cardigan, her caramel hair plastered in wet-look waves.

'Yes, well done then, John. For getting started. You're quite a *talker*.'

Gore was unsure if he was on the horns of another teasing. This odd little woman's whole face seemed to stretch with her broad piano-key smile, but behind chic little slot-like spectacles her almond eyes had a patronising cast. 'Yes, but I must say, I am a little *disappointed* in you.'

'What have I done?'

'What have you *not* done? What about all we talked about at your meeting? What use are you making?'

'Kully, you can see my congregation. It's toddlers and pensioners.'

'You have to *make* it. You don't just go to work on a Sunday, do you? Now, come on. I have an *invitation* for you. What are you doing now? Are you busy?'

'*Right* now?'

'Within the hour. I have my drop-in at the youth centre. Crossman Estate.'

Gore could picture that squat, menacing seventies build, snug to the Gunnery pub, a pile of damp breezeblocks and rusty wire mesh.

'I do a *counselling* session every Sunday, free advice. For the ones excluded from school, mainly. We have Cokes and burgers, yes? So you could come with me? Have a burger. Give a little advice, perhaps?'

'Advice on what?'

'Oh, I don't know, John, maybe drugs? Sexual health?'

Gore put a hand to his brow, trying to massage forth an excuse.

'I'm *joking*, John. Come on. What do you say?'

They walked together out into St Luke's car park, where the day's Coulson-appointed labourer was trying single-handedly to reload the pool table into the back of the transit, wrestling with one tilted end from ground level. Gore recognised him as the affable young dullard from Middlesbrough he had met on that first useful night in the Gunnery.

'Alright there, Smoggie?' Gore called out cheerily as he and Kully passed. The lad straightened, bore the weight of the table awhile, serving up a hard look in return.

'Me name's Robbie, pal.'

The truculence surprised Gore, chastened him somewhat. He paused. 'Sorry, Robbie. That's a tough job you're taking on solo. Can I help?'

'Aw, I doubt that, man. Can't see it, nah.'

Gore was tending by degrees to the sense that he was being oddly and actively slighted. 'Sorry, do you – have you got a problem with me, Robbie?'

'I might do.'

'Well, so you know, I don't actually want any help that's not freely given.'

Robbie snorted out a laugh and turned back to his Sisyphean task. Gore had begun to feel this determined oddness rousing his hackles.

'That's funny, is it?'

'Not so very, no' was thrown back over the lad's hefty straining shoulder.

'Striking, the art,' he murmured to Kully, hoping he sounded approving.

'Better they do it here than out of doors and get arrested.'

Murals in metallic spray paint adorned all four walls of the Centre – cartoon caricatures of scowling pint-sized hoodlums in outlandishly baggy pants and wraparound shades, carrot-like reefers jutting from their lips, some toting Russian assault rifles. Incomprehensible slogans and legends were marked up in bold jagged characters, filled with mists of colour. Still, this was a gloomy shed, rank with the reek of the toilet cubicle by the door: in the circumstance, graffiti were not so very unsightly.

He and Kully sat abreast behind a short table, government-issue leaflets fanned out across its surface, a hot seat opposite currently occupied by diminutive Cliffy, of whom Kully could not seem to get rid, such were his woes. He was pale and freckled, his small eyes wary, a gap between two buck teeth, his sandy hair so thin it already seemed to be receding.

'They just take the piss out of wuh,' he was complaining. 'Doon the Job Centre. Me writin' and that . . .'

I hear you, thought Gore. Like a child new to school he had feared he might be the butt of sniggers. But no one was paying him much mind. He surveyed the dozen or so adolescents loitering with little obvious intent. One pair hunched over a computer that had been dragged from cold storage and set on a shaky table. Through a built partition, a pool table and dartboard were the locus of some rowdier activity. But the chief lures were three moulting sofas shoved into a C-shape. A mixed group sat and smoked, lads with their chins in their hands, girls with their hair harshly scraped back. The wardrobe was all sportswear, firehouse red or aqua blue or canary yellow, yet its wearers looked anaemic. Over chugga-chugga music from someone's improbably toaster-sized tape-player they conversed sporadically in a braying argot, thick and complicit. *Is this how you'd talk to adults*, Gore wondered? *At school? Or work?*

Such energy as there was seemed to emanate from that games room – the clack of balls, vying cries. Gore stood, politely forsook Cliffy and Kully, and wandered through the doorway. Instantly he knew the boy bent over his baize – the hooked nose in profile, the plump and ruddy face, the close-cut hair. Mackers it was, straightening and chewing his inner cheeks. Gore had no trouble imagining him ten years hence, planted on a pub stool, caked in drying plaster, sneaking a lunchtime pint with the lads. Mackers's opponent – cigarette in mouth, his sweatshirt reading **Notorious** – punched him on the arm in passing and settled down to his own shot. Yes, Gore knew this one too. Though his face – sullen, hollow-cheeked but handsome – was newly marked by a blackened eye and a two-inch gash over one eyebrow, extravagantly close to a scar, his narrow eyes were memorably hostile. It was the bloke from whom he had endeavoured to rescue young Cheryl what's-her-name some weeks ago on Scoular. If they had yet noticed Gore, they were ignoring him determinedly, and so he stepped closer.

'Aye aye. Remember me?'

Grey eyes deigned to him. 'Aye . . .'

'Mackers, right? I'm John. C'mon, we've met.'

'Might've done.'

'Yeah, and I've met this one and all.'

Notorious spun his cue in one hand. 'The fuck *yee* deein' here?'

'Well, I was invited.'

'Not by me.'

'Pack it in Jason, man.'

Gore gestured to the table and to Mackers. 'Fancy a game?'

'It's winner stays on, man,' Jason retorted.

'I'll play you then.'

Mackers shrugged, handed Gore his cue and left the room. The subsequent contest was brief. Gore did not presume himself a player, but nonetheless endured near-constant verbal gamesmanship. 'Ahhh! You're *shit*, man.' Six of Gore's red balls were yet afloat as Jason drilled home the winning black and pushed out past him.

Back in the main room Kully had joined the congregants on the sofas. A low-key symposium looked to be in progress. Gore squeezed onto the end of a chair-arm and accepted a glass of Coca-Cola. Kully gestured as if to draw him in. 'Reverend, we were just talking about the *riot* last summer.'

'Call me John. There was a riot?'

'Aye, it were magic,' said a girl with eyes like a low fever.

'Best thing ever happened round here, man,' a boy said, leaning back emphatically as if to invite dissent, or rival nominations.

'What happened, John,' said Kully, 'the police chased a joy-rider into the Blake Estate, and it all turned into a bit of a stand-off.'

Mackers seemed offended. 'Aye, cos the fella ran off and left the car, but the coppaz went knocking on doors like we wuz all of us hiding him. So they get telt to piss off and do summat useful. It was them what started the bother. Cos of that.'

'Aye,' someone seconded. 'They lash into ya for nowt.'

'Some people said they'd been a bit harassed,' Kully nodded. 'And one or two *missiles* got thrown at the police and next thing –'

'Coppers are *cunts*, man, bunch of *fucken cunts*.' This was Jason, muttering into his chest, though clearly for the attention of the group.

Gore winced. 'Come on with that language.'

Jason's head snapped up at him. 'Shut yer mouth, man. What the fuck? How ya *want* us to talk, like? Like me'sel or how *you* want us?'

'I'd like you to talk to me the way you'd want me to talk to you.'

'Ah divvint *care* how yee talk to wuh.'

'You'd want me to show some sort of respect.'

'Why should ah respect you?'

'Why should I respect *you*? "Notorious"? Because of your brilliant fashion sense?' The resultant sniggers, Gore sensed, were on his side. 'Look, I don't expect you to like the police. I'm interested in your view. But that language – it's hard to hear. And among women, you know? And I think you knew when you said it that I would find it so, right? But you said it anyway.'

Jason snorted and stared at him in silence – though he was tapping his foot to the floor with a manic intensity.

'So, yes, we were saying – why you dislike the police.'

'You heard. Even them uns are al'reet, they come round, aye? Act like you're mates 'n' all. Then summat gans off and they steam into you like *bastads*.'

Gore nodded.

'Is "bastads" alreet for ya, then?'

Gore sniffed. 'Yeah, fine, I know a few bastards.'

A few more chuckles, not from Jason. Gore looked to the group about him. 'What do you think about Hoxheath, then? As a place to live?'

'It's ballocks,' said a girl, sadly.

Cliffy chipped in. 'I'm bored shitless, me. There's nowt tuh dee.'

'Nothing to do?'

'Thas what ah said. Do ah stutter, *fool*?'

Gore blinked in surprise, for the half-pint boy had half-risen from his seat to spit the last word with maximum derision. He earned the best laugh of the afternoon. Gore bit his lip. 'No, what I mean is, is there *absolutely* nothing to do?' He looked to Kully but she was staring absently to the window. 'What sort of work would you *like* to do? If you had your pick? What sort of jobs do people you know do?'

'*Bin* man, *bin* man,' intoned Jason, amusing himself.

'I knaa what *I'm* gunna do,' Cliffy piped. 'Gunna work for Big Steve, me.'

For his pains, a torrent of jeering abuse. 'Not in a million *years*, man.'

'You gotta be *rock* to work for Big Steve.' This was grey-eyed Mackers, as if he had now seen it all.

The complicit air in the room bumped the needle of Gore's curiosity. 'Stevie Coulson? Why do you want to work for him?'

'The big man, in't he?' Cliffy scowled. 'Original gangsta.'

'Coulson's a bastad an' all,' Jason muttered, seemingly heartfelt. 'He wants workin' on.'

By who? thought Gore. *You? And whose Panzer division?* 'You know Stevie does a spot of work for me? At my church?'

The youths seemed to try very determinedly to remain doleful and unimpressed. But Kully was attentive to him again. 'Yes, John, what about your *church*? Would you say a little?'

'Oh. Sure. Well. I have a church service on Sunday at St Luke's School. It's just . . . really it's a place to come along and hang out. Be together like this. And talk a little about how we might make things better. No pressure from me, you know? I won't look out for you, I mean. But you'd be very welcome. I'd appreciate it. And if I can ever be of any help to any of you then . . . you know where to find me.'

There, he thought, *you can't say that's not friendly*. And he slapped his palms upon his thighs. 'Well, I need to be off, thanks for your time.'

'Me and all,' declared Mackers. 'Nee rest for the workin' man.' Gore noted that Mackers' alleged friend Jason, now recumbent and toying with the bunched hair of one reluctant girl, was goading him with a masturbatory jerk of his wrist.

Kully followed Gore to the door, and together they saw Mackers zip up his coat, don a helmet and mount a moped, its delivery pillion box decorated in the Italian tricolour and emblazoned BARZINI'S PIZZA/PASTA. Kully shook his hand, her smile still pitying. 'John, John – you've got to sell yourself better. "I'd *appreciate* it." Really.'

Gore shrugged. 'This was useful, thanks. I just don't think they have much use for me.'

'Oh rubbish. Now I will call you, yes?'

'By all means,' he murmured, vaguely amused by her rhino hide. Then he was striding free down the concrete ramp to the gravel parking lot. Then suddenly he was slipping and skittering and nearly falling face first. *Not fucking dog shit, not again*. He hastily inspected his sole, glanced back to Kully – for once, a picture of embarrassment – and heard the laughter of a few lads jabbing jeering fingers at a burst condom and a snail trail of leavings smeared down the ramp.

'*Urgh* man, look. A *dobber*, a used dobber . . .'

'They need men in their lives,' announced Jack Ridley. '*That's* what.' Had he banged upon his placemat with the hub of his stout table-knife, he could not have seemed more emphatic.

They sat as six in the reception of Monica's tidy home in Gosforth – Gore, Jack and Meg Ridley, Monica, husband Stan and their daughter Janet, a quiet dark girl in her twenties. Gore had been recounting his impressions of the Youth Centre for only a few moments, in the course of which Monica had borne to table a stupendous shepherd's pie, its raked and fissured crust bubbling in a dish the size of a paving slab. It smelled wondrous to Gore, and his appetite for conversation receded. Yet Ridley was wrangling him from across the table.

'And this *Indian* girl was the only one in charge? How is it the only ones trying to put any sense into these young men are women?'

'They're not *all* women.'

'Whey, charity and social services and that . . . all a lot of fussy women.'

'Jack, you'll get a clout off Monica if you don't mind your tongue.'

Meg Ridley was silver-haired and ruddy-cheeked and rather handsome, like the wife of a well-heeled Scottish hill farmer, the homely fragrance of the Geordie hearth about her.

'Well, Jack' – Monica made a face – 'I can tell you, there's always vacancies in them sorts of jobs. If any fellas could be bothered. The money's poor, mind, and it's only women's work, so they get stick off their mates.'

'I'm not talking about them jobs. I'm talking about how they've not got fathers, these lads. That's what they need. Set a good example and they'll follow it, sharpish.'

'Like you and our Luke,' murmured Meg, and Ridley glowered at his wife.

Gore decided to capitalise on the injured silence. 'I don't believe all these boys are from broken homes.'

'Oh, some'll have dads but they'll be dead losses and all, I'll bet. The majority won't, but. "One-parent households", eh? I'll bet you any money. That's why we're overrun. Two so-called parents, two nice flats, two lots of benefit . . .'

Gore looked for someone else to intervene, but no one did. Meg looked merely indulgent. They chewed in silence for a moment. Gore was weighing up the potential size of his second helping before he realised that Monica had her eye on him. 'Oh, but John's a big fan of the single mam.'

Meaning what? He set down his cutlery. 'I agree, life would be better if everybody got raised by two happy parents, but I don't think it's essential. Clearly there are kids who get by. With just a mother, say.'

'"Get by",' Jack growled. 'They shouldn't have to "get by".'

'Well, that's just life, couples can't always stay together. It's not a curse falls on the kids' heads.'

'So why are they sitting around, dead losses, not in school, not in work? If you had kids of your own, John, I tell you now, you wouldn't stand to watch 'em piddle their lives away. You'd give 'em a kick up the arse. Well, I say that, maybe you wouldn't, maybe you'd just let 'em run amok.'

The evening was starting to oppress Gore, its mood recalling him to childhood subjection. 'Some of these lads, Jack, they've not got a chance.'

'Why not?'

'Because they're poor. Just that. They get looked down on.'

'Poor, get away. You're dreaming, aren't you? Being poor is having *nowt*. *My* dad's life.'

'Poverty's relative. If you've got so much less than everyone else, you still feel it. The stigma of it.'

'Aw, so that's why they lie around all day, is it? Life's not fair?'

'Well, it's a fact that it's not fair –'

'And what are you going to do about it?'

Gore's mouth stayed closed, his mind yawning wide, suspended helplessly over his own inadequate store of ideas. *Love each other or die?*

'It's the drugs, really, I think.' Janet, so quiet and attentive all evening, was risking an opinion. 'The drugs make them awfully shiftless. They cause most of the crimes too . . . I know what you'll say, Jack, they shouldn't be taking them. And you're right. But I think it's hard.'

'Hard. They want it given to them hard, that's what they want.'

'By who?' Gore rallied. 'The police?'

'Police, no. No policing will ever get it back to how it was in my day, never mind what power you give 'em. It's not *down* to the police, man. It's the *society*. The adults. It starts with the mams and dads, and it bloody well goes to the teachers and the vicars and all.'

'At least John's not afraid to get his hands dirty.' Gore looked up at Janet in gratified surprise. 'It's a fine thing you're doing here.'

Over dessert, a charred and deep-sided rice pudding, Gore felt Monica attempting to draw him further into dialogue with her daughter. It was true that she had read English at Edinburgh, that she now worked for British Telecom, that she indicated a willingness to assist at St Luke's. The problem, frankly, was that she was the image of her mother. It was Janet who escorted Gore and the Ridleys to the door. Jack seemed not to want to talk or even look at John, but Meg smiled faintly and touched his arm.

'I think you might have been offered more than your dinner there.'

Gore gave her a wan smile. He was aware that had he ever found it so easy to manufacture sexual/romantic feeling then he could have been yet marooned in Dorset with Jessie Bradbeer, stepfather to a pair of bespectacled buck-toothed boys. As to Janet's offer of help – well, help was not help unless given freely. This principle Gore felt sure he applied to all things equally. And whatever were Stevie Coulson's flaws, he was not, as far as Gore could see, sizing him up for a shotgun wedding.

Chapter V

THE MYSTERIES

Saturday, 26 October 1996

His finger hovered over the doorbell. Was it really such an irrevocable act? Hardly. And so he pressed. No sound was discernible within. He pressed again, but silence endured. One more piece of needful repair? He knocked, then rapped at the glass, awaiting vital signs. Perhaps he had botched his timing – early, for a change – just a shade after two of a Saturday, time for shopping or lunch or whatever were the weekend's perks.

He was clad in mufti, a seaman's coat of navy-blue wool over a loose tee-shirt and jeans, and he was touting a hand-sorted box of tools he thought fit to accomplish the various tasks for which he had volunteered – hammer, drill and bits, assorted screws and screwdrivers, a full set of Allen keys.

At last he heard footfalls and the door was flung wide by Lindy Clark, Jake hoisted up awkwardly in her arms.

'Hello there. Well, look who's come knocking, eh?'

Her face was bare of its usual slap, and for the first time Gore saw the freckles dotting her nose and cheeks. At last, the secret of her addiction to liquid foundation. *Irish,* he thought. Had she once been a redhead? She wore a fatigued white tee-shirt and tracksuit bottoms; warmth and bed-smell emanated from her. As she stooped and set down her squirming son, Gore saw once more the sharp-tongued snake at the base of her spine. That snake, that sceptical curl of the lip, that knowing youth of hers . . . all things that made Gore shrivel inwardly, deem as daft some of the idle thoughts he had been entertaining. And yet her door was open, he was bade welcome.

*

On his knees in the boy's bedroom, methodical Gore cleared a space for work, slit the polystyrene round the box, dismembered the cardboard packaging, counted and set aside the panels, and turned a drawer out as a receptacle for assorted small bags of bolts. As he unfolded the instructions, Lindy looked in on him. Her face had been reinstated, black lashes and gleaming purplish lips.

'Is it all canny? Y'alright there?'

'Champion. I was wondering, but?'

'Aye?'

'Is your kettle broken?'

'Cheeky bugger. Hark at you.'

'Listen, I'll try and be quick, I won't keep him out for long.'

'Don't worry, he's got the match on the radio, he's happy. Your daddy's there, isn't he?' She was shouting down the hall. 'He'll maybe take you next time . . .' she muttered in a lower key.

Gore kicked on. For the next hour he diligently bolted uprights to boards before he realised, aghast, that he had set about the job back-to-front. With less patience and more grazing of his thumb he undid the original work and recommenced, whistling for his amusement, hearing occasional crescendos in the football commentary. When he had all but the last few screws to dispose of, he took a breather, hands on his crouching thighs, and peered from the window down the alley to where a kid was kicking pointlessly at a brick wall. Then he felt a sharp prod in his kidneys and almost jumped out of his skin.

Swivelling, he saw the familiar challenging pout. 'Oh, Jake. You gave us a start there, kidder.'

The boy wore shiny red foam-filled boxing gloves on his hands, and was proffering between them another matching but larger pair.

'Look at them, eh? What? You want to have a go with me?'

'Aye!'

'Oh, I see. Fancy a dust-up, do you? Bit of a pagga?'

'Aye!'

Gore slid a hand snugly into first one glove and then the other. He shifted his weight onto his knees and made a guard of his two bulging paws. Jake began to throw jabs, left and right, shuffling about in his stocking feet, first tentative, then with vigour. Gore took care to chortle and exclaim in surprise with each blow landed, for it was good fun – a perfectly safe and pleasurable pounding of glove upon glove. The boy too seemed to be relishing it, though he looked terribly intent, not quite smiling, his backside bulging out of his tracksuit trousers as he bobbed and weaved.

Gore blocked again, then popped a weightless jab to the child's belly.

'Gotcha. Left yourself open there, eh?'

Lindy nudged through the doorway with the tea tray, and she was frowning.

'Oh, sorry,' Gore exclaimed. 'Is this alright?' Then he felt a clout to his chin that made his teeth rattle.

'Eee Jake, man!'

Gore knew he had bitten his tongue, but he resolved to tough it out, and made a pantomime of seeing stars, listing over onto the carpet.

Daylight was fading as he wielded the cordless drill to secure the shelf unit to the bedroom wall. He heard the front door rapped, and voices below – Auntie Yvonne, it seemed, taking Jake into her care for the evening. Gore felt something turn over in his stomach, like appetite, or apprehension. Some minutes later Lindy came to the threshold again with a corkscrew.

'So, handyman, will you have a glass of wine with us? For your trouble.'

Downstairs the two of them sank deep into Lindy's faux-leather sofa, nursing their drinks. Gore was tired, but not so much so as to make his excuses and leave. He glanced about him in the quiet. 'Funny, isn't it? These estates, how uniform it all is. Your place and mine, they're the exact same layout.'

'Keep your place nice, do you? Bachelor pad?'

'I wish.'

'You're not, are you? With anybody. Not married, I mean, are you?'

'No, no. Married to the Church.' He offered a small smile.

'Aren't you meant to have a little woman, but? To do all the woman's things . . .?'

'You mean a housekeeper?'

'Nah, I mean a wife. Your lot are allowed to get married, aren't you's?'

'Oh yeah. There's no – injunction, from above. None whatsoever.'

'So you're free to be with whoever you like.'

Gore smiled softly into his chest. If she wished for his company this evening, he decided, she would have to indulge his odd mood.

'What's funny 'bout that, like?'

'Not funny, just a – oh, a feeling of mine. See, I don't think anyone's ever really *free*. In that department? It's more complex. For being mutual. I mean, you can't just choose who you want, can you?'

'Dunno. I've mostly felt like I've had me pick. Within *reason*, like. I've stopped thinking Liam Neeson's gunna gan out wi' us.'

'Who?'

'Liam Neeson? Actor in the films? Irish. Dead sexy. Big hands.'

'Oh, him,' said Gore, none the wiser.

'Any road, but. You're a nice big lad. You could have your pick and all.'

'Oh, that *is* funny. No. Nice of you to say. But it's never worked out. It's a funny sort of job I do.'

'There's funnier, I can tell you. Least a lass would know where she was with a vicar. I mean, you're kind. You're a decent sort . . .' She put her hand on his arm, he felt a light squeeze of her fingertips.

'Oh, well, you see, now you're talking to me like I'm a bit of a *mong*.'

Lindy looked authentically hurt. Gore recalibrated. 'Sorry, no – I mean, look, the way I see it, to be honest – you talk about choice? See, I'm not sure the choice isn't made for us, in a way. When two people . . . get together. I do just think there's – just a bit of an element of the preordained to it.' Her brow was still furrowed. Gore knew very well what he was thinking and decided to say it, as mad as it sounded – indeed because it was mad. 'A good man I used to know would say, "God will have a partner for you." And that's a very powerful idea.'

'Say again? "*God* will have a partner . . ."?'

'God will – gravitate you to someone. And that someone toward you. Because it was meant to be so. In the beginning, before you ever came to be. I just – I *do* think our lives are fated, somehow. They *have* to be. People *present* themselves to you. And it makes sense. It's like this guy Coulson at my church. It's too bizarre otherwise. So I have to trust in it.'

She was looking perplexedly at him. The wonder-working power he felt in the words, the fantasy in which he could almost believe, did not, seemingly, stir quite so much in Lindy. It was hardly a surprise. 'Well, any road. I expect that all sounds a very sort of airy-fairy . . . *religious* way to look at it.'

'No, no. It's – romantic.' Still, she was knitting her brow. 'What about sex, but? While you're waiting, y'knaa? For God to get you's together. Cos you'd have to wait a canny bit, right? It's not going to land on a plate.'

'I suppose. You have to – kiss a few frogs.'

Lindy seemed suddenly most invested in this discussion. 'I mean, people shouldn't go without. Should they? Without sex?'

Gore shrugged.

'It's one of the good things, isn't it? We wouldn't have it if we weren't meant to like it.'

'No. But the Church says, and I believe, it has to be in a loving relationship. Anything else is . . . disturbing, I feel. The meaningfulness of the . . . two people coming together, reduced to a sort of a . . . just a physical spasm.'

She made a face. 'Quick squirt, you mean? Aye, right, that does sound shit.'

He shifted. 'I'm sorry, Lindy. This is a bit of an adult conversation.'

'You're kidding, aren't you? Feels like I'm back at school. Talking about the birds and the bees . . .' She peered at him, mouth wry. He could see her point, and it pressed acutely into his ribs, making him unsure as to whether she was mocking him or else exhorting him toward a declaration of why he was still here, on her sofa, drinking her wine. Or perhaps she was merely running down the clock before her favourite TV show. He found that he didn't want to decide what were his own feelings, and thus he took the simpler, well-trusted option of pretending that nothing was so very serious.

'I know, I know. You're right. I do have some half-baked ideas. You'd think one of these days I'd grow out of them.' He stood, collected the glasses and carried them to the kitchen, set them in the sink, absently found himself refilling the kettle. Always, he knew, it was easier, far easier, to disengage, drift free. He sensed her behind him but did not turn. She dallied closer.

'I'm sorry, Lindy,' he heard himself say.

'It's me sorry. What are you sorry for?'

'Being what I am.'

He felt her arms slip around his waist, saw her hands clasp in front.

'I really like you, but, John. I really do.'

She pressed her face into his back.

'I like you, Lindy,' he murmured.

He took her hands into his and turned them, felt them squeeze, felt and heeded the firm impress that seemed to be saying: be quiet. He turned and she was smiling. He folded her into him, the warmth of her body pliable and cat-like, and he kneaded her, feeling her strain and stretch as they inclined to one another and kissed. As he tasted her perfumed lipstick a deliciousness flooded through him. In this cold kitchen he could feel blood in circulation again, a well-reckoned but long-suppressed uncoiling of desire. Her lips were up at his ear. 'Do you want to go upstairs? Lie down?'

He took her hand and she led him up and across the landing into her bedroom – perhaps fifteen feet by ten, scent in the air, clothes on the floor or hung upon a free-standing rail, russet cotton curtains leaking light onto a carelessly made bed, an ivory duvet fringed with small frills. Lindy perched on the edge of the mattress and yanked off her tee-shirt. He hastily removed his own tee-shirt and emerged to be faced by the hollow of her shaven underarm as she reached behind her back and unclasped a sensible white bra. She bunched the hems of her track-pants and knickers and peeled them down, baring a coppery delta. Gore glanced aside, to the MFI drawers, the bedside table bare but for a lone spent cigarette in an ashtray. And to the framed film poster on the wall, the chiselled features of a male lead. Was this Liam Neeson, he of the big hands?

Then she was unbuckling his belt, unstudding his jeans, drawing them down. He kicked them free of his ankles, slid down, over and on top of her, and they kissed. They lay a while in the gloom, he cupping her face in his hands, she grinning up at him.

'Lindy, I don't have any protection.'

'We'll not make a baby, divvint worry.' She stretched to kiss his mouth, then wriggled aside and reached to his groin. For a sick moment he feared for the stoutness and preparedness of his erection. Some feather-light touches of her fingers dispelled that doubt. Then she steered him inside her, their crotches met, and he began to thrust with all the *tendresse* as he could muster given his entire being was clenched in white-hot concentration. He was lumbering, he knew – short of practice, eager to please. But Lindy was still smiling, and keenly groaning in time, exhibiting – at least it seemed – one hundred per cent of her own capacity for excitation. He had found his rhythm – a gamut of sensations long forgotten – and she appeared keenly abreast of her own, indeed some way ahead of his. Assured that he might also start to enjoy himself, he made his thrusts short and uninhibited, then the stone in his groin dissolved into hers and he slumped to rest on his elbows above her, breast to breast. He withdrew carefully and rolled aside, but she reached and stroked him, idly, trailed fingers across his mons pubis. And so he laid a careful hand in kind upon her. *The precious things of the earth and the fullness thereof* was the thought that struck him, and he wanted to laugh, already short of breath and mildly elated.

*

Lindy reclined on her pillows, taking short draws on a Benson & Hedges, one arm strewn around Gore's neck where she idly stroked and tweaked the short hairs there. He was conscious, disconcerted even, that he lay in the position traditionally occupied by the female at such moments.

'Ahhh,' she exhaled. 'A tab and a big man in wuh bed. If I just had a brew and a bit toast I'd be in heaven.'

'Shall I – would you like me to make that for you?'

'Aw, would you?'

'Of course.'

'You're the best. Masses of butter on the toast, aye?'

Gore shucked off the mattress, extricating his shorts from his tangled jeans, and padded down barefoot to the kitchen, where he prepared the simple repast. Lindy supped and munched keenly. *She's so physical,* he mused, before biting into a slice himself and realising he was ravenous. They snuggled down in the duvet, profile to profile.

'Are y'alright?'

'I'm good, yeah, thanks.'

'You're funny, you are.'

'Funny how?'

'You had us worried a bit. Wasn't quite sure we were gunna get there, y'knaa what I mean?'

'I know. Sorry.'

'Well, we managed.' Her fingers turned around in his sparse chest hair. 'It's alright, you know? To say what you're after. And you were so keen, but, to give us a hand? I knew then, see. That you liked us.'

Gore smiled, inwardly disquieted. Here they were, snug lovers, her sharp tongue now rolled up as she replayed the highlights of the seduction, like instant lore, the story of a romance. *Was* this a romance? He remained, he knew, just a little in shock.

He excused himself and wandered down the hallway to her bathroom, tidy doppelgänger of his own. There he showered hastily and dried himself with her sole bath sheet. He had stepped lightly halfway down the stairs when he saw Lindy, in knickers and a short kimono, scrambling eggs at the kitchen hob, singing off-key snatches of a pop tune. '*But any fool can see they're fallin' . . .*'

He padded back into her bedroom, and there peered more closely at her knick-knacks on the dresser drawers. A couple of framed photos, one of Jake in an unlikely convulsion of giggles, the other of Lindy in monochrome, perhaps six or seven years younger and rather gravely doe-eyed and lovely, her hair cut in a feathery bob. Looking closer, he realised the image had been trimmed out of a magazine.

Around the photos were snaking piles of trinkets, an ashtray like a swan, a pair of gonks, a fat envelope bulging as if with banknotes, and a portable music player flanked by small piles of CDs, the artists all surly, handsome and dark-skinned. He prised open one drawer – full of folded and slightly faded tee-shirts and little tops. The second was all bras and knickers. Her best frocks were suspended on the crowded clothes rail, mixed with skirts, jeans, coats – nothing fancy or startling, save for a short black leather dress which, Gore had to concede, looked sexy. Tucked behind the rail amid a pile of odd shoes was an orange Adidas hold-all, a gym bag, a sniff of testosterone in this otherwise girly haven. Idly Gore reached for the handles, and found the bag heavy as a pair of bowling balls. Curious, he tugged the zip but it snagged, no more than half-exposing a thickly wadded towel. Then he heard a mounting tread on the stairs, and dived for the bedcovers.

At twelve after six they were still abed, watching *Blind Date* in a fuzzy image on her portable television. She snuggled into his chest. Sipping another tea, Gore was starting to feel tolerably hefty and masculine – at least a plausible imitation of the same, he thought, were his picture to be taken in the act. Not something for the church newsletter, admittedly, nor any of his recent media outlets. 'The vicar among the people.' Just another Saturday night for some, a determinedly strange one for himself. *Blind Date* was followed by *Gladiators*, muscle-bound members of the public in athletic contest with pro-bodybuilders. Few of the professionals, he decided, had anything like the forbidding brawn of Steve Coulson and team. He couldn't picture any of *them* in coloured spandex, snarling and clawing the air. A chuckle escaped him. 'Dear me. What posers.'

'Say that to their faces, would you?' Lindy murmured. 'I know you're big and all, but I divvint reckon you'd last in the ring, pet.'

It was perhaps the minor disparagement that told Gore it was past time that he be elsewhere. The feeling grew swiftly and acquired a solidity, the urge to be gone much more resolute than his earlier decision to linger.

'Lindy, I'm sorry but I'm going to have to push off.'

She only looked at him, in some dubiety.

'Tomorrow's Sunday. I'm afraid I've a fair bit to get done.'

'What, have you got a *sermon* to write or summat?'

'I do, actually . . .'

He dressed quickly, as Lindy seemed to remain absorbed in her show. But once he was buttoned up, she sighed. 'Off you go then, thief in the night . . .'

She fastened herself once more into the kimino and led him flouncingly down the stairs. He simply couldn't decide whether or not she was joking. By the door he embraced her, kissed her lips, but felt her withdraw from him first. He measured what should be the parting words. She intervened.

'See you tomorrow then?'

'Are you – won't you be busy?'

'I'll see you at your service.'

'You'll be there? Great.'

'I'll be there. And I'll maybe see you in the week? Maybe do something?'

'Yes, let's.'

She gave him that wry smile. What was she thinking? Gore could not tell, and had no time to weigh it any further. He strode off into the darkness. The evening was crisply cold – he could feel it, most unusually, in his thighs. He spun round at the end of the alley, so as to wave, and found that Lindy had not dallied at the door.

Chapter VI

AN ENCROACHMENT

Saturday, 26 October 1996

'No. No, I'm not best pleased, fellas.'

Stevie looked from Roy – his mien, indeed his whole posture, lugubrious and troubled – to the sludgy heaps of newly tilled earth stretching out for an acre beyond the Maginot Line of the rear fence. They had dawdled a hundred yards from Roy's house, down the full length of the damp landscaped lawn, to this lonely end of the garden shrouded by towering pines, sweet sharp scent in the air, needles crinkling underfoot. It was quiet, unnaturally so. In days gone by, on little strolls of lesser purpose, Roy would tote his shotgun along with him, loose an occasional shell into the air. Not today. For starters he wanted Stevie and Shack to observe this, the ominous ugliness of a soon-to-be new neighbour.

'It used to be an old tip, as I heard. I thought, "Who'd want it?" Didn't think they could ever build. Stupid of me. Prices round here.'

'Did your lawyer not pick it up, like?'

'Aw, probably did. He's good. I just wasn't too fixed on the particulars. See, that's how things slip into the shit.'

Roy shrugged. And Stevie could see him shouldering the burden of matters grave and regrettable, if perhaps ultimately manageable. But Roy wasn't quite the bolshy force in the camel-coat that he used to be. Shack, by contrast – on this his first outing to Darras Hall – seemed brimful of frustration, a bridling lieutenant waiting permission to report. Stevie, for his part, was feeling the cold of the dwindling afternoon, wanting to be elsewhere – another city, another calling, another set of associates.

'Least you've got them trees,' he offered. 'Tall, like. Natural barrier.'

Roy scoffed. 'I doubt I'll ever see the birds in them again. Not once this fucker's a proper building site. No. You can't stop people doing whatever they bloody like if they set their little minds to it – throw enough money at it. As for that fucking Morpeth Council . . . some arsehole's getting paid for this, you can bet. Aye, well.' He sighed heavily. 'If this were the sum of our woes we'd call ourselves happy.'

For the first time that day Stevie saw Roy give Shack the full glare of his foglights. 'So what did the polis say then, Shack? About Teflon?'

'Aw, it was arson, for sure, Roy. They only got in as far as the lobby, then they just dumped a bloody great petrol can. Lit it and ran off. Police reckon it was between three and half-past in the morning.'

Roy blew out his cheeks. 'Christ. Good job somebody talked us into putting all that fucking steel in the foyer. The old velvet would've burned until Christmas. A petrol can, but. Dog-shit way to go about it.'

'Dog shit's about what they're like,' Shack muttered. 'The state of them gadgies come into the Gunnery that night.'

Roy was pensive. 'Aye. Aye. So that was the start of all this, right?'

Steve worried a pile of needles with the cap of his boot. 'Only if you reckon all this is cos of Skinner. Not them Codys.'

'Whey of course it's bliddy Skinner, Stevie man,' Shack snapped.

Roy was switching his gaze back and forth between them. 'You've not had so much bother before, no? Not at Teflon?'

'We've had plenty,' said Shack evenly.

Stevie rounded on him. 'What was that, like?'

'You've not always been looking, Stevie, so you've not been seeing it. If some radgy Manc tells us I'm a dead man, I remember it.'

'So do you just tell us the half of what gans on then, Shack?'

'It's only the half what you listen to, Steve.'

Stevie felt himself knotting up all over his body. They had swung for each other twice before – once as mere lads, then a 'straightener' out the back of the pub Shack used to guard in Hebburn. They had shaken hands over a draw, though Shack had been on his knees at one stage. Round about now, though, it was starting to look like a rematch.

Roy slashed the air with his hand. 'Alright, for fuck's sake. Jesus. I shoulda dug ditches for a living. Like my old man. This is where we are, whether we like it or not. Let's not be dickheads about it.'

Stevie countered Shack's stare until Shack looked to his feet.

'Now, obviously, all this bother – the main slight is directed at me. But you might want to take it personally too, Stevie. People aren't meant to like you, right enough, but all this is pushing it. Who'd be giving the orders? Who's Skinner's man like you are for me? Is there one?'

'This bloke Crowley, I hear,' Shack said quietly. 'The one come in the Gunnery that time. The leader.'

'I put him in the General,' said Stevie.

'Aye, well, now he's out, so he must want putting back.'

'He wants putting in a fucking box is what he wants.' Roy's jowls were newly thunderous. 'We know that, don't we? No use tarting it up. They need a proper wind up 'em, that lot – blow 'em right the fuck back to Moss Side or wherever. No more than what they're giving you, Stevie.'

Shack nodded. 'Givin' all of us. Mickey, like. That was a fucking outrage.'

Stevie glared. 'It was me at his bloody funeral, neither of you's.'

'What's your point?' Roy had produced a cigar, and he jabbed it at Stevie. Stevie well knew that for Mickey he had no deep feeling, nothing much more than the shudder of disgust that such a ten-stone weakling should have been hacked into by a mob, left without a prayer. That was grievous. That was the sort to whose level they were getting lowered.

'Okay.' Roy winced. 'So here's *my* point. There's gotta be some comeback here, fast, or we look like cunts. That's not – it's not *sustainable*. Stevie, I'd have thought looking down a gun-barrel would have cleared your head. You're not just gonna give this guy a bollocking, right? Invite him out for a bit of the old Gentleman Jim?'

Stevie was silent, staring aside into the trees. Roy laid a hand on his arm and he could smell the Cohiba Robusto, like burning leather. 'Are you with us, Stevie? I'm saying it's just where we are. Daddy can't make it go away.'

The tone was anathema to Stevie. But Roy had a hold on him, his voice slipping down into a low burr. 'I can get it done for me, Steve. Someone'd do it for me. But it'd cost me twenty grand I can ill afford.'

Stevie glanced back to the formidable house, to Roy's Donna, worriedly vigilant on the patio, being tugged about by the leashed labrador. All bought and paid for. One didn't acquire such a castle, he knew, through an excess of sentiment. 'You'll be alright,' he murmured at last.

The burr, insistent. 'Steve, my money's not just there to piss into a river. What do I pay you for? Pay him? All your team?'

Stevie had never ever wanted to hear it phrased like so, like this – as if his livelihood were a mere handout, not his own diligent handiwork.

'See, I'm just as concerned about you, Steve, you know that.'

'Aw aye?'

'Aye. You've had a good run. Good years, you and me. But you might have run into a bit of a wall here, personally. That's what I'm seeing. You back away from this one, it'll still be you that'll end up paying for it.'

'He's right, Steve.' Shack had picked his moment. 'They're walkin' all over you, man. It goes on and where's your respect? That's what it's about.'

That word, bandied endlessly, emptily. Stevie's stomach was turned by it. And he had never heard such scant 'respect' from his deputy.

'Look, bollocks, I'll do it,' Shack was saying. 'I've done it. Nowt new to me.'

Roy's eyes evinced a new interest. Stevie shook his head sharply. It was Shack's stock Goose Green story, how as a private he had 'finished' some Argie, pumped bullets into his back and head as he tried to crawl off. Until now Stevie had thought Shack's fleeting Para career an unqualified boon, the likely root of his calm in the gale, his hundred-yard stare, his dependable presence at shoulder. But he didn't want any of that pitched against him now.

'It's my decision,' he muttered.

'But you're not *makin'* it, man. It's not just about you, see. They'll get after us and all – me, Simms, Dougie. They'll get onto your girls, your *bairns*. They're just giving you two fingers, man, they don't care.'

Roy nodded. 'Right enough. It's a what's-it. Gauntlet.'

'You need to get your head on straight, man. You've not got a *choice*. Divvint kid yourself. There's money out on you, right? We know that. Just cos one pair of numpties fuck it up – there'll be *teams* looking for you, man. Lawrie Skinner'll just pay out whenever he has to. Cos one of 'em'll manage. Even if they just get lucky.'

The weight was on him and before him, just as if he were lying recumbent beneath the four-hundred-pound bar, its oppression blindingly obvious. So why lift a finger? No, there was always a choice – always the option to leave it, rise up and walk, disappear. And was there a hole big enough, one where he would never again need to look at himself? Unable to say, he merely nodded.

'I'll have your back, y'knaa that,' said Shack – redundantly, by Stevie's reckoning, for today had seen sedition that would not be forgotten.

Chapter VII

A PROPOSITION

Sunday, 27 October 1996

Gore had imagined he might not sleep through into Sunday, such was the mazy nature of his thought that Saturday night. He had hardly undressed, though, before a concrete heaviness set on him and carried him under. When he awoke – sharply, from uneasy dreams – his telephone was trilling and his alarm clock, untouched from the night, told him it was five after nine. He hared from under the covers as if kicked. Monica Bruce was the perplexed caller. He inserted himself scratchily into his vestments and tore some sketchy notes from the printer.

Bursting through the doors of the school hall he found Ridley, stooped and laying prayer books onto seats. Mrs Boyle sat solo at her piano, seemingly discomfited. A short distance hence Steve Coulson and Brian Shackleton looked to be deadlocked in testy conference – Shack smoking, as was his wont, but Stevie, too, most unusually, puffing away in fidgeting draws. Gore hastened to Ridley's side. Wordlessly Jack transferred the pile of books into Gore's hands and lowered himself into a chair, producing his pipe and tobacco. 'If *them* uns are allowed then so am I.'

'Where's Susan Carrow, do you know?'

'I reckon she might be lodging a protest, that one. You might have lost her. Not best pleased, I don't think.'

'That's responsible of her. Shows real commitment.'

'Aye well, she's not paid for this, John. None of us are. 'Cept you.'

Gore decided there and then to quit Ridley's company. He wandered up to Stevie and Shack with a nod of the head.

'Stevie. How're you keeping?'

'Been worse, John.'

'Shack. How do.'

Shackleton grunted. The mood music was altogether discordant today.

'Aye aye, here he comes, Billy the Kid . . .'

Shack was looking past him and Gore turned to see Mackers striding down the hall toward them – the little working man, visibly straining to appear as pugnacious as sixteen years could permit.

'I didn't know you were pals?'

'Mackaz? Aw aye, he's rock hard, this man,' nodded Stevie. 'We's right then? Let's get shifted, bonny lad.'

And so Gore found himself alone with Shack, who stared fixedly aside, snorting, and sucked at his dog-end tab. Then he laughed, not pleasantly.

'Can't get over this, mind.'

'Sorry?'

'This. Here. It's just weird, isn't it? No *offence*, like.'

'None taken. I'm glad of your help.'

'Divvint thank us. It's Stevie, man. Soft touch, he is. Soft as clarts.'

'That's – well – not how I see him.'

'Whey, even you could walk over him if you wanted. Give it a bash.'

Shack tossed the butt to the lino and trod on it.

If the omens had been poor, the turnout was passable. As they groaned together through 'Rock of Ages', Gore head-counted forty-odd. A slight drop-off was probably inevitable. He had intended to get more dynamic this week. How had time beaten him again? Where had it gone?

He had not expected any of Kully's kids to appear and they had not – save, of course, for Mackers, who sat apart with Steve and Shack, chomping on gum, a raw maquette of the hard man he clearly desired to be, not so tough yet clearly seasoned. Lindy sashayed into the hall, in good time for once, minus her boy. *My sweetheart*, thought Gore.

His sermon was shreds and patches on the page, but he improvised, his chosen text the fifty-first Psalm, 'Create in me a clean heart, O God, and renew a right spirit within me.' He spoke disjointedly of fresh starts, clean slates, revelation and self-transformation, beginning in the bathroom mirror. Surveying his sedentary flock he knew, in his heart, that he was essentially pissing into a stiff wind, and might as well have recited the Hums of Pooh. Yet he stayed his course.

In the aftermath he had half-expected Jack Ridley to make himself scarce, and yet the stalwart came forward, cap in his hand, his bagged eyes yet more dolorous than usual.

'You should know, John – I can't be here for the Sundays nee more. Meg's been missing us for this and that. You'll manage, but, won't you?'

'I suppose. I'll be down to bare bones soon – you, Susan.'

'Well, you've got your extra hands. The heavy mob.'

Reflexively Gore rubbed at one eye-socket. 'Look . . . Jack, I do know your feelings, I'd just rather think you're not going off – I don't know, *vexed* at me.' No sooner said than Gore saw its wrongness in Ridley's obsidian eyes, knew that he sounded juvenile, an impenitent child persisting in folly.

'I'm not "vexed", John. It's your job. You make your choices, they're yours to make. Any road. I'll still see you at the meetings.'

'Well then, thank you.'

'Nee bother. Good luck to you. I'll help finish up here now.'

He put out his hand and Gore took it, accepting the resignation since he had no alternative. Then he studied the scuffed back of the olive-green car-coat as it retreated.

Lindy Clark was waving the fingers of one hand at him. Now seemed the moment to cross the hall, give his regards – a peck on the cheek? – if he could circumnavigate the stern Albert Robinson and friends. Then Stevie Coulson's broad back moved across and masked his sight of her, and her bright laugh carried across the hall. He felt something ever so oddly poignant clutching in his chest, and tried to discount it. Yet he also found himself rooted to the spot, a sensation of detachment building, his will receding like a rope ladder winding upward.

And then who could it be but his sister? She was striding toward him between the various huddles, poised as ever, if dressed down today – jeans and penny loafers, a white shirt, a loose linen jacket. She looked younger, friendlier. He kissed her cheek.

'No cameras today, Jonno?'

'I've maybe had my fifteen minutes.'

'Don't say that. We'll get you back in the limelight. So have you got time for me today, stranger?'

'What have you got in mind?'

'Oh, just a little chat would be useful.'

'We could go for a stroll?'

'I'm in the car.'

'I'd prefer a stroll.'

'Okay. Be like that then . . .'

Gore glanced over at Stevie and Lindy, still engaged in seemingly polite intercourse. 'Shall we?' he said, and hustled his sister toward the exit. No call or quick tread came after him.

They trudged through Hoxheath Park, sticking to the path, nothing much to look at in the grey autumn, though they looked about regardless. She took his arm. 'Is it all going as you want it then?'

'More or less. I suppose phase one's been accomplished.'

'Well, I must say, I'm impressed you've even got it off the ground.'

'I didn't do it alone. I've had some great help off people. People who've really gone out of their way for me.'

'That's people for you,' she shrugged. 'They like doing good turns. Makes 'em feel better about themselves.'

Oh God, thought Gore, *not again*. The Concise Susannah, her patented philosophy of the human heart as a customised engine for private consumption, fuelled by driving self-interest alone. There was no arguing with her. He was about his work now, she about hers, and he didn't intend to resume the hard lashing of a dead horse.

She broke the silence. 'Have you talked to Dad?'

'I saw him. He seemed alright. Offered to give us a hand.'

'Don't let him climb any ladders. Seriously.'

'And how's it with you? Your business?'

'Busy. It's a lot different now. Funny for me, after all the lobbying I did. Working with Marty so much, I do find I'm on the receiving end.'

'"Marty"?'

'That's his name. Don't sneer, kidder. No, it's got more interesting the more he's got on. Changing of the guard, see. I get calls off people who wouldn't give us the time of day before. Not when I started on my own. Old clients from Hook Millard, wanting to make a case. To who they think'll be the next lot in charge.'

'Because of Blair?'

'Aye. People are shy of saying so, which is weird. But, yeah, of course it's cos of Blair.'

'So what do you tell them?'

'To change their thinking. At least watch their language. I mean, see if I were repping Vickers Armstrong now? I'd be telling them to say they're into making *kinder, gentler* sorts of tanks.'

Gore scoffed, as he assumed by her smirk that she wished him to. They walked on.

'He's been asking after you, actually. Marty? Persistently, I have to say.'

'Asking what about me?'

'Well, he's heard about you now, obviously. Seen your stuff in the papers and that. Not on my account. But he's very curious.'

'And what have you told him?'

'That you're red-hot Labour. Hammer and sickle all through your spine. You are, still, aren't you?'

'I think I still pay my Party subs. Direct debit.' Gore picked up a gnarled stick, threw it aimlessly. 'I don't go to meetings. Haven't for an age.'

'Well, anyhow. The thing with Martin is, he wondered if the two of you couldn't maybe meet up sometime? Put your heads together?'

'About what?'

'I think he's after a bit fresh thinking on sort of *grass-roots* work? In the community. The whole "social exclusion" thing.'

'What on earth's that?'

'What you're doing. How to do good work with little groups of people, stuff that's new, different, forward-thinking. Getting people together for a good cause.'

'Suze, that's what we do in churches. We've done it for centuries. There's nothing new about it. It's nothing to do with politics either.'

Susannah shot him a scowl. 'Don't act the clart, John, I know you better. This is serious. I mean, are you not interested? Just a lunch maybe?'

'Suze, I know how you're all into this whole Labour thing of yours now, but I'm just not sure I've the time for it.'

'Make the time, John. You know you can.'

'Well, yes, but, it's not just that. I think you know, in fact, that I don't much care for your friend.'

'Oh, well, that's just *odd*. Far as I can see, you've a lot in common, you's two. If you asked Marty to say what his politics were now, he'd say he was Christian Socialist.'

'Oh, get away, Sue. He was a Trot.'

'That was years ago, man. He goes to church now. A lot of them do these days, you might be surprised. People change.'

'Well, that would be some manoeuvre. He must have smelt it on the wind.'

'That's his job. Having antennae. You don't get going in politics without a good set. Otherwise you'd never have a clue what people want from you.'

'You can always just do what you think's right . . .'

'*Christ* but you annoy me, John. Look, it's not like you'll be injected with a poison if you shake his bliddy hand. Don't be so *snide* all your life. Are you interested in politics or not?'

'I'm not – *snide.* I just don't see the point of him and me talking.'

'Well, that's you all over, John. To be frank. I mean, you act like you're above it. All the rest of us minions. Judging us.'

'I don't. I *do not* judge people. Not out of hand.'

'You judge Martin and you never *met* the bugger. Not in twenty year, any road.'

This, Gore conceded, was a half-decent debating point.

'Eh? I mean, where's the harm? What's one hour out of your weekend? It's just possible, John, just *possible* that you might learn something.'

In his heart Gore already knew he would relent. The proposition was far too interesting. No pastoral chore on his dance-card could compare. Above all, though, he had never before seen his sister express such a need of him, and he would happily see more of it.

Chapter VIII

THE TRIBUNE

Sunday, 27 October 1996

As the afternoon's amblers passed him by, Gore stood perplexed on a corner of Railway Street, peering up and down, checking again the address scribbled on the edge of his *Sunday Sun*. It was a corner office building below the Westmorland Road and Marlborough Crescent, newly refaced and whitewashed, six storeys of smoked windows and bolted glass-and-steel balconies. By the door a shiny plaque proclaimed ST JAMES'S BUSINESS CENTRE. Such was the address of Pallister's constituency HQ – on the very cusp of the constituency, Gore duly noted, for this one could only call the border between the stricken west of town and the prospering centre. He buzzed the fifth floor, and gave the big stiff glass door a shove. On a low armchair in the foyer sat Susannah, restored to a dark blue suit in the two hours since they spoke. She rose to greet him and they entered a mirrored elevator.

'Sorry, but can I ask who *pays* for this?'

'You do, pet. The tax-payer. Don't worry, we get a knock-down deal on the rent. He earns it, but. Who else works their Sunday lunchtime?'

'You do, pet.'

She shrugged. 'I've just got a bit paperwork. Might as well do it here. This way I get his little researcher to fetch us wor coffee.'

Gore waved his newspaper. 'You saw your boy made page three?'

Gore had been amused to read of Pallister's reprimand by the Speaker of the Commons for failing to correctly register a recent trip to Germany, his hotel bill and sundry other costs having been met by a leading local manufacturer of motor exhaust systems. Susannah waved a hand.

'Oh, usual bloody pompous procedure. He just forgot. Wouldn't you?'

They had reached the fifth floor, and Susannah offered him a face so earnest he thought it comical. 'Now you will listen, won't you? You won't just sit there and – I don't know – throw the Bible at him?'

'As if I wrote it?'

'Exactly.'

She steered him through a fire door into a big pleasing open-plan room, new jute carpet and creamy walls, long windows giving vantage over the old Forth Yard toward the Tyne. At one desk a young man with a drooping fringe was bent over an open page and barely acknowledged them. Susannah led her brother round the books to the corner office, its outward-facing windows masked by strip blinds, its door ajar. Within, framed before a French window, in shirt sleeves and tie loose-knotted, Martin Pallister stood upright behind his desk in the act of taking a call. But he grinned and motioned for Gore to take the comfortable chair. Instead Gore stood a while, then sauntered to the office shelves.

'No, look, I've not got a comment on it right this moment. If it's true then it's not good, obviously, but that's for then . . .'

Hobsbawm's histories, various bound *Hansards*, Deutscher's *Trotsky*, Peter Drucker's *Management*, one or two *Viz* annuals. Among wall-mounted photos Gore saw Pallister drinking a yard of ale with some rowdy Teutonics, and a shot of the Newcastle football manager, Keegan, cheerfully alongside Tony Blair, Pallister lurking at his elbow.

'No, I'll give you something before then. Yeah, I've someone here . . .'

At the edge of the MP's desk, between the PC monitor and piles of foolscap folders, was planted a figurine in heavy cast metal. Gore lifted and hefted it – a paperweight of sorts, in the shape of a pitman lugging a coal-truck.

Pallister hung up the receiver and stretched his arms over his head. Still a sportsman's build, his shirt a little damp. Still a cocksureness in his gaze, humour lurking at the corners of his mouth. Still annoyingly handsome, too, though up close he looked a little punchier than his photos, a slight boozer's ruddiness round the nose and eyes – possibly historic. But those eyes were still bright, hair still lustrous, if speckled with salt like his own, and now piled high in a style that put Gore suddenly and joltingly in mind of Pallister's dad, One-Armed Joe.

He pointed at the figure in Gore's hand. 'Like that, do you? I got given it off the fella who makes them, out of scrap. Used to be down the pit himself. Enterprising. You found us okay, then?'

'Yeah. You're just about inside your constituency, aren't you?'

Pallister smiled. 'Well, I tell you, I understand now why Voltaire made his home on the Franco-Swiss border. You never know when you might need a sharp exit. Any road, pleased to meet you, John, thanks for coming in.'

They shook hands across the desk and took their seats.

'We did meet before,' Gore ventured. 'Once, a good few years back.'

'Oh aye?'

'Suze was there too, has she never mentioned? It was one of the big CND rallies in London.'

'She *might* have mentioned . . . I don't recall. God, when would that have been then? Eighty-four? Eighty-three? I would've still been lecturing.' He whistled through his teeth. 'Interesting times, as the Chinese say. You weren't a vicar back then, but?'

'I was still at school.'

'Gotcha. Right sort of age to be on CND marches.'

'It's funny, but – I remember meeting you so well. Mainly because you were so down on Labour at the time.'

'We've all been down on Labour one time or other, it's a rite of passage. I was still a member then, but. Like I've always been. Like you, right?'

Gore nodded.

'And now look at us, eh?' Pallister smiled broadly.

'I was interested, actually, in what I read in the papers about conference?'

'Oh aye? It was different this year, right enough. Odd . . .'

'Not like it used to be?'

'Well, there's that, but it was that rotten business in Dunblane really got to me. How do you legislate for that? Some shithouse loon walks into a school and starts strafing. I mean, I've got a young son myself, school age.'

Gore nodded, deferring to the sentiment, loath to be distracted. 'Dreadful, yes. But what I read in the *Guardian* was you're in favour of splitting from the unions. Is that right?'

'Listen, if the *Guardian* attacks us then we're doing something right. I mean – and we're off the record now, yeah?' Gore pulled a quizzical face. Pallister shrugged. 'Well, you do media, don't you? So, just between us? My view is once you commit to balloting members you're on the way to cutting them ties. Now you'll not hear me defaming the cause of organised labour. *But* – it's been a marriage. Not always a happy one.' Gore could sense Pallister warming to his topic. 'In the past, you know, the unions have been a bit of an abusive husband. Coming back from the pub full of beer, wanting their tea and all else. I mean, you'll have been to the same sorts of meetings as me, right? You always got a lot of macho crap off the brothers.'

Pallister leaned back in the chair, cupped his hands behind his head. Gore rather felt he was witnessing a rival show of testicular authority.

'Now, if you're talking Party coffers – well, the pocketbook is an issue in any marriage, right? The thing is, *now*, Tony's got a real touch when it comes to getting new donors in. Why are you smiling?'

'"Tony" . . .'

'The maximum leader. Aye, I know. It's not like we were at school together. But, that's his name. Like I say – money's always laid us low. We're poor, as a party. So where do we find what we need? To put meat and muscle on the bones? Unions won't do it. Local parties have nowt. If you're not careful you spend half your life at whist drives. Bring-and-fucking-buy sales. 'Scuse my French, but you must find it similar with the church, right? What you're doing?'

Nice try, thought Gore. 'I do. At the same time, I find one has to be careful about the kind of help you accept. The kind of people. What they think they're paying for.'

'I hear you. How keep thyself pure, brother? Look, we're not like them sleazy tossers in power. There's some things aren't for sale. But we have to raise a war-chest, we *have* to. Sure, there's bread-and-butter overheads we should always meet worselves. But, I mean, look at this wanker . . .'

Pallister had rustled up a newspaper clipping from a desk drawer.

'Here's this Todd on his high horse, saying it's an outrage that a supermarket's sponsoring badges at conference. Talk about a matter of state, eh? Come on. Why stump up for forty thousand plastic badges when some fucking *grocer* wants to write you a cheque? Are they seriously calling that "bought influence"? Get away. Hardly cash-for-questions, is it?'

'I noticed you made the paper yourself today.'

And for the first time Gore knew he had touched a wound. Pallister drew breath, made a bridge of his fingers on the desktop before him.

'If I go abroad these days, trust me, it's business. My business is Tyneside. That thing you're on about? I was in Baden-Württemberg, in the Ruhr. I'm interested in regional power, it's a bit of a hobby horse of mine. *They've* got it. Here, you know, it's a mix, regions always clashing with the centre. So you get overlap, waste. Ah, anyhow.' He chuckled. 'What the sainted press don't understand is I'm not in this for my own good. Okay, I've got a mortgage to pay, just like they do – you too, probably. Or the Church pays yours, right?'

'They bought it for cash. Just a little ex-council place in Hoxheath.'

'Blimey. Right, well, I suppose they can manage. But me, it's not like I'm coining it. Otherwise I'd never have gone into politics, I'd have stayed where I was in business.'

'What business were you in again?'

'Well, it was the business of *generating* business. I worked for

TREC, the development company? That was some good years. Taught me a lot, I can tell you. Look at this, I'll show you what I'm talking about, come on . . .'

He beckoned Gore from his chair to join him at the French window, and they stepped out onto a metal balcony shielded by panels of frosted glass. Precipitously below them were the enclosed rubble mounds and brute foundations of Marlborough Crescent's sprawling construction site. Ahead of them, the glinting roofs of the industrial sheds of the old Forth Yard. Further removed, Central Station, and a train from the south rolling home under afternoon sun. On the horizon, the Tyne Bridge, a tall crane placid behind it. Gore found the view wholly lovable, yet he was sharply aware – Pallister, too, surely knew? – how the frame round this picture sliced off the very much less scenic imagery marooned behind them to the west, the run-down ramshackle sprawl of Hoxheath.

But Pallister was grinning at Gore, his eyes highly lively. 'Not bad, is it? Sometimes, but, you know what? I get the maddest urge just to jump off.'

'I'm sure the angels would bear you upward,' Gore murmured, deciding a split second later that he was pushing his luck.

But Pallister only laughed, one short sharp *Ha!* 'Shame we can't see the business park from here . . . but you've got the new science centre going up. Out of a bus station and some derelict land. That's a fifty-million-pound project, right there. TREC, we put money into it.'

'You and who else?'

'Oh, the lottery.'

'The weekly binge . . .'

'It's only a quid. I've made worse punts. And someone's got to win, right? *God*, but.' And he rattled at the balcony's mercifully sound railing. 'I get like a kid when I see a big site. I love demolition, me, I do. Cos it means *construction*. Construction means jobs, it means *property*. That means prosperity. It goes right through the economy, like lightning, it really does.'

'What about your constituents? In France or Switzerland or whichever?'

'What do you mean?'

'I just wonder. Fifty million. What if you drove west from here and threw that money in the air? Do you not think it'd trickle down a lot faster? To them that need it?'

Pallister's smile was rueful, if not indulgent. 'I hear you, John, of course I do. But you know how it is. Industry left this city. The better-offs went with it. Nothing flourishes in stony ground. You've got to lure the money back. That means big-picture thinking. The end *result*, but, is gravy all round.' He thumped the banister again. 'Anyhow . . .' And with the flourish of a hand he directed Gore back indoors. They resumed their seats.

'I think this meeting ought to come to order. I wanted to say, John, what you've been doing, I find it terrifically proactive. Hands-on stuff. Real initiative. You're making something out of nothing.'

Gore shrugged. 'Not nothing. Out of people. That's my job.'

'Is it, though? Is that what all vicars do? It's not what the guy at my church talks about.'

'Right. You go to church? Really?'

'Yeah, for my sins. I meant to ask, in fact, did you by any chance happen to see the hoo-hah over Tony's article in the *Torygraph* last Easter?'

Gore nodded. '"No Christian can be a Tory". That one?'

'Aye. Talk about stirring the pot. You've got to like the cheek of it, but, eh? Obviously some of them godlier Tories were highly affronted.'

'Yes. Well. I don't know if I had a view on that. I don't much like sanctimony. Didn't like it in Thatcher either.'

'Well, one thing you should know, John – he's sincere, is Tony. His faith is solid, really, it's what he's all about.'

Gore was pondering. 'His wife, she's Catholic, right?'

'Cherie? Aye, I think so. What of it?'

'Just, I don't know if I recognise his particular brand. Of the faith. And I should say, I don't know that the public care for politicians who wear that stuff on their sleeve.'

'Oh no, not a bit. That's your job. And that's what Tony says and all.' Pallister wore his own thoughtful look. 'You know what, you'd put me in mind of him a bit. Tony.'

'I'm sorry?'

'Don't blow a gasket there. No, I think you'd get on, the two of you. What with the faith in common. And you're both Durham lads, right? Now I think, you lost your mam quite early too, didn't you? You and Susannah?'

Gore swallowed, unhappy, but nodded.

'How old's your dad again?'

'He's, uh, sixty-two.'

'Really? Mine too. Wartime kids, eh? They'll not die, just you watch.'

The door was rapped and swung wide, Pallister's researcher shouldering in with mugs of tea. Behind him, Susannah, and with her, two bearded men laden with video camera, boom-stick microphone, clapper, cases and the attendant ephemera of the newsgathering crew.

'Sorry, John – Marty, can you do this now?'

'Right now?'

'It's the only time the lads have got before you head back to London.'

Pallister bit his lip. 'Sorry, John. They're doing this little piece on me.'

Susannah had already begun to reorder certain items on Pallister's desk. 'John won't mind being in shot, do you, John?'

'I would, actually. But I'm happy to step outside, leave you to it.'

'That's not what we're after,' the cameraman announced to Susannah. And Gore felt his instincts confirmed as truth.

'God, okay, let's take it outside,' his sister was muttering, driving the men out of doors as quickly as they had come.

Gore kept his eyes on Pallister, who had been unable to keep a shade of chagrin from his face. 'What was that about?' he enquired as the door clicked closed.

Pallister held up his hands. 'Look, there's space out there in the media needs filling. I thought it might as well be us. Just for starters.'

'You mean, "you".'

'Not this time.' Pallister blinked. 'It's funny, you know? I asked you here thinking we could talk.'

'We have been, haven't we?'

'No, I mean, a real conversation. I'm intrigued by what you've been doing, honest. What you've said. I can see you're interested in politics. So I meant a talk like that. But I'm sort of' – he waved a hand – 'I dunno, I'm just getting this *feeling* what you really wanna do is take a swing at me.'

Gore shifted in his seat. 'Can I be frank with you?'

'It's about time, bonny lad.'

'I'm still not clear what you want from me. I'm happy to talk politics. Actually it feels more like you've been deferring to my area. There's no need. By all means get to business.'

Pallister leaned forward, took a breath. 'Okay. Let's talk about Hoxheath. The West End in general. Government money's been pumping into the place for years. I know that from my TREC days. We got a lot of things going there, but it didn't last. It couldn't. Now you'll hear some say it's just throwing good money after bad. That it's beyond redemption – we're just managing decline and we'd be better off razing Hoxheath to the ground. Year zero.'

'Well, that's disgusting.'

'Exactly, John, but that's just how some people think. So I reckon it wants a whole new plan, and a better one – the best people on it, really working with the best of what's there in the community.'

'Who's going to pay for that?'

Pallister opened his hands. 'That's why I'm here, John. Have you heard of the regeneration budget?'

Gore shrugged. 'No, but it sounds familiar.'

'It's a big pot of government money. Cross-departmental. A lot of it's ring-fenced for capital projects but there's a special pot, "challenge fund" they call it, for smaller initiatives. And it's there for the bidding. You just have to put together what they call a board to apply. What they like to see is a cross-section – local people, business people. Unlikely bedfellows. Well, I want to get me a board together and make a project for Hoxheath.'

'Are you allowed to? As an MP?'

'Nowt to stop us. Who better? Listen, we're not talking a fountain of money but it could be put to bloody good use, the right project and the right people. Trouble with these boards is they end up all the usual suspects. Bunch of time-servers. Some fat councilman in the chair. I don't want the same tired old community types neither – people who don't understand *politics*. So what I want is for you to sit on the board and coordinate that whole side of it. There's nowt tired about you. And you can speak and people listen, I can see that.'

'Who's the chairman of this board? You?'

'No, actually, my pick would be someone from business. They run a better meeting. Look, I'm not saying I want you to mastermind the thing, but I want you onboard and behind us.'

'As a driver or a passenger?'

'Fully involved. And fully supportive. But more than that. I mean, you know your Marx, right? "Religion, the soul of a soulless world"? Well, we need some soul to what we're doing. Otherwise it's just numbers. We need you to give us that weight.'

The style of the pitch, at least, had begun to snare at Gore's interest.

'This is what I'm about, see. I can't sit here trying to sell the old state socialism. It was backward, sluggish, it didn't bloody work. There are limits to politics – I've learned that. We can't save the world. But I'm bloody sure what we *can* do is help out the neighbourhood.'

Susannah was at the doorway once more, her face a silent warning.

'That's never the time, is it? Look, we've to get the four o'clock train but I promised your sister lunch. Why don't we continue this over a nice roast?'

'You'll have a bottle of Brown with that?' Pallister offered and Gore acquiesced, though the MP himself abstained. ('I don't drink alcohol any more. Hardly. Get more done that way.') But in the wood-panelled restaurant of the Station Hotel they did not stint on their victuals. Thick moist slices of slow-roasted beef, buttered baton carrots, cauliflower in white sauce, plump Yorkshire puddings sopping in gravy from the boat. 'Geordie Sunday, eh?' Pallister chuckled as he tucked his napkin into his shirt. Susannah, who had opted for a dry sliver of quiche, was less boisterous. But the gents feasted keenly.

'So, John, what about my proposal? What do you say?'

'I don't entirely understand. What my role would be, what the project would be. I need some more specifics.'

The MP stifled a belch. 'We're still just in concept. All I'm asking you for is a handshake deal. Sue and I are working on a proper day's event, a forum. We get all our people together, talk through the options, pick the best idea. Obviously I'd want you in there for that.'

Gore picked at his teeth and sat back. 'I'm still not sure it wouldn't be wrong of me to involve myself too much. To that degree.'

'Whey, I thought you were precisely the "involved" type.'

'The Church can't be just a Band-Aid for bigger problems. And I have to say by nature I'm wary of . . . public relations.' He glanced at his sister, in whose mouth butter would not melt.

'Fine. For a moment I was afraid you'd say you're a bloody Lib Dem.'

Gore blinked to dismiss the levity.

'Will you at least have a think? At least tell me that, eh? You play hard to get, don't you? I heard you'll take a helping hand off all *sorts*. Why not me?'

With that Pallister excused himself for the gentlemen's, dabbing a smear of gravy that had somehow besmirched his red tie. Susannah smiled to herself. 'So he hasn't seduced you?'

'I'm not such an easy lay.'

The terminology seemed to tickle his sister. 'Oh, I know that, kidder.'

'What are you smirking at?'

'You know when I came by your service the other week? And we were talking? And there was that rather fabulously tarty girl. With the bairn?'

'Lindy. Her name's Lindy.'

'Right. You're not by any chance sticking one up her, are you?'

'No, I'm not. She's a friend. She's not "tarty" either.'

'Tarted-up, I mean. For a church service. No, she seemed canny, though.'

'That was a lame trick you tried back there, with the TV people? Ham-fisted by your standards. So was I meant to be caught on camera giving him my blessing?'

'I thought you enjoyed getting your face about the place.'

Pallister was returning. Gore sipped his ale as the MP resettled in front of his still-steaming plate. 'So, are you looking forward to power?'

Pallister rapped the table surface. 'You can't be a slave to polls, but you're daft to ignore them. You know KPMG? Sue tells me they're running seminars for their clients on how to protect their money when we win. *If* we win. No, whatever happens, we've dragged ourselves back. This election I'm actually looking forward to. At last. In the past, you know, we weren't professional. There was just a base area of cunning that we surrendered. Like it were just too tawdry.' He speared a fat carrot, toyed with the fork. 'I mean, they say elections get lost, not won. The Tories are in a hole, right enough. But there's a hunger for us out there, I know it.'

At twenty to four Susannah was shuffling tickets, unfolding Pallister's coat for him while Gore was still mopping his plate. They struggled to their feet as three. Pallister appeared solemn. 'We're gonna keep talking then?'

'Sure.' Gore shrugged, and they shook hands. Pallister retained his grip.

'All I'm saying, John, stick a little bet on me. You won't lose. Next time I'll come see you. On your turf.'

There was something to the man, Gore was forced to concede as he sat back alone at the cleared table, weighing his unfinished half of ale. The quality of assurance was not the mere facade of some nervous wreck. The air of honest business – I give you mine, you give me yours – was perhaps more carefully cultivated. But re-running the tape of the conversation in his head, Gore heard no truly glaring bullshit. The vigour, too, was infectious. And a Labour man, despite it all – not some shameless turncoat, not Susannah. His offer did not appear to carry conditions. Gore looked forward keenly to devising some of his own, prior to what he imagined would be a measured and reluctant acceptance in the very near future. He drained back the ale, the best drink he had enjoyed in a month of Sundays.

Rattling down to London, speeding through darkened provincial towns . . . To Martin it had once seemed the apogee of thrills and vaulting prospects. Never again, he knew, could he entertain such gormless provincialism. He had learned to settle in First Class – not that he wouldn't gladly put up elsewhere. But there was no point pretending it was fun among the griping kids and the gasping lager fiends. This was his business, and his constituents could hardly begrudge the extra working space for he and the impeccable Ms Gore, now perched opposite.

Across the aisle were a well-tended quartet in their fifties, all in waxed jackets – two husbands, two wives, though the game of whose was whose Martin intended to leave for later. Meantime he amused himself in eavesdropping. These ones were Yorkshire by accent, London by orientation. *We are all of us marked on the tongue,* he mused. *Will anyone tell the Bradford man in his new silk hat?*

'Is that your shooting coat?'

'This old thing? Oh no.'

'Ah. What do you think of this awful business? Them trying to outlaw it?'

'Outrage. Pure outrage.'

One of the males, the one with less hair, was a publican, the other – hawk-faced and distracted – a surveyor. One of the wives, it seemed, had briefly sold commodities. Pallister rolled his eyes at Susannah, and she smiled over her papers. They were not her sort either, not any more. But then they never were. This was your actual Tory, and this was why the Tories were and ever would be a nasty little party of the shires and market towns.

Susannah was trying to immerse herself in work, briefings and press rumblings compiled by his researcher, but he knew she was tired and out of sorts. She was making this trip for a variety of reasons, but he trusted he was high among them. She was, as so often, only lightly made-up and in want of a hairbrush. A stray lock caught the light most unfavourably. He leaned over the table and smoothed it down. She flinched.

'Ah, *ah*. Now come on, let me. It's better for you.'

Peering closer still, he frowned, licked a fingertip and began to blend her foundation. They were far enough removed from unfriendly eyes, not that any of that had ever concerned him. Gossip was the devil's work, the no-mark vice of the inadequate and vicarious. They were a long time removed from the two or three – or was it more? – occasions that they had slept together, seven – or was it eight? – years hence.

'So how did I do? With your brother?'

'You tell me. Do you like him?'

'Do you?'

She made a pained face.

'Well, I do, yeah. Seems a bright enough man. On the basis of a few dodgy remarks, I'd say he's *slightly* on the wrong side of the Masturbatory Tendency. Doesn't entirely strike me as the go-getting sort neither.'

'Nor me. But I've been mildly impressed by his persistence.'

'Fair enough.' He gave her some mischief in a grin. 'Bloody vicars, but. When do I get to meet that guy off the telly? The soldier? When do I meet *Alan Shearer*?'

'I've spoken to his PA. She'll see. He's quite careful.'

Martin felt he was now owed a perk in return for his ongoing effort to extend himself in the direction of her pet theory. Susannah was obsessed by the notion that all things were enabled through contacts and associations, and had lately pushed under his nose a proposal for the improvement of his 'intelligence-gathering'. This, as far as Martin could read, was the purloining of phone numbers for blue-chip businessmen, footballers, soap actors, musicians and assorted celebrities. He attributed the fixation to her past relations with advertisers, and she coolly confirmed as much. 'There's a place for endorsement in politics too, you know. If we're talking public awareness of policy areas, it could be golden.'

Fair enough – though Martin had to wonder where was the material gain? Susannah argued that some associations were mere reflected glory, but others offered new stocks of lateral thinking. Martin was comfortable in the company of high-net-worth individuals, and had never been averse to getting his photo in the paper, yet on some humble level he receded before names grander than his own. 'These people like to be listened to,' Sue insisted. 'You do that and they're impressed. You're a good listener. People think MPs are up their own jacksies. You show them you respect their achievement. They want to advise, we want to listen.'

'Oh, do we?'

'Even if it's just humouring them. Once they're onside, who knows what you might get? Down the line.'

This woman had shaken him from the clutch of so many bad habits, taught him to foster his own brand – what she had done for his spirit, he could hardly enumerate. But after such scoldings he wondered – at some length – about the degree to which she truly respected him. Whether, indeed, he was to her a mere rung on a ladder. Since fucking her was now so far off the agenda, it seemed never the time to ask her directly.

Now she peered up from the page. 'You need to look at some of this.'

'What?'

'Mueller aren't sounding too happy. There's some talk of pulling out.'

'Jesus, they've not been there six month. Anyhow, it's not my problem. It's Mike Watt's.'

'You might want to comment. If you still have an eye on Trade and Industry. Oh, and they're talking about a strike at the Freeman Hospital.'

'Strike? For pay or conditions or what?'

'Pay.'

'Oh, right, easy.' Pallister cast a drooping eye over the briefing papers. 'Right. The usual SWP shit-stir. The Freeman, you know that's where my dad got treated? For his arm?'

But Susannah had abruptly crushed her chin into her chest. 'Malcolm Fairbrother, twelve o'clock.'

It was indeed the Liberal Democrat member for Leadgate – tall, suited and white-haired, a trace of rugby league in his build and gaunt cheeks, and the extent to which he clearly fancied himself, even in his fifties. But those same cheeks were blotted red, the berry-fruits of late sessions in Annie's Bar. Even here, in transit, Fairbrother had a glass of red wine to hand.

'Make way there, eh, Martin? Clear some of that muck of yours. Taking up the whole area, well I don't know . . .'

Martin shifted his suit-bag from the aisle to beneath his seat. 'I will always give way to the honourable gentleman.'

Fairbrother was cosying himself down beside Susannah. 'Back to work then, eh? Nose to the grindstone.'

'What would you know about that, Malcolm?'

Mirthless laughter. 'Good weekend, was it? I was up in the Lakes myself. Walking, you know. Good crisp days, frost on the hills. *Marvellous.*'

'A busy one for me. Full surgery, full appointment book.'

'Ah, the humble tribune. His loyal constituents. Did they send you back to the Smoke with a flea in your ear?'

'They know me well enough by now.'

'That's the trouble, eh? No, I must say, Martin, I find the people in Newcastle *fantastic*. Now, this will interest you, I do believe your Mr Keegan's in the next carriage.'

Pallister fought the urge to make demanding eyes at Susannah. *Damn it*, though. A real opportunity. How, then, to get shot of this windbag? Perhaps in a moment or two he might declare the need for a shit? There was just cause, at least, since that hotel roast had turned molten in his gut.

Susannah's mobile rang, she clicked it and cupped it, nodded and frowned. 'Martin, it's the *Journal*. About Mueller? They're probably going to go big on it tomorrow.'

'They want something now?'

'We've got fifteen minutes?'

'God. Let me think. Malcolm, would you excuse us? I find I need to choose some words with care . . .'

'Oh, right-ho, far be it from me.' And he levered himself up and off.

'Thank fuck,' Martin sighed. 'There goes the world's least impressive Yorkshireman. You expect them at least to talk sense, even if they're so fucking *proud* of it.' He didn't bother to glance across the aisle and see onto whose ruffled feathers he had sprayed foul petroleum. Silence from those quarters was quite sufficiently pleasing.

'Okay. Ready? "Obviously, we regret that this has come to pass" – no, "looks like it might come to pass. I'm sure we will work with Mueller and make our views clear. But the unions must make their own case . . ." Blah. You know how it goes from there?'

'Yes, fine.'

Pallister slumped back into the seat, stared absently at the big bottle of sparkling eau minerale on the table between them, then caught the eye of one of his Yorkshire neighbours. 'Water, water everywhere, and not a drop to drink,' he muttered.

They were now approaching Darlington, it seemed. Martin let his thoughts lose their moorings and drift to the sound of Susannah's scratching pen.

Book Four

DR PALLISTER, MP

Chapter I

WAR STORIES

What the fuck are you doing here, Marty?

Thus spake the devil in his ear, the reprobate voice with which he was at war, this day as every other.

May Day of 1996, and he was a bidden guest at a reception, one that demanded his presence and the raising of a fizzy glass. Other guests appeared content to sip their Veuve Cliquot, munch their sweet pepper tartlets. And yet to Dr Pallister, MP, it didn't feel entirely like a day for giving thanks. Droplets of unease clouded his drink.

'How did it come to this, eh, Martin? You've gotta wonder.'

Robson Talbot, grey-eyed stalwart of the regional engineers, clung to his side, doing nothing to lift his spirits. The Member had at least dressed for the occasion – navy suit, scarlet tie, show you mean business, the Suzie Gore credo. Robson wore the same patched tweed coat in which he had lived and worked for three decades.

The two men stood together, apart from the chattering throng, in the conference room of the new Blackwater Hotel. It was a plush space, dapple-grey carpet festooned with hypnotic spirals of dark mauve that matched the walls and became the furnishings – faux Rennie Mackintosh, spidery-black. Abstracted industrial imagery hung in chrome frames. Long windows offered similar if plainer views across the Tyne to Gateshead. Uninspired, Martin sipped his drink and considered a rejoinder to Robson.

They had heard out the announcement of the Mueller Group's acquisition of Alderton Power and its famous Heaton Works – a great acreage of plants and depots on the Shields Road, site since

1890 of the late Sir Thomas Alderton's industrial magnitude. Alderton's chief business down the decades had been the making of steam turbines for electric power stations. Prosperity had come and gone, as had a succession of British owners. Now the cool blue logo of Germany's world-renowned Mueller was to be hoisted over the entrance, stamped all about its perimeters. The takeover, Martin knew, was a sort of a boon for his colleague Mike Watt, Honourable Member for Heaton & Wallsend – though, in the round, it was hard to see it as aught but a pricey PR success for the government, each and every one of a thousand new jobs lavishly subsidised by start-up sweeteners.

Martin chanced a long look across the room, toward the power trio of Mueller executives flown in from Munich this morning, now stood approvingly by the tall nerd they had announced as UK CEO. Their Hugo Boss suits were a bit boxy and square-shouldered to Martin's taste. One of them looked to be of his own vintage, a sandy-haired child of the sixties. Another was a doughy bloke in a wig, run to fat on Bavarian butter and beer. But their boss-man wore his fringe in a razor-keen parting, his lightweight glasses seemingly made of Perspex. It was, Martin decided, the high glint in the lenses that conjured up the war stories. Relenting to his devil, he inclined and whispered to Robson, 'Divvint mention the war, then? None of that "Them's the bastads bombed me granny."'

Robson broke into a smile, finally. 'Aye. They *did*, but, Martin.'

'I know. Me dad never let up about the firebomb came down twenty yard from his old back door.'

'He wasn't fighting age, your dad?'

'Nah, man, he was still at Chilly Road School. I always remember, but, the house where I grew up – his old gas mask, on a nail under the stairs.'

'Whereabouts was that, Martin?'

'Tosson Terrace. North end of the Chilly? Aye. I used to ride past the works every morning, on me bike to school.'

It was for Robson's sake that Martin deigned to coarsen his accent and wax nostalgic. His true memories of those rides were pallid. In the fog of a winter's dawn, his school-bound mood usually tetchy, he had found the works a cheerless sight – sprawling and formidable, but somehow sad, somehow oppressive, a functional hive for drones.

He decided now to test Robson's mettle. 'I remember metalwork teacher of ours took us for a day-trip to the works. Got us shown around. When we got back on the bus he said, "Right lads, now that's why you want to get your exams. So's you don't end up working *there*."'

Robson coloured. 'He never? Of all the bliddy – see, now *that* sort of attitude . . . Thirteen thousand *men* we had at the old works. Your dad among them.'

Martin shrugged. 'Forty year ago now, Robson.'

'What, you think *this* lot are in it for more than a fortnight?'

'Who knows? A buyer's a buyer. There's a case against it. There's a case for it. It's not cut and dried.'

'Whey, tell us what you *think*, man. Not all that politician's talk.'

In a personal capacity? Yes, Dr Pallister respected the principle of the Mueller acquisition. As new supplants old, son supplants father, so Mueller must supplant Alderton. So ran the logic. And it *was* supplanting – not asset-stripping or carpetbagging or any such sneer. It was growth and development, the nature of business, sure as the turning of the earth. Such was Martin's theory, based on long study of the interplay between base and superstructure. But it did not come impersonally to him. It could not have been more personal. He had now lived long enough, by his own estimation, to have seen these forces clash within the bounds of his own life. He had no interest in rehashing such a feud with Robson Talbot.

Excusing himself, he shouldered a way across the room in time to corner the lithe blonde girl in charge of Blackwater Events – dark-eyed and hollow-cheeked, in her compulsory hundred-quid charcoal trouser-suit from Next.

'Tell me, Tessa, do you do a sort of a package rate for this kind of thing? The room and staff and catering and all that?'

'We do a whole range, sir, depending on your needs, if you'd like to see our tariff?'

'I would, thanks. Proctor's a pal of mine, if that's any use.'

'Aw really?' She raised a black-pencilled eyebrow, seemingly respectful of this free and easy way with the proprietor's given name.

'While we're at it, what price are your bedrooms on a midweek? Any more of this fizz and I'll be ready for a lie-down.'

He held her gaze long enough, but no, she was quite oblivious, referring him to her colleague Michelle at front desk. She was – Martin ruled – a bit delicious. But a bit sallow and fretful too, short of spark. A grafter, not the kind to be lured away from her afternoon chores. It was galling, for he couldn't deny his interest in what lay under her layers, what sort of knickers she had on beneath that compulsory trouser-suit.

But Tessa was leaving him, and his reverie was disturbed by the hoving into view of a familiar beaky proboscis, a well-known derisive grin: his one-time protégé Red Paul Todd, wearing his own standard smart gear – some cheap black sports coat shiny with wear, and washed-out black jeans.

'How do, Doc Martin. Not up at the May Day bash then? Thought that's where good Labour members ought to be the day.'

'Bad timing. This had precedence. I'll get up later on.'

'I saw Robson Talbot get himself away just now.'

'And what about you, Paul?'

'The paper wanted me here. Looks more like the story. The selling of Tyneside by the pound.'

Martin felt at liberty to ignore the halfwit jibe. 'And what paper is it pays for you these days?'

'Just a bit stringing I do for the *Journal*. Just trying to get on. Like yourself. You got a line for us then? Good day for the north-east, is it?'

'A fine day for Heaton Works and its workforce. Good day for Mike Watt. And I congratulate the president of the Board of Trade for having helped make the case to Mueller.'

'Oh, the *president*? And is it nice to bow and scrape to that Tory?'

'I'll shake any hand, Paul. That's my job. I'll say this, but, knowing the history of Alderton, and I know it better than you –'

'Oh, I know you do, Martin. Your dad's worth ten of you, mind.'

'You're the judge of that, are you?'

'You know he fancies standing against you next time?'

'My dad can do what he likes. I'll respect him for it. Listen, but, you want to get off up to May Day, Paul, there'll be a bottle of cider there with your name on. What we've got *here* is something that's of actual *use* to Tyneside. Not like you and the comrades, all wanking in a circle. You can print that if you've got the nuts. Excuse us now, will you? I need a piss.'

So hadaway and fuck yourself, Toddy, said the demon in Dr Pallister.

Stalking away down a hushed and spot-lit corridor Martin felt a stab of pain across his shoulder muscles. Maybe the strain of yesterday's fitful squash game, more likely the raw nub of his tethered anger. Someday, this would all have to get settled one-on-one in the back of some car park, because the upshot of these bitchy little verbal battles was never satisfying. He could take the banter and give it back, but he would not stand to be patronised. Yes, by his own admission – he was not the man he had thought he would become. He was newly forty, the feeling every bit as dispiriting as schoolmates had led him to believe. He was on the right stage in life, yet he had envisaged a more central role. So what, though, if it had transpired that his true calling was as a conduit, an enabler for the energies of others? What mattered, plainly, was the material good.

Their house on Tosson Terrace had survived the Luftwaffe, but Martin would not have minded so much had it been targeted and firebombed into cinders. It was of 1920s vintage, a bit of a hutch, lacking the bay-and-lintel bearing of certain nearby Victorian terraces where the neighbouring street names were all posh – Sackville, Craythorne, Huntcliffe – though the standard of construction didn't match the aspiration. Heaton as a whole had once been considered quite fancy, or so the lore went, before the

Alderton Works. For the works wanted a workforce, so much the better if they were housed en masse within its shadow.

In his ambulant boyhood Martin liked to stray from Heaton to the wider space of nearby Jesmond, where the air felt finer. The house rows were elegantly Georgian, and larking students were much in evidence. Jesmond people carried themselves differently too, seeming to work at nicer occupations. Then there was the ample civic parkland of Town Moor, its boating lake and bowling green and gravel tennis courts. Quickly diligent in his practice on those courts, Martin was further gratified to find that the game was favoured by a lot of rosy girls in pristine white, some of a surpassing blondeness, most of whom wore pleated thigh-high skirts that flipped pleasingly in time with their exertions. At courtside he made his first girlfriend, the blushing daughter of a city councilman. Her dad would roll up in his Austin De Luxe to whisk her back home, but he was markedly unfriendly toward her young swain. *Sod you, then,* swore the little devil in Martin. His own father heard out and endorsed his complaint. 'You get some snobs in life, Martin. Even your mother, y'knaa, she's got a bit of it.'

Jenny Pallister – ash-blonde, fine-boned – did seem to carry herself a cut above the norm. 'However did I marry such a madam?' Joe liked to chuckle, throwing a brawny arm round her shoulder. He got away with it, most of the time. Other times, Martin noted his mother's wince.

She was the force behind his admission to the local grammar school, where the classroom windows were black-leaded, teachers affected flowing capes, and certain older boys were designated prefects, with exceptional powers to humiliate. But no bugger ever shoved Martin Pallister's head down a toilet bowl. Though a bright lad and a pretty face, he was a sportsman too, physically dauntless. He embraced the quagmire mud and freezing rain of midwinter rugby, keenly retrieved house-bricks from the chlorinated floor of Chilly Road Baths.

Rugby was no more Joe's game than tennis. It was books, of all things, that helped he and Martin stay pals. Fiercely autodidactic, Joe made sure to share his learning with his lad – 'You want to read *this*, you do.' And so Martin battled through the density of Thompson's *The Making of the English Working Class*, and *God's Englishman* by Christopher Hill. He fancied himself one of nature's roundheads, subduing cavaliers with the flat of his sword. Above all, he fell for the figure of Cromwell, Lord Protector. Joe warned him that history was not about great men, though one might want to recognise certain unsung heroes. Martin couldn't agree. Surely somebody had to do the hard shifting, and so take extra credit? In time he saw that Joe viewed human agency in light of a greater cosmic struggle, due in part to the influence of the man Martin knew as Uncle Marcus.

Joe finished school at fifteen, served an apprenticeship, earned his HNC, and – after national service Down South – got himself hired at Alderton, where he attained the rank of foreman-fitter. Through the society of the canteen and some after-hours meetings he got matey with a design engineer, a pale, intense man called Marcus Chambers who, improbably, was forging a name as an eloquent and unbending orchestrator of strikes, work-to-rules, even an occupation of premises.

Joe had always called himself a Labour man, like his father before him, holding it as an article of faith that the Party had made great strides for the working class in general and the north-east in particular. Yet over pint mugs of tea Marcus Chambers had impressed upon Joe that those strides had not been so broad – and, indeed, were followed by craven retreats. Martin could imagine the effect upon his father once he, too, had been made to hear out Uncle Marcus's stock speech.

'Whatever they promise you in opposition, once they govern they're just the party of business. What'll history say of Wilson? But that he froze wages, cut spending, raised prices? No, under Labour just like anyone else, the boss class get the gravy. Just like Morrison said – socialism is whatever Labour decides to do in power. If that's what we've to settle for, then – I'm sorry – isn't it Labour that's stopping us from ever getting real *socialism?'*

At some point this logic had carried such clout with Joe that he binned his Labour card and joined the Tyneside branch of the

International Socialists. And it became the particular ritual – the very badge of Joe's beliefs – that he and his fellows should sell the *Socialist Worker* paper all round Newcastle, in the commercial thoroughfares, the environs of the university, even outside the gates of the works. On certain evenings after school Martin would tag onto these rounds with his dad, who seemed glad of the company, and the chance to expound.

'This is how you build a party, son. You get out and sell your papers, by *hand*. That way, something gets passed on, between people. It's like, "Take this, pal, read it, think about it, pass it on . . ."'

Martin didn't mind loitering in draughty precincts, was happier still casting an eye over female undergraduates. But what he liked best was following Joe through the doors and into the fray of the rowdy saloon bars of Byker and Battle Field. There, Joe's exhortations were usually met by ribaldry and shouts for a pint. 'Gerrit doon ya, man, it'll dae ya good.' But other times there were sharp words, even outright inebriate hostility. Martin enjoyed watching how his old man handled himself – manfully, patiently – when explaining to some rubicund loudmouth the fine points of the IS position. 'Naw, naw, *listen*, will ye? We've got nee truck wi' Soviet Russia. We call wor'sel Trotskyist. And that's nee small thing to live up to.'

Joe could then segue with ease from how the struggle for a fair wage on Tyneside was much akin to that of the Viet Cong against the US imperium, or of blacks against tyranny in Rhodesia and South Africa. Martin saw the pictures on the news, he knew there were violent things afoot round the world. It impressed him that his dad seemed wise to them. It bothered him but slightly that no one else's dad held anything like the same set of views.

It was not uncommon for them to trudge back to Heaton without a paper sold. But Joe never took the bottom line as his judge. 'It's sad, really it is, son, to see working people sat supping their wages, arguing against their own interest. I mean, look about you, eh? Even *you* see what the problem is, aye?' Martin nodded. One night in Battle Field was sufficient to observe the dismal lot of working people. It offended the eye no less than the spirit of fairness, and someone, clearly, needed to do something about it.

Martin couldn't deny that he liked the look of himself. Encouraged by what the mirror dependably showed him, he developed a crisp diction, a certain bearing, a style of looking down his nose at less able adversaries – all of which he shared with Jenny. She made no claim over her son's endowments, yet seemed to exude satisfaction in the handsome figure he cut. Joe, though, more or less openly regarded his son as a crude work-in-progress, to be coaxed and fretted over, albeit with patience.

If Jenny was Martin's first female devotee, she was soon supplanted. Come 1971 the grammar school and the neighbouring Girls' High underwent a shotgun marriage, a line of air-raid shelters between the two torn down so they might merge as a comprehensive. This was no great novelty to Martin – reliably surrounded by lasses from his early teens – other than that he and his then-girlfriend, a darkly pretty thing called Pamela Stark, now walked together to the same gates rather than parting with a juicy kiss on Jesmond Park Road. In sharing a classroom, though, Martin began to brood on Pamela's deficiencies – the slackness of her jaw, not to say her mind, and the frayed state of her jersey and skirt. 'You're well away from that one, pet,' Jenny observed after Pamela stopped calling round. 'Her *people*, Martin, they're not our sort.'

He knew in his boots he would always have girls on the go, for he was both a fancy footballer and a natural leader for the lads – Titch Harwood, Tony Charnley, Mike Tweddle – who were game to duck out at lunch hour to the pub by Jesmond Dene. There, a rogue's gallery of underage drinkers, they supped Tartan Bitter at half a crown and hogged the table football, drawing a mute but giggly female audience. Martin began to tailor his swagger to their gaze, affecting a silver chain and a long sleek shag for his dark hair. He squired selected girls to see the Who at the Odeon, Roxy Music at City Hall, Rod and the Faces at the Mayfair, and in the sultry aftermath he generally found they had much the same thing in mind as he.

Flushed with erotic success, his appetite for kitchen-table dialectics waned. He agreed less readily with his dad, and tired of arguing the toss. For one thing, Joe didn't *like* anyone – with the qualified exception of Keir Hardie ('After about, 1911? He was sound. Didn't treat his family so well, but neebody's perfect.'). Otherwise, Joe's general line was that someone, somewhere, was forever selling out the good old cause. It wasn't sufficient that the union movement had grown, for history warned that the bigger unions put their own interests before their class. It wasn't enough that working men be MPs, for their heads, too, were all too easily turned.

'If that's how you really feel' – Martin groaned, the devil his advocate – 'then why don't *you* bloody well stand for election?'

'It's nee small thing, standing candidates, son. They don't *make* it easy.'

But who were *they*? The boss class, in league with Satan? Martin's considered response, on turning sixteen, was to join the Labour Party. He didn't much warm to the chore of branch meetings, nor could he persuade Titch or Tony or even his most compliant girlfriend to join him. But it seemed a step further to being his own young man.

As if in spite, Joe's militancy grew yet more entrenched. He had always thrown a slice of his wage into a union pot for men made redundant, but now he was donating to some clandestine 'dispute fund'. Jenny was tight-lipped about the shrinkage to the pay packet, and Martin would have known no better, had it not been for a slow Sunday afternoon when she blew up at Joe within his earshot. 'What about the boy? Do you not think you've a duty to him? His prospects? Have you thought of that? Or are you only bothered for your mates? I hope they're bothered for *you*.'

'That is the whole bloody *point*, Jenny. Martin'll be right as rain.'

Joe then sought out his son in the quiet of his room, and they sat uneasily on his bed beneath the tacked wallposters of Led Zeppelin and *A Clockwork Orange*. 'There's a sort of a *conservatism* you get in women, son. It's almost an instinct. They get so bothered for hearth and home – and I don't mean to say that's nowt.

But it does mean they've not always . . . got the heart, you might say, for fighting a tough corner? On principle, like?'

Martin remained in two minds. The spiel might have carried more clout had it been uttered within his mother's hearing. As it happened, Jenny did not stew in her own juice. Rather, she set about refreshing the shorthand she had last purveyed at age sixteen, and obtained a secretarial job at the giant Purves-McArthur Pharmaceutical. Each morning she would commute to a site in Longbenton where the firm's cleverest men conducted leading-edge research into new types of washing powder and sanitary towel. Joe made no fuss, enquiring respectfully of Jenny's day when the family convened for tea, though he was partial to some sharp asides about low union take-up at the Purves plant. Jenny confined herself to a few quietly glowing remarks about her boss, Dr Colin Honeyman, PhD, whose dignities she carefully observed. New social opportunities came her way, she took up invites to dinner parties and dances, and Joe escorted her without gusto. Some nights they returned in silence, Joe in a high colour, Jenny heading directly upstairs. Martin felt for the slow decline in his father's manly charm. But he could see where Joe had let things slide. He remained sure that his own brand could carry all before him.

Newcastle had begun to feel a little too small for him – dreary, fatally deficient in bright lights and crackle. The idea of London gained a foothold in his daydreams. There were trains leaving daily and nightly from Central Station. What if he just climbed aboard one? Similar fancies were perhaps the undoing of his concentration that day on the wintry school sports field when he raced for a fifty-fifty ball with an advancing keeper, realising far too late – committed to his slide – that he would come up badly short. Before he bit the turf, his ankle was wrecked – a blow for the First Eleven, but an outright sickener for Martin Pallister. 'I hope you've got hobbies, bonny lad,' said the doctor who cast his foot. 'Or it'll be whist for you every Saturday night 'til new year.'

With renewed application he hobbled along to Labour branch meetings, now convened at the Corner House pub, and there, amid the drear standing orders, he found himself stuck on one thought. This Party liked to boast of a thousand members per constituency, yet if Martin's branch were typical then there could hardly be two hundred in all Heaton & Wallsend. Ten-to-a-dozen was the monthly average, no more than two or three so-called 'activists', and they seemed active mostly on their own behalves – garrulous blokes, who had pressed for the move to the pub, the better to suit their favoured level of brow-beating ('You've not a bliddy clue, you'). By a little and a little Martin asserted himself, for he sensed that one need only open one's mouth and keep doing so. He was not anti-machismo – he simply preferred his own brand. One night it happened that one of those bluff activists – the joiner George Manton – told him without nicety to go fetch another plate of the cut sandwiches the landlord had laid on. On his return Martin tossed the paper plate and its fare into old George's face, and held his ground as others then held them apart. 'Aye! Aye! And you're an ill-mannered *twat*,' he shouted across the flailing arms.

By the time the Tories went to the country in February of 1974, Martin was off his crutches and running. He dogged and heckled the rabbit Tory candidate all round the constituency. On election day he was out the door by six in the morning, the better to marshal fellow volunteers, take polling-card numbers outside the stations and ferry old folks to vote in his second-hand Morris. Joe showed no more approval for his son's vigour that day than he did for Labour's victory. And that, frankly, boiled Martin's piss.

He was the first Pallister to get to college, a reader of History at Newcastle. He had daydreamed awhile of the London School of Economics, but the living looked expensive, whereas this way he could live at home, whatever vexation was entailed. Joe made some leaden cracks about 'middle-class playgrounds' and indeed Martin felt uneasily favoured, what with Titch off to clerk at Barclays Bank and Tweddle vanished through the gates of Swan Hunter shipyard. But he couldn't spurn his mother's cash when it helped him out and into a shared flat. He cruised his courses, and made a lightning ascent within college politics and the National Organisation of Labour Students. On a platform he had looks and delivery, he didn't shy from popularity contests, and was firmly of a mind that he could win them.

He was less assured of how to finesse his relations with Joe, an ever more prominent face in hard-left circles and the vanguard of his party, now calling themselves the Socialist Workers. Martin could not always demur from the motion that Labour was a wash-up and a sell-out. And yet it remained the pony on which he was minded to bet. His own investment in marching causes was to join CND and the Anti-Nazi League, neither of which gave him offence. There were, perhaps, too many herbivore hippies in the former, and in the latter too many fans of the scrofulous punk rock. Gamely he tried, nonetheless, to stay abreast of new readings in anarchism and feminism, while keeping up his general studies in the opposite sex. A dilemma arose, in that all too many young women at Newcastle were well-bred and well-mannered southerners, to whom his doggishness proved catnip. It was a treat, he found, to fuck upwardly – to give these debutantes a taste of the North. It was also less bother, on the whole, for unlike his dad Martin was unwilling to take the raw edge of any female tongue. Ladyloves came and went, for many were the nights on the lash when he couldn't restrain his thirst, turning red-faced and lecherous or outright unmanageable. Becky Markham from Kentish Town was the one who suffered longest and yet stayed. Her fair hair pinned up like a nurse, her dark hooded eyes so authentically serious, she betrayed a true concern for his welfare. He realised that she loved him, and he was mildly chastened.

In the spring of 1978 he and Becky took a train to London for a big Rock against Racism concert in Hackney, Martin keen to sample the atmosphere and ready, in principle, to give a fair hearing to the Clash. They stayed overnight with her parents Rodge and Pip, in a darkly shuttered terraced home of bare floorboards, littered with Pelican paperbacks and unpainted furniture, its outer walls assailed by ivy. Rodge and Pip were secondary-school teachers both, and though Martin would have genuinely liked for them to like him he soon quit trying, for he had to adjudge them dour and patronising people. On their kitchen wall they made a proud show of a pair of old miners' helmets, hung from nails, though clearly no one in the house had ever worked with anything heavier than a pen. Martin thought it risible – worse even than the mining museum at Beamish in Durham, where the staff clarted about in period pit-costume. The sacred relics were being collected while the industry still drew breath.

In the morning, after toast and stewed tea, Rodge sent the youngsters on their way with a clenched fist. 'Stick it to the fascists, you two.'

Martin found he could no longer tether his tongue. 'Eh, it's a pop concert, we're not off to fight the *Wehrmacht*.'

Pip tutted. 'Martin, you wouldn't say that if you were Asian.'

'Well, I'm not, am I? Okay, we're not so mixed in Newcastle. But I don't think the National Front's got a Thousand Year Reich on the cards.'

He was aware he might as well have pissed into their tea, but was pleased to have relieved his irritation. For some time he had suspected that his tutor at Newcastle was earmarking him for teaching, and in soft moments he yielded to a certain fantasy of standing up and expounding before a classroom of keen lads and lasses. But the profession itself he disliked instinctively – middle-class fuckers in the main, it always seemed, and nary such dismal proof as that before him now.

He woke with an acrid mouth and a pulsing head. The party had been a late one, and to its arduous end he had been declaiming most eloquently to some wide-mouthed girl about the vulnerable merits of anarcho-syndicalism. It was her bedsheets he was now half-in and half-out of, her humid pit of a room. She herself – Rosie by name, he was reasonably sure – was nowhere in view. But then she was tugging him awake, for he had dozed off again. She seemed unusually troubled. He was prepared to apologise. In fact, her moaning was to do with there being a phone call for him. That he had been traced seemed the worst possible start to the day

– this before his flatmate came on the line, barely coherent, to say that Martin's mother had been trying to reach him all morning. Joe had suffered an awful accident at work.

Martin ran all the way to the General Hospital, cursing himself, dread clasping at his stomach and chest, afraid to imagine what he would see.

He found Jenny seated and still and colourless, the mild Dr Honeyman hovering over her, having driven her from Purves directly on receipt of the news. But Honeyman slipped away as Jenny tried dazedly to talk. Joe had been in charge of an overhead crane that unloaded prematurely, a steel drum crushing his right side against a concrete abutment. As Martin put his arms around her, hoping to instil calm and control the wild spin in his head-space, the registrar was pacing toward them, his mouth set plain in a line of regret.

'Mrs Pallister, we've reviewed all the options, I'm afraid an amputation *is* going to be necessary . . .'

'Is there really nothing else you can try?'

'I'm truly sorry, just – the state of the arm, it's effectively severed. Even if we could re-attach it, he'd never have the use of it. I'm so sorry, Mrs Pallister, this is just the place we find ourselves. So I need your approval.'

Jenny was shaking her head, but Martin knew in his bones that matters had passed beyond redemption.

Joe came around very late that night and was propped up, bloodless and hoarse, an immaculate bulbous cloth bandage midway between his right elbow and where his wrist had been.

'I saw it come at us – saw it all the way . . .'

Jenny tried a hesitant caress of his right flank. Martin stared doggedly downward at the vestiges of the mop-head across the linoleum floor.

'See . . . It's odd, so odd. It wasn't the pain, that wasn't the worst – not like you'd think. I just remember thinking, clear as day, aw God, that's it. That's done for, it'll not ever get mended . . .'

In the silence Martin heard the rattle and squeak of trolley wheels.

'It didn't get this, but, eh?'

He glanced up. Joe was raising and clenching his left fist. His voice had clotted, and the gesture seemed to Martin entirely futile and forlorn. Then he heard his mother's drastic sob, saw her painful smile, and realised that Joe's good thumb was rubbing at the thin gold of his wedding band, which he now pressed to his lips. Martin felt himself rise unsteadily, venture to lay a hand on his father's left forearm, and leave the room. Outside, a pair of slender nurses were trotting past and he managed but barely to bury his face behind his hands.

Chapter II

HEARTS AND MINDS

Sunday, 10 November 1996

'When we start to complain of all the things that aren't like they were in the old days – well, there's a danger we never stop, isn't there? The price of butter. Manners – young people's manners especially. Newcastle United, of course. The Labour Party . . .'

Liven up, John, Gore chided himself. As he had feared in the drafting, he was sounding like an old coot. The intention, yes, was to focus on his core demographic, sticks and liver spots and all. Yet as he spoke, he was counting those mainly stooped and grey heads. Thirty-nine, forty? Undoubtedly a turn for the worse – perplexing too, in light of his rising profile, and thus a slight that he was minded to take personally.

'We can always have a pop at the Church, too. You'll have noticed, I'm sure – scheme after scheme we've seen for reforming it, restoring its unity, making it "relevant". Sometimes the extra effort only brings fresh disappointment . . .'

Like, for instance, today. The late-declared absence of Steve Coulson and crew, purportedly 'busy', had reduced them to bare bones, all the more damnable since the scarcity heightened Gore's awareness of a pair of conspicuous newcomers. Blue-suited Martin Pallister was front and centre, sitting upright, arms folded. But Simon Barlow slouched and rubbed his chin near Lindy, who was minus Jake and looking rather nice in boots of tan suede and a jean jacket over a short jade peasant dress. He would have to address the issue of *her* in due course.

'I do wonder sometimes – with all our talk of schemes and structures – whether we've maybe lost sight of the relationship of God and man? If God seems irrelevant to us sometimes, might it not be because we've

made Him a rather distant notion? Not a living God, his influence present among us. But a God stuck in some Bible-story past? Don't get me wrong, God is God – yesterday, today, and for ever.'

He looked up, paused, enjoying Barlow's over-emphatic nod.

'But God's revelation was not set down once and for all time. Not even in the tablets of stone. Why? Because we are God's children. We grow and change, as children do. And God watches us. Do you really imagine that God's own view of his children doesn't change just as we change?'

Gore didn't bother to check for Barlow's displeasure. What he did assess, and appreciate, was the keen attention of Pallister.

'If I might digress just for a moment – perhaps you'll have heard me on the radio recently, or read the column I've been doing for the local paper, talking about some matter of politics?'

A loud harrumph from the pews – Albert Robinson, ever so easily riled.

'Some say that churchmen shouldn't get involved in these things. But politics are our daily bread, aren't they? We can't escape them even if we wanted to. If God has a purpose for this world, politics must be a part of it. Of course, I don't pretend to know His purpose. But I do know it's a matter of what's right and best for us as humankind. How can politics be free of that?'

'I'll tell you what *I* think, Reverend.'

Gore raised his eyebrows but kept his lips veiled by the rim of his teacup.

'You're over-busy, you are. Excuse me, but on the bloody radio and all, banging on about them bloody Bosnians . . .'

Not your bloody business, Albert, thought Gore. It was annoying, though, that Pallister, next in line for the meet-and-greet, had to witness his being harangued. True, he had got himself exercised at length by Dragan and Dijana, a fretful but pleasant pair of young Orthodox migrants who sought him out for guidance on housing. He had only directed them to the Citizens Advice Bureau, and understood they were to be accommodated in one of the fearful high-rises of the Scotswood Road. But their story had struck him sufficiently as to recount it during another appearance on Chris Carter's show, and in his occasional column for the *Journal*.

'I thought you were for *us*.'

'I am, Albert.'

'I'll tell you, you're *not* – not if you're on the side of strings being pulled for people who've just blown into somewhere and want it all handed them on a plate. You can't be for *everybody*.'

The pensioner waved a snappish hand and turned, nearly clashing into Pallister, at whom he peered with similar contumely before shuffling off. Gore supposed he might just have lost one more punter. He ought then to be working the flagging room, asking after everyone's health. But Pallister could scarcely be expected to wait, nor did he look minded to. Meanwhile, and rather to Gore's irritation, Simon Barlow seemed to be circulating purposefully, chortling keenly, giving the glad hand to one and all.

Pallister whistled through his teeth. 'Tough crowd you get in, John.'

'Oh, some people, they've just got to get their tuppence worth. Thanks for coming, anyway. You didn't bring your camera crew?'

'Naw, man, I thought you'd have one ready for us.' He glanced around the sparse hall. 'No, they weren't wrong, it's a job you've got on here. You deserve every encouragement.' He slotted his folded Order of Service into his jacket pocket and rubbed his palms as if removing a sully. 'Anyway. This was good, thanks, got to shoot off now, pick up my lad for the day.'

'You have a son?'

'I thought I told you. Suzie didn't mention? I'm nowt but an invoice to her, aren't I? Look, so what about my offer? Have you had any thoughts?'

'I'm thinking it over, as we said.'

Pallister crooked a forearm, jabbed at his watch-face. 'Statute of limitations, mind, eh? C'mon, man. I've not got for ever. That forum I told you about? It's this Thursday. If we're doing this, I need you there.'

'I'll talk to you before then.'

'Try and be sharper, eh? I'm not back in London 'til tomorrow night.'

Into Pallister's place stepped Mrs Alison Boyle, sighing as she squared loose pages of sheet music needlessly between her hands.

'Is it all okay with you, John? What I'm doing?'

'Fine, sure. Why wouldn't it be?'

'Oh, just you never say, so I wouldn't know.'

And off she trotted, point made. As he frowned Gore felt a soft hand on his shoulder. 'Oh! Lindy.'

'Aye, *Lindy*. Listen, you. I want a word.' And she threw a light pretend punch at his arm. Fully decorated this morning, mascara and mauve eye-shadow, fuchsia lips and *framboise* rouge, little pink clips in her hair. For November it was a summery sort of ensemble, and he noted she didn't wear a bra either. But then he supposed it was the local custom. She looked nice, for sure, and he knew he ought really to tell her as much.

'John? Are you listening to us?'

'Sorry, can we pop outside?' He gestured to the door, conscious of his own hush. As he took her arm, he saw Monica throw him a critical glance. *Come on, what's to look at?* True, several more able-bodied regulars had already pitched into stacking up the chairs. But the vicar couldn't do everything – not every Sunday, not on top of the prep and the spadework and the diplomacy. Did he not deserve five minutes' grace?

They trotted together down the school corridor in silence, passing the Year Two artboard. He heard her scoff under her breath.

'Ha. Typical. Fanny Blott's taken all Jake's pictures off the board.'

'How is Jake? Where is he today?'

'With his auntie. He's got a bit cold.'

'Oh. I'm sorry.'

Pushing out of the front doors Gore took in the panorama of the car park. Simon Barlow leaned against his Mondeo, in the startling act of puffing on a cigarette. A few berths further away, big Sharon Price was helping her bent grandmother into the rear seat of a hatchback, the slowness painful to behold. Even she seemed to peer at him without sympathy. He turned to see Lindy kicking her square heels under the legend FAITH HOPE CHARITY.

'What, then?'

'Well, yes, what?'

'*You* wanted to gan outside.'

'Yes but you wanted a word?'

'Aw right, and you don't?'

She was shaking her hennaed head in sore wonder. Other parties were starting to trail out of the front doors and past the pair of them – curly Rod Moncur, his usual grin mislaid. No, Gore granted he had not thought this manoeuvre through so very astutely.

'Are we a secret then? You and me?'

'Well, not any more, I doubt. Look.' He beckoned her a little further hence, closer to the wall. 'Lindy, I'm not trying to make a fuss, I just think a little discretion is maybe necessary? It's not – it's just there are various issues. One is I want to have you more involved in this church, and that will be harder if I'm known to be – involved with you.'

'John, if I'm dead honest? I'm not really bothered about your church. It's not why I'm here, is it?'

Gore absorbed this. It seemed quite the day for plain speaking.

'Are you even arsed about us? I mean, do you want to spend time with us?'

'Yes, I do. Look, if we're being so honest, I was more wondering if you wanted to spend time with *me*.'

'Well, right enough, you never pick up the phone so you're probably a wrong 'un.'

'It's just I've got an awful lot on, Lindy.'

'You think I don't?'

'I don't mean it like that, it's more . . . you've got your hours, yes? Your shifts? My commitments are a bit more nebulous. And sort of . . . continuous. But I do have certain specific times that are free –'

'Like when?'

'*And*, listen, *and* those are times I'd gladly spend with you. And Jake.'

'You don't have to worry there, John, you're not his daddy.'

'Well, come on, I don't pretend that, do I?'

Presenting a mask of hurt seemed to buy Gore a moment to measure his feeling. Why was he letting this slide? Work, yes – his mission, it wore a solitary cast. There again, his own company also gave him no offence. It did not, at any rate, entail complications of this kind at every turn.

'Okay, so how's about Tuesday? Can we's do something Tuesday?'

'Blast. I can't.'

'You see?'

'Wednesday, but? I'd love to see you then.'

She swayed. 'Right then, Wednesday. In the day, aye? You'll come round to ours?'

He had earned half a smile, however expensively bought. She offered her lips, and he abandoned caution and brushed them lightly with his own, a hand straying to her hip. Then he watched her wander away, and wondered what they might do to pass the time.

Barlow was sauntering over, stroking his chin, grinning impiously.

'Girl trouble, John? Blimey. Kiss and make up though, eh?'

In the teeth of unwanted scrutiny Gore endeavoured to exude only blankness. Barlow chuckled and looked aside. 'Oops. 'Scuse me for breathing, then. That was old Martin Pallister in there with you, wasn't it? What got him here?'

'Just being the MP, out for the community. Wants me involved in some project.'

'*Oh* yeah? What would that be?'

'God knows. It's written on the wind.'

Barlow wore the aspect of the ravening hound denied its haunch, but seemed resolved nonetheless to divert his energies. 'Huh. Anyway. That sort of half worked today, didn't it? I mean, with the obvious problems.'

'It's been better. Today was a fall-off. I had some support missing.'

'Yeah, I was hoping to see these bouncers of yours. Nah, you've done okay, John. Done it your way. I respect that. We're different, I know, but we both plough our own furrow, don't we? You and me? Lone wolves. The diocesan mob up here, they haven't a clue how to handle me neither.'

'You're maybe not the easiest man to handle, Simon.'

'Oh, I try to fit in. You don't hear me moaning about women priests any more, do you? I don't need the aggravation, it's a waste of time. And energy.' He produced his packet of Silk Cut, extended it to Gore. 'No? It's the workload's got me on these. No, seriously. My thing is, I just want to make my point, have it noted, then get on with my job. Working for the gospel on Tyneside.' He flared up and exhaled. 'Some causes are lost. There's always others.'

Gore glanced behind him. 'Simon, I ought to head back in.'

'Hang on, no, listen. We ought to talk. I wanted to say – do you remember Gavin Knott? From back at Grey?'

'Gavin. Yeah, I do. Augustine fan. Quiet sort, serious.'

'You didn't keep in touch though? I thought you two were matey?'

'No, not so much. I know he went to London. Lewisham, I think.'

'He did, yeah, close to a pal of mine. Anyway.' Barlow sighed. 'The thing is, Gavin, he's – ah well, the bad news is he's HIV-positive is what he is.'

Gore's hand went to his brow. 'No. Oh no. That's awful.'

'Yup. Sad to say.'

'Are you sure? How do you know?'

'This pal of mine. It's not news yet, but it's gonna be. Bound to be.'

The news had dismayed Gore more than he could have anticipated. Casting his mind back now, he was surprised that Knott had ever let himself succumb to an expression of sexuality. His catastrophe then seemed doubly cruel.

'Oh, it's tragic, yeah. Real tragedy, for him.' Barlow sighed. 'But there's an issue there too. Don't you think?'

The amity had slunk out of Barlow's even gaze, as Gore now supposed it had been bound to. 'What do you mean?'

'Well, I don't know how else you dress it up, John. We bang on about these things and no one ever listens. It's just a fact, but. You don't get up to that sort of thing, and you don't get diseases that kill you.'

'Is that what you'd say to Gavin?'

'What would *you* say, John? After all this time? "Sorry, pal"? Look, I didn't want the poor little sausage to suffer. I didn't want people like him to ever get in that jam in the first place. You *know* that, John, I've always said it. It's time to get it out on the table and say "Enough". Our Church wasn't meant to be just a refuge for a load of mixed-up gaylords. Sheepish little closet-cases, always saying "Judge not". All because they've got every reason to fear getting judged. This is serious, John. If they won't go now, it's time they got shown the door.'

'You mean a witch-hunt.'

'This is a broad church, mate, but there are limits. I mean, what you were saying in there – God changing his mind and all that *crap*. Near the knuckle, son. I'd half a mind to get up there and clip you one. So, no, I wouldn't mind the odd heresy trial. It'd weed out the traitors. Shield the faith.'

Replete with his enemy's malice, Gore took a deep breath. 'It's such a *gift* you've got, Simon, to be so cheery when everything out of your mouth sounds like a threat.'

'Oh, don't be taking it personal, mate.'

'Why not, *mate*? You're stood there all twinkly like you've got something up your sleeve to ruin my day and you can't wait to say it.'

'There's no secrets with me, John. At least give me that much, I'm clear as day where I stand. Who I stand with. I've got my own group up here, we're two hundred strong. Not some bunch of loons.' He had drawn closer. Gore could smell that tobacco-breath, and a certain cologne sharp as pine-fresh toilet cleaner. 'Now, it's our view that the Church teach its members to abstain from sex outside of matrimony. Or else pay the cost. *And*, that ministers do likewise. Or else be disciplined. Cos what does Revelation say of Jezebel, John?'

'Simon, I don't give a –'

'"I have given her time, time to repent of her sin, but she is unwilling. So I will cast her on a bed of suffering. Then all will know I am he who searches hearts and minds, and I will repay according to deed."'

'If you could only hear how stupid you sound –'

'I hear myself very clear, John. I have listened to my conscience, I have looked into my heart, like a *laser* I've looked, John. And I am content that I live as God wants. Now I'm looking at you, son. And I'm not impressed.'

Barlow wheeled away and seemed almost to dance the distance back to his Mondeo. The citing of Revelation, Gore supposed, had just made his day.

Monday morning and he dallied by the bulletin board, carefully apart from where Cliffy stood, woeful, before a clerk's window. Gore had Kully Gates to thank for this assignment, and though he hadn't quite mastered the fine print in respect of the new 'Jobseekers Allowance', he accepted her view that his presence might be of vague use to Cliffy. He hadn't seen inside a dole office for a decade either, and the new set-up seemed daunting as well as glum. The carpet was sadly worn, a solitary aspidistra wilted gently by the window to the street. But the security provisions looked very new, new as the navy cable-knit sweater on the burly bored-looking man by the door, whom Gore took to be some sort of bouncer.

He perused the cards pinned under VACANCIES. 'Barperson wanted, £3.60 per hour.' 'Deputy Manager, Call Centre, £7,300 p.a.' 'Catering assistant, £3.20 per hour, 6-day week. Shifts.' Which of these – he wondered suddenly – might he be moved to try his hand at? If he absolutely had to, were he cast out of his living by Witchfinder Barlow?

The thought was dispelled by noises from over his shoulder, and he spun. Cliffy was still by the window, but thumping on the counter. Gore darted to the boy's side. The female clerk had a file cracked open before her.

'Is there a problem?'

'How man, I telt you, she won't let us have me dole.'

'I'm sorry, sir, are you any relation to Mr Petty?'

'He's my friend. He belongs to my congregation.'

'Well, as I've advised him, his entitlement's elapsed.'

'I don't understand, sorry, how can that be?'

'It's policy, I'm afraid. We have to withdraw social security from the claimant for a certain time if instructions have been ignored.'

'What instructions?'

'Mr Petty refused an offer of work without cause.'

'I didn't get me bastad hair cut.'

'That's right, a maintenance post at the Telewest Arena. The employer's conditions were very clear, and I advised Mr Petty there would be a penalty if he chose not to want to satisfy them. He signed a contract.'

'You can't just say – I mean, he must have another chance.'

'Sir, I'm sorry, you don't know the whole story. He's been told umpteen times if he can't show us evidence he's been actively seeking work, and that means paper evidence –'

'Aw, piss off then if you think I'm a liar.'

That, Gore knew, was not a political move.

'Sorry, but if you must shout I'll have to have you escorted off premises.'

'This is *fuckin' bollocks,*' Cliffy protested, slamming the counter again with his feeble fist. Gore flinched, but he did not suppose the gesture could possibly make matters worse – until the hitherto listless security guard loped toward them. Gore placed a proprietary hand on Cliffy's shoulder.

Out in the street, he groped for what might be the paternal response.

'Look, Cliffy, don't worry, I can check into this for you.'

'What can yee do, man? You're *useless.*'

That stung. 'Well, look, I do know somebody who might help . . .'

He patted his coat pockets. The card was there somewhere, with both office and mobile numbers. And this would be a reasonable test of good faith.

'The problem's not your little friend. It's the *really* useless ones who spoil it for the rest.' Pallister sighed and leaned back in his swivel chair, at the end of a day that appeared to have told upon him. 'Frankly, we're concerned about benefit fraud. You'll say that's Tory behaviour, I bet. But it's got fairly clear to me the state shouldn't have to fund certain ingrained habits that are basically anti-social. So – you tighten the rules. But, yeah, they do then tighten on everyone. The just and the unjust.'

Clutching a token cup of coffee, Gore leaned in, and nearly out of his seat.

'Yes, but this system, it's going to put people on a rubbish dump. Kids.'

'No. Everybody gets another chance. Look, John, the way things have got, there just *has* to be a bit of coercion into work. It's called treating people as adults. All of us, at some stage, we've had to just swallow our pride and do things we didn't like – to get on, to show willing. *Test* ourselves, even. I mean, it's an opportunity, really, if you look at it. I don't want to see anyone on the breadline. But I don't want them dependent neither – on "good turns". There has to be provision. But it can't be free, as such. You have to sign up. Get yourself to class in the morning.'

Pallister rose sluggishly and went to his window, refilled his mug from a tepid cafetière, took thirsty gulps. His enervation was truly pronounced.

'Had a day of it, have you?'

'Just the usual. Problems, problems . . . Housing, as usual. Schools, kids having bother in school, or they can't get *into* schools. And then an awful lot of people who are just *depressed*, it seems to me.' Pallister shook his head. 'You must get a lot of what I get. People just stalking up to have a bloody good rant in your face. Pissed off about some rubbish in their lives they can't get shot of, but they reckon *you* can – in some sort of magical way they don't understand but they're sure exists.' The MP slumped back into his chair. 'So. What do you do? You tell them you'll look into it. You'll talk to someone. Maybe go with them to have it out face to face. But there's a procedure. You have to do a bit of checking-up too – just to be sure the grievance is legitimate, right? Before you go barging in. Because some people can see everybody's wrongs but their own.' He threw up his hands. 'But tell *them* all that, and their eyes go narrow like, "Aw right, what are *you* then?" I don't know . . . I mean, what do you say to a woman tells you her boy's gonna get shot? For some drug-related rubbish? A mother's love, it's pitiful, isn't it?'

Gore would have liked to have rebutted Pallister at some point. But he needed some moments to alight on an element that jarred. 'There are times, y'know, when you sound more Geordie than others.'

'I've lived in Newcastle all me life, John.'

'Yeah, but Susannah was the same, after she went to college. Turned posh, but just gave it a little bit Geordie now and again. For whatever reason.'

Pallister massaged his brow. 'John, I tell you, I'm getting weary of you sitting there drinking my coffee, trying to kick my arse all round this office.'

'I don't want your coffee,' said Gore, setting his mug down on the carpet.

'It's not about *coffee*, man. Look – here's what. What you've told us, I'm happy to look into. If I have to, I'll raise this lad's issue with the right persons. So how about a bit of good will, eh? How about getting onboard with me? For a perfectly harmless bit of putting wor heads together?'

'You still want to steal my thunder?'

'What bloody thunder, man? I saw your show, you had what? Three dozen people in your little school hall?'

'There were fifty.'

'You reckon? Well, we start working together and you'll double your numbers. I know you're on the radio and all that, but it's not going to get you closer to the people who can *change* things.'

'What's it about, then? This forum? Where is it?'

'Blackwater Hotel on the Quayside, very nice. It's just a day's conference, a panel, a few speeches, bits on the side. Look, all I'm asking is you sit on a platform with me. Speak your mind. You can do that, can't you?'

'The agenda. What is it? Can we discuss it?'

'Agenda's already done, it's fixed. But I'll get you a copy. Ed!' He shouted through the open doorway to his diligent researcher.

'Fixed by who?'

'Me and some other people I've got onboard. I can't just do it with you, John. Listen, you'll meet them. And your voice is just as valid as anyone's. No one has veto, my mind's not made up and nor is anyone else's.'

'I just want to know what I'm getting into.'

'Well, I can't tell you yet, John. I'm not saying it's all laid out. I *am* saying, give it a whirl. I'd value your input. If not? Fine, let's shake hands and you'll not hear from me again, I promise.'

Gore knew what he would do. He dallied only in the sudden realisation of how much he would have missed these little colloquies had he chosen otherwise. He thrust out his hand.

'Hang on – is that in or out?'

'In.'

'*Right* then.' They shook, Pallister grinning broadly. 'Good man. See, John, I'm telling you, there's no time in this life to be shy.'

Chapter III

BY HAND OR BY BRAIN

1982–1989

'Aren't you going to speak?' The sotto voce of Ms Polly Charlesworth posed a challenge, implied an expectation.

'Not yet,' Martin shushed. Her throaty whisper had a power to excite, but just for the moment she was annoying him.

They sat decorously side by side in the stalls, drinks at their feet, one very blonde undergraduate historian and her doctoral supervisor. The night's business was one more factional meeting, the AGM of the Labour Coordinating Committee. Upon rising this late November Sunday of 1982 Martin had made a sober assessment of the odds that boredom might reign, and so decided to bring a date.

But there were easily a hundred and fifty bodies convened in the lofty Rutherford Hall of Newcastle Poly, a journey from Martin's home of less than a mile. Others had come far, not least the mildly annoying foursome sat behind he and Polly, two youngish couples, nicely dressed, up from London. At a glance Martin imagined them en route to a Genesis gig, but he soon gathered that they were barristers, albeit very bored with the Bar, trading complaints of surly clerks and early hours. In fairness, they were also conferring in hushed, fraught tones about the main debate of the night.

'Order please, let's get started. Item one on the agenda is our debate on the register of groups. The LCC executive has met and commended – in line with Conference, and Clause Two of the constitution in respect of membership – that we support and add our name to the Party's proposed register of internal groupings. Right, I know there's plenty wanting to speak, so let's try to get through this. The chair recognises Phil Conroy, Wallasey CLP.'

Martin bent his mouth toward Polly's fragrant left lobe. 'Here we go then. You're gonna hear all the black arts tonight.'

The dogs in the street knew this 'register' palaver was a ploy to smoke out the Militant Tendency. Even his dad was wise to it, sat like Buddha in his empty bloody bookshop, living apart – to all intents and purposes – from Jenny. 'There's some say now's the time to get in and take over the Party. Fine by me. But my lot want no part of it.'

Martin himself had no time for the Spartan cadres of Militant, their shifty efforts to infiltrate Labour's grassroots committees. He could see the appeal of the subterfuge, were one a doggedly sanctimonious sort of a prick. But as a long-time GC delegate from his own branch, he knew that one only had to attend a few drear meetings to get oneself kicked upstairs – hardly a heroic assault on the Winter Palace.

Thus it pleased him that Ms Charlesworth was witness to tonight's arguments, for they were all good grist to her thesis, provisionally titled 'Splitting Airs and Graces: A History of Labour Defectors from H. M. Hyndman to The Limehouse Declaration'. As an alternative title he had proposed 'The Masturbatory Tendency', and earned a dirty laugh. Her line of inquiry he wholly endorsed, and much else besides. What was the secret of blondeness, its reign over him? A riddle, wrapped in a mystery, inside an enigma. And there was Becky, stuck with her teacher-training homework back at their not-too-grotty flat on Garland Avenue. It wasn't a cushy life but they had all they needed for the moment. She didn't contest his nights with Titch and Tony, or Saturdays consumed by the pub team, the Toon match and a gallon drunk in its aftermath. Her discernible interest in procreation, though, was not a productive line – indeed a reactionary tendency, as his dad had always said. His wage was just about fit for books and beer, and a long way shy of baby's trousers.

Tonight he was struggling to find the passion for proceedings. More than the usual fissiparous Labour business, it was the collegiate setting that depressed him – the grim hall like a refectory, the plastic chairs and fag smoke and unsmiling faces over coat collars.

Still, such was his life, he had made it all himself, vice-chair of Heaton & Wallsend Labour, area convenor for Labour Students, soon-to-be lecturer in history at the university. Already he had a useful little office, with a door that locked.

Up front, behind a small lectern, one more free-speech hero in donkey jacket and dungarees was slashing at the air with a finger. *'Why should we go along with this farce? Why endorse a witch-hunt? We should affirm the rights of Labour members to hold any damn views they want, so long as they're* socialist *views. These kinds of purges, comrades, they have a black history. I know I joined the Young Socialists to stamp out this sort of thing.'*

Martin inclined his head to Polly's. 'I joined the Young Socialists to meet girls.'

She disdained him with her whole face. 'You act like you're above it all.'

'Not a bit. I'm just sick of this game. Leftie versus Super-Leftie.'

'Who do you *like* then?'

'I'm for the register, Polly. I'm not for all these bloody Benn groupies.'

'Wedgwood Benn,' she sighed. 'God, I lost my heart to that man.'

Short hairs of embarrassment distended on his neck. Admittedly, Benn was why Martin himself had signed up to the LCC, indeed the criterion for membership in those days. He had respected the man's principles, his oratory, his fight to divest himself of a hereditary title. It was the obduracy since that had dispelled his charm – the air Benn carried of saviour-in-waiting, a different brand of flighty entitlement. He was a recruiting sergeant for the common-sense brigade of the SDP, and a lightning rod for Super-Leftie tosspots. They had been through all this in the LCC, a million fucking times, and Benn's lot had stomped off in high dudgeon. And yet here they all were, scrapping away still in this dismal chamber. The queue of speakers had dwindled, and on balance there had been far too many northern voices, in praise of Real Socialism, dotingly acclaimed.

'This could go either way,' he murmured distractedly at his po-faced date.

'Well, speak, then. Why don't you get up and speak?'

He did have some notes. And yet – hateful sensation – he found himself torn, shy of this stage. Bollocks about witch-hunts apart, there was no easy way to take the high ground on either side of this borderline question – no straight route to applause. It was a compromise matter, and he was not a compromise man.

'Oh, this is shit . . .'

Well, well. The low mutter came from behind Martin, for one of the Genesis quartet was getting to his feet, shifting along and out of his row.

'I'll let the posh lad from London go first,' Martin whispered to Polly, realising too late that his whisper had carried. One of the posh lad's associates prodded his shoulder over the seat back.

'Actually, Martin, you'll find Tony's a Durham lad.'

Belatedly Martin recognised the Lancastrian accent of the Membership Secretary. 'Oh, he's from *Durham* is he?' was as much as he could muster – a non-vintage rejoinder.

Tony from Durham was giving his name at top table, taking his place next in line, tugging at the colour of his checked shirt, stealing glances at some crumpled crib sheet. A bit nervous? Rightly so. He had clouds of hair, and a rather girlish ruby mouth that cleaved remarkably as he chanced a smile toward his friends.

'The chair recognises Tony Blair, Hackney CLP.'

His figure didn't inspire confidence as he stepped to the lectern, yet he was casting a hard lawyer's look around the assembled. Martin decided he wouldn't mind if the bloke took a pasting.

'I have to say to you – those members who've criticised the register – you talk very passionately about what's right. And I do respect that. I'm sure you're sincere. But I must also say – you're very sure of yourselves. Almost godlike in your assurance. And, I mean – I say that as someone's who's a churchgoer. Though I know that's not so fashionable these days . . .'

He smiled a little abashedly into his chest, as well Martin thought he might.

'You say your socialism's pure. Purer than mine, I'm sure. Fine. But what do you want to do *with that? Other than get people like me to*

admit we're just rubbish, next to you lot? I do wonder, you know, how long we're going to go over these same old arguments. I mean, what's the ordinary Labour member to make of it? All this talk about witch-hunts – I have to tell you, it sounds self-indulgent. It looks *horrendous. And for goodness' sake, what's actually in front of us? A simple request that we abide by the constitution and the decision of Conference. Our constitution says there shouldn't be parties within the Party. That's a fact. Yes, fine, socialists should stand up and argue their convictions. But the biggest party is the biggest party. And I don't happen to think there should be sects within it. Full-time agitators. Whose so-called editorial board meet in secret and send down tablets in stone. There should be debate, yes. But also consent – consent that the majority view is the best view, if that view has prevailed democratically.'*

'Tony' folded his crib sheet, apparently content he had expressed himself.

'If you don't like that – if you hate the rest of us so much – then what are you doing here?'

The applause in the room was muted, if prolonged and stormy at Martin's shoulder. 'There you go,' Martin smiled thinly at Polly. 'No need to speak. The posh lad nailed it.' She looked at him in low esteem, and he could see that this had not been his finest couple of hours.

By days and by inches it crept across Martin that he had been coasting – dallying and waiting, in some dulled manner, for his life to begin. But in the autumn of 1983 the newly enrobed Dr Pallister was, as promised, appointed the history department's youngest ever Lecturer/Researcher. Three weeks on, Becky cautiously told him she was five days late. The slight shakiness he felt in his legs was nothing compared to the quite unheralded sense of well-being. He circulated the news and, hostage made to fortune, swore a private vow to renounce the night, forswear Polly Charlesworth and pitch himself into productive labour. As Becky grew mildly gravid, he began to give classes at weekend schools for trade unionists, funded by the Transport and General. They seemed glad to have such a scholar among them, and the working men he taught were gratifyingly savvier – much less moping – than his workaday students.

His settled area of expertise was the political ambition and mobilisation by or on behalf of the British industrial working class. At times he felt like a professor in the pains of his own family. When the miners went out in March of '84 he groaned inwardly, for he could see no good come of it. A strike was the last thing Martin would have wished on his Party – a forcing of sides, a resurrection of nostrums, old-style class war. But his dad, dependable as a prize pigeon, was up at Grey Monument every Saturday, rattling the tin.

Martin was otherwise engaged, for Alexander Pallister was born without complication on the 1st of September 1984. Becky's exertions astounded him, and when he clutched the infant to his chest he felt yet more of a humble man. Though their quarrels were now incrementally more nerve-stretched, he accepted that he had shouldered a moral and emotional debt. He and Becky were married the following March, in the same week that the miners took the longest walk back, trudging in step behind banners and bands. Rodge and Pip attended the registry service with no apparent acrimony, no mention whatever of helmets or fascists.

As soon as Alex could toddle, Becky resumed her teacher training with the extramural assistance of Martin's mum, and an occasional hand from Dr Pallister himself on such days as he was allegedly grading papers at home. In the run-up to Christmas he drove Jenny and the boy over the river to the Metro Centre, a spanking new 'super-mall'. It was his first visit, for he had political objections to the place. The land for the build had been reclaimed from the mud of Dunston Power Station, and great praise afforded its developer, Cameron Hall Limited. Martin disdained the chorus, for the egregious Mr John Hall struck him as the worst sort of bolshy, made-good, self-adoring Tory, one whose vaunted acumen seemed largely to consist of having flogged his stake at the earliest point, and to the dopey old Church Commissioners at that.

Inside the Metro he pushed his son's chair along the promenades, half-appalled, half-amazed. It was a retailer's paradise of a sort, Marks, Fraser's, Boots, BHS. The masses were crammed in, families fully assembled, grannies and bairns in tow. He heard Scots and Brummie accents. The design seemed a stately conveyor to carry one round and up and down again, past each and every strip-lit shopfront, leaving one so limp and scant of fresh air that a stodgy meal on a tray and a drink in a plastic cup became suddenly enticing. All this, he suspected sourly, was likely why some of his lazier colleagues were writing long pseudo-scholarly papers – toying even with books – about fucking *shopping*.

In due course the Pallisters too rested their feet by a slow-bubbling fountain, and Alex was treated to a drooling ice-cream sundae. 'Good place, isn't it?' offered Jenny, dipping into a small pink paper bag, unfurling a beaded scarf. Martin grunted. He had lingered only over a selection of compact-disc players, repelled by the expense of rebuying *Who's Next* and *Led Zeppelin IV* in the minimal new format.

'I don't know,' he winced. 'I find it ugly. No character, man.'

'Well now, this is Gateshead, Martin, it was never pretty.'

'Aye, but what's this got that Newcastle hasn't?'

'Well, I tell you what I like, you can really shop around. You can't get oversold, not that I can see. Not like Fenwick's. All under one roof. I mean to say, it's *huge*.'

'It was Enterprise land, all this, you know? They're not paying rates, they'll not even pay tax.'

Jenny shrugged as to say that was neither here nor there. 'I know I've had a nice day. How about you, little man?'

Alex nodded shyly, raspberry sauce all over his lips. Martin swilled tepid Coca-Cola round his mouth. Such was the nightmare scenario to his mind – that big ugly wheezes such as these were somehow seen to *work*.

It had gnawed at him for some time – a certain historical notion – that the north-east was a laboratory for this stuff, a testing ground for some spark's obsession with the spanking new and cutting edge. When Wilson had blown hot air about a 'white heat' of technology, no one had taken it seriously, least of all Wilson himself. And yet, somehow, north of York and Darlington, the notion seemed to enjoy breathless respect. Worse, it was open to easy purloin – Thatcher, donning a white coat and a hard hat to open the Nissan car plant in Sunderland.

All this, Martin knew in his gut, was the grist of his own major work. It wouldn't be fucking *shopping*, that was for sure. No, the north-east was living an industrial nightmare, but one from which it might awaken. The crisis was an opportunity, for radical analysis. What would Marx have said? Might new industry render the old no more than a blackened memory? Could the Metro ever employ so many as his dad's works? Doing what? It seemed a lightweight proposition. *All that is solid melts into air.* Yet this mall, these crowds, their custom – you couldn't call it fly-by-night.

Martin wetted a finger between his lips and rubbed absently at his son's smeared and beaming cheeks. Oh aye – happy now – happy he had what he wanted off his grandma. It was a breezily banal thing, family life – it gave and it took away. His energies felt sporadic to him now, his style firmly cramped. At work, where once he had basked, he found himself newly irascible to his students. One above all gave him a keen pain between the eyes, through every profitless tutorial hour. This was Paul Todd, the ex-Durham mechanic, now chasing a mature education for himself after the closure of Sacriston Colliery. A protégé of Martin's union weekenders, and ostensibly a sensible lad, he had somehow fallen in with Joe and mutated into the same species of Trot know-all. It was sufficiently distressing to have lost a fan – much the worse to be rowing with some lanky doppelgänger of his dad every fortnight in a tiny office.

With crushing inevitability Todd had chosen for his thesis the Taff Vale Judgement of 1901, wherein the Lords made the railwaymen's society liable for costs of a strike they hadn't supported. Martin freely conceded this to be a turning point for the fledgling union movement, a spur to their pursuit of representation at Westminster. Todd, though, seemed to see it as a proud and final welding together of a class determined to secure for itself the full fruits of its labour, 'by hand or by brain'. At first patiently, Martin tried to make the lad see the sometime vying interests and concerns of dock workers and engineers, the not always pure desire for political power, the often faint-heard claims of solidarity. Todd only sat there and laughed at him. 'How did a Labour lad like you get so down on the unions, Martin?'

He was Dr Pallister, in point of fact, and for some reason he could not but take it personally. 'Because, Paul, they don't speak for their members. What they do is deliver a nice fat sack of their members' votes to the leadership, all stitched up . . . I've heard it all before, man. If you get bored I could sit here and argue your end too, argue better and all.'

He knew he ought to be generous. It gave him no pleasure to cut that sorriest figure, the poacher-turned-gamekeeper. But such was the straitjacket for which he had got himself fitted – the former firebrand, now to be found down at the shopping mall, his gibbering bairn on his lap, ice cream staining the lapel of his all-weather coat.

The GC of Heaton & Wallsend had dreamed of convening in high spirits at the Rajdoot curry house come the 18th of July 1987. The revel, though, became a post-mortem. There was nothing half-baked about a majority of seventeen thousand for Mike Watt. Newcastle Central, too, had been wrested back to where it belonged. In the country, though, it was the same old waste of breath, for the Tories had said 'Britain is Great Again, Don't Let Labour Wreck It', and they had been believed.

Martin had demanded a free pass for the night from Becky, she more terse than obliging, and he duly planted both feet in the trough, wolfing a scarily red tandoori mixed grill, keeping the pints coming. Mike Watt was an affable moon-faced bloke, yet another lawyer, as seemed obligatory these days. But he sat laconic at the end of the table, surrounded by the women, nodding limply at each hare-brained critique of how Labour had fought. It seemed to Martin that not one in this bunch had the gumption of the late George Manton, at whose hardy forehead he had once hurled a plate of egg-and-crisp sandwiches. And if there was one thing he liked less in Labour than self-pity, it was self-satisfaction.

'It's like what Hatters said on telly the other night, we have to stick by our sermon on the mount . . .'

'That bloke with the moustache, fancies himself. I don't care for him. Didn't care for that red rose, not one bit . . .'

'Come on, don't be so fucking quick to knock Mandelson.' Martin hadn't thought that he would swear, or slur, but such was his mood, and it killed all other conversation. 'I mean, come on. There's nowt wrong with a red rose. It's our policies people didn't want. If you want to think the public are kidding themselves, go on, kid yourself too. It's patronising shit, but.'

'That's not very friendly, Martin.'

'Whey, we're too friendly in this Party. We're afraid to hear what we don't want to. Britain's back on top, we've made it happen, my lot are alright, the rest of you skivers fuck off.'

'Get *away*, Martin.'

'You don't believe that!'

'I'm not talking about *me*, man. I'm talking about *people*, they like backing winners. I've worked for this Party since I was sixteen. We beat the Tories twice that bloody *year*, man.'

It was a heated, intolerable table and he left early without preamble, desirous of different company. He reached Titch Harwood from the payphone in Bob Trollop's pub. Mike Tweddle couldn't be prised from his hearth, but newly divorced Tony Charnley was game. From Trollop's to the Offshore, the Cooperage, Akenside Traders, they got locked in a session. Martin felt some of the old crackle in his strides. Onward! Down to the river, and the pulsating Club Zeus. The fucking lightweights only left him there. But the devil in his ear sang, *Marty, oh Marty, man, you've done it again. In for a penny, in for a pound, get yourself hung for a sheep as a lamb.*

The music was poison but the place was throbbing wall to wall with summertime girls, partially clad, tender flesh kissed by the sun or singed by the sun-bed. Swishing hair and bobbing chests on the dance floor, some of their looks awfully provocative. That was the thing about girls – they walked past you and all of a sudden you pictured other possibilities in life.

He danced gamely with a few, one who stood very tall in heels, her black hair eerily long and straight, Kirsty by name, a bit too mannishly square-jawed for his taste, but clearly keen as mustard. With a meditative succession of vodkas, though, he had grown, he knew, just a teeny bit fixated by a girl with a Betty Boop haircut in a shiny slip of a blue dress. Eighteen, surely – legal and tender? He had no qualms about shimmying up close and slow. Then, to his stupefaction, some lanky arsehole was trying to push him aside.

'Just get *away*, man. Fuck off.'

'Lindy, I'll gan and get big Steve.'

Lindy had liked him, though, she surely had. 'You cheeky get,' she had pouted at some stage, if a good bit earlier. She had her bloke, alright, but plainly she liked Dr Pallister tonight.

A big baldy bouncer surfaced with alacrity, a little keener-eyed than the usual meathead, seeming to think himself a Zen Master.

'Alright, *Steve*, just cool it, eh, kid? Nowt to see here.'

A cuboid hand was planted on his shoulder and he intended to shrug it aside in short order, for through the fog he recalled what Tweddle the boxing fan always said about keeping hands up and chin low, throwing from your hips. Then an elbow struck him like a shovel in the face, a hammer fist fell on his nose, and the lights went down over the Quayside.

Kirsty was his saviour and damnation, helping him up, getting him out and into a cab. Alas, she resolved at some stage to go all the way. Next Martin knew, the taxi was running on Garland Avenue, Kirsty had determinedly inserted herself into his drowsy arms, but Becky – crazily – was standing out in the street in a tee-shirt and flip-flops. He stumbled indoors. He had no explanation. Only with the bathroom closed in his face did it occur to him how he might look. Then the door was open again, Becky hissing, 'Don't you *dare* wake Alex.'

The next day he was a dirty hungover dog, under a loathsome sun. Becky would not look at him.

'Why did you have to get so hammered?'

'Because I'm miserable.'

'*You're* miserable. *Miserable?* You *fucking* child.'

He had nothing else prepared, whereas she had phone numbers and condoms retrieved from his coat pockets. He had expected he would make a pledge to do better. Instead he grew resentful. He could have done a lot worse. And thus he was floored when she asked him to leave. He almost found himself admiring her anew. For sure, she had turned out far braver than he had ever guessed at.

He took Titch Harwood's view on the state of the market and mustered the deposit for an ex-council place on the Blake Estate in Hoxheath, one of the newer, better builds in the area. Fresh magnolia on the walls, beige pile carpet – by no means swanky, but clean and manageable. Tweddle hired the van and helped him shift his chattels from a sadly deserted Garland Avenue. It was only on foot back from the off-licence at dusk, swinging six cans in a bag for them both, that he started to pick up a current in the air, one he hadn't sensed when viewing the place in daylight. Some of his new neighbours had hauled ropy armchairs out into their gardens, the better to enjoy beers of their own. There were kiddies running barefoot, lads hacking about on bikes, little girls smoking. Hardly worth staring at, he told himself. But the lads, loitering in packs, stared straight at him. How did they imagine they looked, skulking like hyenas in a dull documentary? He ventured a greeting, was met by a hail of barked insults. The next morning he judged that something had ran in rivulets down his front-door paintwork, leaving a stain and an odour on the doorstep. The woman next door – Sharon Price by name, grossly overweight, a sad-eyed little girl hoisted up in her sausage arms – seemed to blink with surprise at everything Martin said, at his very presence, though not at his predicament.

'Thursdays, see? They get tha' giro and drink it.'

That night the kids were rowdier yet by twilight – mad shouts, bottles smashing on concrete. Alert at his work desk Martin listened and told himself he was only slightly bothered. But overnight he rose several times from tangled sheets and darted to the window, fearful for his car.

Three cagey weeks in, he returned from a quiet pint with Charnley to find his fanlight jimmied open and his various entertainment systems torn from their housings. He had never suspected he and Mrs Price would have so much to talk about, yet there they were together on his doorstep as he waited for the call-out response.

'Police aren't so bad at coming round, but they can't do shite. Not really. Getting turned over like you's almost nothing. I don't mean nothing by that. Lady at thirty-seven, but, her's got set on fire. Despicable, really.'

He had never wanted his consumer durables to mean too much to him. But his answering machine then fell prey to foul garbled messages, the red light promising much but offering only screeches of crackle and evil juvenile jeering. 'Ahh! We done yah fucken house, man! Yee are fucken *deed*!' His insurer dealt promptly with matters, but advised him matter-of-factly that his premium would vault, which seemed maddeningly unfair in the same week that he received a banger and a paper bag of cat excrement through his letterbox. 'Candidly? You'll struggle to sell that place. I mean, good luck.' Martin blamed himself, for no one had forced him to take the financial advice of Titch Harwood. He struggled, though, to ward off more malign spirits. What were the underlying causes of the presenting problem? Limited prospects, learned helplessness? Bad parenting, broken homes? All of that shit, mixed up together in a bucket? Whatever way it fell, life had deposited him in the selfsame reeking litter tray.

Charnley took him for a drink he actually didn't fancy, since the lads had begun to do little more than sit looking rueful on his behalf. This was what the night-times were reduced to. Somehow, he hadn't had sex in five months. Per recent form, Charnley started twittering about some 'motivational' course he had undergone, crediting it with giving him the nerve to start up his new bedroom-furniture business. Martin was primed to point out that such patent rip-offs were for nerds and rabbits. Charnley happened to have a brochure to hand. *The Compass Course: Get Yourself*

Directed. The pages boasted of instilling transferable skills in leadership, entrepreneurship, communication, all-round personal excellence. It was, on paper, a weekend at a newly refurbished Hampshire hotel with a decent bar and pleasant gardens. Reviewing the application form at the back, Martin realised with dawning relish that the university could pay for him, under a long-unclaimed training subsidy.

Sheets of rain fell on the first day's sessions. The course 'mentor' was a soft-spoken Irishman with a suspicious tan. The other enlisters seemed largely a shower of southern ex-salesmen and journalists. Clad in his customary black, Martin tried to look flinty, though he felt scruffy and sweaty. At coffee breaks he adjourned alone to the bar to watch Wimbledon tennis. The sun broke through, and still he rued the uncharacteristic lameness that had led him here.

On the second morning the Irishman told them they were to play 'trust games'. Martin nearly walked. But, seeing nowhere else to go, he exhaled slowly, got into the circle, and turned to his right as instructed.

'Put your hands on the waist of the person in front of you.'

Before him was the tidy brunette with the vaguely Geordie lilt. Things were looking up, fractionally.

'Now, in a moment, you're each going to lower yourselves down so you're parked on the knees of the person behind you. The person in front of you will be doing the same, so focus on getting them settled, nice and comfy. Do that, and you'll know the person behind is doing the same for you. Ready? Slowly, now! One, two, three . . .'

She shifted her bottom in his lap. Her hair was bottle-fresh.

'Is that nice for you, pet?' he murmured carelessly.

'Is that a chisel in your pocket, kidder?' she murmured right back. 'Or do you really like trust games?'

Susannah was her name, some kind of Tory, yet tolerably bullshit-free. Not Martin's sort of girl at all. They rubbed along nicely, though, whether by some north-east solidarity, or the same sly humour, or maybe her instant attraction to him – he didn't care to speculate. Much could be endured thereafter, even the 'Are You Happy?' quiz, and the lecture on 'Rubbing Your Inner Genie'. He led her into the hotel bar that night without much persuasion, anticipating a simple procession of events, but on his return to their seats bearing the first round he saw that her eyes had narrowed.

'You know what? We've met before. I've just cottoned.'

'Oh aye?'

'It was London. About six years ago. Aye. You were with a girl.'

'Sounds like me. Not a crime, is it? We weren't married, were we?'

'No, but *you* were, weren't you?'

She proceeded to pick what seemed to him a string of gratuitous quarrels – about mortgage rates, homelessness in London, the strength of the pound, what were the better songs of Roxy Music, God knows what else. 'Bloody right I'm for privatising. We should do the whole bloody lot. What makes governments better at running business than businessmen? You get back the revenue in taxes anyway. Howay, man, you're not going to sit there and deny that capitalism's the best way to create wealth?'

'Best way to steal it, maybe.' He grinned into his pint.

'Oh, don't *sneer* like that, you look about *twelve*. If you're so fed up with things, stand for election. Stop wanking about. *I'd* vote for you.'

'Why? Why would you do that?'

He looked at her, feeling careless once more, delighted when she blushed.

'Do you want another?' she said finally.

They repaired to her room and split a bottle of Asti Spumanti, first sitting then lying down. The sex happened mostly clothed, Susannah on top. She was a nice person to have sex with, considerate too, for five months of abstinence had exacted a price on his stamina, and he lasted less than half as long as he would have expected.

'Throw us them tabs, would you?'

'You get up and get 'em. I did all the work.'

No, she didn't need a lot of hugs, this lass. Once they had agreed to agree that the Compass Course was drivel she began to unburden herself of more complicated professional anxieties. 'I've always known I wanted certain things. I'm a bit stuck now, but. Not sure why. Or – I maybe do and I just can't be arsed. I'm good enough, I never worry about that. I'm just maybe not enough of a player, whatever they call it. Maybe not glam enough.'

'Get away. You're lovely.'

'Aw. Aren't you sweet?'

Out of a protracted silence she told him she had been fucking Sebastian Sellars, MP, and he was startled and slightly repelled, most of all to infer that this streak of Tory smarm was fire in the sack. But seeing that she thought herself bold, Martin was emboldened. The tale slipped from him of how Becky had kicked him out – and rightly so, he asserted, for he had been a disgrace, a dead loss.

'This is like confession, eh?'

'Don't start. Me mam was a proper God-botherer, bless her.'

She laughed a touch glumly. 'My little brother and all, he wants to be a priest.'

Clearly she had escaped a peculiarly cloying family. He admired her anew.

The following morning they shared a train journey to London and thence back to the north-east, she bound for a call upon her widowed dad.

'Okay, don't sneer now – three things you'll do with what you've learned.'

'Start giving motivation courses. Three hundred quid a head. I've got the qualifications. Which is none.'

'Don't *sneer*, you. Come on. Three things.'

'Well, okay, I mean – what you said last night? Standing for election?' And she nodded. She didn't laugh. He could have kissed her again. 'I mean, it's a mad idea. The seats, they're occupied for ever. Or kept warm for some bugger. Newcastle's impossible like that.'

She tapped her tin of Diet Coke pensively. 'Does it have to be Newcastle?'

'My roots, man. My people. That's where my passion is.'

'Passion, it's overrated. You have to be sure you're right before you get passionate.' She tossed her bob. 'Actually I heard

Hartlepool could be up for grabs next time. Though Mandelson might have his beady eye on it.'

'You don't think I'd be wasting my time, but? A life in opposition?'

'Oh, you never know. There's always cycles. Even for Thatch. Something always goes wrong, people get mardy about something. You'd probably get a kick out of it anyway. You know what they say, showbiz for ugly people.'

'Eh, come on, I reckon at least I'd drag up the average a bit.'

She snorted. 'You're not bad-looking, Martin. Try not to squander it.'

'What's that supposed to mean?'

'Try not to *piss* your looks away, kidder. You're going the right way about it. You dress like some moody kid at a concert and all. That's do-able, clothes are easy. I can see you wash your hair most days, so why not shave your bloody face while you're at it?'

He tried to grin away her blistering impertinence. But she had prodded a raw nerve.

'You slouch, too. You know that? I bet you were sporty once. Threw back the pints, thought you'd never get a belly. Well you've got one now, kid. There's little broken blood vessels all round your eyes, your nose. Don't look so gutted, mind. *That's* what you want to take off this course, see. "Visualise. The path ahead. See your way to success. Start in the bathroom mirror." Eh? "Not who you are now, but who you might be."'

She chuckled and, done with him, took up her police procedural paperback. Martin had fancied a can of lager, but that treat was now spoiled.

As they trundled into Durham she grabbed her own case, handed him an embossed card, and kissed his cheek coolly. The next day he slunk into Next in Eldon Square, and there assessed some options in affordable Italian-style tailoring. One blue suit in particular fell fluidly from his shoulders and hips. He could see the inkling of an important distinction. And yet it seemed a daunting expense – an awful lot to throw in redress at a reflection he had trusted so long, admired without question.

Chapter IV

TALLIES

Wednesday, 13 November 1996

'I don't entirely like the look of it.'

'You don't say.'

The draft agenda of *Forward to the Future* rested askew on Gore's lap as he shifted the receiver from ear to ear. He had hoped for one more sit-down with the Member, but had grown resigned to the potluck of trying to catch him on the fly, his mobile switched on.

'It's just there seems an awful lot here about "Tomorrow's Company"? Technology and whatnot.'

'Right. That's a given, John. If our business is job creation, and it is, then we've got to be realistic about who the employers will be. That's why we're talking education, training – the new economy. It's all down there. Chris Carter's chairing it, him does Tyne Talk, *you know him?'*

'Yes, but all these panellists. They're all businessmen, aren't they?'

'Not all. Robson Talbot's from the engineers' union, he's sound. They're all worth meeting. Jon Salter's in North Sea oil. Frank Delavel's a developer. Proctor, he owns the hotel. David Chase is high up at BT. Your dad was a BT man, right?'

'Yeah. You've not got anyone from the council, though?'

'No, I don't want them in, not just yet.'

'And nobody else from the voluntary side?'

'As I say, John – you're my guy in that department.'

'Okay. Well, just one thing. I don't know where it fits, but I'd be very keen that we discuss public transport at some stage.'

An audible intake of breath. *'Any reason in particular?'*

'Well, as you'll know, the buses in Hoxheath only run north–south. That's a lot of trouble for pensioners who want to go east–west.'

A blast of silence back down the line. *'Let's just see how we manage, eh? Look, I'm gonna have to get on here, John.'*

'Oh, me too.' Indeed Gore had to be out the door directly, for he had a date.

She led him into the living room and he leaned down to kiss her, but her eyes darted right. Following her gaze, he saw her Auntie Yvonne standing over the sink, Marigolds immersed in the suds.

'Me washing-up fairy, aren't you?' said Lindy.

Yvonne smiled, gap-toothed, looked askance at Gore, then spat into the dishwater.

'Don't mind her.' A benign whisper. 'She does that, she's got a fat tongue.' And with that, Lindy was pulling on her short red jacket. 'Anyhow, it's settled, Yvonne's gunna pick up Jake and give him his tea. What we doing, then? What have you got lined up for us?'

'Oh, I thought we'd – maybe just see where the day takes us?'

'God, you make an effort. There was me thinking wine and roses. More the fool . . .' She put the back of a slender hand to her brow.

'But what about your work?'

'I'm not working. Not 'til maybe late on tonight. I already put a shift in this morning, see. I planned ahead. More than you've bothered yourself.'

'Well, look, shall we take a stroll?'

'Where to? God, no. And you've not got a car, have you? We can bus it into town. I fancy a bite of something first, but. Shall we's gan?'

'Right. Lunch. Where's nice?'

'"*Lunch*",' she mocked him. 'I only want a bite, man. Have you been to the Little Nibble? It's alright.'

The egg and bacon gave no offence, the tea was surprisingly bold and flavoursome. The Nibble was not busy, and they lingered over the smeared plates and condiments, her ankles locked lightly about his beneath the Formica table.

'I used to bunk off school every Monday afternoon, come in here with me lad. Chas. Heartbreaker, he was.' She showed him the line of her jaw, her mouth arch. 'I s'pose you'll want to know about all me other fellas. From the past.'

'No, I don't. Why would I want to know that?'

'Get away. Divvint tell us you've not thought about it. What a slag-bag I mighta been. Me with a bairn and that.'

He had tidied away such thoughts from the start. What did discomfort him was to hear her speak in such hard-edged terms of herself. 'I never thought any such thing, Lindy. I mean – we've all done things we regret.'

She pouted. 'Who says I regret it?'

'It was just the way you said it. What I mean is – I'm not to judge.'

'Fellas do, but. I bet you do. Even though you're cloth. *Specially* cos you're cloth, now I think.'

'All that really matters is now, Lindy. I'm happy to be with you now.'

Those sounded to Gore like words on which he might rest awhile. Lindy, though, sat back, her smile thin. 'You mean you'd rather not hear.' She began to rummage her bag, nodding at the rightness of her own conclusions. 'Aye, that's it. You'd rather *think well* of us.'

'I do – "think well" of you. I couldn't not. I mean . . .'

Gore shifted in the seat. No part of his scholastic past had prepared him to challcngc such logic. At a loss, he leaned in and tried to put his hand over hers on the tabletop. But simultaneously she was reaching up, as if to touch his face. After a fleeting clumsiness, they reset themselves, Gore taking hold of her forearm, stroking its freckles lightly with his thumb.

'Look, I just – if you're asking me what I feel about – your romantic past – then I'm saying I don't need to know the *precise* figure. You know?' He tried a smile. 'I mean, if you really want me to be honest, *one* would be too many, so . . .'

'*One?* Bloody *hell*. Aw, we'd better get off this, then.'

'Well, why not just agree that there's probably a disparity?

Between our respective – tallies.'

'So how's about you, then?'

'What?'

'What's the scores on your doors? Notches on your bedpost?'

'Oh. Well – one, really.'

'*One?* Serious? Hang on, is that us? Or there was one before us?'

'One before you.'

'Right, so two altogether, with us in there?'

Gore nodded weakly. Yet Lindy looked pleased. 'Aww. That's nice. You've saved yourself, haven't you? Is that cos you were waiting on God to find you your dream girl?'

'I suppose I must have been,' Gore shrugged, and mopped up brown sauce and yolk with a last cold slice of toast.

'Dunno how you manage, but. I tried to go celibate once. Made a proper vow to meself, y'knaa? Like, from now on, I'm not getting involved, I'm gunna be very pure and clear about it, and that's that. I managed about three month. It were good, but.'

'How come you . . . fell off the wagon?'

She beamed, hunching her shoulders rather bashfully. 'I like men. Men who've *got* summat, y'knaa? Summat *about* them, I dunno . . . gannin' on *inside* them. Like you can feel. A fella like that, you want to get closer.'

'Closer physically?'

'Well, you canna *get* closer to someone than shagging 'em, can you?'

Gore rested his chin on his hands and rubbed at his eyelids. Her philosophies had become a sort of lunch-break puzzle for him.

'What's the matter, John?'

'Nothing, I'm just thinking. About what you're saying.'

'What? Did it sound a bit slag-bag?'

'No, no, I mean – well, you know, I think I said to you, I've always thought physical stuff between people has to be meaningful – to both parties.'

'Aw aye, and it is to me, John, it means a lot. Same time, but, it's only sex. Once it's out the road y'knaa who you're dealing with, you can be yer'sel.'

'Right. You can get closer? To that person?'

'Aye. If you can be arsed.' She smiled. 'I mean, there were one or two lads, I sort of nearly talked me'sel into being Little Wifey. But nah. Mostly – I dunno – I never fancied just being somebody's lass.'

She had come over wistful, crooking her elbow to support her head, chewing her lower lip. The fresh information seemed to Gore a fruitful line. 'Well, I think I know what you mean. You don't mind your own company. You're sufficient unto yourself.'

'Aye, maybe. For a bit. I get bored with that too, though – after a bit.' She reached around their plates, put her hand on his, beamed once more. 'God, but I have some proper old chats with you, don't I?'

'You started it, Lindy.'

'I know. I like it, but – how you listen to us. So what now, lover man?'

'What would you like to do?'

She rolled her eyes. 'Aw, howay man. I'll make it dead easy for you. Why don't we's gan to the pictures?'

'A film? This evening?'

'Nah man, *now*.'

'Oh, a matinee?'

'Aye, a *matinee* . . .'

They hopped onto a bus down the Hoxheath Road to the city centre and made their way to a multi-screen cinema by the Haymarket. Gore was content to give Lindy her pick from six possibilities, though he was surprised when she chose *Michael Collins*, which looked from its poster to be the most stolid fare on offer. Once they were huddled in the dark with popcorn and giant Colas, the picture did indeed unfold as a sort of Irish history pageant, one that Gore found involving, if a touch overblown. It was as the Collins character began to romance some colleen with a piano-key smile that he suspected the basis of Lindy's selection was much to do with the brawny lead actor. '*Lush*,' she whispered, at one inapt moment. But her eyes were lively as they descended to the street, she working her moist hand into his. Details of the movie were relived and discussed all the way back to Oakwell. Gore expressed some reservations about that love-story element, indeed the film's whole approach to history. 'Howay, man,' Lindy countered. 'It's only a film, like. That's what they do, the films.'

He was slumped blankly into her sofa when she slipped onto his lap and kissed him probingly. In one fluid movement she wrenched her cotton tee-shirt to her shoulders, threw them back and stuck out her chest, grinning, a pin-up girl parody. Her breasts were teardrop-shaped, a little wan and undernourished on her narrow chest, their wide aureoles pimpled and pale. Pulling the top back down, she stuck out her tongue at him.

'Are you cold?'

'Not if you give us a cuddle.'

In this fit of vivacity she was suddenly and heavily arousing to him. He found her lips with his, slid his hands under the tee-shirt, began to sense the needful traction below. Pushing his hand down the front of her skirt, under the band of her knickers, he felt her crinkling hair between his fingers and her pelvis pressing into his touch. His middle digit slid easily inside her. Then they slipped down to the floor and he kissed her belly, delicately, mindful of the hard laminate under them, a touch she seemed to appreciate.

When they were done she bounded upstairs, returned having donned her kimono, and set to brewing a pot of tea. Gore was starting to find these encounters a little more manageable – nice and easy, relatively normal, unexpectedly enjoyable. Their love-making seemed to take a manic edge off her, and he felt some of his own cloudy abstractedness evaporate.

As seven o'clock drew near, it was without trepidation or fear of reprisal that he set down his cup and got to his feet.

'I think I have to get off now – I've a bit prep to do for something I'm doing early tomorrow?'

'Oh aye?'

'Yes, it's just a conference of some sort. With the local MP.'

'Who's the MP again?'

'Martin Pallister. You don't know your MP?'

She shrugged. 'Told you. Do-gooders, all the same to me. What's it you have to do?'

'Just sit on a platform and say how we could all live our lives better.'

'Just the usual, then. Hey, when is it again? Can I maybe come watch you?'

'Oh, I don't think so. It's not open to the public. People have paid money and all that.'

'What, and you can't sneak us in?'

'It'd be tricky . . . I'd be a bit anxious. I'm only an invitee myself, I don't think it's a plus-one situation.'

She was giving him that thoroughly dubious look of hers. He laid his hands on her shoulders.

'Please, Lindy, really, just trust me, will you?'

Chapter V

THE PROCONSUL OF GEORDIELAND

1989–1996

Martin tugged at his shirt collar, instantly rueing the shiftiness of the gesture, a gift to his interrogators. He was just as damned if he didn't, though, for the TREC boardroom, however modishly appointed, was badly in need of a breeze through an open window.

He now knew, uselessly, that he should have worn his loose linen suit, not the tweedy coat and woollen strides. If only there were but one soft-eyed female sat there surveying him – not a row of balding men, smugly stripped to shirts and ties, acclimatised to the fug. The Tyneside Regenerative Economics Corporation had set out its stall – take the heat or get out of the sweatbox, come prepared or not at all. Martin had arrived fully primed to espouse these sentiments, but his enthusiasm was ebbing with each minute that his curriculum vitae got kicked around the room.

'I look at this and I see someone who's been good at exams all their life. That, and ball games. Which is canny, but not a *great* lot of use to us.'

Martin had done his homework, though, could identify his chief antagonist – this long slap-head sourpuss – as Jon Salter of Hart-McGrain, US oil explorer with heavy-duty interests in the North Sea.

'Mr Salter, I've been planning a shift out of academia for a while –'

'Well, bully for you, but what makes you think you can start here?'

'With respect, if you look you'll see, I spent most of last year in a key part-time role for the council, its business centre – an office I helped to expand – offering a complete consultancy to small business.'

'Right. All the big hitters came to you there, I'll bet? Wanting your expertise? Look, Mr Pallister, what we've got here is a major market-driven project, we're not the municipality.'

'Jon, in fairness to Martin – what's the job here? Officer for community development, not chief executive.'

The mild cross-table rebuke was an unexpected boon. Martin looked closer at Frank Ball, a short stocky man who was chomping little pills of nicotine gum, and had seemed stone-faced, bassett-eyed and scary until a moment ago. He now sported a sort of conciliatory smile. 'Martin, you'll have heard, I'm sure, the council aren't happy with us coming on the scene. Cos they can smell there's government money's gunna get spent, and they want it all for themselves. So they're going round saying it's all a big Thatcherite scam. Well, if it was – would I be sat here?'

Martin nodded. No, the chairman of North East Labour, the regional chief of the Transport and General, was self-evidently no man's lickspittle.

'Yes, we'll report to the minister. But, the fact is – whisper it if you want – the government's been almost generous. We've got some money, and some clout, and we're going to use it. Cut some red tape, get some things built. Council can moan if they want, but I'm betting they'll like what they see after we've done it. Cos the plan is to be radical.'

'As reality itself,' Martin murmured, no longer so bothered by the heat, or those few frowns still trained upon him.

'Jon's right, but. We're not set up to be the Samaritans. We've got to follow business logic. Saying that, though, there's no reason we can't help the neighbourhood. Now, I see here you live in Hoxheath? So you'll know the problems there, from a development side?'

Martin nodded keenly, until realising he was expected to exhibit some of the knowledge to which he tacitly laid claim. 'Oh aye. Yes, God knows, Hoxheath needs something radical. The riverside's a wasteland. You've got buildings derelict, old shop-floors emptied for storage, left to rot. Polluted land, acres of it in need of a clean-up. I mean, clearly, from a business angle it's value sitting there to be unlocked.'

Ball beheld him with tolerant rheumy eyes. 'Of course, now, there's people living there too . . .'

'Of course there are. But we need to get *more* people in there. Moving *back* there. Kill this idea that it's just the losers get left hanging on. The local people have to feel like they've got a stake in what we're doing.'

'Right. What we need's a man who's good with people. To – I'll not say *sell* the project, because people should want to buy – it's in their interest. But to *present* the thing . . . Do you get me?'

'I do. That's me. I'm an explainer. I'm a *proselytiser*. I can hold a room, I can talk to people on their level. Make 'em listen, get through to them . . .'

A fart of dissent blared forth, Salter shifting audibly in his squashy chair. 'Says you, my friend. You're not getting through to *me*.'

'Whey then, sit up straight, man, get your fingers out your ears.'

A risk, Martin knew, but noting certain smiles across the panel he didn't think he would have cause for regret. If it came to a vote, right now, he believed he had the numbers.

He convened public meetings, chaired sessions in civic rooms and hired halls and, on occasions, in people's front parlours. He shook hands up and down the Tyne from Hoxheath to North Shields.

'I want us to know each other better. Because we should. I want to help you understand what we're doing, reassure you – if it's reassurance you need. But I need as much from you in return. I have to convince you *to participate. I don't take that lightly. Without you, we're nothing. With you? We'll look a hell of a lot better . . .'*

If this much earned him a laugh, however grudging, he was thereafter at ease.

'They say Tyneside's in decline, gone to seed. Okay, it's in a poor state, and there's reasons for that, you know better than I. Eleven years of this government, for starters. Not soon put right. But I tell you, give us the

tools and tackle and we'll start doing the job. Because this is God's own place, right? And we're God's own people. What else do we need?'

The usual way was that, within the hour, a gratifying number in the audience were ready to buy him a drink. Always there were some who claimed to have seen his sort coming a mile off, but he could turn closely attentive to them at the spin of a heel. If the complaint was that there would be no jobs for local people, he stressed the focus on training. If the fear was that flash new flats and their owners would only embarrass the old, he spoke of his personal commitment to the Housing Associations. At all times he listened and took good notes, though he reserved the right to form his own views, issue his own recommendations.

He was yet more sedulous on occasions when he dined with selected TREC board members at sponsored meet-and-greets. The favoured venue was Altobello, a glowingly understated Italian restaurant on Dean Street, four months old and already the best in Newcastle. He noted the ostentatious impatience of the most prosperous attendees, men who costed their time and scowled at idle chat. He was sometimes baffled when introductions were made and he struggled to connect his work to the ostensible interests of a hotelier or a rep from an American cinema chain. It was explained to him by Jon Salter, originally from Monkseaton, who bore him no grudge over Pinot Grigio and *insalata tricolore*. The heavy hitters were being courted for large-scale 'flagship' endeavours, under which a fleet of smaller projects would sail. 'We're used to all this in Newcastle, Martin,' Salter waved a hand. 'People *care* about the north-east. Top people. Get 'em up here and they love Geordies. The Tories admire us, they do. Not as a job lot, mind you. But they're on the side of any have got *initiative.*'

A silvery gent from Scottish and Newcastle invited Martin to a whisky-tasting weekend by the Tay. TREC's Director of Finance, fresh from KPMG tax & audit, offered to advise him on his 'investments' – an advance on Titch Harwood. The chief executive of Nissan endured his dauntless jests about Sunderland FC and how it felt to shake Thatcher's hand. The red wine was always velvety and heady. Frank Ball, though, stayed stony sober at these functions, and would rise from his chair among the earliest, invariably with a blunt parting to Martin. 'Don't drink too much, y'hear?'

But it was only by lingering late over brandies that Martin got palled up with Proctor Wallace, Altobello's owner. Wallace was a well-tended fifty, still in possession of his black hair and sporty build, and he had a high old tale he liked to tell of his path to glory – from shipyard apprentice to door-to-door salesman, to renovator and developer of a better class of homes for the aged, a business he had built up, floated, and flogged at its peak. 'I'm nowt special, me,' he asserted. 'Just I was in the right place, and I was hungry.' Thus did a Fellgate man come to pass his days in a million-quid pile in Ponteland, suntanned from jaunts to a Portuguese villa, his ambitions still far from fully realised.

Invited out to the Wallace homestead for a World Cup barbecue in high June, Martin ironed a polo shirt and chinos and collected Alex from Becky. Proctor's boy Peter was seven too, and they ran off together like tow-headed twins down the epic jade lawn to where a full-sized football net billowed unattended in a slight breeze. Martin fancied a kickabout too, but the grown-ups were meant to watch Italy versus Ireland on Proctor's monolithic Japanese telly. 'I probably spoil the lad,' Wallace shrugged between sips of lager from an engraved frosted tankard. 'That Sting, he doesn't give his kids owt. What else is it *for*?' Martin nodded, affirmative of Proctor, his largesse, his sleek young Danish wife.

'What you're doing at TREC, y'knaa,' Proctor confided, 'I'm all for it. It's inspiring. I've nee clue what I'm worth now, but if I hadn't got given a bit of start-up cash back when, I'd still be selling plastic windies to pensioners.'

It occurred to Martin anew that he had got himself in gear much, much too late in the day – had applied but a fraction of his capacity for clear thought, and accordingly banked but a pittance of what he might otherwise have earned. His focus, his energies – they had always been there, but had led him down some pointless byways, on the narrowest of principles. Stood beside Proctor, he found that stretches of his past life only embarrassed him – none more so than his ongoing residence at the Blake Estate, Hoxheath.

But Proctor wheedled the story out of him, then got him out of that beleaguered ex-council house by dint of a friendly loan at nought per cent interest. Proctor was big on property, more than happy to be helpful, and Martin would not have refused in a million years. In tandem with his new salary, his funds were adequate to offload the Blake house at a thumping loss and acquire a light-filled flat on the Jesmond fringes, a secluded Georgian terrace nestled amid insurers, accountants and legal services. When the truck came Sharon Price knocked on his door to say cheerio and all the very best, a gesture that cut him unexpectedly. But from the moment he parked his car and closed his new improved front door, it felt right. This was a place that his boy would like, that Becky might covet. That first weekend of occupancy, he strolled up to Town Moor with his tennis racket and smashed a few serves over a net. Regeneration had revived him.

True, the first developer TREC invited for talks at Altobello was discovered to be trading while insolvent. But the firm of Doggett & Delavel stepped into the breach, and Martin was good as his word to the people of Hoxheath, adamant through each and every planning meeting that one-in-four new-build homes be social housing. He was a little sneaky, he knew, in advising Becky to buy one of the smart boxy apartments in the heart of the 'Project Zone'. He wasn't surprised when she frowned through her inspection of the show house. But he knew that the gleaming taps, the duck-egg walls and floor-to-ceiling windows rubbed her the right way.

'Alright for a bachelor boy like you, Martin. Not for me and Alex.'

'Just trust me, eh, Becks? For once in your life?'

'What are you doing? Are you in bed yet?'

'No, I'm fixin' me supper.' Indeed the sound of mashing jaws now assailed his ears. But even after the longest of days that ran into evening, he looked forward still to that hour before bed and the more or less nightly phone call. It was one stable fixture in his life, a prized friendship, an intimacy.

'I like a man who knows how to use the phone.'

'No great skill there, pet.'

'You say that. My dad spent his life up a telegraph pole and you hardly get a word out of him.'

Susannah, too, was pressing on, now a tyro lobbyist. Yet she seemed obsessively interested in Martin's job.

'It's a new sort of culture, I'd say,' he let himself pontificate. 'A new way to mix public and private. I'm not saying it's the socialist dawn. But we're handing out money all over.'

'Don't kid yourself, Marty. You can't slightly *endorse the free market. You can't be* slightly *pregnant.'*

'Says you. Proctor always says he'd never have got on without the state.'

'Oh, "my mate Proctor". If he said jump in the Tyne, would you?' The vying was gentle. She seemed pleased for him. *'So what's next?'*

'Suppose I wait for my boss to get another job.'

'What about Marty Goes to Westminster? I've not forgotten.'

'Aye, well, me neither. I've talked to my mate Proctor and all.'

'You've been talking that long and not doing – I could lose respect for you.'

'It's the *time*, but, Suze. And the effort. And the money. I can't be dragging round church halls for a year trying to get selected. Where's the seat, anyway? I don't see it, Suze.'

'It'll turn up. You've got to be ready for it. Gotta sharpen your odds. I mean, look at you. Okay, youngish sort of a fella, not so shabby-looking –'

'Thank you very much.'

'Party man to the core, put in the hours. Travelled light, never made a fuss. In with the unions.'

'But in favour of one member, one vote.'

She snorted. *'As are all sane men and women.'*

'I've friends in the T and G, sure. But it's GMB pulls the strings up here.'

'You just keep in with Frank Ball. He'll see you right.'

Martin smiled into his chest. The selfsame thought had occurred.

'Now then – what about the bitter ex-wife?'

'Nah, Becky's canny. I've done right by them. I'd worry more about my old man, to be honest, if you're talking about someone showing us up . . .'

'No, that's a blessing, that. Telling your old man to fuck off shows you mean business. Not afraid to dump old baggage. All that leftie shit.'

'Let me stop you there, flower. I know you're a bit ignorant when it comes to how we do things in the Labour Party, but I think you'll find there's principles aren't open for discussion.'

'I'm not saying ditch everything. *Then you wouldn't be Labour. Then we'd miss you. But come on, kidder. Some things are just symbolic, aren't they? Out of date. They've got to go. Got to go* sometime, *so get shot of them now, get it over and done with. You'll feel better. That's Kissinger's Law.'*

'Who? The bomber of Cambodia?

'Whatever. Just say you learned better. Better than clinging on to things you didn't believe in anyway, just for an easy cheer. That's what you like to say, isn't it? Be as radical as reality?'

'It was Lenin said that, sweetheart.'

'Oh, God help us . . .' Her voice dwindled down the line.

After three decades of service Harold Rodham declared that he would retire from representing the people of Newton Aycliffe in 1992. Martin got the news early, and knew what he had to do. He filled his tank with petrol, burned up the phone lines, secured his nominations, fretted over his lines for the selection meeting. Susannah listened to an early draft and let it be known she didn't approve – too 'clever', too 'wordy', insufficiently 'humble'. *Fuck her,* Martin heard his demon jeer. *Who knows how Labour works? You or that Tory?*

And yet, installed in a creaking seat before the panel at Horndale Working Men's Club, he watched his hopes crash, and it was clear that the old guard rankled most at his high estimation of his own powers. They were not impressed by half a lifetime of Party service, for their own counts tallied to more. When he declared he was 'politically savvy', they seemed to mishear, and to openly scoff when he spoke of 'contacts' and 'up-to-date thinking'.

'Look, we're maybe on the wrong foot here, I mean, don't get me wrong, I can talk Labour movement all night long.'

'You may talk it all you want,' the chairman grunted. 'You've not lived it.'

'I may not have come off the shop-floor but what I *am* saying – with respect, on the whole – is that I understand the history of this Party better than you.'

He had not banked on trading verbal blows with a senior citizen, much less coming off second best in the eyes of the assessors. In the cold light of analysis, yes – he had been too clever, too wordy, insufficiently humble. So much for 1992. On election day itself, the 9th of April, Dr Martin Pallister – who had once submitted a paper to the Fabians on the need for compulsory voting – found so many chores with which to occupy himself that he was unable to attend his polling station before closing. Mike Watt didn't need his vote. He was certain, though, that the Party had need of his qualities, and was not so very surprised when they lost in the country yet again.

He didn't speak to her, for weeks that turned into months. But his stance was not so resolute that he failed to keep count. When he parked his pride, he found the voice unchanged at the other end of the line.

'What do you think then? John Smith and old maid Beckett? Is that the Labour dream ticket? See, I thought it was Kinnock and Hatters.'

'Don't mock, Suzie.'

'I'm sorry, pet. Next time, eh? Really. You'll have enough in the tank then. Least there's what you might call talent on the front bench. All northern too. Northern or Scots. That's interesting, isn't it? Something else too. Another little thread – a tip for you.'

'Aye? What?'

'Well, it's funny, but have you noticed? They're all churchgoers and all. Or they say they are. Smith and Brown. Blair, Blunkett, Straw.'

'Oh no.'

'Oh yes, Marty.'

'No, Sue, look, I can swallow nuclear weapons but I draw the line at God.'

He had not hoped that in his lifetime Tyneside West would ever stand in need of a new Labour candidate. But then no one had imagined that Alf Jakes – fifty-nine years of age, married for thirty-five of them, and MP for twenty-two – would be arrested by plainclothes policemen during the routine raid of a massage parlour in Coxlodge. Martin was more or less certain that sex scandals were Tory behaviour until Alf was interrupted in the midst of tender ministrations from a sixteen-year-old Taiwanese. He asked forgiveness only from that wife of his, and would not seek re-election – indeed deemed it wise to stand down and permit a by-election in 1994.

Newly appointed Director of Development at TREC, Martin might not have mustered the will for a second sally had not Susannah harried him onward, goading him for a gutless wonder. She was herself setting out alone as SEG Solutions, a one-stop shop for lobbying, PR, planning and analysis. He chuckled over her brochure, its boast of 'a wealth of experience at the heart of Westminster'. But it was all true, only more so. Now she was ready to work with anyone, public or private, corporation or charity, bookmaker or children's hospice. And she would work for the selection and election of Dr Martin Pallister at a striking discount. The plan she presented to him was almost embarrassingly comprehensive.

It was immediately clear to him that the constituency party secretary preferred him to his chief rivals, the perpetually grey city councillor Bob Muir and some mouthy ex-miner with UNISON backing who stomped round the selection meeting at Hoxheath Civic Centre as if these needful preliminaries were a conspiracy against horny-handed sons of toil. Martin, though, was in his element. It was only a few years since he had shaken every hand worth shaking in Hoxheath. His speech was by some distance the most poised, and when it came to questions from the audience he was much the least awkward in addressing the matter of the debacle of the retiring candidate.

'Look, there's gotta be a moral basis to what we do. I say that as someone who's a churchgoer. I know that's not so fashionable these days. But without that moral base, we're nothing. We're not *Labour*. Tell you what, but, the Church hasn't got a monopoly on the moral high ground. Nor has the hard left neither. It's not for me to judge whether I meet the highest standards, or whether others meet 'em either – just to act morally. To match my deed to my word. And you can bet your life I'm gonna try.'

His sense was that he had moved the crowd. He had almost managed to move himself.

The Mother of Parliaments put Martin in mind of a faded hotel, the pricey-but-dependable choice in a honeymoon city. He thought as much late each night as he walked down quiet corridors of tired carpet, wainscot and striped wallpaper, past closed doors toward his own windowless office.

His maiden speech held no trepidation for him. He had no fantasies about rows of rapt souls on green leather benches – there were just too many buggers there already, settled in their spots, clearly preferring the sound of their own braying voices. But the first address, he knew, offered the tamest crowd he would ever have. Susannah warned him not to showboat, but he knew what he was doing. He saluted Alf Jakes with tact, hailed the spirit of Tyneside West and its proud people. Then he bared his incisors.

'I appreciate how wrenching it must be for Honourable Members opposite when they confront their restive constituents in Wells or Carshalton. They must hear the most piteous cries about stamp duty – indeed the asking prices for second homes. When I hold surgery in Hoxheath, people tell me the roof is coming off their council house, locks unmended since their latest burglary.

'Why do we have this state of urban decay? The answer lies very close. I can smell it from across the floor. The dividend of a failed economic policy. Two dreadful recessions. A north–south divide at which the Tories have kicked with glee until it has gaped yet further. Be it said, I welcome the government's recent efforts to put Band-Aids on long-running wounds. But they are reaping the whirlwind.

'I say, just give up. Get out of the way. Spare us the weasel words, just give us the money. Give the regions themselves the tools and tackle, the reparations they deserve, the independence and the powers to regenerate themselves. Give us a northern assembly, a Minister for Local Government, and then get off our backs. All power, I say, to the regions!'

He strode serenely through the lobby that day, though he noted some smirks among his PLP colleagues. In the tea-room, too, he overheard the drawl of some chinless fatty. 'He's a Geordie Kinnock. Another windbag.' He cared not, for it was now his special pleasure to take Jon Salter and Frank Ball for lunch at the Churchill Rooms. They all drank sparkling water. Martin was religious now about two weeks off the booze for each week on, much as he missed the delicious blurring of the edges. Before their orders were placed, though, Martin sensed he was not quite party to the mood of his fellows.

'So it seems I rattled a few cages on the other side today.'

'That's not all you did,' Salter winced, setting down his menu. 'What the hell was that blather of yours? A "northern assembly"?'

'I was speaking to my area, Jon. My passion.'

'Which is what? Bureaucracy? Thought you knew better than most, Martin, it's the hands-off approach gets things done. Softly, softly.'

'Martin man, it'll never happen.' Ball weighed in. 'That's why you're daft to get involved. Neebody wants it. More politicians clarting up the place.'

Salter was smiling now, but meanly. 'I mean, what's the appeal, Martin? You after another job already? So you can start giving us all what for?'

'I'm just here representing the people voted me in, Jon.'

'Aye, well, *we* voted for you. I did any road. Dunno about Frank.'

'Oh aye,' said Ball, chuckling into his fizzy glass.

'But it seems to me, Martin, you want to be directing your energies to trying to earn your spurs down here. In the big fishbowl. Not trying to get yourself made proconsul of Geordieland.'

'It's not about me,' Martin snapped. 'It's about the neighbourhoods I'm responsible for now. To me I serve that interest by keeping politics local. Joining things up, making the best of your money, getting the best people involved. I'd have expected you two to be onside for all that.'

Ball looked amusedly to Salter, then back to his protégé. 'Loose ties is what we like, Martin. Nice and loose. If you know a politician to talk to, personal, like, why do you need a lot of them sat jabbering in a chamber? And now we've got you.'

Martin could almost smell himself singeing from the flare of black umbrage. And yet, he knew, he would have to douse it down, for the moment. True, he had fought his own instinct in order to recast himself as a compromise man. But they wouldn't make a Judas of him – not today, not tomorrow, not by swords nor staves nor whole cohorts of henchmen.

Chapter VI

COMRADES

Thursday, 14 November 1996

Feeling rain spatter on his brow, Gore hastened his steps down the Quayside promenade, passing under the skeletal steel stanchion of the Tyne Bridge that vaulted up and over his head to the underfloor of the mighty arch, toward great grey slow-shifting clouds in a dirty-white sky. The clocks said it was nearly nine, late again, de rigueur. But the Blackwater had to be close. And he refused to rue the spurning of an offer of collection. He had quailed at the thought of some sleek black BMW rolling up and into Oakwell, some chauffeur rapping at the door of number seventy-three as though he were bought and paid for.

Power House, Titanium, Teflon – the awnings and facades of the waterfront pubs and bars were mute and still at this early hour, though chalked boards left out in the drizzle still sang of VODKA JELLIES, HALF-PRICE DOUBLES, HAPPY HOUR X 2! He passed the row of legal chambers and the Crown Court, the promenade then making a graceful curve lined by new-planted poplars drawing the eye to a granite-faced warehouse building of ten storeys, its revamped awning adorned by silky blue-black flags hanging limply from poles. Cars and taxis were trundling up to the drop-zone of the paved piazza, people in suits and macintoshes making haste up stone steps to a revolving door. This could only be the place. As Gore too mounted those steps, a familiar carnival barker's cry assailed him.

'Socialist paper, get ya socialist paper, all the latest on cash for questions and Tory sleaze, Blair's hobnobbing in Tuscany, where's the difference?'

He saw then, non-too-discreetly to the side of the entrance, the ghost at the feast – the declamatory figure whose existence those preceding him had staunchly ignored. It couldn't be, surely? And yet it so clearly was. There couldn't be more than one uni-dextrous pension-age vendor of the *Socialist Worker* on Tyneside. Gore kept his head low as he ploughed on. To pause for even an affable word would have felt like disloyalty to his patron. The years, too, had given Joe Pallister a craggier, more forbidding look.

'John!' the Member shouted over heads to the threshold where Gore teetered, gripped by shyness in the face of a teeming room. Momentarily his sister had seized his arm and was leading him through the throng. He was plonked into a line-up of smart suits, flashbulbs flaring in a short fusillade. 'Gotcha,' Martin Pallister whispered into his ear.

The conference lounge had a muted grey-mauve elegance, mellifluous piped music, air-con, superfluous art. The top table was illuminated tastefully, FORWARD TO THE FUTURE stamped cleanly upon a flat board behind, place markers and microphones and little blue-glass water bottles lined in a row. Gore kicked his heels in the group of seven being readied to mount the dais, until his hand was seized by Chris Carter, suited and booted but none the less breezy, and he was jostled from one to another in the cluster of substantial men, their names familiar from the literature – Delavel, Salter. Wallace, aged-rock-star casual in sports coat and jeans. Talbot, a querulous older bird. And Chase, a thickset emphysematic American. Now a blonde girl in a charcoal suit was herding them onto the foot-high stage. Gore blinked through the trained lights toward seating set for two hundred, more or less full. Who *were* these people? He fixed on his sister, dutifully leading applause from the front row.

Pallister stepped to a lectern, gave thanks to an alphabet soup of sponsors, exhibitors and unions, then commenced a keynote address that seemed to Gore as if it might have been written by – rather than merely upon – a computer. Leafing his agenda, he drifted in and out of the frequency.

'The nature of work is being transformed . . . what we used to do, what we do now, from production to services . . . outsourcing, downsizing,

partnership . . . information and communication technology, the knowledge economy . . . we need to put these things together. Today is about options for development of our vision.'

Carter introduced an opening session on Education. Gore, unsure of what role he would fulfil, quickly understood that none had been allotted him. For no sooner had all agreed Britain stood in need of 'a world-class education system' and 'best practice in all our schools', than the discussion seemed to turn entirely to computers.

'What the near future offers,' rasped Chase, *'is an information superhighway – an Infobahn, if you will. BT want to see every school in Britain hooked up to it, by cable. And we're exceptionally keen to help in that roll-out.'*

'I'm sure BT would like a helping hand into the cable business too.' This was Talbot, the aged union man in the patched tweedy coat.

'In fairness to BT,' interjected slow-nodding Proctor Wallace, *'if they don't get into that market soon then they'll cease to exist.'*

'Aye, but who's going to pay for all them machines that want "hooking up"?'

Pallister eased into the fray. *'Robson, you can count on a Labour government putting a new computer in every classroom. That's the least we can do. My worry is more about whether the teachers are up to teaching the stuff.'*

There was sufficient rumble among the congregants to persuade Gore that teachers were indeed present – sufficient, too, to embolden him into a contribution: *'I must say, I'd worry more about whether there are enough jobs out there to make the pupils want to do the work in the first place.'*

Pallister winced. *'That's backward talk, John. The skills IT brings, they create jobs. Kids'll write their own ticket. Not wait for jobs to fall out the heavens.'*

That did not seem wholly friendly.

After forty minutes or so, a dull school period, they were invited to the back of the room for cups of bitter coffee. Gore desired a quiet corner, and Talbot seemed the only one desirous to stand with him, though his chat was limited to 'I hate these bloody things' and gripes over the daintiness of the pastries. Already the day struck Gore as one to be endured.

KEY-PUSHING OR METAL-BASHING? That was the question after the break, and Dr Pallister moved robustly to take charge of the agenda.

'To regenerate locally you have to think globally – be more ambitious. That's why I get weary when I see people turn up their noses at inward investment. Effectively we're talking about importing job providers – and huge numbers of jobs. Where's the problem? Just look at Nissan, look at Mueller.'

The flaring of Robson Talbot's nostrils was detected by the microphones. *'It's not like they come for free, Martin. Why should the big boys just blow in and get all that subsidy money? Why not spend it on helping out local business?'*

'But it's not just the "big boys", is it, Robson? Once a Mueller gets set up it's local businesses they employ to make the small parts for them. Do the engineering, or the installing – that's thousands of jobs for your members right there. Now, do you want those "big boys" stationed in Heaton and Sunderland, or do you want them swanning off down south?'

Chase was tapping his pen on the table, and microphones amplified that to a metronomic complaint too. *'I have to say, with respect, I find this argument curious. To even be having it still. This is the world we live in. The nature of business today.'*

Talbot had reddened. *'With respect to our American friend – I'm not a Luddite, but nor am I conned by a lot of corporate blather. Mark my words, Mueller's not gunna last. We've seen it before. These multinationals, they're lured up here for millions off the government, the Queen maybe comes up to cut the ribbon if she's not too busy, then – presto – give it a few years and it's shut. They don't like the costs any more so they're off to Czechoslovakia. Hundreds of jobs lost, jobs of my members, thank you very much, Martin.'*

Bravo, thought Gore. Indeed there was a light shower of applause in the room. Pallister smiled and waited for it to recede.

'Sometimes, yes, they go. The bigger your global operation, the more

sensitive you are to shifts in the competition. But someone else comes in. Look at the Job Centre figures. People get back into work. I have to say, Robson, you think short-term, you're way too pessimistic.'

'Oh, am I now?'

'Aye, you are. Coal, it took a couple of centuries to build to what it was. That's a long game. Things move faster today but still you're talking decades. One thing I know, but – the old manufacturing jobs are never coming back. I was talking to a colleague of mine in the Commons, took over Manny Shinwell's seat. He said Shinwell always said, so long as there was coal in the north-east, we'd get nowt else. Like a curse – that would be all we were good for. Now that was sad, but it's true. What I'm saying is that nowadays we can do more. More and better.'

Listening to Pallister knocking down arguments like pre-set pins, ignored, and preferring anonymity to grudging acceptance – Gore fell first to doodling upon his pad, then to the sketching of a notion, a scheme that descended upon him with unexpected force.

Over the lunch hour Pallister sought him in his corner. 'Not a bad gaff, eh, John? Listen, sorry you've not had much of a day of it yet.'

'At least I got my picture taken.'

'Right. But have you found it interesting?'

'Vaguely. I wonder, though, what any of it's got to do with Hoxheath.'

'Blue-sky thinking, John. Something'll come of it, you watch.'

'Well, as a matter of fact, I've been thinking – all that time on my hands up there – and I've figured out what I want from you. From this.'

Pallister's brow was sceptical. 'What you *want*? Didn't your mam ever teach you, "I want never gets"?'

'Okay, what I *need*. What I think would be *useful*. If you're interested.'

'Go on, then.'

'I need a church, right? A building fit to purpose. My own place. Instead of being stuck in a school hall. The thing is, I'm not sure any more that the Church can afford –'

'John, John, look, that's not going to suit what we're about here –'

'No, but listen, I'm not just saying a church. This could be a proper full-on community centre. Purpose-built. Different rooms for all different functions – a church hall would just be one of them. If someone else built it, the Church could just as happily lease the space, I'd bet on it.'

'Oh, could it now?'

'Yes, or even – the trick of it would be – I mean it doesn't *have* to be this, but there is a rather fine old building within the school grounds at St Luke's that just needs a roof on it and some work –'

'No, hang about, John. I know a guy at Historical Buildings. There's Europe money for that sort of thing too, there's Lottery money. Listen, I'm not opposed to . . . whatever you'd call them, "faith projects". I'm for them. They have to be in their proper place. We can't just do something here that fits right inside your pocket. All for the good of the Church.'

'That's not what I've said. I mean . . . Okay, if not that, then what? What do you actually want the Church to do here? Run soup kitchens?'

'That hadn't occurred but hey, look, if you've a mind to it then I'm right behind you, John. 'Scuse us a minute.'

Susannah was nigh, and the MP stepped aside to loan her his ear. For all her smartness Susannah still scuttled a little as she walked, shoulders hunched and bobbing, as if perpetually late, or apprehensive.

He contributed nothing to the next session on the single European currency. Despite high expectations, he found himself unable to join the discussion of 'A Cultural Renaissance in Newcastle?', which mired into a disagreement from the floor as to whether football and fine dining qualified as cultural pursuits. The room thinned a little of its contingent of schoolteachers, but seemed to fill up anew with print media. Chris Carter was calling for any final questions from the floor. That was when Gore began to notice a fixedly frowning aspect to Pallister's expression, one that had previously seemed imperturbable all day long.

Then a rangy figure clambered to his feet, accepting a baton microphone from an usher. And Gore registered a hawking clearance of the throat, a long and probing nose pointed in the air, a black but washed-out denim uniform – familiar defining lineaments, seeming to make the past a tangible presence even in this very contemporary room, and all before the questioner had so much as identified himself.

'Paul Todd, from the Journal *. . .'*

Pallister leaned to his microphone, planting a fist on the cloth before it. *'Sorry, are you accredited here, Paul?'*

'Whey, I've sat here all day and listened like everyone else. We've heard plenty out of you, Martin. Quite the speaker, you. Does a lot of it, this fella. Nicely paid for it and all. Few grand a go, if anyone's interested? Got a wedding, bar mitzvah?' Todd rocked easily on his heels, as if the floor were entirely his to expound from. *'It pays for his office, maybe. Cos it's a nice flash office he's got. Or maybe it doesn't. Maybe someone sat up there might know how Martin pays his rent?'*

'Paul, have you got an actual question or do you just want to –'

'Oh aye, I've a question for you, Martin, I'm wanting to know if there's a price on every word comes out of your mouth. I've been looking into this man, see. Do you know even half what this honourable gentleman gets up to?'

Todd was brandishing a wad of paper, A4 pages in scarlet, waving them before him. Gore watched Pallister throwing up volatile hands, looking to the ushers, to Susannah.

'Oh, come on, this is just – can we get a serious –?'

Todd, though, had taken to doling out his literature among the seated.

'Take a sheet and pass it on there. Have a look. Some of it's Register of Interests – not all, mind. No, he's not doing badly for an opposition man. Consultant to TronTech Computer Systems. Where are they from, eh? Crooksville, Ohio, how about that? Twenty-five grand a year he gets for that . . .'

Pallister was looking to the sound desk, making cut-throat motions, but the burly technician appeared as if wilfully hard of hearing. Indeed the room had taken on a murmuring attentiveness, a sense of their own money's worth that Gore had not seen all day, and from which Todd seemed to draw sustenance in the manner of a stand-up comic.

'Now, what do you suppose TronTech get for their money? You think they won't come knocking if he's ever in office? "Computer in every classroom", indeed. I'll bet they've a fancy for a nice fat contract out in Crooksville.'

It was becoming, Gore supposed, a security situation. But where was the security? Blonde Tessa was by the entrance and throwing fraught glances into the corridor. Susannah was out of her chair.

'Then you see he gets ten grand off Hart-McGrain oil, you know that Mr Salter, don't you? Another ten off Hook Millard lobbyists in London. And – oh yeah – his researcher's a lad on secondment from Hook Millard and all. How's that work? Well, you might want to look at who he speaks up for, when he bothers to speak – all his early day motions, whose interests concern him.'

Susannah was attempting to budge down the row in the midst of which Todd was holding court. Gore no longer knew where to look.

'Aye, I tell you, they all want a piece of this man. They're buying shares in him.'

Now Susannah was tugging, wrenching, at his microphone arm.

'Oh, and this lady here's his spin doctor, another old hand from Hook Millard. And guess what? That's her little brother sat up there on the platform. The vicar there, the little nodding dog.'

The flush Gore felt in his cheeks was like a slap. Two large men in Blackwater uniform were at last bustling through the lounge entrance.

As they filed from the stage Gore believed he could see extraordinary tension in the MP's mouth and across his broad blue woollen shoulders. Susannah darted to his side, and Gore heard the clenched exchanges.

'I thought you had the accreditation in hand.'

'He only nabbed some other bugger's badge.'

'Well, you'll give the paper fucking *war*, right?'

Now they were spilling out into the tight halogen-lit corridor – and there, appallingly, was Todd, alone and loitering, blithe and untroubled. Gore saw his sister hasten to step before her client, only for the MP to wave an irritated hand, a swatting gesture.

'The spoiler, eh? Spoiling for a fight, are you?'

'Martin, I'm not blaming you for trying to stuff your bank account, just be honest about it, man.'

'Away and pour another drink, Paul.'

'Only if you'll join us, man. I'd always get one in for an old comrade.'

'Get knotted, you snide prick.'

'Aw well now, you're getting personal, I might take offence . . .'

Pallister seemed ballistic now, a hair's breadth short of squaring up.

'Come on then, let's have it. Let's have you. Let's see it.'

But Susannah, yet more incensed, was grabbing and pushing, a little dynamo, exerting enough pressure to hustle Pallister past and out and away toward the lobby. Gore gave Todd a second glance, but the stare he received in return was loaded only with jubilant enmity.

He made his way down more dim and ashen-mauve corridors, past more monochrome photography of moody cranes and pulleys and derricks, until he found Room 102. Within, the wounded man sat on the bed over a bottle of red wine, in his creamy shirt and loosened crimson tie. 'You'll have a glass with me, eh? Go on. Sit down.'

Gore remained on his feet. The long drapes were half-closed against the view to the Tyne, blue light was exuded by a broad flat television tuned to the local evening news. One of Todd's glaring news-sheets lay semi-crumpled atop the queen-size duvet. Rock music blared from a micro-system. Pallister set down one remote control and clicked at another, fruitlessly. 'Here, would you kill that for us and all? Bloody racket.'

Gore did as he was asked, and took up the glass that was poured. The MP was studying the screen, his eyes seeming to burn then cloud over. An item on 'Forward to the Future' was introduced, an anodyne script that Gore imagined his sister might have approved. He glimpsed himself in one brief shot. Otherwise it was Pallister who dominated the highlights package, foursquare behind a lectern, making emphatic shapes with his hands. The man himself grunted, and the bulletin passed on to a report on the installation of CCTV cameras on an estate in Wallsend. Pallister did not attend to his guest, continuing to take unsmiling swigs from his glass. 'Tough on crime. That's bollocks for starters. You can't be tough enough. Not if you did it all day long. Our hands are tied. Everyone's in somebody's pocket, you never get to the top. Just streams running into the same cesspit. You can't shut off one and say you've drained the swamp.' He snapped off the television at last. 'The underworld, John. Always there. Never goes away. When you think, but – it's almost got a right. Being as it's half the world. Half of me, half of you. It's got to have its day and all. Hasn't it? I don't have to tell *you* that, do I? Can't tell you anything.'

Pallister was looking at him fully now and some buried fierceness was wresting to the surface. Gore wondered if there wasn't something inadvisably inciting about his very presence.

'Susannah said you wanted to talk?'

'Aye. Sit down but, for God's sake. Stood there like a bloody teacher.'

Gore lowered himself unamenably to the opposite edge of the bed.

'No, I've been thinking about that sermon of yours. When I came to your place. I mean, most of it was balls, no disrespect. But that one thing you said – how the revelation didn't happen in the past? Once and for all time?'

Gore nodded.

'Right. So let me ask you this. See if you find yourself changing your mind on things – is that cos you're a slippery sod? Or is it cos you've kept your eyes open? Seen how the world changes?'

'It depends, I suppose, on the circumstances,' said Gore, and sipped his Merlot.

'Huh. Put it this way, then. Do you believe in one law, everlasting? Or is it about the greatest good of the biggest number? I ought to know, see. I marked enough fucking essays on it.' He picked up Paul Todd's rap sheet between finger and thumb, chuckled without mirth. 'One thing I've learned, for sure. You only get one go in politics. You have to show one face, say one thing. If you look like you're in two minds on anything – you get murdered. But the trouble with the other, see – you get *held* to things.' The sheet, discarded, fluttered back to the bed.

'I don't know that I follow you, Martin.'

'*Whey*, man. You know what I mean, you *heard* it. These self-righteous arseholes, drives me spare, they think they *own* the Party. Think they bloody *invented* it. It's all *talk*, man.' He was on his feet and grasping for the bottle, voiding it into his bulbous glass. 'That's the brilliant thing about talk, you never have to *do* owt about it. Just keep singing the old tunes. Preaching the old sermon on the mount.' He stood over Gore, his rugby physicality reasserted. 'So, what? It's not quite to your liking, how we do things? Well, somebody has to actually *do* it. You reckon you've not got skeletons in your closet? Fine, you stand where I am for one fucking minute, see how you like it.'

This towering fury ought to have been daunting, Gore knew. And yet he felt himself calm, deliberate, in no mood to be browbeaten. 'I think the charge on you, Martin, is not what you do or say but what you're paid for it.'

Pallister seemed to absorb the blow. It stilled him momentarily, at least. 'We all serve somebody, John. Tell you this much, you'll not hear me saying socialism's a dead loss just cos it's died a bit in me. Better men than me'll keep flogging it. Good luck to 'em. Me, I've come to other conclusions. Based on my experience. And I wish a few others would look a bit harder at themselves before they line up to stick the fucking knife into me.'

He seemed replete, or emptied, and sat himself once more upon the bed, at a remove from Gore. 'Now come on. We need a proper think now, you and me. About today. The board, the project. What we're going to do.'

'I don't know.'

'Don't know *what*?'

'I'm not sure any more that I should be part of this. What do you need me for anyway, Martin? I don't see what use I am to you.'

'John, the whole – I mean, my *purpose* was to be of use to *you*.'

'Why, though?'

'*Why?*' The MP's dejection appeared to have hit a record low. 'And there was me thinking we got on.'

'No, really. That's hardly an unreasonable question. Yes, we've talked. I don't know you've listened to anything I've said. Either that or you feel just this contempt for it. But it seems like you've already made up your mind.'

'And you haven't?' Pallister stared at Gore, then down to his crotch.

'Whatever, then, fine. *Tant pis*, piss off, whatever you want, John.'

And Gore did not tarry. He stepped out into the corridor, there to find Susannah pacing, phone in her palm. Without pleasantry she rolled her eyes, pressed past him, and let the door swing hard behind her.

Book Five

MELINDA

Chapter I

VENDETTA

Thursday, 14 November 1996

'Who called, Steve?'

'I telt you, man, one of wor lookouts.'

'Aye, *who* but?'

'What's it *to* you, Shack man? D'ye hear me askin' you how you got the motor? It's nowt to *dee* wi' ye.'

'Fuck off, man, I'm sat here, aren't I? That makes it wor business and all.'

Shack was driving them, true. But were his hand not on the wheel – were the night and the Coast Road not rain-lashed and treacherous – then Stevie might have lunged from the back seat, seized him by the throat, jabbed a thick digit into his eye. Anything to silence the yack, jam the squawking frequency. This blinded resolve to cavil and quarrel every last little matter had gotten far past a joke.

'I'm telling ye, *Brian*, ye divvint need to knaa every fuckin' thing.'

'And I've telt *you* a million times, man, it's not just about you.'

'*Pack it in*, will ye's?' Thus Simms, riding shotgun, as if to bang heads and boss matters. But the stern look on his big backward face was worse than comical. Stevie heard the rattle in his voice.

'Fuck off, Simms, man, I'm *talkin'*. Naw, this is my business, Steve, you *make* it my business.'

Business, yes. A lovely business this was, sat thighs-pressed-to-crotch in a cold stolen car on a piss-rainy night, haring down the Coast Road toward Whitley Bay, nursing an ex-copper's pistol in a bag. Stevie stared out of the window at Battle Hill and Holy Cross flying by in the dark. Memory came unbidden of something read years before in *Black Belt* magazine, some kung fu master preaching how he learned to moderate his heartbeat, depress his body temperature, by pure exertion of will. It had sounded like bollocks, but richly fantastic bollocks, in the near-supernatural style some martial arts guys had when it came to talking about fighting. And Stevie had come to picture himself as one who could store great drums and barrels of unease about his internals, shifting them from chamber to chamber when needed – head to heart to gut to lower intestine. Tonight, though, he was not in possession of the full grip on himself. A kind of heartburn was throttling his chest, reflux like hot ashes in his throat.

'That's it, man, there.'

A revolving sign on metal legs declared the turn-off to the left for some god-awful retail park forecourt. Shack eased down, turned the wheel. A quiet night – no more than a dozen vehicles scattered unattended around a space for several hundred, this at a few minutes shy of nine o'clock. Looming up on all the four sides were darkened hangar-sized outlets bearing household names – Gala Bingo, Asda Dales, Carpet Rite, Argos. Tucked into the furthermost corner, with pedestrian access to the road, a glaringly lit windowed hutch, BARZINI'S RESTAURANT & TAKEOUT.

'Park us close, man, just not so the windows can see wuz.'

'Aye, I knaa.' Wincing, Shack cruised them to a prudential standstill and killed the engine. They sat for a moment, Stevie mulling over the grim vantage from his back seat. It was in much the same sort of innocuous all-hours supermarket lot that he had waited on Fitzy's hooky pal to deliver him his package. A sort of a joke, it seemed, that car parks should be so integral to the process of putting men into the ground.

There was movement outside Barzini's. 'There's the lad,' he murmured, a scrap of reassurance. The lad was muffled and bulky in helmet and waterproofs, loitering by his bike-stand and the restaurant dump bins arrayed at the side of the hutch. Unstrapping his headgear, he gave a thumbs-up to the car.

'Fuckin' hell,' muttered Shack. '*Mackers*, aye?'

Ignoring him, Stevie wrested his hold-all up to his lap – old faithful, his cracked and careworn orange Adidas gym bag, fifteen years of service. He unzipped it and withdrew the swaddled package, unwrapped the oily cloth, lay bare the dulled blue-black barrel. Shack stared fixedly ahead but Simms fidgeted and stole glances.

'Simms, man, gan on in there, will ye? Do us a quick recce.'

'What do ah do?'

'Just look out the gadgies for wuh, where they're sat at. Order summat, y'knaa, pizza or summat, then get yer'sel back out. Be cool about it, but, aye? Divvint hang about.'

Simms slammed the door behind him. Rain was thrumming still, smearing itself across the windshield, the floodlights of the forecourt flared out and blurred orange amid the inky darkness. Stevie wrapped fingers snugly round the pistol grip. Shack's gimlet eyes were on him now.

'Browning, is it, aye? Is it the high power?'

'What you sayin'?'

'Is it the high-power pistol? Did he tell you, the copper? The trigger, did he say it was double action?'

Stevie grunted. 'I just slide this top bit, right? Then I cock it, then I'm just firing then, aren't ah?'

'Your clip but, is it full?'

'Aye. He telt us it was.'

'Did you check, but? Aw, give us it. Give it *here*, man. Yer safety on?'

Stevie conceded. He hadn't wanted any meddling – had wished for the device to stay primed just as it had been passed to him. But Shack knew well enough how to rattle his cage.

Shack fiddled and finicked, then there was a click and the magazine dropped from the butt into his palm. He pondered its contents. 'Aye, them's yer soldiers . . .' Reinstating the clip, he shifted the weapon from hand to hand below the dashboard, then retracted its slide and cocked it. 'Not bad. That old cunt in Dunblane used one of these, y'knaa? Mighta had a couple on him, even.'

Stevie accepted its safe return.

'You'll want to use both hands, mind? It'll kick on you. It's not so big but there's a canny bit power in it.'

Shack and his own square-inch of expertise. Would he speak once more of Darwin and Goose Green? Or the one about the 'execution' on the road out of Zagreb, back in his bodyguarding days? But Simms was bundling back in, wrenching the door shut.

'Aye, it's them. Them uns from the Gunnery, aye? It's them.'

'All three of 'em?'

'Two of 'em.'

'Two. Where?'

'Right up at the front windie.'

'How many's in? In the whole place.'

'I never counted, man.'

'Just guess, what you saw.'

'Aw, there's maybe ten? A dozen? Few twos. Aye, and like a family?'

'Fuck it,' Stevie winced. A leaden heaviness had settled on him, about his shoulders, in his thighs, his boots. Shack shifted his whole body to face backward. 'Steve, man, see them bullets he give you? They're all soft-tips. You hit them cunts wi' those and they'll not even gan out the other side.'

'If I hit 'em.'

'Just fuckin' get right up to them, man, I've telt ye. Both hands.'

'Aye I heard you.'

'Steve man, fuck sake – you wouldn't still be *walkin'* if they thought like you think. Your bairns'd be goners and all. Right? You hear *that*, Steve?'

'Shut yer hole, man.'

He was walking now, covering tarmac at least, cleaving the air with purpose, the rain easing, the black wool balaclava hot on his face, and it was all getting to be out of his hands and into the realm of timing and how his luck was laid out. He rounded the rear of the brick hutch, past the bins, and saw the back door yawning open, pinned back by another bin, just as promised. He pushed on and in, no let-up, passing straight through the kitchen, some little short-order cook exclaiming in his direction yet instantly shushed by another.

Through, to the fluorescent light of the restaurant and round a serving counter – call it a dozen bodies right enough, Simms wasn't wrong – and before him a lass in black skirt and white rayon shirt, blithely bearing beer bottles and glasses on a tray. He fell in step behind her. And there they were, clear as a stain under the lights, he had heard them before he saw them – Chief Numpty, yes, and the little Squirt, their feet in the trough by the long window, their shiny coats over their chairs, great plates of meaty pizza spread before them.

You, Stevie, are fucking dead.

He was bearing down, and the people now staring at him and ceasing their chatter vanished from his mind as from his eye-line. He reached into his leather, wrapped fingers round the Browning grip.

Crossing the central reservation, into the face of oncoming.

The Squirt saw him, was off his seat and rising. Stevie swatted at the waitress, she crashed aside, and now he was thrusting up the gun into both his hands and squeezing the trigger once, twice, thrice – sharp, barking detonations that coursed up his arms and tossed the Squirt back against the wall, broken.

The Chief was only starting to shift half-free of his chair as if rapt. Stevie jammed the gun one-handed to the side of his head and fired again, a roar that burst open the Chief's face, throwing him off and to the floor like a deadweight sack.

Shrieking chaos all around – chairs scraping, minor bodies running out past him to the forecourt – Stevie took it as his due, knew himself its centre and begetter. His hands had felt heavy as lead until he felt the lancing recoil of those first shots. Now there was energy all through his limbs, the weapon seeming light as a toy. He stepped round the table for a better view of where the Chief's left ankle lay twitching. The eyes in the head strained upward but the bottom of the face was a red crater of gelatinous slime, an abysmal wound. The broad chest made itself an elementary target. He fired again, and again.

Then he turned to where the Squirt was trying to claw his way up the wall, clutching his right flank as if to knit it together. Stevie stepped smartly around the table and fired two-handed at his neck – devastating it – then again and again into the back of the prone figure, bellowing punches that jerked the body about the grey-tiled spattered floor.

Finished, he wheeled round to the tumult behind him, and his kneecap smashed into a table-edge. Cursing through pain, he saw appalled faces – punters, staff, some other pimply-faced slip of a waitress, moaning. Detail was bleeding back into his field of vision – he understood now there was some sort of Roman mural around the restaurant walls, temple girls in togas, pouring water. He waved the gun in the direction of those faces.

'Shut up and divvint fuckin' do nowt, you'll all be alright.'

His knee was throbbing, his pulse felt like a pain in his heart, there was pain too in his gun-hand, but no worse than that of a careless punch. He swapped the weapon to his left, shook out his fingers. He would address it all presently, once he was in motion. *Walk,* he told himself. *Calm, control. Get it all behind you*. He moved to the doorway and beyond he could see his ride, the motor running. Then he sensed a presence, to his peripheral left, and he flinched and spun and levelled the gun again. But it was only Mackers, staring at him, wet as a dog, rigid, seemingly petrified. *Fuck, don't just stand there catching flies, son, get yer'sel offside and all.*

Shack was burning rubber down the Coast Road, the clutch was squealing, Simms was squirming and rubbing his head as if car-sick. Stevie, with as steady a hand as he could summon, slipped the safety on the gun.

'How was that, then?'

Of all the fucking idiot things.

'Steve, man, are they dead?'

They were, weren't they? The doubt reared up, a very sick and sudden fright. He rewound the scene in his head again as best he could. The red crater. The floor, grossly smeared with guts. No. Not a chance, no man got up and walked away from that.

'Aye.'

'Aye? You're sure, like?'

'Aye, they're fucking dead, now slow down, will ye?'

Shack shot him a look. 'Not till we's get on. I'm takkin us through Shiremoor, the garage is in Longbenton.' And he coughed out a short scorning laugh. 'Not their lucky night, then, was it? Them cunts?'

'Not too lucky, naw.'

'Aye, fuck 'em but, eh?'

They travelled then in silence to the roadside service station, nestled between the darkened farmlands of Shiremoor and the concrete industrial sprawl of North Shields. Shack steered them into the hushed cover of the garage and got out to confer with his mate, the proprietor. Simms, too, clambered out, into another vehicle, and zoomed away into the black with a solemn wave. Stevie stayed slumped in the gloomy back seat, adrenalin receded, making inventory of his aches and pains.

He saw now the shocked white abrasion and bright blood in the webbing between his right thumb and forefinger. The firing hammer – it must have snagged at his skin.

He drew the gun from the bag once more – held it to his nose, breathed in the odour of burnt powder. Then he realised that his coat and jumper were as if sprayed with mist. Not rainwater – thicker, globule-like – blood, he realised – still slick on the leather, but drying into flecks on the dark wool of the jumper. He hadn't believed he had stained himself so. He licked his palm and rubbed it across his chest, until a cooler head told him, *What the fuck you doing, man? Divvint do that.*

Who are you, but? Who are ya?

Steven Leonard Coulson.

And he sat back, feeling the strangest current travelling through his body, bearing no relief – more like a hollow premature climax, one that had released toxins into his bloodstream, caused something rancid to settle and congeal, tumour-like, within the vitals. He wanted to drink a bottle of good whisky, tot after tot, straight down to the amber heel. That, or crawl into his pit and lie curled there like a dog. But he couldn't conceive of sleep, not in this new place where his buzzing brain was stationed, stonily bleak.

That's it, done it now. All done for.

Shack was returning – time to change cars, he supposed. He restored the weapon carefully to the bag.

'You want us to get rid for ye? The gun?'

'Nah, I'll get shot of it.'

Get your fucking nose out of it, Shack, man. No question, these had to be the dog-end days of their long association. If he could have had one wish, it would have been to end it right there. *Call it a handshake, eh? Then you gan left and I'll gan right.* But the night shift had an hour to run. He still had need of a ride.

And he would not be losing the firearm, no fear. Waste not, want not. Something in his gut told him its usefulness was not yet at an end. It didn't quite bear thinking. But the thought of discarding it, even sinking it to the bed of the Tyne, seemed lunatic – infinitely less sane than stowing it away in a place of safekeeping. At least, small mercy, he knew just such a place, just such a safekeeper.

Chapter II

THE NIGHT CALLER

Friday, 15 November 1996

They clung to one another, yet neither could seem to find comfort.

'You're manic, you. It's like kipping with a dog.'

'Sorry. Am I keeping you up?'

'Nah, you're alright . . . I'm the same. Got a bit itch.'

In the early evening hours, confined to quarters, he had hankered after her company – was glad of her voice on the phone, glad of her invitation. They had talked of this and that, without consequence. Now, in the dark around midnight, he felt emptied and pensive, resigned to passing the night under her frilled and slightly soiled duvet. On her bedside table lay the wilted latex sheath, his semen bagged and knotted like kitchen leavings and wadded up in tissues – a used dobber, to be dropped, he assumed, into the crowded bathroom bin, there to nestle amid toilet-roll tubes and spent sanitary towels. For the moment, though, Lindy seemed unbothered by housekeeping, and Gore didn't care to be her tidy-up fairy.

She yawned, flipped her pillow, nestled her profile resignedly next to his. 'You never told us how it started with you? Taking the cloth and that?'

'Christ, you don't want to talk about that, do you?'

'Why not? It's what you do.'

'We don't talk about what *you* do. Your many jobs.'

'S'not worth talking about. Yours is a story, like. How, just tell us, man. You'll maybe get us off to sleep.'

He sighed, rolled onto his back. 'I was born in Pity Me. You know? Just north of Durham. I thought for a living I might try and pity other people.'

'Get away. Divvint act the prick wi' us.'

He blew out his lips. 'Well, okay, the truth is – I felt a call. That's the only way to say it. I went to France one summer for work. I was maybe twenty? And I had a, a sort of a religious experience, basically.'

'Like what?'

'A sense of God. That just came at me. And was overpowering.'

'What was it like, but?'

'I don't know. It just felt all of a sudden like – the world was a perfect creation. And there was no way it couldn't have been *willed* that way. I'd never thought that was remotely plausible before. Then it just seemed obvious.'

'And that was it for you then?'

'What else do you need?'

She scrunched her features. 'Sounds a bit mental is all. A bit touched.'

'Well, maybe it was. I'm just saying – I felt God. I'm not trying to sell it to anyone. People have to feel it for themselves.'

'Aye, well. We's can't all gan off around France.' She rolled aside, groped for her alarm clock. 'And have you ever felt the same since? D'you ever look round Hoxheath and think, "Eee man, it's just *perfect*, this"?'

'I do, sometimes.'

'Get away.'

'No, I do. God is here, Lindy. He's on this estate.'

'Hallo, God,' she hooted. 'Divvint mind wuh.'

He shrugged aside the duvet, swung his legs out over the side of the bed, sat up, presenting her with his broad back. And he rubbed at his stiff neck.

'Well – you're maybe right.'

'About what?'

'It's not the same. That time in France, I still remember the feeling. In my whole body. I do wonder, but. If I didn't maybe – read it wrong. Back then? The wrong end of the stick. I was shattered, see, I'd done a hard day's work. For once. Maybe I should have been a stonemason, you know. I maybe missed my true calling.

Honest labour.'

He had decided not to care whether his musings aloud sailed clean over her head. Indeed, turning to look at her, he saw she beheld him coolly from over the bedcover.

'Wouldn't *that* be funny? Eh?'

'*I'm* not trying to be funny, John. If you felt it, you felt it.'

'Thanks. No, but you're right, really. Just in that one moment – I cashed in an awful lot of reservations. Doubts I'd had.'

'Like what?'

'Oh, that Christ was born of a virgin? That God became a man. Died for our sins, all that, you know – it sort of underpins quite a lot of what we do. You've taken communion off me, you should know.'

'I don't think about it.'

'Yes, but if you don't *believe* Christ rose, then what you're doing in the act is a sacrilege. You're just mocking it.'

'No I'm not. I wouldn't do that.' She raised herself from recumbent to her elbows. 'Fuck off, you. I'm not the one wears the dog collar. It's *your* problem, pet.'

He laughed softly into his chest, since clearly there would be no sleep tonight. 'Well. Sorry. You did ask, Lindy, so – that's what you get.'

'Aw, bloody sod *you*, man.'

She threw aside her own share of covers, stomped round the bed and out of the room, flushed in her loose tee-shirt and knickers.

Gore lay back, stretched, heard the crank of the tap running in the kitchen below. There was no point in pretending sweet harmony between them. When she had unrolled the condom upon him – after bobbing with her lips and running fingers quicksilver across his perineum – however undeniable and desired was the effect, he had sensed something tired and perfunctory in her performance. He had to face himself, had to wonder indeed how many others had been privy to her conscientious manners in the act. And he could no more guess now than on prior occasions quite how Lindy felt in its aftermath.

Tonight she had not looked too thrilled – rather more patient, indulgent. Could she have reached the terminus of her curiosity in him? Or had he dismayed her inadvertently once more, as seemed to be his gift? Over a glass of wine he had made the blandest of remarks about time and the demands of childrearing. 'Aw God, I'd love another one,' she had avowed instantly. 'Little brother or sister would be *magic* for him.' He smiled and said nothing, deeming this by far the wisest course. The prophylactics, box-fresh, nestled in his coat pocket, and whilst he would offer them as a gesture of shared responsibility he knew he had acquired them more by way of insurance.

He must have dropped off, for the next he knew he was blinking confusedly in the semi-dark, eyes swimming toward the angle of light through the doorjamb. There were noises below, the front door clicking closed, heavy boots shuffling on the bristly doormat, hushed voices in conference. Groggily Gore lifted himself up and out of bed, and with a crooked finger lightly pulled the door open a little wider.

'Y'alreet? What's the matter wi' you?'

'I need a bit kip, Lind. I'm done in. S'alright if I crash out?'

'Aw not tonight, man, I've got company.'

'You've *company*, pet? Man alive. Anyone I knaa?'

'Naw, man –'

'Got yer'sel a new little friend then, pet?'

'Just a fella I'm seeing.'

'Aw, I see. Well, you've let us down there, like. I get lonely an' all but, sometimes Lind. There was me dreaming of you fixin' us breakfast.'

'Stevie, I canna, man, please –'

'Naw, you're alright. You're alright, divvint get yer'sel het.'

In the silence that followed, Gore could think only of Coulson's pulverising size, the uselessness it made of all resistance, usually.

'Honest, but, what's the matter?'

'Nowt. Just the normal.'

'Just you look really off, man. Peaky, like.'

'I'm canny. Just fucked is all. Here.'

Gore heard a tread on the lowest stair, and his scalp prickled.

'Leave it, Stevie, just leave it there, I'll take it up.'

The stair creaked again, but only in relief, it seemed. Gore stepped back to the bed and slipped back under the duvet. The conversation ebbed in and out of his earshot.

'Lad's al'reet?'

'Canny.'

'You're on for the shop the morra neet?'

'Aye, and Saturday and all, I've talked to Claire.'

'And you'll do ours Wednesday? Aye? Good girl.'

He heard the front door click once more, weighed his options, then rose, pulled on his jeans and trod down the stairs with deliberation. Lindy was curled in her armchair, chewing a fingernail, staring into space. Finally she favoured him with her gaze.

'Thought you'd got off . . .'

'No chance. You had a visitor?'

'Aye. Just Stevie. You know Stevie.'

'What about? This time of night?'

She scoffed through her enervation. 'Peak hours for Stevie, this. Naw. There's a bar I work in some nights. In town. It's Stevie's place. He runs it, his lads on the door and all that.'

'That sounds a bit rough.'

'Naw, it's just like a clubby sort of bar. For young uns. Ravers and that. He wanted checking I was on for doing a night in the week.'

'What's it called, this bar?'

'The bar? Teflon.'

'And it's okay, is it? Okay place?'

'Aye, it's fine. Just the odd night a week I do.'

'Maybe we should have a night out there. Together.'

'Get away.' Her eyes narrowed, as if hostilities had recommenced prematurely after a seasonal ceasefire.

'Wouldn't that be nice, though?'

'I don't think it's your *scene*, John.'

'Can't know 'til I try.'

'Look you, don't be making promises you'll not keep, alright?'

'I thought you wanted us to do more together?'

'Not like *that*. God. It's where I *work*, man. I wouldn't go near it otherwise. It's not my scene neither, not any more.'

'Well then – maybe I could just drop in at the end of your shift one night. Pick you up, bring you home.'

'In what? On your bike? Two in the morning? I'm tellin' you, John, you'd not like it. You'd stick out like an arse in Fenwick's window.'

'I'd only be there to see you, Lindy. See what you get up to.'

'Well I don't *want* you seeing us, not particu'ly, thanks. I'm on my bloody feet all night pulling pints for a load of jakey lads. I'd not be *comfortable* with you there, John, can you not see that? I'd be *shy*, man.'

'*Shy*? You?'

'Aye, fuckin' *me*.' She eyed him blazingly, and it crashed in on him, just how crude he had sounded. 'I mean – what do you *think*, like? Do you think I'm just some *trollop*, John? Do you think it's just fun and games for me all the time? Am I just here for your *pleasure* any fuckin' hour of the day?'

Gore blinked under her barrage, thrown, grasping mentally for some respite, a temporary pause, something to re-exert the force of his silence.

'No, Lindy, no. I don't think any of that. I only want us to have a few things in common. Like you say. Given the . . . the disparities of our lives.'

The line of her mouth was bitter and crumpling. 'It's not a life *I've* got, man. I never know if I'm bloody coming or going.' She thrust a balled fist to her lips. He moved impulsively toward her, open-armed. 'Naw, look, just don't, man, alright? Don't.'

So he lowered himself gingerly onto the arm of her chair. She did not look at him.

'It's just fucking hard sometimes. You know? So hard.'

He nodded.

'I know you're not like a lot of fellas, I do know that, John. It's just sometimes . . . you've stood there like a bloody *statue*, man. I dunno what you're thinking. And – oh, I dunno – sometimes I just can't be *arsed.*' She gave him the full weight of her gaze. 'What I need to know is, am I wasting my time with you?'

'You're not. Of course you're not.'

'Well then, look, you. I'm not just here to tickle your fancy. When you can be bothered. I'm not just gunna be, y'knaa, your little breath of fresh air. Liza bloody Doolittle. Alright?'

Gore would have whistled under his breath, had the moment permitted. Her acuity had come at him from clear out of the blue, and he was abruptly and crushingly embarrassed by himself.

'Do you hear us, John?'

He hazarded a caress of the nape of her neck, a stroke of the thick hair gathered there, tangled and dulled.

'I do, I do. Look I'm sorry. Really. But please don't be thinking any of that. That's not how I feel about you.'

'Oh, it's not, is it?'

'No. You have to believe I care for you. You have to.'

'Oh aye . . .?' She bowed her head, rubbed at her eyes. But there was no more fight. Stroking her still, gently, cautiously, he followed her gaze to the floor. Resting by the coffee table was the orange Adidas sports bag, that now-familiar eyesore of her bedroom belongings. He prodded it idly with a toe.

'Just leave that, man.'

'Sorry, will it explode?'

'It's Stevie's, he must've left it, just leave it.'

There came a creak from the stairway, and they looked together to see Jake descending, one step, two step, his tummy protruding from pyjamas styled in England football colours. Gore smiled wanly at the boy, who stared back, impassive.

'Aw, man . . . Look, it'd be better maybe if you just go, John.'

He looked close at her, surprised – a little put out.

'Then you'll maybe sleep. We'll all sleep.'

She was already getting up, moving past him, taking her boy in hand and back upstairs to quarters. Gore sat for a moment in his discomfort. It was cold outside, and this seemed a sort of banishment – but, on reflection, he had no obvious grounds for appeal.

*

Alone again, her son safely stowed abed once more, Lindy sat and fingered a strand of her straggling hair. Now then, would she? Or wouldn't she? Her late-favoured colour had been growing out awhile, the auburn roots making themselves heard again. Selfish, maybe – so late in the day, laundry unfolded, dishes unwashed, and here was Miss, thinking only of expending some care on herself. But she loathed the thought of creeping back into her pit so dissatisfied.

No, she was resolved. She went to the kitchen drawers, located the big-handled scissors, headed for the stairs. Then she remembered Stevie's magic bag, and plucked it from the floor. It was lighter than usual, rattling a little – clearly not stuffed to the gills, as she had observed once when she dared to peek and found it brimful with ten bagged kilo-weight of cocaine.

What would that fella of hers make of the change she had in mind? He could think what he liked, the sod. In all the years she had finicked and finessed her appearance, she could honestly attest that the work had never been done for the benefit of any man. Quite often, the reverse was intended.

Since they had first kept one another's company, she had been puzzled, miffed, by his perpetual looks to the door, the glances to a wrist where there was no watch, his seeming need for a need to be elsewhere, as if fearful of tumbling into some vortex. It was almost amusing, up to a point – though a girl less tolerant or worldly could have taken the huff. But clearly he was a conflicted sort, and she had developed a mild fascination in watching him dare to shift his weight off the fence.

That interest, she knew, had waned a little. The closing door now afforded her a share of the same relief she presumed in him.

Physically it wasn't what she was used to, far from it, though he smelled nice and was tidy, touched her with delicacy – maybe too much of it. That was part of his manners, and his manners did elevate him.

But his personality – the weird silences, the show-off talk, that private little world, that freezing *look* of this – all of these were a faff and a bother. And now she had to put up with his judgement too. *That* she could have got from anyone, at a fraction of the cost. The lesson, she supposed, was that even when you tried to deal the cards afresh, make the safer or supposedly 'better' choice of a man, they didn't necessarily *treat* you any better. And that, if true, was a glum state of affairs.

In the bathroom she located the electric clippers, long neglected in their box under the sink. She ran the plug to the socket by the skirting, dusted the blades with the small stiff brush, and selected the quarter-inch fitting. Then, setting the tool aside, she took up the scissors, bent over the sink and, eyeing her reflection, seized a long lock of hair between her fingers, close to the roots. She snipped, and she snipped. Curls, soft and drab, began to tumble into the bowl, joined by others, soon a dark matted pile. Violence of a kind, she fancied – but still, it would feel good to get shorn again.

Sixteen she had been when she first stepped over the scored threshold of Bob Craven's the Barber – nominally a cutter only of lads' hair – and asked him to shave her head. The shop was quiet and Bob wasn't fazed by much, so he soon had her cranked up in the high chair, swaddled in a plastic cape, inhaling the tonic and talc. At the very last, she bottled it, unsure she could withstand a grade-one crop – and so settled for number two. It proved to be an error. The visual effect she had sought was a kind of gravity, a strength and serenity, from the crown of her scalp to the nape of her neck. What she wound up with seemed dour and dowdy at first – she looked at best like some punky American lesbian, at worst like one of those fat Mod girls in fishtail parkas who dawdled round Eldon Square scoffing chips.

And yet, it was a change, and that was for the better. She had tried the other route – soft and shiny and girly – and it hadn't paid dividends. She was never set firm on what she thought of her looks – sometimes she despaired, at others she saw certain strengths – but by her mid-teens it was piercingly apparent that her plump lips and downy hair were some kind of red rag, encouraging lads to pull and push her and generally aspire to misuse her. Her first full-on boyfriend – Lee Quint from Sceptre Street, of the sneering smile and the scarred cheek – had seemed a surprise charmer, fiercely absorbed by her every curve and hollow, right up until hours after he first ejaculated inside her. The falling-off thereafter was supremely hurtful, and she struggled for a while to regain her sense of self. In due course she took as some solace that she was possibly fortunate to have skipped an allotted place on the pram-pushing roster.

Now she beheld herself and her handiwork in the mirror awhile – Raggedy Annie, the butchered doll. She pulled the door to, took up the clippers and clicked the switch that made them buzz. Then she stooped, craned her neck and commenced the shearing – up the sides and round the back, blade snug to skin, steering close to the planes and contours, then over the top in good straight rows, and back to the nape to finish. At intervals she shook little snippets like iron filings onto the gathering carpet in the bowl. Shutting off the warm tool, she effected some finishing touches with a disposable razor normally deployed on her legs. Finally she made her inspection – ran her fingers over the fresh bristles, always a pleasing sensation – then scrunched up her face for the mirror, tearing her mouth open wide in a silent shout, just like a warrior woman. The sight had long since ceased to alarm her, for all that it retained its power to appal certain others. 'Oh you've *spoiled* yourself, Melinda.' That was what her mother shrieked, foolishly, on the day she trooped home from Bob Craven's. And that was the name Mairead gave her, one of which she tired, as of so much else besides.

Chapter III

ECONOMIES

Friday, 15 November 1996

She levered herself out of her pit to beat the alarm at eight, had despatched her restorative cuppa and toast and shaken Jake's Rice Crispies into the bowl before trooping back upstairs to shake the boy awake. For some moments after his lids unglued he looked at her as though she had harrowed his own fair head and not hers.

'Do you not think your mam's nice-looking any more then?'

'It's *'orrible*, man.'

'Oh, thank you. Well, your mam's got to have her little ways, okay?'

Fifteen minutes later, cereal untouched, shoes not yet on, he was making a lugubrious face and reporting a stomach ache. 'I don' *wan' oo*!' he protested, and grimly she supposed that his froth and vigour would have floored a lesser female.

'How, Jake man, just get *on*. We've all of us gotta do things we don't want to sometimes. What do you think it's like for me?'

She had a full day ahead, the place was looking more than 'lived in' – it was a sty – on top of which she was starting to feel November-fluey, which always crept over her with maximum charm in a week she was due to menstruate. She had him inserted in those shoes by the time the neighbour rang the bell. She gave herself a cursory seeing-to with lipstick and hairbrush, and was out the door ten minutes later.

Peak-time, then, at Mankad's News'n'Booze. Lindy sold fizzy cans to the schoolkids, twenty Lamberts to the mums, scratch-cards to the pensioners and *Suns* and *Mirrors* to the drivers of transits. This most perfunctory of all her wage-labours was also the least remunerative, but the least bother for all that. The Greek restaurant in town could not be relied on for hours or even custom, and the owner was a red-eyed lech. Tending bar at Teflon was starting to make her feel careworn, spinsterish, though she was by no means the oldest on display – indeed, still a dish next to some of the heifers who piled in. As for the Damask Rose, one or two of the girls there were good sorts, making up in laughs for the nature of the job, but not entirely. Elevenses at Mankad's offered at least the perk of a paddle through the newest *Elle, Cosmo, Vogue, Marie Claire, She, Zest, Company* . . . She chided herself for the curiosity, the ritual succumbing to nonsense – that stuff, it never changed. And yet, it was for her an area of expertise. Her eye was trained to assess the vying claims of models, and she fancied she could tell the better sorts from the scores of kohl-eyed anorexics clearly rating themselves hotter than newly lain shit.

She had only been loitering down Northumberland Street, cocking a snook at the windows of Zara and Next and Hennes, on her way to buy a sandwich that she planned to consume alone at the foot of Grey's Monument. Newly seventeen, she was trying out as a junior in a solicitor's office. The job had seemed a boon, but it amounted only to filing while several haughty blokes cast long looks at her arse. The girls weren't any nicer.

In the dim reflection of Zara's glass frontage her radar sensed a hovering presence – an older bloke in a jerkin of mauve-ish coloured leather, hair like a meringue, casting stealthy looks of his own. He asked her if she'd ever been told she could model? Bollocks or not, she had no fear – and it wasn't like anybody else had asked her a friendly question all morning. He enquired if he might speak to her parents? She muttered that there was only Mairead, and that he'd have to catch her early in the day. He gave her a card, which looked and felt legitimate. Better yet, there was something laconically take-it-or-leave-it in his manner, one that encouraged her to believe. And she wanted to.

Two days later she took a bus to his studio out by Low Walker, overlooking the Tyne. His name was Eric Manners – 'Call us Guv'nor, eh?' – and he treated her carefully, called her 'Miss Clark' as he asked her to tilt her chin, told her categorically that she had what was known in the biz as 'a European body'. He thence conveyed her to Vivian Beer, the hardy old bird who ran the Viva Model Agency, and Viv took her on the books as if routinely. Lindy found herself sitting through classes in skincare, hair-care, maquillage, wardrobe. And this time – so unlike her schooldays, where the kudos came from caring less – this time, she paid attention.

After a few tetchily dreadful styling sessions that made her look ugly, and a live PA for hair-gel where she forgot to smile and was made to feel incompetent, Viva came up with an image for her, and in retrospect it seemed obvious – her hair in a short, inky-black, super-glossy feathered bob, putting Lindy in mind of the one Madonna used to wear when she was acting the peepshow girl. A photographer from Newcastle Poly, a bony lad called Phil, shot some angular black-and-whites that really made her book into something a bit different, and earned her some play in *Blitz* magazine. Phil squired Lindy to Club Zeus by way of celebration, and after two strong ciders he surprised the life from her by lacing his fingers in hers. She let him kiss her mouth, and found it not unpleasant.

Mairead couldn't just be pleased for her – it couldn't be that sweet and simple. Mairead had thought herself a glamour girl back in the seventies, knocking around with all the local bands. Lindy assumed she had been drunk most of the time back then, and that had only got worse, while there was nothing glamorous about scrubbing other people's toilet bowls in West Jesmond. Lindy had never intended to rub her mother's face in it, but nor would she defer to any sozzled pretensions of wisdom. With benefits thrown in to her pay she had enough to get out into a communal flat with two other Viva girls – Jill who'd been cast in a telly drama for kids, Holly who sang and danced. They carried themselves unabashedly as talents, this pair, natural blondes both, but Lindy found them not the worst company. Then she snagged a fashion campaign for British Home Stores, a naff 'hip-hop' range that nevertheless set her upright as life-size cardboard in the window of the Eldon Square store. She began to lead a bit of a mad life. She could waltz into clubs, her drinks paid for, and she met all sorts. She was inherently wary of boozing – that was what Mairead did. But Lindy believed she could do it better, with a bit of flair – a kir royale and a rasping line of charlie. She found it heady, pleasing, to see silly money chucked about for silly and selfish and wholly ephemeral treats.

In retrospect? She had one good year. It was almost cruel, how swiftly the work grew thin. She suspected she was not favoured at Viva, not thought golden, even when her flatmates – the Blonde Alliance – upped and left together for London. Newer girls seemed to have the edge on her within days of signing on. When it was all over, she sometimes brooded. Why hadn't she applied herself? Why did she act as if by one poxy campaign she had 'arrived'? Why did she go on the lash so hard? Why not protect her assets? It wasn't, she knew, for want of advice – but the advice from Viv Beer always came sourly coated, dispensed in an uppity manner. It reeked of the whole 'spoiling yourself' business, and she couldn't but feel it was worth ignoring that stuff, whatever the cost – just to be her own person, sovereign, real, free of airs and bullshit.

In the event she was highly wired, nursing a sharpener of rum and Coke, on the early morning that police attended her flat to inform her that her mother's body had been found in Hoxheath Park, positively identified by Yvonne, stone dead of alcohol poisoning. The officers' cursory manner was a strike against them, one she wouldn't forget. It was nothing, though, next to some of the mingey faces at the funeral – the crowd from the Queen's Head who had kept her mother steeped in drink, acting now as if *she* had driven her poor mam into the ground. They weren't to know her feelings, and it was past time for them all to take a hard look at themselves.

*

She pulled her knees up into the armchair, cupped the cigarette into her palm between draws, and watched him crafting with plasticine, laid out flat on his belly, tip of his tongue pressed against his teeth, his eyes stony with concentration as his fingers modelled a stocky humanoid figure from the laminate floor up. He made her want to cry, sometimes – the little dough-boy, her half-pint welterweight champ. It amazed her, thinking back, that this robust boy-child had come forth from her body. He could be surly, yes, but there was sweetness there too.

She had no regrets. It hadn't been sanguine from the get-go. The dawning blue cross of the test had brought on a lurching, prickling fear. *I'm a daughter, not a mother*, was her first clear fit of panic. Over the ensuing hours she learned to chide herself. The light of day was chilly, and she belonged to no one now. She was meant to know better, too – not to fall to ashen pieces, none of that soft shit. Complete *mongs* had kids, and they managed. A good attitude was called for. She had to view it as a job of work – no, a project, an opportunity to make something special, in her own image, altogether loveable.

Getting great with child was the last thing her clubbing crew had expected of her, back in the Summer of Love. She found herself relishing the outrage. Just how well did those cronies imagine they knew her anyway? Junior among them, she began to feel like the old soul. It all added up to the end of a good time that had been ending anyway. And they duly melted away, those pals. Not a problem. She had not for one minute expected Phil to stick around, not when the kid wasn't his and she wasn't saying whose it was. A hand to grasp in the delivery room, that she could have wished for, but wishes weren't for living on.

Instead she crossed alone into the askew world of fraught nights and grey mornings, smarting breasts, bottle regimens, playgroups and sitters. The fear that stayed plangent was that her precious private time would be consumed, lost – that she was never to be herself ever again. And yet, denied the gallivant, the wired nights on the piss, a new vista of reflection had opened up to her. In that place, though, she found also a new and debilitating tendency to brood.

Then the taxman kicked her with both boots, for she had never quite got round to declaring some of those Viva earnings. It was only that her former and fleeting livelihood had now closed off to her, one more blind doorway. There was no joke, no mere attitude, that could shrug off this burden. Now she had to accept certain charities, swallow down certain unhappy realities, be glad of such friendships as endured. For Jake's sake she knew that much.

And there was the door. Her babysitting fairy, her mother's dowdy elder sister – a little early, but dependable as rain.

An easy walk at this time of night, up the Hoxheath Road, onto the Westgate. She turned the key in the unmarked door and climbed the poor carpet of the stairs to the white-gloss door of the converted flat – a classically creaky Irish bodge job. Into the reception, the little cubby of a kitchen, bounded by the breakfast bar that doubled as front desk. No one visibly manning the fort, though – just Dougie Petrie, his back to the wall, tonight's regulation ox in black bomber and DMs, sufficient to scare off any ditherers by his pudding face, broad squashed nose and monobrow. Preferable, at least, to Shackleton, who made plain his hate for this work.

'Hiya!'

'How, Lind – hell's *teeth*, what you done to yer heid?'

'Jake done it when I was asleep.'

'He never? The little –'

'*Nah* man, grow up. I did it. What, have I spoiled me'sel?'

Claire was emerging from the toilet room jammed in beyond the kitchen – leading with her belly, post-shit fag in one hand, *Chronicle* in the other.

'Aw, fuck me, Lindy, not again?'

Such was the sum of the greetings. Indeed the pair of them looked harassed and grouchy, faces like kicked-down doors.

'What's the matter with you's, then?'

'Friggin' police were round, weren't they?'

'What did they want?'

'Nowt. Just give us a load of bother.'

'Did they *say* they were police? When they come in?'

'Aye, two of 'em, badges and all, bold as a fart. Said they'd had complaint.'

'Off of who, like?'

'Didn't say.'

'So what did they do?'

'Just walked around the place being arsey. We'd nee punters in, thank fuck. Eh, but one of 'em says to wuh, "Funny sort of sauna this is. Where's your steam room?" Aye, he says, "Where's your massage tables at, then?"'

'What did *you* say?'

'I said we did it all just on the beds.'

'Aw, Claire, man, that was a bit fucking mong, wasn't it?'

'What was I *s'posed* to say? I wasn't expecting it. I thought they weren't bothered.'

Lindy's calculations were already more advanced. 'Naw, but they can't have been serious, like. Or they'd have had a watch on us – they'd have burst in the minute they reckoned they'd catch some bloke up to his nuts. Naw. It's just trying to put the wind up wuz.'

'Aye well, you wanna talk to them girls, they got proper rattled.'

'Doug, you'll tell Stevie, aye?'

'Aye, I will. He'll not want to hear, mind.'

'Bloody tough.' She could feel herself taking charge again. She was in the wrong line of work, she knew it. 'Who's on, then?'

'Yulia – she got the frighteners the worst. Leanne's in, Kirsty . . .'

'Right. Anyone else coming?'

'The Thai girl, maybe, she'll call to say. Aw aye, and Liz.'

'Which Liz?'

'Fishwick.'

They'd got a lot of Lizzes. For the customers Liz Fishwick called herself Lana.

'Did you get fed, Lind? Do you want owt?' Claire gestured to the microwave, to a sack of oven chips and a small stack of shrink-wrapped chicken pieces, their pimply skins yellow as jaundice. The house menu. No, Miss Clark would not be having any of *that* shit. 'Just a cuppa tea, eh?'

'Aw, you can get that yer'sel. I'm pushing off then.'

'Wait on, will ya? 'Til I get round the rooms?'

She gestured to her plastic bag of gear from Superdrug. Claire, though, was resolutely collecting her own goods. 'D'ye want the paper?'

'Aye, leave it.'

'Okay. And are you pleased, then? With your lovely hairdo?'

'Aye, I fuckin' love it.'

She checked into the living room – curtains drawn, the faded plush settee where the girls sat watching telly, waiting to be weighed in the balance. *Top of the Pops* was on, some Michael Jackson video. 'Hiya,' Lindy sang. Leanne smiled back. She was in her mid-thirties, fair and fair-looking, if plump – worked in a nursing home by day. Lindy was more or less sure she made in a week at the home what she could pull in here in one night, albeit a grossly crowded one.

And there was Yulia, pushing her wispy hair from her face, prodding the ring in her nose, shifting her girlish carriage on the settee. Lindy motioned for her to come outside, as to step into her office.

'Y'alright?'

'Not so good. Ah . . . okay.'

'Don't worry, about the police, okay? It all gets settled, honest. There won't be bother.'

The girl bobbed her head, unconvinced but seeming to appreciate the effort.

'Listen, can you do a bit in the day for us the morra morning? With Jake? It's just I've got a load of errands to run.'

'Oh yeah, oh sure, Lindy, I love to.'

'Just maybe three hours? I'll give you twenty quid, okay? And here, I've got a bit special.' With two fingers she unveiled the small glossy wrap from her jacket top pocket. Yulia's eyes lit, her hands were greedy. 'Hang on, we'll do it together bit later, eh?'

She found it best to be discreet about these things, in deference to house rules about not getting rubbish in off the street – typical Stevie, his twisted universe of right and wrong.

Pressing on down the corridor to the Red Room – which was, in truth, cerise – Lindy found the door closed, in use. Kirsty, presumably – younger and less to look at even than Leanne, but with a jutting milk-white bosom. The bathroom door, too, was shut, the hiss of the shower audible – one satisfied soapy customer. She hoped he had thrown the window open, for it was getting mouldy round the corners in there. She threw down clean towels at the foot of the door. These always seemed on the small side for the clientele, the lardy blokes they got in – those keen readers of the small ads in the *Daily Sport*, hungry recipients of a dirty secret down the pub.

She set to business in the Green Room – went from the yucca to the aspidistra, the begonia, the spider ivy, watering the soil from a tooth-mug, wiping the leaves. She propped a window ajar, plumped the pillows, threw the duvet afresh and smoothed it, working carefully around the alarm button screwed into the head of the bed. Then she sprayed the air with several squirts of Woodland Pine freshener, refilled the hand-wash dispenser with Forest Glade liquid soap, pulled off the stained hand-towel by the sink and hung a fresh and folded one. The palaver of each room, its allotted scent and branded goods – it made her laugh, for it was all the same shit really. She got down to her knees to change the bin bag, pick up some nearby detritus, in no hurry, for next up was the Black Room – black walls, black quilt, a teenager's haven, but a nest for filth too. Whilst the room was not specifically reserved for anal intercourse, its ambience seemed liable to propose the mood. More troublingly, Lindy was never sure she could properly see what was on the sheets, or strewn about the floor.

'Oi, Lind. There's a fella.' Dougie, bothered, was filling the doorframe.

'Eh? What, man?'

'Claire's off and there's a fella pitched up.'

Lindy got testily to her feet, wiped her hands on the hem of her tee-shirt, and followed Dougie's swaying bulk back down the corridor.

Stood by the kitchen counter with his chin to his chest was a most uncommon customer, clad in a not-bad blue suit. She passed him and rounded the counter, business-like, and now he looked up to her eye – forty, probably, fit and handsome, yes, but a bit of a boozy flush to his cheeks and a challenging kind of a smile. His shirt collar was open, the forked tail of a discarded crimson tie poking out of his jacket pocket. The night seemed made for off-cue surprises, and this one smelled iffy too. Why would a bloke with money and his own hair and teeth come to pay for it here? Fruitless to ponder, she knew – just blokes, dirty dogs, prey to all manner of mad urges, high fevers, nagging and persistent stiffness.

'Hiya. What you after?'

'I can't quite see . . .'

'Well, why don't you step into the lounge there, have a bit shufty?'

'Oh, I've had a look.'

'You've met the girls?'

'Not met, just – it's just I'm not *quite* certain. That's the thing about girls, eh? All these possibilities. Could I maybe have a word?'

'Just talk to the lass you're after.'

He nodded but didn't seem to listen, just grinned slowly. 'That's quite a look you've got. Striking.' He waggled a finger at the side of his head.

'Thanks. Now why not nip back in the lounge there, just talk to the girls 'bout what sort of massage you fancy.'

'Aw aye, then, gotcha.' He was still grinning like an imp. It was giving her the hump. They weren't stood there for the purpose of sharing a joke.

'You a bit shy, pet? No need to be. Everybody likes a bit naughty.'

He didn't seem to care so much for that tone. He could fuck himself. There was a coyness that wasn't really appropriate in one of his years – was, in fact, a royal nuisance – because the facts were not hard to master, even for a novice. Within the kitchen drawer nearest to her, taped to the base, was a list handwritten in blue-ink capitals on a sheet of ruled A4. Twenty quid for the base, a half-hour chat and the so-called 'fingertip massage'. Then the itemised extras. Hand relief, thirty. *Topless* hand relief, forty. Sixty by mouth. Ninety full-on. Up the arse, one hundred and twenty. The gentleman could either extract this much from Yulia or Leanne in his own sweet time, or else Lindy was minded to shove that tariff under his nose and enquire as to exactly how he fancied getting his dick wet this evening.

But he was sidling back in any case, toward and through the lounge door, fingers stroking his chin. Lindy jerked her head and lowered her voice. 'Keep an eye on him, Dougie, will ya?' She mimed the tippling of a pint. Dougie shifted to station himself with a discreet view through the doorway.

Lindy switched the kettle to boil and took up Claire's *Chronicle,* a more than usually startled front-page splash blazed in high capitals. EXECUTED: DOUBLE PIZZA KILLING SPARKS TIT-FOR-TAT FEARS. Nasty. She paddled through the rest of the front-end. PAEDO PRIEST GETS SIX YEARS. Typical, should have strung him up by his mouldy gonads. EX-PIT GOLF COURSE FLOPS. Well, what did they expect? Golf, in Sunderland? FAKE PISTOL STICK-UP. Well, at least it was a fake. But it was all pretty much grim as fuck, as per usual.

She had reached the Entertainment – STING COMES HOME IN GLORY – and the telly schedule spread, when renewed motion disturbed her. That bashful reddish face was hovering nearby once more.

'Actually no, I don't think I will.'

'Aw right, whatever you like.'

He laid a hand on the counter, tapped as if thoughtful. His smile, she supposed, could have won him favour on a happier day. 'You're not by any chance available yourself, are you?'

'Bugger off out of it, man. What does it look like?'

Lindy flashed a harried look at Dougie, who stirred and stepped forward, hand out. But the client was showing some gumption at last, holding up his own hands in penitence, beating a sharp retreat for the staircase.

Chapter IV

KINSHIP

Saturday, 16 November 1996

The alleyways of Oakwell were slick with overnight rain, an odour of dogs and dead leaves in the air as Gore took the long walk, the walk of shame, a hundred yards to Lindy's door. If the day's portents were dank November-dismal, his mood was cautiously hopeful, coloured by a night and a morning of solid self-criticism and resolutions made firmly on the basis thereof. He carried a spray of pink freesias and the semblance of a plan for an afternoon out, one that would see Lindy nicely lunched, Jake escorted to a bookshop and then, he fancied, the swimming baths. Knowing he was overdue to make good, he intended to settle a goodly portion of the debt. There would have to be agreement, though, each to give some designated inch to the other. He didn't have an answer for the full extent of Lindy's charges against him, but he had words as well as deeds prepared. *I know I've seemed distant. Please let me try and show you it's not what you think.*

He rang the bell, prepared a face. No answer. He looked about him. Two doorways down the alley, a woman had come to her stoop for a cigarette, and surveyed him with some mild interest. He took no offence, for this morning he was wearing his clerical suit and collar, precisely so that all might know where he was coming from.

The door before him was flung open, and a wholly unexpected girl was inspecting him also, her slight smile vaguely critical – Slavic-looking, pallid, very young in her black vest and hooded jersey top, drawstring bag over her shoulder.

'Hello?'

'Hallo! For me?'

'Ha. No, I'm here for Lindy?'

'Ah, no, I am sitter.'

'*Sister*?'

'Sitter. Lindy's not here, I sit with Jake. Her son?'

'*Baby*sitter?'

'Yes! She is back soon, you wait?' She motioned for him to step aside.

'Sorry – where are *you* going?'

'No, no, Jake is fine, is good, he upstairs with his daddy. You go?'

She was holding the door for him, so keen to be on her merry way, oblivious to his confoundment. Gore's first impulse was to turn tail, get long gone himself. No, he simply wasn't braced for this encounter.

But wasn't this the day when matters were set straight? Was he or was he not a serious man? Something was instructing him that this had to be so. His uniform, he knew, gave him both pretext and escapeway. He took hold of the handle as she passed him cheerfully, her Saturday newly unburdened. Gore stepped lightly over the threshold, pulled the door closed.

Upstairs indeed was from whence the sound of action emanated – small cries, jarring loud thumps upon the floor. Gore laid the freesias down on Lindy's coffee table, mounted the stairs, wary, breath bated.

'Oh! Oh! Eh? *That's* a good un . . .'

A voice bold as brass, commonplace Geordie, and yet with an emphasis he knew he recognised. On the top stair he lingered.

Your steps were always leading you this way. The need to know, to see. Too strong.

He stepped closer and peered through the open door of the boy's room.

Steve Coulson was crouched upon his knees, packed into his jeans and tee-shirt, playing energetically with Jake. They each sported those shiny red Lonsdale boxing gloves, Jake in football shorts yanked up to his belly button. Stevie was making a comic show of keeping guard as Jake flailed at him, dropping hands at the last minute so the boy could bash the broad target of his grinning face. Hands-on daddying, plain to see.

With a sharp sideways glance Stevie clocked Gore, then looked back in time to weather another haymaker from Jake. Then he planted his gloves vice-like at the sides of the boy's head.

'*Eee*, son. Now *look* who it is. It's the Reverend Gore.'

Jake revolved to face Gore and struck a pose, gloves raised, proud as punch. Gore flicked the fingers of one hand at the boy. Stevie nodded with his chin, then lightly cuffed Jake's jaw.

'Shall we duff him up, eh? The Reverend? Shall we's, Jakey, eh?'

Stevie pushed aside the cut flowers, set a mug of tea and a virgin pack of biscuits down before Gore, then slumped back into the leather sofa. Gore knew he was right to have plumped for Lindy's chair, as Stevie's frame made the long settee look a meagre thing. His countenance, though, seemed odd to Gore's eye – he was red-faced, mildly sweaty, as if from fever or whisky rather than exertion. There was a rent in the crotch of his jeans, and a flap of striped under-shorts protruded.

'You admirin' wor ballroom?'

Gore dragged his eye to Stevie's flashing overbite, and nodded in the direction of the joke. 'How you keeping then, Stevie?'

'Aw . . .' A shrug. 'Not brilliant. You?'

'Not so good, neither.'

'Naw?'

'Just a lot on my mind. Things stacked up. Things not working.'

'I knaa how you feel. Whey, we're having a time of it, aren't wuz?' Stevie sighed and lifted the biscuits from the table, ran a thumbnail round the wrapping, split it in half and set it down again. 'Tell ye, I've been in a mood lately. It's like every morning I get up – I want to give thanks to someone. For every day I've got. Weird, isn't it? Maybe not so weird for you, like.'

Baffled, Gore tried a knowing smile. From the first moment of their acquaintance, he knew, Stevie had shown him this curious gravity – some sort of fancy that they were tough and serious men, struggling through a thicket, a vale of tears, sorely misreckoned by their peers. Moreover, that they had something in common. The decision to play along had seemed more than worth his time. As of this hour, the fancy seemed substantive and rebarbative, the decision foolish. Everything had changed.

He reached to take his mug. Stevie too surged forward and clapped hold of his forearm, vice-like.

'Look, I want you to knaa, John, it's not any of my business, your affairs and that. I've not got any problem wi' you.'

'What do you mean, Steve?'

'What you get up to, your life, y'knaa? Nowt to do wi' me nor anyone else.'

Gore measured a reply. Stevie's grip made clear thought difficult.

'You don't have to come the choirboy, John. Everybody likes a bit naughty.'

The expression was ludicrous to Gore, but Stevie wasn't smiling. 'Naughty . . .?'

Stevie sat back. 'Just a saying. I mean, you're not doin' owt wrong.'

'No, I'm not. Look, you'll have gathered, Steve, Lindy and I have been spending –'

Stevie raised a hand, his mouth set. 'John, I divvint need to *knaa*, man. I *knaa*, like, but I divvint *need* to. That's my *point*. My only business here is that lad up there.' He jerked a thumb. 'She'll have telt ya all that, aye?'

'Well, no, you see. She hadn't said a word.'

'Aw. Right.' Stevie scratched at the frayed knee of his blue jeans. 'Well, she's like that. Keeps all her bits in a box, like. It's good habits, but. Cos people talk, I knaa that. From experience. Your enemies, they talk.'

'Enemies?'

'Look, I'm only sayin' – I knaa what it's like, man. To feel like everyone's out to get you. It's rotten. Now, see if someone said you were like a hypocrite, aye? They'd be right out of order. *Right* out of order. It's just like what you've always said. People want to have their own houses clean before they gan round flingin' stones.'

Gore was tracing a line around the rim of his mug, trying to recall any experience from his past that approximated to this.

'Now, see me, right? I've got my line of work, been at it lot of years now. And I don't say I'm an angel. Cos there's bother in it. There's trouble, aye? All I'm about – all I've ever done – is help people enjoy tha'selves. But where you've got that, you get tossers and worky tickets and – excuse us, John – but absolute fucking *ratbags* who wanna ruin it for everyone. And sometimes I've gotta give it out to them what had it coming.'

Gore nodded as seemed mandatory, dunking a biscuit.

'People I care about, though, them what's dear to me – I do right by. So who's gunna judge us for that?'

Stevie was looking very intently at him. Gore was determined to remain noncommittal. The gaze finally relented, dissolving into that devouring grin. 'So you like her, but? Our Lind? She's a smasher, isn't she?'

'I'm very fond of her, Stevie.'

'Whey, champion. She was too good for me, I'll tell you that.'

Stevie appeared satisfied, gave Gore's forearm a pat with the formidable flat of his palm and tipped back his mug to drain it. Then he picked up the remote control as if this were his own parlour and snapped on the television – *Football Focus*, the picture and sound fuzzy. 'Eee, I tell ya. I only just got her this and she's knacked it already . . .'

Gore was emboldened that it might now be his turn. 'And she works for you, is that right? Lindy?'

Stevie glanced sharply, not so friendly. Then he leaned back as if oblivious – working his shoulders, straining his chest, as though the tea were percolating down through his massive and convoluted internals. 'Not for *us*, nah. Not really. I mean, she'll do the odd night in this club I've got now, club I manage. She's got bits of things with some of the same lot I've done bits for. I've put a bit word in for her, like. Over the years.'

Stevie was rummaging inside his black bomber jacket and he retrieved his mobile phone, becoming very absorbed in its face, punching buttons as if composing a tune. Gore was turning over the wreckage of his plans for the day, and a range of possible parting words. For the moment he let himself tune into the TV show, its prolonged report on whether Man United could turn round a worrying slump against Arsenal.

Then a key was scratching and turning in the front door. Lindy surfaced from around the wall, laden with plastic shopping bags. Clearly she was not happy with the sight that met her, not even the neglected freesias. Gore, for his part, was stunned by what he beheld – a glum dark-eyed androgyne. Stevie clambered to his feet. 'How pet, the hell you done to your heid?'

She looked through him. 'John, what you doing here?'

'I thought I'd drop by. Your sitter let me in. I found Stevie and Jake.'

'Aye, I think he got a shock and all.'

She looked about her, as if trapped. 'So what do you –'

'Perhaps I should –' He moved toward the sanctuary of the hall.

'Hang about there.' From Coulson's lips it sounded like an order. 'I'm just thinking, like. Maybe John fancies comin' wi' us this afternoon? You're a Mag, aren't you, John?'

Strapped into Stevie's Lexus they drove, a family plus guest, down the Barrack Road, past affable milling hordes in multiple variants of black-and-white stripes, and scattered cheery clusters of claret and blue. On another day, Gore was dully aware, he might have been diverted by the sociological view from the soft leather back seat, rather than feeling raw-skinned, tongue-tied, dull and disconsolate.

Stevie parked and marched his troops through a private entrance, up five flights of stairs, and down a strip-lit hotel corridor to the door of an executive box. 'Pal of mine's treat,' he said, pushing in, without elaboration.

There were ten to a dozen bodies thronging the space, a pack of youngish men in good coats, some of them built to Stevie's scale, sporting gold chains, sovereign rings, grade-one crops. They loitered about a table strewn with the remnants of a meaty buffet lunch, and the mood was bullish, a fog of smoke and garrulity, the boys charging their glasses from a wet bar. Gore hung back uneasily at Lindy's shoulder, conscious that she and he were the reserves of silence in this full-throated room, and he the butt of some barely suppressed sniggers. He accepted a bottle of beer from Stevie and sought seclusion, stepped quietly out of doors onto a tight balcony that squatted over the eighteen-yard line, folding chairs arrayed down its length. The fine green checkerboard fuzz of the turf seemed vast, likewise the raked amphitheatre seating and the projecting Perspex rainshield that made a gloomy rectangle of the sky. The hubbub and the thumping chants rising from the standing fans might, it seemed to Gore, have made for a Roman ambience, were it not for the rather shiftless ambling ball-games of the players warming up on the pitch below. He stared at all this for as long as seemed fit, deeming the company indoors hateful.

Back inside, bets were getting loudly placed with a gangly pen-licking youth in a shirt and tie. The banter was of West Ham, today's opponent, and – with near-lurid relish – of having 'murdered' Man United just the other week. A few big dogs were huddled over the team sheet, pulling at it as if for scraps, prominent among them a perma-tanned Scot in a camel overcoat, a rusting tub of a man waving a rank stub of cigar.

'Oi, Stevie, where's your fifteen-million man then? Your Geordie messiah?'

'Not playing, Roy man, he canna, he's under the knife wi' his groin.'

'You what? Fifteen million and you broke him already? Shitting *hell*, Stevie. Good bit of business, that.'

The exterior din rose, for the teams were jogging onto the field and the afternoon sodality hastened to their seats, clutching brimming drinks, packets of tabs and lighters.

As the match got under way, Gore wrestled with the matter of how he should conduct himself. Resigned to his situation, he remembered anew the longueurs of live football. Excitement must have dissipated in others too, for they watched with furrowed brows. To his right Lindy wore a hunted look, chain-smoking, eyes watery, repeatedly wiping her raw nose, a soft black cotton cap pulled about her ears, nursing her vulnerable head. To his left Stevie bounced Jake on his knee, tucking a black-and-white scarf round his neck, keeping up a non-stop verbiage, teaching him a song. '*Phi-lippe, Phi-lippe Al-bert, everybody knows his name . . .*'

Gore supposed that no one else in this bristling company knew him from Adam, or wished to improve their acquaintance. But when West Ham scored, he found himself applauding gently and instinctively, and one of the strangers barked at him. 'Divvint clap the other *side*, man, we divvint fuckin' pay to hear *that*.'

Stevie's riposte was harder. '*Whey*, man, *language*. The bairn.'

Come the half-time whistle and the pensive trudge of players from surface, Gore looked to Stevie, who seemed untroubled by Newcastle's deficit. 'Well, I'm about ready me bait,' he announced, rubbing his hands. 'Lind, will you gan doon the back into the cheap seats and fetch us in a pie?' A few more stray orders got shouted.

'I'll give you a hand,' Gore murmured, rising unheeded.

Back out in the concrete maze she knew where she was going and he followed in silence, until she threw him a look that seemed to implore that he keep in step.

'John, look, I've been wanting to tell you. With Stevie, but –'

'I know. We've talked.'

'You's two? What did he say?'

'Not much more than you.'

They took up places in a slow-shuffling queue before a counter vendor of teas and reheated snacks. Warily she watched him, as he chewed over his intended words.

'Have you *really* wanted to tell me? Or did you just plan on – oh, I don't know – toughing it out?'

'I told you from the start, John, I was happy telling you all about us, any bloody thing. It was *you* told us you didn't wanna know.'

'Yeah, but – God, this – you could have just told me anyway, Lindy. It would have been helpful.'

'It's personal, man, between me and him, it's not summat we gan round shoutin' about. How would it've helped *you*?'

'Because. We've had an association, me and Steve. You know that. So you and me – I mean, it would have saved me feeling how I feel *now* is how.'

'Fine, I hear you. So now you know. Happy?'

'Oh, I'm over the moon, Lindy, it's . . . delightful. There, look, don't miss your turn.'

They threaded their way back through the corridors, blisteringly hot snacks ill-cushioned by napkins in their palms. For Gore the thought of returning to that box in this temper was a prison sentence.

'How the hell did it happen then? The two of you?'

'Aw, *now* you want the story, do you?'

'Don't be like that. I'm just . . .'

'Look, I used to gan a lot to this club. Zeus.'

'I know it. I went to a funeral there.'

She frowned. 'Well, Stevie was doorman, right? There was a crowd of us used to knock about after it shut, we'd gan on to parties and that.'

'You went out together?'

'Nah, it was just one night. One or two.' She sighed. 'We were *pals*, he was like me brother. Used to buy us stuff, little gifts and that. There was just a night we ended up at mine and we were both a bit off it, and . . . that's how.'

'How did you handle it? When you found out?'

'Handle it? I called him up and telt him. He come round and gave us a big speech. All serious, you know what he's like. How he'd always see us right and all, but he wasn't ever gunna be tied down. I said get away, man, as if I'd set me cap on *you*.'

A smile squeezed itself out of Gore. That much, at least, served to recall a girl of whom he had once grown fond. 'So you just managed? Alone?'

'I've always managed. Stevie, but, his big thing – I mean, I can't fault him, not for money, or time. He gets us what we need. I could do it me'sel if I had to, but Jake – I know how it works, he should have a daddy, it's boring but it's just the bloody truth. Stevie'd never let us have it any other way.'

They were too close to re-entering the lion's den for Gore's comfort. He took her arm, arrested her steps. 'Look, you can say. If you're scared of him.'

'Stevie? Naw, man. It's just a set-up we've got, it's fine. Look, we're not like . . . I mean, he's got another one somewhere. Another bairn by another lass? I know nowt about it. 'Cept they don't get on, him and the mother. But with us, he's fine. Fine. Not so clever the day, like . . .' She sighed. 'It's not *important*, but. Jake's got us – he doesn't need owt except us. He likes men, right enough, I *thought* he liked you. But you've not said a word to him all afternoon.'

Gore groaned. 'Lindy, I find this a bit awkward, you know?'

'*You* do? What about me? I dunno, John, you just pitch up . . . then you're sat there like stone as usual, not kissed us or held wor hand or owt.'

'It didn't' – he forced out between teeth – 'seem quite the place.'

'You don't need his permission, y'knaa. What, are *you* scared of him?'

He had felt himself bluster, and now wanted badly to be terse and chilly. But irritation was reinstated on her face, a stronger force.

'Come on, these are burning a hole in us.'

On the way home – the radio cranked up to reports, interviews and supporters' views of the Toon's second-half revival – Gore sat in the back, one eye on the restless boy fastened in at his side, the other on the disparate pair of twitching shaven necks before him. This bizarre domesticity, his ill-sorted place in it, had begun to upset his innards. Worse, in his head, was a kind of vertigo. Who were these people? How had his mission directive brought him to this impasse, this queasy back-seat function?

I'm a missionary – that's it, that's what I am. They told me, 'Take the good word to the natives, just ignore their manners.' And what have I gone and done? Treated myself to the first fuckable native girl. Turned out she was wed to the chief.

At Oakwell Gore helped Jake from the car, seeing that Stevie and Lindy lingered in the front seats for what seemed like a troubled exchange – his hand clamped to her shoulder, her chin on her chest. Uneasily he turned his attention to the boy.

'Did you enjoy the match, Jake?'

'Nah. Was crap.'

'You didn't? Why not?'

'We's just drew. Didn't get seein' who's-his-name.'

'Didn't you like it when Newcastle scored?'

The boy shrugged. 'Liked the noise. That was mint.'

Then the Lexus was pulling away, Stevie offering a thumbs-up.

From the dim upstairs landing he watched Lindy watching Jake grow steadily immersed in the act of scrawling on a page. Then she rose and pulled the door to, and Gore followed her down the stairs. The bunch of freesias remained limp under cellophane on the coffee table.

'John, look, I'm sorry . . . I dunno, if your feelings are hurt I'm sorry. It's my life, but, see? It's just what happened. I can't apologise for that, can I?'

Gore shrugged. 'No. Of course you can't.'

'So what are we gunna do then? You and me?'

'Oh, I don't know . . . Try to get along. Like we've been doing.'

She lowered herself to the arm of her chair, pulled off her soft hat, looked at him ruefully. 'We're a pair, aren't we?'

She rubbed her eyes. He moved to her side and folded her into an embrace – nuzzled and kissed the top of her head, surprised to find it softer than it looked. He felt her clasping on to him with something like feeling.

'Do you still want to see us, like?' She spoke into his chest. 'I mean – what *do* you want?'

'Maybe we just need to give it a bit of time,' he said, staring out through the open micro-blinds into her darkened garden, as desolate as his own.

She freed her face from his front buttons. 'What does that *mean*, but?'

No idea. Time for you to change entirely. You, or me. Time for me to think how to get out of this cleanly. He cursed himself and this quandary of a day, at the outset of which he had fancied that all existing grievances and gridlocks were soon to be relieved by best effort. What was the game plan now?

'I do think – that I need more time with you. The two of you.'

'Me and Jake?'

'Yes, you and Jake. Who else?' He relinquished hold of her shoulders. 'What do you say, shall I fix us all a bit of dinner?'

She bit her lip and glanced disconsolately toward her thin wristwatch.

'Aw, I'm working the night, man. Gotta get me'sel together.'

'Where are you working?'

'Where? Aw, at the club, just.'

'Teflon?'

'Aye, Teflon.'

He was much too familiar with her usual candour to ignore the clear unease, the sudden indirectness in her gaze. *Liar*, he thought, the vehemence of his feeling arriving unbidden.

Before he reached his doorstep he knew what he would do with the evening. He wouldn't call it spying. There seemed no other means by which his curiosity could be relieved. And it didn't seem a terrible subterfuge to discreetly test her word, observe her in her environment. If all was well and the mood right, he could perhaps step from the shadows and surprise her. After such a day, he reasoned, how bad could that be?

He cooked a simple omelette, drank two glasses of white burgundy, listened to a CD selection from *The Well-Tempered Clavier*. For an hour or so he sat at his desk over some notes, though nothing he typed cohered into sense. He was merely idling, waiting for the night-time to deepen. When the hour seemed apt he went to his wardrobe and reviewed his sparse options. A 'clubby sort of a bar', hadn't she said? Generic smartness, would that pass muster? Thus his black suit, a white shirt, a grey tie. He shined a pair of Oxfords, assumed the accessories, combed his hair with tap water, splashed some old pale cologne about his cheeks. It would have to suffice. As ten o'clock ticked round he dialled a local cab firm, then extinguished all his lights and sat waiting in silence.

'I'm after a club called Teflon?'

'By the Swing Bridge, aye?'

They proceeded down the Hoxheath Road, Gore sunk in disquiet, until the driver grunted some words he didn't catch.

'I'm sorry?'

'I'm saying, you want in Teflon you might have a job? Don't mean owt by it, like, but it's a trendier lot than yer'sel, mostly. Least that's what ah see.'

Gore said nothing, only gazed out of the window at the hurly-burly of the night streets as they broached the Quayside – traffic solid, raucous hubbub in the air, lads and lasses in pavement packs, baring a good deal of skin to the cold – insulated, maybe, by the first half-dozen drinks of the evening. The girls teetered on heels, tossing hair and bouncing cleavage, clutching tiny bags, faces thickly veneered, paler thighs flashing – lots of tiny dresses, some on rather large girls. The boys walked the walls, fists in the pockets of heavy-belted jeans, biceps thick in pocketed short-sleeve shirts, big and yet straining to make themselves bigger – so young and full of it, as if they might surge out onto the road and stop cars with the flats of their hands. Gore's reflection met him in the muted glass. *Were you ever that age?*

Paid up and deposited at street level, the wind off the Tyne whipping at his trouser legs, he walked with irresolute tread across the cobblestones toward the entrance of the club, a converted building. A couple passed him, the girl stumbling forward as her four-inch heel snagged between cobbles. Ten yards ahead a rope-cordoned square of six-foot-by-six marked the doorway of Teflon – from within, the metronome thump of bass; without, a smallish queue filing in turn past the eye of a brick-solid doorman. Gore endured some derisive gum-chewing looks to reach the end of the line. But a few of the males seemed to favour dark trousers and crisp shirts. Perhaps his outfit would pass?

'Oi, mistah . . .' A tug on his sleeve. Two girls had edged up to his side from behind a parked car, both of them dark-haired, faces glossily daubed, glammed-up in short dresses, one notably prettier, neither liable to have seen their eighteenth birthday. They were whispering, conspiratorial.

'Oi, mistah, can you help us, like? Please? Help us get in?'

'Just past the bouncer, aye? We can be like your girlfriends.'

'Aye, your bitches, like.' The prettier one giggled.

'How man, we'll make it worth your while, promise.'

The lewd cast of her purple mouth Gore took for mere front. He had made a fast assessment, decided he had been favoured with a certain advantage.

'Okay, alright . . .' Without further deliberation he threw one arm around each of them, so drawing a breath of their cloyingly lacquered hair, and they giggled anew. Shortly the line was moving, they were up to the ropes. The bouncer wore black suit, black shirt, black necktie, like a chain-store Mafia pallbearer. He looked them over, impassive. 'You sure you're in the right place?'

Gore tried a slow would-be worldly grin. 'Aw, help us out here, will you? I've more than I can handle.'

'How old's she?' The bouncer's terse gesture was to the plainer of the girls.

'She's thirty, man. Thirty tonight. I've promised her your best champagne.'

He earned half a smile. The rope was raised. *I am an actor*, thought Gore.

They passed through a foyer of bolted aluminium panels, oddly blackened by phantomic shapes as if licked by flames. A woman behind a glass grille instructed Gore that it was past ten and he would have to pay. The girls shot him hopeful looks. *In for a penny*, he decided. On demand he gave up his wallet to another bouncer, who poked through its folds and clasps.

Through double doors, into a warm dark bath of bodies and noise – shoving room only, a head-splitting four-time pulse. All about him were blithe and curt young faces, eyes clocking and discounting him. Draughts of dry ice oozed through the crowd, a sickly throat-clogging scent, and pink laser-light slashed the fug. Plain Jane lunged up and kissed his cheek, then both his little consorts were weaving off and away.

He let the crush of bodies carry him from one end of the space toward the bar in sight at the other. The distinction between bar and dance floor that he had thought essential to discotheques was negligible here – everybody seemed to be jiggling, their eyes wide and avid. A black man danced alone, his body shaking, trance-like. A girl with her eyes tight shut had a dummy in her mouth, her friend wore a spangly studded dog collar.

The long bar was a brawling convention of cries and cocked banknotes. Darting his head about, Gore could see two harassed girls, chilly in strappy tops, fending off the shouted orders. But no Lindy. The very idea that she could abide this pandemonium seemed fantastical. Jogged and prodded, he waited ten minutes or so to procure a small beer, pulled from a fridge stuffed with rows of bottled water, sloppily voided into a plastic glass. As he battled back out, two young males were throwing up their hands. 'Fuck it man, let's gan the back bar.' He followed them, dodging the manic dancers and waving arms, into the relative cool and calm of a narrow corridor and through another doorway. He found himself in an L-shaped room, a sort of haven, alternate pools of darkness and fluorescence, clientele lounging about on low sofas. Doodling electronic music issued from near the back, and a corner bar was tended by a young male in a tight and glaringly white tee-shirt. Gore saw that his own shirt-front glowed, and his skin was as if dipped in magenta. Feeling foolish on his feet, he noticed some space on a long sofa only half-occupied by an ardent kissing couple, and so crushed himself into its opposite end.

Across the way, a crew of young men were hunched in conference, razor-cut heads ducking and weaving like the corner of a title fight. Two pairs of bare female legs swished past Gore's eyeline. From his living-room sofa to this one – the disparity almost amused him. In this late-night haunt he felt himself a ghost among the habitués. Did anyone see him? Or might he stand up and walk through walls, vanish back from whence he had come? He decided to drain off his beer. The novelty had been short-lived, the mission fruitless, and it was past his bedtime.

Standing, he glanced again at the male group sitting opposite. At its centre, locus of attention – **Notorious**, boldly emblazoned in

Gothic script upon a sweatshirt. Gore knew the face before he had made eye contact, and he ducked his chin to his chest. Then a pair of bouncers were barrelling into the space, his exit barred, and they hustled smartly toward the youths' table, squaring up, obscuring Gore's view.

'You, son, on your fucken feet.'

Gore realised he was sick of these identikit thugs, the sight and sound of them, their thuggish funereal chic: they wanted barcodes on their fathead necks to distinguish them. And now Jason was being dragged from the couch, hard hands on him, and he was being aggressively frisked. Were they after his wallet? His team-mates seemed to wish to disrupt and interpose, get their bodies in the way of the back-up bouncer – a limp effort. For now the lead bouncer was lifting Jason bodily by the underarms, his kicking and cursing all for naught as he was manhandled toward the door, the second bouncer seizing his feet. As they rammed past Gore, Jason's wild eyes met his. They had him in a chokehold, the bulging crook of an elbow round his neck, and he writhed, red-faced.

'You'll kill him,' Gore heard himself shout.

'Fuck off, man, I'll kill *you*.'

He weathered the snarl, for the second bouncer's face he suddenly made out through the gloom – Robbie, the Smoggie, youngest of Coulson's mob, he of the chippy attitude. There was no more favour in the look thrown at Gore before he vanished.

Gore's feet spurred him forward, in pursuit, down the dark corridor and through some FIRE EXIT doors that the bouncers had kicked apart. What did he imagine he would do? He was bent on nothing but what the boy's mates had tried – to get in harm's way, whatever the cost. It seemed to him his only strength. He was in a backway alley behind a high wall, a private parking spot, and at its dead end he saw Jason, shaky on his feet, attempting to spit in the general direction of the bouncer planted squarely before him. The heel of a palm thrust out and the boy's head cannoned back, he clattered against the brick wall and fell. The bouncer delivered a kick into his flank, bringing forth a piteous howl.

'Oi,' Gore shouted, striding toward them. 'Come on, there's no *need* for that.'

'Fuck off out of it,' barked Robbie, standing apart as if refereeing a bout. Gore was past him and poised to lay a hand on the aggressor when an elbow was thrown back, unruly, and he was clouted. He reeled and fell hard onto the cobblestones. *Not again*, was his only pained thought on the ground as he groped to shield his skull, feeling a graze on the torn knee of his trousers. Then he was being hoisted, up and away, the grip almost reassuring, even if by the lapels. 'How man, I'll sort this fucker,' he heard Robbie. He had been set rightways up, dragged yards hence, now he was being prodding and shoved in the chest.

'Come on, take it easy, please . . .'

'The fuck you doing here, idiot?'

'It's Robbie, right? Isn't it? Robbie?'

'What you *playin'* at, man?'

'The boy. I know him, just wanted to help the boy.'

'Keep your fucking nose out of it, *I'll* sort him out.'

'No, look, please, don't hurt him.'

His lapels were seized again, the hard face right up in his own, breath sour, voice low. 'He'll not get fuckin' *hurt*, man. I'm police. Alright? Got it? I'm a copper. Now when I let go of you, you run, you fuckin' *disappear*, right?'

And Robbie turned and jogged back down the alley. Gore wiped his mouth, his blood beating at his temples, then he turned and found his feet beneath him, carrying him clear of the chaos.

Near three in the morning Gore woke up gasping, feeling a weight on his chest as though something squatted there. He knew at once that his dream had been lucid, that he had roused himself by force of will, so as to cease the stream of upsetting images laying siege to him.

He was prone awhile in the dark, hands clasped on his chest. The house was cold, yellow light from the alley leaking under the curtains. Oakwell was uncommonly still. Fragments of the bad dream were returning – some version of himself stood before a long mirror in a dowdy room, but pulling a slip-dress free of his shoulders. For the face, the shape, reflected in the mirror's murk was female, blonde, with a doll's vacant prettiness. He pushed a button beneath a nameplate, a door opened to admit an indistinct shape – something like a man but more akin to a blur of darkness, an evil vapour, full of malediction, forcing him back onto the candlewick spread.

He rose and went to the bathroom, urinated, sidled down the stairs to the kitchen, poured a glass of water from the tap.

It came to him anew that his life was a toy, an indulgence, a special dispensation for the weak. He had never tried – never even begun – to fathom the depths, the true dark. He knew nothing about nothing, and everything about him was, by his own reckoning, risible – even this, his sorry dolour.

When he woke again nearer six, he was stunned to find a sort of calm had descended, his depression dissolved as if by a drug. He recognised anew his own worst habit – a seeming need, when in the doldrums, to lash himself harder, deepen the gloom to pitch black. With so much to do, it was self-doubt and low spirits that were the true indulgence, the devil's work. At the same time, he knew, such knowledge behoved him to take action – strong, plain, and remedial – against the arch enemy.

Chapter V

ABSENTEES

Sunday, 17 November 1996

Hunched inside his elderly anorak Bill shuffled up and down the length of the scuffed school hall, peering critically at the windows, chewing a thumbnail, occasionally scratching with a pencil into a small ring-bound notebook. He had to be indulged, Gore knew, but his presence was a bother on a morning pre-booked for some awkward business. The usual volunteers traipsed about with chairs and prayer books, looking at them oddly, Gore felt – clearly uninterested in meeting the vicar's old man. Such was the odour of decline and dysfunction about the place.

Cogitations seemingly complete, a familiar furrow on his brow, Bill sidled up to where his vestured youngest stood tapping his shoe. 'What I'd do, son? Close all them curtains, then put some up-lighting at the sides with gels on, colour filters? Then up the front, behind where you stand, a couple of cross-lights either side and one on your back. So you stand out a bit.'

'Sounds a bit amateur-dramatic.'

'Whey, not at all. Not when you see it proper. I've got a bit gear in the car, I'll hoy it in and show you.'

'You need a hand?'

'Not to worry, you just crack on with your work.'

For some moments Gore stared absently at the doorway through which his father had departed – until through it anew came the dog-and-pony show. A now familiar sight, a now familiar galumphing struggle, Steve Coulson and lackey Simms heaving through the double doors and across the linoleum, bearing between them some manner of broad wooden table.

Greeks bearing gifts, thought Gore, rubbing at one tender temple, starting to feel the intestinal clench in his bowels.

They plonked their offering down before him. Coulson, though hardly exerting himself by what Gore took to be his normal standards, was looking poor. What was the expression? *Ten pounds of shit in a five-pound bag?*

'What you reckon to that then, John?'

Stolen goods, was Gore's instinct.

'It's an altar table, aye? Better be. Bloke telt us it was.'

The table was smaller than was usual or wholly desirable. Nevertheless the oak retained polish, the legs were stout, the table-top panelled all around its sides. It was a handsome piece, 1920s or 30s, one over which he would have purred were it not now impossible for him to credit Coulson with any authentic kindness.

'No,' Gore murmured. 'He wasn't wrong. Which bloke is this?'

'Lad I knaa deals antiques down in Cleveland. He gets all reclaimed stuff in. Says he's always got people wantin' churchy stuff. For their homes and that? Cos of all the churches getting shut down, like. Their gear sold off.'

Gore felt his lips curl into a smile. The irony was sour, but then why else was he here, in his new model church – downsized, no-budget, made from recycle and scrap?

'Any road. It's all yours, man. Gotta be better than that ratty owld pool table.'

Gore patted his pockets. 'What do I owe you?'

Coulson shrugged. 'You divvint owe us owt, John.'

In reply Gore only grimaced, noting the perplexity this caused.

'Naw, man, I won't have it. You just call it a donation.'

'Well, I don't know what to say.'

'Needn't say owt, man.'

'I hope it's tax-deductible. I'm not sure how much more of your generosity I can take, Steve.'

'There's not a price on friendship, John.' Coulson seemed blithe again, taking a cigarette and a light from Simms. 'Naw, you couldn't put one on it if you tried, man. Any road, like I telt Simms' – he grinned through curling smoke – 'you're black-and-white. You enjoy the match, then?'

'It was an eye-opener. Thanks for that.'

Gore looked about him, saw the customary hard looks coming his way from those volunteers who doubtless felt themselves less-favoured. For what he was about to do he hoped they would be truly thankful.

'No little helper today?'

'Say again, John?'

'Mackers not with you today? The lad?'

'Naw.' Smoke didn't mask Stevie's slight wince. 'Naw, he's let us down, that one.'

Bill was lurching back down the hall toward them, the handles of lamps in each hand, gels and barn-door-shutters jammed under each armpit. Simms made a motion as to unburden the older man, but Bill's brow crinkled. Gore chose not to effect introductions, and so Bill stood blinking impatiently at the trio before turning to business. 'Naw, they're not right, these uns I've got here. But I'll just rig 'em and give you a look and you'll get the idea. It's ten o'clock you start, aye? I'll be out your road before then.'

'You won't stay for the service?'

'Aw no, John, I'll not stop.'

He hoisted up his load and set off toward the nearest sockets. Coulson threw Gore a mocking look and waggled a sly finger at the side of his head. Gore pursed his lips.

'Simms, man, gan and fetch John that bit paper come with the table, will ya? It's in me glove compartment.'

Simms lumbered away. Coulson pinched the tip of his fuming cigarette between two fingers, and slipped the dead butt into his coat pocket.

'Steve,' Gore said to his feet. 'There's something I've wanted to say.'

'Aw aye? Spit it out then, Reverend.'

'I want you to know I've appreciated all your help here.'

The big head nodded. 'Nee bother, that, John. All in a good cause.'

'Yes. I wonder, but' – Gore felt himself take air onboard – 'if we maybe haven't reached a point where the usefulness is – done, really.'

'Useful what, sorry?'

'What I mean is I don't feel I should trouble you any further. It's been a burden. I'm sure you've happier things to do of a Sunday. So maybe you should get back to your thing and I get back to mine.'

'It's only how you want it, John. That's all this is.'

'Well, I just think that's probably how it should be.'

He couldn't quite read Coulson's immobile expression. There seemed no umbrage there, but a possible displeasure round the narrowing eyelids. And yet a forearm was being raised and a fat open hand came down at him. Gore took it, and they shook briskly.

'You're maybe right. Maybe so. We'll see. I'll not hang about then, John.'

And he turned heel. Gore watching him clump down the hall, passing a quizzical Simms. Relief arose in him, for he had pictured one or two other possible outcomes. This one seemed nearly too easy.

He made his head-count, somewhat sickened. Thirty-three bodies, but these including his stock helpers – plus Simon Barlow, sauntering in just prior to the start of proceedings, as welcome as the tax inspector. Distraction had been the colour of Gore's day, and it was uncommonly late when he clapped a hand to his pocket and realised that his sermon was not there. So be it – he had the King James at hand, he would simply have to extemporise.

'In the Gospels – three out of the four, Mark, Matthew and Luke – we read the same story of a certain incident that happened not long after Jesus had chosen his disciples – his twelve good men, the team for the work he had before him.

'He had made camp in a town by the sea with all his followers, a multitude of them by then. But he was sought out there by his mother, Mary, and some other relatives – his "brethren". They stood outside the place where Jesus and his followers were gathered, and they called for him to please come out and speak with them.

'So you can imagine, I'm sure, a rather plaintive scene.

'And the disciples inside, they grew uneasy and said to Jesus, "That's

your family out there, they want you – your own mother, she must need to speak with you very badly." But Jesus only stared them down. He said, "Who is my mother? Who is my family? You are. You're my family now. Whosoever shall do the will of God, the same is my brother, and my sister, and my mother."

'That's rather a stunning remark, isn't it? Jesus was basically saying he would hold no one person dearer than another just because of blood.

'Now, you might say, "But he was the son of God. Born of woman, yes, but that was just . . . expedient. So it's not surprising he could be so detached."

'But is there also a lesson there for the rest of us? Well, think of this. In Matthew's account of the Sermon on the Mount, Jesus says that to be a true child of God you must love your enemies. Love them that curse you. In other words, if you only love those people who love you back – your family, say – what have you done that everybody else doesn't do anyway? With God or without Him?

'I don't think – or at least I find it hard to . . . Well, I mean, I say "I", actually, who cares what I think?'

There was a rustle of dry mirth about the hall.

'No, the question is, what did Jesus *intend? That we honour our mother and father, I'm sure. But maybe not above all others. You've heard it said, I'm sure, you can choose your friends but you can't choose your family. Christ chose his disciples over his family, His followers chose to follow Him over theirs. Clearly, no – we can't choose our families. If we could, we'd probably all be less inclined to murder our fathers.'*

He saw some vexed looks, heard some mutterings, some seat-shifting.

'That's only what old Freud said. What sons want to do. I don't know what he said about daughters. I wonder now, actually.'

But he had lost his mental place, was groping into empty space for an ending.

'I suppose the truth is – the question for us is – the love in a family, is it enough? Is it enough to make us better people if the love stays within those walls, and never gets circulated? Of course, some people have great reason to thank their families. But then what if you never had a family in the first place to give you that love? Is it easier then for those people to go out and

love others? Or are you much the worse off? Or what if you don't ever start a family of your own? As an adult. If you were only ever the recipient of family love? Do you even have the right to speak about any of this?

'I'm not sure. I dare say you've all lived longer lives than me. Maybe you could let me know.'

Afterward he girded up and pressed flesh as diligently as he was able. It didn't hurt. A dwarfish old woman whose name he cursed himself for having forgotten kept hold of his fingers most intently in her dry, calloused hands. 'I want you to know, hinny, it's interesting, the thought you put into what you say.'

'That was one of your better ones, I thought, John,' Monica Bruce echoed a little later as Gore was pitching himself into shifting and stacking the chairs. Heartened, he washed teacups, pushed a broom round the floor, swapped cheerful murmurings with all who drew near.

He felt new vigour commingled with the relief of a burden shifted. If this was a meagre, much-diminished base from which to work, it was nonetheless a manageable one. A certain millstone had been lifted aside and the moment seemed to propose itself for an erasure of the slate, a back-to-basics reckoning of resources, a utilising of old skills alongside the new lessons learned. The lingering concerns of recent days and weeks, those that had clung like dank wet clothes, seemed now as if they might be just as easily cast off and torched.

He stepped out under the awning, stretched and shook out his limbs, suddenly hungry, noting what looked to be not the gloomiest of skies, though sporadic clouds were black as coal-fire smoke. A last couple of parishioners' cars were taking turns to nose out of the gates, and before him on the walkway a girl sat perched upon a concrete bollard, her back to him, her very yellow hair in a ponytail. She wore a pink hooded top with some illegible decal, a washed-out denim skirt, and scuffed white trainers like plastic bricks on her feet. She turned to him, and at once he knew her – recognised her frown, and the sallow bird-like prettiness made by ill-nourishment – remembered too the flare of her underwear as she had been dumped onto concrete by her inconsiderate swain.

'John Gore, aye?' She was up and coming straight at him.

'That's me. It's Cheryl, isn't it? Did your mam tell you to come say thanks?'

'Me mam telt us come get yer. Can you come see her at ours? Only we've got bother, she reckons you can help wuh, it's wor Tony.'

Gore put up a hand to still the wild words. 'Hang on. Tony?'

'Aye. Mackaz, like?'

'*Mackers*? You're related?'

'He's me brutha. Aye, he's not been home, see? Not for two nights. So will you come on with wuh? She's ever so desperate, me mam.'

He wracked his headpiece for a delaying tactic. 'Can I – look, I just need to finish up here first and then –'

'*Please*, but. Please. She's desperate. She's doing all wor heads. Please.'

He really could have wished it otherwise, his newfound equilibrium won at such price. *You have no choice*, a fastidious voice told him straight.

She led him through the barren yard and down the weed-strewn path, under the doorway and through a cramped kitchen smelling of turpentine and browned mince, past a narrow stairwell, steps littered with toys, down which was traipsing a dozy-eyed hulk of a young man, naked but for a bath-towel round his hairy midriff.

'Me brutha Col,' Cheryl drawled. 'He's on nights.'

From the living room the television glowed blue and mute. The carpet was tacky underfoot. Gore took the hand of Mrs Fay MacNamara – her own pasty blondeness clearly kin to her daughter's, albeit run to fat – and accepted the introduction.

'Thank you so much for comin', Father. I'm at me wits' end.'

'Of course you are, of course. Think nothing of it.'

There was nowhere to park himself but on the settee beside her, and he inserted his person next to a slumbering black cat, lowering himself gingerly. Cheryl lingered in the doorframe.

'I'm imagining all sorts, see. I can't get *on* with anything.'

'I'm sure. This will sound pat, Mrs MacNamara, but please remember, people go missing every day. I know it's murder for you.' He saw her eyes pop feelingly, and so cursed his maladroit phrasing. 'But we'll find him. I'm certain he's safe and well.'

She sniffled, seemed almost to crush her fingers. 'Well, you say that.'

'Is it out of character? Has he ever gone off before?'

'Nah, never. Except for the odd mad night.'

Cheryl piped up. 'He went off that time after you and that Gormley bloke.'

'Aye, well, that wasn't this was it, Cheryl?' Frowns were exchanged at this evident filial impiety.

'And what have the police said?'

Silence. Mrs MacNamara's frown had deepened, somewhat guiltily.

'You *have* reported this, to the police?'

'I've not. Only that's why I asked *you* here, Father.'

'But why not the police? I mean, you need to get into the system, get an officer round –'

'I divvint *want* an officer round. That happened to me friend Paula. All they did was turn her place owa. Made her feel rotten. Like she'd done her own lad in.'

'What if *I* went to the police? On your behalf?'

'Aw, don't, they'd still be round. Please, man, I don't *like* 'em. Can we not keep this just between wuh? Can we not?'

Gore bit his lip, weighing the matter unhappily. Slowly, since no other option occurred, he withdrew his notebook from his pocket, and uncapped a biro. 'Well then. When was the last time you saw Tony?'

'Yesterday morning. He'd been in his bed, then I looked in and he wasn't.'

'What was the actual time? When you last set eyes on him?'

'Well, I only *saw* him when he went *up* to bed, like. Midnight mebbe?'

'Midnight, okay. How did he seem? Was he acting like normal?'

Mrs MacNamara looked to Cheryl. It was the girl who spoke up. 'The place where he works, right? There was that shootin'.'

'What shooting was that?'

'D'you not hear? The pizza place out North Shields. There was two of 'em got shot dead, two fellas.'

'My God.' Gore felt his control over proceedings rudely sent packing. 'My God, so that's where Mackers – Tony – that's where he works? He was there when it happened?'

'Aye,' Fay fumbled in her lap. 'I knew there was summat wrang, see, cos he was never home 'til late, and he come in all moody. He was moody, wasn't he?'

'He looked like they'd shot him an' all,' Cheryl muttered at her armpit.

'The men were shot actually sitting in the restaurant?'

'Aye, in front of everyone, like.'

'Is Tony a waiter there?'

'He delivers. Drives a bike.'

'Did he *see* the men shot?'

'Dunno. He didn't tell us exactly. He was just so moody.'

'I'd have thought he would have been traumatised.'

'Say again?'

'An experience like that. He'll have suffered a huge shock, to his system. I mean, it wouldn't be surprising if he was just – wandering the streets somewhere.'

'You think? Suppose he could, couldn't he?'

'It's possible. He's not on any medication, is he?'

Cheryl snorted. Her mother squinted at her. 'He's not, but.'

'Have you rung around the hospitals?'

'*I* did, a few,' said Cheryl.

'Well, now, look, this is already a police matter, isn't it? It's a part of a – of an actual crime, with a crime number and so on. Tony will have been spoken to himself, won't he? By the police, on the night?'

'Dunno. He didn't say. Never says that much, see. He wouldn't, but. Normally. Talk to the police.'

Cheryl was shaking her head adamantly. 'Naw. He said to us he had.'

'He told *you*?' Gore turned his attention wholly to the girl.

'Aye, said he had, but he wished he'd not.'

'Why not?'

'Didn't tell us.'

'What *did* he say?'

'Just what I telt *you*, man. He was in a mood, I couldn't hear half what he said. Just shut the door on us. Heard his mobile ring, but.'

'He has a mobile phone?'

'Aye.'

'I assume you've tried calling it?'

'We've not got the number.'

'Why not?'

'He never give us it. Said it was just for his work.'

For a moment Gore felt his vision swimming in a high swamping wave of fatigue. He rubbed at the corners of both eyes. 'God, this is – let's – let's just try to establish, what are the obvious things to do? Have you talked to his friends? Who are his friends?'

'Cheryl's been round all them, haven't ya?'

'Aye, just like a few I knaa. They'd not seen him.'

Gore looked closely at her. 'What about that boy Jason? Jason Liddell?'

Disdain seized her face. 'I don't speak to him no more, he's an idiot.'

'He is a friend, though, of Tony's?'

'Naw. They'd fell out and that.'

'Why? Any reason?'

'Dunno. It was all like sort of, "You're in with this lot and I'm in with that lot. This is my gang and that's yours."'

'Gang?'

'Aye, like, y'knaa, gangs of lads what knock about.'

'And Tony was in a sort of a "gang", you would say?'

'I dunno with Tony. *Jason* is. There's a whole load of 'em what live in the same flat. Over on Scoular. They think they're that rock.'

'What, it's a flat just full of kids?'

'Aye. But it's Jason's flat. They put him in there when he come out of care, he just lets everyone crash. Neebody stops it.'

Mentally Gore was herding the fragments into a pile, hopeful that some might coalesce or else stick out. 'Maybe – you could show me it, Cheryl? This flat, where it is?'

'Tony'll not be there, man, I tell you he'll not.'

Gore bit at the end of his biro. He had no resources left to hand, other than an offer he fought shy of voicing, namely to tramp the streets of the locality for whatever remained of daylight. Yet he was toying with that offer still when another notion, albeit disagreeable, stepped forward forcibly.

'I wonder – I wonder should I talk to Steve Coulson?' Fay MacNamara ever so slightly flinched. 'Just that he knows Tony, of course.'

Cheryl was laughing mirthlessly into the neck of her hooded top. 'Why would *he* help anyone?'

'I've found he can be a helpful man.'

Fay's MacNamara's mouth was tight and defiant. 'Aye, Cheryl, he's been good to you.'

'How's that then?' the girl shot back.

'Ways you're not to know. Don't listen to her, Father, our Tony always looked up to Stevie.'

Gore nodded tactfully. 'Fay, do you have a recent photograph?'

'Of Stevie?'

'No. Your son.'

Now he was in motion, covering pavement, fighting himself from thinking twice about the wisdom of the mission self-imposed. He knew at least where to start his enquiries, so long as he was in time. Crossman was enlarging in his sights when a BMX bike darted maniacally over the kerb and onto the pavement before him. Even on a small-size set of wheels Cliff Petty looked diminutive, yet he stood up on his pedals, his face supremely surly.

'Oi, you. You said you'd help wuh with wuh dole. Didn'ya?'

'I did, yes, and I've been having a go. Now's not a great time, Cliffy.'

'Aw aye, right, you, wank-wank bollocks. Yer *useless*, man.'

'Listen, Cliffy, you know Tony MacNamara, right? Mackers?'

'What's it to *you*, bollocks?'

'Have you seen him lately?'

But the boy only grasped his handlebars, threw a wheelie, and pedalled away, flicking a V-sign back at Gore.

Nearing the Youth Centre, Gore saw a few more cars than usual parked on the gravel out front, and a smattering of juvenile onlookers. He pressed on up the ramp and indoors, there to be met by an empty stage – a scene of dismantle and removal. It appeared that everything not nailed down had been bagged and piled for shifting. Two unshaven men in loose tee-shirts motioned for him to step aside lest they clout him with a stainless steel sink-top. He stepped across the floor between the detritus, and through the door of the former games room he saw Kully Gates in faded Wranglers and frayed pullover, pensive over some papers spread out atop a solitary table.

She looked up. 'Well now. Hello, stranger. You're late.'

'Kully, what's going on?'

'Oh, you pick your moment. Today's the great day. Today we shut.'

'What, your drop-in?'

'No, no, the whole centre. For the chop. *Bulldozer* time.'

For the first time on this generally confounding day, words failed Gore entirely.

'Oh yes. We got the news not so long after your last little visit.'

'But – God, that's so drastic, isn't it?'

'Oh' – she shrugged – 'forever they've had complaints. "Behaviour issues", they say. Meaning drugs, you know. A *petition* they got up this time. And it worked! They should have a party! Woo-hoo. Now their kids can all get into a taxi to some club five miles away, can't they?'

'They couldn't have just let you try and get rid of the trouble-makers?'

'John, then you have no bugger left. Has to be for all, or else for none.'

'Isn't there a duty, though? To have *something* here?'

'Oh, but they have big plans, John, big plans. You need to read the paper.'

She slid the opened *Sunday Sun* across the table to him and he took it up. Page five was given over largely to a photograph of Martin Pallister, glowing with exertion in shirtsleeves and crimson tie, one arm around a thin clear-faced teenage girl , the other round a sheepishly handsome black boy – both of the youngsters in Newcastle football kit.

MP SEES FUTURE IN BLACK-AND-WHITE

Tyneside West MP Martin Pallister is betting on young football talent to shoot Hoxheath out of the doldrums. The MP today announced plans to lead a regeneration project for the recently closed Hoxheath Youth Centre. Working in tandem with the City Council and Newcastle United FC, the MP will seek a slice of government funds to build a top-class all-weather football pitch on the site of the old centre, with full changing facilities.

'Football breaks down boundaries in our society, and it creates new opportunities,' Pallister told the *Sun*. 'Football is dreams. Right here we hope to make some of these dreams reality.'

'We love watching our sport in Newcastle but we need to get more people *doing* it,' the MP went on. 'Football is now a serious profession in this country. If we get local talent started young and properly encouraged, they could make their fortunes – and maybe save the Toon a few bob in transfer fees down the road,' Pallister joked.

After announcing the project, the MP enjoyed a game of 'head-tennis' with Junior FA hopefuls Sophie Benton, 16, from Town Moor, and Remi Odukew, 15, of Fenham.

Gore looked to Kully, who shook her head sadly. 'God, I should have paid attention when he was banging on about football. I'm sorry, Kully. Is there anything I can do?'

'You? I doubt it. Well, no, I say that, you can give me a hand with some of this rubbish. My car's outside.'

Reluctant to intrude further on Kully's dejection, Gore chose to defer his enquiries into the disappearance of Tony MacNamara. They each took an end of a cumbersome computer monitor, and Kully began to shuffle backward toward the rectangle of pale daylight.

Chapter VI

SIMON BARLOW IS BUSY

Monday, 18 November 1996

Awkwardly stooped, his fingers pudgy in gloves, Gore was chaining his bike to the gate outside the vestry of St Mark's when he sensed a messenger drawing nigh through the dark, be he friend or foe. It was Michael Mercer, the dapper, bespectacled, slight and prematurely snowy-haired archdeacon of the diocese.

'Michael. What's got you all the way out here tonight? Am I in trouble?'

'Not that I know of. No, but I believe we're to hear a paper from Simon Barlow? A little report, on how you've been faring? You didn't know?'

Mercer wore a small smile, his breath materialised about him like an aura in the arctic night air.

'I didn't, no.'

Mercer patted Gore's arm with his own leather-gloved hand. 'Well, never you worry, you're still in a job. For now.'

A portable whiteboard had been wheeled into place at the head of the meeting room. Barlow stood over a humming laptop computer, rocking on his heels, seemingly full of battery power himself as he waited for the councilmen to settle themselves and their coffee cups before them. For once he was rigorously failing to meet Gore's eye.

'Right then. Let me say up front, as I've said before – I am hugely in favour of church planting. It's fresh, it's dynamic, it's the way forward for us. Hoxheath has been a good model. But now we see problems.'

He nudged the mouse, and a graphic blinked onto the screen –

a steep-declining purplish mountain-range on an x–y axis.

'We see here – John starts out with maybe sixty heads? Nice. Close enough to what we'd want week in, week out, if we were in for the long haul. And the numbers stay in that park for a bit. Then – fiftyish here. That's the low end of the national average for Sunday. But then look at this tail-off. And yesterday? Twenty-two, not counting present company.'

Gore was not quite listening, more concerned with the body language on display about him. Jack Ridley looked sombre. Susan Carrow had her arms firmly folded. Fluorescent striplight danced over Michael Mercer's bifocals.

'John hit a ceiling. Now it's looking like he could crash through the floor. The *test* is – how do we respond? After all of our efforts here?'

It was for Gore a dismal sensation to observe how swiftly his against-the-odds triumph was being rebranded a bothersome let-down – shrugs and sighs the order of the day, plaudits in the past, now perhaps regretted.

'Do we just, you know, say "Hard luck"? Wait for the turnout to hit zero, then move on? Do we call that a good try? Or do we look to the failings here and see if there are lessons? So future plants can grow? Or even – and I say this cos I'm an optimist, see – do we try and reverse the decline of John's church? My concern, see, is that we don't get the same mistakes repeated. We don't just say we'll carry on throwing up a lot of little plants that get throttled by weeds.'

Barlow tapped at his computer keys. Bob Spikings, subdued, turned to Gore. 'Sorry, John, do you want to, uh, comment?'

'Well, not if I'm the only one who's finding this all a bit premature.'

Barlow winced. 'John, look, what if you give a service and *nobody* comes? That's what I'm forever trying to get through to people. We can't just assume the Church will always *be* here. I'm not knocking them twenty-odd you've managed to pull in. I'm sure you've fought for every one of 'em. Trouble is, one harsh winter could kill off the whole lot.'

Gore glanced to Ridley, who had closed his eyes – pained, or just weary?

'What's needed,' Barlow ploughed on, 'is a proper *analysis*. If a few people came and stayed, then why not more?'

Gore drummed on the table. 'Go on, I trust you have a theory.'

'Well, first and obvious, John, they might have fancied the idea on paper, but not liked what they heard when they got there. Or else they got there and felt they needn't have bothered. Were ignored, not made welcome.'

Gore grimaced. And yet treacherous heads nodded round the table.

'See, John, your congregants aren't just there to put pennies on the plate. Or do a bit of donkey-work when you whistle. If we're gonna revive our churches, members have to be listened to – actively involved in the service.'

'I do listen to them, I have done. I don't always agree.'

'Oh, I know, John, I've watched you stood there arguing with pensioners, so we know you're an adamant sort.' Barlow rode amiably over the chuckles. 'But a church needs more than a good shepherd. It needs a fisher of men. Doubly so when it's a small church. Okay, easy for me to say – I've got a big one. But *you* try shuffling into some draughty school hall on a Sunday, and there's two dozen gloomy faces you don't know. So much easier to slip in the back of a big chapel where there's a couple hundred. Band playing, happy voices, whole mix of people. And friendly sidesmen, saying hello there, nice to see you, how are you keeping?'

Gore pinched his temples. 'Simon, all that stuff you do isn't going to happen at St Luke's. It can't.'

'No, John. It *could*. With just a bit more thought to presentation. A bit more *care*. For starters you'd look a lot friendlier if your sidesmen weren't ruddy nightclub bouncers.'

'As a matter of fact,' Gore began, feeling himself pitted solo against the room, 'Mr Coulson is no longer involved at St Luke's. Also I've been looking at some proposals for changing the decor – the lighting and so on.'

'Okay. That's one part of presentation. What about your *self*-presentation?'

'What of it?'

'John, think about those old dears – they can just about groan through a hymn on a wonky old piano, but then they have to listen to a sermon from a wordsmith like you. Not a simple story, with an uplifting message. Not you, eh, John? I mean, sorry, but the other day I reckoned you were making it up as you went along. Sigmund Freud? Dear me. I know time's scarce, but you owe it to those people to be properly prepared. It's a courtesy.'

The impression of the scoring jab was much the worse for Gore, silent as he saw the relish climbing up one side of Barlow's face.

'You see, on one hand we've got John's bad numbers, then we've got all his other endeavours out there in the world. The two could be related.'

'What are you referring to?'

'Oh, you know, John. We all see you, running out and about with the locals. Extracurricular activities and that. But it doesn't always look to me like the true work of the spirit. It's possible you're wasting your time. And, by extension, the time of others.' Barlow opened his palms to the table.

'I never asked for your time, Simon.'

'I *think*' – Spikings inserted himself, uncomfortable – 'we're maybe, uh, drifting somewhat here. In fairness to John, his media work, which I assume you mean, Simon, has been quite a success.'

'Nice for John, sure. Nice to be on the radio, in the paper – people like a bit of chat off a tame vicar. But it doesn't seem to have done the trick for your numbers, has it?'

Gore tossed his capped biro onto the blank open notebook before him. 'Right. So, all *talk* aside, what are you actually proposing I *do*?'

Barlow stabbed at his keyboard. 'Let me just tell you a few things about my church.'

An array of pie-charts blinked up onto the whiteboard. Much squinting and leaning forward.

'Fifty-three per cent of people coming every week had never

been inside a church before mine. But *this* one's the stunner. Thirty-three per cent of them travel five miles or more to attend. And – just so you don't say I'm big-headed – seventy-one per cent say they like what we do, but they want *more* of it. More music, more evenings, more events, more youth work. Now, you all know my view. A *vital* church is where the Gospel truth gets preached week in, week out. What my stats show is that a church like that is self-renewing. New people are always coming to the door. Because they've *heard*, see? That this church has something for them – them and them alone – and they couldn't get it anywhere else.'

Salesman of the Year, no contest, thought Gore, as Barlow made exhortative shapes with his hands, sleeves rolled up despite the low thermostat.

'I'm not saying "Everyone back to mine." We're full up. I *am* saying the people of Hoxheath need a bit more encouragement. You can't bring a church to the people. But you *can* bring people to a church. One coachload of my lot could turn the whole thing round. I'm saying let's show Hoxheath what it means to have a righteous congregation, a proper, full-on, Jesus-loving service. A joyful noise unto the Creator.'

Barlow's slow-burning fervency seemed to have arrived at an earnest pause. Spikings clicked his pen. 'Simon, do you – is this a, uh, concrete proposal?'

'Too right, Bob. Let me do a social at St Luke's, a proper fundraiser. I'll provide the bells and whistles. One night only, I'll bring my church to Hoxheath. My bands, my youth team, my sidesmen. They'll be made up, honest, they love to network. Call it maybe two quid on the door, another quid for a raffle ticket? But when the hat goes round at the end, I promise you, you'll see tenfold that. And all for St Luke's, of course.'

Spikings tapped the table, pensive. 'Well. What do you say, John?'

'I don't know where to begin.'

'I must say it sounds rather nice,' offered Susan Carrow. 'Could be a shot in the arm. You can't say we don't need one.'

'Uh, Monica, then – what say you?'

'I'll not be the one to pour cold water on it. It'll need to be a weekend, mind. And all Mr Barlow's lot doing the lifting. I've not got time for it.'

'Oh, you can leave it in my hands, Monica. Lock stock.'

Spikings glanced toward his diligently minute-taking wife. '*When*, though? When are we supposed to do this?'

'Let's not mess about,' Barlow leapt in. 'Call it for this Saturday.'

'Gosh. That quick?'

'Bob, that's how you have to act in a tight corner. Look at the Bob Geldofs of the world. Not everything needs a million boring meetings. Just give me the sign and I'll do it.'

Gore could feel eyes on him, awaiting his next move – and indeed he could see himself rising and walking out, washing his hands of this room, this disapproving convention, dingy old rain-dark Hoxheath. But walking to where? He waved a noncommittal hand at Barlow, then let it fall.

'Okay. So I took the liberty of asking a couple of friends along tonight, they're outside, and I'd like to bring them in. They're youth workers at my place, always full of ideas. I can guarantee they'll drive this train.'

No one demurred. Barlow paced from the room and the air was still in his wake, a mood of general relief, as when – it seemed to Gore – a much-deferred task, an awkward spot of knife-wielding, had been accomplished by other hands. Rose Spikings's pen scratched across the page before her. Gore worried a thumb at the peeling edge of the meeting table. When he raised his gaze it was to observe the entrance of two dimly remembered faces over matching firehouse-red tee-shirts proclaiming THE SHIELD SOCIETY, Barlow the conductor in their wake.

'This is Stuart and Tina Grieveson – John, you've met before?'

Gore lingered by his bike as one by one the councilmen, at whose faces he couldn't stand to look, climbed into their vehicles and made off into the evening. Barlow emerged belatedly, conferring as if affably with the archdeacon. Once Mercer was ensconced in his Volvo saloon and Barlow was jiggling keys by the door of the Mondeo, Gore strode across the crunching gravel and jabbed a finger at the smirk that met him. 'Pleased with yourself, are you?'

'*Whoah*, don't be waving that about, son, I don't know where it's been.'

'I ought to put you through the window.'

'Don't be *ridiculous*, John. With what? You'd need your bully-boys for that.'

Annoyingly, Barlow did not shrink. But nor did Gore's adrenalin-flow cease. 'How big of a *rat* are you, Simon? Sneaking about in my business.'

'Don't talk crap, I'm helping you out. Don't you ever listen?'

'Oh, sure, that's you, all *heart*. And you get nothing out of it.'

'Not much I can see, no, short of some extra legwork.'

'Oh no? Short of maybe weaselling me out of my living?'

'That'll not be my doing, John. You're doing fine on your own. Tell you what, but, it ought to have a new man – poor old St Luke's. Someone who'll preach the Gospel. Not sit counting the hairs on his arse – chasing skirt, palling about with thugs. Or giving off to the MP, for that matter.'

'What fucking *business*,' Gore spat, 'is that of yours?'

'Calm yourself, will you? I've a bit of a stake in it, John, matter of fact. I'm meeting your sister tomorrow.'

'You *what*?'

'Oh yeah, her and Martin Pallister. About this group he's putting together? His board? The one you bottled on, right?'

Gore felt it now – the blade going in between the shoulders, to the hilt, Barlow's pleasure in same.

'Do you never talk, then, you and her? Must say, but, I'd never have picked the pair of you's for brother and sister. You sure you weren't adopted?'

As if involuntarily Gore seized the lapel of Barlow's coat. But the adrenalin had waned, his fist easily beaten aside.

'Oh, piss off, John, either take a swing at me or get out of my face. It's bloody freezing and I've other things to do tonight.'

*

She answered the door wearing a white towelling bathrobe and reading glasses, the ends of her bobbed hair wet.

'Well. What do I owe this pleasure, kidder?'

'I want to talk about Barlow.'

She sighed – 'Fine' – and swung the door wide. The interior of the Quayside apartment did not much surprise him, not in its dim-lit open-plan whiteness nor in the pricey functionality of its furnishing. A glass of red wine sat atop a stack of paper on a low table by a black-leather Mies van der Rohe chair, sited with a certain exactness upon a russet hooked rug. Susannah flopped into this pew. Gore lowered himself onto the edge of the white sofa facing, his topcoat unsurrendered.

'*What's* your problem then?'

'You can't guess?'

'Haven't we done this? You weren't into it. Obviously, *obviously* Marty had me scout other people. We'd a few other meetings. *He* had me get hold of what's-his-face. Marty goes to his church, takes his kid the odd Sunday. As far as I know he finds the guy interesting. Can-do about stuff.'

'Yes. That's how he worms his way into everything.'

'Well, as a matter of fact, he didn't want to know at first. Bit like you. I don't think he's a Labour man by nature.'

'No, he fucking is not.'

She made a moue. 'Well, whatever – he's turned out alright. Unlike you. I guess he's just more our sort of vicar.'

'I just cannot believe . . . you've got in bed with that *arsehole*.'

'Oh, don't be so petty, Jonno. It's just an arrangement. A consultation.'

'Do you actually know what he's like? Him and his sort? He's twisted, Bible-mad – he hates gays. Hates women.'

'He's always behaved himself round me.' And demurely she sipped from her glass. Gore found himself maddeningly short of any more concrete charges.

'The main thing for our purpose is he's got a lot of ideas. About education. Which is Marty's main thing.'

'What ideas?'

'All stuff about new schools. New *kinds* of schools. It's all here.' She lifted and heaved to her brother the brick of A4 paper from her side table. Above the scarlet circle-stain of her glass he saw the letterhead and logo of The Shield Society, a Gosforth address.

'I can't knock it. He runs a good operation. Just five people he's got in the office, but by God they graft. From a fundraising point of view they're shit-hot. I'd hire them in a New York minute if they weren't spoken for.'

Gore flicked the pages – policy document upon policy document, in irksome small type. 'I can't be bothered with this.'

'No? Well, I'll tell you. They've got quite a smart idea for getting shot of the really crap schools. Replacing them with big brand-new builds.'

'And who's going to pay for that?'

'Private funds, kidder. It won't be the begging bowl. Naw, they would be independent schools, these, only they wouldn't charge fees – cos of them being so well-endowed. So they'd pay better for better teachers. And you'd get a damn sight higher standard than some rotten comprehensive. More focus on the useful things, skills that get you jobs. And, you know, they'd be proper godly and all. I mean, it ought to be up your street.'

'What do they get out of it? Barlow? "The Shield Society"?'

'*I* don't know, man. Spreading the good word. It's early days. Just blue-sky stuff for now. But it's thorough. That's one thing he understands, your pal Barlow. Red tape – how much you've got to cut to ever get owt done. Any road.' She sighed. 'We're only talking. Simon'll sit on Marty's board, Marty's going to speak at some event they're doing. Introduce him around . . . Quid pro quo. Just like he would have done for you, kidder. He was all for getting you in with the people he knows. But not you, oh no. You had to take your bloody stand against the wicked world.'

'Everything you told me was bullshit, Susannah.'

'No, it wasn't.' She took a longer pull on her wine. 'Fair enough, but, I see now – it wouldn't have worked. I'll tell you something else about this Barlow. He works a room. He can bring money to the table. Not just whingeing for handouts. I was amazed, actually. Turns out he's tight in with Dick Broke.'

'Who?'

'*Sir* Dick Broke. The ball-bearings millionaire? From Consett? You never read the business pages, do you, kidder? *He's* got Jesus and all, see, Dick Broke. Got a big fat foundation where he puts all his dividend. For his good causes. I know he keeps Simon's office in paperclips.'

Gore set the papers down on the floor. 'Right. And these are the people you want to work with? You think a Labour MP should work with?'

'I bloody do. Tell you what, if you've built up a multi-million-pound company all by yourself, you'll have a strong view of the world, and it's liable to have a bit more heft to it than some bloody vicar's. People might pay attention. They might *care*.'

That seemed unnecessary – vindictive, even. Gore, blinking, found it unexpectedly hard to bear. But his sister's eyes were dry and didn't sympathise. 'Though why you're a vicar I've never understood. Unless you were after an excuse to wag your finger at the lot of us. Well, you can spare me the sermon, kid, I know you better.'

For the longest time Gore sat in the grasp of his living-room armchair, bundled up still in his topcoat, unwilling to unwrap himself from what seemed a kind of cold comfort. The central heating system was clunking dysfunctionally. A pint glass of water stood untouched. Vigour was entirely drained from his limbs, the need for sleep seemed tremendous, yet his eyes would not stay closed. When the telephone trilled at half past nine he expected the worst. At the seventh ring, resignedly, he answered. It was Fay MacNamara. He stumbled into a weary apology.

'It's only we're frantic, but, Father, it's like we've started having things through the letterbox.'

'What things? What . . .?'

'I hardly dare say.'

'Look, you've called the police? Please tell me you've called them now.'

The silence on the line was damning, inexplicable.

'Mrs MacNamara – you put me in a very difficult position. How is anyone supposed to help you? What do you imagine I can do that the police can't? I mean, have you thought about –'

But she had hung up on him.

His eyes were still fixed on the ceiling, the conversation replaying, when the phone rang again. He was not minded to apologise, rather to let the answering machine serve a rebuke.

'Hiya John, it's just me. Lindy. Wondering how y'are. When you want to meet up? Okay, will you call us? Bye . . .'

The red message light blinked at Gore. Yes, he would call her back. But a headache was starting to signal dully through his fatigue, and he needed to self-medicate. He got to his feet, listing somewhat as he veered into the kitchen, rummaged the drawer into which he had tipped much ill-sorted junk on move-in day. Amid spare Allen keys and boxes of dud matches he found a crushed packet of Ibuprofen, and salvaged two pills.

Then his ears pricked, for there were scuffing, scuttling noises coming from the patio outside. Footfalls? Or just the customary night-time garbage thrown over his wall from the alley? Might he have heard some booze bottle clinking and skittering on concrete? Perhaps it was the mangy fox he had seen dawdling down the alley one evening. He was wearily habituated to it, but it snagged at the nerves nonetheless. He peered out of the small kitchen window into the gloom of the yard, then, dissatisfied, swept out to the curtains masking the patio's sliding doors and whisked them aside.

A pale, wretched moon-face stared back at him through the glass. He thought his heart would kick clean out of its cage.

But the spectre instantaneously acquired a shape, a reality, familiar and yet changed – a mere boy, one who had always looked older than his years.

Mackers sat in the armchair picking at the grubby skin of his palms, his silence oppressive to Gore, who found himself standing and buzzing uselessly, wanting to make himself active, talkative, effective – not the crushed figure into whose godforsaken evening this unbidden guest had intruded. He drew the curtains, stood over the boy, hovering, uncertain, until he saw the glum face raised to him. No, this one no longer seemed an apprentice adult – very much a child, somehow profaned and ill-used.

'Have you got owt to smoke?'

'I don't. I'm sorry. But, look. Let me give you something hot to drink. With a tot of brandy. I mean, yes, it'll do you good.'

In the kitchen he poured water to boil, ransacked the cupboard of cooking bottles for the supermarket-brand cognac, glancing backward as deftly as was feasible. Mixing the drink in the mug, he saw the boy had his face in his hands and was rubbing at it, his shoulders twitching. He hastened out.

'Look, Tony, it's okay, it's alright, just let it out.'

The face was raised again, but it was not tearful. The eyes, in fact, had a fury in them. 'Let fuckin' what out?'

Gore reconsidered – pressed the mug into his hand, lowered himself into the smaller occasional chair opposite. The boy slurped and grimaced.

'Your mother came to me, your sister . . . They've been terribly worried.'

'Don't care. It's nowt to dee wi' them.'

'Well, just . . . You should know. They'd love to see you back home.'

'Can't. Nah. No way.'

He slurped again. Gore sat back. 'Tony, what's this about?'

The boy flinched as if stung on the neck. 'Divvint wanna talk about it.'

'Tony, I know –'

'*Mackaz*, man, *Mackaz*. Ye *sound* like me mam and all.'

Gore waited for this fresh ire to fizzle. 'Mackers, I know it must have been an awful shock, what happened. I can't imagine, I won't pretend.' The boy stared at his toecaps, unreactive. 'Whoever did it, whatever it was about – you don't think they're chasing you too, do you? Meaning to hurt you?'

'Might be.'

'What did you see? Did you tell the police?'

His head swung upward, the eyes hostile again.

'Look, it's just that your sister said something.'

'That's *how*, see. That, that's how it *starts*. I didn't tell 'em fuckin' *owt*. No one believes wuh.'

'Do you know something? About why it happened?'

'It was my fault.'

Gore winced, for this much he knew of, the perennial behaviour of victims. 'No, now you mustn't say that. How could that be, Tony? How could it?'

'I canna tell yuh.'

'Why not? What are you so scared?'

'You'd fuckin' be and all. So divvint start on wuh.'

'Is this – look, are you scared of Steve Coulson?'

'Will ya *stop* with aal the fuckin' *questions*, man, pack it *in*.'

This then was how it would have to be – awkward and scant of courtesy, perhaps even abusive. On his part – no severity, no pull-yourself-together.

'Well. What are we going to do with you?'

The boy's response was to cloak his brow in his hands once more.

'I mean – you can stay here, you know? I've got a little room.'

The eyes, at least, emerged through the hands.

'You'll be okay here. Safe. No one comes here.'

'You'll not dob us in? Not to neeone, but?'

'No, absolutely not. You can trust me, you have my word. Okay?'

The boy nodded as if to himself.

'But, Tony. Tony, look, you do need to know – this has got to get settled. This situation? I mean, we can't have this . . . just like this. You can't hide away for ever. We need to come up with something. You need to tell me, what we can do. To right things.'

There was nothing in response, neither motion nor muttering, until 'Can I use your toilet?'

'Of course. It's upstairs. The bathroom.'

The boy got to his feet.

'Would you like to shower? Or bath?'

'Nah. Just the shitter.'

Gore found himself leading the boy up the stairs, gesturing needlessly toward the small room at the end of the landing. It was shut and locked, and shortly from within Gore heard a rude gaseous eruption. He withdrew to the small room he called spare, rifled the fitted wardrobe, located the spare duvet, the one spare pillow, the one set of clean linen. One of everything had always been his life – he had travelled light for as far as he had travelled. It had been an organising principle. It was just going to have to be disturbed.

There was no sound from the locked bathroom, but the light was plain under the door, and he was more or less glad of the respite. He returned downstairs, plucked the barely touched brandy mug from the casual table. The red message light on the phone still blinked at him. But it was past the hour. He pressed down the DELETE button and held it.

Book Six

JUDGEMENTS

Chapter I

CHARITY

Saturday, 23 November 1996

With his one sharp knife he peeled and pared, sliced and diced, studiously sweeping clean the board as he went, dumping each rendered mound of raw cubes into his one chipped and worn stockpot. His own rigour pleased him, but glancing to the oven clock he knew that he was already behind schedule. The boy could wait, but Gore himself could not – not if he were to be dressed and out of the door for seven, as was his lot for the evening.

This much effort, though, he believed he owed as host – something at least marginally more edifying than the carry-out stodge he had fetched home in hot plastic bags each night since the boy took up residence in the 'guest room'. Over the days preceding, Gore assumed, it had been dinner out of dustbins for Mackers – assumed, for details were not forthcoming, conversation still clenched between them. In lieu of chit-chat he had shifted the portable television upstairs, and blue light seeped under the door most hours, materialising blue smoke, for each day too he offered the boy a token of ten Embassy Regal.

Scraping rind and peel into the pedal bin it occurred to him that he hadn't laid a table for anyone but himself since Grey College – the weekly ritual decreed by Lockhart, each staircase of ordinands taking it by rote to prepare and serve an economical meal for students and faculty, chopping and stewing and bearing out the fare to the trestles in the long hall overlooking the courtyard. Gore was turning over this memory, weighing its disparity to what was before him, when he believed that he heard the click of his front-door latch. Jerking his head from the chopping board he sliced cleanly into his left thumb.

'*Ow*, fuck, I didn't *do* that . . .'

He threw down the blade, wrapped a fist round the cut, kicked aside the kitchen door, and was appalled to see Steve Coulson planted squarely under the unshaded lightbulb of his living room.

'Steve, you –'

'Your door's not locked, John. Good job it were us.'

Coulson was in his Saturday-night finery, the dark suit worn with an open black collar, a high shine on patent leather boots. His unsmiling head more than usual bore the stern aspect of a Roman stone bust, and his eyes were murky as they followed Gore from the spot. Gore could hear blood beating in his ears. 'Sorry, I need to get a plaster. Okay? I'll just be a moment. Just need to fetch out the bathroom . . .' He was raising his voice loud enough to carry, even as he moved to get himself between Coulson and the staircase.

'Naw, you get yer'sel sorted out, man. Before you give us earache.'

Gore bolted up the stairs. Through the open door of the small room he saw Mackers framed against the darkened window, as if cornered, plight all over his face. With fraught hands Gore motioned him to be still, and wrenched the door to. In the bathroom, struggling toward composure, he located aertex strips in his toilet bag, staunched the seeping cut with wadded toilet tissue then taped it up. He looked into his eyes in the mirror, then descended the stairs. Coulson had scarcely moved from the spot, his bulk trammelling the space, cutting off all exits. He reached and rapped the bare hanging lightbulb with a knuckle, and it swung askew.

'Looking for us, were you?'

'I'm sorry?'

'I thought you was looking for us?'

'Steve, I'm not getting you.'

'Naw? The other week? I've seen you since, I knaa, we've talked. But I was just with a few of my lads, see. Catching up on stuff. And Dougie telt us you were in Teflon last Saturday. I says, "Never. Not John Gore."'

'No, that's right. I was there. I didn't see Dougie.'

'He saw you.'

'I wasn't there long. Just dropped in. I was curious.'

'Fancied a poke about, did you?'

'Yes. Since – all what I'd heard.'

'You shoulda asked to see us. Long as you were there.'

'I didn't think on. I was only there for the beer, Steve.'

'Enjoy yourself, then?'

'It was interesting. Not my scene, you know.'

'Aye. Cos I hear you got yourself in the middle of some bother. In the way of a couple of my lads trying to do their job. Big Don Boddy, he tells us he's got this little rat outside and some bugger tries to jump on him. And there's Dougie says, "Nah, I saw it, it was John Gore." That Robbie , he says the same. So what I wanna know is, what's that about?'

'Steve, I saw a boy getting – I thought manhandled. That was just how I saw it. I decided I'd have a word, just.'

'A word. Did you reckon that was your business, eh?'

'Like I said –'

'I mean, we've talked, you and me, haven't wuh? 'Bout my business, your business. I've telt you and all, in my line I've gotta deal with bits of trouble. Worky tickets.'

'Like I say, this was just a boy, it looked to me.'

'A "boy". Well, see, that's cos you divvint knaa what you're looking at.'

'No, I maybe don't.'

'This is a ratbag kid brings trouble into my place. Dirt and drugs and rotten attitude. So divvint get all daft about "boys", John.'

'Well, I'm sorry if I – no, I'm just sorry.'

The heavy head was intransigent, until Coulson cast a look about him, offered some wintry version of a smile. 'Funny, but. How yours and Lindy's are the same. Sort of. Least she's got hers so you can live in it.'

Gore shrugged his agreement.

'Mind if I use your bog?'

'No. Go ahead.'

Stevie moved to the staircase. Gore had to recover his voice. 'Steve, the one down here works just fine. In the hall there.'

'Aw right. I'm used to Lindy's, right enough. Blocked for years. Might have been us that blocked it.'

Coulson didn't deign to shut the toilet door, merely unzipped and bowed his knees, drilled at the porcelain, flushed and rinsed. He re-emerged rubbing his hands around each other, staring still at Gore. The silence Gore was finding unendurable – whereupon came there a thump through the ceiling, muted but audible.

Coulson's chin tilted. 'Not wor lass, that?'

'No, no. No, that's my two-bit DIY, I think. Everything I put up falls down again. In the end.'

Coulson shook his head. 'It's poor, y'knaa. Living in a dump like this. Man of your age. Shame.'

'It does me fine, Steve. For what I do.'

'S'pose it might. If that's what you want – just to get by. It's not a crime to want a few of the better things about you, but. It's common sense, that.'

'Well, you don't have to worry about me. It's my life, I chose it.'

'Aw, I won't.' He looked to the door, but not concertedly. 'You'll excuse us for saying, John, you maybe think too much of what's yours. Not enough of others. Wor lass, she's not so happy wi' you, I reckon.'

'Lindy?'

He grimaced. 'Aye, Lindy. Divvint act the prick. Whatever you do, John, you want to be sure you do right about her. I'd count that a favour, in fact.'

'I don't think I –'

'Just a *favour*, John. Just that, eh? You've had enough out of us. Haven't ya, man? Why aye, you've had plenty.' The stare was dead-eyed again. And yet, miraculously, he was shifting at last from his impregnable stance.

'Be seeing you, then, Reverend.'

The intruder gone, the claustral confinement lifted, Gore needed a moment to feel his stomach settled, his feet firm under him again. He locked the front door and hurdled back up the stairs. The boy was pacing, rubbing his face, another Regal pinched between hand and mouth.

'The fuck was that, man?'

'I don't know, Tony, I really don't. He's gone now but, it's okay now.'

The boy, Gore could tell, thought this lame at best – perhaps even ignorant.

'Good evening, sir, may I welcome you to St Luke's?'

'No need, thanks, I'm the vicar.'

Gore spurned the glad hand from the smiling young fucker in the firehouse-red pullover, though he couldn't quite shirk the handful of paper pamphlets pressed upon him by a frog-like girl in spectacles. A lively din was already audible, and through the double doors he found the hall – he had to concede, for all it meant – impressively transformed. His father couldn't possibly have matched such endeavours – mirrorballs, bunting and painted banners laced and draped from the light fixtures, the walls bedecked with streamers, and a small stage freshly erected and flanked by lighting scaffolds, set for a rock show – guitars, keyboards, drums, microphones. Gore had never stopped to contemplate what might be the sight and sound of a hundred-plus grown men and women milling and chattering in this drab space, a dozen couples twirling each other gamely across the badminton markings to some jaunty pop tune.

Baby baby, I'm taken with the notion . . .

Behind a long table at stage-side, Stuart Grieveson was nodding his big head affably over a record deck and a short stack of long-players. Trestles set width-to-width down the left flank of the space purveyed a generous spread of hot and cold savouries. Tina bobbed behind these, attending to a microwave oven, a toothy little girl in a pink dress tugging at her waist. Gore moved through the gathering, raising his eyes to those who raised plastic cups in his direction. It was an incursion, no business of his but that it seemed a victory party at which he was the vanquished, his head already measured for a mounting on the wall. Susan Carrow sidled up to him, fruity punch in her cup, wearing a blouse with a scarab beetle at the neck. 'Well now, Reverend, this is a bit nicer than the normal.'

'Glad you like it. I can't see any of our people, but. Just the day-trippers.'

'At least they've not got tattoos.'

Jack Ridley joined them. Mrs Carrow raised her cup. 'Might we see you out on the floor then, Jack?'

'Whey, these aren't my tunes.' He munched at a slice of pizza. 'Not struck on this neither. Not a bit of what they've got. All I fancied was a sausage roll.' Silently he proffered his paper-plate buffet at Gore.

'No thank you, Jack, I've been fed.'

'My, you're a misery. The pair of you.' And Susan flounced away, presumably to find the fun-loving people.

Ridley and Gore stood awhile. Gore found nothing to say.

'Was a church dance that Meg and I met, matter of fact. 1951. Not a great deal like this un, I might add.'

Gore tried a smile, wondering how long he was reasonably bound to stay.

'Busying yourself, eh, John? I saw you'd an advert in our church gazette. Looking to go freelance, are you?'

'I'm told I might have to . . . I don't know. Sorry Jack, I'm not quite functional tonight.'

Ridley looked on as if unsurprised.

'Fact is, I'm in a – I've got a few bits of bother.'

'Oh aye? Owt I can help you with?'

'You've done more than sufficient. Anyhow. I know your feelings.'

'I see. Heavy mob then, is it? I'm sorry to hear that.'

Ridley was watching him, he knew, as he watched others sightlessly.

'I'd not want to see you stuck. Not if there was summat.'

Gore exhaled. 'I could maybe do with . . . your advice.'

Ridley nodded in satisfaction. 'Well, I'll call on you the morra morning. Good and early, like. Before you start your shift.'

The volume of the pop music had faded out and up on the stage some poodle-headed musicians in shiny shirts and skinny denims were tweaking and plucking their instruments. Simon Barlow skipped across wires and packing cases to grasp the frontman's microphone stand.

'We on? Okay, good evening everybody. Most of you know me, but to one and all let me say a big welcome to St Luke's School, where we've been trying lately to bring God's word to a whole new service. But it ain't easy, folks. And tonight is all about lending a hand to that cause. So thanks a million to you for coming. Special thanks to Stuart and Tina Grieveson, you guys, great efforts as always. And most of all, thanks be to Jesus, praise Him, cos I feel his presence tonight, and I think you do too.'

Gore heard Barlow's dedication being echoed keenly all around him.

'Now I just want to take a moment here, cos I'd like to share with you, if I may, a personal feeling.'

Barlow bit his lip, raised his eyes, nodded as if affirmed.

'Y'know, God was never cool when I was a kid growing up in Essex. My mates, they were mods, punks. Some of 'em wore blouses and girls' make-up. Like that *was cool. Bit confused, you might say. Now don't get me wrong, me and the boys in Christian Union, we didn't look a whole lot better. They said we were a load of spotty Herberts with body odour and bowl haircuts. And you know what? They weren't so far wrong. That was me, oh yes, my brothers and sisters, I was that Herbert . . .'*

Barlow stroked his goatee, acknowledged the warm and encouraging laughter with his own skewed smile. *An actor,* thought Gore, *at the peak of his powers.*

'Tell you what, but – I look back and I think, who looks silly now, eh? Cos the way I see it – atheism is yesterday's thing, it's last year's colour. But one thing that's never out of fashion is God's word. Yesterday, today, for ever . . . I don't want to start preaching here. I see some of you, you're thinking, "Off he goes . . ." No, but I want to say is, it's right that we take some time and care with how we look. We should try to make ourselves more presentable, more approachable. Change the old stereotypes.

But, see, I look around at you people and I see a great-looking bunch. And most of all I want Christian men and women in this country of ours to never, ever be ashamed of who they are in front of their peers. Because you are the silent minority. Good people, hard-working families. I always say, you don't have to be saints to join our church, you just have to want to hear the good word, and want to live by it. So let's not go about it quietly, let's not hide our light in a corner, when it's the culture around us that's the problem. The media doesn't want to hear us, we know that. But we need to let this culture know we reject it. We're going to go our own way, make our own spaces, our own arrangements. Cos our faith is far stronger than the cynics and the trendies. And if the culture's not careful, hey – it's gonna look around one day and find that our numbers *are stronger too. How about that, eh? Can you wait for that day?'*

This struck Gore as vintage Barlow – the switchblade holstered by the cross.

'Now you'll have been given a little something to read about The Shield Society as you came in, and if you've not come across us before and you're interested then please do look us up.'

It was only now that Gore thought to glance at the pamphlets crumpled in his hand. On the front of each was the logo of a red cross within a white shield – a Crusader shield, as the history books would call it.

'Now tell you what, though – all those people who say God's not cool? I tell 'em, "Listen, mate, you need to hear God's rhythm. Alright!"' He punched the air. *'I said* alright!*'*

Fists were aloft in the audience too. Gore ground his fists deeper into his pockets.

'Now, it's my very great pleasure to introduce the band, they're friends of mine, they make a brilliant sound, and if you like what you hear then the CD's for sale at the door. So please give a hand for the mighty Sentinel . . .*'*

Barlow led the clapping as he departed the stage, the drumsticks clicked and the band struck up on a synthesised current of airy rock, the vocalist squinting as he wrapped himself round the mic stand.

Heavenly trumpets, all around, angels singing, do you hear that sound?
Join the queue, at the gate of life, son and daughter, man and wife . . .

He should have walked right then, replete as he was feeling with the teeth-baring self-love of certain parties. And yet he let himself drift into desultory small talk with Archdeacon Mercer, knowing this for a hopeless cause even before Barlow muscled into it.

'A rousing address to the troops there, Simon,' Mercer nodded.

'Well, you know my thing. It's all about the grass roots, that's how we'll thrive. Make the congregation the driving force. Not to usurp your role, Michael. But nobody wants too many straitjackets and committees on high. Give the people their head. My troops know what to do – long as they've been properly rallied.' He glanced at Gore.

'Oh yeah,' Gore murmured. 'Give it another six months and you'll be ready to invade Poland.' And he smiled over the startled brows as Henry March drew near. Barlow seemed to be scowling too at a sparkling stud in Henry's ear, though Gore could see a silver hoop in Barlow's own left lobe.

'John, what time should I stop selling raffle tickets?'

'Uh, whenever you like.'

'No, you want to crack on, mate.' Barlow was testy. 'It's all good money, John. Least another half-hour.'

Henry nodded coolly. 'John, something else. Can I talk to you?'

'Of course, what is it?'

'Just a little problem on the door . . .'

'Oh dear, John,' smirked Barlow, visibly cheered. 'Where's your skinheads when we need them?'

Henry hastened Gore aside. 'John, there's a couple of girls just rocked up and I'd say they've got plenty drink onboard. I only asked for the door fee and they said something a bit unrepeatable.'

'Well, Henry, they probably shouldn't come in. Are they – ?'

'No, but they're already in, see. Thing is, they said they know you.'

The frame very suddenly found focus. 'Did one of these girls have her hair very short?'

Henry nodded. 'Oh yeah. Thing is, they just steamed past us and went off. I'm worried they might be on the loose round the school.'

He wandered the cool and darkened corridors, through patches of clean moonlight on the linoleum, passing each closed and silent classroom. As the hubbub from the hall receded, replaced by the carbolic odour rising from the floors, Gore felt a kind of relief suffuse him – the disappearing act, his favourite trick. And tonight it had a special utility. The illusion of solitude persisted for some privileged moments before his ears picked up exuberant feminine giggles, drifting from around the next corner.

There before the Year Two art board were Lindy and her young Slavic friend, in clingy frocks and high spirits.

As he drew near they were unabashed. Even in the half-light he could see Lindy's self-satisfied slightly inebriate smile as she pushed a drawing pin through one of her son's drawings, so reinstating it in prime position.

'Oh, hi you. What do you think of that?'

There was, he had to admit, a certain justice.

'You've met Yulia, haven't you? Doesn't she look nice?'

The Slav girl was in a pink dress like a shiny tube that pressed her slight figure flat, suspended by spaghetti straps running up to a neck-piece. He recognised Lindy's black halter dress with its ruched tutu-like hem, for he had seen it hanging in her bedroom. Side by side they were like a pair of rowdy cocktail princesses.

'Have you just come to take the piss?' he murmured.

'Whey, naw, John. Come to see you. And to take the piss.' More giggles.

Gore heard squeaking steps behind him. It was Henry.

'There you are. Barlow wants you. The band are finished and he says you need to say a few words?'

Lindy tilted her chin at the younger churchman. 'He's handy at that. Sorry about earlier, mate, no offence. I can be a bit of a *cee-you-en-tee* meself sometimes.'

Playtime over, back to the hall Gore strode, shoulder to shoulder with Henry, the snorting mirth of the ladies audible in his wake. Through the hall he ploughed, toward the stage that lay in wait. From his vantage at its side Barlow offered Gore an unfriendly nod and a hastening gesture.

He grasped the microphone. '*Good evening. One or two of you may know me, I'm John Gore, the vicar of this, uh, this little experiment. I really don't want to take up much of your time – or any of it, really – not with all the fine entertainment. To our visitors I just want to say I do appreciate your efforts and donations on our behalf, and for sprucing the place up. We're a poor man's church and here you're quite turning our heads. And those of you who have come before, well . . . we're up and running now, and I trust we've got accustomed to one another, and in a few places I hope I've made some impact.*'

A whistle pierced the air, eliciting a murmur that wasn't quite approving.

Gore stepped down to perfunctory applause and found the girls pestering Stuart at the record decks, he delving with one hand into a wooden crate.

'Have you not got the Fugees, man? Not got owt good, have you?'

'No, I reckon . . . I've got the single, it's just at the bottom. It's jammed into a bit of a crack, like.'

Lindy laughed hard, causing Yulia too to spit her punch back into her cup.

Gore angled his brow at Lindy. 'Having fun, are we?'

'Fun? Get away. I'm trying, but. Divvint worry, John, I'd never ever not want you to think well of us.'

She had been drinking, undoubtedly, but her exuberance seemed made out of something stronger, some more potent spirit within – an aggression, he would have called it, and a quality quite apart from the razor-cut hair. For her lips had their mauve gloss, her black-lined eyes their brazen sparkle, and in that dress she was irrefutably girly.

The lights were a little dimmer and it seemed that Lindy's record was playing, a slow number, a woman's creamy voice against spare percussive backing – her choice it surely was, for now she was hopping around him, making up to him, swaying and making diving shapes with her hands, mischief in those eyes.

She giggled, grabbed the hem of her cocktail dress and flipped it, then stuck out her tongue.

It was a sort of a challenge, Gore knew, for as usual he could feel unfriendly eyes trained on him. In former days he might have felt the skin prickling all across his body, the dire need to recede into the wall. But to defer to the decorum of these suburban crusaders seemed to offer nothing in return. Whereas this irrepressible woman now courting his attention was one with whom, after all, he had enjoyed some strenuous intercourse. It was with a very sudden relish that he realised the censors and the spoilsports could all take a running jump into the Tyne.

As she weaved about him, he made himself move from foot to foot on the spot. However foolish he felt, Lindy's face seemed puckishly pleased – not, at least, contemptuous. It was only as she veered a little to the starboard side, ramming the rear of an unfamiliar couple, that Gore decided she should probably be escorted homeward. When he wrapped an arm round her shoulder and guided her aside he was relieved to find her willing.

'Not ducking out, are you, John?' was Barlow's curt goodbye.

'Yeah. I expect you'll manage. Good luck in Poland.'

It hardly surprised Gore that tonight's sitter at number thirty-two was a lithe and diminutive Asian girl, Eskimo-like as she zipped herself into a voluminous quilted parka.

'What did Lindy say she'd give you?'

'Ah, she say thirty pound? Cos it Saturday yah?'

This was the extent of what Gore had in his wallet. As he handed over the notes he peered past the girl's padded shoulder to the drained bottle of Smirnoff Red and smudged glasses on Lindy's low coffee table. This, he assumed, was one the cocktail princesses had polished off earlier.

Upstairs he found her in half-light stretched out and slumbering on her bed, one knee raised and lolling to the right so that the short dress rode up and exposed her lacy black crotch. As he knelt upon the mattress she rolled onto her right side. He lay down behind her, heard a low snuffled snore. There were goosepimples running down her bare left arm. The *framboise* brush-strokes on her cheekbones had smeared sadly. He curled his body into hers, wrapped an arm around her. The surface of the duvet was cold and he felt sluggish, a little sick, but consoled by this closeness to her.

It was, he understood now, a gift she had given him, not yet revoked – not quite. For a while he hadn't dared seize it for himself, preferring to hole up in his cloister. But still, she had given this gift of herself – her sweet, somewhat strained, somewhat distraining person. He believed he could now see something of the novelty this had wrought upon her. For a while his imagination had failed to extend quite so far. And yet, casting his mind back across her moods and manners since the first real day of their acquaintance – the earnestness, the demands, the dissatisfaction – he saw it now. She had invested some version of hope in him – had *needed* him, even if that need was never expressed in quite the moment or manner he thought appropriate.

And for his own part, had she not been a vulnerable embodiment of hope itself? Whatever his failings or misgivings, he had, for once in his life, conducted a romance. This strange Saturday night – hateful at times, at others unnerving – now seemed to him a promising turn in the affair.

She stirred a little under his touch, clasped hold of the hand that lay across her breast. He snuggled closer, cradling her head with his free arm, pressed his nose and mouth to the back of her neck. The slight scent was citric, teasing, delightful. In which little coloured bottle had she dabbled this evening? Loulou? CK One? Her head twisted, she half-moaned and found his lips with hers. It was a kind of goodnight kiss, soft, lips brushing, until he felt her tongue fluttering at his, her warm tail shifting into his lap. He reached and ran his fingers up her thigh, under the tutu-like skirt, to the fine mesh. There was a yearning hollow in his stomach, the desire to get inside of her was very suddenly insistent.

She turned her body into him, now fully alert. But her kiss was withdrawn.

'You've still got your costume on.'

'So have you.'

'I mean the head on your Guinness. Get it off, man. Looks daft.'

She tugged at his clerical collar, held by twin studs inside his high-necked shirt. 'Dunno why you bother. With all that lot.' As he groped to detach it she rolled aside, yawning. 'Oh aye, I remember, you had that *feeling* . . .'

As he set the collar on the bedside table he heard it – muted but unmistakeable, the childish jingle-jangle of a mobile phone. She groaned and delved into the clutch bag on the floor at her side.

'I didn't know you had one of those . . .'

'It's just for work. He'd not pay the bill otherwise.'

'Can't you leave it?'

'It's *work*, man.' She was already stabbing a button and pressing the phone to her ear. 'Aye? Aye . . . Aw God. Whass the matter wi' her? . . . Aw fuck . . . No, I'm not saying that, just give us ten fucking minutes, man . . . Alright.'

She sat up, wincing, and rubbed at her eye with the flat of a palm.

'What was that?'

'Bother. He needs us the night. At the club.'

'Teflon?' In reply she nodded. 'Really?'

'*Aye* really. One of the bar girls, Jane, she got a smack in the face off some gadgy. They've had to take her to the General.'

'Right. Lovely. And you're next into the ring?'

She had hoisted herself from recumbent and was rifling her clothes rail, reaching below the hangers where an assortment of footwear was piled up in mounds.

'Lindy, I'm saying, it's ten o'clock at night.'

'I know that, John. Late for you, I know.'

From the rack she plucked the black leather miniskirt and a white scoop-neck top, and tossed them onto the bed next to Gore.

'And how do you plan on getting there?'

'He's coming to fetch us,' she sighed, reaching behind herself to unzip the short dress.

'So you just drop everything? A bell rings and you answer?'

'I've not got a *choice*, John, I need the work, in case you've not noticed.'

Gore got to his feet. 'He *gives* you money anyway, doesn't he?'

'I'm not a charity case. I've gotta earn me keep.'

'And what about Jake?'

'I *fucking know that*.' She hissed. 'He's asleep, isn't he? He'll not be if you can't keep your fucking voice down. What about *you*? You can stop in for us. I mean, you can, can't you?'

'No, I can't,' he said quietly. 'I would, if I'd known, it's just – I can't explain.'

She was glaring, vindicated. 'Right. That's all it ever is wi'you, John.'

'Oh, you say –'

'Just a quick squirt you were after tonight, then?'

'That's not –'

She flounced round him and out. He yanked up the zipper of his trousers and slumped down onto the edge of the bed – heard a door swinging but not quite closing, the hiss of the shower, towels being yanked from a hook.

Stonily he looked around her room. The gonks, the bottles, the trinkets, all the feminalia on which he had no purchase. The clothes rail. Beneath the forest of frocks and tops, amid the detritus of shoes, the Adidas logo stared back at him. The old orange bag, Stevie's bag, its incongruity amid Lindy's frills somehow more brutish than usual.

Without rising he was able to lean forward and hook the bag's handle, dragging it out of its cover, though the unanticipated weight made his lower back shout in protest. He wrestled the bag into his lap, picked a little at its cracked plastic exterior, then drew the zip across. The old wadded wash-towel bristled up at him, and by inches he tugged it out, bringing forth a few rattling pharmacy-issue boxes. He inspected one such, stamped with a sticker that read TESTAVIRON, stocked with ampoules of clearish liquid. Delving back into the bag he withdrew another cardboard carton, this more tightly packed, and thumbed open the top.

The sight he met put him sharply in mind of the back of his dad's old telecom van – the umpteen boxes and buckets of screws, rivets and widgets. These, though, were bullets – stunningly apparent, a glinting cluster of copper-jacketed live ammunition.

He plunged a hand to the floor of the bag, found and withdrew a black-and-white football shirt, mere swaddling for some concealed package, which he unwrapped as delicately as if it were a gift he wished to gaze upon one last time before relinquishing. He was fascinated by his own calm, surprised too as he yielded to the need to trace a finger along the blue-black metal barrel. The slubbed grip seemed also to invite fingers wrapped around it. Some better angel counselled him otherwise.

His first thought arrived in the voice and tone he knew best: *Gently now. Everything now will need greater care. Higher precaution.*

His next thought, near-sneakily euphoric: *I've got him.*

His next thought: *Did she know?*

Attentive to the thrumming from the bathroom he squared all things away as he had found them. Then he lay back on the bed again, his mind clicking over at high speed.

Presently he heard a thump on the stair, flinched, leapt up and swung the bedroom door. Coulson was ascending two steps at a time to the top landing.

'You again, eh? Where's she at?'

Flummoxed, Gore glanced toward the bathroom door. Stevie nodded and grasped the handle.

'Steve, she's –'

'How, man, it's nowt I've not seen.'

He ploughed blithely in. Gore froze, his scalp crawling.

'*Howay*, Stevie, man!'

'How you. You're late. Eh, I remember that. Has it changed colour? You give it a lick of paint?'

Gore kept staring at the closed door for moments that crawled until Coulson made his exit, grinning, and bounded back down the stairs.

Gore padded down the hall, rapped the door.

'Aye?'

He stepped in. She was towelling herself vigorously, her wet skin pink and blotchy, her pale breasts jogging, the snake tattoo scaling her lumbar region. He studied her.

'What?'

'Do you not have a problem with any of this?'

She straightened, he saw the tension in her shoulders, then she turned and her mouth was clenched, babyish, tears being fought back. What came out of her at last was an aggrieved gasp.

'I can't *believe* – can't *believe* you can't see how it is for me. I mean, who are *you*, man?'

'I'm the one who cares for you.'

'Aw, keep trying, John, someone might believe you. One day.'

'Can you never just *tell* him? Tell him to piss off out of your life?'

'Like you have?'

'I have done, yes. You, but, you don't ever seem to get sick of being – I don't know – *indentured* to him.'

'I'm sick to the back *teeth.* Who am I s'posed to count on, but? Eh? You?'

She was past him again, as though he were a cone on the road.

The top barely came down to the band of the skirt, itself about two inches higher than mid-thigh. Hurriedly she slathered on the Lancôme foundation, drew the arches of her eyebrows, brushed at her lips. Gore remained in the doorway, letting the silence deepen.

'Lindy, I know about the gun.'

She half-turned. 'Eh? What you talking 'bout?'

He had expected to scrutinise her face but there was no need, such was its scowling conviction that he was simply the living end of all things. He ducked his chin to his chest.

'No, sure, that's all I need to know.'

'What you *talkin'* about, but? Is that what you said? "Gun"?'

He shook his head and she waved an impatient hand, turned to scribbling on a sheet of drawing paper. 'Well, gan on then,' she muttered without looking up. 'If you're gannin', I've to lock up.'

'Lindy, it's not because I want to.'

'Then what do you want?'

He sat for some time in his dull parlour, under the harsh bulb, leafing his hardbacked notebook. He poured a glass of water, considered the time on the kitchen clock. Then he climbed the stairs, saw the blue light under the door, rapped gently. The boy had his arms behind his head, the rancour of the depressive as tangible as the overflowing ashtray.

'Tony, there's something I have to ask.'

The boy pushed himself to his side, toward the wall.

'Don't . . . ignore me, please. I'm tired of this and I've not got the time. It's a simple question.' He saw the twitch of the shoulders. 'Your mother told me you have a mobile phone. Just for work, she said. Was it Coulson gave it to you? Just say yes or no, will you? Was it from Coulson?'

'Aye.'

'What for? What did you do for him?'

Some answer was muttered into a pillow.

'What?'

'Said you know what. I kept deck. Lookout for him. Watched his place when he were out.'

'Watched for what?'

Now he had the favour of the boy's dour face. 'Just people. He said there might be people hanging about. After him.'

'What people? Police?'

'Anybody. That's what he said. Anybody. Even his lads, like. Said any of his lads come round I'd to call him. Didn't trust none of them.'

Gore nodded, taking this much onboard for solace. The fit course of action had proposed itself to him at first slyly, now forcibly.

Chapter II

CONSPIRACY

Sunday, 24 November 1996

It was in the act of upturning the collar of his topcoat against the perishing wind that he saw himself, all of a sudden, as a sort of third-rate private eye. That had once seemed to him a compelling make-believe of a job – a licence to watch and wait for the moment to intrude upon the guilty and their plans. Now, somewhere past two on Sunday morning, loitering in a low pedestrian tunnel, the numb cold of the cobbles seeping through the soles of his shoes, he felt only shabbiness and misgiving, more vagrant than detective. A few yards behind him in the shadows of the tunnel were two heavy lidded dump-bins on wheels, full to bursting with ill-sorted garbage. In the wait he had toyed with hunkering down between them, parking his backside on a crushed cardboard box. This until he noticed the trampled sleeping bag and the soiled blankets in the shape of a man, and turned to hoping instead that their owner would not be reclaiming his patch before this vigil was done.

The Quayside was still alive with what remained of Saturday night, people streaming to and fro across the Swing Bridge six feet over his head. For a while a certain trickling number – mainly couples clutching one another – had been making their exit from Teflon's front doors, picking their way toward parked cars. But now the thump of the music seemed to have been permanently stilled, punters coming forth in droves, sweaty and part-exposed to the cold, exuberant or truculent, proceeding on foot or stopping to harangue the few parked taxi drivers. Gore tried to recede into the brickwork as an all-male mob came lurching through the tunnel, kicking stray rubbish and clattering tin cans before them. He kept one eye on those main doors, another on the mesh gates before the fire exit at the side. It was with something of a pang that he observed Lindy leaving arm-in-arm with another young woman, not obviously jaded by the night's labours, sliding directly into the back of a cab.

And there, at last, was his man. For one drastic moment Dougie Petrie was there with him too. But it was only a hand on an arm and a muttered farewell before Petrie ducked back indoors. Then Robbie was headed right, and Gore pushed himself out of the shadows in pursuit, keeping a measured distance, dogging his strides across the cobblestones, past the club and the cars clustered under the High Level Bridge, across a small square where two girls huddled on a bench, high heels crossed, one consoling the other as she wept bitter tears.

'He's not worth it, Lisa,' Gore overheard. 'Honest he's not.'

'He *is*, but.'

Gore was close now, but reckoned a hand on the bullish shoulder would be unwise. 'Robbie?' he ventured.

Wheeling, the young bouncer's headlights flared. 'Aw, Christ *alive*.'

'I have to talk to you –'

'No you don't.'

'– about Coulson.'

'Fuck off out of it, man, how stupid are you?'

'I'm serious, it's vital, will you just hear me – ?'

'Shut *up*, man, get back behind us.'

He strode off at high pace, put yards between them – then ducked sharply right, into some form of narrow alley beside a pub. Gore rounded this same corner and there stood Robbie, glaring through the dimness at the foot of steep-rising stone steps. Two flights up ahead a pair of young lovers were wrapped avidly, selfishly around each other.

In the silence of the staring match Gore looked anew at the heavy brow, the broad nose, the thick trunk, the general demeanour of a defensive footballer, and probably a handsome lad when ill temper didn't so convulse his features.

'Look, I'm sorry, to trouble you. But it's important.'

'Fuck off youse two,' came a casual sneer from on high.

'*You* fuck off, dickless,' Robbie roared, turning, fists clenching. It seemed to do the trick. He spun back to face Gore. 'I'm gunna get in me car. You gan up there' – he jerked a thumb – 'and wait for us. Corner of Forth Street and Railway Street, that tunnel under the railway, y'knaa? I'll fetch you from there.'

Then he darted aside, vanished round the corner once more. Gore weighed his instructions for some short moments, then turned and began the stiff ascent of the Long Stairs, giving the widest possible berth to the surly lovers and some broken glass beyond them. After three flights he was breathless. He surfaced on the Forth Road behind the high wall guarding the lines and sidings of the Central Station, and trod the deserted pavement, past a desolate car park and a row of shuttered lock-ups, until he came to the tunnel. He heard a shimmering whistle, saw a late train trundle by overhead. The tarmac of the tunnel floor was all pigeon shit and feathers, the walls peeling and dripping. He looked down the long steep Forth Bank toward the Queen Elizabeth Bridge, and saw a green Saab steadily gaining ground. As Gore grasped the handle of the front passenger door, Robbie was cranking down the window. 'Nah, you get in the back, scooch yourself right down. Flat.'

Gore obliged mutely, resolved to obey any and all such conditions. As they accelerated away, his cheek pressed to a cool padded cushion behind the passenger seat, he could make out the upper facade of Martin Pallister's office block, his very own window, his glass-and-metal vantage onto the city.

'Where are we going?'

'I'll tell ya when we're there.'

From his low cramped vantage Gore quickly understood that they were fleeting over the Redheugh Bridge into Gateshead. Silence prevailed, until Robbie snapped on the car radio – some inoffensive rock station, but the volume was blistering. Recumbent, Gore assessed what he could see of his driver under the strobing light. A heavy fist on the gear stick, a tattoo of twin samurai swords curving elegantly from bicep to forearm. His hair would probably have been curly if not sheared so short. The hostility he could excuse, for a life so divided surely had to be a factory of tension. Whatever the brusque handling and the cramp, Gore felt his nerves at least steadied by this much progress.

He watched roadsigns and motorway lights streak by across the night sky, a strange lunar landscape, all colour leeched from it. It was a canvas he half-recognised from childhood, from trying and failing to sleep in the back of his father's car as they returned late to Pity Me from some call upon an uncle or aunt. Robbie, though, drove very much faster than Bill, played his music louder, bashed at his horn with impunity.

Gore was starting to feel queasy. They had attained the junction for the Western Bypass and the distance covered was unsettling him anew.

'Robbie, I have to know how far –'

'We're here.'

He was taking an exit off the bypass, pulling into a parade of small convenience shops, reversing and parking. Gore looked to Robbie's glowing dashboard clock. It was 3.34 a.m.

'You want owt?'

He raised himself up and followed Robbie's gaze to the bleary yellow lights of Herbie's Hot-Dogs'n'Burgers. A quiet spot for a quiet chat.

'Could I have a tea?'

Gore stretched his stiff limbs and studied Robbie through the glass as he transacted, pacing, unsmiling still, pushing some coins into a slot machine. On his return to the driver's seat he handed back to Gore a lidded polystyrene cup, molten to the touch.

'Do you mind if I join you up front?'

'Nah, just you stop back there.'

Robbie unwrapped his steaming repast, the hot-grease odour strong in the cramped car. Gore sniffed, sipped, and burned his tongue.

'I'm waitin' then. What ya want?'

'Can I ask first? Who you are?'

'Y'knaa who I am, man, I've telt ya.'

'No, look, I've got to know – *exactly* who I'm talking to. For what I want to say.'

Robbie bit, munched and swallowed, before glancing at him grudgingly. 'I'm DC Robert Chisholm, Northumbria CID. All better now?'

'Thank you.'

'Right, so what then?'

'I've got some information, I think you could do with. For what you're doing. What I assume you're doing.'

'Oh aye? What's that?'

'Well, I mean – you're after Coulson, aren't you? Investigating him?'

Another glance, with some amusement discernible there amid the contempt. 'Might be. Some of what I'm doing. What's it to you?'

'Well – you know. He and I have had this association.'

'Aye, been a bit of a star for you, hasn't he?' He laughed shortly. 'So now you want him shopped, do you?'

'I – made an error of judgement. Stupidly. Didn't see things in the round . . .' Gore caught hold of himself. How much did he intend to explain – confess – in this babbling manner? 'Things have got clearer to me. His influence, in my community, people I know. The range of what he gets up to.'

'Oh aye, he's a busy lad is our Steven.'

'I mean, I realise, he's mixed up in drugs and all of that.'

A short laugh. 'You sussed that one out?'

'I've known, I mean – I gave a funeral for a man called Michael Ash.'

'Nice, was it?'

In the silence Gore felt himself reproved and tongue-tied. 'What I'm saying is, I realise my befriending him was a mistake.'

'He's not a pal you'd want, no. You don't want to get wrong off him neither, but. That might drop you right in the shit.'

'I've already been told to – to leave alone, I think.'

'Off Steve?' Robbie whistled. 'Fuck me. You wanna listen to that.'

Gore sat back, rebuffed again, watching the windows fur up with steam from the rancid takeout, this hopeless dialogue.

'I'd have done something sooner if I'd known he was such a . . . a ringleader.'

'He's not, man, he's just a guard-dog. All he's ever been. He's got an owner, a boss-man, pulls his lead. That's the bugger we're after.'

'Can't you just arrest him? Coulson? I mean, you must –'

'Nah, we can't. Thanks for the idea, but.' The lip was curled. 'What, you reckon I should just drop the act, eh? March in, say "Howay, Steve, the game's up so come quietly, eh?" Nah, thanks, I don't fancy gettin' hoyed out a window with wuh balls in wuh mouth.'

They both heard the muffled chime of a phone. Robbie reached into his coat.

'Well I never. You keep it tight shut now, hear? Not a peep.' He clamped the phone to his ear. 'Stevie, man? Aye. Nah, I'm nearly home. Aye man. Nee bother. Nah, I'm there.' He balanced the phone on his knee. 'See? Good doggie, that Steven. Got a thought for everyone.'

'You sound like you think he's alright.'

'You've had his company. He can be canny. When he's not stamping on your face. That's the laugh of it.' Robbie rubbed at his brow. 'Not all that funny, like. Listen, I'm sure you think you can make yourself useful here, being you're that sort. All you'll do, but, is balls things for me. You think you can tell us owt about Stevie? When I'm working for him, every day? What I told you, it was for your own good – to get you out of the shit. Not so you could go pester us in the street. Put *me* in the shit. Didn't think about that, did you? So if you don't mind, just get yourself home abed and leave alone.' He blew on a handful of chips in his palm and then shovelled them into his mouth. 'I mean, fuck sake, man, if it was as easy as you coming up to me all vexed you think I'd be riskin' me arse like I'm doing?'

'No, I'm sorry. Obviously I don't mean to – insult your expertise.'

'Expertise bollocks. I was just the biggest lad in me year.' He finally swallowed what he had chewed. 'Nah, any bugger can see what you see. But you've got to get it nailed down, man, every last fuckin' thing. Or you've wasted years owa nowt. Some little turd of a brief gets in there and your man's off. He's clever, see. Caldwell, the boss man. Stevie's pretty smart and all.' Another sharp glance backward. *Unlike you*, was Gore's inference. 'Keeps everything in its own little strong-box. The body doesn't know what the head's up to. Stevie does, but neebody else. He's got his lads, you've seen 'em, they're thick as clarts, most of 'em, but they're all tight as a gnat's chuff. You can't get him through his lads.'

In the silence Gore saw his moment, and its hated counterweight, the dread implications of where the moment might lead. 'What about his women?'

'Stevie's? Which one?' Chisholm chuckled. 'They're even tighter, them, man. Nah, I stay out of the red-light stuff, me. No point in nicking Stevie for indecency. Him or Caldwell.'

'Red-light stuff?'

'Aw, taught you summat now, have I? Naw, there's a massage parlour on the Westgate Road. It's Caldwell's. Steve keeps an eye on it. One of his old girly-friends minds it for him. Though I reckon he keeps it on so he can help himself to the stock now and then.'

The disquiet Gore felt was a spider on the nape of his neck. 'Which girl?'

'Dunno. There's a few of 'em, mind. I've not been in the place.'

'Does it have a name?'

'The Damask Rose. Interested, are you? You'll find it in the personals.' He wadded up the greasy wrappings of his supper. 'Are we finished, then?'

The proposal had its dour appeal, offered an end to the interminable night. And yet, he had decided, he could no longer face himself if he shrank or flinched from his own logic.

'No, there's something else.'

'Whey then, spit it out, man. I need me pit.'

'The killings a fortnight ago, the men at that restaurant out in Shields?'

Robbie's fingers drummed the steering wheel. 'What of it?'

'You know Coulson was involved, don't you?'

'I said, what of it?'

'I have . . . I've heard something. I know somebody, who could tell you something, I'm certain. And then – there's evidence I think I can obtain.'

For the first time Robbie shifted his whole body in the seat. 'Who? What? Come on, divvint get all shy now.'

'No, it's not that simple. I need – you need to give me a day or so. I can talk it out with these people, then I can bring you something.'

'Fuck off with that shite, if you know summat tell us now, *I'll* talk to them.'

'No, no, you have to understand. These are people who trust me. Vulnerable people. I can't violate that. I have to protect them.'

'You? Get away, man. Protect how? Now I've sat here with you and you owe us for that, so divvint make us lose wor patience.'

There was an irate finger jabbing toward his face. And yet he had seen this quandary coming, was not deterred. 'I want to help, if I'm going to then it has to be done right. We have to agree, you and I. I have to know these people will be protected. Fine, if not by me then you.'

'This isn't for your benefit, man. You carry on like this and I'll drag you in.'

'You'll be wasting your time.'

He couldn't be sure, but there seemed a new level of interest in the look he was receiving, whatever its boiling disgruntlement.

'Okay. Alright. You give us summat proper, and I'll tell you what we can do about it.'

'No, that's not good enough.'

'Listen, you, I've got a control and a senior officer to deal with, it's not down to me. If it stands up – *if*, I say, whatever the fuck you're talking about – then I'll not ask you anything that doesn't need asking. Alright? Now that's a promise. Divvint you tell me what's fucking good enough. That's my word to you.'

Gore weighed the deal, tersely put and wanting, but from behind his back-seat cordon he saw no further room for manouevre in these talks.

'In a day or so then. I'll be in touch. How do I reach you?'

Robbie started reeling off numbers.

'Hang on, I need to write it.'

'No you don't. Remember it.' He nodded, winced. 'Right. This is where you hop out.'

'How am I supposed –'

'There's a taxi firm owa there.'

No sooner had he found his feet on the gravel than Chisholm was tearing out and away. Gore found the pen in his inner pocket, hurriedly etched the phone number on his palm. As he turned to the cab office, he saw the lights in the small premises blink out. He reached the door to see a shutter wrenched down behind the glass.

I have walked a crooked mile, he told himself, as he had been telling himself mindlessly for hours. He was wet with rain and there was nothing left in his legs, his level of fatigue surreal, near laughable. He had seen the sun struggle up over Dunston and Team Valley, the day break upon Gateshead. He had vied with early traffic across the Redheugh Bridge. Oakwell had slept without him. Now his front door was in his sights.

Shoving the key in the lock, he found it unmoving. Uncomprehending, his hand found the handle, turned it cleanly. *Not possible.* Heat rushed into his face. He stumbled over the threshold, down the hall, looked about the still living room, then made for the stairs.

'You needn't bother.'

He spun and saw Jack Ridley, emerging from the kitchen with a mug of tea. Saw, too, and recognised the particular smoker's apparel arrayed on the sitting-room table.

'God, Jack, you gave me a start.'

'Aye well, sorry. I've had one and all. He's gan off. The lad.'

His step unsteady, Gore returned slowly to the foot of the stairs.

'Gone? Did he say where?'

Ridley threw him a chastening look. 'What do you think?'

'How did you find him?'

'How? Whey, your door were open, so I just assumed, and then – y'knaa. He got a shock and all. Not as bad as what I did. He was putting some stuff in a bag, see, I could tell it were one of yours.'

Ridley sat down at the table. Gore could see his shirt cuffs were damp, as though he had been washing up at the sink. Gore, too, lowered himself into a chair. 'What did you do?'

'I asked him who he was, he telt us he'd been stoppin' wi' you but he was headed off now. I says to him, "Howay, I wasn't born last night."'

'No, he was. Staying over.'

'Aye, well, right enough, he seemed quite sure of hi'sel. I just stood and watched him and he didn't panic or owt. Then he says, "Tell Gore he's gotta keep his promise." I says, "Oh aye, am I your messenger?" I let him gan, but. Seemed to know what he was talking about.' Ridley took up his tobacco pouch. 'Mind you, you'll still want to check all your drawers.'

Gore nodded, weighing the damage, his inner calculations in ruins.

'Was that your problem, then? What you wanted to talk about?'

'You might say.'

'Well then, it's gone. You got lucky.'

Gore shook his head. 'No, that was – that was just the start of it.'

'He's in bother, is he? The lad? With Coulson?'

Gore nodded.

'Then he's better off away. Your luck's still in.'

'Is that your answer to everything, Jack?'

Ridley's expression was such as to imply that the folly of Gore's remark carried its own punishment, with no need for rebuttal.

'I'm sorry. I suppose . . . you can say you told me so.'

'I try not to say things that are no bloody use when it's all past helping.'

Gore lowered his head toward his crossed arms on the table. 'What am I going to do?'

'I'd be surprised if there were owt you could. If there's one thing I know, John, it's not to get mixed up in other people's problems.'

Gore jerked up his head, ready with a glaringly obvious rejoinder, and was gripped at the same moment by its glaring redundance.

'I mean, you've got enough to manage, haven't you?' Ridley added in afterthought, and to Gore's mind, needlessly.

They were good clean people, Barlow's lot, no doubt about it, but for all the general efficiency of the set-striking operation certain detritus from the night before lingered in corners. From behind a curtain Gore turned up several piles of Shield Society pamphlets, and tossed them into a black plastic bin-liner. Shifting the chairs from stores, he proposed to Rod Moncur that they make the usual seating grid a good deal smaller, perhaps six rows of six. As it transpired, they could not fill even these.

As advised by Monica, Gore announced that the Saturday dance had raised a sum of four hundred and seventeen pounds for St Luke's coffers. The news seemed to impress a good many of the old folk. There ought to be a party just for them, he decided – a farewell party, the sooner the better.

He felt his own exhaustion turning a touch slap-happy. For his reading he decided, for his own delectation, to preach a little fire and brimstone – just for the sport of it, to read the words as if he had written them. What would it mean, after all, to give oneself such power to judge? He turned to a long-favourite passage from Ephesians.

'Finally my brethren, be strong in the Lord and in the power of his might. Put on the whole armour of God, that ye may be able to stand against the wiles of the devil.'

He had, at least, decided what had to be done. One door closed but another opened, and once one dragged one's feet forward by one step, so many more became obvious, beholden, irreversible.

'For we wrestle not against flesh and blood, but against principalities, against powers, against the rulers of the darkness of this world. Against spiritual wickedness in high places . . .'

He paused and stared out intently at the drooping and the infirm, their weathered scalps and greying heads, some nodding, turning over in their hearts, perhaps, their own definition of the wicked in the world.

'Wherefore take unto you the whole armour of God, that ye may be able to withstand in the evil day, and having done all, to stand.'

Afterward the old lady from Old Benwell whose name he thankfully remembered as Lillian took his hand to assure him he was 'doing very well'. In his nonchalance he suggested she take the lectern for the following week and read a lesson of her choice. She blinked agitatedly behind her heavy lenses, grew shy and flustered.

'No, please, next week. So long as there is a next week, eh?'

And then she looked a little startled, wounded even, and he instantly rued both his restive mood and his thoughtless phrasing. Had they but the time and she the interest, he would have taken her aside and outlined the whole nature of his preoccupation.

He was ready to keel over by the time dusk drew in. But he girded himself and dialled her number. Very soon he had some cause for regret.

'Can I call on you tonight?'

'No you can't. I'm working anyhow.'

'Where?'

'In town. It's not your business.'

'Lindy, I need to see you.'

'I don't want to see you.'

'Lindy, don't – please.'

She replaced the receiver and left him with no choice. He slumped toward the kitchen, intending to brew strong black coffee, something sour and sharp enough to slap his face into the right-facing vantage of what remained to do with this day.

Chapter III

RED LIGHTS

Sunday, 24 November 1996

Was this, then, a customer? He answered all too many descriptions – a pudding of a man in work suit and anorak, bespectacled, briefcase in hand, a shaggy skirt of hair round his bald monkish crown. Even from twenty yards, through the fallen dark, past the traffic lights and across the road, Gore could make out a womanish bulge of white-shirted gut over belt.

He slowed as he reached the end of the presentable Victorian terrace, where the lights glowed homely just as in every other window, and he bent and pushed open the gate, plodded up the steps, buzzed at the door. Within moments he was admitted and out of the cold.

My double, my brother, Gore chided himself.

And then: *No. He knows what he's doing and he just does it, goes about it normally, as if it were normal.*

And perhaps it was – more so than this watching and waiting, this queer and questionable compulsion into which he had lapsed.

Enviable, even. He strolls right on in without a qualm.

At this moment Gore would sooner have walked into freezing waters until they closed over his head. But he had seen her go in, and so he had to follow. Had seen Yvonne go in and her go out of her front door. Had trailed her up the Hoxheath Road, onto the Westgate, a little heartbroken by the unenthused slump in her gait. She was wearing her long skirt and short red jacket, just like their first long afternoon together, save for a knitted scarf at her neck. He was in his seaman's coat and jeans, just like their first tryst, save that he had shoved a claw-hammer down into the deep inner pocket before leaving his door – a lunatic's notion, one over which his conscience still glared at him in disbelief. And yet it seemed the night for such, a night when all fond reason seemed to have fled the house.

His back to the wall, he heard church bells chime. Could it be seven? From this same cold spot he had seen boys tramping home from Sunday sport, seen bored men and women through the windows of cars and buses, hastening home from work. And her, only just arriving for the start of same. All the world was industrious but he. He needed to move his feet.

But it seemed a hard threshold to cross. He couldn't conjure a picture of what lay beyond, knew only that his expectations were at rock-bottom. And still a traitor in his head was poking him with the notion that he didn't have to do what he had told himself he must – that he could yet melt away.

It was true, he could have begun to question his corporeal existence, to doubt he even cast a shadow, were it not for the knot in his stomach, the dragging wreck in his mind that was the pile-up of days, weeks, months of ruined judgement. There was, he knew, nothing left for him, no alternate reality other than the need to finally see what he so long feared – see it under lights with his own two eyes – the evil spirit in the corner.

The choice was made for him, the door opening before he could prod the buzzer, opened by a gentleman making haste and seeking no eye contact. Gore wiped his feet on a bristly mat and mounted the stairs, each of them groaning beneath the poor carpet, a white-gloss door gaining ahead of him. It was ajar and, gingerly, he pushed it open, to be confronted by an unpeopled tableau of modest domesticity.

A small cubby of a white kitchen, deserted, the breakfast bar strewn with papers. Low fluorescent light, modest accoutrements, an aluminium wall clock ticking along, the *Sunday Sun* spread open, kettle on the boil and microwave oven shuddering on full power. Somewhere else in this flat, he knew, a television was on, and a man was expressing himself behind a closed door. He looked to his left, saw a pair of tubular nesting chairs around a low table strewn with pornographic magazines, their corners flipped and frayed. Save for this wrinkle, he could have claimed to have waited for doctors in some less salubrious receptions. But never alone, never so full of foreboding.

He looked over the kitchen counter – drawers half open, an open ring-bound book, names over columns on a ruled page. LEANNE, KIRSTY, SUNEE, LANA, BARBRA.

'You getting seen to, pet?'

He turned as if stung and saw a woman – fixed his eyes instinctively to her face rather than her babydoll nightie and briefs of matching black. Her eyes were small and close around a prominent nose, lacquer making a starched gable-hood of her long black hair. She had the manner of one cosily at home for the evening, but none too bothered by intrusion.

'Is Claire seein' to you, pet?'

In the silence the microwave oven began to ping.

'Aw, bugger.'

The dark woman moved swiftly past him, took up oven gloves, was calling through another archway to this Claire of hers. Then the telephone on the counter was ringing too. Gore sidled into the long corridor from whence the woman had emerged. He was confronted by an open door through which were framed a glum assortment of women, all bare shoulders and pale legs, slumped into a tatty once-plush settee, curtains drawn, television glowing. Heads and eyes slowly revolved to him, sluggish smiles in tow.

'Sorry . . .'

He ducked out, saw nowhere to go but the end of the corridor – took hesitant steps further, past a closed door, past a doorway into a bathroom that exuded a dank odour not quite masked by the sickly deodorant smell he realised he had been smelling since he came through the door. Now he was staring into a gaudy pink-painted bedroom – a bed-and-breakfast option for a teenage female runaway.

''Scuse me?'

Behind him another jaded woman was now filling the corridor, bottle-blonde, sunken-eyed and ballooningly plump in a jumper and sweatpants. She seemed familiar, was giving him a close look in turn.

'Hiya, sorry, I was on the lav. Can I help?'

'I'm not sure.'

'Well, why don't you step back into the lounge there, have a bit shufty? I'm off now, see, but me colleague'll assist you. Lindy?'

'What?' Behind him, that voice, issuing from the final doorway down the hall. No, he realised with a sickening plummet of heart into gut – this part he had simply not braced himself for.

He turned and it was Shackleton who loitered on the threshold, the familiar look of enmity mutating into one of hard amusement.

'Eh, what the fuck are *yee* deeing? Jesus, man. How, Lind, look who's here.'

Gore stepped forward, since there was no turning back. For a moment he believed Shackleton would bar the door with a swell of his chest. But he stepped aside.

There in the midst of some ghastly black-walled room, lit solely by candles, she was down on her knees, a paisley do-rag tied round her head, a wadded J-cloth in her hand, a spreading stain on the crimson tufted carpet and some spray-gun ammonia close at hand.

Was she seeing him as she stared? What was within? He couldn't hazard.

'Dear me. I'll let you's two alone a minute, shall I?'

He heard Shackleton but did not see him. Heard the door close. And he had to look aside, at the black gloss on the walls, the black satin curtains, the black-sheeted bed with its black vinyl headboard – all a dirty sort of a black, fit for a black mass on a wet afternoon. The ammonia odour was mingling with some foul undercurrent.

And she? She was rubbing her hands on the knees of her denim skirt, studying them as she did so.

'Looking for me, were you?'

'Yes. I came to find you.'

He made to help her to her feet but she was launching herself upward, and he saw at once that she was boiling, swelling with temper.

'Look, don't –'

'Why?' She shoved with both hands at his sternum and he was painfully jarred, flung up both his own hands in defence, which she tried to flail her way through still. 'Come *on*, say. Why? Why the *fuck*, man?'

'I had to know. The truth.'

'Happy now, then, are you? Seeing us like this?'

'No, but I understand now. I know I've been wrong.'

'Oh, wrong? *You*, wrong?'

'Yes, wrong, but it's okay now.'

'It's not okay for me. Not for *me*, John.'

His toneless responses seemed to have sapped at her. She rubbed her face, paced away to the darkened window, turned, then thought better, then turned again, her arms crossed in defiance. 'Big kick for you, is it? Slipping around, fucking *spying* on us?'

'No, Lindy, of course not, it's the opposite.'

'Then why do it?'

'Because I care for you. Because you can't go on doing this.'

'I don't *do* this, you know? I don't *fuck* anybody. If that's what you're thinking. Or I dunno, is that maybe a letdown for you?'

'No, God no, you don't understand . . .' He had to lower himself down to sit on the edge of the odious black bed, for it all seemed hopeless, insupportable, unremitting. He could see the livid hurt in her, could feel it under his own skin, wanted so badly to transmit to her how he had lived with the same despondency and still found this path through it.

'What don't I understand?'

'That you can't stay like this. I don't just mean this . . .' He waved a hand. 'I mean this *mire* you're in, Lindy. Because of him. When you only need to take a step out of it. Cut the link. You can. Leave it, just walk away.'

'I can't.' Her voice was flat. 'I've not got a choice. You're a fool if you think that.'

'No. No, that's wrong, you *do*. I've thought that way, but it's wrong, you say it's your life but it doesn't *have* to be. There's another life.' He realised that some part of what was coming from his mouth had been foreign to him until this very moment. 'This one, it's a poison to you.'

'What do you care?'

'I love you. I want to take care of you.'

This seemed the gravest outrage yet.

'Aw look, I just want you to *go*, man. Now. I mean it, really. Before I –' And a stifled shriek came out of her, a painful compound of hurt and frustration.

'I'll go, I'm going. But you're coming with me.'

'I'm fucking *not*.'

'You are, you have to, Lindy I need you to.'

'Don't be *stupid*.'

'I'm not going without you.'

'You're an *idiot*. They were right. I thought you knew better.'

'Who's "they"?'

She almost laughed. 'Whey, everyone, man.'

'I can protect you from them. I can, I promise you. I know what to do now. I love you, and I'll protect you.'

She stared at him as if each word, each phrase, worsened the injury – to her face, to her shaking head, her wounded eyes and sorry mouth, the thumbnail now being worried between her front teeth.

There was a thud at the door and it was thrust open, Shackleton sweating displeasure. 'Lindy, *howay* for fuck's sake, there's a fella, you're wanted.'

'A *minute*, man.'

The door swung to. Gore came forward, got his hands around her arms, and though she flinched and writhed it lacked conviction, for he wrested her into him. His plans had dwindled to nothing, lacking all substance. Feeling had surged up in their stead.

'Lindy, are you hearing me? I love you.'

'Shut up, man, you don't, you just don't.'

He took hold of her head, kissed her brow, took her hands in his and kissed them, laid a hand on her throat. 'I've said, I was wrong, I treated you wrongly. I want to make good. I have to. Because you're everything to me. You are. You're all I have, nothing is anything without you.'

He had said it and, with a force that ran the length of him, he believed it. Then he released her in fright as Shackleton charged back in.

'Right, fuckin' *shift* yourself – you and all, Gore.'

Gore's chest was so drum-taut with feeling he feared he had nothing left for this new assault, this hard-faced bruiser coming right at him. At the last he was redeemed.

'Leave us be, man, we're gannin'.'

Gore followed Shackleton's glare in wonder, for this seemed a small marvel.

'Whaddaya mean, "gannin'"?'

'Home. Gannin' home.' She was untying her do-rag.

'You're fuckin' not, Lindy. You canna.'

'I'm sick, man, I can't do this tonight.'

Shack's bullet-head swung toward Gore. 'This your doing? Eh? Eh, dickhead, I'm *talking* to you.'

He looked as if he could strike, and if this was a fight, Gore knew, he was already doomed: the hammer in his coat would be extracted and lodged in his skull.

'Leave him, Shack man.' Her amazing calm seemed that of profound weariness. 'I'll square it with Stevie, I'll call him, it'll all be on us. Alright? So now you can fuck off an' all.'

Shack was looking from one to the other of them now. In the low candlelight his skull looked as though it had been carved from white stone. But he was blinking, brow tilted, his tongue working behind his teeth. The visible thought process was spectacular.

'Alreet then. Alreet. Run along.'

Gore looked to Lindy. Whatever her self-command, she clearly had not expected this either.

'Thank you,' Gore heard himself say.

'Thank *you,*' came the sneering response, just a little menace exuded, as was this man's wont. And yet their way was unimpeded.

So he walked behind her, legs a little shaky, passing a slack-jawed young man stood gormlessly by the reception. Her calm stunned him, but was a blessing of a sort. The next station could only be worse, probably bitter and ugly, calling for deeper reserves of resolve. She had put him on the spot again, condemned him to try to see it through.

'Steve, are you listening to us?'

Yes and no. He heard her, mostly. But it was an effort of will, and there was a limit to what he could usefully contribute. By his reckoning they had already spoken enough tonight of this difficult juncture in Ally's career.

'I've gotta know what you think, but.'

'About what?'

'Well, should I try it with this other band? Or do I stick with this lot? Or, I dunno, do I just pack it in?'

Stevie saw no doubt – her singing wasn't to the standard of her dancing, and the showband she had been fronting for a few months had clearly told her as much that afternoon. His own afternoon had been spent still drinking down the spoils of a Saturday passed at Newcastle Racecourse, the first meeting of the jumps, where a risky fifty quid at twelves on Take No Prisoners had paid off in spades. He had been on Johnny Walker and Carlsberg ever since, burning through a rare elation rather than slaking any special thirst. Now his tandoori mixed grill was being set down before him, and he realised that his eyes had been a good deal bigger than his stomach.

'Steve. I'm asking you, please. Have you got a view?'

'Aw, have I not fucking said?'

'Don't be so *irritable*, God.'

'I'm *not*, man, I've *said*. There's only way to gan about it – you've just gotta decide what you wanna do and set yer'sel to it. Y'knaa? See where you want to be in the end, do what you need to get there. It doesn't *matter* what any other bugger thinks.'

'Do you not like wuh voice, then?'

'I like everything about you, pet.'

It was no lie. When they first met , when Mickey Ash had started squiring her to Zeus – then she had the same twee powder-pink prettiness, the same flesh-baring compulsion he'd seen in a million Geordie blondes. Now her skin seemed airbrushed, there was copper in her variegated coiffure, her wardrobe was cutaway but classy. She was pure sleek. He had thought her dim, too, in those early days – thought that a fact when she took up with Dougie. But she had shown herself shrewd and attentive, had chose her moment well to tell him she had always been shy of him. There was, he had decided, a certain grace in their being together now, after all this time. She was adaptable, too, fazed by next to nothing, certainly not by his now making camp at her little walk-up flat on Fenkle Street, commandeering her tidy bedroom with several crates of his rough gear.

Something, though, had changed. This night alone had begun all wrong, he saw as much in her face when he pitched up in his pub suit of leather and jeans. He had thought it a night to relax. She had a definite agenda.

'If it's gonna work for me I've got to do it now or not at all. That's if you and me are serious, like.'

'What's not serious about you and me?'

'You know what.'

Decidedness – that was the quality in her he had never expected, just the thing for a nice untaxing evening. He nearly laughed. 'Ally, just – think about it a minute, eh? Do you *want* a kid? Really? Or is it just the idea you've started fancying? Cos of what's-her-face?'

'Don't be bloody rotten. What do you take us for?' She poked at her plate. 'I'll tell you this for nowt, if we'd a child you might give us half the thought you give them others.'

'What you talkin' 'bout?'

'You *know*, man – Karen and Lindy.'

'Ally, divvint go down that owld road. It's just – it's a fact, right, I divvint *need* another bairn.'

'Well, I think you do. Cos it's not like you've got the ones you've *got.*'

'*Bollocks*, man. They're my kids, I see 'em when I want to, and that's all – it's all squared and agreed with the mothers. What?'

'You. "The mothers", like. Is that what they were? Just the little baby-ovens for you? Incubators?'

'Nah. Wasn't a bit like that. It's just how things turned out. Didn't turn out like I was meant to be with 'em. Neither of 'em.'

'Cramped your style, did it? Couldn't live with 'em once they got a bit broody?'

'It were nowt like that. Bloody hell. Tell you what – *you* but, *you're* gannin' the right way about it.'

It was a try at levity, buttressed by a version of the Sharky smile. But she had taken offence and, so decided, would not be shifting. Her fork sifted her plate as if food itself had been the slightest pretext, now indigestible.

'It's like you don't ever think about the future . . .'

He rubbed at his temple, disbelieving. Truly she had picked a strange moment to turn slow-witted. 'Ally, the future's all I *ever* think about. It's just there are times you've just got to get from day to day, nowt else. Deal with what's right in front of you. Can you not see that?'

'Whey, that's what *I'm* having to do – cos of you. I don't know where I am, Steve. You use me flat like a lodging, you don't tell us owt why. If you're thinking of packing in what you're doing, *I've* got to do something, we've got to think where we're –'

'Have I not said? How many times? I'm *not* fuckin' packing in. They're not *real* problems, these, none of 'em. All it needs is time and we'll sort them, man. So will you give it a fuckin' *rest*?'

He was leaking adrenalin, he knew, burning off aggressive carbohydrates, and it was wrong that she suffer the force of this pent-up feeling, the price he was paying for being in a kind of hiding, permanently switched off and shy of attack mode. The fury reared up in him suddenly, he saw himself doing it and still couldn't arrest it.

They ate, then, in silence, until Stevie's phone pulsed in his coat pocket, and he rummaged for it thankfully.

'Do you have to? Answer that?'

'I do.'

The hubbub of the restaurant was hopeless, so he rose and stalked toward the door, only to find a pint-sized waiter darting to his side.

'Sir, excuse me, where do you go?'

'You're kidding, aren't you pal? I just got me *plate*, man. That's wuh lass owa there.'

Outside he paced about the stoop, glancing back through a porthole in the door at Ally, who still wasn't eating.

'Aye, what?'

'Where are you?'

'I'm at a mate's, where are you, *Brian*?'

'The Damask. We've had some bother. Lindy's pissed off, there's nee-body on.'

'Eh? Pissed off where?'

'Off home. It was Gore, see. He come round, started –'

'Gore? The fuck was *he* doing?'

'I divvint knaa, do I? He just showed up. It was him talked her into it, like, pissing off, looked like to me.'

'What, and you just let 'em off, the pair of 'em?'

'Whey, what was I s'posed to do? Give her a smack? Or him, like?'

'You're supposed to use a bit of judgement, man. Jesus, you coulda given fuckin' Gore a clout, that would'na taken owt.'

'Well, see, I didn't know that was your view on things, Steve.'

'Aw, fuck me. So what? What are you doin'?'

'What do you think I'm doing? I'm gunna lock up, send the girls home.'

'Like fuck y'are. Divvint you fuckin' move your arse, Shack, I'm gunna gan fetch her back.'

Silence from the subordinate. *'Aye, well . . .'*

'Aye *right*. You hear us?'

'Aye, I do. Whatever you say, boss . . .'

Some valve in his head had come clean off its thread. Every association in his life now a source of disorder in his house, a cause of calamity. She, perhaps, had been overdue her little revolt.

He? Stevie could not have foreseen the aggravation that was John Gore, not if he'd been given a million years.

Back at table he sat only to spoon up some hasty mouthfuls and swig from the three-quarter pint.

'Listen, I've gotta do a quick bit business, but you stay –'

'Aw *what*, Steve?'

'You stay and finish, here's the money. I'll see you back at yours.'

'Who was it? Was it Shackleton?'

Old Shack – nobody liked him, he didn't care. Stevie thought it almost enviable. He tossed his chin in the affirmative.

'Just leave it, man. Can you not just?'

'Don't tell us to fuckin' leave it. I'll be an hour. Hour tops.'

He threw on his leather and stomped out, cleaving the air, his boots hardly touching the ground en route to the car park off the Gallowgate. There as he left it, the heap-of-shit cut-and-shut Corsa that Shack had secured him from his mate in Shiremoor, where the Lexus was garaged. A joke vehicle, but functional, negligible, permitting him to feel he had slipped into sweet anonymity round town. For that much service, he supposed, he had *Brian* to thank, since *Brian* always had a sharp eye for a deal.

Chapter IV

RECKONINGS

Sunday, 24 November 1996

He sat on the faux-leather sofa beside his subdued beloved, perched on a knife edge of his own forging, quietly going mad. By their abrupt return they had disturbed Yvonne from her planned viewing. Now she slurped at a mug of tea intended to send her kindly on her way. But she seemed reluctant to quit the faux-leather armchair, burbling in her clotted accent of how the boy was no bother but was surely a bit spoiled. Lindy nodded at the news that Jake had been safely abed since eight-thirty, though his toys were all rudely upturned around the laminate floor as though he had been abducted.

Amid the blather Lindy favoured him with half of a smile, a godsend of sorts, for in the taxi she had seemed remote. 'Glakey', wasn't that her word? After a fruitless phone call to her friend Claire, she had slipped down the seat and into silence.

'I'm proud of you,' he said after a while.

'I'm doing this for me, John. For me.' There were pensive moments before she added, 'So I hope you've got a plan, mister.'

Now, though, it was as if little of note had occurred that night, other than what she told her auntie – that she had developed a chill and planned to curl up. Nonetheless they were both smoking cigarettes, sharing the ashtray, the sliding door to the garden shoved aside. Perhaps she had attained some prized sense of relief. It was too bad he had to wreck it. She was putting off her phone call, but he could not delay his. Nor could he be sure of the size of disturbance he was liable to cause in her house. He had toyed with the notion of smuggling it out, and seen that for futile. It would have to be found in its place. She could be no party to his process until it was done. So he would have to do it, then persuade her of its wisdom. He would have to vouch for the integrity of Robbie Chisholm, an unknown, perhaps unknowable quantity. It was a headlong leap into the dark, but the moment had come, was already past, nothing left but the fall.

He smiled, touched her arm. 'I'm just for the bathroom,' he murmured, and rose, went to the stairs, climbed them calmly, but turned right on the landing and proceeded by tiptoe into her bedroom. He crouched and with deft hands drew aside the clothes on the rail. There, he saw only the timeworn mounds of her pumps, heels and trainers.

He felt needles behind his eyes – stood, cheated, despairingly silent, wanting to kick things over, looked about him wildly. Everything seemed messily available to his futile inspection, no other nooks or crannies. He yanked uselessly at the drawers. Why now? When hid for so long in plain sight? Who was thwarting him, laughing at him? He dropped to the floor, on his knees and elbows – and there it was beneath the bed, amid fluff and hair, shoved onto its side. He wrenched it out, pulled the zip halfway, determined that the packing was as he had left it.

He sat down on the bed, by the bedside telephone – then, indeterminate, rose and went to the door, listened and heard still the aimless chatter below. And so he pulled the door closed, retrieved the scrap of paper from his wallet, took up the phone, dialled the number. It rang five times.

'Hallo?'

His voice lurched out of him as a hiss. 'Robbie, it's John Gore. I –'

'Can't bloody hear you, man, speak up.'

He struggled up to a notch just below conversational. 'It's John Gore.'

'Aw aye?'

'I've got what I promised you.'

'You what? What was that then?'

'A gun. A gun, it's Coulson's but I've got it, how do I get it to you?'

There was a pause, a discordant crackle, a new hush.

'A gun. You serious?'

'Yes, it's in front of me for Christ's sake, how do I get it to you?'

'Don't you do a fucking thing, I'll come to you. Jesus. Don't touch owt neither, you hear? Where are you?'

The anticipated question, and yet still it loomed, a giant.

'Where are you, John?'

He was waist-deep, neck-deep, sunk and drowned. No compromise.

'The Oakwell Estate, Hoxheath. It's number thirty-two.'

'Whose place is it?'

'Her name's Lindy.'

'Not Lindy who works at Teflon?'

'Yes, but this is what I meant, she doesn't know anything about this, she has to be kept out of it.'

'We'll sort that all out, she'll be fine. She's there with you?'

'She's in the house. But she doesn't know, see.'

'Thirty-two Oakwell. Right. I'll be there in maybe twenty minutes. Just sit tight and keep your head on.'

Gore set down the phone, feeling the merest euphoric twinge through the knot of trepidation in his gut. He stood, stepped out onto the landing, heard nothing now. Edging to the top of the staircase, he craned over the banister and knew then that Yvonne was being shown to the door. He crept back to the bedroom, sat at the foot of the bed, pushed the Adidas bag to one side, and waited. Then he heard the footfalls on the stairs, and felt some measure of blood and vigour drain from him. She came through the door, and he met her jaded gaze.

'What you doing up here? Were you on the phone?'

'Yeah. Sorry. I just had to talk to a friend.'

'Oh aye? Is this your house now?' She came and sat beside him, gave him a look he thought plaintive – rueful, unimpressed and yet mildly indulgent. 'I'm not just giving you the keys here, y'knaa. Just cos you love me.'

'We have to talk, Lindy.'

She sighed, profoundly. 'I dunno I can manage much more. Can it keep for the morning?'

He laid a hand on hers. 'We know each other now, don't we? No more secrets?'

'If you say so,' she murmured.

With his free hand he hoisted up the hold-all between them. That flare in her he saw revive as if sparked.

'The fuck you doin' with that?'

'Tell me what's in it.'

'What's it *to* you, man?'

'Because no more secrets, Lindy.'

His invocation of principle seemed an added annoyance. 'John, I don't *know* what's in it. It's Stevie's, it's his bloody . . . bag of tricks. I've always kept it for him when he's asked us. Look, he used to sell them drugs for weightlifters, the steroids? He'd ask us to hang on to his stash sometimes, case he got raided. Alright? So that's why. It's not my *business*, but.'

'Okay. That's good.'

'What's good about it?'

'Because we have to get our stories straight.'

She winced at him. He summoned his nerve. 'The man I just spoke to – he's a policeman. Northumbria CID. He's coming here. So we can sort this out.'

'You what?'

'He's a plainclothes man, undercover, he's – you'll see, you'll know him.'

But she was clutching at her lolling head, face purpling. 'Police? Coming here? Aw, what have you *done*, you stupid bastard?'

'We've agreed, it has to stop, Lindy. Well this is how.'

She groped for the bag in his lap and he pushed it aside, to the floor. But she swung an open palm at his face, and he felt the smart of her ring finger on his cheek.

'*Why* did you do that? Why? How can you be so – *stupid*?'

She punched and grabbed at him, and he tried to restrain her yet her vehemence defied him. They were struggling. She had her fingers on his face, her nails scoring.

Now the doorbell was being rung, insistently, angrily.

He managed to rise, aimed at the door, found her still snagged on him, yanking at him. 'You mad? Where do you think you're going?'

He resolved that he would yank her along with him if need be, but the drag was more cumbersome than he had supposed. They were tussling still down the stairs, she flapping and forcing herself in front of him, pummelling him. And then she must have misstepped, for she was tumbling down the last half-dozen steps, thumping and flailing into the facing wall at the foot of the staircase.

He hastened to her. She slapped at his hand – 'Fuck off!'– and he felt himself let go of certain hopes that had lingered. He had not wanted it this way, but the door needed opening, and an amen put to affairs.

Instead he heard a key turning. They both did, and her face was stricken.

He turned and saw Coulson in the doorway – in his hard boots and his leather, his face a mask of rancour.

'The fuck's gannin on here?'

Gore felt all his resolve crash through the floor. Panic had hold of him now as Coulson shouldered his way into the space. Lindy was regaining her feet, very awkwardly.

'Y'alright, Lind? You hurt?'

'Steve, man, you've gotta get on. Get out, it's for your own good.'

'Aw, I'm not leaving. Naw, I'm taking you. Get your bloody –'

'You've *gotta*, Steve. Police are coming.' Gore shot a look at her, and she at him, and he saw her in the act of relinquishing some stake of her own. 'He's shopped you. Your bag, he's shopped you for it.'

He saw it fully now – too late, he knew – her dread, conceivably worse than his own.

'He has, ask him.'

Coulson's dead eyes were trained hard at Lindy's and he was breathing oddly. A bitter dragging cry came down from the top of the staircase.

'Mam, what's happenin'?'

Lindy was bounding up those stairs again. Gore felt Coulson's dense, skin-crawling hostility turned solely upon him. The space was tight and this bull of a man filled it. No means of escape, no possible mitigation.

'She right? Did you, then? Shop us?'

'You have to stop, Steve. They're coming for you.'

'Who's coming? Eh? Who?'

The shove to Gore's chest drove him against the wall and near off his feet. Coulson was shaping his body and Gore flung up his hands, but the flat hard heel of a palm flew out between them and rocked him on his feet, rattled his jaw. The speed and the static before his eyes dazzled him, and as he listed the right fist came at him squarely through his feeble guard.

The pain was as if a rail-spike had been hammered through the meat and bone of his face. His vision crumpled and muddied, his legs were giving way – he grasped a hold of the newel post of the banister, but felt himself lolling round it, hopelessly exposed. He wanted very badly to raise his groggy head, and yet he had the ghastly sensation of his face filling with blood like a wineskin. That, and the grim maddened monster, implacably over him.

'Stop, Steve, please,' he managed to groan, before he sensed the pivot in Coulson's body and saw something of the boot hurtling at him, believing that his head was to be snapped clean off his neck in the fractional second before oblivion.

She had no choice but to try to contain the shrieking boy in her arms as she hurtled back down the stairs. She could risk but a hand to grab at Steve while he kicked the prone, inert Gore repeatedly in the stomach.

'Stevie, *don't*, man, you'll *kill* him.'

'Get *away*, he'll fuckin' –'

'Why did you kick him in the *head*?'

'Shut *up*, man. I oughta kick it the fuck *in*, the *cunt*.'

And he lifted one boot and crashed it down on Gore's collarbone. Jake, whose screams had become whimpers, broke into wails once more.

'Steve, man, please, look, there's blood coming out his *ears*.'

'Shut *up*, you. That doesn't mean owt.' He wrenched Jake from her arms and swung the boy round, dumping him into the armchair. Then he seized the fabric of Lindy's shirt and wrenched her toward him. She could smell the drink on him and her stomach turned, for she had watched him hurt people before but never with such fervour.

'Fucking pull yourself together, woman,' he spat. 'Tell us what he done.'

'He just said he called someone, they were coming.'

'Where's me bag? Upstairs? Your room?'

She nodded and he thrust her aside. She regained her balance, looked at her terrorised son, his livid streaming face, and then at Gore, unconscious, his nose grotesquely flattened amid bluish bruising and shocked laceration. *Don't freeze*, she told herself, even as something heavy and frigid clogged her veins.

Noises carried through the hallway door, from the alley outside, and she turned to see through the frosted panel of the door – a human figure, first one then another, perhaps another. She ran to the door, fumbled out her keys, turned the lock, turned back to the staircase, her panic total. As she looked blindly this way and that, there was a grievous thump on the door that shook its frame, then another, a splintering, and the door swung wildly and battered the wall. Men were filling the hallway, men in black balaclavas and windcheaters. She gaped, turned and ran for the living room and her son.

'Don't hurt us, please.'

But she couldn't reach him, and then there were hard hands over her eyes and mouth.

Stevie heard the unholy commotion and was stock-still for one moment, knowing himself trapped, aware too of a torpor round him like a cold fog. Impulse was his only guide. Instantly he unlatched the window, seized the hold-all and hurled it over the neighbouring wall. In the same moment he resolved to follow, shoved the glass frame as wide as it would go, grasped on to the frame. But he was just too large to go through by any means other than a sickening plummet headlong to the paved patio below. Maddened by his brute plight, he wrenched himself back out in time to see the bedroom door smashed wide, and in that sight of hoods and balaclavas he was deluged by dreadful realisations – his own misreckonings, the nature of his betrayal, the shape of dread – for these were not policemen but soldiers, blades in their hands, two feet of long shining steel.

The first assailant was scrambling at him across the bed, and he threw the right and struck relenting flesh, but his other flank had been taken by a second man, a canister thrust in his face and he received the toxic jet full-on, felt the dire piercing chemical burn, his eyes gushing pain. He bellowed and choked, lumbered and lashed about him. His hands were still on his face when he felt the cleave through his leather arm, through his flesh and to the bone, sick and loathsome and disabling.

That's dead, that's gone.

Sightless, nauseous, in agony, he clutched and his fingers entered the raw wet gaping wound. Then a savage gouge into the meat of his belly tore the breath from him.

'That's for Paul, Stevie, son. This is for Rob.'

The blade was moving in his gut, another hacking at his back. Blow upon blow, ripping through, ripping apart. Blood thick in his throat.

Someone was laughing near to his ear. Evil, pure devilment.

'And this is from guess who? *Brian*. Your old mate *Brian*.'

The next blow bit into the side of his face, then a fireball blazed in his head and burned out his eyes.

Chapter V

THE RECORD

28 November 1996

Dear Sir,

I am writing to you angry past words for what was printed in your paper tonight of STEVIE COULSON. I know what of I speak for Stevie was my friend and a dear one to me for all his life that was ended so cruelly. Do people have no decency in them when a tragedy happens. It is not true and an OUTRAGE all what things are getting said about Stevie, who cannot defend himself now since he is gone. But shame on you and any others who give false witness. One day THE TRUTH will be known, not the lies and 'scandal' people write to sell their newspapers DAMN them.

Yours,
Mrs E. A. Dodd

Date: 26 November 1996
Crime number: 257539w/02
Report of first attending officer: DC Chisholm

Since June 14 1996 I have worked undercover as doorman for the firm of Sharky's Machine Ltd, part of the SCT investigation into Roy Caldwell + Steve Coulson and suspected traffic/supply of narcotics.

On night of Saturday November 24 [2109] I had information by phone from a trusted source and on basis of same proceeded to #32

Oakwell Estate, Hoxheath. My belief was I would gain entry to said address without difficulty and find on the premises physical evidence related to the killings of Messrs Paul Crowley and Robert Donner in North Shields on Thursday November 14 1996 (crime number 980230476, investigation ongoing).

On arrival at #32 [2136] I found that forced entry had been made to the premises by the front door. I entered with caution to a narrow hallway, and was immediately aware of sounds of distress from behind a locked door to my right. Behind it in a small bathroom I found a white adult female and a white male child. The female I identified by prior acquaintance as Lindy Clark, sometime employee at licensed premises managed by Steve Coulson. I established that Ms Clark was the homeowner and that the boy was her son Jake, aged 6. Both were very agitated and I tried to calm them and prevent them from intruding further upon what I now took to be a crime scene. These efforts were difficult, especially with Ms Clark, and my initial requests for details of the break-in were not properly answered.

Proceeding through to a living space, I found evidence of a struggle and then a man lying unconscious near the foot of a staircase to an upper floor. Here I was unable to prevent Ms Clark climbing those stairs with the boy. I inspected the unconscious man, saw he had suffered injuries to face and head, clearly a broken nose, plus swelling and bleeding I thought consistent with a fractured/dislocated jaw.

(I established in due course that this man was a neighbour from the Oakwell Estate, John Gore, aged 31, a minister of the Church of England.)

I tried to rouse Mr Gore. He recovered consciousness but he was breathing with difficulty on account of the broken nose, was not coherent, and in considerable pain and distress.

I had heard cries from the upper floor and as soon as I was able made my way up, turning right into a woman's bedroom (A) which I took to be Ms Clark's. The scene presented as the aftermath of a violent assault (blood on walls, arterial spray). Ms Clark was still with her child though trying to attend to another wounded man, the child now in such a bad way that I saw no option but to insist that Ms Clark take him and herself down the hall to another bedroom (B) while I made my inspection. This was achieved with some difficulty, but it was then I took the basic details as above.

Returning to Bedroom A I used the telephone to make calls to the ambulance service and to my colleagues DI Fitzgerald and DS Henshaw, whom I instructed to alert Forensics and Scene of Crime Officer. I then went quickly to the second man, a white adult male. It was immediately apparent he had died as the result of multiple stab wounds, inflicted, I guessed, by a heavy knife or machete (victim effectively disembowelled, right arm partially severed, deep cuts to the neck, both thighs, and across the left cheekbone, disfiguring). His face looked also to have been scarred separately, a red blister-burn I took for CS gas or pepper-spray. I checked for pulse and found none. By prior acquaintance I could identify the aforementioned as Mr Steven Coulson.

Ms Clark had once more entered Bedroom A despite my warnings, her manner hysterical, and again I had to insist forcibly that she return to her child. I quickly located a bedsheet and covered the body. I then made a further call to Area Operating Room to report the fatality and arrange a second ambulance.

I then took steps to preserve the scene, conducted visual search for DNA and for dangerous items. Inspection of the view from an open window alerted me to a suspicious bag on the lawn of the neighbouring property.

I returned downstairs and stayed by Mr Gore until DI Fitzgerald arrived on the scene [2151]. Having handed over I returned upstairs to Ms Clark. It was clear that much effort was needed to calm her, and that she would need to be removed from the scene for a statement to be taken. I brought her and the child back downstairs, where the paramedics had arrived. Steven Coulson was pronounced dead at 2202. Mr Gore was revived and here I established his details as above. DS Henshaw was now in attendance and I requested he make door-to-door enquiries, and also locate the item I had identified from the bedroom window. At this point Investigating Officer Fitzgerald relieved me of the care of Ms Clark and her child, asking that I accompany Rev. Gore in the ambulance to the General Hospital. I left the scene at 2212. Space was found for the Rev. Gore in A&E at the General and I took his statement at this time (cf. 723-1)

DC R. Chisholm

7 December 1996

Dear Lindy,

I am very much afraid you won't read this. I would not blame you. I am old enough to know there are times when forgiveness can't be asked for, when things can't be undone. This, I know, is how I stand before you.

If I may beg just one thing of you it's that, please, however you are feeling now, don't discard this page but take a moment to read and consider its contents. Please set your proper antipathy to one side if only for one moment and allow me to be of use.

It is your right to understand fully why things took the awful course they did, for which I am essentially culpable, though some matters were beyond my control. For my part it was truly only that I wanted – and so badly – to drive off a shadow from your life and Jake's. Probably the action I chose was not my choice to make, but its undoing was the result of evil misfortune – and other more actively malign motives. It wasn't meant to happen as it did. I was myself let down, by a man from whom I had received certain assurances, ones he later neglected, albeit in 'the heat of the moment'. There are other matters I will never be able to properly explain. But I understand that Brian Shackleton remains part of the police investigation, and please believe me, you must on no account have anything to do with him from now.

With these care proceedings now underway you will need all the support you can get. I learned through a friend at the

Citizens Advice Bureau that you had the services of Mr Redbill, that he is rated a good solicitor, and that legal aid is available. I contacted Redbill and we have agreed that I will provide a substantive written statement in your support. I take it you would feel as I do that for me to appear in person would not be productive. But I dearly hope that I might be helpful when it comes to the final hearing.

The local authority will be a hard opponent. It's possible they will make some effort to discredit you, seek 'expert assessment', use whatever facts suit their petition. You will have to fight, to draw on all your reserves. But for Jake to be placed permanently in care would be a grave assumption of responsibility on the part of the council, and I understand that many judges fear, rightly, that such an outcome can be a disaster for a child. Hence a great deal of evidence and persuasion has to be put. I am certain you can challenge anything that emerges.

Forgive me if I state your predicament as if I were not, in part, a cause of it.

You have been a victim of my failure of nerve. I have been made to pay for it myself, though I don't compare our losses in the slightest. If I could take your place, take on to myself what you have been through, I would do so.

I only want you to know that I never lied to you. My failings are many, but this was not among them. I say so not to claim some useless credit, only so you know that from the first to the last of our acquaintance, whenever I spoke of my feelings for you, it was truly felt, and more so than anything in my life.

With my love,
John

B4/1997/1419
IN THE COURT OF APPEAL (CIVIL DIVISION)
ON APPEAL FROM NEWCASTLE COUNTY COURT
BEFORE: LORD JUSTICE MONCRIEFF, LORD JUSTICE WRAITH
IN THE MATTER OF J (A CHILD)
JUDGEMENT (as approved by the Court)

1. LORD JUSTICE MONCRIEFF: The parties to this appeal are the local authority; the mother Miss C; and the sole relevant child, J, as represented by his appointed guardian.
2. Miss C is the mother of J who was born on 3 June 1990. She seeks permission to appeal against orders made in care proceedings relating to the child instituted by the Local Authority.
3. The involvement of the Local Authority was pursuant to the killing of Miss C's estranged partner and J's father, Mr C, by persons unknown at the family address on 24 November 1996. The killing led to the issue of care proceedings on 27 November 1996, so as to remove J from the home. Social Services were not satisfied that J was safe from harm in his mother's care, owing to the violent circumstances of Mr C's death and the degree to which this episode furnished evidence of the appellant's neglect of J.
4. J was first placed under police protection for 72 hours and housed by Social Services. An Emergency Protection Order was obtained subsequently. A guardian *ad litem* was appointed to represent J in the proceedings by CAFCASS.
5. On 10 February 1997, at the conclusion of a contested first hearing, HHJ Flint placed J in the interim care of the Local Authority for an eight-week term until the final hearing, deciding with the Authority that there were indeed good reasons the child might come to harm. In his judgement he noted the dire events of 24 November 1996, Social Services' report of Miss C's lack of co-operation with them, and the assertion that Miss C had told untruths to police officers that had hindered the investigation. It was further the judge's view that Miss C required a psychiatric assessment.
6. On 24 February 1997 Miss C appeared at an oral hearing contesting the interim care order, her case argued by Mr Redbill, but was not successful.

7. On 7 April 1997 HHJ Middleton presided over the final hearing of the care proceedings, now paying special attention to the issue of the well-known 'threshold criteria'. The document produced by the Local Authority referred to section 31(2)(a) of the Children Act 1989, so asking had Child J suffered or was he likely to suffer significant harm? (Here we understand that harm may include impairment suffered from seeing or hearing ill-treatment of another.) And per section 31(2)(b), would any such harm be attributable to J not receiving the parental care it would be reasonable to expect Ms C to give? The local authority concluded, sub-paragraph (E): 'The past history of Miss C's behaviour, indeed her behaviour in the course of this investigation, do nothing to allay our concerns.'
8. In the final hearing this question of Miss C's personality and temperament, her lifestyle and associations, came under close scrutiny. Moreover a great deal of the judgement was to be concerned with the historic past as well as the relevant present. Miss C was cross-examined by Ms Quine for the Authority, and I can well understand that HHJ Middleton was shocked by aspects of how Miss C managed her life and household, and the role of J's late father in same. An account emerged of a chaotic and unsettled environment, one where the violence of 24 November could be seen in somewhat of a context, and the potential for reprisal also weighed. All these were plainly relevant to the threshold criteria and the welfare of J. The evidence of the child psychologist Dr Motter was also key here.
9. There was no dispute that the threshold had been established. The only issue was the appropriate form of order in respect of the child's welfare: whether a Supervision Order would be sufficient, or whether J's interests could only be protected by the Local Authority assuming parental responsibility through a Care Order.
10. HHJ Middleton's definition of the essential issue comes in paragraph 52 of her judgement, when she says: 'All agree that a risk to J remains, even if quantified as a low risk at the moment. It is my finding that for the foreseeable future the local authority need to assume parental responsibility to minimise that risk.'
11. Thus Miss C sought permission to appeal. The application was settled by Mr Ian Redbill QC and in the interim Mr Philip Leigh, for the

guardian, filed a skeleton supporting the appeal and Ms Quine a skeleton resisting.

12. To the crux: we have seen that HHJ Middleton's judgement is necessarily preoccupied with evaluations of Miss C's behaviour – none of which Miss C can challenge, as they were plainly open to the judge to make. I am drawn to the following remarks in particular: 'I am satisfied that if I were to return this boy to his mother's care, his life will nevertheless be overshadowed profoundly by the effect of her deeply troubled personality. I consider the risk of same to outweigh the benefits of a reunion, this despite their evident bonds of affection.'

13. Mr Redbill's assertion of Miss C's willingness to change her way of life is noted. He also drew proper attention to the extended remarks in the written statement supplied by a friend of Miss C's who is an Anglican priest and clearly holds her personal qualities in the highest regard.

14. I find, however, the first judgement clear and properly made out as to the risk of 'significant harm'. HHJ Middleton has not overlooked an appreciation of Miss C's love for her child and its reciprocation. She dealt with the facts, but also directed herself appropriately as to the law. I find no fault in the care order and see no prospect of success for Miss C's application.

15. The local authority has managed the protection very professionally, for it is indeed a highly difficult case, but one in which the best interests of J have been the first priority. I am satisfied by their considered long-term care plan as presented, and encouraged by their early identification of suitable adopters for J.

16. In these circumstances, therefore, I would respectfully refuse to grant permission to the application.

17. LORD JUSTICE WRAITH: I entirely agree with the Lord Justice Moncrieff, and there is nothing that I can usefully add.

Order: Application refused.

EPILOGUE

Wednesday, 16 April 1997

'Hello there, stranger, mind if I sit?'

She waited for an answer, as others probably wouldn't, and upon his semi-obliging half-smile she slid herself into the facing chair. Shortly she was attended by the waitress – a sweet-looking girl but for a regrettable stud in her nose – and she dithered a little over her choice of cake or tart to accompany the pot of Earl Grey. Thus was she chastened a little by his frugal request for black coffee.

'You'll not have a pastry? I'd have two if I were you, there's nowt on you. I only wish I could keep it off.'

The corners of his mouth twitched. *Come on, pet,* she was thinking, *a little nicety won't kill you.* Her half-dozen colleagues in the canvassing team were sat as one on the far shore of the tea-shop counter, clearly a little mutinous and muttering, and with a certain justification, when their alleged leader – this frowning man whom they hadn't met before today – sat himself apart and alone, perusing the *Mail* and the *Sun*, of all the wretched things.

But Mrs Margaret Deveson was nothing but a trier. Her calling as a hospice nurse was not one that allowed her to hide when she felt less than gladsome. Today – a bright spring day with a chill that put cherries in her cheeks – she was reasonably chipper. She would not rush to judgement. It was generally her view that solitary types wanted saving from themselves, or else they would have made a more thoroughgoing job of their solitude.

She tapped his pile of newsprint, which he had not entirely set aside.

'Don't tell me you're reading for pleasure.'

'Not a bit. Just better to know the enemy's mind. When there's a war on.'

She deemed that worthy of a chuckle. 'Well, maybe so, but you want to watch. You'll lose points off good Labour folk, sat with them dirty rags.'

He was stirring a spoon needlessly round his coffee cup. 'I don't know that my first impression was so great.'

Since he had shown himself not impervious, she favoured him with a more serious tack. 'Listen, you won't take it personal, I hope, but the others? They *are* a bit wary of you. I said to them, I said, "Look – he's got this job, he must be good." But, you know, with people not knowing your face, and you not from round here –'

'I am, in fact. But that's not the point. No, I understand – if it seems like I'm an imposition. A fiat. But I'm only here to help.'

'And, have I got it right? You're sent from the *regional* office? You're one of them organisers?'

'No, no, I'm from HQ. Millbank? The task forces? Have you heard of them? They're only set up for the election, not the long run. So I'm just here to observe and support. Maybe advise if I can, just on presentation. "Message and delivery" they call it.'

'Right, so that's your expertise, is it?'

'No, I just went for the job like anyone else.' He smiled. 'I've done a lot of it, but – presentation, public speaking. Acting.'

'Okay, well – you see, I've been a Labour member all my life, the local parties are very close-knit, you might know. They have to be. So they're not so keen on being given what for.'

He leaned forward and gestured impatiently, rather taking her aback. 'Margaret, I couldn't agree more. I joined when I was fourteen. But you've got to remember, there just aren't so many members any more. Sometimes you have to hire bodies in to get things done. When the stakes are this high.' He stopped, as if mindful of a stridency in his tone. 'I don't say I'm better than anyone, trust me. I'm just here to ensure the message gets over.'

'So what's that, then? The message?'

'Come on, Margaret, you know very well, I'm sure.'

The note of complicity pleased her, and she nestled back cosily with her tea. 'Well, I must say, I told the others, after you'd said your little piece to us this morning, I said, "There's a man can express himself." I was watching you a bit and all, as we went along, you're good on the stump.'

'Well, I ought to be,' he said, in the direction of his chest.

They had passed the morning prior to this short break dawdling through the narrow and well-thronged streets of Durham City, urging the re-election of the sitting MP. The Market Place was to be their afternoon's stall, and it was visible to them now from the upper windows of the Special Treat tea-room on Saddler Street. Mrs Deveson let her gaze rest on the dallying human traffic through the glass. 'It makes me laugh, but, them uns who'd do anything not to stop for you. Looking over your head or at their watches and that. Like they're so busy. I want to shout at them, "I don't want your money." And some of these kids you see, all in black, like death warmed up. I should talk, mind you, my daughter's girl's going a bit that way. No time for her granny any more, oh no.'

He shrugged. 'I'm told you get twelve nice years with them. Then they'd rather, on the whole, you were dead.'

She smiled, though the witticism, if such it was, struck her as off-key. 'I tell you summat else gets up my nose. The students. You'd think they'd have a view on an election. I thought they were all good Tory-haters. They're supposed to be curious, at least, aren't they? About the world? But they act like you're not worth their time either. The accents on them and all. Public school, I suppose. Rugger-buggers. I say that, you're not a rugby man, are you?' His breadth of shoulder and stunningly bent nose had caused her to question her manners suddenly.

'No,' he murmured. 'But yeah, you're right. My granddad used to say there's two sides to Durham. Ne'er the twain shall meet.'

'Oh, your family are from Durham then?'

'*I'm* from Durham. Pity Me.' He jerked a thumb at the window.

'Pity Me! Oh! Know it well. You do get some names around these parts, don't you?'

'You do that.'

Belatedly she was getting interested. 'But you'll not have spent much of your life here?'

'Until I went off to college. Then I started working, you know . . . but I moved back up last year, for a bit.'

'So what were you doing before this? Was it for the Party?'

'No, no. I was a – I was a priest, actually. An Anglican priest.'

'You never were!'

'It's true. I was due to take a post here, but it all fell through at the last. So I was unemployed. But it meant I could get involved with the Party again. Then, you know, the election was called, I heard they were hiring, so . . .'

'And – but – you're still a vicar then, are you? Or not?'

He looked to the window. 'I'm on a bit of a sabbatical.'

'My. Well, this'll all be a bit of a change of pace, I suppose?'

'Not so much. Still a lot of talking to people who don't want to hear. For not much money.'

'Oh but now, that's God's work for you, isn't it?' She savoured the taste of her own wit. 'Right, and that'll be where you get your good voice from then? The old sermons, eh?'

'It's not such a transferable skill, but yes, I suppose.' She could sense his retreat from the colloquy. 'I've not got a watch, is it time we shifted?'

'We've a good ten minutes yet,' said Mrs Deveson.

'It's just I've to run a small errand, before we start up again? But I'll see you back in the Market Place for two.'

'Okey-doke. Long as you're not late for our star guest.'

'He can wait.'

As her new friend John pulled on his coat she dabbled her fingers in the crumbs of her fruit slice. 'So will you stay up here then? After the election?'

'No, I expect I'll troop back to London. See if there's anything else going.'

'Where are you stopping? While you're here?'

'With my dad. Out in Framwellgate Moor.'

'Ah. Nice to have home still, eh?'

They rose, and she turned and shot a look at her colleagues, similarly stirring. He had resumed his frowning over the front pages of the papers.

'What do you reckon to his chances then?'

'Home and dry with a bigger majority, I'd have thought.'

'Not our man, I mean *Blair*. In the country? I've still got my worries, see.'

'I wouldn't. He'll be in by a mile. People should stop flapping.'

'Well, aren't you a little sunbeam?' she clucked. 'A few of the others are a bit down on him, see. I reckon he'll be more radical than they think.'

'Probably best to be realistic about things. That way you're never disappointed.' He smiled, in a manner Mrs Deveson thought apologetic, and drank down his sour-looking coffee.

Gore was chiding himself as he hastened past the shopfronts of Saddler Street. At best, his tale had finessed the truth, and the telling had been its own little humiliation. The urge to reinvent oneself was insistent at times, but a demoralising chore when it came down to the detail. Others, perhaps, had a greater facility for lying to themselves. Gore was not sure he considered such a feat even possible. But it was clear to him that certain aspects of the past had to be forcibly set aside if one were to go on with life. A measure of dishonour was probably his lot. And it would have been much the worse, he knew, had DC Chisholm not duteously kept him apart from the investigation and media scrutiny of same.

The brute fact was that he had been in a hole, had been granted an exceptional favour, and seized the opportunity without scruple. It was Susannah whose phone call had thrown the lifeline, and she who had, to all intents and purposes, both filled out and filed his application to Millbank, subsequently drilling and dressing him for interview in a matter-of-fact manner that he was far too chastened to query. If she had judged him harshly, her verdict had turned out to be not irrevocable. She was loyal, he had to admit, and for that much he was grateful. And so he was a working man again, albeit lodging in his teenaged bedroom – four white walls, a bookcase and a map of the world, his father sometimes shuffling to the threshold with a mug of tea.

Do places really change with time, he was thinking, *or is it only us?* His tread carried him up the narrow steep-winding path of Owengate, from the foot of which he could see the peak of the fortress, its northern face – five hundred feet wide from east end to west and the view over the gorge, dense woods shrouding the river. An impregnable site, this virile promontory, above the loop of the Wear. The Cathedral bells were still for the moment, but the aura of Norman supremacy needed no amplification.

At the north door a tour guide in a purple branded sweatshirt was addressing a loose congregation gathered before the sanctuary knocker. '*Their clothes were taken off them and given out to the poor, you see, because as long as they took shelter in these walls they had to wear a black robe with a yellow cross . . .*'

It was a tale Gore knew well, perfect for the tourists – the old legend of the Cathedral's granting grace to fugitives from the law, lodging for thirty or so days, as long as they confessed to their sins. He glanced at the faces in the tour group – Americans, he guessed, standing attentively with handy cameras and annotated guidebooks and bored kids.

Within, he passed by some strenuous activity by the font, more deckhands in purple jumpers fiddling with the set-up of a silvery movie screen, twenty feet high, while others shifted lamps and a projector. It struck Gore as another little touch of showbusiness, stage management. There seemed no shortage of such notions for renewing this medieval site. A crocodile of boy choristers wended past him, mostly po-faced, a few smirking.

He sat awhile in the pews of the nave, staring up at the great circular rose window high in the east-end wall – muted golden light and Jesus in majesty, hemmed by a ring of saints. A few visitors were lighting penny candles. Many more sat stolid, heads bowed. The sole nuisance was a little blonde-headed girl making a playful mime with a hymnbook – 'La-la-*la*! La-la-*la*!' The pulpit was empty, the morning's rota of hymn numbers still slotted on the wall to one side. It occurred to Gore that he had not been an audience member for some time. He could imagine being up at the front, leading the chorus, yet he could no longer see himself a customer in the stalls.

It made a magisterial case for the faith, this old Cathedral, no question. You could not do without it. It could never be erased, never get sold off for luxury apartments, whatever the prophecies of Simon Barlow. Not yet. People would always come – for the sense of time and lineage, the efforts inscribed in the walls. They would come and fill the place, to visit or study, to be quiet and thoughtful or just to say they had seen it.

What part, though – he wondered – would one sacrifice, if one absolutely had to, to economise, to rebrand, remain current? What was expendable? The service itself, the prayer and the hymnal? Inconceivable. And then the ritual required a professor, a minister, even if the oaken pulpit this afternoon looked fine as it was, vacant and silent. What would go then? The belief in the almighty other? But it had spent so long on last legs. They could not start again, and were in no position to dictate any more. So was it enough that people be polite and kind and well-meaning? Agreeing to defer endlessly the matter of holy decree?

He shivered, for there was undeniably a chill in the air and in the hard seat under him. Then he glanced behind him at the Miners' Memorial, perennially solemn and modest in its alcove. But no, his time was up, he had dallied enough. And so he wandered back down the aisle, over the perfectly inlaid floor, passing those massive drum columns, intricately patterned and round enough to house bodies.

As he drew near the chatty cluster of his team in Market Place Gore found he was not interested in resuming pleasantries with Margaret or launching a renewed charm offensive on those who likely wouldn't thank him for it. Instead he veered toward the new arrival, who sat on a nearby bench with a fizzy can in his lap, chin on chest, swinging his legs.

'Hullo, young master Alex. Is your dad not here yet?'

The boy tossed his blonde mane toward the verdigris statue of the mounted Marquess of Londonderry, twenty feet hence. Gore walked around it and found Martin Pallister leaning against the base, one hand to brow, miniature phone cupped close to his mouth.

'Look, I've got him the Newcastle shirt, I'm getting it signed by all the players . . . Aw, don't even start with *that*, Becky. Twelve years old, I mean Jesus Christ, it's sick you even discuss it.'

He glanced aside, saw that he was waited upon, tugged at the knot of his red tie and concluded his exchanges tersely. Then he nodded to Gore. 'My master's voice. She's decided our son's gay, you see. Based on what, I don't know. What do you think?'

Gore turned and peered back at the listlessly seated Alexander.

Martin came fretfully close to his shoulder. 'She lets him keep his hair that long. Lets him cry off all the team sports.'

'He seems a solid lad, though,' Gore murmured. 'Not one of those speccy types, the ones who thumb their joysticks all hours. Just a regular sort of a boy.'

'Well, you'd maybe tell that to the first Mrs Pallister.'

'Or you maybe need to find her successor.'

'Oh ho. I'll take nee lesson off of you in that demesne, *Reverend*.'

Pallister was giving him that strange small smile he had perfected of late. How much Susannah had confided in him of her little brother's recent debacle, Gore knew not – but some of it, no doubt, for this look was conspiratorial. Yet there seemed a kind of commiseration there too.

'Any road,' Martin persisted, 'I'm as good as married to your sister. It's why you and me are like family.'

Gore winced. 'I'm just saying. If you gave your son more of a home, with a partner – I mean, look, it's not that your wife hasn't raised him perfectly well, clearly.'

'I've had a hand in it, John. Man alive. You the expert on that subject an' all?'

'You asked me, Martin.'

Pallister chuckled. 'That I did. What was I thinking? No, right enough, you've got to have gone through it, really. It all changes with kids, it really does. That's what we're *for*, really. Not winning elections. Or giving sermons. Before *he* come along – all through my twenties – I used to think I was driving forward. Getting on, y'know? Like there'd be a point you got to where life would be different. Then his nibs showed up and I realised I'd hit it. Or it had hit us.'

Gore kept his gaze neutral, not in the mood for the lecture. Pallister's smile had turned sportive once more. 'Do you see, but? All that time I thought I was working my way through life – life was just working its way through me. Y'know what I mean? Are we not but vessels, John? For the great parasite? The worm of the world?' He chuckled. 'See, you can use that. If you ever go back to the preaching. So how are the troops then? And where's Gerry?'

Pallister pressed past him and Gore followed, stooping to take a sheaf of pamphlets from his rucksack, adjusting the rosette in his lapel as he watched the MP give the canvassers the glad hand. He could see a few good citizens of Durham loitering with interest at a distance, as if they might have an active interest in the literature on offer, rather than suffering it to be pressed upon them. Pallister was now standing over his son as they conferred shortly. It seemed a fair enough rapport they had – enviable, in a way. The boy rolled his eyes, stood, yawned and stretched his young frame. Not a bad build, now Gore saw the whole of it – hips and crotch thrust forward with a certain familiar bored cocksureness.

Presently Pallister sauntered back to Gore's side, apparently preferring his company, comfortable with his silence. Gore felt none of the same ease.

'He's at big school now, then, Alex?'

'Aye, he's at my old place. Heaton Manor. Still good. Mind you, they've got buzz-in security gates and all that now, not like my day. But that's the world. It's nice for him, local school, local kids.'

'Right. A pity your friend Tony sent his boy to that Catholic opt-out place. What was it, ten miles from home?'

Pallister shook his head. 'You're just lucky if you've got a good school local. You should see the bloody bedlam where Becky teaches. Failing school. Failing teachers. Any road – it's not an easy choice, so don't be snide. You never bloody give over, do you? I hope you're nicer when you're knocking on doors for Gerry.'

'Of course. I speak plainly to you because we're family, Martin.'

It was as much of a retort as Gore could summon in the hard knowledge that he was bought and paid for.

Pallister grunted amusement. 'Well, as the man said, John, a period of silence out of you would be greatly appreciated.'

Gore sniffed, lowered his head, mutely accepting that the thrust had struck home. Pallister, moreover, had a hand on his shoulder and was pointing a way forward. 'Now look lively, bonny lad, you've a customer.' Indeed one of the hovering circle of would-be voters had edged a few paces closer. Gore clasped his pamphlets to his chest and met the pilgrim's eye.

'Can I help you?'

ACKNOWLEDGEMENTS

There were a number of factual writings that were influential upon this fiction. I owe a particular debt to Andrew Martin for his article 'They Told Me to Plant a Church', which appeared in the *Independent on Sunday* on 20 February 1994 and detailed the work of a vicar in a parish within the diocese of Durham.

The subject of organised crime in Newcastle-upon-Tyne acquired a certain hazy focus after the killing of Viv Graham on New Year's Eve 1993, and a further piece from the *Independent on Sunday* (13 March 1994), entitled 'Death of a Philanthropist' by Richard Smith, gave an account of Graham's demise that was a further stimulus to me.

I am grateful to several books about the recent history of the Labour Party, principally *Tony Blair* by John Rentoul (which provided the anecdotal inspiration for Blair's cameo in this novel), *Gordon Brown* by Tom Bower, and *Mandy* by Paul Routledge. A piece about Blair by James Fenton in the *New York Review of Books* ('The Self-Made Man', 12 June 1997) greatly informed my thinking about the then-prime minister's association with County Durham.

I also found much of value in a pair of published memoirs by ex-bishops: *The Calling of a Cuckoo* by David Jenkins and *Steps Down Hope Street* by David Shepherd.

On a personal level I was much informed by discussions with the Reverend Peter Atkinson, a Durham-born vicar now retired. But I should say that the notional version of 'the living' presented in these pages bears no relation to what was Peter's, or, I suspect, any other churchman's. It is every bit as invented as the emotional lives of the characters and, accordingly, the author's sole responsibility.

I was also greatly guided through the recent history of organised crime in Newcastle by discussions with persons who must remain unnamed, but whose time and insights were greatly valued. Again, the information received was used purely as a springboard for dramatic construction, rather than a documentary template.

Readers may have noticed here, and perhaps with disapproval, a handful of 'moments', pronouncements, and even chapter titles bearing a debt to things they have read elsewhere: namely in translations of the 'big four' novels of Dostoevsky. I readily own up to this *hommage* (or theft, if you like) since it is meant entirely and respectfully as a sort of genuflection to the Master.

The quotation from I. F. Stone used here as an epigraph is taken not from the original but as cited by Christopher Hitchens in an essay for *Vanity Fair* (September 2006) entitled 'I. F. Stone's Mighty Pen'.

At Faber I would like to thank Lesley Felce, Kate Ward, Charles Boyle, Neal Price, Walter Donohue, Neil Belton and Kate Burton. Above all, three individuals supported this project – Lee Brackstone, Kevin Conroy Scott and Rachel Alexander – for which I am dearly grateful to them.

Richard T. Kelly, April 2007